BANTAM BOOKS
NEW YORK TORONTO LONDON
SYDNEY AUCKLAND

THE
TRANQUILITY
WARS

GENTRY LEE

This edition contains the complete text of the original hardcover edition.
NOT ONE WORD HAS BEEN OMITTED.

THE TRANQUILITY WARS
A Bantam Spectra Book

PUBLISHING HISTORY
Bantam Spectra hardcover edition published December 2000
Bantam Spectra paperback edition / September 2001

Library of Congress Catalog Card Number: 00-036087

ISBN 0-553-57338-1

Published simultaneously in the United States and Canada

Bantam Books are published by Bantam Books, a division of Random House, Inc.
Its trademark, consisting of the words "Bantam Books" and the portrayal of a
rooster, is Registered in U.S. Patent and Trademark Office and in other countries.
Marca Registrada. Bantam Books, 1540 Broadway, New York, New York 10036.

PRINTED IN THE UNITED STATES OF AMERICA

OPM   10 9 8 7 6 5 4 3 2 1

For Cooper,
my first adult son.

May your life be filled
with the love and happiness
you deserve.

THE TRANQUILITY WARS

THE MESSAGE

ONE

THE UNTOWARD EVENTS ALL occurred within a few seconds. The two technicians had been sitting in their space suits on top of the long, thick arm of the giant mining machine, just below the bottom joint. They had been having a diagnostic discussion by radio with the supervising engineers, who were watching on video from the confines of the control center inside the enclosed dome. When their conversation was finished, the technicians rose to their knees to finish the repairs on the electronics that controlled the enormous claw head resting on the surface of the asteroid twenty feet below them. Suddenly the mining colossus sprang alive. Its long arm jerked into motion, catapulting the two humans away from the equipment.

They flew in the airless, low-gravity environment of the asteroid as if they had been shot from a gun. Tumbling head over heels, their arms flailing, their terrified shouts resounding throughout the control center, the technicians smashed against the side of a second mining machine two hundred yards away. The engineers under the dome shuddered in horror as their colleagues ricocheted upward and then fell slowly, apparently lifeless, near the lip of a large mining pit.

MR. DAVID BLAKE, the chief engineer on the asteroid Cicero, was sitting in his office when the accident occurred. Just as he finished composing an electronic letter to FISC (Federation of Independent Space Colonies) engineering headquarters in Centralia, on Mars, complaining once again about the shortage of critical parts on Cicero, one of his assistants burst into the office.

"Blake," the assistant said, panic in his voice, "something terrible has happened. Miner #7 moved. Samuels and Turner were thrown off the arm. They aren't responding to our calls."

Blake quickly followed the assistant down the corridor to the main control center in the engineering complex. The control center was a large room at the top of a cylindrical tower near the edge of the dome that covered the inhabited region of Cicero. Half a dozen technicians and engineers were inside the room, along with ten computer workstations and seven large overhead monitors. On each of the monitors, a live image depicting an activity in process outside the dome was projected. When the two men entered the room, the huge central monitor showed a close-up picture of the two men in space suits lying motionless near the mining pit. In the image background stood one of the gigantic, silver, robotic mining machines, the bold, black letters FISC clearly emblazoned on its side.

Nicholas Cruz, the earnest young man who was in charge of outside operations activities on the current shift, walked over to Blake. "The biometry readings are garbage," he said. "Their transmitters must have been crushed during the accident." He paused a moment. "I assume you would like to see the complete video?" he said.

Blake nodded. The large central monitor filled a moment later with a still image of the two men sitting on the arm of Miner #7. The recording that began to play included the last snippets of conversation prior to the sudden movement of the arm, as well as the horrible cries of the technicians during their short flight. Blake winced as he watched his friends carom off the adjacent miner and then fall to the asteroid surface.

"We'll need an emergency rescue team," a visibly shaken Blake said as soon as the video was finished.

"Yes, sir," Nick Cruz said. "We've already begun the preparations." He paused a moment. "Please, sir, I would like to volunteer."

"All right, Nick," Blake said. "You lead the team. Take Lucy, Julius, and Hiro. No diagnostics on the miner. Just bring Samuels and Turner inside as fast as you can. Every second counts."

Nick quickly left the control center. Blake told one of the technicians to reconfigure the screens so that the central monitor would always show the activities of the rescue team. For the next several seconds, he gazed idly at the other screens, his mind deep in thought about the possible repercussions of the accident. Three of the screens showed other, similar mining machines at work in different locations outside the dome on Cicero. The remaining monitors in the control center depicted scenes inside the robotic factories where the raw ore was taken for processing after it was extracted.

There had never been a work fatality outside the dome on Cicero. For a decade eight of the mammoth mining drones, considered to be triumphs of human engineering, had been in nearly constant operation on the small spherical asteroid. The machines ripped into the ground with their enormous claws, tapping the rich lodes of iron and nickel that were very close to the surface. The material was then deposited in the open beds of large, all-terrain robot trucks and carried to four widely separated processing factories, each located about a mile outside the enclosed town.

Inside the vast, translucent dome, which covered twenty square miles in the equatorial region of Cicero and provided an Earthlike atmosphere for the asteroid's three thousand inhabitants, all the mining activities were carefully monitored from the control center. Regular maintenance on the mining machines and trucks, or on any of the equipment in the unpeopled processing factories, was provided by robot technicians dispatched from the inside.

The entire system was designed so that human activity outside the enclosed dome would be reduced to an absolute minimum. In fact, during the four years immediately prior to Engineer Blake's decision to recertify each of the mining machines, only three human sorties "outside" had been required to repair or maintain any of the mining system components.

Over the past year, however, as incident after incident had increased the tension between the FISC and its rival space power, the UDSC (United Democratic Space Colonies), efficient management of its mining operations had become a low priority for the Federation. The engineers on Cicero and the other mining asteroids had been ordered to sharply reduce maintenance activities on the existing equipment and key personnel were transferred to the defense effort. As a result, serious failures in the mining system on Cicero had begun to occur more frequently and productivity had dropped off markedly.

To mitigate these problems, Blake had decided in early 2408 that only a thorough, component-by-component recertification of all the mining machines had a chance of significantly reducing the failure rate. For over a month, human technicians had been going "outside" on a daily basis, carrying with them field-testing apparatus as well as all the requisite spares, replacing any and all components that did not meet the original machine specifications. The previous outside sorties had all occurred without incident. More than forty major parts had been replaced. There was reason to believe that the entire complicated and possibly dangerous procedure was going to achieve its desired result. Only two days had been left in the recertification process when the arm on Miner #7 had moved unexpectedly.

Still deep in thought, Blake watched from the control center as the rover carrying Nick Cruz and the rest of the rescue team passed through the airlock and into the vacuum outside the dome. Nick was driving. The rover was bouncing wildly across the barren, rocky terrain as it sped toward its destination about ten miles away.

INSIDE THE CICERO Hospital, Hunter Blake, the twenty-year-old son of Engineer David Blake, was chatting comfortably with a couple whose son was about to undergo a routine tonsillectomy. "This particular robot surgeon," he told them, in response to a question, "has only performed five tonsillectomies in the past. However," Hunter said, calling up data on the large monitor on his desk, "as you can see from these statistics, this release version of the surgeon has successfully completed over two hundred similar procedures at hospitals all over the Federation. With no complications worth noting."

"I would just feel better," the woman said, "if a human being were doing the operation. I know it's simple, but Jimmy's my only son and . . ."

"Even if you were on Earth," Hunter interrupted her pleasantly, "it would be very unlikely that your son's tonsils would be removed by an actual person. The operation is too straightforward to justify the expense of a real surgeon.

And the risks are minimal. If the robot surgeon sees anything at all that is not completely standard, it will simply abort the procedure and wait for instructions."

"Are you a doctor?" the man suddenly asked.

"No," Hunter said, "I'm a certified paramedic. I recently finished my eighteen-month course here at the hospital." He smiled. "I've applied to one of the Federation medical schools on Mars and am waiting to hear if I've been accepted."

"Hunter," an electronic voice intoned over the network audio system, "I am now ready to proceed. I have finished all the self-tests required by procedure 226A and everything has checked out positively."

"Thank you, 4G19," Hunter replied. As he turned to ask the boy's parents if they had any more questions, Hunter's personal pager sounded, its urgent tone indicating a top-priority message. During his few months at the hospital, he had received only one such message before, when a high-ranking Cicero official who had had a heart attack was being rushed to the hospital and the mayor wanted to be certain that all preparations would be complete before his arrival.

The small monitor on Hunter's pager flashed the sentence "Stop whatever you are doing and report immediately to the central hospital office."

"Excuse me," Hunter said to the couple, "but I have just been summoned to an emergency meeting. I apologize for the inconvenience. Unfortunately, unless you wish to sign a waiver and proceed with the operation with no human monitor, we will need to reschedule Jimmy's tonsillectomy to tomorrow morning."

The woman shook her head vigorously. "As I said earlier this morning, it's very important to me that there be somebody in attendance during his operation."

"All right," Hunter said, "we'll reschedule Jimmy for

ten o'clock tomorrow." He headed for the door. "The robot orderlies will escort your son to the dressing room," Hunter said hurriedly. "You can meet him there."

The woman started to ask Hunter a question. "I'm sorry," he said, interrupting her, "I really must leave right now."

A moment later Hunter was walking rapidly down the hospital corridor. In his haste at one point he took both his feet off the floor and became airborne in the near weightlessness. Struggling to remain upright, Hunter drifted slowly downward for a few seconds. When one of his shoes was again in contact with the floor, he continued, this time at a more even pace.

Within a minute all eight members of the hospital's human staff had arrived at the central office. "There's been an accident outside," the hospital director, a thin, sallow man in his early fifties, told the staff. "An emergency sortie has been dispatched to bring the two injured technicians back as soon as possible. Because their biometry transmitters have failed, we have no explicit knowledge of their condition. It seems unlikely to me, after viewing the video of the accident, that they are still alive. Nevertheless, we must be prepared to do whatever we can.

"I have called Dr. Wallace and Dr. Chen," the director continued. He started the recording of the video of the accident, which played on the monitor on the wall behind him. "They will be here in twenty minutes. They have asked me to make certain that all reasonable preparations are complete before they arrive. . . . Kim, make sure that all emergency room equipment is operational. Blake, check our inventory of replacement organs and other biological subsystems, both hybrid and all-engineering. Singh, review the blood types of the two men and check our supplies, in case transfusions will be required. . . ."

While he was listening to the director's instructions,

Hunter studied the short video of the accident, which was playing for the second time on the screen. He watched in horror as the two figures struck the other mining machine, bounced upward, and then seemed to hang in the air before falling to the surface. *They couldn't possibly have survived,* Hunter thought. *If they didn't die from their injuries, failure of their space suits would have killed them.*

The director had finished his assignments. "Any questions?" he said. "All right, let's meet back here in fifteen minutes. Please be on time."

Hunter returned to his work area to perform his task. He quickly verified in detail what he already knew—that the hospital's inventory of human replacement parts, including all the critical organs, was woefully lacking. Three times in the last year the hospital had received long requisition lists from the FISC defense ministry. All types of body parts—biological, hybrid, and all-engineering—had been their top-priority requests. In spite of the director's protestations, the mayor of Cicero had ordered the hospital to comply. *Even if the technicians are still alive, by some miracle,* Hunter thought as he quickly scanned the list of zeros on the inventory list, *our transplant options are virtually nonexistent.*

The hospital staff members all assembled again in the office at the appointed time. While they waited for the director, they groused about the shortages and their inability to perform their required functions. "I have five robot orderlies out of service now," said the operations chief, "waiting for parts. And Mars can give me no schedule for when they might arrive.... I have been delivering meals MYSELF for the last two months."

The director was almost ten minutes late for the meeting. When he arrived, he looked even more wan than usual. "Our crisis is over," he announced with a heavy sigh.

"The two technicians are dead. They are being transported to the crematorium."

He paused and looked at his staff. "I have decided we're going to prepare a report for the mayor's office anyway. I want him to know how ill-equipped we are at present to deal with any similar kind of emergency." He forced a smile. "Not that it will do any good—I'm afraid the needs of an outpost hospital are not very important when compared with a possible war—but I couldn't live with myself if I said nothing."

TWO

HUNTER WAS IN A terrible mood when he returned to his desk half an hour after his work shift was supposedly finished. It had been a very bad day for him at the Cicero Hospital. Following the fruitless emergency scramble, one problem after another had occurred. The robot surgeon that had been scheduled to perform a gallbladder removal failed self-test twice, once after the hospital's diagnostic equipment had spent twenty minutes presumably verifying that the surgeon was working correctly. Hunter had made a mistake by starting to prep the patient for the operation before the robot surgeon failed its second self-test. Not only did he receive a tongue-lashing from the harried hospital director, but he was also rebuked by the patient's wife. Later, when Hunter tried to complete a routine biometry scan of the patient, a hospital requirement for dismissal, he discovered that the entire biometry system had crashed again. Hunter waited for five minutes for the director to return his page before reluctantly deciding to dismiss the patient on his own authority. His action was soundly criticized afterward by the director, who reminded Hunter that only doctors and hospital executives were allowed to vary the rules.

Hunter slumped into the chair at his desk and looked at the two monitors, both of which were indicating that he had messages. The hospital intranet contained his updated schedule for the next day, including Jimmy's tonsillectomy at ten o'clock in the morning, as well as a recent, upbeat vidmail from the hospital director. The director told Hunter that in general he was doing a fine job, and not to be too discouraged by the day's events.

His other monitor, which was connected to the external network, had three vidmail messages for him, one from his mother, one from his friend Calvin Dobson, and the third from a young lady, Linda Overton, whom Hunter had dated a few times. The message summary gave the lengths of each of the vidmails. Since Linda's was the shortest, he accessed it first.

"Hi, Hunter," a cheery blonde said. "I thought I'd let you know that Elaine, Jerry, and I are watching the new concert from Desperate Fish tonight, over at her apartment around eight-thirty. Why don't you join us? Jerry's bringing some of that dark Centralia beer that came on the last cargo ship. Hope to see you tonight."

His mother's message had been transmitted only an hour before. She was not her usual sunny self. His mother first told him that the planned family dinner for that evening would be late, around eight o'clock, and that although Hunter's sister Amanda, her husband Octavio, and their infant daughter Danielle would all be attending, as planned, it was not certain if Hunter's father would be able to join them.

"I am worried about him, Hunter," she said. "I have never seen him so exhausted. Your father has been working long hours every day for almost a month and was looking forward to a break next week after the recertification was finished. . . . This damn accident has torn him apart. He feels responsible, and nothing I said this afternoon seemed to help. . . . If he does make it home tonight for dinner, please don't get into any political arguments with Octavio—you know how family tension distresses him. Please, I want tonight to be as relaxing as possible for your father. He deserves it."

Hunter watched the vidmail from his mother twice. The second time, he chastised himself for having been so wrapped up in his own affairs during the day that he hadn't even thought about his father. *Dad must be devastated*, he thought. *Those technicians were his colleagues and friends. In addition, Dad put his professional reputation on the line with the recertification process. . . . Yet here I am, feeling sorry for myself because I made some mistakes on MY job. Get over yourself, Hunter.*

He was still thinking about his father while he was watching the vidmail from Calvin. His friend made some comments about how terrible the accident was, and then invited Hunter for a drink at Lucky Luigi's after work. Hunter almost turned Calvin's message off before it was finished. However, just as he leaned forward to stop the recording, Calvin said something that made Hunter pay attention.

"Oh, yeah," Calvin said. "I almost forgot. Guess who Wayne and I saw at Luigi's a couple of nights ago? One of Cicero's most famous ex-citizens, your old high-school girlfriend Tehani. She was having a beer with some of her old friends. Tehani looked absolutely gorgeous, just like she does on the net. And sexy . . . Anyway, Wayne and I tried to talk to her but she was surrounded all night by so many people—fans, I guess—that we eventually gave up. Belva told us that she had come home for a short visit with her mother and little brother. . . ."

Hunter's interest was definitely piqued. He had intended to tell Calvin that he was tired tonight, and might have a drink with him later in the week, but the thought of possibly seeing Tehani at Luigi's made him change his mind. Hunter activated the video camera on his desk and sent two short messages, one to Linda, telling her that he would see her some other time, and one to his mother, saying that he was going to stop off for a drink with Calvin and would be home later than usual.

"Tehani Wilawa," Hunter said out loud as he left his desk and headed for the transportation area adjacent to the hospital. "The name itself," he said, quoting one of his close friends who had been obsessed with Tehani since childhood, "conjures up exotic images."

FOUR OTHER PEOPLE were waiting on the transportation platform. Hunter entered the control kiosk and placed his name and destination on the computer. He then grimaced when the monitor told him that his car would arrive in between sixteen and eighteen minutes. "Terrible, isn't it?" a middle-aged woman who was standing behind him said, noticing his reaction. "Before all this tension with the Dems you never had to wait more than three or four minutes for a car."

"And they never broke down," a gray-haired man out on the platform added. "My wife was headed for the beauty salon last week when her car just stopped. The mechanic appeared in a few minutes, but he couldn't fix the problem because he didn't have any spare parts. It was almost an hour before the path was cleared and my wife reached the salon. Fortunately, she had phoned ahead and her appointment was rescheduled."

A crowded car arrived and Hunter watched as two people squeezed inside. "Please reverify your destination immediately after boarding," he heard the electronic voice say as the car pulled away. Another couple climbed up to the platform from the office building next to the hospital and entered their destination in the control kiosk. Hunter could hear them talking about the accident as they moved over toward him.

"Working outside with machines that large is just too dangerous," the man was saying. "In a hostile environment, the slightest error can be fatal."

"But they operated without any problems for so many years," the woman said. "Willis told me that they are the most reliable large robots he has ever seen."

"What does your brother know?" the man rejoined. "He's not a designer, or even an engineer. He just transmits the daily schedules to the mining machines. . . . Maybe they should consider shutting them all down, before someone else is hurt. At least until the experts can come back and fix them properly."

Hunter grimaced. As he often did, he interpreted such comments as criticism of his father. A few months earlier, he might have engaged the man in a conversation and attempted to change his mind. Now, however, especially after the accident, he knew that it would not be wise to say anything.

He walked over to stand by himself at the edge of the platform. Hunter did not even realize that he was thinking of Tehani until a picture of her appeared in his mind's eye. *She was the only girl who ever made my heart skip,* he admitted to himself, remembering a moment when they had been together two years earlier. *I might have fallen in love with her if she hadn't . . .*

Hunter didn't complete his thought. His car came. He boarded and stood next to the door, aware of a vague disquiet that he didn't understand.

CALVIN WAS AT a table with two girls Hunter had seen before but did not know. Before approaching them, Hunter carefully scanned Luigi's twice, searching for Tehani. He was disappointed that she wasn't there.

As Hunter drew near the table, both girls sat up straight in their chairs, arranged their hair, and smiled. "It's the man himself," Calvin said when he was within earshot. "Hunter Blake, meet Doreen and Numi."

Hunter said hello and sat down in the vacant chair between the two girls. Doreen was a large-breasted young woman with long, strawberry blond hair. Numi, the more attractive of the two, had short dark hair and dark eyes. She looked as if she was a combination of several different Oriental ethnic strains.

"Doreen and Numi were both in my socialization group the year I finished my diploma," Calvin said. "They've been telling me about the shortage of eligible young males here on Cicero."

"I actually met you once before," Doreen said to Hunter. "Do you remember? It was at that going-away party for Ahmad a couple of months ago."

Hunter shook his head. "There must have been sixty people at that party," he said. "And the rooms were all dark and noisy." He laughed. "Actually, I don't remember very much about anything from that night."

Hunter studied the drink menu embedded in the center of the table and made a beer selection. The message WAIT THREE MINUTES flashed.

"I understand why Calvin is still here on Cicero," Numi then said. "His family has political connections. But why hasn't the government called for your services? From what I've heard, you're bright, healthy, and unattached. I would think that Chairman Covington's recruiters would have stolen you away long before now."

"I'm working in the hospital," Hunter replied. "I finished my paramedical certification three months ago and am hoping that I'll be accepted to medical school."

"In Centralia?" Numi asked. "Or did you apply to the university in the Free Zone?"

"Both, actually," Hunter said. He grinned. "My father's afraid I'll be corrupted by the uninhibited life in the Free Zone. He would prefer that I go to Centralia."

"My cousin is studying robotics at Centralia and he says that life there is wild enough," Doreen said. She leaned forward and lowered her voice. "He's having an affair with the wife of his group project director."

The robot server appeared at the table and handed Hunter his beer. Hunter placed his thumb in the required port in the server's abdominal area and the cost of his drink was deducted from his bank account.

"Did you do well on the medical-aptitude tests?" Numi asked.

"I did all right," Hunter said. "But I'm a little worried—"

"All right?" Calvin interrupted. "Is that what you call it?" He put his arm around Hunter and addressed the girls. "You are sitting with the man who made the highest score in Cicero history on the medical-aptitude tests."

Hunter pulled away, embarrassed. As he did, he happened to look at one of the many television monitors that were scattered around the drinking area in Lucky Luigi's. Across the top of the screen was written, in big letters, SPECIAL REPORT FROM THE MAYOR. Hunter glanced quickly at the other monitors. All channels were carrying the special report, preempting everything in the network system.

Mayor Hoffman had just begun to speak. Hunter's father was sitting beside him in front of the table in the mayor's office.

"Excuse me," Hunter said, "I want to hear this." He quickly grabbed a pair of earphones from under the table. After Calvin explained that the man next to the mayor was

Hunter's father, the two girls and he also reached for earphones.

"As I'm certain you all know by now," the mayor was saying, "a tragic accident occurred outside early this afternoon. Two of Federated Engineering's best technicians, Jefferson Samuels and Warren Turner, were killed as a result of a sudden, unexpected movement by one of the large mining machines . . ."

While the mayor described the accident in words, the television monitor displayed the video recording that Hunter had seen earlier at the hospital. The portion of the video showing the two men impacting the other mining machine, bouncing up, and falling to the surface, was shown in slow motion.

The noise level in Luigi's dropped appreciably. Almost all the patrons were now watching one of the screens. "For the last four hours," the mayor continued, "Chief Engineer David Blake and his team have been investigating the cause of the accident. What they have discovered is very disturbing."

Under Hunter's father's face on the screen was written, "David Blake, Chief Engineer, Federated Engineering, Cicero Division." The camera moved in very close as Blake began to speak. Hunter could tell from his father's wrinkled brow and his facial expressions that he was under enormous stress.

"All motions of the miner result from commands issued by its central processor," David Blake said. "As part of the recertification process of Miner #7 that has been under way the last three days, the entire motion module of the miner's software was supposedly redundantly inhibited. This action was taken to preclude the kind of accident that occurred today. We only lift those inhibits during special procedures that are necessary to verify that specific repairs have been completed. The inhibits are never removed if any human beings are outside working on the miner. When today's activity began, we verified that the redundant inhibits were indeed in place."

Hunter's father paused and took a drink of water. "Within an hour after the accident," he continued, "a full readout of the history buffer of the miner was transferred to our control center. Our initial assumption for the cause of the failure that resulted in the terrible accident was that somehow the control software had malfunctioned and managed to override the inhibits in the motion module. But a detailed analysis of the readout indicated no software malfunction. In the implemented instruction set, however, we did find commands to the arm to lift upward.

"Where did these instructions come from? To our astonishment, we discovered that this morning at 9:43, while the technicians were already outside dismantling the claw electronics box, an external command message was received by the miner. This transmitted message, encrypted just as if it had been sent from our control center, removed the inhibits on the motion module and stored four delayed commands in the processor. The first of these delayed commands caused the arm to lift abruptly, dooming our technicians. The other three commands were scheduled for implementation this afternoon and evening, but have been canceled by our recent action. Needless to say, we have checked and rechecked to see if we somehow mistakenly transmitted that message ourselves. We have absolutely verified that the message this morning did NOT originate from our control center."

"Thank you for that explanation, Blake," Mayor Hoffman said. He looked back at the camera. "In layman's terms, what we apparently have here are acts of sabotage and murder. Someone, somehow, transmitted commands to the miner that resulted in the action that caused the accident. The transmission could have originated here on Cicero, or it could have come from somewhere in space. At present, we have no way of knowing. What we do know, however, is that whoever sent those signals was intimately familiar both with the coding of our miner commands and the operations of the miner software."

The mayor shuffled some papers on the table in front of him. "We have referred this case to the Anti-Sedition Police," he then said. "ASP headquarters in Centralia has informed us that several of their computer experts will be dispatched to Cicero in the very near future to continue the investigation.

"We have also had a call from Lester Sackett, the FISC Minister of Defense. He has asked us to place all Cicero on a first-stage alert, beginning immediately. Minister Sackett believes that this incident may be part of a Dem strategy to claim Cicero as one of their own territories. Since we are now inside the orbit of Mars, and will spend the next four months here, the Dems MIGHT claim that they have territorial rights to our asteroid. The Treaty of Tranquility is vague on this issue. Asteroids that CROSS the orbit of Mars are not specifically mentioned in the codicils that established the domains of the Dems and the FISC . . ."

"What does he mean?" Doreen asked, the tone of her voice betraying her concern. "Cicero has always been a Federation territory. How could the Dems claim . . . ?"

"The Treaty of Tranquility gave the Dems all territories INSIDE the orbit of Mars," Hunter explained. "We have everything outside. Cicero spends five months every two and a half years inside Mars's orbit. Nothing was explicitly said in the treaty about asteroids that are sometimes inside and sometimes outside . . ."

"But how could they have done that?" Doreen protested. "We're left . . ."

"I guess we're just not that important," Numi said. "Our

population is only one-tenth of one percent of all the space settlements."

"There are only two other inhabited asteroids in our situation," Hunter added. "And the treaty makers had many more important issues to decide."

The mayor was concluding his address. He reminded the citizens of Cicero that violation of the curfew associated with the first-stage alert could be considered treason, and urged everyone to learn and follow all the temporary rules. "This additional regimentation is designed to protect us," the mayor said, "in case of an attack. I hasten to add that there is absolutely no evidence, other than this act of sabotage this afternoon, that the Dems are planning to attack Cicero. The FISC defense minister just believes that it is a prudent act for us to establish a first-stage alert at this time."

After the mayor was finished, Hunter excused himself from his companions and, after checking one last time to make certain that Tehani was not in the room, left the bar.

THREE

HUNTER STOOD IN FRONT of his apartment door for a few seconds until the security system recognized him and released the lock. "I'm home," he shouted as he opened the door. His mother greeted him in the hallway almost immediately.

"Hello, darling," she said, kissing him on the forehead. "How was work today?"

"Not good," Hunter replied with a pained look on his face. "Let's just say it was not one of your son's better days."

The gentle alarm bell of the biometry scanner reminded Hunter that he was overdue for a scan. He took a step back and stood in front of a black device, roughly two feet long, a foot wide, and six inches high, that was resting on a shelf at chest level in a small alcove just inside the door.

"What happened?" Mrs. Blake asked.

Hunter waited a few seconds for the dozens of tiny probes inside him to dump the contents of their microscopic recorders into the biometry scanner and the ALL PARAMETERS NORMAL message to flash on the small screen on the front of the device.

"Mom," he said in a mildly unfriendly tone. "I really don't want to go into it just now. I'm tired and . . ."

Mrs. Blake's smile disappeared. "Sometimes you are so much like your father, Hunter," she said. "He never wants to talk about his work, either." She turned to walk toward the living room.

"I'm sorry, Mom," Hunter said, following her. "How is Dad, anyway? Have you spoken to him in the last few hours?"

"He called about half an hour ago from the mayor's office," she said. "He sounded really depressed. He didn't have time for a conversation. He only told me that the mayor had promised he would be home by eight-thirty at the latest. . . . I reprogrammed the dinner to be ready at eight forty-five."

Mrs. Blake sat down on the couch in the living room. Hunter stood just inside the door. "If you don't mind, Mom," he said, "I'd like to go to my room."

His mother shrugged. "Suit yourself," she said, "but please remember what I said about arguing with Octavio." Mrs. Blake activated the monitor that filled one wall of the living room. As he departed, Hunter heard a news reporter giving the details of an incursion by Dem armed forces into the Free Zone on Mars.

Hunter's bedroom was small, but well organized to take advantage of the space available. His desk, shelves, computer, monitor, and ancillary equipment were just inside the doorway, on the right. Hunter's two dressers sat against the opposite wall, on either side of the small, solitary window. Both the closet and the entrance to his personal toilet and washbasin were on the left as he entered the room. His bed was against the right wall, the foot almost touching the stack of electronics on the left side of his desk.

Hunter took off his shirt and went into the toilet area to wash his face. When he returned to his bedroom, he sat down at his desk and turned on his computer. His wrist communicator indicated that he had not received any new messages since he had left work, so Hunter bypassed the mail section and accessed the entertainment menus. Several seconds later Hunter's choices resulted in his monitor being filled with a dazzling video advertisement for Sybaris, the adult destination resort in the Free Zone that was operated by Federation Entertainments. FedEnt, as it was called by everybody, was actually one of the largest branches of the FISC government. The enormous annual profits from its resorts, network gambling, virtual worlds, and music and video enterprises significantly reduced the taxes that citizens of the FISC were required to pay.

"Whatever your pleasure," a beautiful feminine voice intoned as the camera panned around the many different venues of the resort, "you can find it at Sybaris."

Hunter watched for half a minute as the narrator peppered her quick tour of Sybaris with superlatives. Hunting, fishing, golf, tennis, skiing, food, music, dancing, beaches, theater, virtual worlds, gambling, and "unparalleled physical pleasures"—all these attractions were available inside the fantasy world of Sybaris. All the visitor had to do was simply express his or her vacation desires, and a "vacation counselor" would set up the holiday of a lifetime.

Sybaris vacation counselors were available twenty-four hours a day. If the potential visitor would fill out a simple one-page survey, he or she would receive a personal vidmail from an experienced counselor in less than two hours, and the vacation planning would commence. Hunter did not follow the prompt, choosing instead to access the Guides area on the submenu list.

"The guides at Sybaris are trained to maximize the quality of your vacation experience," another female voice said, as a video played showing groups of varying sizes, accompanied by guides in their distinctive red coats, enjoying the wonders of Sybaris. "We have guides for groups, ranging in size from three persons to thirty, and we have our famous Sybaris hosts and hostesses, who are companions to individuals or couples throughout their entire stay in our spectacular resort. Group guides are assigned by our Guest Relations Department, depending on the characteristics of the vacationing group. Reservations must be made for the individual hosts and hostesses."

Hunter selected the "Hosts and Hostesses" category. On his monitor he was provided with seven options. He could View Gallery, Read Mail, Send Mail, Make a Reservation, See Male Private Escorts, See Female Private Escorts, or Exit. Hunter chose to view the gallery. An alphabetical list of the hundred or so hosts and hostesses who were available as guides for individuals or couples appeared on his screen. Hunter quickly scrolled down the list to the bottom. Tehani's name was not there.

He next attempted to access See Female Private Escorts. A beautiful, casually dressed blond woman in her mid to late twenties, sitting behind a simple desk, with Sybaris posters on the wall behind her, appeared on Hunter's monitor.

"Because of the overwhelming demand for access to this particular site," she said, "your network account will be charged five dollars for each minute that you are browsing. If you do indeed make a reservation with one of our private escorts, and spend a vacation at Sybaris, your browsing charges will be credited to your account. Please enter your personal password and you will be transferred to the desired location."

Hunter paused a moment, thinking about the cost, and then entered his password. Sixteen thumbnail photographs in four rows and four columns were immediately displayed on his screen. Underneath each of the photographs was the pictured woman's name. Tehani was next to last in the alphabetical list, in the bottom right-hand corner of the page.

"I am Tehani Wilawa," the video began a few seconds later, "and I would be delighted to be your private escort at Sybaris for a vacation you will never forget." Tehani was standing beside a couch in the living room of a beautiful suite in one of the resort's hotels. She was wearing a long purple cocktail dress that was slit up one side, and matching solid purple high heels with single ankle straps. The dress was cut low enough that her ample cleavage was visible, but not so low that it would have been considered tawdry. As Tehani walked toward the camera, turning slightly, her magnificent long black hair could be seen cascading down her back to below her waist. The subdued background music, a soft string concerto, increased in volume while she was moving forward.

Hunter took a deep breath. This was a new video, expensive and expertly done. Tehani was more beautiful than ever. He didn't hear much of what she actually said during the forty-five-second presentation. Hunter just listened to her voice, watched her move gracefully around the room, and fantasized that he was there, with her, in that hotel suite.

The camera came in for a close-up near the end. Tehani smiled warmly, showing her perfect white teeth, and explained that she was committed to giving her companions the "experience of a lifetime." Hunter was staring fixedly at her almond-shaped brown eyes when they disappeared from the screen.

A number of choices confronted Hunter on the monitor after Tehani's image vanished. In the upper right-hand corner, a digital display counted the seconds since the special site had been entered. Hunter started to select a repeat of Tehani's video, but he decided that he would watch it at another time. He exited, and the screen reminded him of the amount of money that was being removed from his bank account.

HUNTER SAT IN his desk chair for over a minute without moving. A montage of images flooded his mind in no particular sequence. The pictures had one thing in common. Tehani was in all of them. Hunter's thoughts during this time were jumbled. He was being bombarded by so many different emotions and sensations that he couldn't possibly make any sense out of them.

He reached into his bottom desk drawer, into a carton of used data cubes, and found one labeled "Ti." He pulled out the cube and inserted it into his computer. Several seconds later an image of Hunter and Tehani, together at a party, filled the monitor. Under the picture were the words DIPLOMA CELEBRATION: JULY 2406.

They were both laughing in the photograph. They had laughed most of the night. Hunter and Tehani had made the two highest scores in Cicero on the secondary-school final examinations that year. They had just found out that day that both of them had won the Covington Medal of Distinction for their outstanding scores, the only time in Cicero history that two new graduates had earned the Covington Medal in the same year. No wonder they had celebrated. Hunter and Tehani had danced for hours, and had drunk almost every kind of beverage available at the party.

I was wildly, deliriously happy, Hunter remembered as he sat at his desk. *I had exceeded my expectations on the exams and I was with the most beautiful girl in the solar system.*

They had left the party at about three o'clock in the morning. On the transportation platform, holding on to each other for stability, they had nearly slipped and fallen together. "I know what you're doing, Hunter Blake,"

Tehani had slurred, in between bouts of laughter. "First you got me drunk, and now you think you're going to take advantage of me."

"Who got who drunk?" Hunter had protested. "Or is it who got whom?" He had then burst into silly laughter himself.

"I like whom got whom," Tehani had stammered. "It may be wrong, but it has a certain poetic ring to it."

A couple in their thirties had joined them on the platform while Hunter and Tehani were still laughing nonsensically. "I apologize," Tehani had said with difficulty to the couple, "both for my behavior and for this strange character with me. We're celebrating, and I'm afraid we're both a little drunk."

When we reached her apartment, though, Hunter remembered, *she didn't seem so drunk. She told her mother that we were in the living room, made us some coffee, and curled up in my arms. Then she kissed me. She REALLY kissed me.*

Hunter and Tehani had been together a couple of times before the diploma celebration evening, but always in the company of others. They had held hands, and exchanged perfunctory good-night kisses, but nothing even mildly sexual had ever occurred. That early morning in Tehani's apartment, Hunter was completely overwhelmed by her kisses and affection. He had become aroused and aggressive.

Wait, my darling, she told me. There will be a better time and a better place. My mother or my little brother could walk in at any moment.

Still deep in his memories, Hunter absentmindedly called up other items from the data cube and displayed them on the screen. He quickly scanned through all his correspondence with Tehani from the time period, comparing the intimacy of their daily vidmail messages after the diploma celebration with the friendly, but almost formal, nature of the messages before. They had had dinner with his family the following week, and Tehani had charmed everyone. Because of their part-time work and busy schedules, an opportunity for Hunter and Tehani to be alone had not occurred until the beginning of August. One evening her mother was scheduled to take Tehani's little brother to a birthday party in the adjacent apartment building.

"Darling," her written message to Hunter on August 2 had begun. "I didn't want to send you vidmail because I'm a mess. But I have some very good news. Mom and Tesoro will be out at a party tonight. For two or three hours. She told me I can have you over to the apartment for dinner."

Reading the note from Tehani again catapulted Hunter back in time to that pivotal day almost two years earlier. *I thought it was going to be the best day of my life,* he remembered. *But it turned out to be one of the worst.*

The evening had started out well enough. Tehani had greeted Hunter at the door with an incredible kiss. She had then backed away quickly, with a little-girl grin on her face. "Patience is a virtue," Tehani had said laughingly, as she had danced away from Hunter's outstretched arms.

He had pursued her into the small living room, but she had been too quick for him. "After dinner there will be plenty of time," Tehani had said when Hunter had finally calmed down and sat down on the couch. "Mom and Tesoro won't be home for at least three hours. Besides, I want to prove to you that I can serve a fantastic meal."

Hunter had laughed. "Your mother probably set up everything before she left," he had said.

"She did NOT," Tehani had replied immediately, acting offended. A few seconds later her expression changed to a wry smile. "Well, maybe she helped me a little bit," she had said. "I wanted everything to be perfect for you."

The meal had indeed been marvelous. Hunter and Tehani had talked easily about a wide range of subjects. After they had eaten, Tehani had quickly cleaned up and joined him on the couch.

"What would you like to do now?" she had asked Hunter coquettishly as she had snuggled softly into his arms.

"As if you don't know . . ." he had replied, bending down to kiss her.

The next ten minutes were unmitigated ecstasy, Hunter thought, surprised at the clarity of detail in his recollection. *Never before, and never since, have I experienced anything even remotely similar. She seemed to know how to make me unbelievably comfortable and drive me wild with passion at the same time.*

With Hunter disheveled and consumed with desire, Tehani had then risen from the couch, holding his hand, and backed up slowly into her bedroom. In quick succession she had gently tugged his pants down and taken off her blouse and bra. In her bedroom, Tehani had walked slowly toward Hunter, her eyes smiling with love. She had pressed herself against him, and kissed him insistently, her tongue tickling the inside of his mouth to heighten his longing. Hunter had picked her up off the floor and carried her to the bed. For several minutes he had straddled her, kissing her furiously.

Finally Hunter had sat up and yanked off his underpants. Tehani had effortlessly slid out of her pants and underwear. She had been lying there waiting for him, a naked goddess, his for the taking, when her telephone rang.

Tehani had reached up and kissed Hunter, ignoring the phone. He hadn't been quite as able to block out the intrusive noise coming from beside the bed. He had broken the kiss, put his arms around her, and waited for the sound to stop.

"Miss Wilawa," Hunter had then heard a woman's voice say from the recording device, "this is Rebecca Davis, the night communications manager at the mayor's office. I have just received an urgent vidmail from Personnel at FedEnt. Apparently they have sent you several messages in the last few days and you have not responded. They are concerned that perhaps your personal communications system has malfunctioned. Would you please verify to me, and to them, that you have indeed received their correspondence. My number is 3682–9144. Thank you."

At first she wouldn't answer my questions, Hunter remembered. *She just laughed and told me that the call was about a job with FedEnt. But I kept pressing her. Eventually Tehani informed me that she had already accepted the job as a private escort at Sybaris. I went wild.*

She told me as I stalked out in anger that she had intended to tell me about Sybaris before I went home, but not until after we had made love. She hadn't wanted anything to ruin our first time together. Hunter closed his eyes and heaved a huge sigh. *I acted like a prima donna, an absolute ass,* he said to himself. *I said nasty things I didn't mean. I called her names. I wouldn't let her explain anything.*

Another message from the past, the last file from the same data cube, soon filled Hunter's monitor. It was dated August 4, 2406, and was signed by Tehani.

"Hunter," it began, "do you by any chance remember this quotation from Dostoevsky's *The Idiot*? I believe it was one of Natasha's responses to Prince Myshkin."

You know nothing but the truth, and have no tenderness, and thus you judge unjustly.

HUNTER WAS EXHAUSTED. He couldn't have explained all the things he was feeling, but a sense of loss and a desperate yearning were certainly components of the complex emotions that were engulfing him.

He turned off his computer and rose from his desk chair.

He walked slowly over to his bed and plopped down upon it.

Hunter fell asleep immediately. Tehani was in all his dreams. His sister Amanda's voice outside his bedroom door awakened him half an hour later.

FOUR

"CATCHING A SHORT NAP, were you, little brother?" his sister Amanda said. She gave him a warm hug when he opened his bedroom door.

"What time is it?" Hunter asked, still groggy from the abrupt awakening.

"A little after eight," Amanda said. "We just got here. Octavio and I are having a drink. Would you like to join us?"

Hunter nodded and followed Amanda down the hall. His sister was five years older than he was, and had been married for almost three years. Hunter and Amanda had not been that close when Hunter was a child, but in the last two years they had become better friends. Amanda had been having difficulty with her marriage and had occasionally even sought Hunter's advice.

"Danielle fell asleep right after we arrived," Amanda said. "She'll probably wake up and scream all through dinner."

Octavio Gonzalez, Amanda's outspoken husband, was twenty-six. He was a cargo agent for Federated Shipping. His main responsibility was planning incoming cargo shipments. With the escalation of the tension between the two rival space powers, his job had become a nightmare. Scheduled freighter arrivals at Cicero had dropped markedly and the number of containers allocated for "nonessential" items was only half what it had been a few years earlier.

Octavio spent most of his day dealing with people's complaints. He was unhappy with his job, but unfortunately he had not been able to find any other employment on Cicero that was satisfactory. Octavio wanted to move, either back to North Mars where he had grown up, or even to the Free Zone. Amanda, however, was not willing to leave her family home on Cicero. The issue produced constant friction in their marriage and remained unresolved.

Octavio was in the kitchen when Hunter and Amanda reached the living room. "Can I get you something to drink?" Octavio asked.

"A beer, please," Hunter said.

Octavio came into the living room carrying Hunter's beer. He sat down in the chair on the other side of the coffee table that was in front of the couch. "Your mother told us you had a bad day at the hospital," Octavio said. "Welcome to the club. Now you know how most of us feel when we leave the office."

"Actually, it wasn't THAT bad," Hunter answered. "Our schedule was kind of screwed up by the accident. . . . Then this afternoon I made a couple of mistakes."

"What?" Octavio said, taking a drink of his beer. "The golden boy made a couple of mistakes? Are my ears deceiving me?"

Amanda shot a disapproving glance at her husband and turned to Hunter. "I don't understand," she said. "I thought the men were dead before they were back inside the dome. Why did the accident affect your schedule?"

"At first, nobody knew for certain they were dead," Hunter said. "The hospital was asked to prepare for any contingency."

Octavio scoffed. "Didn't any of you medical types watch the video?" he said. "How could they possibly have survived?"

Hunter ignored the unpleasant tone in his brother-in-law's voice. "We all thought the technicians were probably dead, Octavio," he said, "but we proceeded, as requested, with our preparations to take care of them if they were still alive."

Mrs. Blake walked into the room. She was not aware that there was an ongoing conversation. "Did any of you see that special segment on *Today* about the pirates?" she asked. "Mrs. Griffith swears she saw Chelsea Dickinson in one of the sequences. I watched it hurriedly this morning, but I'm not sure I would recognize Chelsea after all this time."

"Was she that short girl who helped you prepare for your math finals?" Hunter asked Amanda.

His sister nodded. "Chelsea was really smart, but a little on the weird side. She apparently did very well her first two years at Centralia University. Then she dropped out, for some reason, and went to work as a cocktail waitress in the Free Zone. I lost track of her after that."

"Her older brother's still here on Cicero," Octavio said. "He works in some trivial job in the network office. Rumor says he's an undercover agent for the ASP."

Amanda turned on the wall monitor. "Was it the most recent segment of *Today*, Mom, or one of the earlier ones?"

"I think it was posted on Monday," Mrs. Blake said, "but I'm not certain."

Octavio went to the kitchen for another beer while Amanda located the *Today* segment they had been discussing. Mrs. Blake was sitting on the couch between her son and daughter when the program began.

The host of the magazine show was a handsome, polished Oriental man in his mid-thirties. He explained that

Today had obtained some "sensational video footage" from a young woman who had renounced her life as a pirate and somehow managed to return to her parents' home in a small city on North Mars. This video, which would be presented later in the segment, was taken over a two-year period, the host asserted, and showed life among three different groups of the pirates.

A lovely female reporter provided background information on the pirates. Using maps and other visual aids, she showed the hundred or so abandoned space stations or asteroids that were possible habitats for the various pirate groups, and estimated that the total number of "these renegades," including their many sympathizers in the Free Zone, could be as high as ten thousand. "They are mostly disillusioned young people under thirty," she added, "with both Dem and Fed backgrounds, who have chosen their outlaw lives either because they have been in trouble with the law or don't want to conform to the rules of the two established space societies."

"Bullshit propaganda," Octavio interrupted in a loud voice. Amanda temporarily paused the video. The three Blakes on the couch all politely looked at Octavio.

"Would you like to say something else?" Amanda asked, an acerbic edge to her voice. "Or should I continue with *Today*?"

"I just get tired of the crap the government feeds us, day in and day out," Octavio said. "Everything about the Dems is bad; everything about the FISC is great, or at least as good as it can be. No reasonable young person would want to escape from monitoring, or conscription, or fear of the ASP. Of course not . . . It's just possible that some of these young 'renegades' are idealists, and don't want their lives controlled by old farts."

Nobody said anything for several seconds. Then Mrs. Blake spoke. "Excuse me, Octavio," she said, "and please don't take offense, but could you please not make statements like that after Mr. Blake comes home? He's had a very tough day and—"

"And you don't want me to upset him," Octavio rudely finished her sentence. "Okay, Mrs. Blake, I'll curb my tongue, and act like everything is peachy-keen in my life. I'm guessing you also don't want me to mention that my résumé is in circulation on Mars and that I can't wait to say good-bye to this hunk of iron and nickel."

"Honey," Amanda said, making no attempt to conceal her displeasure and embarrassment, "could I talk to you for a minute? In private?"

"That won't be necessary," Octavio said. He heaved a sigh. "I'm sorry, Mrs. Blake, you're a nice lady and don't deserve my harassment. I'm frustrated, that's all. I'll just sit here and drink my beer and keep my mouth shut."

Amanda wasn't satisfied. "Please forgive him, Mother," she said. "Octavio sometimes says things just to shock people. He probably doesn't even believe all the things he says."

Octavio glared at his wife and took another drink of beer. "On with the pirate show," he said.

THEY WATCHED THE next several minutes of the *Today* segment on the space pirates without comment. In the rest of her brief background piece, the reporter explained that the pirates preyed on unprotected interplanetary cruisers, primarily privately owned vessels, stealing computer equipment and even weapons and spare parts as well as water, food, and other essentials that supplemented what they were able to produce themselves. "Because of the tensions between the two great space powers," the reporter concluded, "the pirates are currently enjoying an extended period of benign neglect. The FISC Minister of Defense,

Mr. Lester Sackett, has described them as a 'pesky nuisance' and has warned that they will be 'eradicated' if their actions compromise Fed lives or property."

The supposedly sensational video footage was of poor quality. The snippets of pirate life really didn't reveal much, except that the pirates existed in disparate groups, sometimes wore strange clothes, often carried weapons, and were mostly young men. One of the short pieces showed a communal nursery at an undisclosed location, with four women and two men taking care of ten or eleven small children. The children were unkempt and uncontrolled, causing Mrs. Blake to wince.

In one sequence an armed female soldier, wearing some kind of identifying insignia on her blouse, handed what appeared to be a rocket weapon to a male colleague. Amanda immediately recognized Chelsea Dickinson as the armed soldier and stopped the program. She used the controls to zoom in on the image until Chelsea's face filled the monitor. Amanda requested a hard-copy printout of the selected image. The small printer in the corner of the living room was stirred into action.

"It is Chelsea," she said. "There's no doubt about it."

"Her parents seem to be such nice people," Mrs. Blake said. "Why in the world would Chelsea do something like this?"

"Hundreds of reasons," Octavio replied, finishing his beer. "Adventure, love, money, anger, a desire to be different—there's no logical explanation for human behavior, especially for teenagers and postadolescents."

"Why, darling," Amanda said, "that's the closest thing to wisdom I've heard out of your mouth in a long time."

Octavio smiled. "As much as I talk," he said, "I'm bound to say something intelligent sooner or later."

The phone rang and Mr. Blake's tired visage appeared on the main monitor in the living room. "Hello, dear," he said, addressing his wife. "I apologize, but it looks as if I'm going to be another hour or so. Maybe you and the kids should go ahead and eat."

"We'd like to wait for you," Mrs. Blake said. "As long as we know that you will indeed be coming home at a reasonable time."

Blake sighed. "I can't imagine that we can last that much longer. Everyone is hungry, and the mayor has said twice that we will not work through dinner."

"I have some munchies to keep us from starving to death," Mrs. Blake said. "Why don't I program dinner to be ready by nine-thirty? If you're not home by then, we'll start without you."

"Thanks," Blake said. "That sounds like a good compromise. I'll try to make it by then."

Mrs. Blake went immediately into the kitchen after the phone call was over. Amanda stood up from the couch. "So we have an extra hour, and Danielle is asleep. I know what I want to do. . . . Mom," she yelled, "is it all right if I use the kiosk?"

Mrs. Blake gave an affirmative response. "Back to the land of chivalrous knights, dragons, and damsels in distress?" Octavio asked in a sarcastic tone.

"As I have told you before, Mr. Gonzalez," Amanda said defensively, "there are no damsels in distress in 'Camelot.' The world is an authentic reproduction of the age of King Arthur. The visuals are glorious, the music is fantastic, and the possibilities almost limitless. In the latest edition of *Virtual World* on the network, both the magazine's regular reviewers referred to it as a work of genius. FedEnt spent over a hundred million dollars on its design."

"That's for the fully interactive version with all its bells and whistles," Octavio said. "Most of the capability is superfluous for a user on Cicero, because you can only interact in real time with avatars of people who are currently on this asteroid."

"Why must you always be disparaging about something I like?" Amanda said, showing some pique. "The entire Leicester Castle subworld has been allocated to Cicero, and we do interact with each other in real time. We correspond with the other players active in the game by electronic mail. . . . This is stupid. I don't need to explain myself to you. I ENJOY Camelot. For the most part, my life there is more interesting than the real world. And the people I meet are a whole lot nicer."

"That's why FedEnt makes the big bucks," Octavio said, trying to have the last word as Amanda left the room.

Octavio stood up. "Do you want another beer?" he asked Hunter.

Hunter shook his head. "Why don't you leave Amanda alone about 'Camelot'?" he asked his brother-in-law. "It obviously gives her pleasure. . . . What harm does it do?"

"Do you want the short or long list of my objections to this virtual-world crap?" Octavio said.

"The short list will do," Hunter replied.

"First, it's expensive. Every minute Amanda spends in the kiosk in the plaza costs us half a dollar. Sometimes, if I'm at home and Danielle takes a long nap, Amanda will remain immersed in that fantasy world for more than TWO hours. And usually she doesn't come home until I signal her pager that the baby has awakened. And that's just the usage cost, and doesn't begin to cover the special clothing, or electronic gear to 'enhance' the verisimilitude."

Octavio loved to lecture anyone who would listen. The two beers he had drunk added to his volubility. "Second," he continued, "virtual worlds are psychologically addicting and, in my opinion, make it more difficult for people to deal with reality. Why shouldn't Amanda be happier in

'Camelot'? She's a duchess in that fantasy world. She has ladies-in-waiting. Handsome young men pay homage to her when her husband, the duke, is off dealing with his minions. No babies cry, or need to be diapered. No bills need to be paid. No husbands criticize you for not having accomplished anything all day. And that's just the beginning. . . .

"Have you ever seen what Amanda's avatar looks like in 'Camelot'? Well, I have. The Duchess of Leicester is stunning. She has huge breasts and a small waist, both attributes that Amanda will never have in the real world. The duke looks like a model. In reality, he's probably some wimpy nerd with a runny nose and bad breath, but hey, in the imaginary world of 'Camelot,' he's the quintessential Prince Charming."

Hunter had started to laugh. "I'm sure glad that you don't have a strong opinion on this subject," he said. "I'd hate to see how excited you would become then."

"Hey, this is serious shit," Octavio rejoined. "Especially on Mars. A recent article indicated that more than a quarter of the people there spend over six hours a day as alter egos, or avatars, in the virtual worlds created by FedEnt. People aren't living their real lives, Hunter. They're escaping into fantasy. . . . I can't get Amanda to express an opinion about any political issue. I'm not sure she cares whether our great leader Covington is a dictator or not, as long as she has access to a kiosk where she can take on another identity."

"I think you're overreacting, Octavio," Hunter said. "Amanda's just fascinated with the virtual world for the time being. Right after I finished my school exams, I spent at least an hour every day in the Rama world. It helped me unwind."

"Now THAT use was legitimate," Octavio said, preparing to launch another tirade. "On the other hand, your sister doesn't have enough hours in the day to take care of everything. She can't afford to be sitting on her ass, assuming she's the Duchess of Leicester or some other bullshit. . . ."

Hunter realized that nothing he could say would soften Octavio's stance significantly. His brother-in-law was like that. He stubbornly adhered to his opinions, even if they proved to be absolutely wrong.

TRUE TO OCTAVIO'S prediction, Amanda did not emerge from the kiosk in the game room until after Blake arrived home. Soon after entering the apartment, where he was greeted in the entryway by his wife and son, Chief Engineer Blake stopped in front of the biometry scanner, as he dutifully did twice a day, and four yellow warnings were triggered by the recorded data dumped from the probes inside his body to the biometry processor.

Blake tried to dismiss the warnings. "They're just telling me what I already know," he said to his wife, "that I'm tired and need more rest. I had three yellows this morning, and two last night."

"One of the yellows is from the probe near your left ventricle," Hunter said, examining the data on the screen closely. "According to hospital recommendations for people your age, after five yellows in any forty-eight-hour period, you're supposed to report to a physician for a checkup."

"Thanks, son," Blake said in a slightly patronizing tone. "As soon as I'm caught up on my work, which will be never, I'll stop by to see Dr. Ekanayake."

"When the full biometry system is back on-line," Hunter continued, "your yellows will be tabulated, and a report will be sent to Dr. Ekanayake. He'll probably call you."

"Can we drop this subject now?" Blake said. "I'm

hungry, and I want to see my granddaughter. We can worry about my health later."

Mrs. Blake and Hunter exchanged concerned glances as the three of them walked into the living room, but neither of them said anything else about the biometry results.

"Hi, Dad," Amanda said a few minutes later, coming out of the game room and giving her father a big hug. "It's good to see you." She paused for a moment. "I'm sorry about the accident. I know how much this recertification thing meant to you."

"Not as much as those technicians," Blake said, sitting down in his chair after accepting a beer from Octavio with a thank-you. "One of them, Jefferson Samuels, has been working in my department for almost eight years. . . . I sent his wife a vidmail, expressing my sorrow, and volunteered to drop by to offer my condolences in person. She thanked me but said that she was too devastated to see me."

Blake sat silently on his chair for several seconds and drank his beer. Then he suddenly stood up. "Now where's my granddaughter?" he said, walking out of the room.

As if on cue, Danielle began to gurgle. She was resting in what had once been Amanda's bedroom, but had since been converted into Blake's home office. Hunter's father picked her up and cradled her in his arms. "How are you, little one?" he said.

The baby girl responded to his attentions with a huge, innocent smile. "She always smiles for you," Amanda said proudly. Octavio and she had followed her father into the room where the portable crib was stored. The three of them exchanged small talk for a minute or two while Blake rocked the baby back and forth. Octavio thanked Blake for having them over for dinner and even said, in response to a question, that his day had been "all right."

"Dinner is served," Mrs. Blake shouted from the dining

room. The members of the family washed up and took their seats at the table. Blake opened the meal by requesting that there be no more discussion of the mining accident until after dinner. "We don't have an opportunity to eat together like this very often," he said, "and I want it to be as enjoyable as possible."

"Have you seen Tehani yet?" Amanda asked Hunter when they were halfway through the soup course.

"Not yet," Hunter said. He quickly shook his head while Amanda was looking at him, hoping she would understand that this was not a topic he wanted to discuss.

"Is she here? On Cicero?" Mrs. Blake said. She turned to Hunter. "Why didn't you tell me? When did she arrive?"

"Now that is one beautiful girl," Blake said before Hunter could answer. "And smart . . . She went to work for FedEnt right after her diploma, didn't she? What's she doing these days?"

"She's still working at Sybaris," Hunter answered matter-of-factly. He then abruptly changed the subject, complaining about how impossible it was for the health-services people on Cicero to do their job when the main biometry processor was always crashing. This discussion carried into the serving of the main course.

"There was a fascinating segment featuring Tehani on *EXPOSURE* last month," Octavio said during a subsequent break in the conversation. He smiled and looked across the table at Hunter. "Didn't any of you see it?"

"No, I didn't," Mrs. Blake said with obvious interest. "I almost never watch that program. . . . Hunter, darling, why didn't you tell me?"

Hunter squirmed in his seat. His emotions were in turmoil. He had a powerful desire to strangle Octavio and, at the same time, an inner voice was telling him not to overreact or he would make the situation worse.

"I don't remember," Hunter said. "I think it was when I was working night shift and was only seeing you for a few minutes each day."

"Still," Mrs. Blake said, "a special feature on Tehani on *EXPOSURE*? I would have thought you would have insisted that I watch it."

"They said she's the most in demand of all the hostesses at Sybaris," Octavio said, ignoring the looks he was receiving from both Hunter and Amanda. "Apparently people reserve her services as much as a year ahead of time. . . . And they had testimonials from satisfied customers who praised her as if she were a queen."

"My goodness, Hunter," Mrs. Blake said, turning to her son. "I can't believe you didn't tell me about this. I would think you would be so proud. . . ."

"Is Tehani a private escort at Sybaris?" Blake said sharply, finally understanding the undercurrent at the table.

Hunter swallowed hard. "Yes, she is," he said in a near mumble.

Mrs. Blake was in denial. "A private escort?" she repeated. "That lovely girl who had dinner at this table with us is a private escort at Sybaris? Isn't that . . . don't they . . ."

Hunter could take no more. He stood up, fighting to control his emotions. "If you don't mind," he said, his voice trembling, "I'd like to excuse myself. I'm not feeling very well."

He didn't wait for a response. Hunter heard Octavio say the words "glorified prostitute" just as he opened his bedroom door.

HUNTER THREW HIMSELF on his bed, facedown. He was as miserable as he had ever been in his life. He was angry with himself for not having stopped the conversation about Tehani soon after it started. Hunter was also absolutely furious with Octavio. In his mind's eye, he uncoiled a vicious punch and smashed Octavio's smiling face to smithereens.

But the primary emotion he was feeling was overwhelming embarrassment. Hunter knew that his mother's look of startled disbelief was indelibly burned into his memory. *My parents now know,* Hunter thought, recoiling in agony on his bed, *that the only girl I ever told them was special to me has become a high-priced whore at Sybaris.*

"Whore." Hunter said the word twice out loud, the second time twisting it with a nasty sneer. *Whore,* he remembered, *that's what I called her that night in her apartment. That's what made her start crying. Tehani told me that I didn't understand.*

A sudden heartache, so powerful that he was temporarily unable to breathe, engulfed Hunter. *Oh, Tehani, why why why?* he thought. Tears sprang into his eyes and he felt as if he was going to sob. Hunter checked himself just in time. He calmed his unbridled emotions with long, deep breaths and a resolute will. *I will not cry for her,* he told himself. *She is not worth it.*

Hunter continued to lie on his bed. His eyes were open, but he was not seeing anything. *I never should have said anything about her to my parents,* he thought. *I never should have invited her home for dinner.*

He realized that someone had been knocking softly on his door for several seconds. Puzzled, Hunter crossed his room and opened the door. It was his father.

"May I come in?" Blake asked.

Hunter backed up as his father entered the room. "I hope I'm not intruding," Blake said awkwardly, "but I thought maybe I could be of some help."

Hunter's father walked over next to the window. He gazed out at the nearby apartment buildings for several seconds before turning and looking at Hunter. "Son," he said, "I'm not very good at these things . . ."

His voice trailed off. Blake blinked a couple of times, then looked out the window again. "I know you're suffering," he said softly. "And there's really not much anybody can do to make it easier for you. . . . I apologize for Octavio. Deep down, I don't really think he wanted to hurt you. He's just young, and confused, and frustrated."

Hunter's father turned around and walked back toward his son. "But that's not what I really wanted to tell you. . . . It's about Tehani. You know, her father died only six months or so before you two . . . before she came over to dinner that night. Roger Griffith was the probate officer for Mr. Wilawa's estate. Tehani's father had been a compulsive gambler for many years. Apparently he gambled on the network nearly every day."

Hunter was staring at his father with a bewildered look. He did not yet understand why his dad was talking about Tehani's father. "When he died," Blake continued, "Mr. Wilawa owed FedEnt an enormous amount of money. He had made FedEnt the beneficiary of all his life insurance, but even that wasn't nearly enough. The family was technically bankrupt. Roger shared all this with me because he was so concerned about Mrs. Wilawa and the children."

Hunter sat down on the side of his bed. His mind was exploding with questions. "Under FISC law," his father said, "FedEnt can attach all the assets of the family to secure payment for the unpaid debt. Roger offered to find someone to help Mrs. Wilawa, but she turned him down when she realized that any benefactor would need to know about her husband's gambling problem."

Blake put his hand on Hunter's shoulder. "I don't know if any of this information is worth anything to you," he said gently. "But it might have something to do with Tehani's choice of employment, and I thought . . ."

Hunter stood up and hugged his father. This time he didn't suppress the tears that started flowing from his eyes. "Thank you, Dad," he said.

HUNTER STAYED IN his room after his father left. He sat at his desk, in front of the camera, and composed half a dozen different vidmail messages to Tehani, none of which was transmitted. He recorded a couple of them, hoping that maybe after the fact they wouldn't seem so stupid. But unfortunately none of them satisfied him.

Hunter was in his bathroom, still thinking about Tehani, when the alarm sounded. At first Hunter thought that there was a fire in the apartment building, but when he listened more carefully, he realized that what he was hearing was the emergency siren. He jumped up quickly and joined the rest of his family in the living room.

Mrs. Blake was in a panic. She could only find two of the emergency packs that all Cicero families were supposed to keep fully equipped at all times. "There's SIX of us, David, including Danielle," she said as she feverishly stuffed extra supplies into a box that she had found in her closet. "What are we going to do?"

"Extra water is the most important thing," Blake said. "Don't worry about more food—we can survive on what we have if necessary."

The wall monitor was blinking the word EMERGENCY every three seconds. A man's voice kept repeating that the Cicero mayor would have an announcement "momentarily." The sirens continued to wail and Danielle, sensing the tension around her, was crying uncontrollably.

"Help Octavio check the packs," Blake said when he saw Hunter. "Make sure we haven't pilfered anything essential from them."

The wall monitor suddenly showed a picture of the

mayor in his office. "Citizens of Cicero," he began, "three unidentified spacecraft are approaching our asteroid at a very high speed. During the last hour, we have attempted to contact these spacecraft by a variety of methods. We have had no response. The spacecraft have also failed to follow the accepted interplanetary protocol of periodically broadcasting their identification information.

"Recently, after conferring with FISC headquarters, we warned the intruders that if they continued on their current course, we would be forced to fire our defensive missiles. Since that warning, the spacecraft have increased their speed in our direction. They are now on a trajectory that will place them within range of our missiles in forty-five minutes. We will commence firing at that time if the spacecraft do not change their flight paths.

"Therefore, evacuate your living units and go to your assigned shelters as quickly as possible. Take your emergency supplies. It is our intention, for safety reasons, to seal all the shelters thirty minutes from the end of this transmission. Good luck to all of us."

FIVE

THE BLAKES WERE OUT in the apartment corridor five minutes later. Octavio was carrying Danielle and two of her blankets. Amanda had a diaper bag into which she had stuffed, at the last minute, some toys for her daughter. Hunter and Mr. Blake were each carrying one of the two emergency packs on their backs and Hunter had his mother's extra box in one of his hands.

A dozen people were already in the corridor, most heading for the elevators in the center of the apartment. Mr. Blake led the family to the left, toward the emergency stairs on the outside of the building. "The elevators will be jammed," he said in a loud voice. "We're better off using the stairs."

The Blake apartment was on the fourth floor of an eight-story building. Each floor had ten units, five on either side of the elevator. Altogether just over two hundred people lived in their building. The assigned shelter was below the surface of the asteroid, halfway between the Blakes' building and its twin companion. It was designed to accommodate a maximum of five hundred Cicero citizens.

An eerie scene, like something out of a nightmare,

confronted the Blakes when they opened the door to the stairway. The sound of the emergency siren, which had been attenuated by the walls of their apartment building, became almost terrifyingly loud. People were everywhere, above and below them on the stairs, on the outside stairways of the companion building, and on the grass in the park that separated the two apartment structures. Across the way, two teenagers were floating to the ground after jumping from the third-floor landing. Although the Sun was currently shining on the other side of the slowly rotating asteroid, there was sufficient illumination that it was not dark. In addition to the lights on the outside of the apartments and other buildings, the great lights on the underside of the inner dome were also lit, because of the emergency, adding a surrealistic aura to the entire townscape.

An elderly couple was standing in the middle of the fourth-floor landing. Slightly up the stairs, a man, woman, and their two small children were descending toward the same platform. "Remember to keep one foot on a stair at all times," the man was saying sternly to his children, "or you could float away and bang into somebody else."

There was a traffic jam on the fourth-floor platform. Octavio and a wailing Danielle were at the front of the Blake family, standing just beyond the door. Hunter was next, wedged into the doorway. Everyone else was behind them. The elderly couple, their packs neatly adjusted on their backs, were still not moving, and there was not sufficient room to go around them safely.

"Excuse me," Octavio said in a loud voice, trying to be heard above the siren and Danielle's cries, "would you please move to the side so that the rest of us can pass?"

The man turned around haltingly, looking first at Octavio and Danielle, and then at the impatient family descending the stairs from above. "My wife's frightened and out of breath," he said slowly. "We stopped here to let her rest."

Octavio softened. "In that case," he said pleasantly to the elderly man, "why don't you and your wife stand over here, against the rail, so that everyone else can go by?" He turned to the woman. "Would you like for me to help you?" Octavio said.

Both Octavio and Hunter could tell from the woman's eyes that she was in bad shape. She was either in shock, or very close to it. The woman clearly saw them, but she neither responded nor acknowledged their existence. At length Hunter gently took her arm and nudged her slowly over to the corner of the landing. Her husband followed. "Thank you, young man," the elderly man said. The family of four hurried past them, followed by the contingent of Blakes. Mr. Blake was at the rear of the group.

"Go on," Hunter said to his father as he passed. "I'll find you inside the shelter. This lady won't make it on her own."

Mr. Blake checked his watch. "Okay," he said, "but remember, the shelter will be sealed in twenty-two minutes."

"I'm Kurt Nordquist," the elderly gentleman said to Hunter several seconds later, when the landing was temporarily empty except for the three of them. "This is my wife, Brigitte. She's ninety-four years old."

Hunter introduced himself. For over a minute Mr. Nordquist made small talk while his wife stared over the rail at nothing in particular. Seven more people passed through the fourth-floor landing during that time. "Sir," Hunter then said, "you do understand, don't you, that Cicero may be under attack and that we're all supposed to be in the emergency shelters twenty minutes from now?"

"Yes, young man, I understand," Mr. Nordquist answered. He moved closer to his wife. "Brigitte, darling, are you ready to go now?"

She shook her head. The man turned to Hunter. "She's still resting," he said.

"Wally!" a woman's voice shouted from above. Hunter turned around in time to see a portly boy, about ten years old, floating out of control down the stairs from the fifth floor. He bounced off one of the rails and caromed into Mr. Nordquist's shoulder, knocking the old man to his knees.

"Are you all right, Mr. Nordquist?" Hunter said, bending down to help.

"Okay, yes, okay," the man said, standing up slowly.

The boy Wally was lying on his back near the beginning of the descending stairs. His mother rushed down to see if he was all right. When she confirmed that her son was unhurt, she gave him a scolding and told him that he would be required to hold her hand for the rest of the descent. The woman then looked briefly at Hunter and the Nordquists, but never said a word of apology. Hunter shook his head in angry disbelief as Wally and his mother disappeared from view.

Hunter waited as long as he dared. Then, just after another family passed their landing, he approached Mrs. Nordquist. "I am here to help you to the emergency shelter, Mrs. Nordquist," Hunter said gently. "We need to start now, for the shelter will be sealed before too long. . . . I will guide you carefully down the stairs."

Hunter touched her arm. The woman's only response was a frightened look. Mr. Nordquist came over to help. "Brigitte," he said, "don't be afraid of this nice young man. He is going to help you."

The next several minutes seemed like an eternity to Hunter. Slowly, steadily, he guided Mrs. Nordquist down the three flights of stairs. It wasn't easy. People pushed past them in a hurry, often brushing either Hunter or Mr. Nordquist. Nobody stopped to offer help. Twice Mrs. Nordquist nearly fell and Hunter had to catch her. Both times, she refused to take another step again until her husband entreated her to do so.

On the final stairway, with time running out, a teenage girl soared by them, passing close enough to Mrs. Nordquist to unsettle her. This time not even Mr. Nordquist's pleas could convince her to move.

Hunter glanced at his watch. It was less than three minutes before the shelters were scheduled to be sealed. Apologizing to both of them, Hunter picked up Mrs. Nordquist and cradled her like a baby. As he carefully climbed down the final steps with the startled woman, Hunter urged her husband to walk as "quickly as he safely could." He also told Mr. Nordquist that he would return to pick him up after he had made certain that his wife was inside the outer doors of the shelter.

When he reached the bottom of the stairs, Hunter turned to his left and increased his speed. Because of the almost insignificant gravity on Cicero, Mrs. Nordquist was not heavy. She was, however, an awkward package and Hunter had to be very careful not to lose his balance.

He deposited Mrs. Nordquist on the landing just inside the thick outer doors of the emergency shelter and placed both her hands on the railing. Hunter then hurried back for her husband. The two men reached the shelter with no time to spare. As Hunter and the Nordquists slowly descended the long, broad stairway above the inner shelter doors, a civil servant in charge passed them, going the other way to seal the outer doors. Five more people, barely escaping being locked outside, made it into the shelter behind Hunter and the Nordquists.

The scene inside the emergency shelter was unmitigated chaos. People were moving in all directions. Even though the siren could barely be heard, the noise in the shelter was deafening. Four hundred people were in one large, rectangular room, the size of a highschool gymnasium. Cots were arranged in rows and columns from one end of the building to the other. Placards designating coordinates for the cots were hanging down from the ceiling. Fifteen to twenty large television monitors were scattered strategically around the shelter. Just inside the entrance, three harried Cicero officials were checking off people's names, making cot assignments using a computer, and trying to deal with the many complaints.

Hunter stood in the processing line with the Nordquists. A dozen people were in front of them when they arrived, and the line was moving very slowly. "I want you to know, young man," Mr. Nordquist said as they were standing, "that Brigitte and I are grateful to you for helping us." His wife said nothing. She simply stared around her with a look of total bewilderment.

There was no cot available for Hunter anywhere near his family. The processing officer apologized profusely, and admitted remembering that Mr. Blake had specifically requested that one bed next to them be set aside for Hunter, but somehow ... Hunter shrugged it off, took the card with his cot assignment, and set off across the room toward his family.

"ALL I'M SAYING," Octavio said, "is that there exists no hard evidence that we're really being attacked."

Hunter was losing patience with his brother-in-law, who was in one of his worst argumentative moods. "What possible reason could the mayor have for making this whole thing up?" Hunter asked in an exasperated tone. "It just doesn't make sense."

"I don't believe the mayor would have done it on his own," Octavio said. "But suppose the FISC had plans to use

Cicero as a major base in the next phase of the war, and needed to tighten up security here, what better way—"

"That's preposterous," Hunter interrupted. "You're suggesting that the mayor and other Cicero officials would deliberately lie to us—"

"You're naive, Hunter," Octavio interrupted back. "Governments have been lying to their citizens for centuries. Study your history more closely." Octavio leaned toward Hunter and his voice rose. "Compared to the tight security that exists today everywhere on North Mars, life on Cicero is a virtual paradise of freedom. Our location-monitoring system has never been implemented, for example. We have no curfews. We still have freedom of speech, and ostensibly freedom of the press. No sedition code has ever been defined. According to Raoul, who spent the last four months in Centralia, the ASP there is more in evidence than the normal police."

Hunter and Octavio were sitting on opposite ends of the same cot. They were both unaware that people around them in the shelter were starting to listen to their discussion. Blake was temporarily away from the area, visiting with a colleague. Both Amanda and Mrs. Blake were becoming uneasy about the growing audience, but were reluctant to intercede in the conversation.

"Okay, Octavio," Hunter said, passion now in his voice. "Suppose you're right. Suppose the FISC does want to tighten security here. Then why didn't the FISC and the mayor simply announce more stringent security measures today, after the sabotage incident outside? It would have been easy to justify, based on the fact that Cicero is now in what could be construed as enemy territory." Hunter waved his hand in a big circle. "Then we could have all been spared this colossal inconvenience."

"That's where you're wrong, brother-in-law," Octavio

rejoined, convinced of his superior position in the argument. "People do not give up their freedoms willingly. It takes a significant threat before people accept limitations upon their lives. Whatever happens during this supposed attack tonight, I bet the citizens of Cicero will gladly embrace new constraints on their freedoms. Mark my words. Tomorrow there will be an executive proclamation significantly changing our daily lives. And nobody will object."

Octavio's tone had become more and more strident with each sentence. By the time he was finished, everyone in the area was listening to him. Hunter had already looked around, wondering why the noise and activity around them had suddenly diminished. Octavio forced an awkward smile, acknowledging the attention.

Amanda sat down on the cot beside her husband. "That was not smart," she said quietly. "This is not the time and place for such a discussion."

Octavio was unrepentant. "Nothing I said was wrong," he argued. "We're all so damn gullible, it amazes me."

Hunter had walked away, and was standing next to his mother, who was holding the sleeping Danielle. "You promised me no arguments," Mrs. Blake said, shaking her head.

"I know, Mom," Hunter said. "I'm sorry—but at least Dad wasn't around." He glanced over at Octavio. "Sometimes he can be so damn irritating. And he always has to be right."

"One of these days," Mrs. Blake said, still concerned, "that mouth of Octavio's is going to get him into serious trouble."

THE REST ROOMS were across the shelter from the Blake family cots. Hunter stopped several times to talk with friends before he reached his destination.

When he was leaving the rest room, Hunter heard a young boy's voice calling his name. He turned and saw Tesoro Wilawa approaching him. "I thought that was you," the boy said with a smile.

"What's up, Tesoro?" Hunter said, returning the smile. "Are you still tearing them up at math?"

"I'm doing okay," Tesoro grinned. "I just passed my algebra exam last week."

"Congratulations," Hunter said. "That's really good. And you're not even twelve yet, are you?"

"Next month," Tesoro said. "I had to beat Tehani," he confided proudly to Hunter. "She passed algebra the day AFTER her twelfth birthday. . . . When did you do it?"

"I don't remember exactly," Hunter replied, not wanting to spoil Tesoro's moment.

"Tehani's here for a visit," Tesoro said after a brief silence. "It's great to see her, but she's hardly had any time to play with me. The phone rings all the time. And I bet she gets more vidmail than the mayor."

"I heard she was here," Hunter replied casually.

"Would you like to see her?" Tesoro asked ingenuously. "Our cots are over there, next to the wall." The boy pointed at a far corner, at the exact opposite end of the shelter from where the Blakes were staying. "I bet she'd love to talk to you," Tesoro said, "instead of all those strangers who keep pestering her. . . . Mom says it's because she's so famous."

Tesoro started walking away from the rest rooms, down an aisle among the cots. Hunter hesitated. The boy turned and waved his hand. "Come on," he said.

Hunter thought his heart was going to jump out of his body as he followed Tesoro through the array of people and cots. Yes, he wanted to see Tehani. But what was he going to say to her? Hunter had started at least twenty conversations with Tehani in his mind before Tesoro and he finally reached the other side of the shelter. As they approached,

Hunter forced himself to calm down. *Just be casual,* he told himself. *Act as if it's no big deal.*

Mrs. Wilawa saw them first. Tehani was sitting on her cot, surrounded by six or seven people. "Guess who I found?" Tesoro said in one of his loudest voices.

Tehani's mother walked over and greeted Hunter warmly. "It's good to see you," she said. "How have you been?"

"All right, Mrs. Wilawa, thank you," Hunter answered much too formally. For a moment, he had no idea what to say. "Tesoro says he's already passed his algebra exam," he said awkwardly. "You must be very proud of him."

"But not at the age of ten and a half," a familiar voice said from behind him, "like someone I know."

Hunter turned around. Tehani was coming toward him. "Hello, Hunter," she said with a warm smile. She gave him a brief, casual hug, then pulled away.

Hunter was completely discombobulated. Tehani was standing right in front of him, waiting for him to speak. But he couldn't even breathe, much less remember any of the conversation starters he had practiced while he was crossing the shelter with Tesoro. All Hunter could do was stare at her. *She is so unbelievably beautiful,* he kept thinking.

Tehani turned to the group that had been surrounding her when Hunter and Tesoro arrived. "If you don't mind," she said graciously, "this is one of my dearest friends. I haven't seen him in a long time."

"I found him in the bathroom," Tesoro said proudly, as the group slowly dispersed. "I knew you'd want to see him."

"You did well, little brother," Tehani said, giving him an affectionate pat on the back. She turned to Hunter. "Can you sit down for a minute?" she said. "I'd love to know what's going on in your life."

Hunter sat beside her on the cot. Tesoro hung around

for a few seconds, until Mrs. Wilawa called him. By that time Hunter had more or less composed himself.

"You look beautiful, Tehani," he said.

"Thank you," she replied. "You look pretty good yourself."

Hunter had promised himself that the first time he saw Tehani, he would not, under any circumstances, talk about anything serious. Certainly nothing about anything that had happened to them two years earlier. She spoke while he was trying to decide what to say next.

"I understand you're working at the hospital," she said.

He nodded. "I've applied to medical school," he said, startled by the sound of his own voice. "Both at Centralia and Masursky."

"I'm sure you'll be accepted," Tehani said. "Julie told me that you destroyed the entrance exams." She smiled easily. "I wasn't surprised. I think you'll make a terrific doctor."

Her face was not more than an arm's length from his. Hunter could not take his eyes off her. In spite of his resolve to act as if she were just another girl, he felt himself losing his composure. He turned away and looked across the shelter.

"So how are things with you?" he said stiffly.

"Mostly okay," she said. "I've met some nice people. But I miss my mother and Tesoro."

A young girl, perhaps fourteen, was standing about ten feet in front of them, watching Tehani with rapt attention. "You are really beautiful," she said admiringly, when she noticed that Tehani was looking at her. "I've seen you on the network."

"Thank you," Tehani replied just as the girl's mother, a plain woman with a scowl on her face, appeared behind her.

"Come along, Darla," the woman said, grabbing her daughter's arm. The woman cast a furtive, unpleasant glance at Tehani and Hunter as she hurried her daughter away, ignoring the girl's protests.

Hunter became aware of all the eyes pointed in their direction when Tesoro came over to ask Tehani a question. "Is it always like this?" he asked Tehani after her brother left. "I mean, do people always just sit there and gawk at you?"

"Sometimes," she said. "At first it really bothered me, but now I tell myself that they don't mean to be rude, and try to ignore them."

Hunter looked at her again and lost himself in her eyes and her smile. Powerless to resist Tehani's beauty and charm, he abandoned his plan to keep the conversation light. "Are you happy, Tehani?" he asked.

A different look came into her eyes. She had just opened her mouth to answer when the ground below them jumped and then swayed from side to side. Tehani's look turned to one of alarm. A couple of objects fell off Tesoro's cot. Someone screamed.

No more than two seconds later, the ground moved again, this time violently. Two cots over from them, a sleeping girl was thrown on the floor. The screaming became widespread and loud shouts could be heard on all sides. Hunter grabbed Tehani's arm. "Are you all right?" he said.

She was looking for her mother and her brother. Tehani found them nearby and stood up to go in that direction. Another strong jolt shook the shelter, then another. Tehani stumbled. Hunter caught her before she fell. They headed for Mrs. Wilawa and Tesoro together. Moments after the four of them had huddled against the nearest wall for support, a new series of powerful motions shook the shelter. Several of the placards fell from the ceiling, fortunately floating down harmlessly in the low gravity. Two of the monitors crashed to the floor. The next five minutes the jolts and shakes were nearly continuous. The four hundred citizens of Cicero inside the shelter became a quivering, screaming, terrified crowd, desperately holding on to each other and anything else that was stable.

When the jolts subsided, at first nobody moved. After about a minute, some of the people in the shelter started milling around. "I must go see my family," Hunter said to Tehani.

"I understand," she replied. Tesoro was still holding on to one of Hunter's thighs. "Please let go," she said gently to her brother. "Hunter has to leave."

The terrified boy looked at Tehani. "Is it over?" he said.

"I think so," she said, gathering him in her arms. She reached up and kissed Hunter on the cheek. "Thank you," Tehani said softly as he departed.

S I X

HUNTER RESISTED THE IMPULSE to stop and help others as he wound through the disorderly crowd toward his family. He didn't see anybody who was seriously hurt, but there were a lot of minor injuries. When Hunter was still thirty yards away from his family, he heard Danielle's characteristic wail. Amanda was cradling her baby daughter in her arms, trying to comfort her. Octavio and Mrs. Blake were standing nearby, looking concerned. Mr. Blake was on his knees, sifting through Hunter's pack.

"Can you help Dad find some medicine?" Amanda shouted when she saw Hunter. "Danielle has a nasty scrape on her forehead."

Hunter found the antibacterial unguent quickly and applied it to the baby's forehead after cleaning and inspecting her wound. He then carefully placed a bandage over the entire scraped area. "She'll be all right," he assured his sister when he was finished. "It'll hurt for a few days, but that's all. Babies heal very quickly."

Amanda and Octavio thanked him. "How about the rest of you?" Hunter said. "Are you all okay?"

Nobody said anything. Hunter grabbed his pack. "In

that case," he said, "I'm going to see if there's anybody else who needs help."

For the next fifteen minutes or so Hunter moved around the shelter, helping wherever he could. Minor wounds, like Danielle's, he bandaged himself. The one serious injury he encountered, which Hunter thought might be a broken ankle, he left for the two doctors who were circulating among the Cicero citizens. Hunter was delighted to discover that neither of the Nordquists had been hurt. Mr. Nordquist was gratified that Hunter was concerned enough to seek them out. His wife, Brigitte, seemed more bewildered than ever.

By the time Hunter returned to his family's area, a semblance of order was returning to the shelter. People were no longer crowding the aisles and the noise had diminished considerably. Some of the citizens were already stretched out on their cots, ready for sleep.

Mr. Blake and Octavio were engaged in a quiet conversation when Hunter came back. "We must have been bombed," Blake was saying. "I can't imagine what else could have caused the large jolts and shocks. Firing our defensive missiles would barely have shaken the ground."

"What if the bombs destroyed the domes?" Octavio asked.

Blake frowned. "That would be the worst-case scenario, of course," he said. "The domes are essential for our life-support system here on Cicero. If they have been destroyed, or seriously compromised, we may be forced to stay in this shelter for a month or longer."

"I thought the inner dome was virtually indestructible," Hunter said.

"It's supposed to be," his father replied. "But if the outer dome was blown away early in the attack, a direct hit by certain kinds of bombs could conceivably cause a tear in the inner dome that would take weeks to repair. We have an emergency repair procedure, using squads of robot technicians and engineering personnel, that we partially practice every year or two. But I'm not certain we even have enough space suits on hand right now to implement it in a reasonable amount of time."

"May I have your attention, please?" one of the civil servants said over the shelter's loudspeaker system, interrupting their conversation. "Would Mr. David Blake and Mr. Julio Franco please come to the communications center?"

Hunter's father prepared to leave. "I was expecting the call," he said to his family. "I was going to go without being summoned in another few minutes. The preliminary damage assessment by the drones must have been completed."

Blake kissed his wife. "I should be back fairly soon," he said. "Unless we have a major life-support emergency."

IT WAS ALMOST an hour after Blake's departure before the television monitors throughout the shelter carried the message that an announcement from the mayor of Cicero was imminent. By that time, most of the children had gone to sleep on their cots. The majority of the adults, however, remained awake. They talked quietly in small groups, their grave faces reflecting their understanding of the tenuous situation.

Hunter had stretched out on his father's cot. He was lying on his back with his eyes closed, but he was not sleeping. In spite of the situation, Hunter's thoughts were focused on Tehani. *She was definitely friendly,* he told himself, reviewing the details of their earlier encounter in the shelter. *Maybe I should call her tomorrow.*

For a few minutes Hunter allowed his imagination complete freedom. He saw himself taking Tehani out for dinner, and then to one of the two clubs in the plaza area.

Afterward they were laughing and she invited him into her apartment. It was late and both her mother and brother were already in bed. She kissed him. Hunter shuddered slightly, remembering how wonderful Tehani's kiss had been two years before.

But the imaginative fantasy did not continue. Instead, the Tehani of the Sybaris video intruded upon his daydream. This Tehani, seductive and alluring in her purple cocktail dress, was not the innocent, passionate teenager who had once led Hunter into her bedroom. Hunter became confused again. *She makes love to men for money,* he said to himself. *Men who are rich and experienced. And knowledgeable about sex and pleasure. . . . I would be just another insignificant name on her list.*

Hunter's emotions were in turmoil. Every few seconds he changed his mind completely. One moment he wanted to race across the shelter, apologize profusely for his behavior two years earlier, and pledge his undying affection to Tehani. The next he never wanted to see her again and cursed her for having stolen his heart.

He sat up on his cot and looked across the shelter. Hunter strained his eyes but couldn't quite see Tehani on the far side of the large room. He stood up and started walking in her direction. "Where are you going?" his mother asked.

"I think I see somebody I knew in school," Hunter answered vaguely.

Halfway across the shelter he realized that he had absolutely no idea what he was going to say to Tehani. Hunter stopped for an instant, right in front of one of the large television monitors. At that moment the mayor appeared on the screen and began to speak to his constituents.

"Citizens of Cicero," he said, "tonight we were attacked by three unknown spacecraft. Our initial assessment indicates that their bombs destroyed two of our processing factories and three of the large mining machines. Fortunately, none of their many bombs struck the domes that protect our living area. Nevertheless, one or two of the bombs did explode close to our habitat and we have decided that, as a precautionary measure, we should do a detailed check of all the key life-support systems in Cicero before allowing you to return to your homes."

The mayor paused. "I have just completed a meeting with my engineering and security staff," he continued. "We have developed a plan which, if we don't find any new problems, will permit you to leave the shelters eight hours from now. During this time, we ask each of you to please cooperate with the shelter officials as much as possible. We realize that your circumstances in the shelters are far from ideal, but we believe it is prudent that we do a detailed assessment of any possible damage before you return to your living quarters. Thank you for your patience and understanding."

The video immediately repeated. Hunter, like most of the people in the shelter, watched the first part of the mayor's speech a second time. As his attention began to drift, however, he heard a familiar voice behind him.

"It's the perfect cover-up," Octavio was saying. "Suppose you were Minister Sackett, or that goon Tyson who runs the ASP, and you needed to implement a major tightening of security here on Cicero. What would you do? Faking a Dem attack is brilliant. You could even destroy a few factories and mining machines, if necessary, for they're not important to the war effort. Then there would be absolutely no resistance to heightened security."

Hunter turned around. Octavio was sitting in a group with half a dozen young men and women about ten yards away. Octavio's back was toward Hunter.

"I don't know, Octavio," one of the women said. "Faking this raid tonight seems like a lot of effort just to have an excuse to increase security. I don't really think the people of Cicero are that rebellious. If the mayor simply announced new security measures, I don't believe there would be that many complaints."

"You don't understand how they think, Belinda," Octavio said earnestly. "On Dante three months ago, there were several days of demonstrations against the new rules. Covington was embarrassed. He probably ordered Sackett and Tyson to make certain that nothing like that ever happened again."

He paused for a moment. "Covington and his minions think we're all stupid anyway," Octavio continued. "Look at the way they govern. They provide us with technological marvels, and unbelievable efficiency, but completely ignore human rights and all social problems. From a sociological point of view, the Federation is no more advanced than the governments on Earth in the twentieth century. And nobody protests. At least not for long."

"Is the ASP a part of the Defense Ministry?" a young woman asked Octavio. "Or is it a separate agency?"

"Until last year it was part of Defense," Octavio replied. "But then Tyson decided that Sackett was hampering his style. He petitioned Covington for a separate cabinet post. Fortunately for him, his petition coincided with the Tanakawa scandal. Six key members of the Defense Ministry had just been indicted for accepting bribes, and Sackett was in Covington's doghouse. Now Tyson and his Nazis are only accountable to the chairman himself."

During the discussion, Hunter had unobtrusively walked over toward the group. "Uh, Octavio," a young man named Raoul de Silva said, after recognizing Hunter, "I think you have a visitor."

"Hello, brother-in-law," Octavio said in a friendly voice after turning and seeing Hunter. "Why don't you sit down and join us? You might even learn something."

"Do you think having political conversations in such a public place is a good idea?" Hunter asked pointedly.

Octavio glanced around his group. "Why not?" he said with a rebellious grin. "According to what I have read in our political science texts, the Federation supports freedom of speech among its citizens."

Hunter shrugged. "Okay," he said, "suit yourself." He started to make another comment but saw his father walking across the shelter heading for the family area. "If you'll excuse me," Hunter said to Octavio and his companions, "my father is finally out of his meeting."

David Blake was having a hard time making any progress. Most of the citizens of Cicero knew that he was the chief engineer of the outpost and that he had just been engaged in a long planning session with the mayor. Every few steps he was stopped by someone with a question. Blake was already growing tired of politely refusing to comment by the time Hunter intercepted him.

"How did it go?" Hunter asked his father.

"I'll tell you later," Blake said in a low voice. The two of them reached the family area after another minute or two. Danielle and Amanda were both asleep. Mrs. Blake greeted her husband but did not ask any questions.

Mr. Blake and Hunter sat down together on Octavio's cot. "It was a strange raid," Blake told his son quietly when he was certain that nobody was listening. "Apparently the only targets were the two factories and three mining machines that were destroyed. There were no bomb impacts near the other two factories or the rest of the mining machines. Nor anywhere else for that matter."

"What does that mean?" Hunter asked.

"We don't know for certain. We sent all the data back to Sackett's intelligence department for analysis." Blake sighed. "There's more to the story, but unfortunately much of the information is classified. What I can tell you is that we could not uniquely identify the types of attacking space-craft from the radar data. And that we didn't hit anything with our phalanx of defensive missiles."

"All of them missed?" Hunter asked incredulously. "I thought Cicero was protected by the best weapons the Federation could design."

"I can't tell you anything else," his father said. "But more than one person in the security department thinks that our attackers had special, inside knowledge about Cicero and its defenses. Especially when the mining-machine disaster earlier today is also considered."

"Do you think the two are related?" Hunter said.

"I don't know what to think," Blake replied. "Commander Tyson has already dispatched a new cadre of ASP officers to Cicero to investigate the whole situation. They'll be here in two weeks. In the meantime, he gave orders to round up everyone with even mildly suspicious behavior. Since an official first-stage alert has already been declared, many of the normal rights of our citizens have been suspended."

"Wow," Hunter said, shaking his head. "This could be serious."

"That's an understatement," his father replied.

HUNTER WAS SLEEPING on his cot in another part of the shelter. He was dreaming about Tehani. She was standing on a beautiful beach about a hundred yards away from him. Tehani smiled, and beckoned to Hunter. In his dream he began walking toward her at a slow pace. In her white bikini, the copper-skinned Tehani looked like a goddess. Her smile was radiant. She continued to beckon. Hunter felt himself becoming aroused as he drew closer to her.

A man suddenly walked into Hunter's dream screen

from the right side. He was a handsome man in his forties, in good physical condition. He was carrying gifts for Tehani. She turned and smiled at him. The man placed a diamond bracelet on her wrist. She thanked him with a long, intense kiss. In his dream, Hunter cringed and called out Tehani's name. She didn't hear him. The man began removing Tehani's bathing-suit top. Hunter couldn't watch. He woke up abruptly, extremely distressed.

Hunter sat up and glanced around the darkened shelter. The only lights still illuminated were over near the door. Almost everybody was sleeping. The dream was still fresh in his mind, unsettling his emotions. He tried to clear his head. *What am I going to do about Tehani?* he thought. *I'm not going to know how I REALLY feel about her until we spend some time alone together,* he answered himself.

The noise of activity in the vicinity of the shelter door caught Hunter's attention. The civil servants managing the shelter were clustered around four or five uniformed men who had apparently just entered. After some animated discussion, the chief civil servant turned on the lights throughout the shelter. Fifteen seconds later he activated the monitors and spoke over the loudspeaker system.

"I'm sorry to disturb your rest," he said politely, "but I really have no choice. I would like for you to wake up for some very important announcements." He paused. "Please, all of you, wake up and pay attention."

Music began playing over the sound system. Around Hunter, people began to stir. Some complained about being awakened. Most just looked in the direction of the door and wondered what was happening.

"Now that you're all awake," the shelter chief said about a minute later, "I would like to introduce Captain Marco Bonesio, of the Anti-Sedition Police."

The face of a young, handsome man in an ASP uniform

appeared on all the monitors in the shelter. His uniform was kelly green, with the image of a snake embroidered on the outside of the right shoulder. "Citizens of Cicero," Captain Bonesio said in a sharp voice, "the ASP is charged with the responsibility of making certain that no disloyal elements undermine our Federation from within. As unbelievable as it may seem, the events that occurred yesterday, both the mining accident and the bombing raid, may have been surreptitiously supported by a few citizens of our own community.

"The mayor yesterday announced that Cicero was under a first-stage alert. One of the provisions of a first-stage alert is the granting to law-enforcement agencies, including the local police and the ASP, of the right to retain and interrogate citizens without a warrant or even a specified reason. In other words, definitive evidence of wrongdoing is no longer a prerequisite for us to question a member of the populace about his or her activities."

Captain Bonesio stopped. In spite of his forced smile, he looked cold and menacing. "Without all the bureaucratic paperwork," he said, "it will be easier for us to protect the loyal citizens of Cicero."

He turned away from the camera and spoke briefly with another of the uniformed men. "This morning we are detaining forty-eight individuals altogether," he continued, "including nine from this shelter. Before allowing my subordinate Lieutenant Nelson to read the list of detainees from here, let me stress that these citizens are NOT, as of this moment, being accused of any crimes. Based on our analysis of their dossiers, however, we believe that there is a chance that one or more of them may have some information that will allow us to find anyone who may have collaborated with an enemy of the FISC."

Captain Bonesio stepped away from the microphone

and the video camera. Lieutenant Henry Nelson, who had been one of Hunter's close friends during secondary school, next appeared on the monitor. He was clearly nervous.

"It will expedite the process," he said in too loud a voice, "if each of you will come forward when your name is called. Bring your toiletries and other personal possessions with you, for we do not know, at this time, how long you will be detained. . . . I will now read the list."

The young man cleared his throat before proceeding. "Mr. Raoul de Silva," he began, "Ms. Belinda Washington, Ms. Rachel Goldberg, Mr. Octavio Gonzalez . . ."

Adrenaline surged through Hunter's body when he heard his brother-in-law's name called. He was in motion in less than a second. Hunter hurried down the aisle toward the Blake family area.

Amanda was crying when Hunter arrived. Octavio looked stunned. "There must be some mistake," Hunter said when he reached the family.

On the monitor, Lieutenant Nelson was reading the nine names a second time. As Octavio's name was read again, an attractive young brunette, carrying a small pack slung over one shoulder, approached the Blakes.

"Well, Senor Gonzalez," she said with a wry smile, touching Octavio gently on the forearm, "it looks as if we've been selected."

Octavio glanced from the woman to Amanda, and back again. "This is Rachel Goldberg," Octavio managed to stammer eventually. "Rachel, this is my wife Amanda, her parents David and Elizabeth Blake, and her brother Hunter. . . . The little tyke lying on the cot, sleeping peacefully, is my daughter Danielle."

Everyone stood in awkward silence for a few seconds. From the look on his sister's face, Hunter surmised that it was likely that Amanda had never even heard Rachel Goldberg's name before this moment. "Rachel is the chief purchasing agent for Brown and Hong," Octavio explained. "She's often in my office complaining about late deliveries."

"Please gather your belongings quickly and come forward if your name was on the list," Captain Bonesio was saying on the loudspeaker. "It will make everything much easier."

Octavio seemed to be paralyzed. Amanda and Rachel Goldberg stared at each other without speaking. At length Mr. Blake came over beside his son-in-law and whispered something in his ear. Octavio quickly bent down next to one of the packs and started going through it, pulling out toiletries and a few articles of clothing. Hunter, aware that all eyes in the vicinity were on his family, walked over beside Miss Goldberg.

"Would you mind giving us a few minutes alone with Octavio?" he said to her. "This is a shock to all of us and we'll need to do some fast planning as a family."

The young woman smiled bemusedly at Hunter. "Okay," she said after a few seconds' hesitation. "See you soon, Senor Gonzalez," she added, glancing at Amanda one last time as she departed in the direction of the shelter door.

Hunter went over to comfort his sister. "I know Henry Nelson well—he's the ASP lieutenant who read the list," he said to her in a low voice. "He was in my socialization group in secondary school. I can talk to him and maybe they won't need to take Octavio . . ."

"That's not a good idea," Mr. Blake said forcefully, overhearing what Hunter was saying. "Nobody but Octavio should go forward. Otherwise, it may look as if we're hindering the process. . . . I'll talk to the mayor tomorrow or the next day, after things have calmed down a little."

"I've told him, over and over," Amanda said bitterly to Hunter as Mr. Blake walked over beside his wife, "that he needs to watch his goddamn mouth. Now look what's happened. Even if they release him, he'll probably be fired from his job. Federated Shipping has been looking for an excuse." She glanced at Octavio, then turned back to Hunter. "And who the hell is she?" Amanda said, raising her voice.

Hunter put his arms around his distraught sister. "Now is not the time for anger, Amanda," he whispered. "Octavio needs your support. He must be scared to death."

Octavio finished his hurried packing and stood up. He forced a smile. "Well," he said, "I guess I'd better go."

Amanda stared at her husband and shook her head. Suddenly she rushed forward and threw her arms around him. "Please be careful, Octavio," she said, as a new set of tears flooded her eyes and rolled down her cheeks. "Remember that whatever happens, Danielle and I both love you."

Octavio leaned down and kissed his wife. "I love you, too, Amanda," he said. He looked directly into her eyes. "I'm sorry, darling," he said. "I really am. . . . I promise you that I haven't done anything wrong except say a few unflattering things about our illustrious leaders."

He bent down and picked up his daughter from her cot. He held her close against his body for almost a minute. The little girl woke up from her sleep. "Da-da," she said softly. He gave Danielle a kiss and then hugged Amanda again.

Visibly shaken, Octavio Gonzalez hoisted his pack to his shoulder and walked between the cots toward the door to the shelter.

SEVEN

HUNTER WAS EMOTIONALLY EXHAUSTED by the time the officials were moving through the aisles of the shelter passing out a simple breakfast. Although it had been two hours since the ASP had left with Octavio and the eight others, and it had been dark in the shelter for the entire time, none of the Blakes had slept again.

Hunter and his parents spent the two hours trying to comfort Amanda. Although she did express some concern for what might happen to Octavio, for most of the time Amanda was either complaining about her husband's irresponsibility, or questioning his relationship with Rachel Goldberg, or feeling sorry for herself. In the end, all her family's attempts to console her were unsuccessful. Amanda remained hopelessly miserable.

While he was eating his breakfast with his family, Hunter thought about Tehani Wilawa for the first time since the ASP had entered the shelter. He finally decided that he would seek her out after breakfast and test his feelings in her presence. If everything was going well, he intended to invite Tehani to dinner the next day. Unfortunately, before Hunter finished his meal, the mayor appeared again on the monitors and announced that all the citizens of Cicero could return to their homes.

Immediately the aisles were filled with people. Hunter picked up Danielle and one of the packs. Because they were so far from the shelter door, it took the Blakes almost half an hour to reach the exit. During the short waiting periods as they were moving slowly toward the door, Hunter scanned the shelter for Tehani and her family. He never saw them.

The Sun was shining brightly through the domes when the Blakes passed through the outer door. As soon as they were outside and their mobile phones were again operable, Blake started calling his key staff members, making plans for the day. Hunter phoned the emergency line at the hospital. A recording made by the director defined the shifts for the day. Hunter was due at work in three hours.

Danielle began to fidget in Hunter's arms. He gave her to Amanda and walked alongside them, a few paces in front of their parents. His sister had been uncommonly quiet during their exit from the shelter.

"Sometimes I think that marriage is impossible," Amanda suddenly said, without turning to look at her brother. "After the passion fades, it becomes banal and boring, especially if you don't have much in common." She sighed. "Octavio and I quibble and pick at each other about small things," she continued. "It can't be much fun for him. . . . There's never enough money, and Danielle is so demanding. . . . I guess I'm not that surprised that he has another, uh, friend."

Hunter put his arm around Amanda. "You shouldn't jump to conclusions, sis," he said. "As Mother said, they know each other from work—"

"Come on, Hunter," Amanda interrupted. "Did you see the way she looked at him? And that touch when she walked up was a dead giveaway. . . . You don't develop that kind of familiarity from an occasional work encounter."

"They're both interested in politics," Hunter said. "That gives them a common ground for the development of a friendship."

Amanda chuckled slightly and shook her head. "You're so naive, little brother. You think the best about everyone. Even Tehani—"

"Now let's not start on that subject," Hunter said easily. "I heard enough from Octavio at dinner last night."

Amanda stopped and turned around. Their parents were almost twenty yards behind them. Blake was still talking on his mobile phone. "What about them?" she said to Hunter. "Do you think they're happy? Do you ever wonder what keeps them together after all these years?"

Hunter looked puzzled. "I never think about things like that," he said honestly. "I mean, they're my mother and my father. They're together because, well, that's the way it was meant to be."

Amanda couldn't keep herself from laughing. "You are priceless," she said eventually. "How can somebody so smart be so unaware about people? Are you telling me that you have never once wondered if Mom and Dad are happy?"

"Nope," Hunter shrugged. "I've always assumed that if something was wrong in their marriage, somebody would tell me."

"You're something else, little brother," Amanda said, shaking her head again. "Are you riding the elevator or walking up the stairs?" she said to her parents as Mr. and Mrs. Blake drew near them.

BACK IN HIS room, Hunter started composing a vidmail message to Tehani. "It was great to see you last night," he said, looking directly at the little camera icon on his monitor. "You really looked sensational." He paused and forced a smile. "I was thinking that it'd be fun to get together for dinner, and maybe catch up with one another. It's been a long time and so much has happened to both of us. There's a new restaurant in the plaza that opened a couple of months ago . . ."

Hunter stopped. He was acutely aware of his own nervousness. Hunter replayed the short video snippet and laughed at himself. His tension was obvious.

He stored the video in a file on his computer and stood up in his room. Then Hunter went into his bathroom and stared at himself in the mirror. *My hair is too perfect,* he said to himself. *And I look like I dressed up just for this vidmail.* He tousled his hair and changed into a more casual shirt before sitting down again at the monitor.

"Hi, there, beautiful," he began his second composition. "Hey, wasn't it great that I ran into Tesoro in the shelter and he brought me over to see you? Anyway, it's been way too long since you and I spent some time together. Why don't we have some drinks and dinner tonight, after I get off work? There's a new restaurant . . ."

Again Hunter stopped the video. *That's too impersonal,* he thought. *Tehani might be offended. After all, we were almost lovers. . . .*

Hunter sat at his desk for another five minutes and tried several more times to compose the vidmail message. Nothing he created satisfied him. One was too serious, another tried humor and ended up being ridiculous, in a third he expressed his feelings a little too openly. Discouraged, Hunter gave up temporarily and walked into the living room of the family apartment.

His father was almost ready to leave for work. "I'm certain that I won't be home for dinner tonight," Mr. Blake said to his wife.

"Will you at least phone Dr. Ekanayake and set up an

appointment?" Mrs. Blake asked. "You know he'll be calling here soon."

"All right," Mr. Blake said, "if it'll make you feel better. But I don't know when I'm going to have time—"

"Dr. Ekanayake can probably come check you at work," Hunter said. "We can send a portable van and a robot technician from the hospital. The mayor will certainly authorize the extra expense."

The wall screen, which had been switched off, suddenly was illuminated. "That's odd," Mr. Blake said, moving toward the control panel built into the coffee table. He tried unsuccessfully to turn the monitor off again. A moment later, a bold banner proclaiming PRIORITY ONE MESSAGE WILL ARRIVE IN 54 SECONDS streamed across the screen.

As the quantitative part of the banner counted down the number of seconds before the message would arrive, the Blakes tried to imagine what the message would be. They were all certain that it would have something to do with the mining-machine accident, or the raid the previous night, or both.

"My guess is that it's from the ASP," Mr. Blake said. "The mayor told me yesterday that they would be contacting me directly with specific questions about the report we submitted on the accident. Their special investigative team is on the way here and I would bet they want to start on the task while they're still on board their spacecraft."

"You don't think then," a worried Mrs. Blake asked, "that the message has anything to do with Octavio?"

"Almost certainly not," Mr. Blake said.

The banner faded away from the monitor when the countdown completed. What appeared on the screen next was a luxurious executive office. A man dressed in a dark blue business suit was sitting behind a large desk. The camera zoomed in on his face. Hunter and his parents were all three dumbfounded. The man behind the desk was none other than the leader of the Federation of Independent Space Colonies, Chairman Marshall Covington himself.

"Hello and congratulations," Chairman Covington said. "It is a distinct and singular pleasure for me to inform Mr. Hunter Clarke Blake that he has been selected for one of the Federation's most coveted honors. Hunter, you and eleven others from around the FISC have been handpicked by my staff members as the next group of Covington Fellows. As I'm certain you know, every other year the Federation senior staff selects a dozen of our most outstanding young citizens and trains them for high-level civil-service positions with our government. Many of the current FISC cabinet members, as well as a majority of their deputies, were once Covington Fellows. Congratulations again, Hunter, to both you and your family. This is a very special day in all your lives."

Hunter could hardly believe what he had just heard. His astonished mother was hugging him. His father, beaming proudly, was shaking his hand vigorously. They both were talking but Hunter wasn't paying attention to what they were saying. He was deep inside his own mind, listening to his own questions. *Did I hear that correctly? Was that Chairman Covington telling me that I had been selected as a Covington Fellow? Is this really happening, or is it a dream?*

A Mr. Hans Langenbahn, who introduced himself as the Covington Fellow coordinator, was now on the wall screen. He, too, offered his congratulations before launching into details about the selection and its ramifications. Hunter heard Mr. Langenbahn say that the fellowship appointment was for a period of two years, that Hunter would be booked on the next available interplanetary transport between Cicero and Mars, that he would be living for at least the next year in Centralia, the capital city of the FISC, and that in addition to his formal schooling, Hunter would be apprenticed to a senior official in the government from the outset. Not only would Hunter be reimbursed for all expenses from this day forward, Mr. Langenbahn said, but also he would earn a generous stipend, the exact amount being a function of how well Hunter performed on both his scholarship and apprenticeship duties.

Hunter was overwhelmed. He moved through the next half hour in a daze. The mayor called immediately after the vidmail from Centralia was over. He offered his enthusiastic congratulations and pointed out that Hunter was the first Covington Fellow ever from Cicero. The mayor then mentioned that this was exactly the kind of news the colony needed, and that he had already ordered his chief of protocol to suspend the curfew and plan some major function honoring Hunter in the next few days. The Cicero television station was next. Could they send a reporter and a cameraman out to the apartment immediately? Would Hunter be available for a live appearance on *Cicero Today* that evening?

Hunter was an instant celebrity. His vidmail queue was up to a dozen by the time he returned to his room to dress for the television interview. The hospital director sent a message of congratulations and reminded Hunter that he should drop by before he departed and properly terminate his employment. Magazines were requesting interviews and background information. Friends were sending encouragement and congratulations.

One of the vidmails was from Tehani. "I just heard the news," she said with a radiant smile. "Congratulations, Hunter, I'm so proud of you. But I'm not surprised. You deserve anything wonderful that happens to you."

The vidmails were piling up faster than Hunter could read them. A bank official from Centralia offered him a line of credit. Linda Overton told Hunter that a bunch of friends wanted to celebrate with him at Lucky Luigi's. When would be a good time? Hunter scanned the remainder of the vidmails in the queue, then decided to watch Tehani's short message a second time.

Smiling to himself, and thoroughly enjoying the surge of elation that he was feeling, Hunter crossed his bedroom and plopped himself down on his bed. *Wow,* he said to himself, *this is really amazing. My life will never be the same again.* He began to fantasize. He was a famous, powerful leader who was universally admired. People recognized him wherever he went. At parties Hunter saw himself as the center of attention, surrounded by beautiful women who threw themselves at him and proclaimed his genius. He thanked them all for their praises, but told them that his heart had already been claimed. Coming forward in the center of his fantasy screen was Tehani Wilawa. She was now Hunter's wife.

KIDNAPPED

ONE

THE NEXT FOUR DAYS were a whirlwind for Hunter. Every waking minute was filled with some kind of activity. Two nights before his departure, the curfew was suspended and a huge party was held in his honor. Nearly everyone in the colony attended. In his long speech the mayor acted as if he had personally overseen Hunter's development from infancy. His father's remarks brought tears to Hunter's eyes. He had never seen his father so proud, or so emotional.

Hunter remained sober for most of the party. It was difficult, for every time that he finished a drink, three or four more were offered to him. A camera crew that had been hired by one of the leading network magazines followed his every move.

Tehani showed up, fashionably late, when the party was already well under way. Hunter had never sent her the vidmail asking her out to dinner. Two hours after the announcement of his selection as a Covington Fellow, Hunter had received another message from Centralia, telling him that he had been booked as a passenger on an interplanetary freighter that would leave Cicero the following Monday. Hunter's schedule during those last few days did not have any room for a private evening with Tehani. Besides, there would have been no way that they could have been together without everyone on Cicero knowing about their date. In addition, Hunter, behaving like a normal twenty-year-old suddenly thrust into the limelight, had been so swept up by a temporary sense of his own importance that he had really not been thinking that much about Tehani.

Seeing her across the room at the party in his honor, however, reminded Hunter of the special place that Tehani occupied in his mind and heart. He chastised himself for not having sent her the vidmail, and resolved that he would find some way to spend some time alone with her before the night was over. As the party reached the point where many of the celebrants were at least partially inebriated, Hunter was trying to invent a plan to allow him to speak with Tehani in private. It was not an easy task. Hunter was followed by a group of well-wishers everywhere he went. Tehani was always surrounded by admirers, most of them young men.

Hunter had almost given up on his plan when Tesoro and Mrs. Wilawa, who were preparing to leave the party, approached Hunter while he was talking to a group of his parents' friends. Hunter politely excused himself, graciously accepted congratulations from Tesoro and his mother, and then pulled the boy aside.

"Will you do me a favor, please," he said in a low voice to Tesoro.

"Sure, Hunter," the boy said eagerly. "What do you want?"

"Will you go tell your sister that I would like to see her outside, around the corner on the left side of the transportation platform, in five minutes," Hunter said. "And please whisper the message—I don't want anyone else to hear."

"I can do that," Tesoro said, beaming with pride.

Hunter watched as the boy skillfully wound his way

through the crowd. When he was standing next to his sister, she bent down so that Tesoro could whisper in her ear. Tehani glanced up and saw Hunter looking at her from across the room. She smiled warmly and nodded slightly. *Good,* Hunter said to himself, *now all I need to do is avoid conversations and then slip out unobtrusively after Tehani has left.* He temporized, making small talk with people he didn't know, until Tehani had departed. Then Hunter excused himself and went into the rest room not far from the exit.

After several minutes, Hunter opened the rest-room door partway to see if the camera crew was waiting outside. They weren't. He made a beeline for the exit. He had one foot out the door when he heard the mayor's booming voice behind him. "There you are," the mayor said. "We've been looking everywhere for you."

Hunter turned around. The mayor and a cadre of leading Cicero businessmen were bearing down on him quickly. There was no way he could escape.

"We've just been talking, Hunter," the mayor said, "about how all the talented young men and women leave Cicero and never come back. We understand that your fellowship will last at least two years, maybe more, but Brown here suggested that we should make certain you know now how welcome you will be in Cicero after your term is completed. In fact, we are prepared right now to make you an unconditional offer of employment upon your return."

The mayor spotted Hunter's father out of the corner of his eye. "Hey, Blake," he shouted. "Come over here, you'll want to hear this."

Everyone waited while David Blake walked across the room. "We were just telling your son," the mayor said, putting his arm around his chief engineer, "that we are very proud of him, and we want to induce him to return to Cicero after he has finished with his fellowship. We are going to make him an offer that is absolutely unprecedented. Winston Brown has found no fewer than seven leading businessmen here tonight, all of whom are willing, RIGHT NOW, to offer Hunter employment at DOUBLE his hospital salary, beginning the day of his return to Cicero. What do you think about that?"

Blake exhibited genuine astonishment and thanked the mayor and the other men. Hunter also expressed his appreciation, but all he could think about was the fact that Tehani was waiting for him. When there was a lull in the conversation, Hunter put his hand on the exit handle and started to open the door. His father looked at him disapprovingly. Hunter sighed and released the door.

The mayor was so excited about the employment offer being made to Hunter that he decided he had to make the news public. Grabbing Hunter forcefully by the arm, he dragged him over to the platform at one end of the large room. It took the mayor several seconds to catch everyone's attention. He then launched into a speech that not only highlighted the offer that had been made to Hunter, but also laid out a series of proposals that would increase the probability that gifted young citizens of Cicero would return home after their university training on Mars was completed.

Hunter rudely jumped down from the platform before the applause for the mayor's speech was even finished. He dashed across the room, out the exit, and then down the corridors that led to the transportation platform. But he was too late. Tehani had already left for home.

IT WAS EARLY the next morning by the time that Hunter arrived back at his apartment after the party. He was exhausted. He promised himself that he would either phone Tehani or send her an apologetic vidmail after he woke up.

In the morning, however, he was awakened by his sister. "Octavio is coming home soon," she said. "Dad went to pick him up."

Amanda and Danielle had been living with the Blakes since Octavio's detention. True to his word, Mr. Blake had asked the mayor to intercede on Octavio's behalf the very next day. As a result, Amanda's husband had been one of the first detainees to be interrogated by the ASP, and was now being temporarily released into Mr. Blake's custody. The terms of Octavio's release were strict. He was confined to work and the Blake home, unless he received prior permission from the local ASP for some other kind of activity. And he was not to associate with any of the other people who had been detained until he had been formally cleared of all suspicion.

The homecoming was warm. Octavio smiled broadly while he held Danielle in his arms. He profusely thanked Mr. Blake for helping him, and told each of the members of the family how much he appreciated their support. Everyone sat down together and had breakfast in a convivial mood. Octavio said that the ASP interrogators had been surprisingly courteous, but that they had warned him that the investigative team on the way to Cicero from Mars might not be so polite.

When breakfast was over, Amanda asked the family if she could have some private time with Octavio. Mr. Blake departed quickly, saying that he was late for work. Hunter went back into his room to dress for a late-morning video interview on the network. Mrs. Blake took Danielle out into the corridor. Amanda and Octavio remained in the living room of the Blake apartment.

After taking a bath and dressing, Hunter tried unsuccessfully to phone Tehani. She wasn't at home and the message on her mobile phone told Hunter that she was temporarily unavailable. Hunter left a message for her, apologizing for not showing up at the platform and explaining that he had been waylaid by the mayor on his way to the exit. He asked Tehani to please call him when she had a chance.

Amanda knocked softly on Hunter's door twice during his video interview with a youth magazine. When he was finished, Hunter went into the living room. His sister was sitting on the couch by herself. Her eyes were red and swollen.

"What's up?" Hunter asked casually.

"Would you be willing to sleep out here tonight?" Amanda said. "I know it's rotten of me to ask, since this is your last night at home, but Danielle and I need to sleep somewhere and your room is the best candidate. We could sleep out here, but you know how easily she wakes up. . . ."

Hunter sat down beside her on the couch. "Well, okay, if it's really important," he said in a measured tone. "Do you want to tell me what this is all about?"

Amanda averted her eyes. "Octavio and I have some major problems," she said. "Under the terms of his probation, he must stay here with Dad. I don't want to go back to our apartment, and I don't want to sleep in the same room with Octavio."

Hunter waited, but Amanda didn't say anything else. "All right," he said at length. "I'll be finished packing in another hour or two." He stood up to return to his room.

"Thank you, little brother," Amanda said. Her eyes were full of tears again. "I'm sorry to be like this," she added. "And I do want you to know that I also am very very proud of you. I just haven't been able to show it properly."

Hunter walked across the living room and gave his sister a hug.

———

ON HUNTER'S LAST night on Cicero, the mayor appeared on television to summarize what had been learned about the mining-machine accident and the raid from space. He admitted that very little progress had been made in the investigation, but reiterated that FISC experts were convinced that there had been some "inside" help in the sabotage of the mining machine. The mayor also indicated that although there were many reasons to believe that the Dems had staged the raid, perhaps just to unsettle an isolated Fed colony, no incontrovertible evidence yet existed that could pin the attack on the UDSC.

"The FISC government has lodged a formal protest with the Dems," the mayor said, "but they have denied any knowledge of the raid. The defense minister of the UDSC, Nolan Garrett, has suggested that perhaps the raid represents a new kind of operation by the space pirates, designed to increase tensions between the two major powers. Our defense minister, Lester Sackett, however, has dismissed that idea as fatuous, saying that the technological prowess exhibited by the raid is way beyond the capabilities of the pirates."

Hunter's father did not come home until just before bedtime. Blake told his family that many unexplainable peculiarities were surfacing in the investigation of the accident, and that it didn't look as if definitive answers would be available in the near future. Looking troubled, he also said that Dr. Ekanayake had met him at his office that afternoon, and had given him the results of the medical tests that had been conducted two days before.

"Nothing truly pathological was found," Hunter's father said, "but there are many indications that my overall health is not good. My heart parameters are not inside the generally accepted limits, my blood pressure is a little higher than it ought to be, and I have some unexplained jaundice. Dr.

Ekanayake believes these symptoms are all stress-related. He is going to recommend in his report to the mayor that I work no more than twenty hours a week until my indicators return to the normal range."

Blake sighed. "Of course, the doctor can't propose who will manage the accident investigation, or supervise the design of the new factories."

"You need more rest, David," Mrs. Blake said. "It's as simple as that."

"Dad," Hunter said, "if you have a heart attack, or a stroke, or some other debilitating illness, you won't be able to work at all. This way at least you'll be able to contribute something."

"I know," Blake said. "I've finally admitted to myself that I'm really tired. I have to learn to delegate responsibility—and accept the fact that nobody else will do the job exactly the same way that I would."

Before he went to bed in the living room, surrounded by his packed bags, Hunter tried to phone Tehani again. When he still couldn't reach her, he sent her a vidmail saying that he was sorry that they had not had a chance to spend some time together during her visit home.

Hunter hardly slept that night. He woke up three or four times, always astonished to see that the clock had made such little progress. He had not expected that he would be so excited.

When Hunter disembarked with his parents at the station near the spaceport, he purposely set his bags on the platform and walked slowly to the end, watching the train disappear in the distance. He took a deep breath and struggled with his surprisingly strong feelings. He was leaving the asteroid that had been his home for all of his twenty years. For the first time, Hunter was aware of the full magnitude of that event.

As his eyes wandered aimlessly around the station,

Hunter wondered how long it would be before he would return. In his twenty years he had only been away from Cicero one time. When he was eight he had accompanied his father on a business trip to another asteroid as part of his birthday present. That trip had taken three days of travel each way, and Hunter had been bored beyond belief after he had finished exploring the small freighter that transported them back and forth. On this trip, since Mars was currently on the other side of the Sun from Cicero, the transit time alone would be almost twenty days.

At length, Hunter returned to the vicinity of his patient parents and picked up his bags. A couple of minutes later they entered the spaceport itself. Hunter was immediately surrounded by a couple of Cicero officials and the media. He stopped to answer a few questions before heading for the processing room.

Entry to the processing room was limited to passengers and two family members. A pair of spaceport employees greeted the Blakes in the small atrium outside the main door. One of the employees verified their identities, and the other, after first asking Hunter to indicate which bags he wanted in his cabin during the journey, took the baggage away to be inspected.

Hunter and his parents walked across the nearly empty room to the huge observation window that was a part of the side of the inner dome. Outside, the long, slim freighter, gleaming in the sunlight, was parked with its nose mostly facing the dome. The spacecraft was much larger than Hunter had expected. Back in the middle region of the somewhat ungainly vehicle, robot machines were placing giant packages onto a conveyor belt. The belt and the packages then disappeared inside huge rectangular containers wrapped around the main structural truss.

"That's the unpressurized cargo that's being loaded now," Mr. Blake commented. "This freighter can probably carry half a million pounds or so." He pointed at a fore-ground cylindrical structure. "Cargo that requires pressur-ization will be stored in the outer annulus of that cylinder just behind the nose. The living quarters and the flight deck are inside, or underneath if you prefer, the pressur-ized cargo hold."

In the distance, at the back end of the spacecraft, three peculiar-looking machines were attached to the freighter. "What's going on back there?" Hunter asked.

"Automatic checkout and final preparation for the flight," Mr. Blake answered. "That rear cluster contains all the vital engineering systems—the reactor, the propellant tanks, the thrusters, and most of the ancillary subsystems. They are located as far away from the passengers and crew as possible. For safety reasons."

"How long is the freighter altogether?" Mrs. Blake asked.

"I'd guess about two hundred feet," Hunter's father said. "I don't know the exact dimensions."

The spaceport employee who had handled the bags now approached Hunter. "Would you please come with me," he said, "it's time to check out your space suit."

Hunter gave his father a puzzled look. "It's an extra safety precaution," Blake said. "Because of the parts short-age, many of the elements of the spaceway are now single string." He laughed slightly. "We wouldn't want any of our important passengers to die because of the failure of an in-significant part."

In an adjacent small room, Hunter first stood, as re-quested, in front of a biometry scanner. All his data were within normal limits. Next he was fitted with a space suit and a pressurized helmet. Then Hunter was asked to take a few steps while fully dressed. He was surprised at how mo-bile he was.

Two more passengers came into the room for their space suits as Hunter was leaving. A dozen people were now in the processing room as Hunter rejoined his parents in front of the observation window. "Those are the drone fighters," Mr. Blake was saying to his wife as Hunter walked up. He was pointing at sleek, black, elongated vehicles out on the asteroid surface, a hundred yards or so beyond the freighter. "The freighter itself has only minimal combat capability. These days drones accompany every interplanetary flight. Otherwise, the insurance costs would be too high."

Mrs. Blake greeted her son. "Did it fit?" she asked.

"Uh-huh," Hunter replied. He glanced at the clock on the wall. It was only an hour before the scheduled departure time.

"Are you excited?" his mother said.

Hunter smiled. "Very," he answered. "I'm still having a hard time believing all this is really happening."

Hunter and his parents silently watched the preflight preparations for the freighter for a minute or so. "We're going to miss you very much," Mrs. Blake said.

Hunter could tell from the expression on his mother's face that she was about to cry. "Don't worry about me, Mom," he said. "I'm going to be all right. And I'll be home sooner than you think."

"Oh, Hunter," Mrs. Blake said, reaching out to hug him.

At that moment the processing-room door to the main spaceport area opened and Tesoro Wilawa entered. He immediately saw Hunter across the room and started running in his direction. Hunter broke his embrace with his mother to greet the boy.

"Tesoro," he said, with a puzzled frown on his face, "what are you doing here?"

"Mom and I are saying good-bye to Tehani," he said.

It took a moment for Hunter to understand. "You mean Tehani is leaving now also?" He pointed out the window. "On that freighter?"

Tesoro nodded. "Yep," the boy said. "The same one as you."

Hunter looked up toward the door. Tehani and Mrs. Wilawa entered the processing room. Tehani saw Hunter staring at her and waved. Without thinking, Hunter walked over toward her.

"Surprise!" Tehani said with a wonderful grin when Hunter was within earshot.

"You *knew?*" Hunter said a little too forcefully. "And you never told me?"

"I only found out yesterday for sure," Tehani replied with a coy smile. "But I was fairly certain the day of the announcement of your fellowship. The next flight to Mars is not until two weeks from tomorrow."

"But why didn't you say something?" Hunter continued, now aware that his emotions were out of control. He paused for a moment, realizing that he was being rude, and said hello to Mrs. Wilawa. Then he turned back to Tehani. "I sent you vidmail and you never even answered. I thought—"

"I'm sorry, Hunter," Tehani interrupted. "But how could I have replied without telling you the truth?" She laughed. "You are surprised, aren't you?"

"Yes, I mean, of course I am," Hunter stammered.

Tesoro and Mr. and Mrs. Blake joined the group. "Hello, Tehani," Mrs. Blake said. "It's so good to see you. You really do look marvelous."

"Thank you, Mrs. Blake," Tehani said sincerely. She touched Hunter lightly. "It looks as if I'm going to be traveling with your son."

"Why, that's wonderful," Mrs. Blake said. "And I was

worried that he would be bored on such a long journey. It will be twenty days before you reach Mars, won't it?"

Hunter nodded in response to his mother's question. Tehani introduced her mother and brother to the Blakes. During the ensuing small talk Hunter did not utter a word. It was doubtful that he could have answered even if someone had asked him a direct question. Simply to breathe required his maximum effort. As he felt Tehani's hand upon his arm, and heard her melodious voice, the little boy in Hunter was shouting inside his head. *Yes, yes, yes,* he said.

TWO

THE NEXT TWO HOURS or so were a blur for Hunter. Later he would remember saying good-bye to his parents, putting on his space suit, and walking behind Tehani down the spaceway that was deployed to take the passengers to the freighter. He would also recall meeting Derek Sanchez, the engineer and chief service representative of the *Darwin,* as the freighter was named, listening to all the safety instructions prior to takeoff, and eating the buffet lunch that was spread out on the dining table in the common area when they boarded. But at the time that these events actually happened, Hunter was definitely not completely present. An overwhelming giddiness possessed him, and he was concerned that he might break into uncontrollable laughter at any moment.

In his most creative fantasies he had never conceived that he would have such good fortune. The Covington Fellowship, by itself, was beyond Hunter's wildest imaginings. Since the announcement of his selection, he had felt he was a participant in an unbelievable dream. Often, during the days before his departure, Hunter would wander into his bathroom and stare at his image in the mirror, saying out loud, "You, Hunter Blake, are a Covington Fellow." To discover, in addition, that one of the other eleven passengers on his voyage to Mars was none other than Tehani Wilawa, without a doubt the one person he would most have preferred to accompany him on the trip, added a decidedly surreal component to his unmitigated joy.

Hunter's elevated mood did not break until the *Darwin* was several miles out in space and all the passengers, after finishing their preliminary unpacking, gathered on the flight deck for a last look at Cicero. Their home asteroid looked ridiculously small in the observation window. Only a small part of the asteroid was illuminated, since the freighter's initial trajectory was away from the Sun. As they watched, the domed colony where they had all been an hour before moved through the terminator, as it did several times each day, into darkness. The passengers stood silently and watched as the lights in the colony came on automatically and sparkled against the dark background of space.

"It's beautiful," Tehani said beside him.

"Good-bye," Hunter mumbled quietly. A wave of emotions engulfed him. Somewhere in the mixture was sorrow at being separated from his parents and the familiarity of his life on Cicero. Equally poignant was a combination of anticipation and fear about what lay ahead of him. There was a moment when Hunter thought he was going to cry. Then the electric touch of Tehani's hand on his abruptly changed his mood.

Hunter turned to look at her. "I know," she said quietly. "I remember the first time I left, almost two years ago."

The *Darwin* changed attitude and Cicero vanished from the window. Derek Sanchez, their affable host, came out of the small cockpit on one side of the flight deck and asked for their attention. He requested that the passengers follow him to the common area for general introductions and a discussion of schedules.

The dozen *Darwin* passengers dropped down a step

from the spacious flight deck and filed into a wide passageway that led to the rear of the spacecraft. On either side of them were the food and equipment compartments, the engineering room, and the crew quarters. A thick glass door separated this front part of the *Darwin* from the main passenger section of the pressurized compartment. On the other side of the door was the dining area, behind which was a lounge with two couches, a small rectangular game table with four folding chairs, and half a dozen additional, more comfortable chairs scattered around the room. Except for the folding chairs, all the furniture was anchored to the floor. The virtual-world kiosk, a futuristic module that could accommodate two people comfortably inside its sealed confines, was just inside the glass door, over in the corner on the left-hand side facing the door from the dining area. One exercise station and one work desk, with a computer terminal, were against the walls of the lounge on each side. Between the exercise station and the work desk on the left-hand side was the spacecraft entrance through which everyone had come when they boarded the *Darwin* originally. Along the walls near the back of the lounge were the passenger lockers, where items that would not fit in the cabins were stored.

Farther toward the rear the common area narrowed until it became no more than a wide corridor. The four showers and the six passenger cabins were on either side of this corridor. Behind the cabins, in a small section just in front of the back wall of the compartment, six more work desks and terminals were arranged symmetrically around a large door leading to the nonpressurized areas of the spacecraft.

The cabins themselves, each of which was occupied by two persons, were tiny. Each passenger had a small twin bed, a closed shelf behind the head of the bed for toiletries and a few accessories, and drawers to hold enough clothing for two or three days. A single washbasin was against the outside wall at the end of the aisle between the beds. Above the basin was a little round window that afforded a glimpse of space outside the spacecraft. The minuscule toilet closet, virtually concealed when the cabin door was open, filled the remaining space in the room.

Once everyone was gathered in the common area, the gray-haired *Darwin* pilot, Captain James Pollack, appeared and introduced himself. He explained to the passengers that except for takeoffs and landings, the freighter essentially flew itself, according to a predetermined program, and that very little manual intercession was necessary unless there were problems outside the bounds of those that could be handled automatically by the fault-protection system.

"Most of the time," Captain Pollack said, "the cockpit will be unoccupied. Please do not be alarmed by that. All three of us who are certified to pilot this spacecraft, including the charming Derek Sanchez here, wear pagers that activate when any significant parameter is out of its normal limits. Each of us knows when it is our turn to respond to any signal. . . . For your information, this particular crew has flown together already on seven interplanetary journeys similar to this one."

When Captain Pollack was finished, he mentioned that the other two crew members were sleeping. "Derek and I will basically live on the same diurnal cycle as you passengers. Lieutenant Wong and Major Belinsky will be shifted from us by exactly twelve hours."

Captain Pollack prepared a cup of coffee for himself from the automatic dispenser against the wall in the dining area, then passed through the glass door. Immediately after the captain departed, Derek Sanchez stood up and began the general introduction process by explaining that he was thirty-four, an engineering graduate from Centralia, and that he had been working for Interplanetary Transport, Incorporated, or ITI as it was known, for four years.

There were eight men and four women among the passengers. Two married couples, both elderly Cicero natives traveling to Mars to visit their children and grandchildren, occupied the cabins closest to the common area. One of the married men, who had introduced himself to Hunter as Calvin Thorpe in the processing room on Cicero, informed everyone else during his introduction that he had been the Protestant minister on the asteroid for twenty-three years prior to his retirement the previous March. He mentioned that he would be conducting church services for those interested on the two Sundays of the flight.

Most of the introductions were short. George Slovikovski, a tall, athletic man with gray hair, announced that he was a retired businessman. A Mr. Ali Khan introduced himself as an investment counselor. Rohan Weerasinghe, a middle-aged FISC official who had just completed a one-year tour of duty on Cicero, mentioned that he had immigrated to Mars from Sri Lanka on Earth when he was a young boy. An unkempt man in his thirties with extremely long hair simply gave his name, Carson Bagwell. Tehani's roommate, an attractive black woman with a rich, expansive smile, identified herself as a fashion designer.

Hunter and Tehani were tenth and eleventh in the introduction sequence. Hunter debated briefly whether he should include the fact that he was a Covington Fellow in his introduction, but decided against it as being too immodest. He just said that he had most recently been employed as a paramedic at Cicero Hospital, and that he was on his way to Mars to start a new career.

"I'm Tehani Wilawa," she said after Hunter was finished. "I was born and raised on Cicero, and I now work at Sybaris."

There was a curious silence after Tehani's introduction. Hunter looked around at the other passengers and thought, or imagined, that all of them were already familiar with

Tehani. The faces of the two married women were cold and distant, or so it seemed to Hunter, and he found himself growing angry at what he perceived to be their silent disapproval. If Derek had not called on Hunter's roommate, a middle-aged attorney named Everett Peabody, to complete the introductions, Hunter might have said something that he would have later regretted.

After the introductions were finished, Derek handed out a set of forms containing, among other things, the meal choices for the voyage. "Please select a maximum of twenty breakfasts, lunches, and dinners," he said, "and also indicate all meals that you would consider to be acceptable. Wherever possible, we will feed you what you have chosen. However, we have a limited number of each kind of meal, as you would expect, so please try to understand that each passenger may not be able to have his or her choice at all times.

"Two other items which are shared resources," Derek then continued, "are the exercise equipment and the virtual-world kiosk. We have two exercise stations containing state-of-the-art apparatus for keeping bodies fit during extended weightlessness. One twenty-minute exercise period per day, plus two doses of antiatrophy medication each week, is usually enough that there are no bad health effects from a trip like this. After you have identified your food choices, please clarify your exercise desires, especially the times of day that you would prefer.

"As for the kiosk, let me remind you right now, before the trip begins, that its use is not included in the fare for the voyage. FedEnt has supplied the kiosk with updated versions of several of the newer worlds, and we have an entire closet full of peripheral apparatus that you can rent, if you desire. However, it seems only fair that I warn you that the temptation to use the onboard kiosk is very high, for those of you who like that kind of entertainment, and we have had passengers run up enormous bills during longer duration flights like this one."

Derek glanced around the room. "Are there any questions so far?" he asked.

Mrs. Thorpe raised her hand. "What do we do if medical attention is needed? Are any of the crew members doctors?"

"Thanks for asking that question," Derek said pleasantly. "I sometimes forget to explain how we handle medical problems on the *Darwin*.... First, there are no actual doctors onboard. However, all of us received extensive paramedical training as part of our certification to become flight crew members. To deal with a medical issue requiring expert advice, we keep an open emergency line to Centralia Memorial Hospital."

Derek looked around the lounge. "One of the documents you were each required to sign when you purchased your ticket from ITI was a medical waiver, stating, in part, that there existed no known physical conditions that should require a doctor's attention for the duration of our flight. Your personal doctor has separately attested to the same fact. Nevertheless, medical emergencies can and do arise. We treat them as top-priority items. I assure you, if some unexpected problem occurs, the crew will do everything we can to make you comfortable and to obtain the best possible advice from a physician."

Derek paused. "Oh, yes, before I forget, the biometry scanners are attached to the bottom of the dining table. All of your personalized data was uploaded from the Cicero Hospital. You are automatically scanned each time you eat. Out-of-tolerance parameters are recorded in the main flight computer—one of us, most likely me, will let you know if there are any significant problems.

"Okay," Derek said, starting to sound a bit weary, "anybody have anything else?" Nobody responded. "In that case," Derek added, "let me make one or two comments about weightlessness. The slippers you were given when you boarded the *Darwin,* which I see all of you are now wearing, will keep you on the floor unless you inadvertently lift both feet at the same time. If you find yourself floating, please do not panic. Eventually you will reach a wall or someone will be able to give you a hand."

Derek smiled. "All right," he said, "you've been a great audience. The baseline meal allocations and equipment schedules will be finished in a matter of minutes after your inputs are complete. They can be accessed from any of the computer terminals."

HUNTER AND TEHANI spent a few minutes chatting after the group meeting was finished. After deciding what time they would have dinner together, Hunter returned to his cabin to finish unpacking. When he entered, Mr. Peabody was meticulously wiping the washbasin with a cloth. Hunter watched, without saying anything, as the man put the cloth back in a sealable bag and returned the bag to his shelf. Mr. Peabody then picked up the suitcase that he was going to place in his locker. "Please don't leave your things scattered around," Mr. Peabody said as he walked out the cabin door.

Hunter was going to ask Mr. Peabody what he was talking about, but the man didn't stop. Puzzled, Hunter looked carefully around the room. There was nothing of his in the area around the now spotless washbasin, or in the toilet closet. He had no idea what was bothering Mr. Peabody. Prior to being called to the flight deck, Hunter had spread most of his clothes across his bed, trying to decide what to keep in the drawers in the cabin and what to store in his locker. The clothes were still where he had left them. Were they the problem?

Disturbed, Hunter sat down on his bed. Looking across

at Mr. Peabody's bed, he noticed that the blanket had no wrinkles and had been neatly tucked in everywhere. On a hunch, Hunter rose and looked through the glass front of Mr. Peabody's shelf at the head of his bed. What he saw was amazing. It wasn't just that everything appeared to have been carefully placed in a given position. Mr. Peabody had also affixed printed icons to the back surface of the shelf, indicating where each item should permanently reside.

Ohmygod, Hunter thought to himself, *I'm going to spend twenty days with a neatness freak.* On impulse he picked up the phone and called Tehani in her cabin. "Do you have a second?" he said. "Come on over here, there's something I want you to see."

Since Tehani's cabin was just across the corridor, she arrived almost instantly. "What is it?" she said.

"Look at this," Hunter said in a low voice, pointing at Mr. Peabody's shelf. "You remember our conversation about obsessive behavior? This man has printed icons that he carries around with him so that his toiletries can be arranged properly. A few minutes ago he wiped the washbasin clean after he used it. . . . How am I going to live with him for almost three weeks?"

Tehani inspected the shelf more closely and started laughing. "Good luck," she said, preparing to walk out the open door. "I'll tell Veronica that you may be visiting us often."

Mr. Peabody returned just as Tehani left the room. He didn't look happy. "Blake," he said to Hunter in an unpleasant tone, "I guess there are some things that we should get straight right from the beginning. Your girlfriend has her own cabin. She does not belong here. If you want to see her, then do so somewhere else."

Hunter was so shocked by the man's comments that at first he didn't say anything at all. A minute or two later, however, after he had finished arranging his clothes,

Hunter spoke to Mr. Peabody, who was now sitting rigidly straight on his bed, his back against the wall, completely engrossed in his handheld computer.

"Excuse me, sir," Hunter began politely.

"What is it, Blake?" Mr. Peabody said tersely.

"Sir, we're going to be cabinmates for twenty days," Hunter said, "and I think it would be better for both of us if we didn't develop an adversarial relationship. . . . Now I recognize your right to have a say in who does, and who does not, come into our cabin. But I think you could have chosen a different way to approach the issue."

Mr. Peabody forced a smile. "How old are you?" he asked.

"I'm twenty," Hunter replied. "But that really—"

"My sons are twenty-seven and twenty-four," Mr. Peabody interrupted.

"Sir," Hunter started again, struggling to suppress his growing anger, "my age is really irrelevant here. What I'm trying to say is that we are going to share this cabin for a long time. Neither of us has the right to unilaterally set the cabin rules. These are things that we need to discuss together. Now, I'm trying to be accommodating about this, Mr. Peabody, but I must tell you that I don't like being ordered around."

Mr. Peabody stared at Hunter for a few seconds before closing his hand computer. "All right, Blake," he said without smiling, "let's have a discussion of rules. I propose the following. Rule Number One: No visitors in the room, ever. Rule Number Two: No lights and no noise between eleven o'clock at night and six in the morning. Rule Number Three: No personal objects in the shared space—by that I mean the washbasin, the toilet closet, and the floor. Rule Number Four: The basin and the toilet shall be cleaned after each use." He paused a moment. "So, young man," Mr. Peabody continued, "what do you think?"

Hunter's first inclination was to point out to his pompous cabinmate that his proposed rules contained a glaring inconsistency. *What if one of us needs to go to the toilet in the middle of the night?* Hunter wanted to say. *How are we going to clean it in total darkness?* He held his tongue, however, and waited until he had settled down a little. "Give me until after dinner," he said at length. "I'll let you know then."

THREE

"SO IT WAS YOUR mother's mother who was from Thailand," Hunter said to Tehani. "I thought I had remembered that it was your father's mother."

Tehani shook her head. "Both my father's parents were from French Polynesia," she said. "They immigrated to Mars right after they were married. My grandfather, whom I saw only one time, when I was six years old, was a direct descendant of the early kings of Bora-Bora. He died when I was eight."

Hunter and Tehani were enjoying a drink before dinner. They were sitting by themselves in the two lounge chairs closest to the passenger cabins.

"Okay," Hunter said. "I think I have it straight now. Your mother's father was originally from Italy and was working at the New Earth Amusement Park when your grandmother, who was some kind of international model, went there on a goodwill tour. They fell in love, and she returned to Mars to marry him the next year after she completed her contract with the modeling agency."

"According to Mom, my grandmother was the most famous model in Southeast Asia," Tehani said. "I'll show you some of her pictures after dinner. She was a true beauty. . . . Still is, even though she's almost seventy."

"I'm always happy to look at pictures of beautiful women," Hunter said with a grin. He took a sip from his drink before continuing. "Now as I recall, your mother was born a year after their wedding. Your grandfather was promoted to an executive position at New Earth, but soon thereafter the marriage faltered—"

"Because my mother's father was insanely jealous," Tehani interjected. "He didn't want her to do anything but stay home all the time with my mother, unless she was with him. Even when they were out together, if she was just a little bit friendly to another man, my grandfather would go wild and cause an embarrassing scene. Eventually she couldn't take it anymore."

"There's always two sides to every story," Hunter said. "It would be interesting to hear your grandfather's version. . . ."

"I believe my grandmother," Tehani said. "After the divorce, my grandfather moved back to Italy and married again. According to my mother, his second marriage ended in a similar fashion."

"Have you ever met your mother's father?" Hunter asked.

"Only on video," Tehani said. "He wished me happy birthday when I was eighteen." She sighed. "The only man in my family who was ever in my life was my father."

Hunter broke a protracted silence. "Are you hungry?" he said.

Tehani stood up. "Yes, I am," she said. She discreetly pulled on the straw to finish her pressurized drink and took Hunter's container from him. "Where did Derek say to put these?" she asked.

"On the other side of the dispenser," Hunter said. He smiled. "In the bin labeled DRINK CONTAINERS."

Tehani acted as if she was going to throw the empty drinks at him. "Don't do that," he admonished with a laugh. "They could ricochet off the wall and hit somebody."

Hunter and Tehani walked over to the dining table and sat down at the opposite end from the two elderly married couples, who were almost finished with their meals. Only one other person was at the table, a man in his forties named Ali Khan, who had referred to himself as an investment counselor during the general introductions. Mr. Khan acknowledged their arrival with a smile and a courteous nod. The Thorpes and the Broughers, who had appeared to be engaged in a lively conversation moments earlier, stopped talking and stared at Hunter and Tehani without any comment.

Hunter and Tehani studied the keyboard built into the dining table at each seat. Following the instructions, they each entered their names and received the printed message that their dinners would be served in less than five minutes.

"What did you order for tonight?" Tehani asked.

"I'm not sure," Hunter answered. "I think it was the chicken."

"I'm having the fish with stir-fried vegetables," Tehani said with a laugh. "After all the conflicts were resolved, I think I'm having it every other night of the whole trip."

A few minutes later the two elderly couples rose from the table. One of the two robots from the kitchen came to clear away their plates. After they were gone, Mr. Khan leaned toward Hunter and Tehani and smiled. "I don't think they know what to make of you," he said.

"Excuse me?" Hunter said pleasantly, not understanding Mr. Khan's comment.

"Before you sat down," Mr. Khan said, "the lady with the great smile—I believe that's Mrs. Brougher, but I could be mistaken—was telling her husband and the other couple about seeing a local television interview with Miss Wilawa last week on Cicero." He laughed. "Mrs. Thorpe wanted to know why you were so famous. Apparently she knew little or nothing about Sybaris except that people go there to have fun."

Neither Hunter nor Tehani said anything. "I'm sorry," Mr. Khan added genuinely several seconds later. "I didn't mean to offend you in any way. I just thought you ought to know, since we're a small family on board this spaceship, that you have been recognized. . . . As for me, I hope it's all right if I tell you, Miss Wilawa, that you are even more beautiful in person than in your video."

"Thank you," Tehani said politely.

Mr. Khan continued to talk while the robot served Hunter's and Tehani's meals. "I'm ready for this trip to be over," the man said. "That night in the shelter on Cicero completely undid me. I kept thinking about what would happen to my wife and daughters if I died on a remote asteroid in a bombing raid."

"How many daughters do you have?" Tehani asked in between bites.

"Two," Mr. Khan replied. "They're sixteen and fourteen. . . . We had applied with the Ministry of Health for a son as our second child, but while we were waiting for approval . . . Well, you know how these things are."

Soon thereafter Hunter asked Mr. Khan why he had traveled to Cicero, since all his work certainly could have been accomplished over the network.

"My wife always asks the same question," Mr. Khan replied. "Interestingly enough, statistics show that people are far more willing to invest their money with people they have actually met face-to-face. Because our counselors are personally accessible to our clients, our firm in Centralia is far and away the most successful with Federation citizens who do not live on Mars. . . .

"I'd give up the travel in an instant," Mr. Khan commented a little later, "if I could find another way to produce the same amount of income. I've already decided I'll never come to Cicero again when it's on the opposite side of the Sun from Mars. Spending twenty days in transit is not my idea of fun. Last year the trip only took nine days, and that's too long for me. . . ."

Mr. Khan talked continuously while he remained at the table. When he finally excused himself, leaving Hunter and Tehani alone, they looked at each other and smiled. "He seems nice enough," Tehani said, "even if he does talk a lot. At least he's friendly, not like your roommate Mr. Peabody or the two older couples."

Hunter took a bite from his dessert. "I don't like myself when I suspect other people's motives," he said, "but I bet there are good reasons for his friendliness."

"What reasons?" Tehani said. "I think Mr. Khan's just lonely and wants to talk to somebody."

"Miss Wilawa," Hunter said after an extended silence while they both finished eating, "has it occurred to you that perhaps Mr. Khan might view you as a prospective client? In that *EXPOSURE* article about you, there was clearly an implication that you were making one hell of a lot of money."

Tehani frowned. "That article was nothing but tabloid journalism," she said, "full of the worst kinds of innuendo. They never really said anything that was libelous, but they certainly stretched the truth to make their story more sensational."

Hunter and Tehani both fell silent. In all their conversations since Tehani had returned to Cicero, the subject of her work had never been directly addressed. She had never mentioned it, except in passing, and Hunter had avoided the subject for many reasons, not the least of which was his uncertainty about what he might say. He quickly decided now was not the time for an in-depth discussion.

"Well, beautiful," he said lightly, standing up from the table, "what now? A game, a movie, or a walk in the park?"

Tehani rose, smiling, and put her arm through his. "A walk in the park sounds great," she said.

WHEN HUNTER MADE a brief stop in his cabin later that evening, he found a sheet of paper on his bed. At the top of the page was written, in all capital letters, "PROPOSED AGREEMENT BETWEEN MESSRS. PEABODY AND BLAKE." Hunter read the first paragraph of the document and nearly doubled over with laughter. A few seconds later he was pounding on Tehani's cabin door.

Veronica opened the door slightly and stuck her head outside. "Tehani is indisposed," she said with a bemused smile. "She told me to tell you that she'd be out in a minute or two."

Hunter thanked Veronica and continued reading the sheet in his hand. Twice he laughed out loud.

"What is it?" Tehani said, puzzled, when she finally joined him in the corridor.

"You must read this," Hunter said, handing her the paper.

"WHEREAS," the text of the document prepared by Mr. Peabody began, "Messrs. Everett Peabody and Hunter Blake have been assigned to the same cabin on board the ITI freighter *Darwin* en route from Cicero to Mars; and WHEREAS, said two gentlemen acknowledge the necessity of an agreement including, but not limited to, the common space that they share and their conduct within; THEREFORE, be it agreed by both parties that the following regulations shall govern. . . ."

Tehani was in stitches before she even started reading Mr. Peabody's very formal codification of the rules he had suggested before dinner to Hunter. She kept laughing, shaking her head, and looking up at him. "This is priceless," Tehani said when she finally caught her breath. "It must be a joke."

"*Au contraire, mon amie,*" Hunter said, using one of the two or three phrases he remembered from his brief introduction to French during his survey course in other languages several years before. "I'm certain that it's not a joke at all. This guy is that serious. I bet he spent an hour in our cabin drafting this agreement."

"Nobody is *that* anal retentive," Tehani said.

"Peabody is," Hunter replied. "How would you like to work with someone like that? I bet he rushes into the bathroom in his office five times a day and carefully folds the next sheet on the toilet-paper roll."

Tehani was laughing again. "So what are you going to do?" she asked. "Are you going to sign it?"

Hunter shrugged. "Maybe I'll see if Derek can arrange a cabin switch. I'll take anybody, even the garrulous Mr. Khan, over this Peabody character."

A split second after the mention of his name, the tall, angular body of Hunter's cabinmate appeared at the other end of the corridor, heading in their direction. Hunter said a quick good-bye to Tehani and ducked into his cabin.

Mr. Peabody walked inside and carefully closed the cabin door behind him. "Excuse me," he said brusquely, as he went into the toilet closet. Not a sound was heard during the half minute that Mr. Peabody was inside. Hunter found himself wondering what was happening. What was the man doing? If he was urinating, why wasn't there any sound? Did he have some special sound-suppression system so that nobody could hear him? At that thought Hunter almost broke into audible laughter.

"Well, Blake," Mr. Peabody said as soon as he emerged from the toilet closet, "have you read the draft agreement?"

"Yes, sir, I have," Hunter said, still fighting his laughter.

"Do you have any proposed amendments or suggested clarifications?" Mr. Peabody asked.

"Yes, sir," Hunter responded, feigning seriousness. "I'm particularly concerned about the second rule," he said. "I believe it unduly restricts my freedom. I can't agree to be inside this cabin every night between the hours of eleven and six. What I will accept, however, is a provision that our cabin lights be extinguished during those periods—except when one of us is using the toilet, of course—and a no-noise codicil as well."

Mr. Peabody, who was sitting on his bed across from Hunter, pulled out his tiny computer without comment and began making revisions. After about a minute he looked up at Hunter. "Anything else?" he said.

"I think that cleaning the toilet and/or the washbasin after a use in the middle of the night is in conflict with the second rule. It seems unlikely that the cleaning can be done in the darkness, and without any noise."

Mr. Peabody responded with an approving smile. "I hadn't thought about that," he said. "That's an excellent point, Blake. It's possible that you might have a career in the law."

Not in this lifetime, Hunter said to himself. Mr. Peabody was busily making another set of revisions to the agreement on his computer. Hunter suddenly felt pity for the man. *How does somebody let himself become like that?* he wondered. *What happened to the child in him? Did the world, or his parents, somehow destroy it?*

Mr. Peabody stood up. "I'll just dash outside to one of the terminals and print out copies of the amended agreement for both of us," he said cheerfully. "Good work, Blake," he added. "I was worried that we might have some fundamental disagreements."

HUNTER AND TEHANI were sitting at the computer terminals in the back of the lounge, beyond the passenger cabins, the only location in the common area where there was a modicum of privacy. They had been watching an old movie together for a couple of hours. Intermittently they had held hands, and occasionally they had exchanged a comment, but for the most part it had been an easy, relaxing evening that they had enjoyed together. As the credits began on the two monitors they were watching, Hunter reached for the keyboard to stop the program.

"Not yet," Tehani said quietly, touching his forearm. "I like this song."

The woman singing the song that was playing over the credits had a superb voice. The song itself was about dreams and yearning. The lyrics for the plaintive melody told of reaching for, but never quite attaining, the perfect love, or the perfect state of happiness.

"Sometimes I wish I were seventeen again," Tehani said when the song was over.

"Why's that?" Hunter asked.

"In those days I believed in Prince Charming," she said, "and in living happily ever after." Tehani sighed. "That was before my father died and my fairy-tale life came crashing down around me. Before I found out that reality can be very painful."

Hunter looked at her and took her hand. " 'There was a time when meadow, grove, and stream,' " he remembered, " 'the Earth and every common sight, to me did seem appareled in celestial light. . . .' "

" 'The glory and the freshness of a dream,' " Tehani continued without missing a beat. " 'It is not now, as it hath been of yore. Turn whereso'er I may, by night or day, the things that I have seen, I now can see no more.' "

She forced a smile. "You recited that Wordsworth poem in our declamation competition. You finished first, and I was second. As usual." She paused, deep in her memory. "How old were we then?"

"Fourteen, I think," Hunter said.

"God, it seems like so very long ago," Tehani said. "Did I still see that celestial light when I was fourteen? I must have. I spent all day long immersed in my dreams."

In the soft light Hunter saw a sorrow in her eyes that he had never seen before. He was seized by a powerful impulse to make that sadness go away, to restore hope in the only woman who had ever been the center of his universe. He leaned toward her.

Tehani parted her lips and they kissed. It was a light, sensitive, exploring kiss, nearly devoid of passion. Their lips touched and then moved ever so slightly, finding a new location and an even richer sensation.

The kiss endured for over a minute. She reached up and caressed his cheek softly with her hand. Hunter didn't dare break the kiss to breathe. His heart was pounding so violently that he thought it would jump out of his body. And whatever doubt he might have had about his feelings for Tehani vanished in an instant.

They didn't say anything after the kiss. They stood up, holding hands, and walked slowly toward their cabins. In the corridor outside her door, Hunter and Tehani kissed again. This was a powerful, passionate kiss, full of promise for the future. The dazed Hunter mumbled good night to his beloved Tehani and stumbled into his cabin.

FOUR

HUNTER WOKE UP VERY early the next morning after a dreamless sleep. Being very careful not to disturb the sleeping Mr. Peabody, he dressed in the dark and slipped out of his cabin. The common area was empty. Hunter went to one of the computers in the back and accessed the extensive spaceship library.

During his hectic final days on Cicero, Hunter had received many transmissions from Hans Langenbahn, the Covington Fellow coordinator. One of Mr. Langenbahn's vidmail messages had informed Hunter that soon after he arrived in Centralia he would be given a full battery of examinations "to assess the status of his education and knowledge." The ostensible purpose of these tests was to provide updated information that could be used for the design of his "personal development." Although Mr. Langenbahn had stressed that no preparation was required, and that the results from the examinations would influence only his training regimen, and not his eventual work assignments, the highly competitive Hunter intended to do as well as he possibly could on the tests.

He was quite certain he would have no trouble with any

of the math or science elements of the tests. Hunter had kept his math skills current by tutoring students studying for the secondary-school examinations, and his job at the hospital regularly refreshed his knowledge of biology, chemistry, and computer technology. What worried him were the fact-based humanities subjects, especially space history and government, which Mr. Langenbahn had indicated the tests would particularly emphasize.

The *Darwin* database contained a wealth of information about space history. Hunter spent an hour or so scanning a somewhat random selection of the entries, noting in his mind which articles were the most interesting, or seemed to be the most accessible, before selecting an illustrated survey article to read thoroughly. The article was an excellent starting point for his study—it summarized the entirety of space history, and contained hypertext identifiers leading to other, more detailed entries in the database.

The Space Age began just after the middle of the twentieth century with the launch of the first Earth orbiting satellite, called Sputnik. The launching of this satellite kicked off a frantic space competition between the two major powers of that era, the United States of America and the Soviet Union, who were in an intense struggle for global supremacy. The goal of the competition, which would confirm to most of the world the technological and ideological superiority of the winner, was to safely land a human being on the Moon. The United States, with its vast economic resources and superb systems engineering, won the competition handily, landing a spacecraft carrying two astronauts on the Moon on July 20, 1969.

A magnificent full-screen video of the first landing on the Moon, complete with the audio interactions between Mission Control and the astronauts, was automatically triggered as Hunter read. He paused, wondering what it must have felt like, almost five hundred years previously, to have been watching on television as a human being stepped on another planetary surface for the first time.

Hunter read quickly through the early paragraphs of the survey article, noting the astonishing gap of over fifty years between the initial human forays to the Moon and the subsequent, more orderly exploitation and colonization of Earth's satellite under the aegis of the fledgling ISA, the International Space Agency. He had forgotten that a major factor enabling the human colonization of the Moon was the discovery by robotic spacecraft, just before the beginning of the twenty-first century, of large quantities of water ice near each of the Moon's two poles. Once techniques for economically accessing and transporting that water were developed and validated, no significant impediments to the establishment of permanent human settlements on the Moon remained. By the end of the twenty-first century, several hundred ISA scientists, along with the engineers required to keep the bases operational, occupied the two small towns that had been built, one in the Sea of Tranquility, and the second on the dark side of the Moon, where astronomical observations were not corrupted by Earth interference.

Also in the twenty-first century robotic spacecraft completed the characterization of the solar system, human exploration of Mars began in earnest, and the capability of the species to live and work in space was thoroughly cataloged as a result of experiments conducted in association with progressively larger, and more sophisticated, space colonies that were established in orbit around the Earth.

In the twenty-second century, space colonization expanded rapidly under the steady guidance of the ISA.

Economic support was provided by the new, multinational federations on Earth. Tranquility on the Moon, and then Centralia on Mars, developed into small cities. The mining of the near asteroids began. The first human exploration of the moons of Jupiter occurred. Dozens of permanent colonies in space were created, mostly in Earth orbit. Smaller outposts, some designed only for temporary occupation, were established throughout the region from Venus to Jupiter.

Early in the twenty-third century events on Earth set the stage for a paradigmatic change in the way the space colonies would be governed. Earth was beset by a host of problems—the outbreak of a major war, a severe worldwide depression, environmental degradation, and a devastating epidemic from a new strain of virus—all of which significantly reduced attention to what was happening in space. Funding for the ISA dropped precipitously, so much that the agency was no longer able to provide proper governance for the nearly one million humans who were living away from the Earth. In addition, the difficulties on Earth prompted a massive new immigration into space, just at the time when the colonies were least able to deal with newcomers.

Out of desperation, colony after colony empowered its local government to make decisions previously relegated to the ISA. To deal with issues such as intercolony trade, transportation, and personnel movement, agreements were drawn up among the colonies that created new agencies outside the purview of the ISA. From 2257 until 2260 a series of meetings took place on the Moon, attended at least in part by representatives of virtually all the existing space colonies, that resulted in the establishment of the United Democratic Space Colonies (UDSC). When the UDSC charter was ratified by its founders, clearly defining what powers would be centralized and which would be distributed to the individual colonies themselves, the de facto transfer of authority from Earth to space was officially complete. The ISA stamp of approval on the UDSC charter was simply a formality. By that time the ISA's only significant role in space was the coordination of immigration from the Earth to the colonies.

Hunter felt a gentle hand on his shoulder. "Good morning, Mr. Blake," Tehani said with a warm smile. "Have you already eaten breakfast?"

He swiveled in his chair. "No, I haven't," Hunter said. "And good morning to you. Did you sleep well?"

Tehani was looking at his monitor. "I slept okay," she said. "Wow," she added, "this is pretty heavy stuff for pre-breakfast reading. I didn't know you were that interested in space history."

Hunter smiled. "I haven't even thought about the subject since the secondary-school exams two years ago," he said. "But it's one of the major items on the set of tests I'll be taking when I arrive in Centralia, and I don't want to embarrass myself."

"That would never happen," Tehani said. "Even if you didn't study at all, with your memory you would do better than almost everyone else."

"Don't be so sure," Hunter said. "The Covington Fellows are an elite group. According to the material I was sent, every single one of the selected fellows scored in the upper one percent on the standardized exams during school."

Tehani sat down in the chair next to Hunter and turned the monitor so they both could see it. "I have always loved history," she said, reading a part of the article. "It's the only subject that explains why things are the way they are." She looked at Hunter and laughed. "I guess that's not a very profound statement, is it?"

"No," he replied, "but it communicates, and it's accurate." He watched Tehani reading from the monitor. "Maybe you could help me prepare," he said. "It would certainly make studying space history much more interesting."

"Maybe," she said. "I wrote my term paper on the causes of the civil war that produced the FISC. At least in that area I could be of some help."

He turned to face her. "All right," Hunter said, grinning mischievously, "I'm all ears. It'll be a hell of a lot more exciting listening to you than staring at this monitor."

Tehani laughed again. "The early space history stuff is easy, and reasonably straightforward," she said. "Where it gets confusing is around the time of the civil war, just before the middle of the twenty-fourth century. At that time the space population, especially on Mars, was growing rapidly. There were many conflicting pressures on the UDSC leaders. An acrimonious election resulted in a coalition government that was anathema to the individualists of North Mars. Soon after the new government increased taxes, an armed rebellion spread quickly from province to province north of the Martian equator. The central government was slow to respond."

Tehani stopped and shrugged. "Was the FISC created by impatient, power-hungry renegades who were frustrated by their inability to change a system that was good, but not perfect? That's what the Dems say. Or was the civil war a legitimate, justified act by a bunch of heroes who realized that only by overthrowing the established UDSC regime could they achieve the kind of laissez-faire government they desired? My history discussion leader in high school told us that if the schism had not occurred, and the FISC had not been established as an alternative space government, then the UDSC would have become a complete welfare state by now, with no incentives of any kind to reward individual excellence."

Hunter was looking at her with a mixture of awe and appreciation. Tehani smiled and stood up. "And that, Mr. Hunter Blake, is all you're going to get from me until after I've had some breakfast. I'm absolutely famished." She looked at her watch. "And besides, if we don't eat in the next fifteen minutes, the robots will all be on their coffee break."

HUNTER AND TEHANI were the first passengers to be given the full guided tour of the *Darwin*. They met Derek soon after breakfast and then followed him through the large, thick door at the back of the common area into a windowless room full of equipment storage compartments. Derek closed the door behind them and spent thirty seconds operating the keyboard and the monitor built into the back side of the door. After he had finished verifying that the pressurized region of the *Darwin* was again properly sealed, he pulled their space suits out of one of the compartments. The suits had all been labeled back on Cicero when they were first issued and checked.

"Once I open the door on the other side," Derek said, "we will be in a vacuum. We will revalidate the integrity of your space suit here, before we leave. Please remember that you will be in a hazardous environment. Avoid all sharp objects that could pierce your suit. Take no chances. A leak in your space suit could mean death in a matter of a few minutes."

"Should I be frightened?" Tehani asked through the microphone in her helmet.

They heard Derek's characteristic laugh. "No," he said. "I've never lost a passenger yet. But I have had a couple of close calls. It's just important that you be aware of what you are doing."

Three levels of security prevented the unauthorized

opening of the outside door. Derek had had his retina scanned prior to donning his space helmet. He had also entered a special code, identifying for record-keeping purposes that he was taking passengers on a guided tour of the *Darwin*'s engineering systems, into the processor to the right of the door. The third and final key was an eight-digit alphanumeric password.

"The password changes every day," Derek informed them. "It's stored in the computer on the flight deck and requires a special call sequence known only to the crew. We have no a priori knowledge of what it's going to be the next day."

On the other side of the door it was pitch-black. Derek pushed a button on the small controller he had in his hand and Hunter and Tehani saw a tunnel stretching thirty or forty yards in front of them. "The unpressurized cargo is stored in containers mounted on all sides around the thick walls of this tunnel," Derek said as they began to walk. "The walls have been purposely overdesigned to isolate and protect the structural integrity of this link between the pressurized compartment and the engineering systems. In the worst case, even if an explosion destroyed one of the containers and caused it to be ripped away from the spacecraft, the *Darwin* would still remain spaceworthy."

"If this conversation is supposed to be making me feel better," Tehani said, "it's not succeeding."

"You don't have anything to worry about yet," Derek said. "Wait until I start telling you about what can go wrong with the engineering systems."

As they neared the end of the tunnel, Derek turned around to face Hunter and Tehani. "We're about to enter an area that's open to space," he said. "It's possible that you may become disoriented out there. Without gravity or visual cues for your eyes, your body has no sense of direction." He hooked a line onto a small ring at the back of the waist of their space suits. "If, for any reason, you lose immediate physical contact with the spacecraft, don't panic. I'll be able to pull you back with this line."

Tehani shuddered at the thought of floating away from the *Darwin*. At the end of the tunnel, on the right-hand side, there was a small metal box built into the wall. Waving them onto the large, uncovered platform beyond, Derek attached the other end of each of the three lines to one of the rings protruding from the box. It was actually comforting to both Hunter and Tehani to feel the slight tug of the line on their backs when they took each step.

The view from the platform was spectacular. Huge, dark, geometric silhouettes, connected to the platform by lattice ladders, were visible in every direction. In the gaps among the structural elements the stars shone with an overwhelming splendor. Neither Hunter nor Tehani had ever before seen the stars so clearly. About twenty yards from the end of the tunnel, they both stopped at the same time.

"This is magnificent," Tehani said, slowly craning her neck so she could see directly above her.

"That's an understatement," Hunter replied. He turned his head quickly from one side to the other and suddenly felt giddy. His knees began to buckle, and he had a powerful feeling that he was going to fall. Hunter closed his eyes and reminded himself that he couldn't fall unless there was gravity. He also remembered that there was a powerful adhesive on his shoes that was holding him on the platform. His attempts to reassure his body were a failure. As soon as he opened his eyes, his head began to spin.

"Whoa," Hunter said, extending his arms to grab on to nothing.

"What is it?" Tehani asked, alarmed by the tone of his voice.

"His balance system is confused," Derek said, coming over to steady Hunter. "Even though we're weightless inside the spacecraft, our eyes keep reminding us of the direction to the floor and the ceiling. Out here we have no reference."

Hunter knelt down. Having the extra body attachment to the platform made him feel more secure.

"Let me know when you're feeling better, Hunter," Derek said. "I don't want to turn on the lights until you can appreciate them fully."

After about twenty seconds Hunter stood up slowly. His head had stopped spinning and his knees no longer felt as if they might collapse at any moment. He resolved to move his head in small-angle increments in the future.

"Okay," he said. "I think I'm ready."

Derek activated the lights. The geometric silhouettes became real objects. Four gigantic spheres surrounded them. In front of them, beyond the end of the platform, was a huge, gray ellipsoidal box with a thin ring around it.

Derek pointed first at the spheres. "These babies are the propellant tanks. They are approximately twenty feet in diameter. If filled to capacity, they could carry one million pounds of propellant, which is slightly more than the total dry weight of the *Darwin*. . . . On an ordinary voyage like this one, we actually use only a small fraction of the propellant capacity. Nevertheless, because we fly with a requirement that any two of these tanks can be nonoperational without any untoward impact, we always launch with more than twice the propellant needed for a nominal trip."

"I hate to sound like an ignoramus," Tehani said, "but what exactly does propellant do?"

Derek laughed. "I'm sorry. Propellant is essentially fuel. It provides the impetus to the spacecraft to make it change direction, or attitude. Without any propulsive maneuvers, we fly according to the laws of gravity, like we're doing at the moment. I don't bring passengers out here when the thrusters are active."

"Have you ever had a malfunction that caused you to operate with less than four tanks?" Hunter asked.

"A couple of times," Derek said. "Two trips ago, we had a pair of leaky valves in the lines between one of the tanks and the thrusters. The fault-protection system couldn't uniquely diagnose the problem. So we had to seal off that tank."

Derek turned and pointed at the ellipsoidal container. "That's where the really high-tech stuff is located," he said. "An aneutronic fusion reactor, and its supply of helium-three, is inside. The reactor provides power for the space-craft, and for the operation of the plasma thrusters, which extend out the back side of the *Darwin,* on the other side of the ellipsoid. The power-conversion and regulation system is also inside that box." He gestured at the annulus around the ellipsoid. "The ring is essentially a radiator, dumping the waste heat from the power-conversion system into space."

"Are we supposed to understand what you just told us?" Hunter asked.

Derek chuckled. "Only the general idea," he answered. "And please don't ask me to explain how an aneutronic fusion reactor works. I barely passed my nuclear-engineering course at the university."

He walked over to an edge of the platform that was not close to any of the engineering subsystems. "Now we're going to have some fun," he said.

Derek made a small leap into space. Tehani gasped. He sailed out twenty yards or so, the slack line trailing behind him. The line pulled taut, inducing a spin in Derek's body, and then reeled him in. He was back on the platform in less than a minute.

"Every now and then these safety systems have to be

tested," Derek said. He looked at Hunter. "Would you like to jump?" he asked.

"Uh . . . I don't think so," Hunter replied.

"Not on your life," Tehani said, before she was asked. She shook her head vigorously.

Derek laughed. "It's really quite a rush," he said.

"I'm sure it is," Hunter said. "But I think I'll save that thrill for another time."

Derek gestured for them to follow him back to the pressurized part of the spacecraft. Hunter and Tehani both thanked him when they were back inside.

FIVE

"WELL, BLAKE," MR. PEABODY said. "Mr. Khan tells me that you are a Covington Fellow. I must say I am very impressed."

Hunter had just entered the cabin. He had finished his thirty minutes on the exercise machine and taken a quick shower. When Mr. Peabody spoke to him, Hunter was preparing to put on a fresh shirt.

"Thank you, sir," Hunter replied, a little surprised by the comparatively friendly tone of Mr. Peabody's comment.

"The founder of our law firm was one of the first Covington Fellows," Mr. Peabody said, "almost twenty-five years ago, soon after Marshall Covington was first selected as our chairman by the parliament. He told me it was an invaluable experience. You're a very fortunate young man."

"I know that, sir," Hunter said. "I'm really looking forward to the next two years."

"Unless you really screw up," Mr. Peabody said, "you'll be set for life. Drew Reynolds—he's the founder of our firm—has high-level connections in all the ministries. He probably generates thirty percent of our business just from the people he knows." Mr. Peabody almost smiled. "Say," he then said, "if you don't mind my asking, what have you done that allowed you to win such a prestigious fellowship?"

"I'm not really certain," Hunter said. "Of course I scored very well on the secondary-school exams, and on my medical-school aptitude tests last spring, but other than that, Mr. Peabody, I can't cite anything specific. As far as I know, the actual criteria for Covington selection have never been published."

"So you will be assigned to the Ministry of Health?" Mr. Peabody asked.

"I would assume so," Hunter said. "Although I haven't been told for certain."

"My older son was an excellent student," Mr. Peabody said. "We had heard that he was being considered for a Covington—I know that information is supposed to be carefully guarded, but one of the members of the selection committee was a client of ours—and we were just a trifle disappointed when the announcements were made and his name was not on the list. Randy did receive a full scholarship from Centralia University, however, where he had an outstanding academic record, and he is now already a high-ranking officer in the ASP. Although I don't know exactly what he does—it's all top secret, you know—he says he works directly with Commander Tyson. One time the commander even called our house while Randy was visiting his mother and me. I came out of the bathroom and there he was, one of the most important men in the Federation, talking to my son on our vidmail system."

"It sounds as if you're very proud of him," Hunter said.

"Yes, I am," Mr. Peabody said, beaming. "In fact, I just had a video conversation with my wife and we were both remarking how lucky we were that at least one of our sons had turned out all right."

"Has your younger son graduated from the university yet?" Hunter asked.

Mr. Peabody hesitated before replying. "No, he hasn't," he finally said tersely. "By the way, Blake," he added quickly. "Do you have any specific plans for dinner? Would you like to join me?"

"Tehani had mentioned something about seeing me at dinner," Hunter said, sensing that accepting his cabinmate's dinner invitation could make life much easier in the days to follow, "but we didn't make any specific arrangements. . . . I would enjoy eating with you, Mr. Peabody. Let me just step across the hall and tell Tehani."

"WHAT DID YOU two talk about all that time?" Tehani asked after dinner, as Hunter and she were sharing a drink in the lounge.

"Nothing in particular," Hunter said. "The usual sort of stuff—families, work, sports, women. He's not nearly as stuffy as I first thought he was. But the man does have a few idiosyncrasies, to say the least. He did not eat a bite of his vegetables until after he finished his chicken and waited three minutes for it to digest. Mr. Peabody said that heartburn is caused by mixing different kinds of food in the stomach."

Tehani laughed. "What's his wife like?" she asked.

"I can't really say," Hunter replied. "I still don't have a clear picture of her. Mr. Peabody told me that he met her while he was in law school and that she was a student at Centralia University at the time. They married after she graduated. Apparently she stayed home to raise their sons while the boys were small. She's working again now, Mr. Peabody said, not because they need the money, but so that she can be doing something useful with her life."

"It was kind of you to have dinner with him," Tehani said.

"I think this was Mr. Peabody's way of apologizing for

being rude in our initial encounters," Hunter said. "And although he would never admit it, I think he's a little bit lonely. He's been away from home for over a month already."

"Did he ever say anything more specific about the younger son?" Tehani asked.

"No," said Hunter. "He waxed eloquent about Randy several different times. But the younger boy, Darrell I think his name is, was barely mentioned."

They finished their drinks. "So what's up for tonight?" Tehani said.

"I'm going to study the Treaty of Tranquility for an hour or two," Hunter said, "while I'm still in the mood for space history. Then I thought I'd call home and say hello to my family—I signed up for the videophone system at nine o'clock. Would you like to watch a late movie after that? Or should I see if the kiosk is free?"

"I've never understood the fascination with those virtual worlds," Tehani said. "My real life occupies all my time and energy. But a movie sounds great."

THE TREATY OF Tranquility was signed by Chairman Marshall Covington of the FISC and President Nathaniel Tennyson of the UDSC on March 1, 2394. It was ratified by the legislative bodies of the two powers the following month. The treaty ended three decades of turbulent struggle between the two governmental entities over hegemony in space by establishing territorial boundaries for each regime.

Under the terms of the long and complicated treaty, all settlements on the Moon and South Mars, below a latitude of fifteen degrees south, as well as all space colonies orbiting either Earth or the Moon, are part of the UDSC. The FISC domain includes North Mars above the fifteenth northern parallel, the colonies in orbit around Mars or

Jupiter or any of the Jovian moons, and all settlements, either existing or planned, on those moons of Jupiter.

Asteroid outposts, as well as space colonies in heliocentric orbit, were divided by the treaty according to the nature of their orbits. If the orbit of the asteroid or colony is INSIDE the orbit of Mars, the settlement belongs to the UDSC; those asteroids or space colonies with orbits OUTSIDE the orbit of Mars are part of the FISC.

The treaty also created the Free Zone in the equatorial region of Mars, between the Martian territory of the UDSC and the FISC. The establishment of this neutral, demilitarized zone, covering thirty degrees of Martian latitude, to be governed by a single legislative body selected by the citizens of the Free Zone, was one of the critical compromises contained in the Treaty of Tranquility. The two Martian moons, Phobos and Deimos, with their transportation centers and resorts, were also included as part of this nonaligned domain.

Hunter read the short treaty summary twice, referring on a separate computer monitor to a space atlas, before he thought he had a thorough understanding of the general provisions of the treaty. He was about to start reading the many pages of the treaty defining the political specifications for the Free Zone when Tehani walked up behind him.

"Ah, yes," she said, reading over his shoulder, "the famous Treaty of Tranquility. It's either a work of political genius, or a nightmare of horrendous proportions, depending upon whose opinion you believe."

Hunter turned around. Tehani looked unusually beautiful. Since dinner she had freshened up and changed her clothes. She was wearing a flowered blouse with many rich colors and a pair of pleated black pants. Her magnificent black hair was hanging free down to her waist in the back.

"My," Hunter said appreciatively, "don't you look stunning tonight."

"Thank you," Tehani said. She took one of his hands and then leaned down and kissed Hunter softly on the lips.

"What was that for?" Hunter said several seconds later, when he had recovered from the surprise.

"No reason," Tehani said coquettishly. "I just felt like it."

She held one of his hands and started reading the monitor again. "I don't think there's a single one of the original Free Zone guidelines that hasn't been violated by one side or the other," she said. "The permanent bilateral commission that was established by the treaty to oversee the implementation of the provisions has become a joke."

"You're going to kiss me like that," Hunter protested, "and then begin a political discussion?"

Tehani laughed. "We women are able to do multiple things at once," she said, caressing his hand. "Unlike you men, who are limited to one activity at a time."

Hunter stood up for another kiss, but Tehani deftly moved out of position and glanced at her watch. "Don't you have the videophone system reserved for nine o'clock?" Tehani said mischievously. "That's only a few minutes from now."

Hunter, at first frustrated, eventually smiled and shook his head. "Okay," he said. "I'll wait. But not happily," he added.

THE DARWIN WAS still close enough to Cicero that the signal delay in the video transmission was not significant. The Blakes had been alerted that Hunter would be calling at a specified time. Mr. and Mrs. Blake and Amanda were all sitting in the living room, facing the built-in videophone camera, when the call was initiated.

After the usual pleasantries had been completed, Hunter asked where Octavio and Danielle were. The two Blake parents looked at Amanda. "Hunter," his sister said, "things have happened pretty fast since you've been gone. Octavio is living somewhere else, with a friend of Daddy's, and Danielle is with him tonight."

Amanda didn't say anything else. Hunter was torn. Should he ask the obvious questions? His father made it easier for him by suggesting to Amanda that maybe she should elaborate a little.

"We've officially separated," Amanda said, her voice trembling with emotion. "The day before you left Octavio admitted to me that he had been . . . that he had had what he called a 'dalliance' with that Rachel Goldberg. While Mom and Dad were accompanying you to the spaceport, he confessed that he still had strong feelings for her." She paused a moment, struggling. "He really didn't give me much choice," she added.

Hunter didn't know what to say. Eventually he tried to console his sister by saying "I'm sorry," but nothing else he could think of seemed appropriate. After a lengthy silence, his father asked him a few questions about his accommodations on the *Darwin*, the food on board, and other issues that were easy to handle.

"And how is Tehani?" his mother asked, during a brief lull in the conversation. "Are you seeing a lot of her?"

The subtext in her questions was certainly not disguised. "Mom," Hunter replied, "there are only twelve passengers on this freighter. Tehani and I are the only two under the age of thirty. It would be astonishing if we were not spending a lot of time together. And, yes, she's fine."

Before the end of the call, Mr. Blake told Hunter that everyone had agreed that he would cut back his work schedule as soon as the investigation into the accident was over. "By the way, we have completely ruled out any possibility that the commands that caused the arm to move came from here on Cicero," his father said. "The Defense Ministry is now virtually certain that both the accident and the raid were some new kind of Dem mischief."

After he had said good-bye and the screen went blank, Hunter felt a vague disquiet, as well as a sense of inadequacy. *What do you say to a sister whose marriage is disintegrating?* he asked himself. Hunter thought about Tehani. *I bet she'll know something I could do to comfort Amanda.*

MUCH LATER THAT evening, after the common area was empty except for Mr. Carson Bagwell, who was still in the virtual-world kiosk where he had been since shortly after dinner, Hunter and Tehani were sitting together on one of the couches. He had not said anything to her about Amanda immediately after his videophone call. When they finished watching a movie, Hunter gave Tehani a brief synopsis of his sister's situation, and asked her if she could provide him with any advice.

"From what you've told me," Tehani said, choosing her words carefully, "it's not clear to me that the best solution for your sister's happiness is a reconciliation."

Hunter looked puzzled.

"In general, especially when there are children involved," Tehani said, "I think that it's best for the parents to try to work through their problems. But sometimes, they have to face the fact that maybe the marriage was not a good choice originally, for either of them. It sounds to me as if your brother-in-law Octavio delights in belittling your sister, or at least putting her in her place. That's a form of abuse. And I haven't heard anything that indicates Amanda and he have much in common, except for their daughter. . . . On the other hand, perhaps their interests have grown apart because neither of them has made a concerted effort to find some common passion. In that case . . ."

Hunter listened carefully to Tehani, as she continued to

weigh the pros and cons of a possible reconciliation between Amanda and Octavio. Twice she pointed out to Hunter that there was not really anything he, as Amanda's brother, could do except offer support and remind his sister that he loved her very much. After a few minutes Hunter found himself growing increasingly more amazed that Tehani had accumulated so much understanding about issues that he had hardly even considered. When he complimented Tehani on her insight, she sighed deeply and fell silent.

"Mr. Blake," she said at length, reaching over and taking his hand, "there is a reason why I know so much about relationships between men and women. If you think about it for a minute or two, you'll realize why."

There was a seriousness in Tehani's expression that Hunter had not seen before. "Because of your work?" he said at length, unconsciously averting his eyes.

"Yes," she said, "because of my work." She paused deliberately. "A subject about which you and I have not spoken one single time since that difficult evening two years ago."

Uh-oh, here it comes, Hunter thought, as he felt a queasiness rising in his stomach. *But what am I supposed to say?*

"While you were studying the Treaty of Tranquility tonight," Tehani said, "I was sorting through my electronic mail and working on my schedule for the next two months. Some mistakes were made by my assistants during my absence. I needed to resolve those. Toward the end of the time, it occurred to me that you and I have been purposely postponing coming to terms with some very important issues."

Tehani reached over and gently turned Hunter's head so that he was looking at her. "My darling Hunter," she said, "I am not the innocent high-school beauty queen you once knew. I am a successful private escort at Sybaris."

Hunter felt as if his insides were going to rip apart. As he stared at Tehani's magnificent eyes, and searched for words that would express what he was feeling, the tumult inside overwhelmed him. Tears forced themselves into his eyes. Embarrassed, he turned away again.

"I know what you are," he said very slowly. "What I don't know is how I really feel about it." Hunter took a deep breath. "But there are some things that I can say for certain." He suddenly had no control over his emotions and the tears rushed down his cheeks. "I'm sorry, Tehani," he stuttered, "really sorry, that I acted like such an asshole that night at your apartment two years ago. I was hurt and confused and lost. . . . I've been trying to figure out how to apologize for a long time now, but nothing I came up with ever seemed good enough."

Hunter stood up. An enormous sense of embarrassment was telling him to leave. "If you don't mind," he said, still not looking at her, "I think I'll go to bed now."

Tehani reached out and grabbed his forearm as Hunter was starting to walk away. "Please don't leave yet," she said. "Wait just a minute."

He stood in place, but did not turn around to look at Tehani. "I appreciate your apology very much, Hunter," she said. "I know how difficult it must have been."

Tehani paused. "Now if you're still too uncomfortable to talk to me about this," she said, "then I will not force you. But we've finally touched on the real gut-wrenching issue in our friendship. Until we talk it out, our relationship will remain superficial. . . . Immensely enjoyable, I can say, but still superficial."

Hunter still did not move. Tehani pulled slightly on his arm. "Why don't you sit down?" she said in her least threatening tone. "If, at any time, you don't want to continue, I will not ask you again to stay."

He sat back down on the couch. They started the conversation with Tehani's explanation for why she had taken the job with Sybaris in the first place, the explanation that

Hunter had refused to hear two years earlier. She told him how terrible it had been for her to watch her mother suffer after the double blow of her father's death and the discovery of his overwhelming indebtedness. Tehani described in detail hurrying home from school every day, worried that perhaps her mother might have committed suicide.

"She was alone in a remote place," Tehani said, "miles away from her family. She was responsible for two children, and she had no money and no job. I can't imagine how depressed she must have felt."

Tehani took both Hunter's hands in hers. "I heard her crying every night. As I was lying in my room, I promised that I would do whatever I could to lift that terrible burden from my mother." Now it was Tehani's turn to have tears in her eyes. "When you came into my life, I had already accepted the position at Sybaris. I was terrified that you wouldn't understand, and I would lose your wonderful love. I kept putting off telling you, and I kept hoping that some miracle would occur and I wouldn't need to take the job at Sybaris. I told myself that if I could just make love to you, one time, that you would know how I felt and would understand why I was doing what I was doing."

They talked for hours. Hunter and Tehani didn't really resolve anything, but they both felt they were making progress toward reaching a common understanding. At length, exhausted, they started to leave the lounge. As they passed the virtual-world kiosk, Carson Bagwell stepped out, bleary-eyed, and stared at them blankly before trundling noisily toward his cabin.

After Bagwell was gone, Hunter and Tehani slowly walked hand in hand down the corridor, shared a light good-night kiss, and went to sleep.

SIX

TWO DAYS LATER, WHEN Hunter knocked on Tehani's cabin door just prior to their arranged dinnertime, there was no response. He walked down the corridor toward the common area, smiling to himself and thinking about the previous evening. Tehani and he had spent the evening at the back computers, behind the passenger cabins. She had helped him gather study material from the *Darwin* database about the organization and operation of the FISC government. About midnight, they had started kissing. After a few minutes, their passions had exploded. Hunter was fairly certain he knew what would have happened if Lieutenant Wong, performing a routine check of the spacecraft, had not inadvertently come upon them.

Tehani was sitting beside Mr. Khan on one of the couches in the common area. Mr. Khan was speaking, and Tehani was leaning toward him, listening politely. Hunter felt an absurd spark of jealousy, which he instantaneously suppressed, reminding himself that it was perfectly natural for Tehani to talk to the other passengers.

She glanced at Hunter and smiled warmly as he approached the couch. Mr. Khan was still talking animatedly. At her first opportunity to speak without rudely interrupting the man, Tehani thanked Mr. Khan, excused herself from the couch, and joined Hunter.

"Hungry?" she asked as she approached him.

Hunter nodded. "What was that about?" he then added, gesturing in Mr. Khan's direction. "I hope he wasn't trying to set up an appointment with you at Sybaris."

Tehani frowned slightly. "No," she said, "he wasn't. It was just what you predicted—he wanted to talk to me about investments." She stopped before they reached the dining table and turned to face him. "But Hunter," she said calmly, "even if Mr. Khan WAS trying to arrange an appointment at Sybaris, it's no big deal. As I told you the night before last, it happens all the time, everywhere I go. Men are always telling me about some difficulty they have had arranging a session with me, and asking me to intercede on their behalf. It's a standard flirtation device. I just smile pleasantly and tell them that all scheduling is handled through the control center in Sybaris."

Hunter was silent. He was struggling with some difficult emotions. "Has anybody on THIS flight asked you for a date, or a session, or whatever it's called?" he asked.

Tehani took his hand. "Yes," she said.

"And while you were home on vacation on Cicero?" Hunter asked. "Were you propositioned there?"

Tehani gave him a quizzical look. "I'm not exactly certain I understand your question, or why you are asking it," she said patiently. "It's very rare that I am really propositioned, as you put it. But yes, every day I was on Cicero at least one person approached me about making arrangements at Sybaris."

"Who?" Hunter suddenly blurted out. "Anyone I know? And who aboard the *Darwin* has asked for time with you at Sybaris? One of the other passengers? A member of the crew?"

Tehani glanced around, a little concerned that someone

else might have heard his outburst. Hunter and she were out of earshot of the others.

"My dearest Hunter," she said softly, squeezing his hand, "do you really want to know these things? Why? Isn't that knowledge going to make it much more difficult for us to enjoy this time together? Wouldn't it be better if you didn't know any of the specifics?"

He didn't answer. He couldn't. In many ways, Hunter knew she was right. But a part of him wanted to know who around him was longing to have sex with Tehani.

Almost everyone, a voice inside Hunter answered his question. *That's what you're having a hard time accepting. Tehani is desired by almost every man.*

THEY DIDN'T KISS that evening. Even though they did spend some private time together in the back of the common area, in front of the computers, Tehani stopped Hunter when he tried to kiss her. She explained that she had been embarrassed the night before when Lieutenant Wong had seen them in a passionate embrace.

"Public displays of affection have never been my style," Tehani said. "I'm not blaming you for the other night, you understand. I was every bit as ardent as you were, maybe more. But I wish it hadn't happened. And I realized today that anybody could have suddenly appeared back here, even one of the two old ladies, who would have had a field day with such a discovery."

Tehani acknowledged that privacy was a very scarce commodity on the *Darwin*, and that their situation pretty much precluded spontaneous passion. "So if we're going to have some romantic time alone, we'll have to arrange it ahead of time. That probably sounds fairly mechanical to you, but I don't see any other options."

Hunter's initial response was negative. *If I schedule an appointment to kiss you in private,* he thought, the evening that Tehani first mentioned the subject, *then I'm just like one of your clients.* But by the next day his yearning for her, combined with his youthful lust, was much stronger than his distaste for a scheduled assignation. He asked Tehani how they would make the arrangement.

"I have broached the subject with Veronica already," she said. "She indicated that she would be more than willing to help. I will talk to her tonight before we go to bed."

Tehani told Hunter at breakfast the following morning that Veronica had agreed to be out of their cabin for two hours immediately after dinner. All day Hunter had difficulty focusing on anything. He tried to study, but kept looking at his watch every ten minutes or so. Time seemed to move at a snail's pace. More than once, he replayed with great clarity the night two years previously when Tehani and he had almost . . . The surge of desire that accompanied Hunter's recollections was overpowering.

He could not believe how radiantly beautiful Tehani looked at dinner. They ate early, at a time when many other passengers were at the table. Hunter wondered, as he looked around, if his excitement and anticipation were transparent, if somehow the others could tell from the permanent grin on his face that he was about to make love to one of the universe's most outstanding creations.

WHEN HUNTER AND Tehani were finally alone in her cabin, he was surprisingly tense and anxious. Only a few seconds after she closed and locked the cabin door, he grabbed her and kissed her awkwardly.

Tehani sensed his nervousness. She pulled gently away after the kiss and walked around him between the two beds. "We're not in a hurry, Hunter," Tehani said easily. "Veronica will not be coming back until we return to the common area."

Hunter stared at her as she sat down on the far end of her bed with her back against the wall. He felt foolish and inept. Tehani smiled warmly at him and patted the bed next to her. "Come over here and sit down," she said.

Hunter walked over beside her and sat down on the bed. Tehani took his right hand and began rubbing it lightly. "We have all the time in the world," she said several seconds later, reaching up and kissing him softly on the lips.

In spite of the voices inside his head, telling him to remain calm and to enjoy every moment, and to save his explosive passion for later, as soon as Hunter started returning Tehani's kiss he was overpowered by lust. He put his arms around her and squeezed much too forcefully. She broke the kiss at the first available opportunity.

"It's better for me, my darling," Tehani said, moving her shoulder as if it was hurting, "if we go a little more slowly."

"I'm sorry," Hunter said, embarrassed. "I guess . . ."

She put her finger to his lips and stood up. "I have an idea," she interrupted. Tehani reached under the bed and pulled out a small black device the size of her palm. She pushed a button and tranquil instrumental music began to play. "Take off your shirt," Tehani said. "I'm going to give you a relaxing back and neck massage."

A minute later Hunter was stretched out on her bed on his stomach, shirtless, listening to the soothing music, and thoroughly enjoying the feel of Tehani's talented fingers on his back. Little by little, the tension that he had been feeling began to fade. He closed his eyes and started breathing more deeply.

In the beginning of the massage, Tehani was standing up beside him. After several minutes, however, she climbed up on the lower part of Hunter's back and began to rub his neck and shoulders. Every now and then she leaned down and kissed him gently on the neck or ear. When Hunter tried to move, to respond in some way to her kisses, she told him softly to lie back down and enjoy his massage.

At length Tehani stood up with one of her feet on the edge of the bed and the other against the wall. Hunter rolled over as she requested. She sat back down and began to massage his chest. He watched her contentedly. His eyes were filled with her smile and her beauty. Her hands ran all over his chest for several minutes, gliding lightly over his nipples in passing. A little later Tehani began to focus more on Hunter's nipples with her fingers, leaning down to kiss him each time she felt his arousal growing. He would hold her against him, trying to prolong the kiss, but Tehani would sit up again and continue the massage.

At the end of one of these kisses Tehani whispered in his ear, "Close your eyes, my darling, and don't open them until I tell you."

She slid off his chest, and a few moments later, Hunter heard a new musical selection playing in the cabin. Still dutifully keeping his eyes closed, Hunter felt his pants being undone and pulled slowly off his body. After rubbing his feet and his legs, Tehani's caressing hands explored his upper thighs, around his genitals, and Hunter's desire grew stronger and stronger.

Then her open lips were on his, with her tongue a tantalizing treat both on his lips and against the tip of his tongue. Toward the end of a long, passionate kiss, Tehani climbed back on the bed, placing her knees on either side of his body. "You may open your eyes now," she said, ending the kiss and dropping her naked buttocks on his bare stomach.

What Hunter saw was a goddess or an angel, smiling lovingly at him in the last several seconds before intercourse. Tehani took Hunter's hands and placed them against her breasts. She then reached behind her and caressed his genitals with her adroit fingers. Moments later Tehani rose slightly and took Hunter inside her.

"Don't move," she said softly as Hunter started to thrust with his pelvis. "Let me do it this first time."

He felt her squeezing against him. With each rhythmic squeeze an intense surge of pleasure coursed through his body. After a long minute of ecstasy for Hunter, Tehani began to move up and down ever so slightly. Hunter surrendered to his passion in less than another minute, struggling not to scream with joy at the moment of his release. Tehani was kissing him immediately afterward. He felt her lips on his eyes, his cheeks, and on his mouth.

HUNTER DID NOT want to return to the common area with Tehani. He couldn't imagine talking with anyone about anything. He wanted to be alone, to bask fully in the afterglow of the most incredible pleasure he had ever experienced. Tehani understood. They embraced in the corridor and Hunter entered his cabin.

He stopped in the toilet closet before falling on his back on his bed. After staring blankly at the cabin ceiling for several seconds, Hunter closed his eyes and relived every precious second of his sexual encounter with Tehani. The music played again in his mind and he felt her touch on his back, his neck, and his shoulders. He opened his eyes, half expecting to see her magnificent, naked body above him. He felt her firm, full breasts pressed against his hands. Hunter shuddered as he recalled the intensity of his pleasure after he was deep inside her and she was squeezing against him.

Hunter also remembered holding Tehani, her head on his chest, her legs straddling his body, for several minutes after they had finished. From time to time they had kissed, simple, affectionate kisses without passion or insistence. He had almost fallen asleep. She had laughingly given him a forceful hug, stirring him out of his stupor, and reminded him that they needed to clear the room for Veronica.

For some reason, as Hunter lay on the bed in his cabin on the *Darwin*, the memories of his two earlier sexual experiences came into his mind. Both paled beside what had just occurred with Tehani. *I have never really made love before,* Hunter told himself. *This was something altogether different.* He smiled as a particularly vivid recollection of Tehani's face drove the other memories away.

Hunter was amazed at how calm he felt. No thoughts of tasks to be done, or anxieties about the future, entered his head. As he was drifting into sleep, a few dark questions about Tehani crept into his consciousness, but he pushed them out of his mind and allowed himself the full measure of postorgasmic bliss.

Tehani was beside him in a dream that followed a deep and restful sleep. Hunter was in a huge, ornate ballroom he had never seen before, but he knew instinctively it was in Centralia. Tehani and he were talking to a middle-aged couple when Chairman Covington approached them. The FISC leader shook Hunter's hand, and gave Tehani a congratulatory hug. Tehani flashed a marvelous smile, and reached up to kiss Hunter. "Oh, darling," she said in the dream, "isn't this unbelievably wonderful?"

Hunter watched her walk away, crossing the dance floor on Chairman Covington's arm. Within seconds a pair of middle-aged men had joined them. From his vantage point in the dream, Hunter could tell from the lip and body movements that both these men, senior officials of the FISC, were complimenting Tehani. She smiled at each of them, and allowed them to kiss her hand. She glanced at Hunter, waved with her free arm, and turned around. Still walking beside Chairman Covington, Tehani disappeared from Hunter's view into the crowd of people on the other side of the dance floor.

Hunter stirred and opened his eyes. He was aware of a vague disquiet that he couldn't quite pinpoint. He heard a noise in his cabin. Hunter turned and saw Mr. Peabody placing something on the shelf at the end of his bed.

"Sorry, Blake," Mr. Peabody said when he saw that Hunter was sitting up. "I hope I didn't disturb you. I was trying not to make any noise."

"You didn't wake me up," Hunter said, yawning. "Goodness," he said after glancing at his watch, "I've been asleep for over an hour."

"I'm not surprised," Mr. Peabody said in a friendly tone. "You've been staying up very late every night."

Hunter walked over to the basin to wash his face.

"I just finished a long video conversation with my wife and older son on Mars," Mr. Peabody said. "It was a little awkward because of the long delay between each segment, but I was glad to talk to them. They were impressed that my cabinmate was one of the new Covington Fellows."

"And how was everything at home?" Hunter said, turning around to face Mr. Peabody.

"Mostly okay," Mr. Peabody said. He hesitated for several seconds, as if he was uncertain about whether to say anything more. "Although my wife is worried about Darrell," he added at length.

"That's your younger son, isn't it?" Hunter said.

"Yes," Mr. Peabody replied. "He's been living in the Free Zone for a couple of years now. Sometimes he's not very good at communicating. Marlene says she hasn't received any kind of mail from Darrell now for over a month."

"Has she tried calling him?" Hunter asked.

"She has sent several mail messages, both video and standard," Mr. Peabody said. "She can tell from the system that Darrell has received her messages, but for some reason he hasn't had time to respond." Mr. Peabody glanced at Hunter. "I'm afraid he's a very headstrong, self-involved young man. It's just not a high priority to him to check in with his parents periodically to keep them from worrying. He's not like Randy at all. I can't remember a single time when Randy has gone more than a day or two without sending us some kind of message."

Hunter looked at his cabinmate. He was astonished that Mr. Peabody, who Hunter had originally assumed was too stiff to ever discuss anything personal, was actually sharing something meaningful with him. *Human beings come in all kinds of packages,* Hunter remembered his psychology facilitator saying. *It's important not to make snap judgments based on superficial data.*

"I'm afraid that young people, boys in particular," Hunter said, "are too occupied with themselves to think about their families very often." He grimaced, remembering his mother's comment about Hunter's not discussing his work at the hospital with her. "I'm even guilty of not communicating with my parents sometimes."

"I've only seen Darrell one time in the last eighteen months," Mr. Peabody said wistfully. "I was in the Free Zone, consulting on a case, and I took him out to dinner. He insisted that his girlfriend come along even though I was opposed to the idea. . . . It wasn't a very comfortable evening for any of us. We argued most of the time—about politics, lifestyles, you name it." Mr. Peabody sighed. "His girlfriend Chelsea was quite outspoken, which I thought was a bit odd, considering this was the first time that she had met her boyfriend's father."

Hunter suddenly recalled the discussion in his home about the space pirates in general, and Chelsea Dickinson in particular. "A girl named Chelsea from Cicero, who was one of my older sister's friends, is also working in the Free

Zone," Hunter said. "Do you happen to remember her last name?"

Mr. Peabody shook his head. "I don't think so. It was something common, like Thompson or Dixon, I believe. . . . I don't understand why Darrell is with her. Oh, she was smart enough all right, I'll give her credit for that. But she looked a fright. She wore no makeup, her hair was in braids . . . She sure talked a lot."

"What does Darrell do in the Free Zone, Mr. Peabody?" Hunter asked. "If that's not too personal a question."

Hunter's cabinmate was silent for a long time. At length he sighed again. "Right now I believe he's a bartender at a club," Mr. Peabody said, his pain showing in the expression on his face. "But he never seems to keep the same job—or the same address for that matter—for very long. He says he gets bored easily and likes change."

The dejected Mr. Peabody looked down at the floor of the cabin. Hunter struggled to find something to say that would cheer him up. He moved over closer to his roommate and almost touched him on the shoulder, but decided not to at the last second. "It's probably just a phase, Mr. Peabody," Hunter said to reassure the man. "More than likely, he'll grow out of it in another year or two."

"Just a phase," Mr. Peabody said, still looking at the cabin floor. "I've heard that before."

S E V E N

THE NEXT MORNING AT breakfast, when the others left the table, leaving Hunter, Tehani, and Veronica alone, Tehani's cabinmate looked at her companions with a conspiratorial smile. "So how are the lovebirds this morning?" she said in a low voice.

Hunter blushed. "Fine," he said, a little brusquely. Regaining his composure, he thanked Veronica for providing them with "the opportunity" to be alone.

"It's my pleasure," she said. "I'm certain Tehani would do the same for me if there was anybody I wanted to spend some private time with." She glanced around the lounge, where three of the male passengers were engaged in various activities while sipping their postprandial coffee. "Unfortunately, that's not going to happen on this trip," Veronica said, laughing. "These pickings are pretty slim."

"What about Derek?" Tehani said lightly.

"He has potential," Veronica said, "but he reminds me too much of my ex-husband. Too cocky, too smooth. He would probably expect me to thank him for the privilege of his company."

"You may have misjudged him," Tehani said. "I agree

that Derek exudes self-confidence. But I think that underneath that polished exterior is a genuine human being. He might at least be a reasonable distraction on this long trip."

"You could be right," Veronica said. "And goodness knows, in your line of work you need to be a good judge of men. . . . Which brings me to an interesting question. How do you avoid spending time with men who are flakes, or weirdos, or those who will bore you out of your mind in less than a minute?"

Tehani laughed. "First, they have to fill out an application, including a short essay on why they want me to be their private escort at Sybaris and what they are expecting from their vacation. If they pass that screening, I insist on a video interview prior to confirmation of the reservation. It's not a perfect process, but most of the time I end up with decent clients. However, I will admit that I have been very wrong a couple of times."

"And what do you do when you make a mistake?" Veronica asked.

"Each client signs a contract before he comes to Sybaris," Tehani answered. "It gives me the unilateral right to terminate his vacation experience whenever I want, for any reason whatsoever. The client then has a choice of having all his money refunded, or moving to the top of the priority queue for a reservation with another private escort."

"And have you 'terminated a client' often?" Veronica said.

"Three times during my first year," Tehani said. "But none since then. I think my judgment is getting better. Besides, I now have so many requests for my time, I can reject potential clients whenever I have the slightest uncertainty."

Hunter had been growing increasingly uneasy during the conversation between the two women. He rose abruptly, without saying anything, and left the table, heading in the direction of his cabin.

Tehani excused herself several seconds later and hurried after him. "What is it, darling?" she said, when she caught up with Hunter outside of the shower room.

"What do you think it is?" he said, with a trace of rancor in his voice. He avoided looking directly at her. "Do you think I enjoy sitting there listening to a discussion of the details of your business?"

"Uh-oh," Tehani said. "I think we need to have another talk. I thought we had already covered this territory." She paused. "I'll ask Veronica if we can use the cabin now for a few minutes. . . . Wait here, I'll be right back."

Once they were inside the cabin, Tehani asked Hunter to sit on the bed. "I'm going to make a little speech, my darling Hunter Blake, and I want you to pay careful attention. When I'm finished, you can say anything you want and I will listen."

Tehani stood up in the aisle between the two beds. "My intuition tells me that it was not simply my conversation with Veronica that was bothering you a little while ago, but more generally the nature of my 'business,' as you called it." She stopped for a moment. "I'm going to start by reminding you, again, that I am a special escort at Sybaris, and that I earn my living by being a companion to men. Part of that companionship involves sexual activities. We talked about all this last week."

Hunter nodded, but still looked uncomfortable. "All right," he said. "Please get to the point."

"When I am with my good friends—and Veronica has become one already during these days we have been sharing a cabin," Tehani continued, "I do not try to pretend that I am not what I am. I talk about my business in the same way that anybody else would. If someone asks, I tell her that it would not be my first choice as an occupation, but that the job pays handsomely, and I will be able to free my family from an onerous debt in a short period of time."

Tehani stopped again. She approached Hunter, bent down to his level, and took both his hands in hers. "Hunter, my darling, you must understand that I will still be a private escort AFTER this flight is over, no matter what happens between us. I really have no viable alternatives. I must repay my father's debt and, at present, I am the sole support of Tesoro and my mother. There is no other job I could get that would pay me even half as much."

She took Hunter's hands in hers. "I hope that we can continue to be intimate friends, for nobody makes me as happy as you do. But I don't want to mislead or delude you. And if you can't live with the knowledge that your girlfriend is a private escort at Sybaris, then I will understand. But please, please, don't try to make me ashamed of myself, or unworthy of you in some way. I went through all that two years ago and I will not do it again. It hurt too much."

Hunter was incapable of sorting out all the emotions he was experiencing. Fortunately, he had the good sense not to say anything in his confusion.

"So you have basically three choices," Tehani said, "depending on what you want and how you feel. If you can accept me for what I am, knowing that the intimacy I share with you is unique and special, and contains true affection for you as my chosen companion, then we can continue to be friends and lovers after this flight is over. If the fact that I am a private escort at Sybaris, and will always openly admit it to anyone who asks, makes me not a woman with whom you wish to have a long-term relationship, then we can enjoy this wonderful interlude in our lives, and part with great memories of our mutual pleasure. Or, you can select choice three, in which we terminate the intimate part of our friendship right now, this morning, before we become any more dependent upon one another. In that case, I will be sad, but I will still cherish forever the looks of joy and happiness on your face last night."

Hunter didn't say anything for many seconds. In some ways, he was angry with himself for not having foreseen that the natural outcome of their liaison would be his being forced to select among unsatisfactory choices. *What did you think?* he asked himself. *That Tehani would fall madly in love with you, abandon Sybaris, and come to live with you in Centralia? On a Covington Fellow's stipend? Are you that stupid?*

In all honesty, however, Hunter wasn't certain that he was a big enough person to acknowledge to the world that the woman he loved had sexual relations, or even HAD had them, with other men for a living. But what should he do? The thought of not making love with Tehani again was out of the question. And if they were lovers only on the *Darwin*, and then said good-bye when they reached Mars, would he pine for her for the rest of his life?

He swallowed hard and gazed at her beautiful face only a few inches away. "I really don't know, Tehani," he said slowly. "I'm confused, to say the least, and I can't make any decision. I'm simply overwhelmed by everything."

To Hunter's surprise, tears welled up in his eyes. "I'm going to leave now," he said, "because I don't want to continue the conversation until I get pissed off and say something irrational. But I do want to tell you two things before I go. First, you are the most exceptional person I have ever known. And second, beyond a doubt, last night was the most wonderful experience of my life so far."

Tehani gently touched both Hunter's cheeks with her hands and kissed the tears in his eyes. "Thank you, my darling," she said.

HUNTER AND TEHANI made love again that night. The pleasure was even greater the second time. He was more relaxed and comfortable. At times Hunter was even the initiator of sexual play. Tehani gently coaxed him to do things that she liked, and Hunter discovered the joy of being the stimulating partner. She orchestrated their sexual progress expertly. Their orgasms occurred within a few seconds of one another. Entwined in each other's arms, they fell asleep after intercourse and apologized profusely to Veronica for having exceeded their allotted time.

Hunter and Tehani watched a late movie together at the back of the common area. They held hands throughout the show. Occasionally Tehani put her head down on Hunter's shoulder, or absentmindedly caressed his leg or his chest. Hunter felt a closeness to Tehani that he would never have thought possible. He had a powerful desire to hold all of her next to him, and somehow zip her up inside his own skin. He knew he was falling hopelessly in love.

They stood in the corridor between their two cabins, kissing softly, for what must have been another half hour. Every time that Hunter turned to open his door, his hand would not function. He could not bear the thought of being away from Tehani. The peace and harmony that he felt when he held her in his arms was so unbelievably rich and wonderful. How could he possibly deny himself that feeling simply to sleep?

Only moments after he parted from her, lying in the dark in his cabin, Hunter felt bereft. Part of him was gone. Where were her eyes, her smile, that magnificent face? Why was he here, and Tehani over there? What possible rules and societal conventions forced them to sleep apart? They belonged together, whether waking or sleeping. He longed for her only minutes after they had shared a final good-night kiss. Hunter knew that he would wake up in the morning yearning for her.

In the dark solitude of his cabin he recalled the outstanding moments of the evening. There had been many of them. Whenever the overwhelming questions about the destiny of their love affair tried to impose themselves on his thought process, Hunter forcefully pushed them aside. He was not going to permit anything to dampen the joy he was feeling. He was a truly happy young man.

THE NEXT DAY was Sunday. At breakfast, while six of the passengers were eating, Mr. Thorpe showed up and reminded everyone that he would be conducting a short Christian church service at ten o'clock. Tehani astonished Hunter by telling Reverend Thorpe that both Hunter and she would be attending. After breakfast she told Hunter that even though neither of them was a practicing Christian, it would almost certainly make the rest of the trip much easier if they flattered the Thorpes by making an appearance at his service. Hunter would never have considered attending the church service if the choice had been his alone, but he did not argue with Tehani. He was content to be beside her, whatever it was she wanted them to do.

Just before ten o'clock all the passengers except Mr. Khan and Carson Bagwell gathered in the common area. Mr. Weerasinghe confided to Hunter that even though he was a Buddhist, he thought he might be able to learn something from Reverend Thorpe's service. Derek Sanchez represented the crew. He sat on the three-person couch with Hunter and Tehani.

Reverend Thorpe was clearly pleased at the turnout. In his introductory prayer he first beseeched God to guide the *Darwin* safely to its destination, and then he asked Him to stand beside each of the passengers in their "many and varied" endeavors after they arrived on Mars. Reverend Thorpe had just announced that the topic of his sermon was going to be the statement "Do unto others as you would have them do unto you," when suddenly the lights throughout the spacecraft went out.

It was pitch-black in the common area. On the couch,

Hunter and Tehani could hear the vibration of Derek's pager. "Don't be concerned," Derek said almost immediately. "We have a complete backup electrical system. If you will all please just sit tight, I will go forward and see why it did not kick in automatically."

In the dark, Tehani reached over and grabbed Hunter's hand. A moment later they could all hear Mr. Khan stumbling through the corridor that separated the passenger cabins. "What's happening?" he said, his voice full of concern. "Can anyone hear me? Please tell me what's going on."

"We've had some kind of electrical failure," George Slovikovski said. "Derek has gone forward to the engineering room to fix it."

Mr. Khan managed to find his way into the common area and, with help from others, locate an unoccupied chair. Then for almost a minute nobody spoke. As each moment passed and the lights did not come on again, a palpable but unspoken terror began to spread around the room. The facts were inescapable. They were all passengers on a solitary space vehicle that was miles from anywhere. Any significant engineering failure on the *Darwin* was life-threatening.

"Tehani," Veronica said, breaking the silence.

"Yes, Veronica," Tehani answered in the darkness.

"Isn't there now an open spot on the couch?" Veronica asked. "I think I'd feel better if I was sitting over there with Hunter and you."

"Come on over," Tehani said. "But be very careful."

Moments after Veronica reached the couch, the door to the crew compartment opened and Derek entered the common area. He was carrying an illuminated flashlight, plus a container in his right hand. "For some reason that we have not yet determined," he said calmly, "our backup electrical system has not been activated. Captain Pollack has awakened Lieutenant Wong and we will be working on the problem until we have it solved. In the meantime, I have brought flashlights for each of you. Please use them sparingly, for we don't know for certain how long they will be needed."

Derek fielded questions as he handed out the flashlights. "No," he said, "I have never experienced a blackout on a flight before. But they are not that uncommon. We trained for this contingency at flight school."

"What happens if you are unable to fix the problem?" Mr. Slovikovski asked.

"I can't imagine that would happen," Derek replied. "But in the worst case, we would radio the emergency transportation center and they would dispatch a repair vehicle in our direction."

"How long would it take to get here?" Mr. Peabody asked.

"The design of the FISC emergency network is to be able to reach any spacecraft inside of the orbit of Jupiter in a maximum of sixty hours," Derek said. "Emergency vehicles are constantly deployed in a pattern that permits achievement of that design criterion."

"Didn't I read somewhere," Mr. Slovikovski said, "that the emergency fleet had been seriously depleted as part of the war-preparation effort?"

"Look," Derek said, now finished handing out the flashlights, "this kind of conversation is not going to help anyone. There is no reason for panic, or even undue concern. You have a seasoned crew on the *Darwin,* and the most likely situation is that this electrical problem will be resolved shortly, probably in less than an hour. It might be best if you return to your cabins and wait for the lights . . ."

He was interrupted by Captain Pollack, who had just opened the door to the crew area. "Derek," he said sharply, "when you're finished, we need to talk to you." He closed the door without saying anything else.

There had been nothing reassuring in Captain Pollack's tone. For the first time, Hunter began to feel uneasy. "All right," Derek said after an uncomfortable silence. "You all heard that I'm needed in the engineering room. I suggest that each of you take a water bottle from the rack beside the coffee machine and go to your cabins. We will keep everyone informed on the intercom. . . . I recognize that this is a disturbing situation. Please try to remain calm and let us troubleshoot the problem without interference. I promise we will let you know as soon as we understand what has happened."

AT TEHANI'S REQUEST, Hunter joined Veronica and her in their cabin. About ten minutes later, when it was still dark in the spacecraft and the passengers had heard nothing from the crew, there was a knock on their cabin door.

"Blake," they heard a voice say. "It's me, Peabody. Would you guys mind if I came in there with you? I'm not doing so well over here alone. . . ."

"Come on in, Mr. Peabody," Tehani said.

"Sit here on my bed," Veronica said, directing him with her flashlight.

Mr. Peabody sat down and heaved an audible sigh. "You know," he said, "I don't think it's such a good idea to be alone in a situation like this. The mind starts playing tricks, or at least mine was. I was becoming quite frightened."

"We understand, Mr. Peabody," Tehani said. "I don't know if this will help you any, but all of us are also a little scared."

"What could be taking so long?" Mr. Peabody asked. "And why haven't they told us anything?" He used his flashlight to look at his watch. "It's almost twenty minutes now since the lights went out."

They sat in total darkness, trying to make small talk, as time continued to pass. After another ten minutes there was another knock on the cabin door. Tehani switched on her flashlight and opened the door. George Slovikovski was outside in the corridor. "Are all four of you in there?" he asked. "I became worried when nobody answered at Peabody and Blake's cabin."

"Yes, we're all here," Tehani said. "What is it?"

"The rest of us have decided that we can't wait any longer to find out what's happening," Mr. Slovikovski said. "Two of us, myself and Reverend Thorpe, are going to go forward to talk to the crew. We'll bring back a report, or ask Derek to make one over the intercom."

"Don't you think we should give them a little more time?" Hunter said. "Certainly having passengers in their midst will hamper the troubleshooting activities."

"We thought about that," Mr. Slovikovski said, "but I don't think we can wait any longer. Mrs. Brougher is hyperventilating and is close to a total breakdown. Mr. Khan is running around like Chicken Little, talking crazy and scaring the hell out of everyone."

"Don't send him down here," Veronica said. "That's all I need to lose it altogether, some lunatic telling me that disaster is imminent."

"Please let us know what you find out," Tehani said.

Mr. Slovikovski left and Tehani closed the door. When she sat back down on the bed next to Hunter, she took his arm and put it around her back. "Just hold me," she whispered in his ear. "It makes me feel better."

A flash of light outside their porthole temporarily illuminated the room. All four of them started toward the window over the washbasin. Hunter was the first one there. "What do you see, Blake?" Mr. Peabody asked.

"It's hard to tell," Hunter replied. "It looks as if there has been some kind of explosion."

"Oh my God," Veronica said. "We're all going to die."

Tehani touched her cabinmate on the shoulder. "Don't jump to conclusions, Veronica. We really don't know for certain what happened."

A moment later there was another brilliant flash outside, in the vicinity of the spacecraft. This time Hunter saw the event in its entirety. It was definitely an explosion. But what could be exploding a quarter of a mile or so away from the *Darwin*? Puzzled, Hunter turned and tried to answer some of the questions the others were asking.

"The only thing I can think of," he said slowly, "is that the drones must somehow have blown up."

In the ensuing minute, he explained to Veronica and Tehani and Mr. Peabody that the drones were unpiloted, armed spacecraft that flew in tandem with the *Darwin*, offering protection against intruders. Hunter was careful to say that of course he couldn't be certain that what he had witnessed was a drone explosion, but that was the only explanation that made any sense to him. His next sentence was interrupted by a voice speaking over the intercom.

"Passengers and crew of the *Darwin*," the male voice said. "We have seized control of all elements of your spacecraft, including both the flight computer and the life-support system. We have also destroyed the drone fighters that were supposed to protect you. In a few minutes, we will board the *Darwin* and give you additional instructions. It is imperative that you cooperate with us and offer no resistance. If you do as you are told, you will not be harmed. If, however, you do not follow our orders, or commit any act that we interpret as hostile, you will be summarily dispatched.

"Each passenger is to go to his cabin. Failure to be in the

proper cabin will be viewed as a hostile act. The crew is ordered to gather on the flight deck and to do nothing to impede our entrance into the spacecraft. Any attempt to delay our boarding, or to make it more difficult, will be considered grounds for execution."

EIGHT

HUNTER WAS NOT ABLE to offer Mr. Peabody much solace during the several minutes that they were alone in their cabin. The man was convinced that his orderly world was being irrevocably destroyed. "This is the beginning of the open war, don't you see, Blake?" he said. "We're probably just one part of an elaborate, coordinated, preemptive strike that the Dems are making. Centralia may be under attack at this very moment. And we're almost certainly going to be prisoners of war."

The lights on the *Darwin* came on again only a few seconds before Hunter heard a knock on his cabin door. Telling himself to remain calm, he opened it slightly. A young man, about thirty, with a beard, wearing a UDSC armed forces uniform and carrying a small gun, was standing in the corridor. "Are you Hunter Blake?" he said, consulting a palm computer.

"I am," Hunter replied.

The man opened the door farther and stepped across the threshold. "Then you must be Everett Peabody?" he said.

Mr. Peabody nodded. He was sitting on his bed with his hands folded. Hunter could tell that his cabinmate was absolutely terrified.

"Remain here, with your door closed, until you receive our instructions over the intercom," the man said. "Any attempt to leave your cabin, or to contact another passenger or a member of the crew, will place your life in jeopardy. Do you understand?"

Both Hunter and Mr. Peabody said, "Yes." As the man was closing the door, a shot rang out in the common area. The soldier spun around in the corridor, his gun ready. Hunter and Mr. Peabody did not move. The intruder hurried down the corridor and returned in a few minutes. "One of your crew members was uncooperative," he said, closing the cabin door.

Hunter wanted to stand next to the door, to listen to sounds coming from the corridor. Mr. Peabody, however, was desperate to use the toilet. Hunter stepped aside. His cabinmate threw up repeatedly during the next minute. "Is there anything I can do to help?" Hunter said at one point.

"No, Blake," Mr. Peabody answered with difficulty. "But thank you."

Mr. Peabody looked very pale when he returned to the main part of the cabin from the toilet closet. He sat down on his bed. "I'm sorry, Blake," he said after several seconds. "I made a bit of a mess in there."

In spite of their tense situation, Hunter almost laughed out loud. He checked himself, however, realizing that Mr. Peabody's feelings would definitely be wounded. "Don't worry about it," Hunter said.

"I knew it, I knew it," Mr. Peabody said a little while later. "It's the damn Dems. They just can't stand it that we're making so much more money than they are."

Before Hunter could comment, the intercom sounded. "We are now going to call you to the common area, cabin by cabin," the same male voice that they had heard earlier said. "Do not enter the hallway until your names are called. Do not speak at any time unless you are asked a direct question by one of us. Walk slowly, single file, your arms away from your body, and follow our instructions once you are in the common area."

Hunter and Mr. Peabody were the first pair called. They eased into the corridor. The soldier who had visited their cabin stood at the other end, beyond the passenger cabins and the shower room. He gestured with his gun for them to walk forward. "Arms out," he shouted, as Hunter and Mr. Peabody proceeded down the corridor.

Lieutenant Wong was lying inert, facedown on the floor next to the virtual-world kiosk. An angry-looking Captain Pollack and Ms. Belinsky were sitting on one of the couches. Two other soldiers, both men in their late twenties or early thirties, both brandishing guns, were standing in front of the glass door to the crew compartment. Hunter and Mr. Peabody were ordered to sit in the chairs around the dining table. After Hunter sat down, he saw that there were four space suits stacked on the work desk just inside the spacecraft entrance.

Tehani and Veronica were the next pair of passengers to enter the lounge. "Well, well," said one of the soldiers, the leader whose voice was instantly recognizable from the earlier intercom messages, "it is indeed the infamous Tehani Wilawa." The two women were also told to sit down at the dining table.

Over the next several minutes the rest of the passengers filed slowly into the common area and took their designated seats. Everyone was quiet except Mr. Khan, who was desperately pleading for mercy, and Mrs. Thorpe, who sobbed intermittently. Mr. Khan was told to shut up twice, then warned by the leader that he would be shot if he opened his mouth one more time. Mrs. Thorpe's sobbing was ignored.

Hunter realized before too long that Carson Bagwell was missing. The mysterious Mr. Bagwell, now dressed in a

UDSC uniform and carrying a half-dozen space suits, entered the room from the back part of the spacecraft soon thereafter. He informed the leader that all the space suits had been located and that he would return with the rest of them in a few minutes.

"Listen up," the leader of the soldiers said to the passengers and crew of the *Darwin*. "Most of you are being transferred to another spacecraft. You will be allowed to take with you only those personal items that can fit in one of these small bags I am holding. That is all. There will be no exceptions. When my associate calls your name, come forward, take one of the bags to your cabin, and return in less than five minutes."

Mr. Khan and Reverend Thorpe protested and tried to ask a few questions. They were angrily silenced and told to follow the orders they had been given.

No more than three passengers, and no cabinmates, were permitted to be gone from the lounge area at the same time. While the first group of passengers were collecting their most important belongings, Carson Bagwell returned from the airlock at the back of the passenger area with the remainder of the space suits. Hunter noticed, while he was waiting to be sent to his cabin, that Captain Pollack and Ms. Belinsky already had their small, packed bags beside them.

Hunter made a prioritized mental list of the items that he would take. He realized, with some sorrow, that he would be forced to leave behind all the mementos from his childhood and early adolescence that his mother had insisted he take with him to Mars. Hunter was thinking about what he would be losing when the leader of the intruders came over to him.

"You're Hunter Blake, aren't you?" the man said.

"Yes," Hunter answered.

"Come with me," the leader said.

The soldier opened the glass door and led Hunter into the crew area. Through the window of the engineering room, Hunter could see Derek Sanchez talking to a uniformed woman. The man he was following stopped when they both reached the flight deck.

"You worked in a hospital on Cicero, is that correct?" the soldier asked.

"Yes," Hunter said.

"And you have recently been named as a Covington Fellow?"

"Yes," Hunter answered.

"Stay here," the man said.

Without saying anything else, the soldier walked back toward the passenger compartment. Hunter was left alone on the flight deck. His mind was flooded with a hundred questions he couldn't answer. He was worried about what was going to happen to him, and to Tehani. Even so, as Hunter gazed out the huge observation window at the brilliant dark sky of stars, he found himself moved again by the beauty and the vastness of the universe.

His temporary philosophical contemplation was shattered by the sound of two shots from the passenger area. His immediate impulse was to move in that direction, to find out what had happened. But Hunter restrained himself, realizing that he would be risking his own life if he left the flight deck.

He was alone for a long, agonizing five minutes. Hunter restlessly paced back and forth in front of the observation window, fighting against his fear that something terrible had happened. At length the leader of the forces who had seized the *Darwin* appeared again in the corridor between the crew quarters and the engineering room. Tehani was walking behind him.

The leader opened the door to the engineering room. "Chelsea," he said, "can you spare a moment? The off-loading is under way and I have both Wilawa and Blake here on the flight deck."

A petite brunette with savagely cropped hair came out of the engineering room and spoke briefly with the soldier. He then returned to the passenger area. Hunter recognized the woman immediately. She was Chelsea Dickinson from Cicero. Chelsea greeted Tehani as they were walking toward the flight deck and then extended her hand to Hunter when she reached him.

"So Amanda Blake's little brother is a Covington Fellow?" she said with a friendly smile. "Tsk, tsk." She shook her head. "You probably have no idea that the purpose of that program is to indoctrinate the young geniuses of the Federation and inculcate them with undying loyalty."

"Hello, Chelsea," Hunter said. He glanced at Tehani and smiled. "Am I allowed to speak now?" he asked.

"I guess so," Chelsea replied, "although technically I'm supposed to prohibit all communication between Tehani and you until I am informed that all the off-loading has been completed and the connection with the other spacecraft has been severed."

Hunter was going to ask about the two shots he had heard, but after what Chelsea had just said, he had a bigger question. "Are Tehani and I staying here, on the *Darwin*?" Hunter asked.

"It looks like it," Chelsea said with a peculiar smile. "Unless among your many talents is an ability to fly through the vacuum of space."

"Are we prisoners then?" Hunter said.

Chelsea smiled and put her right hand on the bottom of her chin. "Let me see," she said coyly. "Hey, I think that's probably correct. You guys are prisoners, and I'm your guard, or warden, or whatever. So you'd better be nice to me, and do what I say. Otherwise, there will be no more hanky-panky."

She laughed. "Oh, we know all about the two of you. We've been getting daily reports from Bagwell. . . . Actually, Hunter, the fact that the two of you are lovers added a complication that we didn't want. We almost decided not to take you as a captive. But our band is desperate for medical help, and a Covington Fellow might eventually be worth some kind of ransom, so we decided to kidnap you anyway."

Hunter next asked what they had done with the dead bodies. Chelsea looked puzzled at first, then laughed again. "Oh, they're not dead," she said. "We're not that vicious. We just shot them with tranquilizing darts. They were off-loaded in a space bag, along with their suits, and will be okay, although a little groggy, by tomorrow."

At this point Chelsea received a transmission from Bailey, the leader of their team, announcing that the off-loading was complete, and that they were now officially in Phase C of their mission. "Roger," Chelsea answered him. She turned to Tehani. "As for you, Miss Wilawa," she said in a teasing tone, "I must say that your beauty is absolutely disgusting. You may bring a fantastic ransom, but our women are not going to be happy you're among us, even for a little while. You make the rest of us look bad."

ABOUT FIVE MINUTES later Tehani, Hunter, and Derek entered the common area with Chelsea. They were introduced to the rest of the small pirate band that had hijacked the *Darwin*. Bailey was the leader of the group. His two male accomplices who had boarded the spacecraft that day were Snyder, the bearded pirate who had first knocked on Hunter's cabin door, and Franklin, a lanky, taciturn young man who never smiled. Of course they already knew Carson Bagwell.

Bailey explained that although Tehani, Hunter, and Derek were technically captives, they would be allowed to move freely about the passenger area as long as they were cooperative and followed instructions. Their locations would be permanently monitored by the pirates, however, on their network of palm computers. Bailey used a weird-looking gun to blast a small chip into the upper right arm of each of the prisoners. Hunter was then asked to wander all around the pressurized part of the spacecraft, including up to the flight deck, to verify that the monitoring system was working properly.

Bailey also informed them that Chelsea was their interface with their band. She was both their guard and their representative, if they had any issues they wished to raise. The three prisoners would reside in the passenger cabins; Chelsea and Bagwell would live there also. The other three pirates would occupy the crew quarters and spend most of their time in the front part of the spacecraft. "We had a long debate," Bailey said, "when we were planning this mission, about how much freedom to grant to you captives. After studying the detailed information about the three of you provided by Bagwell over the last few days, it was decided that we should start by trusting that you would have the good sense not to do anything hostile."

He paused for a moment. "Let me make this perfectly clear. We could have placed each of you in solitary confinement in a cabin for the duration of our flight. If any of you makes a single suspicious move, or disobeys one of our instructions, we will rescind our liberal policy and impose strict constraints on your movement and activities."

Bailey asked Franklin to bring him a bottle of water. He took a drink, cleared his throat, and continued. "We will all eat our meals together, at seven in the morning, twelve-thirty after noon, and six-thirty in the evening. You will have access to the exercise stations and computers, including the information in the *Darwin* database and the entertainment selections. The virtual-world kiosk, however, is off-limits to you at all times. We have also inhibited the communications capabilities of the workstations with a software block. Under no circumstances are any of you to make any attempt to override that inhibit and communicate with the outside world. One more thing—if by any chance we encounter an emergency situation, you will be told immediately to go to your cabins, where you will remain until we inform you explicitly that you can come out."

The lead hijacker now addressed each of the captives individually. "Derek," he said, "you will be available at all times to provide whatever information we may request related to the engineering systems on this spacecraft. Hunter, starting tomorrow, you will be working by video with other members of our band on the design of a portable medical facility. Miss Wilawa," he said with a smile, "we don't have any specific duties for you. But I do want to assure you of one thing. You and your person are in no danger from us. We are pirates, opposed to the two unjust space governments, not depraved monsters."

Bailey rose from his chair. "Chelsea will remain here with you and answer whatever questions you may have." He smiled. "At least those that she is free to answer. For obvious reasons we will not divulge where we are going, or how long it will take, or why we chose to capture this spacecraft." He glanced at his watch. "Lunch will be served by the robots in twenty-five minutes."

The four pirate men left the common area. The first question that Tehani asked Chelsea was about the fate of the passengers and crew members who had been off-loaded. "They have been placed in an old, reconfigured UDSC fighter craft," Chelsea said, "about the size of this common area. Ample provisions have been supplied. The flight computer has been preprogrammed to take them on a trajectory in the general direction of Mars. Although their communications system is not currently operational, after forty-eight hours their spacecraft will start transmitting a continuous distress signal."

Chelsea spent a few minutes clarifying what Bailey had said earlier, and then told the three captives that they were free to choose their cabins, and to clean up for lunch if they wanted. "Is it all right if Hunter and I share a cabin?" Tehani asked.

Chelsea laughed and shook her head. "I don't see why not," she said, "if Hunter is agreeable." She looked at Hunter, whose wide smile gave her the obvious answer. "All right," Chelsea said then, "but let me check with Bailey before giving you final approval."

When they reached the corridor the three of them stopped to discuss which cabins they were going to occupy. Carson Bagwell was apparently staying where he had been during the first days of the flight, so they had five cabins to choose from. While they were talking, Derek glanced around, and lowered his voice.

"What they did was positively brilliant," he said. "They must have some computer geniuses among their band."

Hunter looked puzzled. "First they sent commands into our system to turn off the electrical system," Derek said, "and to inhibit the activation of the backup. Then they waited. They KNEW that while we were troubleshooting, we would lift the write-protect portions of the flight computer. They couldn't have accomplished that with an outside command. Only a manual command, from the keyboard, can lift write protection. Somehow they were monitoring what we were doing. As soon as we removed the write protection, they fired off commands that changed all the keywords in the executive structure. We couldn't do anything with our own computers. They were in control."

Hunter frowned. "I didn't understand very much of that, but I gather that these guys are fairly clever."

"Brilliant," Derek repeated. "Absolutely brilliant."

THE PIRATES

ONE

"I'M CERTAIN THAT MY being from Cicero was a big factor in my selection for this mission," Chelsea was saying, "but nevertheless it was quite an honor. It showed that my efforts have been appreciated."

Chelsea, Hunter, and Tehani were sitting in the common area. They had finished their first dinner fifteen minutes earlier. Chelsea was wearing normal clothing, a blouse, jeans, and comfortable shoes, the UDSC uniform having been discarded soon after the passenger off-loading was completed. Derek and the rest of the pirates were on the flight deck or in the engineering room, continuing the detailed tutorial on the operation of the *Darwin* that Derek had begun that afternoon.

"For some time we have been singling out ITI and DTC cargo freighters as targets," Chelsea said. "Because they are the major interplanetary suppliers, their manifests are published on the network well ahead of time, giving us plenty of time to plan. Our quartermaster has a superb inventory program—several of the other bands have even adopted it—and knows where shortages are going to occur three to six months in advance. Generally, however, we just intercept the freighter and remove one or more of the large containers." Chelsea laughed. "This is both our first hijacking AND our first kidnapping. At least for the Utopians. I believe that the Crusaders have hijacked a couple of Dem spacecraft en route from the Moon to Mars."

"Your pirate band is called the Utopians?" Hunter said.

"Yes," Chelsea said. "The first chief, a guy named Reginald, was an avid Sir Thomas More fan. Lance can still remember him, even though he was only five when Reginald died. He says that Reginald was quite a scholar. Apparently he loved anything historical—including plays and novels that fictionalized the characters from history."

"Why did this Reginald become a pirate?" Hunter said.

"Apparently he violated one of the obscure Federation antisedition rules inadvertently," Chelsea said, "and was sentenced to two years in prison. After he was paroled, Reginald fled space civilization at his first opportunity."

"Who's Lance?" Tehani asked.

"He's our chief," Chelsea replied. "He's almost forty, which is old for a pirate. Lance was born a Utopian. He is one of only a couple of dozen in our band who have never lived under either of the two space governments."

"How many Utopians are there altogether?" Hunter asked.

"About five hundred," Chelsea said, "counting all the children. Right now we're one of the fastest-growing bands."

"I must say," Tehani said, "that you are being remarkably open with us. I would never have expected you to have been this forthcoming."

Chelsea shrugged. "These are all things that you would have learned sooner or later. Lance and I had several long discussions after the decision was made to kidnap you. We knew that you would of course recognize me—as I said earlier, that was one of the reasons I was selected. Lance and the subchiefs made a list of proscribed information, based on security considerations. He told me I could talk about anything else with you."

"Why did you decide to kidnap Tehani?" Hunter said.

"That was one of the proscribed topics," Chelsea said, laughing again. "But I can tell why we decided to kidnap you."

"I understand that already," Hunter said. "You're short of medical help. And somebody thinks the Federation might be willing to pay for my release. Although I find that very difficult to believe."

"Chairman Covington makes a very big deal out of his fellows," Chelsea said. "He will be embarrassed, and therefore angry, that you have been snatched away. And his ego is gigantic. He will not ignore what he will perceive to be a personal insult."

Chelsea paused, thinking. "Actually, Hunter, I don't want to mislead or unduly flatter you. The decision to kidnap you was very much an afterthought. When we set out on this mission our targets were, in prioritized order, the *Darwin* and its cargo, Tehani, and Derek Sanchez. We only decided to add you to the captive list after we saw the final passenger manifest." She laughed. "We also had to alter our procedures at the last minute, so that I was never seen by the passengers who were going to be off-loaded."

"Why was Derek a target?" Hunter said.

"I'm not at liberty to tell you," Chelsea replied.

Tehani had a puzzled look on her face. "What is it?" Chelsea asked.

"I'm confused," Tehani said. "You knew that Hunter and I would recognize you. Why did you have to stay out of sight until after the other passengers were off-loaded?"

"It's something personal," Chelsea said.

"I think I know," Hunter said.

"That would be extremely unlikely," Chelsea said.

"Perhaps your boyfriend or husband," Hunter said, "is none other than Darrell Peabody, the younger son of my erstwhile cabinmate, Mr. Everett Peabody?"

Chelsea was silent for several seconds. "That's pretty amazing, Hunter," she said. "It would never have occurred to me that anybody, especially not you, could have become close enough to that stuffed shirt in a few days to learn any details about his personal life."

"Then Hunter is right?" Tehani said.

Chelsea nodded. "Darrell Peabody is my husband," she said. "He's one of the Utopian subchiefs. Darrell is as fine, intelligent, and gentle a man as I have ever met. But his father thinks that he's a piece of worthless trash, just because he's not a Nazi like his older brother."

"Uh-oh," Tehani said. "I think we hit a sensitive nerve."

"Yes, you did," Chelsea said. She stood up. "Speaking of Darrell," she added, "I have a scheduled video call with him just about now." She glanced at Hunter. "And weren't you supposed to continue your discussion of that portable medical facility with Packel this evening?"

"Oops," Hunter said. "I'm already a couple of minutes late."

HUNTER HAD ALREADY worked up quite a sweat bicycling on the exercise machine when Tehani, who had been using the other exercise station, walked over beside him. "Are you almost finished?" she asked.

"With this module, yes," he said. "But I still have ten minutes of arm work to do. . . . What's up?"

Tehani put a hand on one of his shoulders. "I thought we might take a shower together," she said.

"Now?" Hunter said, feeling his pulse rate jump over its already elevated level.

"Uh-huh," Tehani said. "Chelsea's in bed, Bagwell's

back in the virtual-world kiosk, and Derek took a shower before we started exercising. Besides," she added, "there's nobody left on board that doesn't know we're lovers, or will be offended."

Hunter turned off the exercise station. "Lead the way, my princess," he said.

They stopped by their cabin to pick up some fresh clothes to take with them to the shower room. After they entered, Tehani locked the door. "This should be fun," she said, grinning at Hunter.

Hunter watched her undress with a combination of lust and admiration. When she was naked except for her adhesive slippers, he approached Tehani and tried to kiss her. "Not yet," she said with an impish grin, "we can do that after we're in the shower."

They carefully set up the inner and outer curtains of the shower, zipping them both tight across the top, before selecting their shower temperature and turning on the spigot. "Not so much pressure," Hunter said immediately. The water was spouting out of the faucet with a lot of force, first bouncing off the bottom of the shower, and then ricocheting many times off the curtains, the wall, the floors, and their bodies. Fortunately, since the curtains absorbed some of the energy, the water drops did not bounce around forever at a high velocity.

Laughing uninhibitedly, Tehani adjusted the pressure to a more modest level. They still had to wait a few minutes before they could start soaping each other, for the droplets kept hitting them in the eyes and face. At length the water projectiles were no longer a dire threat and Tehani squeezed a tiny amount of soap gel out of a pressurized container. They stood just out of the main stream of the shower. First Tehani scrubbed Hunter all over, front and back, and then Hunter returned the favor.

He was completely aroused by the end of this soapy

massage. Surrounded by water and mist at all levels, Hunter took the naked Tehani in his arms and kissed her passionately. His sexual longing was so intense that he started to pull her down on the shower floor and make love.

"We must rinse off the soap first, darling," Tehani said. "Or else we'll just slip and slide around on each other."

Taking a deep breath, Hunter let Tehani rinse him with the shower attachment. He then did the same for her. "Now back up," she said seductively, after turning off the main shower stream, "right in front of the faucets, so I have something fixed I can hold."

The water droplets from the earlier shower continued to cascade around them, their velocity slowly falling with successive impacts on the curtain. Hunter was standing up when they made love, with both his hands on Tehani's buttocks and her legs wrapped around his midsection. She held on to the shower faucets to stabilize them in the weightlessness.

Hunter had never even conceived of having sexual intercourse standing up, much less in a watery environment. Tehani squeezed and rocked, back and forth, at the same time kissing his neck and ear with her wet lips and tongue. After a few minutes Hunter had a shuddering climax. He even yelled, for the first time in his life.

Tehani released the faucets, lifted herself with her hands on his shoulders, and gently placed her feet on the shower floor. Hunter sat down in the shower and crawled over to the corner, against the bottom of the soggy curtains.

Tehani activated the vacuum pump that pulled the water into a drain on one side of the shower. Then, smiling, her body shimmering with water, she came over and caressed Hunter.

"That was absolutely unbelievable," he said.

"**YOU'LL BE HAPPY** to know," Bailey said to Hunter and Tehani one morning at breakfast, after they had been traveling for six days, "that your fellow passengers have now been safely rescued. Chairman Covington has accused the Dems of a deliberate act of war, which they have vigorously denied, and demanded retribution. An emergency meeting of the bilateral commission has been called. It will convene next week.

"Of more importance to us," Bailey continued, "our intelligence agents say that there is not the slightest indication that any military action against us is under way, suggesting that at least for the time being, our identity is still safe."

The pirate contingent on board exchanged congratulations. "I also would like to take this opportunity," Bailey said, "to commend our captives for their exemplary behavior thus far. Derek, you have done a marvelous job of explaining the workings of this spacecraft. I may be deluding myself, but I believe that Franklin and I could almost fly the *Darwin* by ourselves if required. Hunter, your contributions to the design of the new portable medical facility have been fantastic. That facility is vital if our pirate band is going to expand and grow. As a result of your inputs, we now have a specific list of all the equipment we must, uh, obtain, to make that facility a reality."

Bailey looked at Tehani and smiled. "As for you, Miss Wilawa, I can't cite anything specific you've done that is worth a commendation. But I must say that just having you on board gives all of us a lift."

"Thanks, Bailey," Tehani said. "I can't imagine how being a prisoner could be any nicer."

Everyone laughed. "I guess I should point out, however," Bailey said, suddenly becoming serious, "that there is not unanimous agreement in our band with the liberal way that we have treated you. There is a faction among the council of subchiefs that has already complained to Lance that we are setting a dangerous precedent, and that there needs to be more general discussion about the handling of political prisoners."

There was a protracted silence around the dining table. "What exactly are you telling us, Bailey?" Hunter asked. "That we should be prepared for something different after this flight is over?"

"I guess so, Hunter," Bailey said. "You are under my jurisdiction now. But when we arrive in Utopia, I will no longer have any say about your treatment."

"But I don't understand," Hunter said. "Are we going to be incarcerated? That doesn't make much sense to me. How can I help with your medical problems if I spend all my time in a jail cell?"

"The Utopian band does not have jail cells, at least not as they would be defined by the Federation," Bailey said. He paused for a few seconds. "Look, I don't want to make a big deal out of this. Our discussions are continuing. I just want you to realize that you have been granted certain freedoms and privileges aboard this spacecraft that may not exist after our flight is concluded."

THAT NIGHT, AFTER Tehani and he made love, Hunter was in an uncharacteristically pensive mood. "Has it occurred to you how incredibly perfect our entire situation is?" he said while he was holding her in his arms. "Could you possibly define a more conducive scenario for falling in love?"

Tehani rolled over and rose up on her elbows. "I think about it every day, Hunter," she said. "Every hour I tell myself, 'Tehani, enjoy this time to the fullest, because life will never again be like this.'"

"Have I told you how much I love you?" Hunter said.

Tehani smiled. "Several times," she said. "But I never tire of hearing it."

"I love you," he said, "now and forever."

Tehani scooted over next to him on her elbows and kissed him softly. "The now I believe, my darling," she said. "The forever part, however, is a little on the iffy side."

"I will," he protested. "I will love you forever."

Tehani cuddled up in his arms. "Now is easy," she said. "How could you not love me now? There are no complications, nothing that detracts in any way from our sharing everything. Every night we hug and kiss and make fantastic love. We have no arguments, no outside responsibilities of any significance, no bills, no families to interfere." She looked at Hunter. "Now is a piece of cake."

"You don't believe me," he said.

"About forever?" Tehani said. "I want to believe you, Hunter, more than anything that I have ever wanted. I have never in my life been as happy as I have been with you these last days. I want it to be like this forever. But I know that it will not. Change will come. Our situation will change. You'll change. That's why it's so very important that we enjoy every single moment of this time together and not let worrying about the future take away from our joy and pleasure."

"So you don't want to talk about what we're going to do if we're separated when we reach wherever we're going?" Hunter said.

"And spoil our fun?" she said. "Absolutely not."

"Carpe diem," Hunter said.

"Exactly," Tehani said. "With every fiber of our being."

" 'Gather ye rosebuds while ye may,' " Hunter said.

" 'Had we but worlds enough, and time, This coyness, lady, were no crime,' " Tehani said.

" 'But at my back I always hear, Time's winged chariot

hurrying near,' " Hunter said, laughing and leaning over to kiss her.

"Would you like to make love again?" Tehani said.

Hunter smiled and shrugged. "I don't know if I can," he said, "but I'll certainly give it a try."

Tehani pulled herself on top of Hunter and started kissing him.

"And I WILL love you forever, Tehani," he said between kisses, "whether you believe it or not."

"LATE TOMORROW MORNING sometime, if all goes well," Bailey said, "we should reach our destination."

"Are we arriving at Utopia? Or whatever your main settlement is called?" Tehani asked.

"Not yet," Bailey said. "We have an intermediate stop to make first. We will proceed to our home colony afterward."

"Where are we stopping?" Hunter asked. Chelsea, Tehani, Bailey, and he were sitting in the common area. It was about two hours after dinner. Hunter and Tehani had been watching a movie when Chelsea had interrupted them.

Bailey reflected for a moment. "I will tell you that in the morning," Bailey said, "when the plans are more solid. There are still some uncertainties remaining."

Bailey and Chelsea looked at each other. "We interrupted your movie tonight," Chelsea said at length, "because of a discussion that occurred during our video debriefing with Lance and the council of subchiefs after dinner. Our whole mission team was criticized for not having spent ample time talking with the two of you about our Utopian way of life."

"I'm not sure I understand," Tehani said with a puzzled look.

"Although Franklin, Snyder, and I have had many conversations with Derek about how we live, and why," Bailey said, "none of us could cite a single example of an extended serious cultural or political talk that we had had with the pair of you."

"Part of the difficulty," Chelsea chimed in, "is that the two of you have been sort of in your own world for these fifteen days. You've done your work admirably, Hunter, and we thank you for it, but the rest of the time Tehani and you have basically acted as if the rest of us didn't exist. I don't fault you for that, please understand, but it has made interaction difficult, and Bailey and I have been reluctant to impose ourselves upon you."

"I don't know if it helps any," Tehani said, "but Hunter and I have read every entry in the *Darwin* database that has anything to do with space pirates."

"We know that," Chelsea said, smiling. "We've been monitoring your activities closely. But reading encyclopedia articles prepared by biased Federation writers and editors certainly cannot tell you what we're all about. Besides, there are significant differences among the various pirate bands. The Eastenders, for example, are completely vegetarian. They are also pacifists. The Whales, with whom we deal often, practice a rigid, band-sponsored monogamy. Marriages are arranged by the matchmaker, who is one of the most important subchiefs. Public marital discord results in automatic expulsion from the group. Sexual infidelity is punishable by death."

"Goodness," said Tehani. "I don't think I'd be very comfortable there."

"Exactly," said Chelsea. "But because of what I just told you, you know almost as much about the Whales as you know about the Utopians. I agree with Lance. It is inexcusable that none of us have had a detailed talk with you about our band before now." She glanced over at Bailey. "You want to handle the political stuff? And I'll try to do the culture?"

"Sounds reasonable," Bailey said.

For the next two hours Hunter's and Tehani's ears were filled with information about the Utopians. Bailey pointed out in the beginning that the first and foremost challenge their band faced was survival, and that it was therefore necessary that the Utopians have some kind of organized hierarchy for dealing with other pirate bands and, when necessary, the two space governments. Lance, their chief, was technically an autocrat by the standard definitions of political science, although he seldom made important decisions without conferring with what was called his council of subchiefs. In reality, the council was more like an advisory board, Bailey explained, for the so-called subchiefs were responsible for specific functions, like defense, or intelligence gathering, or housing, rather than being managers of some specific group of people. As a matter of practice, both Bailey and Chelsea agreed, each Utopian reported to one of the subchiefs for his or her work tasks, but only to Lance with respect to daily living issues.

"When disputes occur between or among members of the Utopian band," Bailey said, "they are submitted to Lance for resolution. He either rules on the issue himself, or, depending on the nature of the disagreement, delegates it to a subset of the council. A set of codes, generic statements about how Utopians should live, define the governing principles for our band. Since principles rather than specific laws are the highest level of authority in our society, there is not necessarily a consistency in the rulings of the judges. Lance is aware of this problem, but doesn't want to start promulgating a set of precise laws to mitigate it. Too many laws would be a violation of the fundamental tenet of Utopianism defined by our founder Reginald."

"And what is that fundamental tenet?" Hunter asked, struggling to keep up with the dense flow of information.

"Freedom with responsibility," Bailey said. "Basically, Reginald was opposed to any rules and regulations that tell people how to live, or prefer one lifestyle over another. But he was equally adamant that all members of a community must make a significant contribution, and accept full responsibility for whatever tasks they have accepted."

"I understand the general concept," Tehani said, "but can you be more specific about what it means?"

"Certainly," Bailey said. "For example, there are Utopians of every sexual orientation." He laughed. "Including a few I had never even heard of until I joined seven years ago.... Religious tolerance is absolute, although zealous proselytizing is discouraged.... Marriage can be between two people, of the same or different sexes, or among more than two if they all accept mutual responsibility for one another and their offspring. Drugs of all kinds are permitted, provided the user still fulfills his or her tasks and commitments. In short, you can live however you want, as long as you are a responsible member of the band."

"Both the articles in the database," Hunter said, "and the short network vignette I watched on Cicero emphasized that there were more men among the pirates than women. Is that true with the Utopians?"

"Yes," Chelsea offered. "I believe that the most recent ratio is three to two. Lance is very concerned about recruiting more women, especially young ones."

"So how does that work?" Tehani asked. "I mean, if there aren't enough women to go around, how does that impact families?"

"As Bailey said before, in our band we have many different kinds of marriage," Chelsea said. "The only guideline in the codebook is that there must be a simple, written contract between or among the marital participants covering such issues as sexual fidelity, care of the children, ownership of the possessions, and a few other things. Many Utopian women have two husbands. I know one especially attractive young lady who has four."

"How many husbands do you have?" Hunter asked Chelsea.

"Just one, now," she replied. "But since I haven't conceived during the almost one year that Darrell and I have been regular sexual partners, I am under considerable pressure to find an additional husband. Producing offspring is second to survival in the prioritized list of Utopian goals."

"Wow," said Tehani, shaking her head. "I must say that I'm really glad we're having this conversation. I would have been utterly confused without it."

Bailey nodded. "That's what Lance said. He pointed out that the cultural shock was going to be difficult enough for you guys even if we provided you with basic background information. He was really quite concerned about your welfare. That's one of his trademark characteristics."

There was a brief lull in the conversation. "Let me make certain I haven't misunderstood," Tehani then said. "If I apply that fundamental tenet, I would assume that extramarital sex between consenting adults is completely acceptable."

"Absolutely," said Bailey. He laughed. "Some of the other pirate bands believe that we encourage sexual promiscuity. We do not. Responsibility is as important as freedom. By the way, a Utopian is considered an adult at the age of sixteen, at which time he or she becomes a responsible member of the community, with both the duties and the privileges. Reginald believed that modern human society created a huge problem for itself by extending adolescence for years and years."

NEITHER HUNTER NOR Tehani could fall
asleep that night. Their lovemaking, although satisfying,
had an element of desperation that had never been present
before. They were both well aware that their lives were
about to change irrevocably.

"Hunter?" Tehani said after they both had been lying
awake for over an hour.

"Yes, my love," he said.

"What are you thinking about?" she said.

"Tomorrow," Hunter replied.

Tehani rolled out of his arms, over on her back. " 'Tomorrow, and tomorrow, and tomorrow, Creeps in this petty
pace from day to day,' " she said.

" 'It is a tale told by an idiot,' " he said, " 'full of sound
and fury, Signifying nothing.' "

"Do you believe that?" Tehani asked after a short silence.

"Sometimes," Hunter replied.

"But not most of the time?" she asked.

"No," he said.

This time the silence was longer. "When my father died,
and we discovered his debts," Tehani said, "my mother and
I cried together until we were exhausted. I couldn't imagine ever being happy again. Then, like a godsend, you appeared in my life."

She reached over and took his hand. "After I lost you,"
she said, "I was devastated. Yet, in a way, our brief romance
was the spark that gave me strength to continue, to face the
future with hope. I told myself that being with you had
proven that I could be happy again."

Tears suddenly flooded her eyes. Tehani put her arms
around Hunter. "But never ever, not in my wildest dreams,
did I imagine I could be as happy as I have been these last

fifteen days with you. Yes, I'm afraid of what might happen tomorrow. But nothing that happens then, or in a million tomorrows, will ever take this time away from me."

She kissed him. "Hold me, Hunter," she said. "Hold me as tightly as you can."

"I love you, Tehani," he said.

TWO

"GOOD MORNING," CHELSEA SAID cheerfully as Hunter and Tehani walked into the common area for breakfast the next day. "We were starting to wonder if you guys had slept through your alarm."

"No," said Tehani. "We're just a little slow this morning—we didn't sleep well last night."

"I didn't either," Derek said. "I had a premonition that something terrible would happen today." There was an anger in his eyes that Hunter and Tehani had not seen before. "And based upon what I was told an hour ago, my premonition was correct."

"Derek," Bailey said sharply, "this is neither the time nor the place for this kind of discussion."

Derek rose from the table. "Watch your backs," he said to Hunter and Tehani, "and remember your status, or lack thereof." He stormed off toward his cabin.

"What was that all about?" Hunter asked after Derek was gone.

"We had a disagreement this morning," Bailey said. "Unfortunately, Derek was not happy with the way the dispute was resolved."

Hunter and Tehani sat down at the dining table. Soon

thereafter a robot shuttled out from the kitchen with their breakfast. "What are the patches for?" Tehani asked, noticing that each of the pirates was wearing the same large cloth patch, with the letters "UT" prominent in the center, on the upper-right arm of his shirt.

"They identify us as Utopians," Chelsea said. "We're going to be stopping today at a trading post used by a lot of different pirate bands. The accepted protocol at the post is to wear some clear, unambiguous external identification of band origin. Most of the pirates use patches like these."

There was a brief, strained silence at the table. "All right," Hunter said after several seconds, "is someone going to tell us what's going on?"

"We've had a slight change of plans since last night," Bailey said. "Originally we had expected to stop here at the trading post for only a few hours, to exchange a few containers of the *Darwin* cargo for items that were of greater value to our band. However, during the trade negotiations, we received a generous offer for the *Darwin* itself. We have tentatively accepted this offer, pending inspections on both sides of all the items involved in the deal."

"We had expected that the three of you would remain on board," Chelsea said, "while the cargo containers were being exchanged. Now, obviously, it will be necessary for you to disembark with us."

"Let me make certain that I have understood correctly," Hunter said. "Another pirate band is going to take possession of this spacecraft?"

"Yes, assuming that the inspections are satisfactory," Bailey said.

"Is this what Derek is so upset about?" Tehani said.

"Yes, partly," Bailey answered.

Hunter and Tehani looked at each other. "Okay," Hunter said, "I guess we'd better start packing right after breakfast. How long do we have before we disembark?"

"About two hours," Bailey said. "Unfortunately, the vehicle that we will be using when we leave the trading post is not very large. We will only have room on that vehicle for one small suitcase for each of you. Chelsea will show you which of your suitcases is all right."

"And what will happen to the rest of our stuff?" Hunter asked.

"Snyder will try to trade your articles for items of use to our settlement," Chelsea said. She smiled. "Essentially you will be making a donation to the welfare of the Utopian band."

Hunter did not find Chelsea's response amusing. When Tehani saw that Hunter was going to protest, she reached under the table and grabbed his thigh. He understood the look in her eyes. *Remember,* a voice inside his head said, *you are their prisoner. You don't really have any rights*.

"That's fine with me," Tehani said, rising from her chair. She looked at Snyder. "I'll go pack my one suitcase now and then go through the rest of my stuff with you, pointing out what I think might be valuable trade material."

"That would be much appreciated," Snyder said.

Soon after Chelsea left their cabin, and Hunter and Tehani began packing, there was a soft knock on their door. It was Derek. "May I come in?" he said.

"I can't stay long," he said several seconds later. "Franklin will be back shortly and I'm certain they wouldn't want me to be talking to you right now." Derek took a deep breath. "Whatever you do," he said, facing Hunter, "don't ever trust these people. They're snakes. They may act nice, and sound nice, but they'd cut your balls off if it would benefit them."

"Are you this angry because they traded the *Darwin*?" Tehani asked.

Derek spun around. "You don't know?"

Tehani shook her head. "Know what?"

"They didn't just trade the *Darwin*," Derek said, "they traded ME as well. Snyder said it was one of the critical elements of the agreement." Derek was really agitated. "In a few hours, I'm going to be handed over, as if I were a slave, to someone I have never even seen. When I protested, reminding Bailey that I had been a model of cooperation from the moment I was captured, he told me that he was sorry, but that the interests of the Utopians came first. I blew my top. I threatened not to give the other pirate band any useful information about the *Darwin*. Bailey said that the Draconians would then simply execute me, and Franklin and he would teach them how to operate the spacecraft."

"Good grief," Tehani said.

"I'm fucked," Derek said. "No matter what happens. Even if someday, somehow, I make it back to Mars, I'll be indicted for treason. The antisedition codes are explicit. Sharing classified technical knowledge is considered conspiring with the enemy." He glanced at Hunter. "You should worry about that, too. You've given these bastards information that is privileged, even if it's not classified. They could get you for being too cooperative."

The cabin door swung open abruptly. "Oh, here you are, Derek," Bailey said. He looked at them all with a hard stare. "The three of you are not to be together again without one of us around," he said. "That's an order."

Hunter and Tehani shared a hug after Bailey and Derek left. "Wow," Hunter said, his mind overwhelmed by everything that had already happened. "I guess a lot can change in just one day."

Tehani kissed him before turning back to the open suitcase on her bed. "I'm afraid this is only the beginning," she said.

SNYDER QUICKLY UNDERSTOOD the value of most of the articles Hunter was leaving behind. He did not need much additional explanation. Tehani's overflow possessions, however, were mostly shoes and clothes, some of them quite expensive. Snyder knew a little about materials and fabrics, but absolutely nothing about style. Tehani was trying fruitlessly to explain to him why one pair of her shoes was worth three times as much as another when Bailey informed them that they were docking at the trading post.

Everyone gathered on the flight deck in front of the observation window. Derek was in the engineering room handling the controls. In front of their slowly moving spacecraft, the Sun illuminated a large, rectangular, windowless gray box about twice the size of the *Darwin*. On the side facing them, the box had six long, slender extensions, with gaps in between like the tines of a fork, where all the visiting spacecraft docked. On its top, the space trading-post structure had half a dozen antennas of varying technologies, shapes, and sizes. The largest of the antennas was a gigantic circle, made of mesh, mounted on a short, stubby base.

The nose of the *Darwin* was approaching the end of its pair of docking tines when Hunter and Tehani arrived on the flight deck. Three other spacecraft, all much smaller than the interplanetary freighter that had been their home for almost three weeks, were docked in the adjacent bay. As Derek continued to ease the *Darwin* forward into the tight space, and the first attachments to the trading post were secured, the almost imperceptible rotation of the space structure brought the Sun into the observation window. Hunter glanced at it briefly, noticing immediately that the solar system's source of heat and light was larger than he had ever seen it before.

Only the front third of the *Darwin* would fit in the docking bay. When the motion of the spacecraft had essentially ceased, Hunter and Tehani followed Bailey and the others back to the common area. Their space suits and suitcases were neatly arranged in the vicinity of the spacecraft entrance. Following instructions, Hunter and Tehani put on their suits.

"You will be in open space after you leave the airlock," Bailey said through the microphone in his suit. "Take your time and be very careful on the ladder. If you fall off, it is not certain that you can be rescued."

The door between the *Darwin* and its airlock retracted. After Franklin and Bagwell had finished loading all the luggage into the small airlock, Bailey motioned for Hunter and Tehani to follow him. She turned around briefly, taking one last look at the common area.

Once they were all crammed into the airlock, Derek activated the pressure-control algorithm from a panel mounted on the wall. The entryway to the *Darwin* closed tight, and air started venting into space. A digital readout on the panel showed the steadily decreasing pressure. When it reached zero, the red light on the panel turned to green.

Derek opened the door to space. Sunlight flooded the airlock, causing each of them temporarily to shut his eyes. When Hunter could see again, he saw that a deployable ladder, whose housing was mounted on a portable structure sitting on the landing dock, was uncoiling in their direction. Bailey, on his knees at the edge of the opening, reached out and grabbed the ladder, securing it on the floor of the airlock.

"Franklin, Bagwell, and Snyder will unload the bags first," Bailey announced. "When they are finished, the rest of us will cross. Hunter and Tehani, since this is not an everyday experience for you, watch how my men use small, controlled steps, and avoid all jerky motions."

The pirates formed a chain on the ladder. Bailey would hand a piece of luggage to the first man, who would take one careful step down the ladder before handing it to the second man, and so on. In less than a minute the luggage was all safely on a cart on the dock. Almost immediately the cart was wheeled away by a dockhand.

The total distance from the *Darwin* to the trading-post dock was no more than thirty yards. Nevertheless, remembering his vertigo on the spacecraft tour with Derek, Hunter was uneasy as he edged out of the airlock onto the first rung of the unsteady ladder. He paused before taking another step. Chelsea noticed his timidity. "Drop down on all fours if you're having trouble," she said.

He took another step standing upright. Then, with his head starting to spin, Hunter placed his knees on one rung and reached for the next rung with his hands. He missed. His hands plunged through the ladder, and his chest continued its forward motion until it struck against the rung. The recoil temporarily separated his entire body from the ladder, but Hunter managed to grab a rung with his hands on the bounce. Slowly, carefully, he used his arm strength to bring the rest of his body back into contact with the ladder.

"Are you all right?" he heard Tehani say behind him.

Hunter's heart was pounding so fiercely that he could almost hear it. "I'm fine," he managed to say. But he wasn't. He was completely disoriented and having difficulty breathing. He made a mistake and glanced to his left. Sunlight poured through his helmet and temporarily blinded him. A few seconds later he felt a hand on the arm of his space suit.

When the spots vanished in front of his eyes, Hunter saw that Snyder had crawled up the ladder toward him.

"One rung at a time, Hunter," Snyder said. "I'll help you if you like."

Hunter shook his head. "I can do it," he said. "Just give me a moment."

He closed his eyes and took three slow, deep breaths. When he opened his eyes again, Hunter fixed them on the ladder rungs in front of him. Then he started to crawl with very small individual motions.

He reached the safety of the dock with no additional difficulties. "Well done," Snyder said, after Hunter stood up beside him. "Most neophytes would have panicked and we would now have an emergency retrieval under way."

"Thanks for coming to help me," Hunter said to Snyder.

Tehani was now crossing, also using a four-point approach. She reached the dock without any trouble. Tehani took Hunter's outstretched hand on the step from the last rung to the dock. He could see her quizzical expression through her helmet. "I don't think I would have made a very good astronaut," Hunter said with a smile. Tehani, Snyder, and the other pirates all laughed.

On the other side of the airlock was a small, enclosed room containing a long, dilapidated table, half a dozen chairs, and a pair of file cabinets on one side, against a wall. On the opposite side of the room was a set of large storage bins. The two men in the room were both sitting in chairs at the table. One was operating a computer. Each wore a patch with a large five-sided star on the shoulder of his shirt. While they were removing their space suits, and Bailey was talking with the two men, Snyder explained to Hunter and Tehani that people wearing the star patch were employees or temporary residents of the trading post.

"Are they pirates?" Tehani asked.

"Technically, using the UDSC or FISC definitions," Snyder said, "I guess they are. But they are not members of any specific band. They are hired by the pirate consortium to operate this trading post."

Hunter was about to ask a question about the pirate consortium when he noticed that one of the two men with the star patch was handing Bailey three sets of plastic handcuffs and keys that he had retrieved from a file cabinet just behind the table. Alarmed, Hunter pointed at the handcuffs. "What are those for?" he said.

Snyder turned around. "Bailey will explain them in a minute," he said.

"These handcuffs are for your protection," Bailey said when he returned to the group. "While we are here at the trading post, each of you will be handcuffed to one of us. Derek, you will be with Franklin. Tehani, with Chelsea. Hunter, with me."

Bailey approached Hunter with the handcuffs. Hunter stepped back, clearly angry. "This is a dangerous place," Bailey said, first speaking to Hunter and then addressing both Derek and Tehani. "You could easily be killed, kidnapped, or raped if you wandered around here alone. None of you belong to any pirate band, and therefore have no status with the consortium employees. The trading-post security officers might protect me, for fear that a complaint from the Utopians might cost them their jobs. But they would look the other way if someone attacked you."

"Why didn't you tell us all this before we docked?" Hunter asked.

"What purpose would it have served?" Bailey said. "It would have made everything that much more difficult."

Chelsea cuffed her left hand to Tehani's right hand and tested the key. Derek and Hunter still refused to extend their arms forward for the handcuffs.

"Look," Bailey said, his impatience showing, "I really don't have time for all this. You can either cooperate, or we'll tranquilize you and leave you temporarily in one of those empty bins across the room. Either way you end up handcuffed."

Hunter realized that resistance was futile. Inwardly seething with rage, he thrust his right arm forward for Bailey to handcuff it. Derek, mumbling profanities, did the same. A minute later the whole troupe entered the security room on the other side of a small door.

"Supposedly," Bailey said, after handing over his guns and passing, attached to Hunter, through both a metal detector and an X-ray gate, "all weapons are checked here with the security officers. But don't count on it. Gun battles have occurred inside pirate trading posts like this one. For a small bribe you can keep a knife. For a larger bribe you may even induce one of these security officers to murder someone you don't like."

"All right, keep it moving, wise guy," one of the three security officers said. "And can the chatter."

At the far side of the security room they picked up their luggage. The long corridor outside the room was empty. Hunter's contingent turned to the right and headed for the main part of the structure.

"I have a feeling that this is not going to be one of my favorite places," Tehani said to Hunter as they were walking.

He didn't reply. Hunter was not in the best of moods.

TRANSIENT ACCOMMODATIONS AT the trading post consisted of four large dormitory rooms, three for the men and one for the women. Toilet and shower facilities were communal, with set time periods reserved for the women. After registering at the transient desk, establishing a time for everyone to meet together for lunch, and leaving a message for the Draconian pair who were going to inspect the *Darwin,* Bailey, Hunter, Franklin, and Derek went to the dormitory to select their beds.

Each room had sixteen twin beds, eight on each side of a wide middle aisle. The rooms were adequate, and reasonably clean, although the bare white walls had indentations of various sizes scattered here and there. Occupied signs were hung on the edges of those beds that had already been claimed.

In the first room there were no unoccupied bed pairs together. "You mean we're going to sleep with these damn things on," Hunter said, jerking the handcuffs.

"Absolutely," Bailey said. "I have a friend who was raped by three bullies when he got up to take a piss in the middle of the night." Bailey looked at Hunter. "And you're younger and a lot better-looking than he was."

"Jesus," Hunter said, "this is really a fabulous place."

Bailey and Hunter found a pair of beds in the second room and claimed them with the tags they had been given by the clerk at the transient desk. Derek and Franklin located another pair in the same room. After storing their luggage in combination lockers, Bailey suggested that they have a drink in the bar.

"Suits me," Hunter said. "I don't think I've ever had alcohol this early in the day before, but after this morning I could definitely use a drink."

On their way to the bar, they passed half a dozen other pirates, including a trio of burly-looking men all wearing what appeared to be a permanent scowl. "Who were they?" Hunter asked, after they were out of earshot of the threesome.

"Saracens," Bailey replied. "One of the nastiest of all pirate bands. Many of them are convicted murderers and rapists."

At the transient desk on the way to the bar, Bailey

stopped to see if the Draconians had responded to the message he had left. They had. In fact, they had asked if they could begin the inspection of the *Darwin* before lunch. Derek and Franklin went to meet the Draconians in the trading-post lobby while Bailey and Hunter continued to the bar.

There were eight other people in the large bar, all men. Two handcuffed pairs were sitting at a table just inside the door. The other four were sitting on the stools at the bar itself. Bailey and Hunter chose a table off to one side, away from everyone else. After they entered their drink selections on the keyboard built into the table, which Bailey charged using a card he had obtained when they had registered for the rooms, Hunter asked about the plan for the rest of the day.

"This afternoon, the Draconians will finish inspecting the *Darwin* with Franklin and Derek," Bailey said, "while Snyder and Bagwell are at the trading center with all the personal items from the passengers. Unless something comes up that requires a decision from me, the rest of us have nothing specific planned, although I guess I should go with Franklin at some time to look over the spacecraft we'll be taking when we leave here."

A very young waitress with a star on the shoulder of her shirt and a face full of piercings brought them their drinks. Bailey thanked her. "I thought that after lunch," he then continued, "that maybe Tehani, Chelsea, you, and I would go to the entertainment center. This post has a superb theater with a modern stage and all the technology for a full holographic movie projection. And they almost always have the newest releases from FedEnt." He smiled. "In general, it's better to go to the theater at one of these posts in the afternoon. Evening shows can be a bit rowdy."

THREE

AT LUNCH SNYDER AND Bagwell complained that
there was no way they were going to be able to make good
trades for Tehani's clothes and shoes without her help, so
she volunteered to accompany them to the trading center
that afternoon. Franklin had also encountered some problems with the Draconians. He needed Bailey onboard the
Darwin. While the two Utopians negotiated the details of
the agreement transferring the *Darwin* to the other pirate
band, Hunter chose to sit in the clearing room, unhand-
cuffed, and read a used book that he had picked up at the
trading-post commissary. He had not read more than a
couple of actual physical books in his entire life. At home
on Cicero, he had either read directly from his computer
monitor or downloaded the book or magazine onto a data
cube that he put in his hand computer.

For most of the time, Hunter was alone in the clearing
room. After reading for about thirty minutes, he became
drowsy and stretched out on the floor. When Bailey and
Franklin awakened him, Hunter was astonished to discover that he had been asleep for almost two hours.

Bailey activated a system that summoned the officials
back to the clearing room. Handcuffed to Bailey again,

Hunter and the two pirates passed quickly through security and into the corridor that led to the main part of the trading post.

"Where's Derek?" Hunter said suddenly, surprised at himself for not having asked the question earlier.

"He is going to remain on the *Darwin,*" Bailey replied, "with the Draconians. They want to leave as soon as possible. If they can load all their cargo in the next few hours, they'll be out of here before the dock closes."

"But I wanted to say good-bye to Derek," Hunter said, stopping. "And I'm certain Tehani would have wanted to also."

"Unfortunately, it's too late for that now," Bailey said.

Hunter thought for a moment and then started walking again. "Is Derek all right?" he asked.

"He's not happy, if that's what you mean," Bailey said. "But I think that the Draconians will treat him fairly. Eventually. If Derek stops being such a pain in the ass."

"He's angry," Hunter said. "He has every right to be. No human being likes being treated like someone else's private property."

"At some point," Bailey said, "a wise man stops fighting what he cannot change."

It was thirty minutes before the trading center closed for the day. Bailey, Franklin, and Hunter went into the crowded bar, which was the place designated for them to meet the others. After first checking to make certain that Snyder and Bagwell had not already arrived and selected a table, the trio sat down and ordered a drink. Within a couple of minutes after their drinks were served, the three Saracens they had passed in the hallway earlier in the day approached their table.

"Are you Bailey?" one of them said. He was an enormous, imposing man, at least six-four and weighing over 250 pounds, all of which appeared to be solid muscle. His face was pockmarked and his long, dark hair was plastered down on the sides. He looked as if he was in his mid-thirties.

"Yes, I'm Bailey," was the reply.

"I'm Rango," the man said, extending his hand and forcing a smile that was almost as threatening as his scowl, "chief of the Saracens. Your man Snyder, over at the trading center, said you were in charge."

"I am the leader of this particular expedition," Bailey said.

"I want that girl," Rango said. "The beautiful one. She's handcuffed to one of the women in your band."

Hunter felt his blood run cold. "What are you offering?" Bailey asked after a momentary silence.

Rango smiled again. "More than you can afford to turn down. I haven't seen a girl I wanted to fuck so much since I left Mars five years ago."

Hunter was outraged. He stared furiously at Rango for a brief second, then realized that he had made a tragic mistake. He averted his eyes and looked down at the floor.

Rango moved toward Hunter. "What's his problem?" the Saracen chief said menacingly.

Bailey lifted the handcuffs above the table where they could be seen. "He's an unhappy prisoner," Bailey said. "That's all."

"If he even so much as glances at me again," Rango said, "I'll tear his head off his shoulders."

"I promise you," Bailey said, "that this prisoner will not take his eyes off the floor until we have finished our business." He paused for only a second. "Now what's your proposal for the girl?"

Rango pulled a small sack out of his pocket. "Do you know what these are?" the Saracen chief said, pouring some of the contents into his hand. Bailey shook his head. "These are top-quality diamonds," Rango continued, "only the three highest grades and coloring. I'll give you six carats, with no stone smaller than a carat, for the girl. I take her tonight, and you never see her again."

His two Saracen colleagues exchanged knowledgeable looks. At the next table, where four members of the Crocodile band were sitting and following the conversation with avid curiosity, two of the pirates stood up to see better the diamonds that Rango was holding.

"I'm sorry," Bailey said, "I really don't know anything about diamonds. I have no idea what they're worth."

"They're worth a fucking ton, man," one of Rango's Saracen colleagues said. "Ask anybody. Go ask the chief trader, now, before he closes."

"Six carats just for a girl?" one of the Crocodile pirates who was standing nearby now said. "She must really be something special."

"Nobody asked you," the other Saracen said truculently to the Crocodile. "Sit down and shut up. Unless you want some trouble."

The Crocodile, an immense man himself, glared back at the Saracen for a few seconds before finally sitting down. The waitress bringing drinks to Hunter and the Utopians witnessed the entire scene, and scurried quickly back to the bar. Within seconds a security officer appeared next to the table.

"What's going on here?" the officer said.

"Nothing," Rango said, with another of his forced smiles. "I was trying to conduct business with this Utopian and that fat Crocodile asshole over there decided to open his mouth. Everything's under control now."

The security officer glanced at all the pirates. "Let me remind you," he said, "that taking part in a disturbance at this trading post results in an automatic suspension of your post privileges for six months, regardless of who initiates the action."

"We all understand that," Rango replied with an irritated expression on his face. He moved over and stood beside the smaller security officer. "If you wouldn't mind," Rango said, "could you leave now? I'd like to finish my business."

The intimidated officer hesitated a few seconds and then departed, returning to his post on the far side of the bar. Rango glowered at the Crocodile band members until they all turned their eyes away. During the entire time Hunter had been sitting motionless, listening carefully to the conversation, with his eyes on the floor.

"Now, do we have a deal?" Rango said impatiently to Bailey moments later.

"Not yet," Bailey replied. "I must make a quick check with my chief on Cicero."

"Your chief?" Rango sneered. "What are you, some kind of wimp?" he then said in a loud voice. "Or is that beautiful girl prisoner your private snatch?" He thrust the diamonds into Bailey's face. "Look at these, man. They're worth more than you'll make the next ten years. You can tell your fucking chief she was stolen from you and pocket them all."

Bailey was silent for a few seconds. Hunter, still staring at the floor, was in absolute agony. He wanted desperately to do something, but could not think of anything that would help the situation.

Before Bailey could reply, a growing murmur spread through the mostly male crowd that had gathered around their table. The crowd moved aside, making room for Snyder, Chelsea, and Tehani to approach the table. Rango's eyes hungrily followed Tehani as she walked toward them. "All right, goddamnit," he growled quickly at Bailey. "I'll give you *EIGHT* carats. You have her here, outside the bar, at nine o'clock tonight."

Rango and his Saracen companions departed just as Snyder and the two women reached Hunter and the other two Utopians. "What was that all about?" Chelsea asked, glancing at both the Saracens and the crowd that had already started to disperse.

"Rango wants to buy Tehani," Bailey said. "He is offering eight carats of high-quality diamonds."

Chelsea whistled. "Are you certain you heard correctly?" she asked. "Did he really offer eight carats?"

Bailey nodded. Hunter could contain himself no longer. "Surely you're not going to sell her?" he desperately entreated Bailey. "That would make her nothing but a slave."

Bailey ignored Hunter's comment. "Where's Bagwell?" he asked the others.

"He found a poker game starting at six," Snyder said. "You know how he is."

"Eight carats of diamonds would certainly buy everything we need for the portable medical facility," Franklin said after a short silence. He was speaking for the first time since Rango had come to the table. "As well as several months' worth of food, clothing, and other essential supplies for the settlement."

"You're right," Bailey said. "The offer is very generous. And tempting."

"Shit," said Hunter. "I can't believe . . ."

"Excuse me," Tehani quickly interrupted, frowning at Hunter. "Do I understand correctly that the big man who just left, the one with the long hair and the pockmarked face, is trying to buy me from you?"

"Yes," Bailey said. "That's Rango, the chief of the Saracens. Apparently he saw you at the trading center this afternoon and decided that he wanted you." Bailey turned to Snyder. "What happened over there?"

Snyder looked perplexed. "Nothing much," he said. "Tehani was explaining to the chief trader why her clothes were worth so much money and he asked her if she would model some of them. He said they would help us get better values in trade. She put on a couple of the outfits and everyone applauded. . . . Rango was there, trading his diamonds for food and clothing. He came over for a minute, while Tehani was dressing, and asked me who was in charge of our group here. That's all."

The four Crocodile pirates at the table next to them had finished their drinks and were ready to leave the bar. The large man who had angered the Saracens with his comment touched Bailey on the shoulder.

"I have known Rango for a long time," he said. "He gets what he wants. Take his diamonds and be thankful that he offered you a deal at all." The man turned to Tehani, his leering eyes running up and down her body several times. "So you're the one who has Rango in such heat," he said. He eventually smiled approvingly. "You are a beauty, I'll admit, but you'd have to be the best fuck ever born to be worth eight carats to me."

The waitress finally brought the drinks that Franklin, Bailey, and Hunter had originally ordered. "Why don't you three drink these?" Bailey said, motioning to Chelsea, Hunter, and Tehani while he was pulling the handcuff key from his pocket. "Chelsea," he then added, "would you mind staying with the prisoners while the rest of us have a private talk? I'll give you a briefing later."

Chelsea nodded. "I understand," she said, as Bailey temporarily cuffed Hunter to her other hand.

THE EXASPERATED HUNTER wasted no time. "Chelsea," he said as soon as the three Utopian men were beyond earshot, "you can't let them do this. It's . . . it's obscene, as well as being unbelievably immoral."

Chelsea shrugged. "Immorality and obscenity are relative terms," she said. She smiled and looked at Hunter. "You must remember that from your studies of philosophy in secondary school." She took a deep pull from her drink container. "Besides, Rango almost certainly wants Tehani to be one of his wives," she continued. "He wouldn't be paying that much otherwise. She'd probably have a pretty decent life as long as she didn't cause any trouble."

"How can you be so cold and insensitive?" Hunter said, almost shouting. "Did you see that guy? He'll treat her like an animal."

There was fire in Chelsea's eyes when she replied. "Lower your voice, Hunter," she ordered, "and remember what your status is here. Tehani and you are our prisoners. You have no vote in what's going to happen. If you know what's good for you, you'll follow Tehani's example and keep your mouth shut."

Hunter glanced at Tehani. "Aren't you going to say anything?" he asked, the frustration apparent in his tone.

"What do you want me to say?" Tehani replied evenly. "And how would that make the situation better?"

Hunter shook his head and looked away from the two women. He struggled unsuccessfully with his growing anger.

"What do you think, Ellis?" Hunter heard a male voice say. "Is that a face that's worth eight carats? Do you think she could launch a thousand ships?"

Hunter turned and saw two men approaching their table. They were very obviously staring at Tehani, who, like Chelsea, had not seen them yet. On the shoulders of the two men's shirts were patches featuring a dozen or so eggs arranged so that they resembled a human head.

The two men stopped only a foot or two from the table and simply stood there, looking at Tehani from behind. "Don't you two have something better to do?" Hunter said irritably.

"Why, Chelsea," the other man said, "I do believe that one of your prisoners is disturbed by our presence. Have my powers of observation deserted me, or is this young man enamored of this peerless beauty beside me, the one who has been the subject of so much discussion in the last hour?"

Chelsea turned around, saw the two men, and started laughing. "August," she said, "you always amuse me. How in the hell are you? Did you talk that girl I saw you with last year in that bar in the Free Zone into becoming your wife?"

"Alas and alack, no," August replied. "To my bed she went, with great joy and alacrity. She shattered the quiet of that night with a tremendous scream of orgasmic pleasure. But when I extolled the virtues of being a pirate's wife, she simply laughed."

"August was a graduate student during my freshman year at the university," Chelsea explained to Tehani, who was now also smiling. "It was he who first introduced me to Darrell. . . . August and his companion are Eggheads, a small pirate band that trades their consulting services to other bands for food and essentials."

"And what services do they provide?" Hunter asked in an unpleasant tone.

"Information primarily, young man," August replied, holding up the small computer dangling from his waist. "For example, tonight, if the Utopians had cared to ask, we could have given them the details about the last ten trades made involving diamonds, not just here at this trading post, but at any of the posts frequented by the various pirate bands. I believe, incidentally, that the eight carats offered for this beauteous lass is the highest price over offered for a woman in pirateland."

"How thrilling," Hunter said, turning away.

"Is he always this pleasant?" August asked.

Chelsea laughed again. "He doesn't like being a prisoner," she said. "And he's worried about what's going to happen to his girlfriend."

"Ah-ha," August replied, "so I was right. Ellis," he then

said to his companion, "I believe that this handsome young man does not much like the thought of Rango's making the beast with two backs with his girl. I bet it bothers him also to imagine her beautiful lips parting to take Rango's giant shlong into her perfect mouth."

Hunter rose angrily, his free hand cocked into a fist. Chelsea jerked hard on the handcuffs, pulling him back into his chair. Tehani looked over at Hunter with a pained expression and shook her head. Hunter went into a sulk.

"What are you doing these days?" Chelsea asked August a few seconds later.

"I'm spending three months here," he replied. "Ellis and I are basically freelance consultants, selling our services to the itinerant traders. And you?"

"We've just finished a daring hijacking and kidnapping," Chelsea said proudly. "It was my first. We picked up an ITI freighter out of Cicero—we've already traded it to the Draconians for a mountain of loot."

August looked first at Tehani, and then at Hunter. "And these two?" he asked. "Why did you kidnap them?"

"The girl apparently has friends in high places," Chelsea said. "I don't know the details. But Lance said Cooperman thinks we can obtain a very large ransom." She gestured toward Hunter. "As for him, he has some medical skills that we sorely need. And he was just named one of the Covington Fellows. We may be able to ransom him, too, eventually, once we have enough other medical help."

"A Covington Fellow! You nabbed one of the bastard's pride and joys?" August said. He glanced again at Hunter. "This one must be smarter than he looks," he said. He then touched Chelsea on the shoulder. "What a great caper. . . . By the way, how's Darrell doing?"

Before Chelsea could answer, the other four Utopians at the trading post returned to their table. Bagwell had joined Bailey, Snyder, and Franklin during the time they had been gone. Bailey greeted both August and Ellis. They had apparently met before. The Utopians and the Eggheads exchanged small talk while Bailey unlocked Hunter's handcuffs and then recuffed Hunter to himself.

"Let's go have dinner," Bailey said as soon as Hunter's handcuffs were secure.

"Good-bye, young man," August said to Hunter in a taunting voice as the Utopians rose to leave. "It's certainly been a pleasure meeting you."

Hunter gave the man a nasty look but did not say anything. "As for you, my beauty," August then said to Tehani, "I suppose the next time we meet you'll have a new little Rango in that nice, firm midriff of yours."

"ARE YOU GOING to tell Tehani and me any of the particulars of the conversation?" Hunter asked, after Bailey informed Chelsea that the four male Utopians had had a video call with their chief while they were away from the bar.

"Not yet," Bailey said after a moment's hesitation. "We are going to have another conference with Lance at eight. He wanted to obtain some more information before making a final decision."

They had finished most of their dinner in the trading post restaurant and were waiting for dessert. Bailey glanced at his watch and then reached in his pocket for the handcuff key. "Franklin," he said, "I'm going to ask you to stay here with Chelsea and the two prisoners. I'll feel better knowing that Chelsea has some help."

"But, Bailey," Franklin protested as Bailey removed Hunter's handcuffs from his own wrist and started to affix them to Franklin's. "I want to take part in the conversation with Lance. I have strong opinions on this subject and . . ."

"You made your position very clear during the last

conference," Bailey interrupted. "Lance knows how you feel. But ultimately the decision is his."

Bailey clamped the other end of Hunter's handcuffs on the unhappy Franklin. "We'll return in no more than fifteen minutes," he said. The three Utopians walked out of the restaurant.

"What about the handcuff key?" Franklin yelled after them.

"We won't be gone that long," Bailey yelled back.

"Crap," Franklin said as soon as the others had left. "Now I'm a goddamn baby-sitter." He looked around the restaurant nervously and then turned to Chelsea. "It's incredible to me that Lance is putting so much faith in that nerd Cooperman," he said. "To turn down eight carats of diamonds, a sure thing, because we MIGHT be able to obtain an obscure political advantage . . ."

"Don't forget," Chelsea said, "Cooperman is a genius. He has been right many times before."

"About computers and all that sort of shit," Franklin said agitatedly. "I agree that Cooperman's a genius. But what does he know about politics? And why won't Lance tell us why . . ."

Chelsea suddenly realized that their prisoners were listening to the conversation. She started vigorously shaking her head and drawing her finger across her neck in a cutting motion. Franklin finally saw her and stopped in midsentence.

Across the restaurant, one of the Saracens who had been with Rango earlier was eating alone. The man rose from his chair and crossed the room, heading out the door.

"I need to piss," Franklin said, abruptly standing up and jerking Hunter with the handcuffs. "I'll be back in a minute."

Franklin dragged Hunter to the rest room. Inside, the Saracen was standing at one of the covered urinals, being careful that all his liquid waste was indeed being deposited inside the bag. The vacuum flusher removed the urine when he was finished. Franklin walked over to the urinal right next to the Saracen and unzipped his pants.

The other pirate started to say something but Franklin gestured with his head in Hunter's direction. "Nothing's decided yet," Franklin said in a low voice a second after he activated his vacuum flusher.

"We're expecting you to deliver," the Saracen said in a menacing tone a moment later. Hunter had not heard what Franklin said, but did hear the Saracen's comment. Watching the interaction of the two men, Hunter suspected that Franklin had made some kind of side deal with the Saracens.

"I owe them some money," Franklin said in explanation as he led Hunter back into the hallway.

Yeah, Hunter thought to himself, *and you must think I'm blind and stupid.*

BAILEY, SNYDER, AND Bagwell were back in less than fifteen minutes. "All right," Bailey said in a low voice, soon after he sat down, "everything's all set. We just paid off the dock foreman and two of his men. We'll be out of here in half an hour."

"I don't understand," Hunter said.

"Lance has made his decision," Bailey said. "We're not selling Tehani to Rango and the Saracens. And we're leaving the trading post before nine o'clock, just in case Rango decides that he won't take no for an answer."

"That's the stupidest goddamn thing I've ever heard," Franklin said. "What cunt is worth more than eight carats of diamonds?"

"We don't have time for second-guessing, Franklin," Bailey said sharply. "We have our instructions and we must move quickly. You and Chelsea take the prisoners to the embarkation dock. Snyder, Bagwell, and I will gather up our luggage, make certain all our new cargo has been loaded as we arranged, and conclude all the paperwork."

"You mean you're leaving me handcuffed to the prisoner?" Franklin asked.

"Someone has to be," Bailey replied. "And I can be more efficient if I don't have an extra body attached. We don't have a lot of time."

"All right," Franklin said unhappily. "But at least give me the key. I don't want to have someone in the stall with me if I need to take a crap."

"Here's the key," Bailey said, handing it over, "but you are not to unlock those handcuffs unless there is a dire emergency. Going to the bathroom does not qualify in that category. Is that clear?"

"Yes, boss," Franklin replied in an irritated tone.

Bailey hurriedly reviewed the details of everyone's assignment. Tehani interrupted once, to thank Bailey for not leaving her with Rango, but he cut her off quickly by stating simply that it was not his decision. Hunter considered mentioning his suspicions about Franklin to Bailey, but there was never a decent opportunity. He also had misgivings about saying anything in front of the whole group of Utopians.

As soon as he was finished talking, Bailey immediately stood up and left the restaurant with Snyder and Bagwell. The two handcuffed pairs, as instructed, departed a few minutes later in a leisurely manner. They walked out of the recreation area of the trading post, eventually turning into a corridor that led only to the embarkation zone.

After they had walked about thirty yards down the hall, Franklin suddenly stopped. "Oh, shit," he said. His free right hand was frantically searching his shirt and trouser pockets. "I must have left my identity card in the bar or the restaurant."

"Are you certain you've lost it?" Chelsea asked. "I don't remember even seeing it out. And Bailey paid the bill."

"It's definitely not here," Franklin said, still searching. He thought for a moment. "I left it in the commissary," he then added, brightening. "I bought a couple of shirts."

He pulled out the key to the handcuffs. "Look, Chelsea," Franklin said, "I don't want to hold everybody up. I'll just cuff Hunter to your other arm and dash back for my identity card. I'll meet you at the dock."

"I don't know, Franklin," Chelsea replied. "Bailey was very specific in his instructions. He wanted Hunter to stay handcuffed to you."

"But it would be silly for all of us to walk back—" Franklin started.

He was interrupted by Hunter, who deftly slid his free left hand into one of Franklin's rear trouser pockets and pulled out the Utopian's plastic identity card. "Is this what you're looking for?" Hunter said.

Franklin was surprised for only an instant. "You asshole," he then snarled, "don't you ever touch my body again."

Hunter turned toward the two women. "Chelsea," he said hurriedly, "I believe that Franklin's made some kind of a deal with the Saracens. There was a strange encounter in the bathroom . . ."

Before Hunter could finish, Franklin hit him hard in the back of the head with his right fist. The force of the blow knocked Hunter into the corridor wall. He spun around just in time to dodge a second punch. As Franklin's fist hit the wall, Hunter's anger exploded. Jerking on the handcuffs, Hunter turned the Utopian's face directly into a lethal left hook that destroyed Franklin's nose and sent blood flying everywhere. In the next two seconds, Hunter pummeled his adversary with three more powerful punches, knocking Franklin unconscious and leaving his face a bloody mess.

Franklin was dangling from the handcuffs that were attached to Hunter's right arm. Hunter bent over and pushed him to the floor. Chelsea snatched the handcuff key from the air near where Franklin had let it go.

There was blood in the air, on the walls, and on all their clothing. "What are you going to do?" Tehani asked Chelsea.

The Utopian woman thought for a second. "We're in big trouble if the security officers see this mess," she said. "We'll be held at least overnight so a hearing can be conducted."

"There's a room of some kind just up there, on the left," Hunter said, motioning farther down the corridor. "We can carry him inside and talk this over."

Tehani and Chelsea each picked up one of Franklin's legs and followed Hunter, who had his arms under the man's torso, to the small utility room off the corridor. Once inside, a kneeling Hunter told Chelsea about Franklin's suspicious encounter with the Saracen in the restaurant rest room. Chelsea clearly did not know what to do. "I must find Bailey," she kept saying. "I must find Bailey."

Suddenly, Chelsea reached into her pocket and pulled out her handcuff key. "Look," she said, as she freed Tehani, "I can't make this decision on my own. I'm going to look for Bailey." She pointed at a vacuum hanging on the wall and some rags over in a basket in the corner. "Do the best you can to clean up out there in the corridor, and then stay here until I return. There shouldn't be anyone coming this way, except for our crew, because the embarkation zone is generally closed at night."

"What should we do if Franklin wakes up?" Tehani asked.

"I don't care," Chelsea replied. "Just make sure he stays in this utility room."

WHEN CHELSEA LEFT, Tehani bent down toward Hunter and they kissed briefly. "Are you all right?" she asked, gently touching the swelling on the back of his head.

"All things considered," he said, "I guess I'm fine." He took a deep breath and glanced over at Franklin's body stretched out beside him. "But I'll feel a hell of a lot better when we're out of this place."

"Thanks for being so concerned about me," she said.

"We'll talk about it later, if we have a chance," Hunter said. He motioned with his free left arm in the direction of the vacuum and the rags. "Why don't you try to clean up what you can?" he said. "I don't relish the idea of being held here overnight."

Tehani kissed him again, grabbed the vacuum and a couple of rags, and eased out into the corridor. She was gone for about five minutes. Franklin did not stir during that time. Hunter sat on the floor, thinking about everything that had happened on what had been the longest day of his life.

Tehani darted back into the utility room with a concerned look on her face. "Someone saw me," she said. "I did most of the cleaning with my back toward the rest of the trading post. But just now, as I was finishing, I was facing up the corridor. A pirate looked in my direction and stopped." She paused. "Hunter, I think it may have been one of the Saracens."

"Great," Hunter said. "That's all we need."

Fortunately, Chelsea and the other three male Utopians arrived at the utility room not more than a minute later. Bailey bent down immediately and freed Hunter from Franklin. Tehani told Bailey about possibly being recognized.

Bailey put Franklin's luggage on the utility-room floor beside his body. "I saw Franklin talking with one of the Saracens earlier today," he said, "before Rango came to our table at the bar. At the time I didn't think anything about it. But after our first videoconference with Lance, when Franklin made such an uncharacteristically impassioned plea for selling Tehani to Rango, I began to wonder. That's why I left him handcuffed to Hunter at the end."

Bailey looked at his watch. "Now let's get out of here while we can. Each person is responsible for his own suitcase."

They moved out into the corridor. Nobody was there. At the other end of the hall, the dock foreman and the security officer the Utopians had arranged for the special evening departure were ready. All the necessary formalities were completed swiftly. The group was finishing putting on their space suits when they heard shouts coming from the other end of the long embarkation corridor.

"Get in the airlock quickly," Bailey said. "That might be Rango."

Inside the airlock, it seemed as if the pressure change was taking forever. They could see back into the clearing room through a window. Rango had indeed arrived, and was in the process of bribing the security officer and the foreman with small diamonds.

On the illuminated dock, the boarding ladder was already in place. "Hurry, now," Bailey said through the microphone in his helmet. "The foreman may order the dockhands to withdraw the ladder."

Hunter didn't have time to be afraid. His feet barely

touching the rungs of the ladder, with his small suitcase firmly in his grasp, he scampered across the thirty yards of space. At the end of the ladder he actually jumped into the entrance to their tiny spacecraft, hitting his helmet slightly on the overhang. Tehani was right behind him. The whole group was onboard before the dockhands understood they were supposed to impede the departure.

Snyder freed their spacecraft from the ladder just as Rango, who looked monstrously large in his space suit, came out of the airlock with the trading-post dock foreman. The Saracen waved his arms and gesticulated angrily, but it was too late. Bailey didn't even stop to take off his space suit before he fired up the engines. A minute later, Hunter and Tehani hugged as the trading post disappeared from the window.

FOUR

LIVING CONDITIONS ON THE small, antiquated spacecraft that transported Hunter, Tehani, and the Utopians away from the trading post were far from ideal. There was but a single cramped bedroom, with eight bunks stacked in pairs and no drawer space for clothing or incidentals. The only bathroom had two tiny toilet closets and one shower that worked intermittently. There were no entertainment or communication devices on board, except for the required radio and multispectral monitor on what was called the flight deck, no common area or lounge, and no equipment to prepare hot food. The processed wafers and other uninspired, cold meals were arranged by type in one large container—each person on board simply ate whenever he or she was hungry.

The entire vehicle was no more than fifty feet long. Most of the length was the unpressurized cargo compartment, a peculiar, bulbous afterthought affixed to the back end of the spacecraft. This compartment was filled to capacity with critical supplies the Utopians had obtained at the trading post, primarily in exchange for the *Darwin*. The total living and work space for the people on board was only about half the size of the three-bedroom apartment that

Hunter had occupied on Cicero for the first twenty years of his life.

Both the Utopians and Hunter and Tehani breathed a sigh of relief as soon as the trading post was no longer visible from their small observation window and it was obvious that they were not being followed. "If we had made a deal, and then abrogated it," Bailey said, "then Rango would be after us with vengeance on his mind. But we didn't agree to his proposition, and we didn't take any of his diamonds, so legally he can't claim that he was injured. I'm certain, however, that Rango will not forget this incident. He'll be looking for some way to even the score."

Everyone went to bed once the spacecraft trajectory had been established and verified. It had been an exhausting day. Soon after waking up, the group had a videoconference with Lance, the chief of the Utopians. Bailey provided him with the details of their last hour at the trading post. Lance was upset by Franklin's betrayal, fretted about losing another capable space pilot, and waxed philosophical about the corruption of human beings by greed. Then he asked to be introduced to Tehani and Hunter.

Tehani graciously thanked the Utopian chief for not selling her to Rango and the Saracens. Lance, a handsome, slightly balding man with a hearty laugh, stroked his salt-and-pepper beard and smiled with his powder-blue eyes. "I will tell you honestly that I was sorely tempted to take his offer, Miss Wilawa," he said on the video. "Eight carats of quality diamonds could purchase an enormous quantity of needed material for our band." Lance paused briefly before continuing. "I must admit that I am now incredibly curious to find out what kind of woman could cause Rango to make such a staggering offer."

The Utopian chief talked to Hunter about all the medical needs of his band. "Not many doctors become pirates," Lance said, "as you can probably well imagine. I'm afraid you're going to find our clinic hopelessly primitive, and severely lacking in modern equipment and other essentials. I apologize for interrupting your life with this kidnapping, but I hope you'll be willing to help us out."

Hunter said that he intended to cooperate, but reminded Lance that he would like to be repatriated as soon as possible. "That's understandable," the Utopian chief said. "I guess as a Covington Fellow you have a very bright future ahead of you—if anyone can truly have a bright future in the service of that tyrant. It never ceases to amaze me how successful his propaganda machine is. The man has committed heinous crimes against humanity, yet he is generally revered as a visionary throughout the Federation."

When the videoconference had concluded, Bailey informed Hunter and Tehani that their trip would last five days. "I think you'll feel right at home in Utopia," he added. "Our asteroid is a little larger than Cicero, and the rotation rate is slower, but the landscapes outside the enclosed area will all look familiar to you."

The first evening on board, Hunter and Tehani had a long and pleasant chat with Chelsea, first about growing up on Cicero, and then about her slow but steady disillusionment with the FISC and its government during her university years. "Fortunately," she said, "I didn't take precipitous action and join the Dems as a turncoat as so many others have. While I was living in the Free Zone, where the news was reported more honestly than on either side of the fifteenth parallel, I discovered that both systems are corrupt, and equally responsible for the repressive conditions under which space citizens are living."

Chelsea leaned toward Hunter and Tehani and became quite animated. "Old people run both governments. They are committed to continuing the status quo, to justify their own existence and to preserve their money and power. Young people and new ideas are a threat. They are to be resisted at all costs. The refrain is the same both north and south of the Free Zone."

"But don't you have the same problem among the pirates?" Tehani asked gently. "Whenever anyone has something they want to keep and preserve, whether it's a loved one, or a decent lifestyle, or possessions, or even power, they tend to become more conservative and resist change. I bet Rango wouldn't like it too much if someone openly challenged his being the chief of the Saracens."

"Actually," Chelsea said, "just last year a young Saracen warrior named Grendel tried to foment a rebellion. Grendel was pissed off that Rango had accepted a favorable negotiated settlement in a dispute with another pirate band, instead of destroying that other band altogether in the best pirate tradition. Grendel managed to recruit twenty-five percent of the Saracens, or so we've been told, to his side. Rango handled the challenge to his leadership brilliantly. To keep the Saracens from splintering into opposing factions, with each falling below the critical population threshold necessary for a pirate band to survive, Rango offered to engage Grendel in hand-to-hand combat, with the chiefship of the Saracens at stake. Grendel had no choice but to accept. Rango decapitated Grendel during their fight, and hung his head on the entrance gate to the Saracen headquarters. But he also offered amnesty to the rest of Grendel's followers, and quickly resolidified his position as their leader. . . . The man clearly has qualities you wouldn't suspect from his appearance and manner."

There was a brief silence. "He's still an asshole in my eyes, Chelsea," Hunter said, shaking his head. "I'm also a little confused." He paused. "Was the Rango story your response to Tehani's last comment?"

"In a way, yes," Chelsea replied. "She's correct in her general statement that anyone who is in power, or even just happy, resists change. But many more mechanisms for change exist in our unstructured pirate world than exist in either the UDSC or the FISC. Young people under the jurisdiction of either of the space governments see terrible wrongs that need to be corrected, but see no way of really making any difference. They become pirates out of powerless frustration."

Hunter did not agree with most of the things that Chelsea was saying, but her passion and her logic were both very appealing. Hunter himself had never really gone through a rebellious phase in his life. His family had always been warm and supportive, and he had been able to achieve what he wanted by hard work and self-discipline. Would his life have been markedly different if, as Octavio had once suggested, Hunter had had slightly less natural talent? He found himself wondering about that question as he listened to Chelsea's comments about the young being disenfranchised by the space establishment.

HUNTER AND TEHANI quickly discovered that their opportunities for privacy on their new spacecraft would be few and far between. The tiny vehicle in which they were traveling did not have all of the automatic modes that the *Darwin* possessed. Someone needed to be in the command cubicle at all times, checking various readings, manually updating parameters based on outputs from the navigation computers, and performing other tasks.

On the third evening of their flight Chelsea, after having been prompted by Tehani, convinced the three Utopian men that giving Hunter and Tehani a few hours alone in the bedroom would be a decent gesture to their prisoners. Hunter felt surprisingly awkward as they undressed. Tehani sensed his tension during their first kiss and asked what was wrong.

"I don't know, exactly," he said. "Maybe I just feel funny

because four people are out there, on the other side of that thin wall, knowing what we're doing in here."

Tehani smiled. "How could it be otherwise?" she said. "Can't you just forget them for the time being, and enjoy this chance for us to be together?"

Their lovemaking was slow and satisfying, but Hunter did not ever fully surrender to his passion the way that he had virtually every night on the *Darwin*. They held each other softly afterward, without either of them saying anything for a long time.

"You're disappointed, aren't you?" Tehani said finally.

"No," Hunter answered quickly. "Well, maybe a little," he added after a few seconds of thought. "But it's not your fault. You were wonderful, as usual."

"What's bothering you?" she asked.

"I'm not exactly certain," Hunter said. "I feel somehow sad. As if I've lost something very special that can never be found again."

Tehani sat up on the bed. "Do you remember that conversation on the *Darwin*, when I told you that it would never be quite like that again? And that we should enjoy what we were feeling to the fullest?"

Hunter laughed. "I think we had that conversation almost every night."

Tehani caressed his face gently with her fingers. "We are now in a different situation, Hunter," she said. "Basically, we have two choices. We can be thankful that we have an opportunity to renew our love, in a less-than-perfect environment, or we can spend our time mourning the loss of something that can never be recaptured."

Hunter pulled Tehani to him and they kissed. She then moved over on top of him and Hunter held her as tightly as he dared. "Sometimes," he said in a very low voice, "I wish that time and the world would stop, and that I could simply hold you like this forever."

She kissed him again. "I have that wish every time we're together," she said.

For many minutes Hunter and Tehani again held each other without speaking. At length Hunter, concerned that their private time might be running out, decided it was time to talk to Tehani about a subject that had been on his mind intermittently since their last day at the pirate trading post.

"This is probably not the right time or place for such a question," Hunter said, "but I don't know when we'll have a chance to be alone again."

"That's a somewhat ominous beginning," Tehani said, sitting up. "What is it?"

"While we were in the bar at the pirate trading post," Hunter said, "that obnoxious Egghead pirate named August asked Chelsea why we were kidnapped. Do you remember her answer?"

"Sort of," Tehani replied.

"Chelsea told him that you have 'friends in high places,' and therefore might yield a 'very large ransom,'" Hunter said. "Can you explain what she was talking about?"

Tehani sat on the bed, staring at Hunter while idly caressing his chest with her fingers, for several seconds. "Yes," she said at length, "I can explain it. But I don't think it would be a good idea."

"Why not?" Hunter said.

"It's complicated...," Tehani said with difficulty. "Let me just say that I believe you are safer if you don't have certain information. That way you can always say, without lying, that you don't know such and such."

Hunter sat up beside her, his brow knitted in a frown. "So you have known, from the beginning, why you were kidnapped? And have never told me?"

"I have had suspicions about the reasons for my kidnapping," Tehani said defensively, "but I didn't really know, in a sense, until I heard the conversation between Chelsea and the Egghead pirate."

"And yet you still said nothing to me?" Hunter said.

"What was I going to say?" Tehani said. "Oh, darling, I think that I now know for certain why the Utopians wanted to kidnap me, but, honey, I really don't believe it's in your best interest for me to tell you the reasons. That would have gone over great."

There was a banging on the outside of the bedroom door. Tehani slipped off the bed and started putting on her clothes. Hunter, becoming angry, turned and put his feet on the floor. "It looks to me," he said, "as if you've been lying to me all this time. What was all that bullshit you were telling me on the *Darwin* about love and trust and honesty all being part of the same basic package?"

Tehani stopped dressing. "I have not lied to you, Hunter," she said deliberately. "And I'm not lying to you now. It would have been a lie if I had told you that I had no idea why Chelsea had made those comments to the other pirate. I'm telling you something altogether different. Listen to me carefully. I believe that it is better for YOU, my love, if you do NOT know why I have been kidnapped. Can you understand that?"

"No, I can't," Hunter replied. He was almost shouting. "A lie by any other name will smell as foul. Who are you to decide what's safe or unsafe for me to know?"

"Please, darling," Tehani said entreatingly, "can we drop this subject for now? We must leave this room and I don't want to continue this conversation in front of the others. It could be dangerous for us."

Hunter put on his clothes without saying anything else and without looking at Tehani. His anger and frustration grew stronger every time he thought about their conversation. He was an unhappy young man when he departed from the bedroom. Throughout the rest of the trip he remained convinced that Tehani's failure to share her information with him was a violation of the trust between them. By the time they reached Utopia, Hunter was starting to become bitter, and was even questioning his proclaimed unconditional love for Tehani.

THE SUN HAD moved behind the asteroid about ten minutes before their spacecraft reached Utopia. Under the small, translucent dome, which Bailey explained enclosed only four square miles of surface, or approximately one-fifth of the area under the pair of more modern domes on Cicero, the lights were dense in one region, but were more or less uniformly scattered throughout the rest of the settlement.

All of the occupants of the spacecraft except Snyder were standing together on what passed for a flight deck at the front of the vehicle, trying to look out the tiny square window that was two feet on a side. Snyder was in the pilot's seat, verifying the flight profile before turning the manual controls over to Bailey for the final descent.

"This was never a major mining outpost," Bailey said to Hunter and Tehani. "The four permanent buildings down there, where the brightest lights are, were constructed in a hurry to house the scientists and engineers doing the mineral survey. After it became apparent that there were no accessible significant deposits of critical metals here, the post was quickly abandoned."

"When was that?" Tehani asked.

"A long time ago," Bailey said. "I'm not certain exactly, but it was before the schism between the Dems and the Feds. It had been uninhabited for over a hundred years when our band moved here five years ago." He paused, caught up in a memory. "That was a harrowing time. Our previous home had been in an abandoned artificial space colony, not too much different from the trading post we visited. We were attacked by surprise one night by the Tarantulas, who had fled their own colony when they discovered a fleet of Fed warships approaching a week or ten days previously. The Tarantulas gained control of all the key elements of our settlement before most of us knew they were there. They seized our women and children, and gave the adult male Utopians an ultimatum. We could either remain there, and become Tarantulas, initially without rank or privileges, or we could leave and find a new place to live.

"Forty-five of us departed in three vessels like this one, including two women who managed somehow to convince the Tarantulas they were men. We had virtually nothing but the clothing we were wearing during the attack, the three spacecraft, and a generous supply of barely edible food that the Tarantula quartermaster, a kind-hearted scoundrel, allowed us to take from their stores. For almost ninety days we journeyed in space from location to location, using up favors and trying to find a place to start over. Several bands would have accepted us, but only if we gave up our identity and pledged our loyalty to their group. No matter how desperate we became, Lance insisted that we remain Utopians. Once, when our future seemed especially bleak, we even voted thirty-seven to eight to hand ourselves over to Dem officials at the first reasonable opportunity. Then a miracle occurred."

"What kind of miracle?" Tehani said.

"While we were wandering through space, we came upon a single, disabled spacecraft," Bailey said. "It had no lights and did not respond in any way to our attempts to communicate. In spite of our situation, Lance insisted that we rendezvous with this apparently abandoned spacecraft. To our astonishment, we found ten young women inside. Their power system had malfunctioned, they were out of food—in another twenty or thirty hours they would all have been dead. The girls had been members of the Margaritas, but had become disillusioned with pirate life, mostly because of mistreatment by the male pirates in their band. They had stolen the vehicle as part of their escape attempt. Unfortunately, none of the women had much knowledge of spacecraft engineering, and the vehicle they had chosen was desperately in need of maintenance and repair. They had had one terrible problem after another."

Snyder stood up from the pilot's seat and informed Bailey that everything was ready for the final descent. "My wife Renee was one of those girls," Bailey said, sitting down and doing a quick reverification of the key spacecraft controls. "Her best friend, Tricia, who had been the primary instigator of the escape attempt from the Margaritas, was the only child from a very wealthy Dem family. At that time she hadn't yet learned that her parents had both been killed only two months earlier in a tragic entry-vehicle accident, while they were returning from a vacation on Phobos."

Bailey looked up at Hunter and Tehani, both of whom were following the story with rapt attention. "Sorry," he said, "but I must stop the story now. If I don't watch what I'm doing with this buggy, we could end up dead as well."

"Come on, you can't stop now," Tehani said, her disappointment obvious. "At least give us a quick summary."

"Okay," Bailey said, firing the spacecraft thrusters, and then starting to talk very quickly. "How about this. Tricia fell in love with Lance, went back to Mars for six months to claim her inheritance, gave most of it to the Utopians, and Lance bought back almost all the Utopian women and children who had been seized by the Tarantulas. Lance vowed to have nothing but the best defenses, and soon thereafter convinced Cooperman to become a Utopian."

"Bravo," Tehani said with a laugh. "That was great."

Bailey adroitly landed the spacecraft on a flat, dimly illuminated plain a couple of hundred yards from the edge of the dome. Chelsea, Snyder, and Bagwell applauded, and then began to put on their space suits.

"Home, sweet home," Bailey said. He turned to Hunter and Tehani. "We must walk across the surface to the dome in the dark," he told them. "There are many sharp rocks along the way. If you slip and fall, and your suit's integrity is violated, you will die immediately. So be careful."

He smiled. "And welcome to Utopia."

LANCE HIMSELF HEADED up the small delegation that greeted them on the dirt surface on the other side of the crude airlock. Inside Utopia's dome, the illumination was dim. The only light in the airlock area was provided by a large lantern on the top of a tall pole fifty yards or so inside the habitat. Lance embraced each of the returning Utopians, congratulated and thanked them repeatedly, and even helped them bag their space suits. After Hunter and Tehani had removed and bagged their suits, Lance walked over in their direction.

"Mr. Blake and Miss Wilawa, I presume," he said with a warm smile. Lance extended his hand.

"Just call me Tehani," she said, returning his smile and shaking his hand.

The Utopian chief shook Hunter's hand as well, and then turned back to Tehani. He stood only a few feet away and openly stared at her for several seconds. "Forgive me for being so rude," he said at length, another broad smile spreading across his bearded face, "but as I told you during our video call, I have been extremely curious about you ever since Rango made his offer at the trading post."

"I forgive you," Tehani said simply. She stared back at Lance, smiling and unflinching, not intimidated by either his directness or what she recognized in his eyes.

Hunter did not like what was happening beside him. A

new burst of jealousy and anger added to the confusion that he was already feeling about Tehani. In pique he turned his eyes away from Lance and Tehani, and looked off into the distance, where he saw a group of large tents on the far side of the huge lantern.

"I presume that you've been treated properly," Lance said to Tehani, his eyes never leaving hers.

"Yes, I have. Thank you very much," Tehani said politely.

Lance, Hunter, and Tehani were standing slightly off to the side of the rest of the group. Chelsea now approached them, holding hands with a handsome young man. "Hunter and Tehani," she said, "this is my husband Darrell."

"It's great to finally meet you," Tehani said immediately, stepping toward Darrell and Chelsea and away from Lance. "Your wife has said so many nice things about you."

"Really?" Darrell said in a friendly, but sarcastic tone. "Now that's a switch." He glanced at Chelsea and grinned.

He turned to Hunter. "Chelsea said that you shared a cabin with my father for a few days. That must have been an interesting experience. How is the old fart?"

"Fine," said Hunter. He smiled. "He is definitely an unforgettable character."

"Now that's an understatement if ever I heard one," Darrell said.

Lance walked over to the four of them and commanded their attention. "We've planned a huge celebration to honor your successful mission," Lance said in too loud a voice. "It will begin in the main plaza in about an hour. We thought we'd give you weary travelers a chance to clean up a little before we started."

The rest of the greeting delegation came over at Lance's request to be introduced to Hunter and Tehani. After a few minutes, Lance suggested that the group disperse so that everyone would have plenty of time to prepare for the celebration. "Darrell," he said to Chelsea's husband as everyone started to move away from the edge of the dome, "since we're right here, why don't you stop briefly and show Hunter the clinic, and where he'll be staying?"

The Utopian chief turned to Tehani. "As for you, lovely lady," Lance said, "I will personally escort you to your quarters. It happens to be right on my way."

Hunter felt another surge of jealousy as he watched Lance and Tehani depart. He suppressed the feeling immediately, however, reminding himself that it was futile for him to expend energy about something that was completely beyond his control. *Besides,* Hunter told himself, rationalizing, *even in the best of situations, I'm not certain that Tehani and I could have a future. She's a beautiful woman and an unbelievable lover, but I don't think I could deal with her on an everyday basis. She's just too stubborn.*

THE CLINIC WAS not at all like anything Hunter had envisioned. Essentially, it was a group of seven large tents spread out in no definable pattern on the bare ground. The main tent, in which Hunter would reside in a corner separated from the rest of the space only by a heavy swath of canvas that hung from the ceiling, contained all the patient files and other administrative records, such as they were, as well as the supply cabinets. On the far side of the main tent from Hunter's residence—which consisted of a bed, an open bin for his clothes and other possessions, a small chair, a washbasin, and a latrine—were two large tables, upon which futons were spread. The tables were surrounded by the only electronic-monitoring devices the clinic possessed. Darrell told Hunter the tables were for serious operations.

After the short tour of the main tent that was the hub of the clinic, Hunter and Darrell talked briefly about personal matters. Hunter gave Darrell a summary of his conversations with Mr. Peabody on the *Darwin,* accentuating the pertinent facts he could remember about what was happening in the lives of the other members of Darrell's family. The mention of his brother Randy's name made Darrell bristle. "Now there's a true fascist," Darrell said. "He would sell his mother if he thought it would be good for the Federation."

Darrell seemed genuinely interested in his father's words and attitudes, especially anything Mr. Peabody had said about either his brother or him. Hunter apologized several times for not remembering the exact words his ex-cabinmate had used. After a few minutes of amiable conversation they continued their tour of the clinic.

The maternity ward was a tent with five beds. One of the beds was occupied by a young woman named Clarissa. Hunter chatted with her about her pregnancy for about a minute, and then followed Darrell to the adjoining tent. An attractive blonde girl who appeared to be about sixteen was holding a sleeping child of two years or so in her arms. The child's mother was lying on a cot about ten feet away, moaning intermittently.

"What's the matter?" Hunter asked the woman.

"I have terrible stomach cramps," the woman said.

Hunter turned to the girl holding the infant. "Why don't you give her something to ease her pain?" he asked.

The girl, who had a radiant smile and magnificent blue eyes, looked over her shoulder at the opposite side of the tent. A young man named Winston, in his early twenties, crossed the room and introduced himself as the pharmacist. "We have only limited amounts of pain medicine," he said. "We encourage people to bear their pain if possible. Uletha is simply having a difficult menstrual period. The doctor told me not to give her anything unless the pain endures for six to eight hours."

Hunter walked over to the lone basin in the tent and wet a cloth with warm water. He brought the cloth back to Uletha and gently swabbed her forehead. "Thank you," the woman said gratefully.

"Is your pain unusually strong, Uletha?" Hunter asked her.

"Not really," Uletha replied, grimacing as another cramp seized her. "This is more or less typical—I just have nasty periods."

Hunter talked to her for a minute. The girl holding Uletha's baby came over beside the cot. "Renton is still sleeping soundly," she told the child's mother.

"Is the doctor here now?" Hunter asked the girl.

She shook her head. "No," she said in a low voice, trying not to wake the sleeping child. "He's home, getting ready for the party. We're all celebrating tonight." She flashed one of her big smiles. "I can hardly wait. My mom said I could get high and spend the night with my boyfriend if I wanted."

The infant opened his eyes and the girl began to rock him back and forth. "Are you the new doctor from the Federation?" she asked.

"I guess so," Hunter said, "although I'm not really a doctor. I'm just a trained paramedic."

"Dr. Townsend is not really a doctor either," the girl said. She laughed. "He told me that he was kicked out of medical school for stealing drugs from the university pharmacy."

"What's your name?" Hunter asked the girl.

"Ursula," she said, reaching across the cot with her free hand. "I'm one of the two clinic interns."

"I'm Hunter Blake," he said.

"I know," Ursula said. "Lance was here yesterday and told us all about you. He said that you were really really smart. And we're supposed to call you Dr. Blake."

Darrell reminded Hunter that they both still needed to get ready for the celebration. Hunter bade Ursula good-bye and told her he would see her soon. He then walked out of the tent with Darrell and thanked him for his time.

"No," Darrell said, "it's I who should thank you. For bringing me all the news about my family. And for being kind to my father . . . I really appreciate it."

He stood next to Hunter, staring off into space through the dome.

"Did our conversation make you homesick?" Hunter asked.

Darrell turned, surprised, and looked at Hunter. "A little," Darrell replied after some hesitation. "But not enough to make me think about going back. My life there was much too painful. And I burned too many bridges."

LANCE, HIS IMMEDIATE family, and his most important advisors lived in the permanent buildings in Utopia. The structures also housed the band's computer and communications equipment, as well as their most advanced weapons. Tehani's small apartment was in a small outlying building that the rest of the Utopians called the hotel. Distinguished visitors to the asteroid were often housed there.

What Lance had designated as the plaza was on the other side of the structures from the airlock and the clinic. It was a broad, open, empty rectangular plain, perhaps two hundred yards long and a hundred yards wide, that separated the permanent buildings from the array of tents that housed the ordinary Utopians. It was in the plaza that the entire band met for major ceremonies, parties, or Lance's occasional speeches. On the night of Hunter and Tehani's arrival in Utopia, a large bonfire had been built in the center of the plaza. An elevated platform had been erected a safe distance from the bonfire, and when Hunter showed up at the celebration, fifteen minutes or so late, the five musicians on the platform were already playing loud rock-and-roll music with flair and gusto. A couple of dozen pirates were dancing directly in front of the platform. Most of the rest of the celebrants were in line for the food and drink, which was being dispensed from two long tables on the opposite side of the bonfire from the platform.

Hunter glanced around briefly, to see if he could find anyone he knew, and then entered the drink line. A taupe-colored, bubbly liquid was being served out of a huge container. "May I ask what this is?" Hunter asked, holding the large cup he had picked up from the table toward the ladle that the young man was wielding.

The Utopian looked at him with a mixture of curiosity and puzzlement. "Oh," he said finally, "you must be the new doc." He smiled and dumped a generous portion of the liquid in Hunter's cup. "We call it grog," the young man said. "It's kind of like beer, but stronger."

Hunter took a sip. It wasn't bad. He took another drink and started walking in the direction of the musicians and the dancing area. He passed a group of five happy young Utopians, standing in a circle, passing a crude smoking pipe around. "That's Dr. Blake," he heard one of the young people say.

He turned to look at the group again and saw Ursula coming in his direction. The other four teenagers were right behind her, including a tall, slightly heavy girl, and a gaunt, pimply boy who must have been six and a half feet tall. Ursula was wearing a tiny bikini top that didn't cover much more than the nipples on her small, round breasts, and a pair of tight white shorts that accentuated her slim, trim figure. Thin, oblong, golden ellipses dangled from her ears, and two gold rings adorned her navel.

Hunter waited for them to reach him. "Dr. Blake,"

Ursula said, grinning like a Cheshire cat. "Let me introduce you to my friends. This is Janie, who is, without a doubt, the smartest girl in Utopia—she works with Cooperman and he says she's a computer genius—and this beanpole is my boyfriend Monroe. The other two characters," she said, glancing over her shoulder at two boys who were busily refilling the pipe, "are Ralph and Buzz."

"Shit, man," Monroe said. "You don't look like no doctor. You don't look much older than me."

"Lance told us at the clinic," Ursula said, slightly cuffing Monroe, "that Dr. Blake is super smart. That's why he's perfect for Janie. When they're not screwing, they can talk about all kinds of intellectual stuff."

Ursula put one of her arms around Hunter. "I'm completely ripped," she confided. "This stuff is dynamite—you've gotta try it."

Ralph and Buzz rejoined the group with the pipe and passed it around. Ursula, Janie, and Monroe took huge hits before handing the pipe to Hunter. "Not just yet," he said politely, holding the pipe in front of him. Hunter smiled. "I might forget to eat, and I'm really hungry."

"Shit, man," Monroe said. "That's what it's for. Food, music, and sex. The big three. Dope makes them all better."

Ursula took the pipe from Hunter and took another huge hit. "Come here, Doc," she said in a tiny voice, holding her breath and pulling Hunter toward her. Ursula put her hand behind his head and kissed him, open-mouthed, expelling the smoke forcefully into his mouth. The surprised Hunter dutifully inhaled, held it, and then coughed slightly.

"Way to go, Doc," the boy named Buzz said. The permanent grin on his face stretched from one ear to the other. He grabbed the pipe from Ursula, placed it in his mouth, and pulled for several seconds.

"Hey, Janie," Ursula said to her friend. "He has terrific lips. I might not let you have him after all." She still had one arm around Hunter. "In fact," Ursula said to the others with a flourish, "I think I'd like to have a real kiss right now."

Hunter could tell that Monroe was not particularly enjoying Ursula's show. As she started to kiss him, he lifted his cup of grog to his mouth. In the ensuing confusion, a little grog slopped out of the cup on Ursula, and everyone laughed heartily.

Hunter felt a hand on his shoulder. "I see that you're already making friends," Snyder said. "That's good, very good." He paused for only a second. "Lance asked me to bring you over to the platform for a minute. He wants to introduce you officially to everyone in our band."

"Right now?" Hunter said.

Snyder nodded. "It will only take a few minutes," he said. "Lance is not in the mood tonight for a long speech. He has other things on his mind."

"MY FELLOW UTOPIANS," Lance began, "this is a great night for all of us. Our mission to hijack the ITI freighter has succeeded beyond our wildest expectations. All of our courageous friends have returned unscathed, and they have brought with them the spoils of their mission. At the Andromeda trading post they successfully traded the ITI freighter for food, clothing, new tents, and tons, yes tons, of other items that we have been desperately needing."

Lance paused while the Utopians applauded. "Bailey and his crew have also returned with two visitors. At this time I would like to formally introduce them to you, and ask you please to make them feel at home here in Utopia."

He gestured at Tehani, whom Hunter had not yet seen

at the party, and she climbed up on the platform beside the Utopian chief. She was wearing a simple white blouse and dark pants, with her hair hanging freely down her back.

"This beautiful girl is Tehani," Lance said. "If Cooperman is correct, we should be able to obtain a huge ransom for her in the near future." He laughed. "I'm certain some of you may have already heard that Rango, the Saracen chief, offered eight carats of top-quality diamonds for Tehani when our crew stopped at the Andromeda trading post." Lance shook his head. "It may have been a mistake, but I turned Rango's offer down."

Tehani acknowledged the mixture of whistles and applause with a big smile and a wave. Lance then found Hunter in the crowd and motioned for him to come up on the platform. Tehani greeted Hunter warmly, but did not embrace him.

"This is Dr. Hunter Blake," Lance said, "who will be helping Dr. Townsend and his staff in the clinic. I don't need to tell any of you how much his help is needed. Dr. Blake will also be living at the clinic, and will be available anytime anyone has a medical problem."

Hunter was received with polite applause from the partygoers. He returned their waves and then turned to say something to Tehani, but Lance and she had already stepped down from the platform and were moving through the crowd. The Utopian chief had his arm around Tehani's waist. Hunter took a large gulp from his grog, stared briefly at the bonfire, and stepped away from the microphone. One of the musicians grabbed the mike to place it closer to their instruments. The loud music began to play again.

SOON AFTER HE had eaten, Hunter was approached by a tall, handsome man in his early thirties wearing an outrageous shirt with bold, colorful decorations. On his arm was a buxom young brunette who looked as if she was about sixteen. "Hello, Dr. Blake," the man said with a silly grin. "Welcome to Utopia."

Hunter extended his hand and politely greeted the pair. "I'm Dr. Townsend," the man said, "the chief of staff at the clinic." He laughed exuberantly. "And this magnificent hunk of nubile flesh is Clea." Dr. Townsend pushed her forward. "Have you ever seen anything so wonderful? Clea is just discovering the excitement of sex. And she's driving me absolutely crazy."

Before Hunter could say anything, Dr. Townsend lifted his arms toward the dome and did a full pirouette, saying, "Crazy, crazy, crazy" as he turned. He then wobbled a little before looking at Hunter again. "As you might have suspicioned, or suspected, or guessed," the doctor said with a foolish grin, "I am a little high. Clea and I smoked some of that stuff that Snyder brought back from the trading post. He got it from the Urchins and you know what kind of shit they grow. Whoopee, damn it's good."

At this point Clea, whose eyes were having difficulty focusing, kissed Hunter on the cheek. "Anyway, Hunter—I assume it's all right for me to call you Hunter, and you can just call me Jake," Dr. Townsend continued with difficulty, "I live over in the building next to Lance. There's a button on the wall in the main tent that's marked Dr. T. That rings an alarm beside my bed. Cooperman rigged it up. When you really need me, ring it three times. That way I'll know it's from you and not just a panicky intern."

Jake Townsend turned and kissed Clea. "Ummm," he said. "That was delicious." He took her by the hand. "We're going to my apartment now," Jake said. "We'll talk when I come in tomorrow, probably about ten o'clock."

He stopped about ten feet away. "Oh," he said, "I almost forgot. You'll probably have half a dozen or more visitors tonight. We always do after parties. The headache medicines are in that big light-brown container on the far right of the middle cabinet."

Hunter watched the pair disappear and shook his head. For some reason, he suddenly felt lonely. He wondered if it was because of the grog and the dope that he had inhaled when Ursula had kissed him. Trying to shake off his gloomy feelings, Hunter picked up another cup of grog and wandered in the direction of the dancing.

It seemed to Hunter that most of the Utopians at the party were now inebriated. Radical, uninhibited motions on the dance floor suggested that the dancers were completely oblivious to their surroundings. One woman in her thirties was shirtless and rubbing her breasts suggestively against her partner as they gyrated to the steady beat of the rock music. Another couple had fallen while dancing and were kissing passionately on the ground while other dancers dodged their bodies.

Janie, Ursula, and Monroe approached Hunter and included him in their group dance. The three teenagers were clearly in an altered state of consciousness and were completely unable to carry on a conversation between the musical numbers. The irrepressible Ursula kissed Hunter a couple of times coquettishly, and then mollified the jealous Monroe with passionate embraces that included some arousing fondling.

Hunter did not see either Lance or Tehani during the rest of the celebration. After another half an hour, as Janie, Ursula, and Monroe began to share a new pipe of dope that had suddenly appeared in Ursula's hands, Hunter decided that he was ready for bed. He declined to participate in the smoking, telling his companions that he had a headache. Following one more dance number, he politely excused himself and started walking quickly toward the edge of the group.

When Hunter reached the first of the permanent structures, he heard his name being called. He turned and saw Ursula coming in his direction. "Dr. Blake," she said when she approached him, "you shouldn't be going home alone. This is a night for pleasure. And Janie's still available for tonight, if you want her."

He surmised from the tone in Ursula's voice and her facial expression that he had offended young Janie by his precipitous departure. "I'm just not feeling well," Hunter said, forcing a broad smile. "Please apologize to Janie for me. And thank her also."

Ursula lingered for several seconds, causing Hunter to think that perhaps she, too, was available, but was not going to make the first move. At length Hunter kissed her hand. "See you tomorrow in the clinic?" he said.

The teenager smiled. "I'll be there at nine o'clock," she said.

"Good night," Hunter said brightly. He turned and started walking in the direction of the clinic. As he passed the building that was the home of the Utopian chief, Hunter found himself wondering if Tehani was in there with Lance. He suppressed a burst of anger as he thought about how quickly Tehani had responded to Lance's flirtations. *Anything to save your ass,* he muttered to himself. *But are you completely without scruples now?* Hunter shook his head and forced all thoughts of Tehani out of his mind as he trudged toward his new home.

FIVE

HUNTER'S FIRST NIGHT'S REST on Utopia was interrupted seven times. Most of his visitors were sick pirates who had drunk too much grog, or whose bodies had been overwhelmed by some kind of recreational drug. One laughing group of five, however, who showed up around midnight, was in serious need of medical attention. The three young men, apparently all good friends, had been involved in a scuffle that had obviously escalated into a fistfight. Two of the boys had broken noses, and eight stitches were required to close a laceration around the left eye of the other. The two young women with them, both clearly drunk, had also been in the melee. Each of them had a nasty swelling on her face.

Hunter had had a maximum of three hours' sleep by the time Ursula, the pharmacist Winston, and the other clinic intern, named Gina, a brunette of seventeen, showed up for work at nine o'clock the next morning. While treating patients during the night, Hunter had discovered that the clinic was in desperate need of organization. His first task for Winston was the compilation of an inventory of all the medicines that the clinic possessed. Ursula and Gina were assigned to straighten out the chaotic files and the sparse reference materials. Both the girls turned out to be extremely eager and competent. They were delighted to have something important to do.

Jake Townsend did not arrive at the clinic until after one o'clock in the afternoon on Hunter's first day. By that time Hunter had already prepared a prioritized list of serious deficiencies in the clinic. He discussed the list with Jake and found out, much to his dismay, that the man who was the primary doctor for the pirate band was both woefully ignorant about the practice of medicine and not particularly concerned about the shortcomings of the clinic.

"These pirates are mostly healthy young people," Jake Townsend said to Hunter in a rambling, elliptical defense of his methods. "They don't really need much in the way of doctoring. Their bodies take care of minor problems. As for serious problems, hey, there's not much we can do anyway, because we just don't have the capability."

Jake was more than willing to let Hunter take over all the management of the clinic. He was also happy for Hunter to see most of the patients. The new doctor's presence allowed Jake Townsend more free time to spend with his current obsession, the brunette teenager named Clea whom Hunter had met at the party.

During the first four days Hunter worked every waking hour. He revised and documented the clinic's procedures, lengthened and staggered the schedule for the interns, and oversaw the organization of all elements of the clinic. Word spread quickly in the band that Hunter was competent and dedicated. Many pirates who had physical problems they never would have brought to Jake Townsend came into the clinic for Hunter's opinion and advice.

On the fifth day Hunter had his first major crisis. In the middle of the morning Clarissa, the twenty-year-old woman who had been in the maternity ward the night Hunter had arrived in Utopia, began having serious contractions. Hunter, Ursula, and Gina moved her into the main tent for the birth. During the early labor, the talkative and winsome Clarissa explained to Hunter and the two interns that she was an unwed mother from the UDSC who had fled her comfortable life in one of the larger cities of South Mars after her parents had demanded that she abort the unwanted child.

Unfortunately, Clarissa endured a seemingly endless and excruciatingly painful labor. Even after her water broke and her contractions increased in frequency to every two and a half minutes, her dilation did not progress. After fifteen hours, with the woman's blood pressure rising dramatically and her terror apparent, Hunter concluded that both Clarissa and her child might die unless he delivered the baby by cesarean. He consulted with Jake Townsend, who had been handling the walk-in patients while Hunter and the two girls were attending to Clarissa.

Jake had watched the progress of the labor intermittently. He agreed with Hunter that something was very wrong with the birthing process, but wanted no part of any significant procedure like a cesarean. He made it clear that the responsibility for the decision rested entirely with Hunter, and that he would not even assist in such a dangerous operation.

Clarissa overheard some of the discussion between Hunter and Jake. In between contractions, she called for Hunter. "I can't go on like this much longer," she said to him tearfully. "I'm completely exhausted."

Hunter reached down and held Clarissa's hand. "I understand," he said. She could see the concern etched on his face. "Dr. Blake," Clarissa said passionately as another contraction began, "I have nothing in the world except this baby. I gave up my family, my friends, and my whole existence to give it a life. Please, please, help my baby to live."

She almost crushed Hunter's hand during the contraction that followed. At its peak Clarissa screamed with pain. As soon as the contraction ebbed, Hunter turned to Ursula. "Can you get Gina, please?" he said. "We'll need all three of us."

Even though she was tired from the long day, Ursula's smile could not have been any broader. "You're going to do it?" she asked. Hunter nodded. Ursula hurried off to find Gina.

Hunter had never done a cesarean before. He had, however, studied the procedure very carefully during his preparations for his paramedical final examination. Hunter had also watched two cesareans performed during his time at the Cicero Hospital. He was extremely thankful for all his experience, for there were no reference materials at the Utopian clinic to give him any guidance.

The enthusiastic Ursula retrieved Gina very quickly, but she also caused a mild uproar in the pirate band by reporting to everyone she passed that the new Dr. Blake was about to perform an operation to save the life of Clarissa and her unborn baby. By the time Hunter had finished sterilizing the implements, making certain that blood of the proper type was available if a transfusion was required, reviewing with his interns their responsibilities during the procedure, and administering the anesthetic prepared by Winston, word of what he was doing had spread throughout Utopia.

Before starting the actual procedure, Hunter closed his eyes and tried to visualize the two operations he had witnessed on Cicero. His biggest concern was properly locating the incision. Once the cut was made, and it was apparent that it was more or less in the correct location,

Hunter was confident that he could complete the operation. He took a deep breath and tried to calm his racing heart. Using the scalpel the way he had seen the robot surgeons and physicians do it on Cicero, he started the incision.

Even though Hunter had warned Ursula and Gina to expect a lot of blood, both of the girls recoiled when they were confronted by the profuse bleeding. Hunter stopped for a moment, and quietly reminded the girls of their duties. They responded immediately. He then completed the incision, commanding the interns in a balanced, soothing tone throughout.

After pulling the layers of skin back to make the largest possible opening, Hunter reached into Clarissa's body with his gloved hands. The baby was upside down and extremely large. It was clear that a natural birth would have been an unmitigated disaster. Carefully, tenderly, Hunter pulled the infant through the incision he had made and held the baby boy aloft while the trembling Ursula cut the umbilical cord. He hit the child lightly on the back, and the boy filled the tent with a surprised cry. As they had planned, Hunter handed the baby over to Gina, removed the placenta from Clarissa, and began the process of preparing to close the incision.

It was only then that Hunter noticed the presence of Lance and a few others, who had apparently witnessed much of the operation from the far side of the tent behind Hunter. The Utopian chief offered him congratulations and stopped to inspect the newborn boy that Gina was holding. Clarissa's baby was still crying in occasional bursts when all the visitors left.

Hunter closed the incision using almost half of the suturing material left in the clinic's inventory. When he was finished, he was not pleased with his handiwork. *She'll have a nasty scar,* Hunter said to himself, *but I guess that's really not that important. She has her life, and a wonderful little boy.*

After the postoperative procedures were completed, the emotional Ursula came over to Hunter and threw her arms around him. "Is it all right if I cry now?" she asked.

Hunter nodded. The teenager hugged him fiercely. He could feel her body shaking as she wept. "That was unbelievable," Ursula whispered in his ear. "You are a wonderful man."

HUNTER BECAME A hero in Utopia overnight. By the end of the next day, almost every member of the pirate band had heard the details of the story from someone. People dropped by the clinic to introduce themselves and offer their congratulations. Many of the Utopians invited Hunter to dine with them in their home tents.

Clarissa's recovery was swift and without complications. The baby boy, whom Clarissa promptly named Blake, was as healthy as he could be.

In spite of Ursula's frequent reminders that Janie was available for him whenever he had the time or inclination, Hunter continued to fill his days with work. But the limitations of the clinic frustrated him more and more each day. After he had been on Utopia for two weeks, Hunter decided that he would seek a special meeting with Lance, to appeal for significant upgrades to the clinic. He was preparing to leave the main tent, intending to go over to Lance's quarters in the permanent structures, when he had a surprise visit from Bailey.

After exchanging greetings, Bailey told Hunter that they both had been invited to dinner with the Utopian chief. "When?" asked Hunter.

"Tonight," Bailey said. "At seven o'clock."

"But I already have a dinner engagement this evening," Hunter said.

"I would advise you to break it," Bailey said. "Invitations to dine with Lance do not come very often."

Hunter started to protest that he disliked being discourteous to anyone, but realized quickly that his decision was obvious. *Besides,* he told himself, *this will give me a chance to talk to Lance about the needs of the clinic.*

"Okay," Hunter said. "I'll be there."

Bailey didn't say anything for several seconds. At length he looked Hunter directly in the eyes. "I have some additional advice if you want it," he said. "It's about Tehani."

Hunter felt his pulse rate rise. He hadn't seen Tehani since the party. His work had been so consuming that he had almost stopped thinking about her every day. "All right," he said to Bailey. "I'll listen."

"Lance has really fallen for her," Bailey said. "Even in our open society their affair has already created considerable talk, as well as some unwanted tension. Lance has been neglecting his work since Tehani's arrival. Cooperman is becoming afraid that Lance will be unwilling to release her, even if fantastic terms are negotiated for her ransom. And Lance's wife Tricia has complained to Renee that her husband has ignored her and the children since 'that witch' arrived."

Bailey paused. Hunter, who was struggling with his emotions, didn't know what he was supposed to say. "And the advice?" he eventually said.

"Don't pay very much attention to Tehani tonight," Bailey said. "I'm sure she'll be at the dinner. I'm equally certain that Lance will be watching how the two of you interact." He stopped for a moment. "Lance is a funny man. Even though he is an extraordinarily capable and intelligent leader, he still has some astonishing insecurities. Three years ago, Lance became convinced that his wife Tricia had a crush on an extremely bright young man whom Cooperman had recruited for us from the Free Zone. It didn't matter that all of Lance's key advisors, as well as Tricia, swore that he was imagining things. Lance made life so unpleasant for the young man that he was forced to leave Utopia."

"And why are you telling me all this?" Hunter said.

"To avoid what could become a significant problem in our band," Bailey said. "I saw how you reacted when Rango wanted to buy Tehani at the trading post. Your outrage and jealousy were apparent to everyone. If you make even a remotely similar display of your emotions tonight, your days here on Utopia will quickly be over. At the least, we would lose good medical help that we desperately need. At the worst, you, and perhaps even Tehani, could have your lives ruined. Lance has that kind of power."

Hunter reflected for several seconds. "Thanks, I guess, for the advice," he said finally. "But there's still something I don't understand. Doesn't Lance know that Tehani and I were lovers on the *Darwin*?"

"He knows that the two of you are close friends, and were secondary-school buddies on Cicero," Bailey said. "Lance also knows that Tehani and you shared a cabin on the *Darwin* after we kidnapped you. When he queried all of us last week about the extent of your relationship, we all told him the same story—that we suspected the two of you may have been at least casual lovers. We didn't think it wise to say more."

HUNTER DIDN'T KNOW what to expect when he showed up for dinner at seven o'clock. He had decided, after some thought, to wear a clean shirt and his only pair of dress pants. Corinne, Lance's extremely able assistant, met Hunter at the door of the Utopian chief's quarters. She ushered him into a small, tastefully furnished room where Chelsea, Darrell, Bailey, and Renee were already having drinks. All four were dressed in smart, casual clothing. Everyone greeted Hunter heartily and asked him how things were going at the clinic. Nobody mentioned Tehani.

Corinne brought Hunter a drink, then disappeared. Since Bailey, Darrell, and Chelsea soon became engrossed in a conversation, Hunter visited with Renee for about ten minutes. From her, he learned that Bailey was the subchief in charge of "external affairs," which Renee laughingly said meant that Bailey captained all the dangerous expeditions to steal cargo. Of more interest to Hunter were Renee's comments about her Utopian family. Bailey, Eiki, and she had four children, she explained, and Eiki helped her take care of them during the long periods that Bailey was away from Utopia. Eiki, who was twenty-two and Renee's other husband, also worked four hours a day in the children's center.

"He's wonderful with kids," Renee said, "very tender and patient." She glanced briefly at Bailey and smiled. "My older husband would rather read than play games with imaginary people or creatures." She shrugged slightly and laughed. "It's a good situation for me. One of the two of them has everything I could want. And I never have to spend a night alone."

Renee was explaining to Hunter that Eiki was clearly responsible for their youngest daughter, because she had Asian features, when Lance's wife Tricia, wearing a gorgeous long black-and-white dress with a low neckline, came into the room by herself. She did not look happy. Tricia glanced around briefly, then left the room to make herself a drink. When she returned a minute or so later, she picked up a chair and set it right next to Hunter.

"Well," she said, "you've certainly made a name for yourself quickly. Everyone all over the settlement is singing your praises." Tricia was an attractive woman, in her late twenties, with long, curly blonde hair, cobalt-blue eyes, and nearly perfect teeth.

"Thank you," Hunter replied.

"I'm sorry," she said with a laugh, "I forgot. I guess we've never been officially introduced. I'm Lance's wife Tricia."

She took a long swig from her drink. "Now do I understand correctly that Tehani and you were schoolmates on some backwater asteroid?" Tricia asked.

"Yes, that's right," Hunter replied.

"Isn't it a small universe?" she said. "Who would have ever expected that the two of you would be kidnapped together and would end up here with our pirate band?"

Tricia was clearly headed somewhere with her questions of Hunter, but she was interrupted by the arrival of Lance and Tehani. Tehani looked magnificent. Her red cocktail dress perfectly accentuated her dark eyes and long hair, which hung freely down her back almost to her waist. Tehani greeted the dinner guests warmly and gave Hunter a brotherly hug. Hunter noticed that Lance was watching their hug closely. After an awkward minute, Tricia left the room, returning shortly with drinks for the two newcomers. Tricia did not even look at Tehani as she handed her the drink.

Accustomed to dominating all the conversations in which he took part, Lance, who was in an exuberant mood, delivered what was essentially a monologue for most of the remaining ten minutes before dinner. He told the group that some exciting plans were in the offing, and that four or five other pirate chiefs would be visiting Utopia the following month to discuss them in more detail.

"Our hijacking and kidnapping has really put us on the map," Lance said proudly, saluting Bailey and Chelsea. "We're no longer considered an insignificant band."

Hunter hardly said a word during the conversation. He spent most of his time studying Lance and Tehani. The chief's body was always turned toward Tehani. He also appeared to be addressing all his questions to her. And Tehani, perhaps out of politeness, never turned her eyes away from Lance while he was talking.

Beside him, Hunter could sense that Tricia was fuming. *Bailey was right,* Hunter said to himself, *Lance has fallen in love with Tehani. This situation could be even more dangerous than the one at the Andromeda trading post.*

Just before dinner, Hunter focused his observations exclusively on Tehani. Once, her eyes met his briefly, then she turned back in Lance's direction. *She is truly elusive,* Hunter thought. *I can't tell if she is genuinely interested in Lance, or if she's just acting. And I bet he can't either.*

"THE ANTIBIOTICS, THE simple pain and fever medicines, the immunization vaccines, and the basic hospital supplies are extremely important," Hunter was saying, "but the most essential items the clinic is lacking are a computer and a good communications link to the existing medical-reference database. The clinic simply cannot perform its function without them."

They were near the end of the dinner. Lance and Hunter were sitting on opposite ends of the rectangular table, with the other six diners along the sides. Tehani, Bailey, and Chelsea were on the right of Lance, in that order. Tricia, Darrell, and Renee were on Hunter's right.

During most of the dinner Hunter had conversed privately with Tricia, who turned out to be as articulate as she was attractive. He had asked her a question about her escape from the Margaritas and Tricia had regaled him with a humorous, fascinating rendition of the tale that Bailey had told Tehani and him just before they arrived at Utopia.

Tricia's story about the ten young women, none of whom had any flight experience whatsoever, trying to figure out how to operate an antiquated, malfunctioning spacecraft had been hilarious. When she had described their relief and elation after Lance and his band of Utopians had come onboard to rescue them, Tricia had glanced down the table at her husband. Hunter had expected that Tricia was going to say something affectionate to Lance at that time, but her smile had vanished abruptly when she saw how deeply involved he was in his conversation with Tehani.

Toward the end of the dinner, Lance had asked Hunter how his work at the clinic was progressing. Hunter had immediately seized the opportunity to talk about the clinic's deficiencies and to lobby for support.

"The two space powers have a bilateral agreement in place with respect to medical information," Hunter continued to explain, "and grant unlimited, free access to their reference material. All the doctors at isolated outposts use it, for nobody can possibly be an expert in every medical field. It should be a straightforward process for us to access that database."

"Have you met Cooperman yet?" Lance asked Hunter.

"No, I haven't," Hunter replied. "But I've certainly heard his name enough."

Lance laughed. "Cooperman is an original," he said, "absolutely one of a kind. Everyone acknowledges that he's a genius. But he's also, well, you can make your own judgments." Lance paused. "I'll set up a meeting for you with Cooperman tomorrow morning. He'll handle your computer and communication needs. As far as your list of medicines and supplies the clinic lacks, why don't you go over it with Bailey? He'll be able to advise me on how difficult it will be to fill your requisition list."

Lance looked as if he was ready to leave the dining table. "Anything else?" he said to Hunter.

"Yes," Hunter said, emboldened by his initial success. "I would like to request your support for a project to have every member of your band have a physical checkup at the clinic. In organizing the files, my interns and I have realized that we do not have one single piece of medical data on slightly more than half of the Utopians, including thirty of the children. Modern medicine now defines 'normal' not in terms of class parameters, but only in terms of a specific individual. Without any data—"

"I don't like that idea," Lance interrupted. "It sounds like an invasion of privacy to me, and it would take people away from their tasks." He pushed his chair back from the table and stood up. The dinner was officially over. "All right," Lance said with his best public smile, "shall we play a game of Intellego?"

INTELLEGO HAD BEEN invented in the twenty-third century. The game, which required strategic skills much like chess, had quickly achieved universal popularity among intelligent game-players because as many as eight people could play at once, and every playing configuration offered different challenges. There were no teams in Intellego. Each player always played against all the other competitors.

The common focus for the game of Intellego was a large, electronic, cubic playing field, with 512 possible locations for the individual pieces, which was usually mounted in the center of the playing room. At the beginning of the game every cell in the cubic field was empty. Each player also had his own square, secret board, displayed on the monitor of his individual hand computer. The private board contained sixteen locations. The player's eight pieces, each of which followed a different set of movement rules, started each game in exactly the same position. Throughout the game, each player followed the deployment of his pieces on his personal display.

The sine qua non for the game was the master Intellego computer that not only tracked the movement of all the playing pieces, but also made certain that each player followed the rules in maneuvering the pieces on his own private board. The computer was networked to the cubic playing field, as well as each of the individual hand computers. When a player made a move that resulted in an individual piece occupying a cell on the cubic playing field, the computer called out the move audibly, and illuminated that piece in the specific cell of the cube. At any time during the game, each player could use his hand computer to interrogate the master computer and determine the entire layout of the cubic playing field, including which individual pieces were at each location.

The object of the game was to capture pieces from other players. Once a piece was captured, it was removed from the game. In theory, the game could be continued until all but one player had had all his pieces captured. In practice, however, the game was not played that way. The master Intellego computer contained a complicated algorithm, slightly modified over the years, that assessed the state of each player's game at every juncture during the play. When a player's chances for winning were reduced below a certain level, that player was required to resign. The threshold level was generally set by player consensus, depending on how much time was to be allocated for the game. Once a player resigned, his pieces on the cubic playing field flashed intermittently from that point forward in the game, disappearing after one full cycle of moves by the other players.

The play of the game was straightforward. Each player had to move a piece on each turn. Play proceeded in a clockwise sequence. A player had five options: He could move a piece from one location to another on his own private board, without the other players knowing anything except that he had completed his move; he could move a piece from one cell to another on the cubic playing field in full view of the others; he could transfer a piece from his private board to the cubic field, with both the end result of his move and the piece that was moved being known to the others; he could return a piece from the cubic field to his own private board according to the rules of movement for each piece; or he could transfer from the cubic field to a location on another player's private board in a capture attempt. Capture attempts in another player's domain were all-or-nothing maneuvers. If nothing was captured, the piece that was attempting the capture was automatically lost. Only rarely did a skilled player attempt a capture in another player's private domain unless he knew with complete certainty that a piece was located at his destination point.

Blind moves, where a player simply rearranged his pieces on his own private board, were limited by the game. After a certain number of moves by any individual piece, or a total number of moves by a player, a move to the cubic playing field had to occur. This prevented long and boring games in which the cubic field remained empty for too long.

Both Hunter and Tehani had played Intellego on Cicero. Hunter, in fact, had occasionally played the game in network competition when he was fifteen and sixteen, and had achieved a significant ranking before he had concluded that really mastering the game required far more dedication and patience than he would ever have available.

The room where the drinks had been served, prior to the dinner, was reconfigured for the Intellego game. Renee asked Hunter if he knew how to play the game while Lance was making certain that the master computer was properly initialized. Hunter replied modestly that he had played "a little," and Tehani, who flashed a knowing smile at Hunter for a second or two, did not add anything. Lance suggested a threshold level for required resignations and nobody objected. While each of the players was choosing a color for his pieces, Tricia left the room for a minute and brought back mugs of grog for each of the guests.

The early part of the game moved quickly and was accompanied by light banter throughout the room. Renee made a bad early mistake and was the first to resign. Chelsea's husband Darrell exposed his pieces on the cubic playing field too early and was unable to protect them from the onslaught of the others. He was gone from the game in less than half an hour. Tricia and Chelsea both played defensively and lasted until the game was almost an hour old, but once they were forced to show their pieces on the cubic field, they were quickly defeated.

Hunter spent the first hour assessing the strategies and strengths of the other players and sipping his grog very slowly. When Tricia refilled the mugs, only Hunter and Tehani had not yet drunk most of theirs. Hunter had purposely played a very passive, but solid game. His tactics had worked. Based on the way Lance was playing, Hunter had concluded that the Utopian chief saw Bailey as his primary competitor in the game. Without giving away his overall strategy, Hunter assisted in an attack on Bailey's pieces that lowered Bailey's winning probability below the designated threshold and forced his resignation. That left only Hunter, Lance, and Tehani in the game.

At this point Bailey and Renee excused themselves, explaining that they wanted to go back to their home to say good night to their children and give Eiki the rest of the night off. The game stopped for about five minutes while everyone said good night to Bailey and Renee. Tehani stepped out to the rest room while Tricia poured more grog for Lance, Chelsea, Darrell, and herself. Lance started to leave the room but Chelsea reminded him of the rigorous Intellego rule that no two active players could ever be out of the playing area at the same time. When Tehani returned, Lance excused himself and departed.

While Lance was gone, Tricia sat down beside Hunter. "It looks to me as if you've played Intellego before," she said with a flirtatious smile.

"A few times," Hunter answered.

"And do you have other hidden talents that none of us have yet discovered?" Tricia asked in a voice loud enough that everyone in the room heard her.

"I doubt it," Hunter said, not looking at his hostess. He didn't want to say or do anything that she might misinterpret.

Tricia put her hand on Hunter's shoulder and leaned toward his ear. "I want you to win this game," she said in a low voice. "It will really piss him off."

When Lance returned, he suggested to Hunter and Tehani that they put a time limit of one more hour on the game, and let the master computer determine the winner by position assessment if two or more players were still remaining when time ran out. There was no disagreement. The game resumed immediately.

As play continued, it became obvious to Hunter that Lance was employing a dual strategy. He was trying to protect Tehani's pieces and outmaneuver Hunter at the same time. Hunter's play was designed to force Lance to choose one strategy or the other. After Hunter captured one of Lance's pieces with a clever combination, Lance temporarily abandoned providing Tehani with additional defense. Hunter then quickly moved his last three pieces into the cubic field and unleashed a juggernaut that prompted Tehani to resign voluntarily.

"You aren't yet below the threshold," Lance said, after quickly interrogating the master computer.

"That doesn't matter," Tehani said. "My position is hopeless. In another move or two I'll be forced to resign anyway. It makes more sense for me to quit now and let you two fight it out for the championship."

"Suit yourself," Lance said, entering the voluntary resignation into the computer and waiting for Tehani's three remaining pieces in the cubic field to start flashing.

Meanwhile, Hunter studied the playing field carefully. He was one major piece ahead of Lance. No matter where Lance's other piece was located on his private board, Hunter had an overwhelming advantage. There was really no sense in continuing the game for another twenty minutes.

"Lance," Hunter said in a pleasant voice, "Tricia and you have been most gracious hosts. I thank you for inviting me to dinner, and especially for setting up the meeting with Cooperman tomorrow. But it's late, I'm tired, and I may have patients to see when I return to the clinic. Why don't we just stop the game now?"

"Are you offering me a draw then?" Lance asked.

Hunter was astonished by the question. He didn't respond for a long time.

"Darling," Tricia said during Hunter's silence, "I'm no expert, but it certainly appears to me that Hunter has a vastly superior position."

"As you said," Lance replied curtly, "you're no expert."

Hunter was a born competitor. He loved winning more than almost anybody he had ever met. But as he looked across the table at the Utopian chief, and all the things he knew or had heard about Lance flashed through his mind, Hunter knew what he should do. "Yes," he finally said with a smile, "I'm offering you a draw."

Lance stood up and extended his hand. "I accept," he said. "You're a damn fine Intellego player. We'll have to do this again sometime."

As Hunter was preparing to leave, Darrell and Chelsea crossed the room together to speak with him. "This will probably be the last time we'll see you for quite awhile," Darrell said. "I wanted to thank you again for the news about my family."

Hunter looked puzzled. "We're leaving the day after tomorrow," Chelsea said. "On an extended recruiting trip." She laughed. "No, we won't be kidnapping anybody this time, if that's what you're thinking."

"Good luck to both of you," Hunter said warmly, shaking Darrell's hand. "Have a safe journey."

Lance was saying good night and good-bye to Darrell and Chelsea when Hunter actually reached the door. Tricia's parting kiss was aimed at Hunter's lips, but he turned aside at the last moment and accepted it on his cheek. Tehani gave Hunter a brief hug. She also whispered a soft, quick, but unmistakable "I love you" in Hunter's ear.

Hunter was in a surprisingly buoyant mood as he walked back to the clinic. He was, as he had been for days, completely confused about Tehani. But he was pleased about almost every other aspect of his life. At least as pleased as a prisoner of the pirates could be.

S I X

HUNTER WAS STILL IN a good mood when he awakened the next morning. After stretching his muscles and eating the oatmeal that he made from mixing hot water with the packaged cereal, he dressed and went into the clinic. He picked up a pad and began making sketches of how he would rearrange the main tent to accommodate a new computer and its peripherals.

Ursula arrived at seven-thirty. The always cheerful girl greeted Hunter with a big smile, and the two of them conversed about the previous evening. She was especially interested in the interactions among Lance, Tehani, and Tricia.

"In my village everyone's talking about them," Ursula said. "My mother thinks that Tehani is the most beautiful girl she has ever seen, but that Lance is making a terrible mistake by making his infatuation with her so obvious. She also says that he's setting a bad example for the band. He encourages all the men to share wives, because there are not enough women to go around, but he monopolizes two for his own purposes. And Tricia's never even had a baby."

"How many husbands does your mother have?" Hunter asked.

"Two officially," Ursula said. She grinned. "But it's a totally open marriage for everybody. . . . My mom really likes sex. She's in her mid-thirties, and at least temporarily doesn't have any little kids around the tent. . . . She has plenty of free time and energy." Ursula paused. "Last week, after I complained that Monroe didn't know anything about pleasing a woman, she volunteered to teach him a few lessons."

Hunter's brow knitted. "And how did you feel about that?" he asked.

"Oh, fine," the girl said nonchalantly. "Mom and Monroe spent a couple of nights together. She came back from the second night shaking her head, saying that some men 'just don't get it.'" Ursula laughed. "She suggested that I find a new boyfriend."

Hunter picked up his clipboard and prepared to visit the six overnight patients in the clinic. As he started to leave the tent, he noticed that Ursula was staring at him.

"What is it?" he said.

"Are you gay, Hunter?" Ursula asked. "If you are," she continued, not waiting for Hunter's answer, "well, I have three friends who are also gay or bisexual. . . . Buzz, for example, you met him at the party, he has both a girlfriend and an older-man lover. Then there's Bernardo—"

"Hold it, hold it," Hunter said, interrupting her. He started to laugh. "I'm not gay, Ursula," he said, "but I am curious about what prompted you to ask that question."

"Well," Ursula said, "you've been here almost two weeks now and as far as I know, you haven't had sex with anyone. At least, I've never seen anybody leaving your part of the clinic, or any signs that you've had a visitor. And you've turned down Janie two or three times." Her smile broadened. "And I sort of hinted that maybe I might be available and you didn't seem very interested."

Hunter was shaking his head and continuing to laugh. He put his arms around Ursula. "You are a dear girl," he said. "I guess I'm touched that you're so worried about me. But please don't spend your time on such an unimportant subject. I assure you that I have a very healthy interest in sex and women. When I have my work at the clinic here under control, I'm certain that I will find someone to share the nights with—"

"But don't you get horny?" Ursula interrupted. "My mom says that young men need to have orgasms at least once a day to keep from being frustrated and uptight. What do you do, masturbate every night after Gina and I leave?"

"Ursula," Hunter replied, unable to suppress a blush, "I know it's hard for you to understand, but the way I was raised, these kinds of issues, sex and masturbation, are more private matters." He sighed and laughed to himself. "If it will make you feel any better, yes, I masturbate occasionally, but certainly not every night."

"I think that's sad," Ursula said. "Surely I would be more fun than masturbation."

Hunter laughed heartily. "I'm sure you would," he said. "Undoubtedly." He gave her another quick hug. "I've put my notes from last night after you left on the table next to the first bed," he said. "Please file them for me while I'm making my rounds."

"Okay, Dr. Blake," Ursula said with a fake pout. "Hey," she then added, "I hope I didn't offend you."

"I don't think that would be possible," Hunter said as he headed for the next tent.

COOPERMAN LIVED IN a large one-story building directly behind what once had been the main base headquarters on Utopia and was now the residence of Lance and four of the subchiefs. The first door to the building that Hunter approached was locked, and had a large sign indicating that it was a warehouse for electronic parts and subsystems.

Above the other door there was also a sign. "Abandon hope, all ye who enter here," it said. On the door itself was a beautiful but frightening picture painted by a talented artist. The bottom part showed a man, a dog, and a ghostly figure dressed in black. They were together in a small rowboat crossing a river. On the far side of the river angry flames were consuming what looked like a city. Skeletons, decapitated bodies, anguished, ghostly faces, and other gruesome scenes were strewn amidst the flames, covering the top half of the door and spilling onto the adjoining concrete blocks.

A button beside the door said "Push me." Hunter followed the directions. In about five seconds he heard a deep voice that sounded as if it were in an echo chamber. "Who are YOU?" the voice said. Before Hunter could respond, the voice repeated, "WHO are you?" with the emphasis on the first word, and then "Who ARE you?" with the emphasis on the verb. That was followed by wild, hysterical laughter.

"I'm Hunter Blake," he said after the laughter subsided.

"Never heard of you," an electronic voice shrieked from the tiny microphones that Hunter had finally located just above the top of the door.

Nothing happened for several seconds. Hunter decided to push the button again. "Why are you here?" the deep voice in the echo chamber shouted angrily.

"It's about computers for the clinic," Hunter said. "Lance told me last night to come see you this morning."

The door creaked open. *"Entrez, s'il vous plait,"* the deep voice said.

Hunter took a hesitant step inside. "Please move out of the doorway," the electronic voice said.

Hunter complied. The door closed behind him, immediately triggering the playing of the first few bars of a full orchestral version of Beethoven's Fifth Symphony at a volume level just below the threshold of pain. The startled Hunter looked around at a scene that could best be described as electronic chaos.

He was standing in a large room filled with computers, monitors, virtual-world kiosks, keyboards, speakers, game-playing machines, projectors, printers, televisions, holograph machines, audio recorders, and dozens of other types of electronic equipment that Hunter didn't even recognize. There was no arrangement of any kind in the room, except for the narrow aisle that meandered among the stacks and piles and boxes jumbled helter-skelter from front to back and wall to wall. Beethoven was no longer playing, but Hunter could discern at least three different kinds of music coming from distinct sources in the room. Movies were playing on two of the monitors on one side of the aisle, toward the back. In front of those monitors was a couch on which there was room for three people to sit between stacks of data cubes.

As Hunter moved slowly down the aisle, he heard the tiny clicking sound of a video camera moving on a rail over his head. On the left wall his realtime image was projected on a thin screen of huge dimensions that he had not seen from the door. While he was staring at the screen, what appeared to be a large red bird flew over his head and perched on top of a pile of printers between the screen and Hunter. "Cooperman will be here shortly," the bird said in distinct English. "He is brushing his teeth."

Before Hunter recovered enough from his shock to say anything, the bird was aloft again, flying toward the back of the room. A large young girl, wearing a gargantuan shirt and apparently nothing else, appeared briefly in a doorway on the opposite side of the room. "Good morning, Dirk," the girl said.

"Good morning, Marlene," the bird said. It landed on her shoulder and the two of them disappeared down a hallway to Hunter's right. Moments later a short, blond, mustached young man in his underpants came out of the doorway and walked down the aisle toward Hunter at a rapid pace.

"Hello, hello," he said as he walked up. "I am Cooperman. You must be the doctor who beat Lance at Intellego last night." His words came out quickly, as if they had been fired from a gun.

"Actually, it was a draw," Hunter said, shaking Cooperman's extended hand. "And yes, I'm Hunter Blake. Technically I'm not—"

"That's bullshit," Cooperman interrupted, "and you know it, unless you were playing out of your ass with blind beginner's luck. I pulled the game from the recorder about midnight, before my mind was pulverized." He looked at Hunter intently. "What would you have done if Tehani had moved her interplanetary cruiser to the same spot on the cubic field two plays earlier?"

"I would have captured it with my missile launcher," Hunter said after a moment's hesitation.

"Then Lance would have destroyed your launcher with a raid from his fighter group," Cooperman said.

"Which would have left him vulnerable to a phalanx attack from my three pieces on the top of the cube, above his unprotected fleet."

Cooperman paused for half a second, thinking. "Good, very good," he said. "I might have to be semisober to beat you." For an instant Cooperman looked puzzled. "Oh, yes, I remember now. You want a computer for your clinic and a tie-in to the two networks so you can access the medical database. That's easy as pie. . . . Although, if I remember correctly, your power network is almost saturated now. I'll probably have to provide a new PDS as well."

A different large young girl, this one a mixture of Asian and African extraction, approached them from the back of the jumbled room. She also was wearing only a huge shirt and nothing else. Even at a distance Hunter could tell she had enormous breasts.

"Where's the rigatoni, Cooperman?" she said. "Marlene and I are starting to come down and it's a bummer."

Cooperman turned around. "I told you last night, Loretta," he said. "Rigatoni is too expensive, and too dangerous, for regular use. Besides, I promised Arthur I'd have you home before noon." He looked at his watch. "Get yourself something to eat out of the fridge, help yourself to the shower, and get dressed."

Loretta continued to walk in their direction. "You're mean, Cooperman," she said with a pout. "You take me to nirvana and then you tell me it has to stop. I heard you howling from pleasure, little man. Only Loretta can give you that kind of trip."

She was a giant, taller by several inches even than Hunter. Loretta towered over Cooperman. She pulled him roughly to her breasts. "Now where can you find a pair like these, Cooperman? Huh? Nowhere is the answer. No sir, not on Utopia. And you can fill your mouth again and again, just for a little rigatoni."

Not even trying to extract his head from its comfortable resting place, Cooperman turned in Hunter's direction. "This is Dr. Blake, Loretta," he said in a muffled voice. "He's the new man at the clinic."

"Whooee, he's cute," Loretta said, releasing Cooperman from her powerful grip. "Hey, Doc, do you have any rigatoni for Loretta? I guarantee it will be a morning you'll never forget."

Hunter shook his head.

"Okay, Loretta," Cooperman said, "that's enough. It was great, but now I have work to do. You and Marlene clean up and head back to your tents."

Loretta leaned down and kissed Cooperman on the top of his head. "You're a lot of fun, Mr. Gadget," she said. "Let me know when you want to play again."

She turned to Hunter and grinned. "Glad to meet you, Doc," she said. "With any luck I'll be seeing you soon with a little Cooperman in here." She rubbed the lower part of her stomach. "He exploded in me early this morning and I'm at just the right time of the month."

"Dirk, come here," Cooperman shouted as Loretta was walking away. The red bird appeared a few seconds later and zoomed down to a spot on Cooperman's outstretched palm. "Go wake Woodsy," Cooperman told the bird, "and tell him to get his lazy butt in here. I have a job for him."

Cooperman saw the consternation in Hunter's eyes. "State of the art," Cooperman said proudly. "Hottest product in the solar system. I sell them for thousands through the catalogue and our store in the Free Zone. Dozens of sizes and colors. Vocabulary of five thousand words plus. Amazing scanning capabilities. Better syntax than a five-year-old kid. Would you like to see my lab?"

Cooperman's sentences came out so fast that Hunter had difficulty following them. When the diminutive genius did finally pause, however, Hunter nodded vigorously. Cooperman turned immediately and started walking down the aisle.

"They're the perfect pet for the rich and famous," Cooperman said as he hurried along. "They don't shit or need to be fed. They don't make noise at inappropriate times, unless you screw up their training. And their personalities can be shaped by the owner."

Dirk reappeared just as Cooperman and Hunter turned

right behind the couch and the monitors playing the movies. "Woodsy says he'll be out in ten minutes," the bird said. "He still hasn't taken his morning crap."

"Now THAT'S really useful information," Cooperman said, laughing and shaking his head. "I couldn't have lived one more nanosecond without it."

Cooperman stuck his head in some weird kind of rectangular device mounted on a wall, and the door to a nearby room opened. "Nobody, but nobody," he said, "can come in here without me. I have the highest-level security check that anybody's ever put in a small lock. It not only scans both my retinas, it matches the full pattern of my nose." He grinned, waiting no more than half a second before continuing his rapid-fire conversation. "We'll make a few million from this thing, too. Tyson and Sackett are arguing about which agency should have the right to buy it. Meanwhile, I may sell it to the Dems. Hey, isn't capitalism great?"

Cooperman switched on the lights. *"Voilà,"* he said. "This is the research division of Electronic Birds, Incorporated. I spend most of my evenings here when I'm not stoned or in need of a squirt." He glanced at Hunter. "My days are saved for more nefarious pursuits, cloak-and-dagger and outwitting the idiots in the space governments and all that garbage."

A long counter filled the left-hand side of the room. Four stools were staggered along the counter. At each position was a small computer and a monitor, some additional electronic gear that Hunter did not recognize, and one or more birds, some complete, some opened up with their chips and other parts scattered about. Against the back wall of the windowless room was an open cabinet filled to the brim with electronic circuits. On the right, affixed to the wall, was a railing, on which half a dozen birds were perched. More computers, monitors, and other electronic systems were arranged under the railing.

"Getting the navigation right was the toughest part of the original design," Cooperman said, "especially accounting for all the different gravity fields." He walked over to one of the stools and picked up a pair of bird wings to show to Hunter. "I'm really not that much of a mechanical engineer. The sensors and the algorithms were a snap, but finding the right materials to implement flight for all the different sizes of birds, and designing the actual control surfaces, that was tough." He laughed. "I found a confused, antisocial genius at Catholic University, in the middle of the Dem outpost in Argyre, who was only one conviction away from being screwed for the rest of his life. We moved him to the Free Zone. He was only too happy to work with me on the mechanical subsystems in exchange for a nice home, a sweet young thing, and access to the smoothest dope he had ever used."

There was a knock on the door. Cooperman pushed a button underneath the counter and Woodsy, a short, fat man in his mid-twenties, entered the room. "This is the new doc at the clinic," Cooperman said. "He needs a computer, with full local networking capabilities, and a hook to the main Fed and Dem nets. Lance wants us to do it right away. I'll come out in a minute and show you which equipment to install." He paused a moment. "We also need to upgrade the clinic's power system. I'll build that here and you can take it over when you go."

Woodsy started listing the other tasks he had been assigned. Cooperman cut him off abruptly. "This is top priority," he said. "Janie can do the upgrade on Tricia's kitchen. It's a no-brainer anyway."

Cooperman explained a few details to Woodsy before he departed, then commanded Dirk to find Janie and tell her of her new assignment. "So," Cooperman said to Hunter, "would you like to have a bird?"

"Of my own?" Hunter asked.

"Yep," Cooperman replied. "They're great companions, and who knows, you may even find a use for the bird in your clinic. Assuming of course that you train it properly." He crossed the room and brought a printed manual back to Hunter. "Read these instructions carefully before you start. Otherwise, the bird will be all screwed up."

"Yes," Hunter said after an uncharacteristically long silence. "I think I would like one of your birds. That could be fun."

"Which one?" Cooperman said, pointing at the birds sitting on the railing. "The most capable one is that white bird with the blue head. Her name is Camille."

"She would be fine," Hunter said, still overwhelmed by everything he had seen and heard since entering Cooperman's living quarters.

"Of course, all gifts have strings," Cooperman said after retrieving the bird and showing Hunter the activation button beneath the fake feathers on Camille's neck. "You now owe me an unlimited number of games of Intellego," he said with a smile. "I'll always give you a day or two of warning, but I expect you to show up unless you have a damn good reason."

"That sounds fair enough," Hunter said. He extended the hand not holding Camille in Cooperman's direction. "Thanks for everything," he said.

HUNTER'S NEXT THREE weeks were unbelievably full. When he was not working with Ursula and Gina to transfer all the patient records into the computer, or printing out basic medical information from the databases to expand significantly the available reference material at the clinic, or restructuring the operation of the infirmary at the children's center, or seeing one of the increasing number of patients, Hunter was studying the manual Cooperman had given him on the training of Camille.

He worked on his pet bird's capability slowly and methodically. Hunter loved to stand outside the tent and watch Camille soar away, following his instructions by flying almost up to the dome itself before returning to his palm. Camille spent the night on the perch next to his bed. She started every day by flying through all the tents of the clinic and correctly reporting whatever the patients told her in response to the question "How are you feeling this morning?"

As his duties mounted and the workdays lengthened, Hunter requested, and received, approval to acquire both an apprentice assigned to him and another clinic intern. After interviewing several poor candidates for the apprentice position, Hunter decided that Ursula had all the intelligence and compassion necessary to be a good doctor. When he told her that he had selected her as his apprentice, she burst into tears of joy. Ursula walked around with a gigantic smile for days after her selection. She also helped Hunter pick the two new interns, both sixteen, a boy named Raymond and a girl named Mariah.

Ursula worked indefatigably, sometimes putting in eighteen-hour days without any push from Hunter. Jake Townsend, unfortunately, did not have the same kind of dedication. He was in no way jealous of Hunter, for he had never felt comfortable as the clinic supervisor in the first place. He was perfectly willing to see patients three to four hours a day, in the afternoon if possible, to give Hunter an opportunity to do something else, but he wasn't interested in a more involved duty cycle. Since Jake was marginally competent at best, once the clinic instituted an appointment schedule, the routine complaints were assigned to him.

When Bailey made an excursion to a nearby trading post, Hunter managed to have some of his requests placed at the top of the priority queue. For the first time, there were ample antibiotics and everyday pain medicines in the clinic, as well as the necessary vaccines to immunize all the children properly. Hunter was justifiably proud of his accomplishments after he had been on Utopia for a mere five weeks.

He kept his part of the bargain with Cooperman, showing up twice for Intellego games. In the first game just the two of them played. Cooperman told him later that he had used the game to calibrate Hunter's skill. What Hunter learned was that Cooperman's talent at the game was fantastic. His mind was photographic, for immediately after the game he could recite every single move either of them had made on the cubic playing field. Cooperman told Hunter that he was definitely the second-best player on Utopia, but Hunter knew that he was not even close to Cooperman in skill.

For the second game, Cooperman invited two young women to play with them, and encouraged the other three players to coordinate their pieces in an attempt to defeat him. The women, both in their mid-twenties, were decent players, but even with the overwhelming odds Cooperman still won. After the game Cooperman invited Hunter to stay and smoke some dope with the women and him, but Hunter declined. After he left Cooperman's quarters, Hunter felt some strong sexual urges and briefly debated returning to share in the fun. But he decided against it. Except for Tehani, Ursula was the only woman on Utopia for whom he had any real feeling, and he had pointedly avoided accepting any of her occasional offers. Hunter felt that having a sexual relationship with Ursula might interfere with their working together.

Hunter still thought occasionally about Tehani, with whom he exchanged insignificant small talk twice at public functions, both times with Lance within earshot, but he forced himself not to yearn for her. He also concluded that he did not understand Tehani at all. She appeared to have settled comfortably into her role as Lance's mistress. *How could she possibly love me,* he asked himself, remembering her whispers after the game of Intellego, *when she has made no attempt to contact me at all?*

Late one afternoon, just after Jake Townsend had completed his short daily stint, Lance's wife Tricia showed up at the clinic. Hunter had not spoken with her since the dinner party. "And to what do I owe the privilege of this visit?" Hunter asked after they had exchanged pleasantries.

"You should check your appointment book more often, Doctor," Tricia said. "I've had this slot scheduled now for over a week."

"Okay," Hunter said, his embarrassment showing, "what can I do for you?"

"I'd like a normal female checkup," Tricia said. "And I have a few questions I'd like to ask you."

Hunter asked Tricia to follow him to the tent where he conducted the gynecological examinations. Ursula and he had systematically rearranged everything in the clinic during the last month. One of the results was that a woman no longer had to stand in full view of other clinic patients while her private parts were being examined.

Tricia removed her clothes and sat on the small examination table without any prompting from Hunter. Even though he had previously examined forty or fifty of the Utopian women, Hunter definitely felt nervous as he started touching the lithe, shapely body of the chief's wife. They talked casually during the exam, a mixture of normal doctor's questions and light remarks about daily activities. Hunter's nervousness did not abate. Once, he glanced up at her face and saw that Tricia was smiling as if she realized how much difficulty he was having treating her as a routine patient. Hunter concluded that she was definitely flirting with him.

When he felt her breasts for lumps, Tricia's response was definitely nonclinical. A moment later, when Hunter was very close to her, Tricia leaned over with her hands, touched his cheeks lightly, and brought his face to hers. They kissed. It was a soft, enduring, sensuous kiss that the surprised Hunter did not try to truncate. Tricia stopped the kiss briefly, turned her naked body so that more of her was against Hunter, and put both her arms around his back. The second kiss was passionate and insistent. Hunter did not resist in any way.

Tricia pulled away slightly, still gently caressing Hunter's face with her hands. "I thought the night you came over that we might enjoy one another," she said. "And I know now that I was right." She slipped one hand into his pants. "You are ready right now, Hunter," she said with a seductive smile, "and I certainly am."

She started to pull down his pants. Hunter, torn by conflicting emotions, did not grab one of her arms until he was completely exposed. Tricia continued to fondle him with her other hand. "What is it, Hunter?"

"Not now, not here," he stammered in his confusion. "I can't. I mean, my assistant might come in at any time. And it's too dangerous."

"You don't have anything to worry about," Tricia said softly, her expert hand work adding more to Hunter's confusion. "Under the circumstances, Lance has agreed that I can choose anyone I want as a lover. Or even as another husband. After all, your little friend from Cicero is certainly making his juices run."

Tricia kissed him again, hard, and slid around on the table. She guided Hunter into the proper location and inserted him as she came off the table into his arms. They had just started moving together when they heard his name being shouted.

"Hunter, are you in here?" Ursula was yelling. "I need you."

Hunter was seized by panic. He decoupled himself from Tricia hurriedly. "What is it?" he shouted.

"A little girl," Ursula said. "She was hit by a rock. I think she needs stitches."

Discombobulated completely, Hunter stuck his head around the insubstantial curtain screening off the examination area.

"I'll be there in a few seconds," he said.

"Oh," said Ursula, staring at him with her mouth open.

Puzzled, Hunter looked at the expression on his apprentice's face, then down at himself. His male organs were clearly in view.

He frantically grabbed at his pants, but inadvertently pulled hard on the curtain he was holding in his hands. The curtain ripped off its railing. Tricia pulled her clothes up to cover some of her naked body just a second before Ursula saw her.

"Oh, OH!" Ursula said, her eyes as wide as saucers. She stood still, looking at the two of them, for a couple of seconds. Then she grinned. "I'll see you in the main tent in a little bit," she said. "Please hurry, the girl is really upset."

URSULA SAID NOTHING about the incident while Hunter was taking care of the distraught little Utopian girl. She had been hit right above the left eye by a rock thrown by her older brother. The girl's mother's mood vacillated back and forth from anger at the boy to concern about her daughter. "She's not going to be blind in that eye, is she?" the woman asked Hunter at one point.

"Oh, no," Hunter replied after applying a mild topical

anesthetic to reduce the pain during the stitching. "She'll be seeing fine as soon as the bleeding stops. But she'll be sore for several days. This is a very sensitive area to suture."

After the little girl and her mother had left, Hunter helped Ursula clean up. At one point he noticed that she was staring at him. "What is it?" he said, starting to feel uncomfortable.

For once, the usually garrulous Ursula was reticent. She didn't say anything for several seconds. "What?" Hunter said again with a little irritation.

"Why didn't you tell me you were having an affair with Tricia?" Ursula said. "I wouldn't have told anybody."

Hunter sighed. "I'm not having an affair with Tricia—" he said.

Ursula broke into laughter and interrupted him. "I'm sorry," she said while she was laughing, "I must have made a mistake. I forgot that you always have your pants down and a hard-on when you examine a woman patient." She smiled. "If that's really true, then I know at least a hundred women who will want appointments tomorrow."

Hunter was going to reproach Ursula for her comment, but somehow, as he looked at his adorable teenage assistant, he just couldn't be angry. In spite of himself, Hunter began to laugh. "Ursula," he said, "you are absolutely impossible."

Her eyebrows raised above her smile. "I guess that means you like me," she said.

"Of course I do," Hunter said. "Even if you are a pain in the ass at times."

They finished cleaning up the operating area with no further comment. Ursula removed the gown that she always wore while she was working at the clinic and picked up a folder containing twenty or so sheets from the reference cabinet.

"My homework for tonight," she said, waving the folder at Hunter as she headed for the exit from the main tent.

"Ursula," Hunter said, "we both know that I am not required to explain anything, but I do think it's important to clear the air."

He paused. She stopped in front of the exit and turned around.

"I had never been with Tricia before today," Hunter said slowly. "It just sort of happened, I guess . . . And we had barely started when you called for me."

"Thanks for telling me," Ursula said. There was a short silence. "Just be careful," she said as she departed. "I'd hate for us to lose you as our doctor."

SEVEN

THAT NIGHT HUNTER'S DREAMS were filled with
sexual overtones. During his sleep Tehani, Tricia, and Ursula each suddenly appeared out of context, seductive and
beckoning, in otherwise insignificant dream sequences.
Hunter awakened the next morning feeling unrested and
uncharacteristically cranky.

Ursula noticed his malaise right away. Hunter showed
no interest in talking with her about Camille's training, a
subject usually near and dear to his heart. Later, during one
of his morning appointments, Hunter was decidedly unfriendly to a patient who asked him to repeat his tentative
diagnosis twice.

"I think you're burned-out," Ursula said while consulting the appointment sheet during a brief hiatus in the
morning schedule. "Why don't you take the afternoon off?
There's nothing special happening today. Jake and I should
be able to handle everything."

In spite of his initial protestations, Hunter realized that
Ursula was right. He had worked every single day since his
arrival in Utopia, sometimes until late at night. He needed a
break. But what could he do? If he hung around the clinic,
Hunter knew that he would end up becoming involved

with the patients. Under the circumstances, it was highly unlikely that he could show up unannounced and visit with Tehani. At length Hunter thought of Cooperman.

For some reason, it had not occurred to Hunter that Cooperman might occasionally have regular duties like the rest of the Utopians. Hunter imagined Cooperman as a freewheeling genius, doing whatever he wanted, whenever he wanted, and always being located inside the walls of the world he had built for himself in that nondescript building where he lived. Hunter was therefore surprised when he pushed the button beside Cooperman's door and nobody answered after he twice identified himself.

Hunter had started to walk away when the door opened slightly behind him and Dirk flew out. "Cooperman's in the engineering area, Hunter," the red bird said, hovering eight feet off the ground in front of the door. "He told me to bring you over."

"If he's working," Hunter said to the bird, "then I don't want to bother him. I can come back later."

For a few seconds, Dirk did not respond. Hunter thought that perhaps his response had exceeded the bird's capability. He was about to say something simpler, when the bird flew down and landed on Hunter's shoulder. "No," Dirk said, "it's fine. You can come now. Cooperman would like to see you."

Dirk flew off Hunter's shoulder in the direction of another building a couple of hundred yards away. Several times the bird turned around to see if Hunter was still walking behind him. Dirk landed on a ledge next to the door of the other building and waited until Hunter was only a few yards away. Then the bird hovered in front of the security system for several seconds. When the door opened, Dirk started to fly away.

"Thanks," Hunter said.

"You're welcome," the bird said, pausing momentarily in its flight.

Janie greeted Hunter inside the engineering complex. She told him that Cooperman was in the conference room, meeting with some of the software specialists, and would be free in another five or ten minutes. Janie led Hunter over to what she defined as the break zone, where a couple of tables and half a dozen chairs were grouped in front of a refrigerator and an open, stocked pantry, then left him alone after explaining that she was involved in a task with a tight deadline.

Although Hunter was aware, from bits of conversation that he had had both with patients and Cooperman himself, that one of the prime assets the Utopians possessed was a large number of talented computer scientists and engineers, he had never imagined a scene like the one that was spread out before him. The huge square room, which must have been at least 150 feet on a side, was divided into two main sections. The side closest to Hunter was more or less a standard work environment. It occupied about two-thirds of the total area of the room. Around this work area Hunter could see more than a dozen individuals, all of them young, engaged in interactive activities with computing systems on their desks. In contrast to the chaotic scene beyond the door in Cooperman's living quarters, the engineering work area seemed to be carefully organized. Each individual workstation had all its equipment mounted in a similar arrangement, and there were actually identifiable aisles in the room.

On the other side from Hunter, stretching to the opposite wall, he could see half a dozen virtual-world kiosks, most of which seemed to be occupied, judging from the illuminated red lights on their tops. Hunter was initially puzzled by the presence of these advanced game machines, but assumed that they were in the engineering complex to provide additional recreational opportunities for the software personnel.

A black woman in her early twenties, short, stocky, wearing glasses, walked into the break zone and opened the refrigerator. She pulled out a soft drink, opened it, and sat down near Hunter. "You're the doc at the clinic, aren't you?" she said pleasantly.

"Yes," he said, "I'm Hunter."

"I'm Nadine," the woman said, extending her hand. "I'm going to come see you one of these days," she said, "about my headaches." She laughed easily. "If we're ever out of the crisis mode. That damned Cooperman seems to think we can accomplish anything. He just committed us to another big job, even though we're shorthanded for the tasks we're already doing."

Nadine stood up and opened the pantry. "Want a cookie?" she said. "We have oatmeal, chocolate chip, shortbread, and butter. All homemade right here on Utopia. We even export the ones that we don't eat." She grinned at Hunter. "My second husband, Wally, says they're a hot commodity at the trading post."

"Sure," Hunter said. "I'll try a butter cookie. And a glass of cold, fresh milk."

Nadine laughed. "There's not a lot of cows on this asteroid," she said, "so I'm not sure how fresh it is." She poured him a glass of milk and handed Hunter both the cookie and the milk as she sat down. "So what brings you over here, Doc?" she said.

"I came to visit with Cooperman," Hunter said, "although I'm afraid I may have come at a bad time."

"He's always busy with something," Nadine said, "no matter when you find him. Now's as good a time as any. If he let you in the complex, he intends to see you."

"What do you do here?" Hunter asked, after taking a bite of his cookie.

"I'm in the spy department," Nadine said. She glanced over at the puzzled Hunter and laughed heartily again. "I'm really a systems programmer," she said. "I develop and test the algorithms and routines for intelligence gathering that the genius himself designs. It's a fascinating job, a hell of a lot better than the grunt work I was doing for the Dem government on the Moon."

A door opened along the wall forty feet from where Hunter and Nadine were sitting and four or five people filed out. The last one was Cooperman, who was involved in an intense conversation with an unusually tall, skinny young man of mixed Oriental descent who was wearing his incredibly long hair in a braided ponytail. Cooperman saw Hunter and waved. His companion and he, still talking animatedly, moved slowly toward the break zone.

"Uh-oh," Nadine said, gulping the last of her soft drink. "The boss is coming. I'd better return to work." She glanced at Hunter. "Now I bet you never thought you'd hear a pirate say something like that," she said with a laugh.

Cooperman was so engrossed in his discussion with the tall young man that he didn't even acknowledge Nadine's greeting as she passed him. "I just don't think it will work," Hunter heard Cooperman saying as he approached. "They're stupid, but not THAT stupid. It's too obvious. We need something much more subtle."

"What's up?" Cooperman said to Hunter after saying good-bye to his colleague.

"Nothing, really," Hunter said. "I just decided I needed to take an afternoon away from the clinic. If you're too—"

"Good for you," Cooperman interrupted, putting his hand on Hunter's shoulder. "I was worried about you the last time we played Intellego—I thought you were working too much." He glanced quickly at his watch. "Let me show you around this place."

They walked down the aisle until they were standing in the middle of the room. "This is one of the most productive work areas anywhere in space," Cooperman said proudly. "I handpicked this entire group over the last five years," he said, "either rescuing them from trouble with the law or their families, or removing them from the boredom of routine jobs either in the UDSC or FISC. There is no remotely comparable assemblage of computer and software-related talent anywhere else."

He pointed at a giant of a young man, sitting in a chair specially designed for his huge girth. "That's Larry," Cooperman said. "He was one unhappy dude three years ago. He flunked out of the University at Tranquility in his first year, failing basically because he thought that the required courses were stupid and the work assignments boring. His family criticized him relentlessly and forced him to see one psychiatrist after another as a condition for continuing to feed and clothe him. Meanwhile, demonstrating his brilliance, Larry hacked into the Bank of the Moon's central processors from his personal computer and purloined over a million for his own use."

Cooperman laughed, and then continued his staccato monologue. "Do you know what Larry did with the money? He ate every day by himself at the best and most expensive restaurants; filled his room at home with state-of-the-art electronic equipment, ordered outrageously expensive jewelry from the catalogues, and reserved three different private escorts at Sybaris, back-to-back, for his next vacation. It didn't take a rocket scientist to determine that something peculiar was going on. But what Larry had done was so clever, and carefully disguised, that none of the authorities could figure it out. If he hadn't bragged about what he had done to another programmer friend, then he might never have been caught."

Cooperman shook his head. "Can you believe that they were going to imprison him for two years? What kind of justice is that? An eighteen-year-old kid, who has never done anything wrong in his life, figures out how to beat his elders on their own computers and manipulates their money. For that he is severely punished. You're a bad bad boy, Larry. . . . I just happened to be on the Moon at the time his conviction and sentence were announced. Rhonda and I quickly studied what the boy had done, admired its elegance and logic, and whisked him away. He's been happy ever since. He implemented the entire Cicero caper almost by himself, with only the slightest guidance from me."

Hunter was slow to respond. Cooperman talked so fast, sometimes it was easier not to try to pay attention. "Excuse me," Hunter said. "Did you say something about a Cicero caper?"

"Yep," Cooperman said, "I thought that would pique your interest. We were demonstrating our capabilities for some, well, for some other people. Larry overrode your mining-machine command code, countermanded your defense system, and made your missiles go awry. He also developed an ironclad plan for remotely shutting off the power inside the *Darwin,* and then taking control once the write-protect portions of the spacecraft computer software were disabled. All in one month's work. Now is that genius, or what?"

Hunter didn't say anything for a few seconds. It was incomprehensible to him that Cooperman was chattering in such an offhand way about an activity that had resulted in the death of two people.

"We never intended to hurt those two engineers," Cooperman said in his unique rapid-fire way, apparently reading Hunter's reaction. "Actually that particular mining machine was scheduled to be dormant on the day of our attack. But your father and his colleagues changed the plan that morning on Cicero and we didn't have time to alter our commands."

Cooperman shrugged. "I sent some money anonymously to each of the two families," he said. "It was a shame that anyone was hurt." He paused a moment and then brightened. "But our capability demonstration was an overwhelming success."

Hunter started to protest, to remind Cooperman that the two lives that had been lost were far more important than any possible "capability demonstration," but they were interrupted by a young woman. She handed Cooperman an encrypted note. "He says it's an emergency," she said.

Cooperman's brow furrowed momentarily. "Excuse me a second," he said to Hunter. Cooperman walked across the room and entered the closest of the virtual-world kiosks. He didn't even close the door. Hunter thought he recognized the music coming from the kiosk. Cooperman returned in a minute or two.

"Now where were we?" Cooperman said. Before he could say anything else, a programmer approached and asked him a complicated question concerning the instruction set for one of their newer, specialized processor designs. Cooperman answered immediately, firing off a detailed technical response at an incredibly high rate. The programmer's eyes indicated that he hadn't understood the answer. Cooperman started into a second explanation, then sent the programmer toward Larry's desk. Larry had temporarily stopped work and was about to bite into some kind of a sandwich.

Cooperman glanced at his watch again. "Let's get out of here and go to my place," he said to Hunter. "I have time for a quick lunch."

"So what you need is a relaxing afternoon, huh?" Cooperman said as soon as Hunter and he were outside. "Take the edge off?"

They started walking toward Cooperman's quarters. "Was that the Rama music I heard when you went into the virtual-world kiosk?" Hunter asked.

"Yes, it was," Cooperman answered. "That's incredibly observant of you. Do you spend much time in the Rama world?"

"Not a lot," Hunter said. "But it is fun. Very imaginative. I enjoy talking in colors with the octospiders." They reached the door to Cooperman's home. "But I must admit that I'm quite puzzled," Hunter said. "I thought you had some kind of work problem, yet you went away to play a game for a minute. Were you helping a friend out of dire straits in the virtual world? Was that the emergency?"

Cooperman hesitated. "You could say that," he said at length, opening the door to his home and personal laboratory.

"THIS IS WHERE I come when I want to drop out of the universe altogether," Cooperman said, switching on the lights and adjusting them to a low level. "The sound system is unbelievable. You can totally lose yourself in the music."

Hunter and Cooperman had left their shoes at the door and entered a small, windowless, rectangular room, maybe twenty feet long and twelve feet wide, off to the side of Cooperman's chaotic bedroom. The walls were covered with a thick black material that looked and felt like velvet.

"Sit or lie down anywhere," Cooperman said. "The floor will conform to your body. It's a very special ergonomic design."

Hunter tentatively sat down. The carpeting material did

indeed shape itself for his comfort. He glanced around the room. In one corner was a small black box with a screen on its top. In another was a closed cabinet about two feet high.

"You can listen to almost any music that has ever been recorded, over a million selections altogether," Cooperman said, displaying the top-level menus on the box monitor. "The high-density data-storage array in this box contains a perfect reproduction of the entire music catalogue in the Library of the Federation in Centralia." Cooperman smiled. "I borrowed it from them a couple of years ago while I was mapping all the protected-information databases in the FISC."

Hunter grabbed a couple of the dozen or so small black pillows strewn around the room and stretched out on the comfortable floor with the pillows behind his head. He took a deep breath and curled on his side. "This sure beats my cot by a long shot," he said. "How often do you sleep in here?"

"Once or twice a week," Cooperman replied. "More often if I have a regular girlfriend. It's divine for lovemaking."

"I bet," said Hunter. He relaxed and yawned. Cooperman activated the sound system and Hunter was surrounded by the clearest version of Tchaikovsky's Sixth Symphony that he had ever heard. Hunter thought that he could actually feel the yearning expressed by the music.

Cooperman closed his eyes. "Everything is here," he said. "Classical, new age from each of the last five centuries, computer compositions, rock and roll, even tribal music from the Earth. There are over a thousand sound nodes, or speakers, embedded in the walls. No matter where you are in the room, you have practically perfect sound."

Hunter knew that Cooperman was talking, but he wasn't listening. He was overwhelmed by the beauty of the music, played by the great Berlin Symphony of the early twenty-second century. Each time the prime melody recurred in the first movement of the Tchaikovsky composition, Hunter came closer to tears.

"And in this corner," Cooperman said, opening the cabinet, "you have a delectable combination of munchies. Chocolate bars, salty snacks, cookies, even a few different flavors of popcorn. There's also beer, wine, pop, and of course water."

Cooperman took a bottle of water out of the cabinet and came over beside Hunter. From his shirt pocket he produced an oblong orange pill about half an inch long. "This, Dr. Blake," he said with a broad smile, "is what is called a loppie. It is the finest creation of the greatest recreational-drug makers in the solar system. The loppie produces a predictable high that is damn near transcendent. It has many of the characteristics of the best THC, with no risks for a bad trip. The loppie high is so good, in fact, that only truly stable, achievement-oriented people should ever use it. It could easily become a permanent habit for those without self-discipline."

Hunter's first impulse was to decline the drug. But his curiosity, and his need for a break from his everyday routine, won the debate over his traditional conservatism. Hunter acquiesced and accepted the loppie and the water.

"Good for you," Cooperman said. "You're in for a treat. By the way, there's real food in my refrigerator in the kitchen. Help yourself to anything."

Cooperman looked at his watch again and apologized for having to rush off. "Dirk," he shouted as he stood on the threshold of the room. The red bird appeared in less than a minute and landed on his shoulder. "I'm going to leave Hunter in here alone," Cooperman said to his bird. "If he should need anything, please come get me."

Hunter settled back into the soft floor with the pillows behind his head and listened to more of Tchaikovsky's

Sixth Symphony. By the time the music reached the fourth and final movement, an unusual adagio, the loppie had lifted Hunter's hearing to an acuity level he had never before experienced. Without difficulty he was able to discriminate among the many instruments of the orchestra. At his choosing, he could follow the violins, or the cellos, or the oboe and the clarinet.

There were no barriers to the music. None of the usual daily concerns, or anxieties about past or future events, impeded Hunter's access. Without knowing it, he began to cry. He had read many times that Tchaikovsky had known his death was imminent when he wrote the Sixth Symphony, but Hunter had never felt that prescience before. In Cooperman's black room, surrounded by perfect sound and distracted by absolutely nothing, Hunter communed with both the dying Russian composer and the talented Berlin orchestra's exquisite interpretation of his final symphony.

He was in a classical mood. Hunter played Rimsky-Korsakov's joyous "Russian Easter Overture" and attacked the munchies in the food cabinet. He ate and ate and ate. He had never tasted cookies or potato chips that were so divine. His mood changed. Suddenly he wanted to listen to rock and roll. Hunter started singing along with the artists, something he almost never did.

Time was a paradox. A minute was forever, yet when he finally looked at his watch the afternoon was almost over. Hunter was so focused on the music that he barely noticed when Loretta entered the room. He started to speak but she put her finger to her lips. She kissed him once, for what seemed like an hour. Hunter thought that he could feel the papillae on her tongue.

They undressed each other. Slowly, with full appreciation for each step. Hunter stared with undisguised amazement at Loretta's enormous breasts. He touched them, moved them from side to side, placed the nipples in his mouth. She fondled him adroitly after his pants were off, watching his desire grow stronger and stronger.

Loretta and Hunter kissed again after they were both naked. She seized the initiative, pressed him gently down beneath her, down into the comfort of the floor. He saw her towering over him, felt her all around him. *Oh my God,* he thought, *I can feel every movement.*

Hunter surrendered to his pleasure. He allowed himself to be transported to an alien world where no moment existed except the present. Hunter knew it was the loppie's gift. But that did not diminish the incredible delight.

His climax endured forever. It was almost surreal, for he knew that in reality it was only seconds long. A broad smile spread across Loretta's face as Hunter's muscles relaxed and he sank back into the lush carpeting. She leaned down and kissed him. He heard a few bars of a current popular song, and remembered nothing after that.

Cooperman woke him two hours later. "How was it?" he asked Hunter.

Hunter tried to find words to describe what he had experienced. It was impossible. At length he simply smiled. "Thank you," he said.

"You're very welcome," Cooperman replied.

HUNTER WAS SURPRISED to find that Ursula was still at the clinic when he returned. She was sitting at her work desk in the main tent, making computer entries based upon the standard appointment forms they had designed together.

"How was your afternoon?" Ursula asked.

"Very nice, thank you," Hunter replied.

"You had a visitor about four-thirty," Ursula said coyly. "She stayed for almost an hour. I think she left you a note."

Hunter's first thought was that the visitor had been

Tricia. In that case, he was glad that he had been absent. He had been deliberately avoiding Lance's wife since their sexual encounter during her examination.

"It wasn't Tricia," Ursula said, as if she were reading Hunter's mind.

His brow knitted. "Who was it?" he said.

"Tehani," Ursula said. "She seemed quite upset that you weren't here." She paused. "She asked me several times if I knew where you had gone." Ursula smiled. "The way she was acting, I might conclude that the two of you were more than just friends from secondary school."

Hunter didn't respond to Ursula's comment. "You said that she left a note," he said. "Do you know where it is?"

"No," Ursula said. "I admit that I did look for it—not to read it, you understand, but just to be able to give it to you—but it wasn't in any obvious place. I guess it's possible that she decided not to leave it."

Hunter went into his quarters and looked around. He didn't see a note anywhere. When he returned to the rest of the main tent, Ursula was ready to depart. As usual, she had a folder of reference material to study that evening.

Hunter took the folder from her hand. "What did you tell me today?" he said. "About working too much."

Ursula reached out and gently retrieved the folder. "I have so much to learn. I can't help you the way I want until I have the knowledge to do so."

"That's admirable, young lady," Hunter said, "but much too serious. You're not even seventeen yet. You should be having fun with your friends, and enjoying life."

"Working here at the clinic with you is fun," she said. "Being able to help people is fun. . . . Besides, all my friends want to do is get stoned and listen to music."

"What about Monroe?" he asked. "I thought you liked him."

She shrugged. "He's just a boy," she said. She looked directly at Hunter for a few moments. She started to say something but caught herself.

Ursula walked toward the exit. "Good night," she said. "I'll see you in the morning."

"Good night," Hunter replied. "Thanks for filling in for me. You were right, I did need some time off."

"Anytime," Ursula said.

After Ursula left, Hunter washed his face and sat down on his bed. An image of Tehani came into his mind. *Why did she come to see me today?* he asked himself. *After all this time, how did she manage to pick the one afternoon that I was away from the clinic?*

The more Hunter thought about Tehani, the more he realized how many unresolved feelings he had about her. For weeks he had deliberately forced himself not to think about her, for that was much easier than dealing with whether or not he loved her, or a host of other issues involving her behavior since they first arrived on Utopia. Hunter had actually developed a special mechanism for avoiding thinking about Tehani. Whenever her image, or some feeling for her, intruded into his daily life, Hunter would deliberately choose some complex reference material from the clinic files and force himself to study it until everything associated with Tehani had vanished from his mind. Now, acutely aware of his disappointment that he had missed her, Hunter could no longer avoid his powerful and ambiguous feelings about her.

He became possessed with an overwhelming desire to find the note. *Yes,* Hunter told himself, while he was thoroughly searching both his own room and the clinic, *it would be typical of Tehani to write something in this kind of situation. But she would never write a note and then not leave it. It must be here somewhere.* He found nothing after looking for half an hour. Hunter was about to conclude that Tehani had indeed, for some strange reason, taken the note with her, when he remembered a twenty-third-century novel they had studied together in school. In that story, the heroine had left an all-important secret note for one of the other primary characters inside his pillowcase. Smiling to himself, Hunter reached inside his pillow. The note was there.

My darling Hunter, you can't possibly know how distraught I am that I did not find you here at the clinic this afternoon. It never occurred to me that you might be somewhere else and not even your assistant would know where. Since yesterday, when I finally received Lance's blessing to have a private good-bye with you, I have been dreaming of holding you in my arms and kissing your wonderful lips. And now, you're not even here. It's almost more than I can endure.

I wanted to tell you my big news face-to-face. I think it's good news, although I realize that you may not at first agree. The negotiations for my repatriation have been successfully concluded. I will be leaving for Mars in the next few days. Yes, my darling, I am unhappy that I will be separated from you. But my situation here has been very precarious. By returning to Mars, my worst fears will be precluded.

I have sensed, from what I have seen in your eyes the few times that we have been in social situations together, that there may have been some change in your feelings for me during the time that we have been on Utopia. I hope not. My love for you remains as "constant as the Northern Star," to quote one of our favorite poets. If you are upset with me either because of my affair with Lance, or because you feel I have not made enough of an effort to visit you, then please read the rest of this note with an open mind and an open heart.

The Saracen chief Rango has continued to bargain for me since the day we arrived here. I have actually seen two of his video transmissions. The man is obsessed with me, and wants to make me his number one wife. He has raised the stakes considerably, to the point where it has become increasingly difficult for Lance not to accept his offer. Only Cooperman, among Lance's principal advisors, has suggested that it might not be in Utopia's best interests to hand me over to Rango.

Last week Lance actually reached a tentative decision to make the deal with Rango. Only when I pleaded with him did he give Cooperman five more days to conclude the negotiations with the FISC for my repatriation. Even now, if forced to choose between the offer from the FISC and Rango's, every one of Lance's subchiefs except Cooperman would almost certainly select Rango's.

Mea culpa, my darling. To reduce the probability that I would become a Saracen trophy, I admit that I deliberately used all my wiles and skill to win Lance's heart. My next worry of course was that Lance would try to keep me here with him in Utopia. I constantly reminded him, when Lance was unhappy with the progress in the negotiations with the FISC, that my mother and brother would have no support if I was not repatriated. Fortunately, Cooperman explained to Lance several times that retaining me here in Utopia as a wife or a mistress was not an option, and that his status with all the rest of the band would be seriously undermined if he did.

In the meantime, I promised myself that I would not say or do anything here that would cause Lance to have the slightest doubt about my love for him. He was wary of my affection for you from the beginning, and by avoiding you altogether, I could guarantee that nothing would occur that would cause him to suspect the truth. Yes, my love, I have been performing a delicate tightrope act, and I realize that you may have suffered as a result. But it now looks as if my plan has been successful.

My hand is trembling even as I write you this note, for if it fell into the wrong hands, I know what would happen immediately. Please destroy it as soon as you have finished reading it.

I believe that when you think carefully about the predicament that I have been confronting, you will not judge me too harshly. It goes without saying that if I were to become Rango's number one wife, there would be virtually no chance that you and I would ever be together again.

I love you, Hunter. I hope that your love for me is strong enough to withstand all the difficulties that it is certain to encounter.

Your Tehani.

Hunter read the letter over and over. His emotions oscillated wildly during his many readings. Hunter did not even understand himself everything that he was feeling. At one point he rebuked himself savagely for having criticized Tehani's behavior with Lance. A moment later, however, Hunter was angry again because she had never made any attempt to contact him.

Hunter went into the main tent and found the matches in their proper place in the cabinet. He took the letter over to the wastebasket in the corner and set it on fire. Tears flowed down his cheeks as Tehani's letter turned into ashes.

EIGHT

"UNFORTUNATELY," HUNTER SAID IN response to Nadine's question, "there are no universally accepted ways to define psychological addiction. Physical addiction is easy. The user simply cannot function without the drug, and will do absolutely anything to obtain the next dose. Marijuana and the other members of the THC family are not physically addictive, per se, but all of us know people who use THC drugs regularly and seem to be high virtually all the time. To me, a person is psychologically addicted when he or she believes that the drug is necessary for him or her to perform everyday functions. Necessity is the key. Suppose, for example, a young woman feels that her personality is boring unless she is stoned or high. If she is convinced that she MUST be high before she can make herself appealing to a possible boyfriend or mate, then she is psychologically addicted. The key words, again, are 'must' and 'necessity.' "

Three more Utopians arrived, bringing the total in attendance to twenty-eight. One of the new arrivals was a young woman who looked vaguely like Tehani. Hunter wondered briefly, remembering the party on the night before her departure, if his erstwhile girlfriend had reached

Mars yet. He felt a dull ache in his heart for a few moments, and then forced himself to return his attention to the meeting.

The attendance for the drug discussions had increased each week since they had started. This was their third meeting, and almost everyone who had attended previously had returned. Ursula's idea to hold the gatherings out on the plaza, rather than in the clinic itself, had turned out to be brilliant. People were more comfortable in the open than in the confines of a tent.

Ursula handed the newcomers the three sheets of printed material that Hunter and she had extracted from the major medical databases. The two of them had spent an entire week reading everything that was available on the subject of recreational drugs on both the Dem and Fed medical sites. They had consciously selected those tracts that contained essential information and were free of sermonizing. The purpose of the discussion sessions was not to stop or even reduce drug use in Utopia. What Hunter wanted to provide was both a venue where the Utopians could obtain the scientific facts about each of the drugs they were using, and a forum for people to discuss the role drugs played in their lives.

The motivation for the sessions had been straightforward. Once Hunter had established himself as a doctor who genuinely cared about his patients, more and more of the Utopians discussed with him, during examinations for routine physical ailments, the patterns of drug use in their immediate family or circle of friends. The questions were generally the same. What was healthy use? What defined abuse? How could they know when it was justified to intercede with a friend or family member? At the same time, after her curiosity caused her to start seeking information on the medical-reference sites, Ursula had become increasingly alarmed about the ubiquitous use of drugs among her teenage friends, and their total lack of understanding of the damage they might be doing to themselves. Both Hunter and Ursula thought the discussion sessions would be a perfect way to address the many drug-related issues confronting the Utopian society.

"All right," Hunter said, as one more participant arrived, "we decided last week that after today we would change the frequency of these gatherings to biweekly, and that Ursula and I would circulate a rough agenda ahead of time to bring focus to the discussions. It's important to point out, however, that it is not our intention to force undue structure on these meetings. We are all here to discuss whatever is on your minds. No questions are out of order. No subject is off-limits. Drugs are an important part of life here on Utopia, and the more we understand about them, the better off we all will be."

Hunter paused for a moment to collect his thoughts. "Last week Mwanda asked me if I could state succinctly what, in my opinion, were the critical factors that separated acceptable drug use from drug abuse. I was not happy with my response last week, so I've been thinking about the subject some since then. Let me say right at the outset that I don't think there exists any foolproof quantitative criterion that can be used to define abuse. Oh, sure, if someone is high eighty percent of his or her waking hours, then it's easy to say that person is abusing drugs. By the same token, someone who uses a drug to become slightly intoxicated once a month would almost certainly be characterized as a nonabuser. In between is a gray area with no clear demarcations between use and abuse.

"For me, in addition to frequency, there is another critical element that separates use from abuse. It is purpose. Why is the person using the drugs? To help put aside temporarily all the worries of his or her hectic life so that it's easier to relax? Okay, that makes sense. In my mind that person is not abusing drugs. To suppress emotional pain, or to escape from difficult unresolved issues with a wife or husband or close friend? That sounds like abuse to me. That baggage, the pain or the unresolved issues, will not go away. If the drug use allows the person to avoid dealing with important facets of his or her life, then there is a danger that a pattern will be established that will shortly become abuse. To summarize, I don't think we can define ironclad measures on this issue. Each case is different, and the purpose of the drug usage is just as important as the frequency."

Hunter surveyed the group. "Are there any questions?" he asked.

A young man named Bradley, in his late twenties, raised his hand. Hunter nodded. "Does the issue of dependency play a role, in your mind, in the separation of use from abuse? I mean, if someone believes that she needs to be stoned to enjoy sex, for example, and doesn't want to have sex unless she is high, isn't she dependent on the drug, and isn't that abuse?"

Hunter shook his head. "Boy, that's a difficult one," he said. "In the generic case, to answer your question directly, dependency is indeed a major factor in separating use from abuse. And if the activity that cannot be performed without drugs is something that is required in order to exist, or to be a contributing member of the band, like eating, or working, then I think we have a clear case of drug abuse. On the other hand, even though we may all want to enjoy sex, it's not a necessity for living. I would think that drug use to enjoy sex is more of a personal choice, and I would be unlikely to categorize it as abuse."

Hunter was a natural interlocutor. His easy, engaging style put people at ease, and encouraged them to ask questions. He was neither didactic nor pedantic, and he very seldom dealt in absolutes. If the answer to a question was factual, Hunter provided the information without embellishment. If, as was most often the case, opinion played a major role in the answer, then Hunter made it very clear that he was offering only his own view, and that it should not necessarily be accepted as the final word. More importantly, Hunter went out of his way to treat each question as if it were significant, so that no member of the audience would ever feel that he was inadequate or stupid.

Ursula was the moderator for the last twenty minutes of each session. It was intended that this portion of the discussion be aimed primarily at teenagers. Adolescent attendance, however, had not grown as quickly as Hunter and Ursula had hoped. At this third session, there were only four teenagers present, and two of them were there only because they had serious crushes on Ursula.

"One of the things that fascinated me when I started learning more about the subject," she said with her usual infectious enthusiasm, "is how much is known about the physical effects of the various drugs. Even the first couple of times that I got stoned, I noticed the next day that I had trouble remembering what had happened the day before. Scientists have shown that a lot of THC—that's the most important mind-altering component in marijuana, hashish, loppies, and reddies—ends up being stored in a part of the brain called the hippocampus, which is where our short-term memory is centered. Regular, excessive intake of THC, especially by adolescents like me, can result in permanent damage to short-term memory function." Ursula grinned, and then suddenly looked as if she were lost. "Now what was I saying?"

The audience laughed easily. Hunter admired the way the girl, who had had no previous practice of any kind in public speaking, was rapidly developing a very effective style. *Just another of Ursula's latent talents,* Hunter said to himself. He had been impressed as well by how quickly she was learning about medicine. She still took a reference folder home to her tent every night. *Intelligent, attractive, enthusiastic,* he thought. *She'll make somebody a fantastic companion.*

Ursula and Hunter were together almost all of their waking hours. They now had breakfast together at the clinic virtually every morning. She seldom left before eight o'clock in the evening. Ursula's duties had expanded considerably. To create time for Hunter to focus on the serious medical problems that arose, such as the rehabilitation of a pirate who had suffered a minor stroke, Hunter had delegated many tasks to Ursula, including the supervision of the interns. He also let her deal with Jake Townsend, whose dependability showed no signs of increasing. Ursula was the main reason that the clinic was functioning smoothly and efficiently, and Hunter knew it.

What Hunter didn't fully realize was that it was Ursula's presence that prevented him from being upset about Tehani's departure. By the time of the third evening discussion session about drugs, she had been gone slightly more than a month. Although Tehani had never played any significant role, except perhaps a fantasy one, in Hunter's life on Utopia, it is very likely he would have sorely missed Tehani if Ursula had not been around so much. As it turned out, Hunter seldom thought any more about Tehani. His life was fine, and Ursula was one of the primary contributors to his contentment.

HUNTER HAD TAKEN off his gown and was preparing for bed. It had been another long day. Ursula and he had seen three patients after dinner, all minor burn victims. There had been a fire inside one of the tents in the far village and the three pirates who had extinguished it had each suffered burns on their hands and arms. Now that the clinic was well supplied, it was a more or less routine matter to cover the burns with the healing unguent and wrap them in bandages.

Ursula had gone home about ten minutes earlier. It was the time of the day when Hunter was almost always alone in his quarters in the main tent. He was therefore startled when he glanced up and saw Bailey standing just outside his bedroom.

"Don't undress," Bailey said. "You're wanted in the hotel conference room."

"Now?" Hunter said. "What for?"

"It's important," Bailey said.

Hunter put on a fresh shirt and followed Bailey out of the tent. The Sun was directly overhead and shining brightly through the dome. Hunter remarked to himself that he had never seen the Sun so large. Although he didn't know the exact orbit of the Utopia asteroid, he had inferred from snippets of conversation that its perihelion was coming soon, and was just barely outside the orbit of the Earth.

As he walked behind Bailey, Hunter felt a rush of nervous excitement. Four visiting pirate chiefs had been meeting in the hotel for more than a week, planning some kind of unique cooperative mission. Three nights before, at a party celebrating the conclave, Lance had proudly introduced the other chiefs to the Utopian band. Goldmatt, the Israeli chief who was widely revered throughout the pirate world, had made a short, impressive speech in which he indicated that an unprecedented, unified pirate endeavor was about to occur. Rango, the Saracen chief, and the chiefs of the Crusaders and the Crocodiles had also spoken briefly. Hunter had been surprised to discover that Rango was actually reasonably articulate.

Just inside the doorway of the hotel, Bailey told Hunter to wait and disappeared down a long hall to the left. Less than a minute later, Lance came around the corner. His demeanor was all business. "Goldmatt wants to talk to you," he said to Hunter.

"Me?" Hunter said, his pulse rate surging. "Why does he want to talk to me?"

"You'll find out soon enough," Lance said. The Utopian chief stared at Hunter for a few seconds and then gave him a friendly pat on the back. "You're doing a hell of a job for us, young man," Lance then said. "I'm embarrassed that I haven't come over to the clinic to tell you that before now."

"Thank you," Hunter said. His mind was jumping about like crazy, trying to figure out what it could possibly be that Goldmatt wanted to talk to him about.

Lance turned around and started into the corridor. "Follow me," he said.

Goldmatt was sitting by himself at the long table in the conference room. Spread out on the table in front of him were maps of the Moon, including a detailed, topographical quadrant around the Aitken crater in the lunar south polar region. The Israeli pirate chief was studying some particular feature on one of the maps when Lance and Hunter entered the room. Goldmatt stood up when he noticed the visitors.

"Come in, come in," he said warmly. "You must be Hunter, the young doctor I've heard so much about. I'm Goldmatt."

He had a firm, meaningful handshake that was bracing. The thirty-seven-year-old Israeli chief was about six feet tall, the same height as Hunter, with a powerful, stocky build and immense forearms. His jet-black beard and mustache were both neatly trimmed. But it was the intensity of Goldmatt's eyes that attracted Hunter's attention immediately. Hunter felt as if the man's dark, expressive eyes were seeing into his soul.

Lance departed and Goldmatt invited Hunter to sit down beside him. "Would you like a cup of coffee, or perhaps something else to drink?" Goldmatt asked.

Hunter shook his head. "No, thank you, sir," he said. Hunter squirmed a little in his chair, belying his nervousness, and then wished he hadn't moved.

Goldmatt took a sip from his coffee, his eyes continuing to gaze at Hunter. "You're probably wondering why I've called you in here, aren't you?" he said.

"Yes, sir," Hunter answered.

"As you heard at the gathering the other evening," Goldmatt said, "we are planning a major mission, an event which, if it occurs, will be of significant historical importance. I am pleased with the progress we have made with most of the plans, but I am not satisfied with the medical support that has been outlined. Both Cooperman and Lance have mentioned, in passing, the terrific job that you have done with the clinic here on Utopia since you arrived. It occurred to me that you might be a valuable asset on our mission."

Hunter didn't say anything. He wasn't certain if he was supposed to speak, or to wait until Goldmatt asked him a direct question.

"I know," the Israeli chief continued, "that you are intelligent, or you wouldn't have been selected as a Covington Fellow, and that you are organized, for that's the kind of skill it takes to run an outstanding clinic. What I don't know is what kind of a man you are. Do you keep your word? Can you perform under pressure? Do you have that elusive attribute called courage?"

Goldmatt now seemed to be waiting for Hunter to speak. "Sir," he said haltingly, "I can't really answer the last two questions, for I've never been either in a pressure-filled situation, or one that really required courage. As for keeping my word, yes, sir, I do. If I tell you that I'm going to do something, I will do my best to complete the task."

"Tell me about your last half hour at the Andromeda trading post," Goldmatt said, taking another sip of coffee.

Hunter took a deep breath, and then recounted the story of his scrape with Franklin in the embarkation corridor and the subsequent close escape from Andromeda. He did not embellish anything, simply stating what occurred in a matter-of-fact fashion.

"Some people might say there was some pressure in that situation, and that what you did required courage," Goldmatt said.

"Not really, sir," Hunter replied. "I didn't have any choice. To me, courage implies that you will deliberately choose danger, for a principle or for a friend, when other options are available."

The Israeli chief liked Hunter's answer. He smiled and toyed with his coffee cup. "How old are you, Hunter?" he asked.

"I'll be twenty-one in another couple of months."

Goldmatt shook his head. "So young, so inexperienced. No wonder you're not politically keen."

"Excuse me, sir?" Hunter said.

"The only negative report I've had on you," Goldmatt said, "was that you're politically naive. I'm just saying that's probably normal, given your age, your experience, and the fact that you were raised on an asteroid out in the boondocks."

Hunter didn't think it was appropriate to say anything in response.

"What do you think of our pirate world?" Goldmatt asked after a brief silence.

Hunter thought for a little while. "I'm not exactly sure I know what you mean, sir," he replied.

Goldmatt chuckled. "Very diplomatic," he commented. "I mean, are you happy here? Or do you want to return to what might be called normal life?"

"I miss my family, sir," Hunter said after a brief hesitation. "And I was looking forward to being a Covington Fellow."

Goldmatt's eyes flashed with anger. "You do know, don't you," he said, "that Chairman Covington is a power-hungry megalomaniac, and a bigot to boot? His social attitudes are directly out of the Dark Ages. In all his years as chairman of the Federation, he has never had one single black person, or a Jew, or a woman as a member of his cabinet."

Goldmatt paused. It was an uncomfortable silence. "I didn't know that, sir," Hunter finally said with difficulty.

The Israeli chief shrugged. "Covington knows," he said, "that if you give the people a strong economy, efficiency, entertainment, and all the newest technological gadgets, they won't be concerned with social issues."

Goldmatt looked away for several seconds. Hunter did not speak. When Goldmatt turned back toward Hunter, kindness was again in his eyes. "I'm considering making you a proposition, Hunter," he said at length. "I'm thinking about asking you to serve with us in a noncombatant role on a very important military mission. If I make the request, and you and I have an understanding that I will do everything in my power to see that you are repatriated after it is completed successfully, would you be able to commit to doing your very best? Even if you do not share our political point of view?"

Hunter didn't respond right away. He realized how important his answer was. "Yes, sir," he said eventually. "I could do that. As long as the mission itself was not something that violated my principles."

Goldmatt smiled and stood up. "All I can tell you is that we are planning a coordinated pirate strike against one of the space powers." He extended his hand. "Will you help us?"

Hunter nodded and shook Goldmatt's hand.

LANCE TOLD HUNTER that he was not to dis-
cuss his possible involvement in the mission with anybody,
for it was not a foregone conclusion. Hunter understood
that other than Lance, only Bailey and Cooperman among
the Utopians even knew that Hunter had spoken with
Goldmatt. His meeting with the Israeli chief was to remain
a secret. Lance told Hunter to continue with his normal
duties at the clinic, and he would let Hunter know when,
or if, he was going to participate in the mission. Lance
didn't indicate any timetable for the decision.

Hunter's excitement didn't subside for several days. Ursula, who had learned to read him well, commented that he
seemed to be different, more energetic even than usual, but
Hunter laughingly told her that she was imagining things.
As part of their plan to conduct physical examinations of all
the Utopian children, Hunter and Ursula started going
daily to the children's center, and if a child happened to be
there for whom they had no medical data, they simply examined and immunized him or her on the spot. Eiki and
the other members of the children's staff gave their full
support.

The children loved Camille. Hunter expanded his training of the bird to include capabilities that would be especially pleasing to the children at the center. With Hunter
and Ursula's help, Camille learned to recognize most of the
children, and to speak their names. One of the children's
favorite games was to scatter throughout the center, and
then see if Camille could find each of them and correctly
identify them.

As it happened, the examination of the children uncovered some health problems that had not been previously
known. In each case, Hunter went to the parents of the

child and explained what had been learned. The father of a five-year-old girl with a leaky heart valve was irritated with Hunter for having examined his daughter without his or his wife's permission. He complained to his subchief, who in turn complained to Lance.

Lance and Hunter had a bit of an argument about the boundaries of Hunter's jurisdiction as a result. Hunter was properly deferential to the chief, but pointed out that he felt it was his duty to make certain that the children of the band were properly cared for. He reminded Lance that he had not again requested permission to conduct a general physical examination of all Utopians. In the end Lance asked Hunter to try to obtain prior permission from the parents in the future, but if that was impossible for some reason, to go ahead and examine the children anyway. At the conclusion of their meeting, Lance informed Hunter that the mission with Goldmatt had been delayed a few weeks for logistical reasons, but he should know about its exact scheduling, and Hunter's possible participation, in ten days or so.

TRICIA HAD DROPPED by the clinic a few days after Tehani left Utopia. Fortunately, Hunter had been very busy at the time and hadn't needed to create a reason why he couldn't be alone with her. Tricia had flirted casually, made some vague reference to her husband's being "inconsolable after losing his plaything," and had left after about half an hour. After Tricia's visit, Hunter had taken Ursula aside and made her promise that she would remain very much in evidence if Tricia ever appeared unannounced again.

Two weeks later Tricia had made another visit to see Hunter at the clinic. Even though Hunter had not been that busy personally, for Jake was on duty handling the scheduled patients, the creative Ursula had kept reappearing with tasks for Hunter that prevented any long, intimate interactions between Tricia and him. Eventually Tricia had grown frustrated and departed.

Roughly six weeks after Tehani had departed, Tricia showed up at the clinic again. It was late in the day; all the scheduled appointments had been completed. Ursula and Hunter were in the process of doing an inventory of their supplies, in preparation for making a new requisition list for Bailey's next trip to the trading post.

"Excuse me, young lady," Tricia had said to Ursula after a few minutes, "would you mind giving me a few minutes to talk in private with Hunter?"

Ursula, knowing that it would not be wise for her to ignore a direct request from the chief's wife, excused herself and left the main tent. Tricia wasted no time. She started kissing Hunter immediately. Hunter, however, did not return her kisses.

"All right," Tricia said, both disappointed and slightly angry, "what's wrong, Hunter? Why are you holding back?"

Hunter smiled wanly and took Tricia's hands in his. "You're a beautiful, intelligent woman, Tricia," Hunter said, "and I find your interest in me very flattering, but if I really kiss you, I will want to make love to you. And if I make love to you, my chances of being repatriated will be significantly reduced."

"You don't know that for certain," Tricia said stubbornly. "Lance will not punish you if I tell him that our affair was my idea."

"I can't take that chance," Hunter said. He came forward and kissed her on the forehead. "If Tehani were still here on Utopia," he said, "I might risk it, for I know that it would be very enjoyable to share some nights of passion with you. But Lance is not in the best of moods these days. He might decide that I am the cause of all his gloom. . . ."

They talked for another ten minutes. Hunter handled the entire conversation very maturely. He injected humor at just the right time, and managed to convince Tricia that she was not being rejected. At the end, at Tricia's request, Hunter kissed her one time. They parted amicably.

When Ursula returned to the clinic, she apologized to Hunter for having left him to deal with the situation on his own. "It worked out all right," he said with a smile. "I don't think she'll be coming back."

The next day, during their breakfast together, Ursula told Hunter that her family was planning a celebration dinner for her seventeenth birthday the following evening. She invited him to attend and he said that he would be delighted.

Ursula showed up for work on her birthday full of energy and excitement. On the top of the computer was a package for her, wrapped in printout from the medical database. The handwritten card accompanying the gift said simply, "To an amazing girl. With affection. Hunter."

Inside the package was a lovely necklace of colored beads that Hunter had found the previous night when he had visited the craft tents in Utopia. He had not had any particular gift for Ursula in mind when he had left the clinic after closing hours, but he had been certain that he wanted it to be something special. A month earlier he had performed a hysterectomy on Wilma, the supervisor of the craft village. She had urged Hunter then to come visit her sometime and see their wares. The necklace had actually been Wilma's suggestion.

Ursula was thrilled with Hunter's gift. She wore it proudly over her clinic gown, explaining to anyone who asked that the necklace had been given to her by a "very special friend." During their lunch break, Ursula asked

Hunter if it was all right for her to go home early so that she could "make herself beautiful" for her special night. Hunter laughingly told Ursula that she was always beautiful, but that she could certainly take the afternoon off if she wanted.

Hunter had visited Ursula's home tent twice before, once to drop off some things she had left at work, and once for dinner at her mother Rebecca's invitation. Ursula's family lived in one of the larger tents in the far village. Both her mother's husbands lived there, as well as Ursula's two siblings, a ten-year-old sister named Clare and an eight-year-old brother, Fernando. Ursula's father was Drake, who had been one of the earliest Utopians and was now over forty. Rebecca's second husband was Luis, a dark, handsome man now only thirty, who had married Ursula's mother eleven years earlier only months after joining the band. It was certain that Luis was the father of Fernando. It was unclear who exactly was Clare's father, for Rebecca freely admitted that around the time of her second daughter's conception she had been having sex with both of her husbands as well as a visiting Crusader.

Hunter arrived while Rebecca and Luis were both outside the tent, tending to the large fowl that was slowly turning as it roasted over one of the community cooking pits. Hunter stopped. "Is that a duck?" he asked.

Luis nodded and smiled. "Where did it come from?" Hunter said. He was aware that chickens were raised in the farming area of Utopia, but he had never before seen a duck on the asteroid.

"Lance loves duck," Rebecca said. She laughed. She was obviously in good spirits. "Apparently a container full of frozen ducks was just one of the items in the deal for your beautiful friend from Cicero. We won this one in a drawing last week."

Ursula came out of the tent when she heard Hunter's

voice. Hunter did a double take when he saw her. Her long blonde hair, which was always tied in some kind of bun on her head at the clinic, had been washed and combed. It fell down her back to a few inches above her waist. She was wearing a simple powder-blue dress the same color as her eyes. Hunter had never seen Ursula in a dress before.

"Wow," he said. "You look great."

Ursula grinned. "You like it?" she said. "Mom and I have been working on it for a week. I was afraid you might not, I mean you're not used to me—"

"It's fantastic," Hunter interrupted.

Ursula took his hand. She led him over to the tent, where the rest of the family and her friend Janie were already inside. Hunter said hello to Ursula's brother and sister, both of whom giggled, and he shook Drake's hand. He then glanced around at the cushions laid out in a circle around the floor of the tent.

"You sit here," Clare said, "next to Ursula." She giggled again.

In the center of the circle were two closed pots containing a vegetable soup and a salad that had been previously prepared. In front of each of the cushions was a large empty bowl, with a spoon inside.

"Would you like something to drink or smoke?" Drake asked Hunter.

"I'll have a grog, thank you," Hunter said.

"Rebecca, Ursula, and I just smoked a joint," Janie said. "Ursula hasn't had any dope for over a month and it damn near blew her head off."

Ursula squeezed Hunter's hand and laughed. "I was nervous," she said. "You know, it's my seventeenth birthday, I have a new dress, and I wanted the evening to be perfect." She looked at Hunter knowingly. "I don't think this would qualify as abuse."

Rebecca and Luis returned to the tent. "The duck will

be ready in five minutes," she said. "Why don't we go ahead and start with the soup before it gets cold?"

The soup was delicious. Made from the fresh vegetables and spices grown under the dome on Utopia, it was hearty with many different tastes. Hunter complimented the cooks. "Actually, Ursula made the soup," Rebecca said. She winked at her daughter. "She has a lot of talents you haven't yet discovered."

Rebecca pulled a joint from a cylindrical container on a shelf in the corner. "This is a night of celebration for me," she said, lighting up and taking a big hit. "My oldest daughter is now seventeen. That only happens once in a lifetime. I intend to have a good time, even if I don't have access to the private tent."

"Why won't you be using the private tent?" Hunter asked innocently, taking a bite of the fresh salad that Ursula had placed in his bowl.

"Because someone else has reserved it," Rebecca said with a randy laugh, "for the whole night. Now that's an optimist, in my opinion."

Out of the corner of his eye Hunter saw Ursula looking at her mother and drawing her finger across her neck in a cutting motion. He understood immediately. Once, at the clinic, he had asked Ursula about the sexual dynamics in her family. Did her mother make love with one of her husbands while the other one was lying on a pad next to them? Did the unchosen one simply sleep out under the dome for the night? Ursula had explained that the family had what they called a private tent, barely large enough for two, and out of consideration for the other spouse, and the children as well, intimate sex acts were constrained to take place there.

Rebecca and Luis brought the roasted duck into the tent. It smelled divine. Luis deftly sliced the meat and laid it on a platter that had been made and fired in the pottery kiln on Utopia. Rebecca carried the platter around and offered it to each of the diners. Hunter asked if it was all right for him to have one of the drumsticks. He took one, placed it in his bowl, and handed Fernando the other. Everyone ate slowly, savoring the food. The conversation was quite lively during the dinner.

"We're going to have a full evacuation drill sometime in the next two weeks," Drake said. "Lance says that if the contemplated mission is successful, we may be attacked by one of the space powers."

Hunter knew that Ursula's father was involved in some way with the security of the band, although he didn't know the specifics of her father's job.

"What are the target parameters?" Luis asked. Luis was a mechanical engineer whose primary responsibility was maintaining the system that purged and conditioned the air under the dome.

"Six hours, everyone near the airlock, priorities assigned and understood," Drake said. "But it'll never happen. We haven't had an evacuation drill in five months. Everyone has become soft." He paused. "I'll be writing discrepancy reports so fast my hand will be hurting for days."

"We don't have the removal capacity, do we?" Rebecca asked. "Wouldn't we need some additional vehicles?"

"That's Cooperman and the communications department's job. Spacecraft from other bands would supposedly be here before the attackers. At least that's the idea of the multiband survival treaty." Drake took a bite of his duck and chewed slowly. "Anyway, our job is to be ready to depart as soon as the vehicles show up."

Rebecca sighed. "It would really be a pain in the ass to have to leave this place," she said. "I'm sure with the allocations we wouldn't be able to take even half our stuff."

"That's the pirate's life," Drake said. "It's very unusual that we have been able to stay in the same place for five years."

"Have you met any of the nine new recruits who came back with Darrell and Chelsea?" Janie asked several seconds later. "They arrived yesterday, six from the UDSC and three transfers from other pirate bands. One of the guys is absolutely gorgeous, but Cooperman says he's gay."

"When's the welcoming party?" Luis asked.

"Sometime next week," Janie said. "Five of the recruits are computer nerds and we need them to start work right away. Lance doesn't want to have a party until we have had a chance to check them out."

After the meal was over, Hunter excused himself and took a trip to the village toilet facility. On his return, he ran into Rebecca, who was halfway through another joint.

"You know my daughter's madly in love with you, don't you?" she said.

Hunter smiled. "I think that may be a slight exaggeration," he said, "but if it's any comfort, I can tell you that I'm reasonably fond of Ursula myself."

Rebecca gazed at Hunter through her dilated eyes. "I hope you're not going to disappoint her tonight."

"Not purposely, Rebecca," Hunter said. He laughed. "Not purposely."

HUNTER AND URSULA left the others and went to the private tent about an hour or so after dinner was over. The sun had just gone down, making the setting more romantic. Ursula was not yet a skilled lover. Her previous sexual encounters had all been with young Utopian males who were not interested in the finesse of lovemaking. But what Ursula lacked in knowledge and experience was unimportant. Her enthusiastic attitude, her genuine affection for

Hunter, and her lack of inhibition more than compensated for any technical shortcomings she might have had.

Ursula was so eager to please that a couple of times during the night Hunter had to ask her gently to desist and explain to her that he was on the threshold of pain from the constant sexual stimulation. At one point, when he didn't respond quickly to her attempts to arouse him, Hunter laughingly suggested that perhaps she should read some of the passages on male sexual capabilities in the medical databases.

Her own pleasure was of no importance to Ursula. She was focused entirely on giving her love to Hunter. Only after many hours, when he finally convinced her that he was utterly incapable of performing again, did she allow him to bring her to a climax. Then she collapsed from nervous exhaustion and fell asleep with her head on his chest.

NINE

THREE DAYS LATER LANCE himself came to the clinic in the late afternoon. "The mission's set," he said excitedly, "and you're part of it. You have a video from Goldmatt."

Ursula looked at Hunter quizzically as he walked out of the main tent with Lance. "I'll explain later," he said. "If there are any serious problems, send one of the interns to find me. Otherwise, handle the patients yourself."

"From this point forward," Lance said, "your work on the mission must take precedence over everything else. Ursula and that lazy bastard Jake can take care of the clinic. It's about time he earned his keep again anyway."

They went to the hotel. "All our planning and coordination for the mission will be carried out over here," Lance said, "away from the rest of the band. That way each of us can give our effort the highest priority."

Lance and Hunter passed Cooperman on the way into the hotel conference room. He greeted them, but walked on by without stopping. Cooperman looked preoccupied.

"He has the second biggest job on this mission," Lance said, referring to Cooperman. "He's the intelligence officer. Only Goldmatt himself, who is the ultimate commander, has more responsibility. And if Cooperman can't deliver on his promises, then we're all dead meat."

Inside the conference room, Lance handed Hunter a data cube. "This is the only decrypted version of this video in existence," he said. "It's not to leave this building. Is that understood?"

Hunter nodded. Lance departed. Hunter inserted the cube in the video player. Goldmatt wasted very little time with a preamble. Hunter's first task? To define the full range of medical equipment and supplies that would be needed to provide optimal support for the operation. Goldmatt also provided a set of baseline allocations for volume and weight for the medical equipment and supplies.

"Start working on this immediately," Goldmatt said on the video. "Of course you will have questions. Ask them as soon as you are certain they are legitimate. We must have the medical-support design completed in one week, so that we have ample time to locate everything that we need."

The second time he watched the video, Hunter took notes. Seventy-five pirates and nine spaceships, including a small two-person medical shuttle, would be involved in the mission altogether. The medical-support planning should cover combat injuries as well as normal medical maintenance to support a two-week journey to the target and back. Goldmatt presumed that each spaceship would be equipped with a standard, low-level survival kit, and that the important and sophisticated equipment and supplies would remain in the medical shuttle. Was that a reasonable assumption? If so, how much volume and mass needed to be allocated to these survival kits?

"What about redundancy?" Goldmatt also asked in the video. Suppose the medical shuttle was itself interdicted. Or that the two medical officers were killed. How should either of those contingencies be handled? Was there some equipment and/or supply set that was so critical that duplicates needed to be carried on another ship, just in case the medical shuttle was destroyed? All his questions were pertinent and thought-provoking. None of them could be answered quickly.

"I am asking these same questions of the other mission medical officer," Goldmatt said at the end of the video. "It is a management technique I discovered long ago. Not only does it increase the likelihood of obtaining the correct answer, but it also allows me to calibrate my personnel. Good luck, Hunter. I'll be waiting for your transmission."

Hunter watched the video a third time and took some more notes before leaving the hotel and returning to the clinic. A patient with a respiratory infection was sitting in the waiting tent when he arrived. Ursula was in the main tent scanning through the medical database for information that would help her select his medication. Hunter stopped and examined the patient, confirmed Ursula's diagnosis of acute bronchitis, with no lung involvement yet, then conferred with her. Their supply cabinet contained two inexpensive all-purpose antibiotics, neither of which was particularly effective against the kind of bacterium that usually caused bronchitis. They had only four doses left of the expensive and difficult-to-obtain bromatine, a genetically engineered antibiotic that could reputedly kill any microbial infection in twenty-four hours with a single dose.

Should they use the bromatine and make certain that no pneumonia developed, even though it could be months before they would have a chance to get a new supply? Or should they recommend rest and one of the standard antibiotics, hoping that the body's natural defenses would do their job? It was the kind of resource-allocation problem that Hunter and Ursula dealt with every day. This time they decided not to prescribe the bromatine and to ask the patient to return for another examination in forty-eight hours.

Hunter handled the next two scheduled appointments while Ursula entered the day's patient records into the computer. When they were finished with the appointments for the day, Ursula waited impatiently for Hunter to explain to her what Lance had wanted. She was not in her usual sunny mood. Her euphoria over her birthday night with Hunter had finally worn off. Ursula was also a little disturbed because Hunter had not yet given her any indication if the evening was simply an isolated event or a major change in the nature of their relationship. Not wanting to hear an answer that she wouldn't like, Ursula had been reluctant to ask him outright.

"So what's up with Lance?" she said while Hunter was removing his gown.

"I don't know yet what I'm allowed to tell you," Hunter said. "To be safe, I think I should say nothing for the time being."

"I heard Lance mention something about the mission," Ursula said, pressing the issue. She knew that she was being difficult.

Hunter looked at her for a few moments and smiled. "I think I'm going to change the subject," he said, "for I certainly don't want to quarrel over this matter." He leaned over and surprised Ursula with a kiss. "How would you like to spend the night with me here tonight?"

Ursula's mood abruptly changed. A broad smile spread across her face. "I think I'd like that very much," she said.

HUNTER AND GOLDMATT exchanged video transmissions for the next five days. At the end of that time the medical-support requirements for the mission had effectively been established. Based on what Goldmatt asked him every day, Hunter was able to infer both in which areas he and the other medical officer were in agreement, and where they had a significant difference of opinion. Hunter showed his flexibility, yielding without argument on what he thought were comparatively insignificant differences. On what he perceived to be major items, however, Hunter defended his position persuasively. Sometimes Goldmatt accepted his recommendations. Sometimes he did not. At the conclusion of the exercise, Goldmatt thanked Hunter, and told him he had handled his responsibilities in a "very adult, professional" manner.

During the almost three weeks between the time that Hunter finished his major planning work and his actual departure from Utopia, Goldmatt contacted Hunter only twice, both times to ask him about specific replacements for medical items that could not be requisitioned for one reason or another. Hunter's primary work focus during this time period was preparing Ursula and Jake to handle the clinic for the three or four weeks that he would be absent. No matter how hard he tried, however, Hunter could not convince Jake that organization and efficiency were critical in the operation of the clinic.

"The interns and I will work around Jake," Ursula said one evening, trying to alleviate Hunter's frustration. "Don't worry. The place will not be a complete mess when you return." She smiled and kissed him. "Besides, I certainly don't want a grumpy bed partner the first few days after you come back."

Ursula and Hunter spent almost every night together during the last week before he departed. Because he didn't really know the details of the mission, and the dangers that were involved, there was no sense of urgency, or fear, in their time together. Ursula never once thought that perhaps Hunter might not return to the clinic and her.

Twelve Utopians, including Lance, Cooperman, Bailey, and Hunter, were taking part in the mission. Of the five bands involved, the Utopians were contributing the least in terms of manpower. Their overall importance to the endeavor was, however, incalculable. Without Cooperman and his four computer wizards, one of whom was the tall, Oriental man with the braided hair named Cho, the mission had absolutely no probability of success.

Until he reached the airlock, and put on his space suit, the reality of what was about to happen had not really struck Hunter. For some reason, in spite of all the video exchanges with Goldmatt, and conversations about the mission with Lance and Cooperman, Hunter had not truly accepted that he was about to leave Utopia to participate in a major pirate operation in space. Suddenly, as he looked through the translucent dome at the space cruiser parked on the dark plains of Utopia, Hunter's stomach began to churn furiously. *Oh my God,* he said to himself, *this damn mission is really going to occur.*

He hugged Ursula, aware that his heart was beating at twice the normal rate. "Are you all right?" she asked. Hunter nodded through his space suit.

The good-byes were short and sweet. Lance had decided not to have a big send-off from the entire Utopian band. Just the families were present near the airlock.

A few minutes later the Utopians were spaceborne. Looking out the observation window, Hunter watched the asteroid recede into nothingness. Cooperman came up beside him in the cramped cruiser.

"So, Tiger," he said with his customary bonhomie, "I bet you never thought you'd see a pirate battle firsthand."

THREE CENTURIES EARLIER, the space satellite in which the pirates met for their final coordination meeting had been one element of a major system designed to protect the Earth from a possible oncoming asteroid or comet. It was located in a trailing heliocentric orbit, a few million miles from both the Earth and the Moon. Its purpose, in those ancient days, had been to scan the heavens for distant objects, using state-of-the-art optical devices of incredible accuracy. The results of its sky survey were then sent to other satellites in the system. These latter soldier satellites were armed with awesome weaponry designed to prevent any asteroid or comet from wreaking havoc and destruction upon the Earth.

The Utopians were the last pirate contingent to arrive at the rendezvous satellite. Less than an hour after their docking was completed, Lance and his men were ushered into the largest room of the satellite, which had been converted by other pirates half a century before into a makeshift auditorium. At the front of the room, beside large boards containing maps of the south polar region of the Moon, Goldmatt stood in his space suit. A bright blue star of David decorated the chest of his suit.

"For most of you," he began, "what I am about to say will be your first exposure to the details of this mission. We have purposely kept the number of people who have had knowledge of our specific goals and objectives to a minimum, to increase the probability that our attack would be a surprise. Based on our monitoring of Dem intelligence during the last week, there is no indication that our presence has been noticed. So far, so good."

Goldmatt walked over to the maps and used a pointer during the next part of his briefing. "This is, of course, the Moon. Our target is here, the Edison engineering complex in the Aitken Basin near the south pole. The Dems have a large ice-processing facility at this location, near an extensive, permanently shadowed crater containing huge deposits of water ice left over from the early cometary bombardment of the solar system. Forty percent of the water used in the Dem cities south of the lunar equator comes from this facility.

"The immediate area surrounding the Edison site is unpopulated. These cold polar regions are inhospitable and don't make good locations for settlements. Edison is, however, often in sunlight, which makes it easy to generate solar energy to supplement the nuclear-power stations.

"The Dem ice facility at Edison is operated mostly by sophisticated robotic machines, which extract the ice-and-rock mix from the craters, transport the material across rugged terrain to the site, heat the combination in a pressurized environment into a slurry that allows easy separation of the water, and then refreeze and store the pure ice. Later the ice is shipped north in mammoth cargo containers. A skeleton human crew of a dozen or so is permanently assigned to the Edison site. These personnel oversee the scheduling of the machines and provide whatever maintenance is required on the equipment."

Goldmatt turned back toward his audience. "For almost a decade, the Dems have been planning a major upgrade of this Edison complex. Over the next year, they plan to replace virtually every significant element of the facility with newer and better components designed in their technological institute in the suburbs of Tranquility." He smiled. "For the past two months the Dems have been shipping all that sophisticated equipment, plus the life-support supplies needed to sustain a hundred-person team for three or four months, to the Edison site in preparation for the work. It is virtually all there now, waiting for the arrival of the engineering personnel who will do the upgrade installation and perform the final readiness tests."

Goldmatt paused to let what he was saying be absorbed by the seventy-odd other pirates in the room. "The great English playwright and poet, William Shakespeare, wrote in his play about Julius Caesar, 'There is a tide in the affairs of men which, taken at the flood, leads on to fortune.' It is a wonderful and fortuitous circumstance that at the very moment all this magnificent booty is sitting there at the lunar south pole, essentially unprotected, no fewer than seven different major pirate bands are within striking distance, three of them because their home asteroids are at or near their closest approach to the Sun. Otherwise, the logistical complexities of a raid such as the one we have been planning would be impossible to overcome.

"Our goal is to load three of our cargo ships with everything they can hold. Our top priorities are the many life-support modules, which contain food, medicine, and extra space suits, and the computer-support containers, with dozens of new processors and all the needed peripherals, plus thousands of spare electronic parts and subsystems. We intend also to take any and all weapons we find, the entire redundant nuclear-power-generating system, the new and improved small robotic rovers and manipulators, and the most portable and widely applicable subsystems from the new ice-processing machines."

Goldmatt grinned and raised his arms. "Are we being ambitious enough?" Most of the pirates saluted him back by raising their arms. "Oh, sure," Goldmatt continued, "we may end up taking several containers full of ice as well, but in terms of value per pound, the rest of the stuff is far more important."

He paced back and forth one time on the slightly raised stage. "Most of you are probably now saying, okay, how are we going to do this? Our plan has four phases. The first phase is a cyberattack that will leave the Edison site without power or any communications capability. According to our plan, the Dem intelligence and defense establishments will not even know anything is wrong during this time, for they will still be receiving what they believe to be the normal stream of housekeeping data from Edison. The chief designer of this entire first phase is Cooperman, a Utopian whose name you probably have all heard mentioned at one time or another. He is without doubt the most creative, brilliant electronics genius I have ever met. Stand up and take a bow, Cooperman."

The pirates applauded in their space suits as Cooperman bounded up on the stage, shook Goldmatt's hand, waved to everyone, and then returned to his seat in the first row. "The attack will not proceed," Goldmatt then continued, "until we have a solid confirmation that virtually all of the goals of the first phase have been met."

Goldmatt outlined the rest of the plan in ten to twelve more minutes. In the second phase, a decoy spaceship would fly directly overhead the Edison complex and fake a crash landing about half a mile away. If the Edison personnel reacted normally, most or all of them would come to the aid of the distressed spaceship. At that point, the third phase would begin. Two warrior ships would land on the opposite side of the complex, move forward, and secure the site for the pirates. In the fourth and final phase of the raid, after the available booty had been cataloged and inventoried, the three giant cargo ships would descend to the surface, one at a time, where they would be filled to capacity by all available hands.

"Each of your chiefs," Goldmatt said at the conclusion of his briefing, "has detailed assignments that they will be going over with you during the next forty-eight hours, as well as a master timetable for the entire mission. I will meet with them the day after tomorrow at noon, Universal Time, here in the station. Assuming that none of the problems that are identified are insurmountable, we will depart from here together, with the official mission clock already in its countdown, six hours later. The estimated time for the decoy overfly, the true beginning of the combat portion of the raid, is slightly more than three days after our departure."

The Israeli chief paused one last time for dramatic effect.

"We are about to embark upon what is clearly the most significant pirate raid ever undertaken. Its ultimate success depends upon each of you. You cannot overprepare for this momentous event. I ask each of you, in the few days before we reach the Moon, to concentrate fully on your personal assignment, and to think about how our lives, and those of our families and friends, will be improved by what we do here. Good luck and Godspeed."

ACROSS THE ROOM, Hunter saw a pirate who reminded him of Derek Sanchez. He was the right size, and the way he moved in his space suit seemed very familiar. Hunter had started to walk in that direction when he was intercepted by a pirate wearing a star of David on her chest.

"You must be Hunter," she said into the microphone in her space suit. "I'm Julie, the other medical officer. Goldmatt told me to find you right away."

"Have you known Goldmatt long?" Hunter asked pleasantly after they shook hands.

"Since I was a little girl," Julie replied. "My father was Israeli chief before Goldmatt." She spoke quickly, without smiling. "Look," she added, "we have a lot of work to do before tonight. Why don't we—?"

Julie was interrupted by a medical question from another Israeli soldier who had walked up beside them. She answered the question hurriedly, her impatience showing, and turned back to Hunter.

"Anyway," she said, "why don't I take you to our cabin on the *Solomon* now, so you can get settled? Then we'll inventory the spacecraft supply kits and prepare for our meeting with Goldmatt and the other chiefs." She glanced at her watch. "Damn," she said, "we have less than five hours remaining."

Hunter looked puzzled. "I'm sorry," he said, "nobody told me that I would be bunking on the *Solomon*."

"Of course," Julie said brusquely. "The medical staff always reports directly to the mission commander. Didn't Lance say anything?"

Julie was shaking her head when Hunter felt a touch on the arm of his space suit. It was Lance. "Good," the Utopian chief said, "I see you've already met Julie. I forgot to tell you before we left our spacecraft to pack your things—you'll be staying on the *Solomon* for the duration of the mission and taking your orders directly from Goldmatt."

Lance apologized to Julie for not having adequately briefed Hunter prior to their arrival at the rendezvous satellite. "We have been spending all our waking hours," he explained, "reviewing the cyberphase with Goldmatt by video, and going over the contingency procedures for the decoy mission."

"How long will it take you to pack your bags?" Julie asked after Lance departed. She was clearly irritated.

"Only a few minutes," Hunter said. "Where should I meet you?"

"Here, at the back of the auditorium," she said. "And please hurry. I don't want us to look like fools in our first big meeting."

On his way to the gangplank that led to the Utopian spaceship, Hunter heard his name being called. He stopped and looked around. Derek Sanchez was approaching.

"Well, I'll be damned," Derek said into his space-suit microphone. "It really is Hunter Blake. What in the world are you doing here?"

"I could ask you the same question," Hunter replied with a grin.

"My answer is easy," Derek said. "The other pirate bands put pressure on the Draconians to contribute the

Darwin to this mission. I am their best, and most expendable, pilot."

Looking over Derek's shoulder, Hunter could see that Julie was watching him. Her body language, even in her space suit, was not difficult to read. "Look, Derek," Hunter said quickly, "please don't think I'm rude. I really would love to talk to you, but I'm in a hurry right now. . . . I'm one of two medical officers on this mission and the other, an uptight Israeli woman, is standing over there waiting for me to return."

Derek turned around and waved at Julie. Hunter winced. "Okay, friend," Derek said, "we'll catch up some other time. But just answer one question before you go. What happened to Tehani? I heard a rumor that she was sold to some obnoxious pirate chief for a handful of diamonds."

"The rumor's not true," Hunter said quickly. "The Saracen chief Rango, who is on this mission incidentally, did try to buy Tehani but the Utopians wouldn't sell. She was repatriated to North Mars eight weeks ago for a large ransom."

"A large ransom?" Derek said with a quizzical look on his face. "Why would the Feds pay a large ransom for a girl? There must be more to this story . . .".

"I really must run," Hunter said, starting to move away. "I'm sorry, Derek. I hope to see you again soon."

WHILE HUNTER WAS unpacking his clothes, Julie read him her compilation of the tasks the two of them needed to complete before their flotilla of pirate spaceships reached the Moon. She was organized and thorough. One of the items on her list was to check Hunter out in the pilot's seat of the small medical shuttle that would be under their control during the mission. When Hunter informed

Julie that he had never flown any kind of space vehicle, she groaned and looked exasperated.

"I told Goldmatt from the beginning," she said, "that this mission required a minimum of three capable medical officers. So what does he do? He assigns two, one of whom is a boy with no pilot training and limited medical experience."

Hunter found both Julie's remark and her general tone offensive. Already he was starting to have a negative attitude about working with her. Hunter knew it would be impossible for them to support the mission properly if they had an adversarial relationship.

He stopped unpacking his clothes and turned around to face the Israeli woman. She was pacing behind him, staring at her hand computer. A scowl was etched upon her face. Hunter guessed that Julie was about thirty years old. He waited until she looked up at him.

"Yes," she said sharply, "what is it?"

"Whether you like it or not," Hunter began slowly, his eyes never leaving hers, "you and I are the medical-support team on this mission. I intend to do the best damn job I can. I presume that's also your intention. It goes without saying that we will be more effective if we cooperate and work together. My limited experience tells me that people are more likely to cooperate if they are treated with respect."

Julie returned Hunter's stare, saying nothing for fifteen seconds. "You are right, of course," she said eventually, almost smiling. "Perhaps I have been a little overbearing. It's just that it's very important to me that this job be done correctly."

"I understand that," Hunter replied. "It's also important to me. . . . By the way," he added, "I consider myself a medical professional. I don't need to be coddled. I do expect, however—"

"Okay," Julie interrupted. "I've got it." She was clearly anxious to finish what was for her an uncomfortable conversation. "Now," she said a few moments later, after consulting her hand computer, "let's talk about the training we're going to give the medreps on the other spacecraft tomorrow. I propose that we lay all the items in their medical kits on a table, then demonstrate and explain each and every item. Many of the medreps will already be familiar with the kits, but this way we preclude any oversights. What do you think?"

"Sounds good to me," Hunter replied.

TEN

THE MEDICAL SHUTTLE WAS a solitary traveler against a magnificent backdrop of sparkling stars. It had been at least five minutes since Hunter had last seen any lights from their flotilla.

"All right," Julie said, turning off the thrusters, "this flying machine is yours. Take it back to the *Solomon* and park it in the bay."

"Do you think I'm ready for this?" Hunter asked nervously. He was surprised by the tension he was feeling.

"No, not really," Julie said. "But we're running out of time. We're scheduled to leave the satellite this afternoon. The cyberphase begins the day after tomorrow. You must solo at least twice before we reach the Moon."

Hunter changed the scale on the navigation display until the radar blips indicating the pirate ships appeared. They were about fifty miles away. On the display the pirate spacecraft were clustered near the abandoned satellite that was their temporary headquarters. Hunter marked a target spot in the vicinity of the flotilla. The flight computer informed him no more than a second later that it had finished computing a fuel-optimal trajectory. After looking at a graphical representation of the attitude time history for this flight path, and verifying that no thermal or other shuttle system constraints would be violated by the proposed profile, Hunter activated the automatic control system. The thrusters on one side of the shuttle first turned the spacecraft around. Soon thereafter the remainder of the thrusters started operating and the medical shuttle accelerated toward its destination.

Hunter's initial excitement subsided as the vehicle automatically followed the trajectory stored in its computer. The small, two-person cockpit was silent for almost a minute as the shuttle zoomed through the blackness of space.

"Goldmatt is certainly an amazing man," Hunter said at length.

"He's an absolute original," Julie responded. "My father recognized his exceptional talents right away. That's why he stepped aside and handed Goldmatt the chief's mantle almost six years ago."

"Is your father still alive, then?" Hunter asked.

"Oh, yes," Julie said. "Very much. He's Goldmatt's chief advisor and manages most of the day-to-day activities of our band. It's a good thing, too. Our mission commander is not very interested in the minutiae of everyday existence. His forte is grand, sweeping projects like this one."

A soft bell began to ring in the cockpit, indicating that one of the shuttle subsystems was not operating inside its usual engineering limits. Hunter immediately moved all the pertinent information about the suspect subsystem to his primary monitor. The left-front thruster pair was depleting fuel at an above-normal rate, suggesting that perhaps there was a valve leaking propellant out into space.

Interactively interrogating the flight computer, Hunter learned that the estimated leakage rate was not large, and that the thruster pair would still have ample fuel to complete the nominal flight profile. He took no other action.

"Would you have shut down the left-front thruster pair?" he asked Julie after a few seconds.

"Probably," she said. "But I'm a pessimistic pilot. Whenever any subsystem even sneezes, my first reaction is to pull it off-line if I can. I'm always afraid that the underlying condition will rapidly worsen."

Hunter moved the information about the suspect thruster pair off his primary monitor. Fifteen seconds later he heard a different soft bell, this one indicating a possible problem with some element of the communications subsystem. By the time Hunter had the communications display in front of him, the bell had become a Klaxon siren. A major failure had occurred. The display indicated that the nominal radio receiver had failed and that the fault-protection system in the shuttle had automatically switched to the backup receiver.

Hunter acted immediately. "Hello, CCC," he said after switching on his radio transmitter. "This is the medical shuttle on a training run. We now have an alert condition. Our primary receiver has failed."

"Copy that, medshut," was the response. "I'll inform engineering and have them ready. Are you coming right in?"

"ETA three minutes and ten seconds," Hunter said.

"OK, medshut. Watch out on the way. The Utopians are testing contingency procedures in the decoy vehicle."

"Thank you, CCC. Medshut over and out," Hunter said.

Hunter requested a diagnostic analysis of the failed receiver from its own self-test algorithm, but he didn't understand either the displayed schematics or the summary of the malfunction. He told himself that this was not a major issue, since they were not far from their destination.

Julie said nothing during the receiver anomaly. Nor did she say anything a minute later when a navigation alert sounded. Another space vehicle, presumably the decoy mentioned by the pirate command and control center, was flying an active, unpredictable trajectory in the volume of space through which the medical shuttle was programmed to fly. The display informed Hunter that he had several choices, including moving the target point to another location and recomputing the nominal flight profile, or even assuming manual control of the vehicle.

Hunter studied the navigation display and turned on his transmitter again. "CCC," he said, "medshut here, coming in to dock with the *Solomon*. Would you please patch me through to the decoy?"

"Roger that, medshut. Go ahead."

"Bailey, can you read me? This is Hunter in the medical shuttle."

"Hunter, you asshole. Are they really letting you fly?" Bailey laughed. "I guess I'd better warn everybody."

"This is my first sortie," Hunter replied. "I'm headed for the *Solomon* to dock. Would you mind hanging back a minute or two so I can safely approach on auto?"

"For you, I'll do it," Bailey said. "Be careful during the manual docking. On my first time I almost ripped the door off my vehicle."

Five minutes later, when Hunter was back inside the Israeli spacecraft and had removed his space suit, he realized that he was exhausted. He had expended an enormous amount of energy on his test flight. During the docking, in fact, when he had scraped the shuttle lightly against one of the walls, his pulse rate had jumped so high that a biological out-of-tolerance bell had sounded.

"Not too bad," Julie said to Hunter as he finished folding and bagging his space suit. "Do you want a detailed debriefing now, or do you want to wait a few minutes until you've had time to relax?"

"Go ahead," Hunter said.

"My overall observation is that your progress is exceptional," she said. "There's no doubt that you would quickly become an excellent pilot if we had time for a proper training regimen. Unfortunately we don't have that luxury. You may be required to fly in combat conditions in only a few more days."

She paused for a moment. "I have only two significant criticisms of your test flight. First and foremost, Hunter, you need to learn to relax. Pilots who are as physically and psychologically stressed as you were during this flight tend to panic more readily in combat. I realize that this was your first flight and it's understandable that you were nervous. But next time concentrate on staying calm.

"Secondly, you must manage your time more efficiently. Prioritize your tasks. Don't try to stay busy all the time—if you do, you might miss something important. It wasn't necessary, for example, for you to try to troubleshoot the failed receiver. That was a waste of time."

Julie smiled. "Overall, as I said, it was pretty good. Better than I expected in fact. You clearly learn quickly."

"I HAVE NOW received reports from all the chiefs on your preparation status and I must say I'm impressed. From every point of view our readiness is excellent. Thank you all very much."

Goldmatt was sitting in his chair in the command and control center aboard the *Solomon*. His video message was being transmitted to all the pirates participating in the mission. The battle network had been implemented by Cooperman and his team the first evening after everyone had gathered at the satellite.

"The night before the battle of Agincourt a thousand years ago," Goldmatt continued, "the English king Henry V supposedly made a brilliant, motivational speech to his troops that was a major factor in their victory over the French the following day. I am not going to make such a grand speech this evening. It has been obvious to me, during my interactions with many of you over the last few days, that no additional motivation is necessary to spur this group into battle. In fact, I am a little concerned that some of you may be too focused on our forthcoming action. For that reason I recommend that tonight each of you try to push thoughts of our raid temporarily out of your mind. Read a book. Play a game. Listen to music. Try to obtain a peaceful night's rest."

Goldmatt smiled. "For myself, I intend to divert my attention by playing a game of Intellego with Cooperman. I understand that his colleague Cho has made it possible for all of you to follow the game on our spacecraft computers. Maybe some of you will be able to point out my mistakes to me later."

Goldmatt became serious again. "As I told you when we first arrived at the satellite, what we are beginning tomorrow, if successful, will have a major impact, both on each of our individual lives and on space history. Never before has any pirate military action been attempted on such a grand scale. I believe we are ready. I thank each of you for the discipline and focus you have demonstrated these last several days. Have a good evening."

ON BOARD THE *Solomon,* the six Israelis who gathered to watch in the small lounge area unanimously predicted that Goldmatt would trounce Cooperman in the Intellego game. "I don't think Goldmatt has been beaten in a two-person game in the last ten years," a young man named Menachem said, "not even in network competition against Fed and Dem grand masters."

"He'll wipe Cooperman out in less than an hour," another Israeli proclaimed confidently.

Hunter was the lone non-Israeli among the kibitzers in the *Solomon* lounge. His colleagues in the audience were eager to bet on the outcome. Although Hunter was not a gambler by nature, he had personally witnessed Cooperman's skills at Intellego and could not imagine how anyone could defeat him. Much to the delight of the Israelis surrounding him, Hunter accepted a few bets on the game.

The monitors in the *Solomon* lounge allowed the audience to follow all aspects of the game, including both Cooperman's and Goldmatt's private boards. The early portion of the match was uneventful, as each player made primarily positional moves, conservative in style, waiting for the other to make an obvious mistake. There was no advantage for either player at the time of the first break, forty-five minutes after the start of the game.

The Israelis pressed Hunter to raise his bets. He eventually agreed, even though he barely had enough money on hand to cover all the wagers. Just before play recommenced, Julie entered the lounge. "How's it going?" she said to nobody in particular.

"About even," Menachem replied. "Cooperman is definitely not a pushover."

Hunter stood up to give Julie a place to sit. "Do you play Intellego?" he asked her.

She nodded. "Goldmatt taught me when I was a teenager," Julie said.

"She's a superb player," one of the other Israelis said. "One of the best in our band."

Fifteen minutes deeper into the game, with almost all the pieces deployed on the cubic playing field, Cooperman made what appeared to be a mistake. Three moves later, after a couple of exchanges, Goldmatt emerged with what looked like a clear advantage. The Israelis around Hunter crowed.

"Do you want to pay now?" Menachem said. "Or wait until Cooperman resigns?"

"I'll wait," Hunter replied, astonished that Cooperman had overlooked a combination that even he might have foreseen.

Julie leaned over to Hunter. "Don't give up yet," she whispered. "Did you notice how little time Cooperman took making that last move? Although I can't see where he's headed, I wouldn't be surprised if that was some kind of clever sacrifice."

Julie was exactly right. Cooperman had enticed Goldmatt into overextending his offensive. After another ten moves, during which Cooperman deployed his remaining pieces on the cubic playing field and consolidated his attacking position, the overwhelmed Goldmatt resigned.

The kibitzers in the *Solomon* lounge were amazed. "That was unbelievably brilliant," one of them said. "Whatever else this Cooperman is, he's certainly an Intellego genius."

"After watching that game," Menachem said, "I must say I'm glad the guy's on our side in this battle."

Hunter accepted the payments for the wagers gracefully. The Israelis wanted to know more about Cooperman. Hunter told them about the electronic birds, the security systems, and the attack on Cicero. "I guess you're pretty confident that the cyberphase of our mission will be a success?" an Israeli pirate asked Hunter.

"In a word, yes," Hunter replied.

ALL ELEMENTS OF Cooperman's cyberattack worked perfectly. Long before the pirate flotilla reached the Moon, the observational defenses of the UDSC had been completely vitiated. The Dems manning the control center outside their capital city of Tranquility never had an inkling that an attack was taking place. Until several days afterward, in fact, the Dems didn't realize that the telemetry they received throughout the raid from their far-flung network of antennas and orbital observation posts had, in fact, actually been generated on board pirate spacecraft. Cooperman and his team hacked into the processors at each of the Dem observation stations, rendered them useless, then substituted new outgoing data streams, with proper telemetry formats, of course. At the Tranquility Control Center, it looked as if everything in the observational network was working properly, and no untoward events were recorded.

A similar technique was employed as the flotilla drew within striking range of the Edison complex. First a complicated command signal was transmitted from the pirate spacecraft to the receivers at Edison. This signal was coded to look exactly like a command generated at Tranquility and routed to the polar engineering site through a lunar satellite. Embedded in the command constructed by Cooperman and Cho was a virus designed to disable all internal Edison power and communications systems at a specified future time. When that specified moment arrived, and the site lost all power and communications capability, the pirates began transmitting a data stream to the Dem satellite stationed over the lunar south pole. This data set mimicked the normal telemetry usually generated at Edison. Again, back at Tranquility, there was no indication that anything unusual was occurring at the south polar site.

After Cooperman verified that the cyberattack had accomplished all its goals, Goldmatt delivered another video message over the network connecting all the ships in the pirate flotilla. "I am delighted to inform you," Goldmatt said, his excitement obvious, "that every part of our cyberphase has been completed successfully. We are now ready to strike. Prepare to descend to the Moon."

BAILEY WAS THE pilot of the decoy vehicle. Three other Utopians were with him, all heavily armed. As planned, Bailey flew the small decoy directly across the Edison complex at an altitude of only a few hundred feet, purposely wobbling in roll and yaw during the actual overflight, and made what looked like a crash landing half a mile beyond the primary engineering structures of the site.

As predicted, a pair of Edison residents were outside in their space suits during the overflight, working to determine what had happened to their power and communications systems. The two Dem engineers immediately rushed back into the large structure that was their residence. No more than five minutes later seven individuals in two open, all-terrain vehicles hurried in the direction of what they believed to be a crashed spacecraft.

Goldmatt followed all this activity from the mission command center on board the *Solomon*. A pirate raid the previous year on an interplanetary transport had yielded delicate sensors capable of observing objects a few feet in size from a distance of a thousand miles. It had been a straightforward systems-engineering task for Cooperman to provide the rest of the electronics to build a multispectral telescope using the sensors. From the *Solomon,* everything occurring at the Edison site could be viewed in both the visible and infrared wavelengths.

Soon after Goldmatt saw the two vehicles leave Edison, he ordered the two warrior ships to land on the opposite side and secure the site. One of his assistants reminded Goldmatt that the last personnel manifest from Edison had indicated thirteen people in residence. "There should be six people left in the buildings," Goldmatt said over the network to the chiefs of the Saracens and the Crusaders. "Flush them out and contain them in an open area. Try to avoid violence, if possible, but make certain that your orders are followed."

Standing on the observation deck of the *Solomon* in his space suit, Hunter watched the two warrior ships break from their formation, one at a time, and depart for the surface of the Moon. "Let's go," Julie said to him a short while later. Hunter followed Julie to the back of the spacecraft. The medical shuttle was in the parking bay just on the other side of the airlock.

Julie strapped herself into the pilot's seat and went through her preflight checkout routine. When she was finished she took a slow, deep breath. "Are you ready, partner?" she said.

Hunter had adjusted the small telescope mounted on the panel in front of him while Julie was checking out the shuttle. "I guess so," he said. He grinned. "As ready as I'll ever be."

Julie glanced at Hunter and smiled behind her faceplate. "I have a few butterflies, too," she said. "But I'm certain they'll disappear as soon as the action begins."

She waved at the pirate on the platform next to them and the attachments were released. The bay door opened and they eased out into space using the small vernier engines underneath the shuttle. Julie turned slightly to the left and flew parallel to the body of the *Solomon*. When they passed the nose, she turned on her transmitter.

"Medshut under way," she reported. "Headed for observation post."

"Roger that," was the reply.

The Moon was directly in front of them. The two warrior ships were tiny dark dots between their shuttle and the Moon. Julie activated the main thruster sets, selected their target destination from the navigation display, and put the shuttle on autoguidance.

The Moon grew steadily larger in their view as the

medical shuttle flew toward its assigned location roughly two thousand feet above the Edison complex. There the spacecraft would hover for the duration of the mission, ready to be dispatched on short notice. From that vantage point Julie and Hunter would have an excellent view of everything that was happening.

By the time Julie and Hunter reached their hovering point, the warrior ships had landed safely and two separate platoons of pirates were cautiously approaching the outbuildings of the Edison site. There was no sign of activity anywhere else. To their right and below them, several hundred yards away, Julie and Hunter could see the mission commander's shuttle. Goldmatt and half a dozen Israeli pirates, all battle veterans, formed the contingency team. Their assignment was to handle any unexpected developments during the raid.

Hunter turned the telescope so that it was focused on the area where the decoy ship had landed. The two Edison all-terrain vehicles were parked nearby. Zooming the lens, Hunter saw that a group of people were tightly clustered in an area between the decoy ship and the Dem land vehicles. Surrounding them were three figures with weapons extended.

"It looks as if Bailey has accomplished his part of the mission," Hunter said to Julie. "I can't tell for certain but—"

"This is your mission commander," they heard Goldmatt say on the battle network. "Bailey reports that he has seven prisoners in custody at the decoy site. Rango and Tristan, proceed to secure the main complex."

Hunter watched as the Saracens and the Crusaders moved into the area around the large building where the Edison permanent staff lived. Rango and four other pirates approached the structure, their weapons in their hands.

Rango pulled out a large flashlight, opened the door, and disappeared inside. Two more pirates with flashlights followed the Saracen chief, while the other two remained outside guarding the door.

"Look," Julie said suddenly. Off to their right, the commander's shuttle was streaking toward the surface of the Moon. Hunter hurriedly adjusted the telescope to see what was happening. Near the decoy site, one of the all-terrain vehicles was racing back toward the Edison site. Behind the vehicle, Hunter could see three bodies lying on the ground. Goldmatt's spacecraft fired two missiles at the speeding Dem vehicle. The first exploded harmlessly several meters in front of the ATV. The second hit the front of the vehicle, the force of the explosion temporarily lifting it off the surface. Moments later the ATV was lying on its side with its driver, unconscious or dead, stretched out on the ground nearby.

"Medshut," Julie and Hunter heard Goldmatt say, "get down here. We have casualties."

Julie flew the shuttle to the surface manually, landing on a flat area between the Edison site and the overturned ATV. Before the medical team reached any of the bodies, they were joined by Goldmatt and Bailey.

"Ernest has a broken leg, or worse," Bailey said, pointing at a Utopian pirate lying on the ground forty yards away. "His suit is fine, but he's in a lot of pain. He was run over by that idiot over there."

"Two of the Dems are dead," Goldmatt added, "but this driver still appears to be breathing."

"We'll take Ernest back to the *Solomon* right away," Julie said. She hesitated a moment. "What do you want us to do with the Dem driver?"

Goldmatt thought for a few seconds. "Rango," he then said over the battle network, "status update, please."

"The four prisoners are now outside with the Crusaders," Rango replied. "We're completing our search of the living area."

"Are all the life-support systems there functioning properly?" Goldmatt asked.

"Yes," Rango said. "The captives were not wearing suits when we entered. One of them did say something, however, about the emergency life support lasting only a day or so at the most."

"All right," Goldmatt said, "we're bringing in one of their injured. How long before you're finished with the search in that building?"

"Only a couple more minutes," Rango said. "Then we'll spread out and search the rest of the site, building by building. If those other two are here anywhere, we'll find them. Based on what we found here, however, my guess is that only eleven staff members spent last night in the residence structure."

"Thanks, Rango," Goldmatt said. "Let me know if you find anything else."

The mission commander switched off the battle network. "Take Ernest back to the *Solomon* and make him comfortable," Goldmatt said to Julie. "We'll put the injured Dem in one of his own beds and have Hunter look at him. Everything here seems to be under control for the time being."

Julie examined Ernest and concluded that Bailey had been correct in his assessment. Ernest's leg was broken in two places. His other injuries were minor. Julie administered a painkiller through the suit with one of the injection guns and waited a few seconds to verify that the self-repair functions of Ernest's suit were working properly.

Hunter, meanwhile, confirmed that the unconscious Dem was indeed breathing. He then helped the others load

Ernest into one of the compartments at the back of the medical shuttle. After stuffing as many supplies as he could into his medical bag, Hunter pulled one of the cots out of the rear of the shuttle and hauled it over to where the injured Dem was lying.

Bailey stayed to help Hunter carry the unconscious Dem back to the main Edison complex. Along the way, Bailey explained that his prisoners near the decoy vehicle had bolted simultaneously on a set signal, almost as if they had had an established procedure for dealing with the situation. "The two dead Dems attacked us, forcing us to kill them, while the others fled. One of them reached the ATV and ran over Ernest, who was trying to stop the escape."

BY THE TIME Hunter and Bailey reached the main part of the Edison site, the final phase of the raid was already under way. A dozen pirates were systematically dismantling the nuclear-power-generating station and loading it, part by part, into the first of the cargo ships. Tristan and his Crusaders were guarding the eight prisoners. The Dems had been herded into a makeshift corral between their residence and the electronic warehouse.

Cooperman and Cho, who had recently come to the surface, had just finished their quick inventory of the contents of the warehouse. They were excitedly detailing what they had found to Goldmatt. "This is a fantastic bonanza," Hunter heard Cooperman say. "It's beyond my wildest expectations. This stuff must be worth more than a hundred million dollars."

One of the Crusaders helped Hunter carry the cot containing the injured Dem, who had still not stirred, through the door and the airlock of the Edison residence structure.

Once inside, Hunter removed his space suit. The Crusader departed after the unconscious man was placed on a bed in the first available apartment.

Hunter stationed his flashlight on a shelf, so that the beam covered most of the man's body. Slowly, carefully, he removed the man's space suit and gave him a thorough examination. His vital signs were more or less normal. There were no broken bones. The Dem did have three nasty bruises on his head, however, including a huge swelling an inch above his left temple. Hunter's tentative diagnosis, which he reported first to Goldmatt and then to Julie on their special audio channel, was that the man had at least a severe concussion, with possible internal hemorrhaging.

"If there's not anything else you can do for the guy," Julie said, "then why don't you leave him, and let one of the warrior pirates stand guard? You might be needed outside at any time. And it's going to be another fifteen minutes before I finish setting Ernest's leg. It's broken in two places and really is a mess. I'll let you know as soon as I'm done."

Hunter followed Julie's suggestion and phoned Goldmatt. Five minutes later one of the Saracens entered the residence structure. Hunter recognized the man as soon as he removed his space suit. He had been one of Rango's colleagues at the Andromeda trading post. The man introduced himself as Hammer and then stared pointedly while Hunter checked the patient a final time.

"Don't I know you from somewhere?" the man asked when Hunter was finished. "Your face looks very familiar."

"It's possible," Hunter replied, starting to put on his suit. He decided not to say anything else for the time being.

While Hunter finished dressing, the Saracen watched him with a perplexed expression on his face. At length Hunter excused himself and headed back outside. Goldmatt greeted him almost immediately. "I have a job for Julie and you," he said, "as soon as she returns to the surface. The infirmary storeroom is full of medical supplies and equipment, far more than we anticipated. I don't think we have enough cargo capacity to take everything. I'd like you two to check what's there, and tell me what we could leave behind if we only had room for two-thirds of the stuff. Can you do that? I'm assuming, of course, that we won't have any need for medical support somewhere else."

"Yes, sir," Hunter said. He was about to inform Goldmatt that Julie wouldn't be back for another twenty minutes or so when Rango walked up beside Goldmatt. The Saracen chief looked directly at Hunter but showed no sign of recognition behind the faceplate of his helmet.

"We have completed our search," Rango said to Goldmatt. "And have found no sign of any other residents. Should we make a second sweep?"

"No," Goldmatt replied. "I don't think that will be necessary. I'd prefer that you and your men lend a hand with the loading of the cargo. Even though I'm fairly certain nobody knows we're here, the faster we finish loading all this booty, the better I'll feel."

Rango returned immediately to his men. Hunter also helped with the loading until Julie returned. By that time the first cargo ship was filled to capacity and prepared to depart from the surface. Julie checked in with Goldmatt, then met Hunter near the infirmary.

"We have only thirty minutes, partner," she said. "Goldmatt wants all the medical stuff to go on the second ship."

"All right," Hunter said. "Let's get started."

ELEVEN

THE INFIRMARY WAS A squat, metallic, rectangular building on a small rise about fifty yards from where the Edison personnel lived. The small atrium, just beyond the door, served as the airlock. Julie and Hunter passed through the atrium and then, after checking the ambient environment to make certain the building's life-support system was working properly, deposited their space suits near the door.

The front part of the infirmary looked like a typical hospital room, with three twin beds, surrounded by the usual monitoring equipment, on either side of a central aisle. On the right side were three thick windows with an unobstructed view of most of the site. Dim light filtered through the windows. At the back of the large open room was an area for the doctors and nurses, with workstations on one side, and washbasins, refrigerators, and small supply closets on the other. The storeroom was in the back half of the building, separated from everything else by a wall that ran from the floor to the ceiling. Access to the storeroom was through two doors, one on either side of the room.

Julie and Hunter opened the left storeroom door first. All they could see were the sides of two metallic shelf cabinets, which had been pushed together so that they blocked the entrance entirely. They next crossed the room and opened the door on the right side of the infirmary. The storeroom was completely dark. A wide aisle led from the door into the storeroom. Julie and Hunter turned on their flashlights and illuminated the aisle.

The dark aisle extended all the way to the back of the building. On both sides were sets of shelf cabinets that rose to the ceiling. Each individual shelf was protected by a transparent plastic cover that had been zipped shut. Julie and Hunter walked a short distance into the storeroom and unzipped one of the covers. Drugs were neatly arranged in columns, starting an inch or so behind the edge of the shelf. Each bottle or container had its own label. There was also a small placard affixed to the shelf at the front of each column, indicating generically what was stored in that particular location.

Julie and Hunter browsed down the aisle separately for a minute or two, unzipping a few more covers to examine the shelf contents in greater detail. "Look at these anesthetics," Julie said excitedly to Hunter, shining her flashlight on one shelf. "There are some here I've never even heard of."

"This entire section," Hunter shouted back, gesturing at a rack of four shelves in front of him, "is all eye medicines. Can you imagine that? I bet this storeroom has a broader inventory than any of the pharmaceutical supply houses in Centralia."

Julie walked back to where Hunter was standing. "Everything is so neat and well organized," she said. "It's obvious that it was recently stocked."

"I agree," Hunter said. He glanced down the dark aisle again. "But how are we going to decide what to leave behind in the next twenty-five minutes? Everything here could be useful."

"I suppose we begin by canvassing the entire storeroom,"

Julie said, "and categorizing what we find. Maybe during that process some kind of prioritization will become obvious."

She pulled out her hand computer as Hunter and she moved slowly down the aisle toward the back of the building. They turned left after checking the contents of the shelf cabinet against the back wall, and then left again into an aisle that ran parallel to the aisle leading to the door. Julie and Hunter followed this second aisle all the way back to the front wall. Hunter stopped at each group of shelves and described the contents. Julie made notes on her computer. At Hunter's suggestion, she also used a mapping subroutine to create a diagram of the storeroom as they went along.

The two pirate medical officers, both of whom were accustomed to dealing with severely limited supplies, expressed continual amazement at the completeness of the storeroom inventory. Each time they encountered a new supply of medicines, they would comment to each other on the variety of the contents. "I feel a little like Alice in Wonderland," Julie said at one point.

The fourth aisle over from the door did not reach all the way to the back wall. Roughly halfway down the length of the storeroom, this aisle was blocked by a large, deep shelf cabinet containing a variety of medical electronic systems. A narrow aisle leading to the left ran almost to the far wall, where it, too, was blocked by another large shelf cabinet similar to the one in front of them. Julie and Hunter followed this aisle to its conclusion, continuing to categorize the contents of the shelves. At the end, they stopped and shined their flashlights in each direction. This new aisle, which ran parallel to the original long aisle in front of the doorway, was very short and extended no more than one-third of the way along the length of the storeroom.

"This is bizarre," Hunter said. "I feel as if I'm in a maze.

I know that there have to be different-size cabinets and shelves, but surely there must have been a more orderly way to lay out this storeroom."

Julie looked at her watch. She was becoming increasingly nervous. "We've been in here for fifteen minutes and we haven't even started on the details of our assignment. If we continue at this pace—"

"I have a suggestion," Hunter said, gently interrupting her. "Why don't I finish the mapping and the categorization? You can backtrack slowly, examining the shelves in more detail and thinking about how we'll determine what not to take." He smiled, sensing Julie's anxiety. "Remember one possible solution, admittedly not the best, is just to take a fixed percentage of what's on each shelf."

Julie returned his smile and gave Hunter her hand computer. "Goldmatt would love that," she said. "Can you imagine what he would say to us?"

"Just trying to be helpful," Hunter said puckishly. He was already on his way down the aisle.

"I AM ABSOLUTELY certain that I didn't make a mistake," Hunter said to Julie. "I was so shocked that I did the entire mapping a second time, from scratch. I ended up with the same result."

They were both staring at a diagram on her hand computer. "If your map is correct," she said, pointing off to the left, "then somewhere over in that direction roughly fifteen percent of the storeroom is sealed off with shelves on all four sides. With no entry from any of these aisles."

Hunter nodded and raised his flashlight beam to the ceiling. "Look up there," he said. "What do you see?"

Julie stared above her for several seconds. "I give up," she then said. "What am I supposed to see?"

"Even though the tops of the shelf cabinets are touching

the ceiling," Hunter said, "there's nothing in the design pattern of the ceiling that suggests a particular layout for the storeroom."

"Okay," Julie said with a frown. "So what?"

"I believe we're in a reconfigurable room," Hunter said with youthful enthusiasm. "On one or more of those workstations in the hospital area, I bet there's a design subroutine that automatically moves these cabinets around."

Julie almost started laughing. "Hunter," she said, "we're running out of time and you're being obtuse. Why are you making such a big deal out of this?"

"Why would doctors," Hunter said, pointing at the computer diagram again, "or better still, a medical director, deliberately configure a storeroom with an area sealed off like that?"

"Because he or she wanted to limit access to certain kinds of medicines or supplies," Julie answered, "and didn't have a large enough vault or secure area."

"*Voilà,*" Hunter said with a huge smile.

"So I guess you don't want to give Goldmatt our report," Julie said, shaking her head, "until we at least try to find out what's in that blank area on your map."

"Exactly," Hunter said. "The best stuff might be there."

Julie thought for a moment, then smiled at Hunter as she activated her transmitter. "Goldmatt, this is Julie," she said.

"Go ahead," was the answer.

"This storeroom is a gold mine," Julie said. "We're having a hard time determining what to leave behind. If we're not going to be able to take everything, we'll need a few more minutes."

"Our cargo capacity is definitely oversubscribed," Goldmatt said. "I just told Cooperman to ditch ten percent of his electronics horde and I thought he was going to cry. . . . I'll give you fifteen more minutes."

"Okay," Julie said. "We'll be finished by then."

Julie looked at Hunter after she switched off her transmitter. "So what is it that you propose we do?" she asked.

"Why don't you inspect the perimeter of the sealed-off area," Hunter suggested, "looking for any breaks, or switches, or security locks. I'll go back in the other room, fire up one of the computers, and see if I can find anything."

"Talk about looking for a needle in a haystack," Julie said.

"I know," said Hunter. "But what if something really spectacular is in there? Isn't it worth a try?"

Julie glanced at her watch again. "Ten minutes," she said. "No more. Then we spend the last five minutes agreeing on what we're going to say to Goldmatt."

"Okay by me," Hunter said.

HUNTER CHOSE THE workstation that was closest to the storeroom door on the right. Fortunately, the operating system on its computer was a familiar one. For a few minutes Hunter conducted a normal search through the files and found nothing related to the storeroom except a map, which was exactly like the one he had developed on his own, and an exhaustive inventory. He noted that the inventory modification history indicated that it had been updated and expanded three times in the last two months.

Julie reported that she had searched the entire perimeter without finding anything and was going to spend the rest of her time marking the shelves with colored tape. Hunter and she had agreed on a three-level priority system on a shelf-by-shelf basis. Sixty-five percent of the shelves in the storeroom would be marked with white tape, indicating top priority. Twenty percent would have blue tape, second priority, and the remaining fifteen percent would be marked with red tape. Julie and Hunter would try to convince Goldmatt that only the contents of the red-marked shelves should be left on the Moon.

Hunter sat at the computer trying to figure out what to do next. Reasoning that it was likely that the physical configuration of the storeroom had recently been changed to accommodate all the new items that had been shipped from Tranquility, Hunter accessed the diagnostic database where historic information was always stored. Eventually he managed to find a timed listing of recent computer activities described by meaningless alphanumeric references. With his time running out, Hunter began searching through this list, item by item, looking for anything associated with the configuration of the storeroom.

At length he found a juxtaposed pair of storeroom diagrams dated three weeks before the pirate raid. One of the maps showed the storeroom as it currently existed. Hunter assumed that the other diagram represented the previous configuration of the storeroom. He noticed immediately that in the other diagram there was also a sealed-off area, but it was in a markedly different location. Unable to read the alphanumeric gibberish that probably described the computer operations that resulted in the changed configuration, Hunter created a generic "Undo" command and tried to link it to the diagrams in many different ways. One of his attempts worked, for he suddenly heard the sounds of mechanical motion coming through the open door to the storeroom.

"Julie," he yelled on their private network. "I've done it. Watch out. The shelf cabinets are moving."

When Hunter repeated the call and Julie still didn't reply, a terrible picture of her being crushed between two metal cabinets surged into Hunter's mind. He raced into the storeroom, realized that he didn't know where he was going, and dashed back to the computer to print out the two configuration diagrams. Hunter then returned to the storeroom, flashlight in hand, and headed for the location where he thought Julie had finished her perimeter survey.

Every few seconds he tried calling Julie on the network and yelling her name in the dark. As time passed, Hunter began to fear the worst. He chastised himself mercilessly for not having said something to her before he made any attempt to change the configuration. His shouts for her became more and more desperate.

"Hunter," he heard Julie say at last, "I'm over here."

"I'm coming," Hunter shouted, his excitement surging. He raced down a dark aisle, heard her voice again, and zoomed around a corner. Suddenly everything went black.

THE WATER WAS cold on his face. As soon as he was conscious, Hunter was aware of a horrible, throbbing headache. He reached back instinctively and felt the huge knot on the back of his head. His hand was covered in blood.

There was a light in his eyes. Hunter realized he was lying on a floor somewhere, but he had no idea where. "He's waking up," he heard a voice say.

He tried to sit up but everything went black again and Hunter fell back on the floor. More water splashed on his face. "Get up," the same voice commanded. Hunter managed to sit up and lift his head. The pain was excruciating.

"You're pretty damn clever," the voice said. "Too clever for your own good."

Hunter put a hand out to shield his eyes. The light moved a little. Hunter could see a man in front of him. He was in his late thirties or early forties, with a full head of hair that was graying at the temples. Hunter couldn't recall ever having seen him before.

"Where am I?" Hunter said.

"Where you shouldn't be," was the answer.

Slowly his mind began to function again. Hunter remembered that he had been in the infirmary storeroom at the Edison site on the Moon. "Julie?" he said with difficulty. "Is Julie all right?"

"For the time being," the man said. "As long as you do exactly what we tell you." He had a thick wooden chair leg in his hand.

Hunter closed his eyes and tried to concentrate. *What is happening here?* he asked himself. He had no answers. Hunter opened his eyes again and turned his head slightly to the side. In the dim light he saw Julie sitting on the floor in front of another man. This man had his left arm around her waist and appeared to be holding something against her throat with his right hand.

"This scalpel is razor-sharp," the second man said nervously. "One wrong move out of you and I'll slit her throat."

Hunter focused on Julie and the second man. He was young, in his twenties. He had blond hair and an average build. Hunter's impression was that the man was near panic. Julie seemed remarkably composed, considering the circumstances. "They were hiding in the sealed-off area," she said. "When the shelves—"

"Shut up, bitch," the man holding Julie said. "We'll do the talking here." He pressed the scalpel against her neck. Hunter saw a trickle of blood run down.

"Stand up," the man opposite Hunter said. He was now brandishing a large scalpel in his right hand. The wooden club was in his left hand. "We need to move to where we can see the door," he added. The man turned to his colleague. "Martin, you go first with the woman. If this guy makes any trouble, kill her."

The four of them wound their way through the dark

aisles of the storeroom and into the front section of the infirmary. Along the way the two men argued inconclusively about what they should do with their prisoners. It was obvious from both their voices and their mannerisms that both men were very frightened. Hunter, whose headache was starting to subside, concluded that the men were probably professionals, doctors or engineers or pharmacists perhaps, and had never been in a situation like this before.

The man with Hunter walked over to one of the windows as soon as they were back at the front of the infirmary. "God damn it," he said angrily, "there must be a hundred of them out there." He stared out the window for several seconds. "They're loading our new equipment and supplies into containers and taking them away." He turned to Hunter. "Who are you, anyway? Fed commandos?"

"They're probably both trained killers, Ed," the man named Martin said in an agitated voice. He was already starting to sweat profusely. "That's why we should strap them to the beds right now."

"In a minute," the older man replied. He returned to the aisle between the beds where the other three were standing. He waved his scalpel at Hunter. "Call your commanding officer," he then said, "or whoever is in charge of your bunch of thieves. Tell him that if anyone so much as opens the door to this building, we'll kill both of you."

Hunter didn't move. "Go ahead," Ed admonished, moving closer to Hunter with the scalpel, "make that call now."

"Don't do it, Hunter," Julie blurted out. Ed walked over and slapped Julie hard in the face while Martin held her. "We told you to keep your mouth shut," he said.

"Before I call," Hunter said in an even tone after he had calmed his anger, "I would like to recommend that you assess your situation. If you go back to the window, and look outside again, you'll see that all your associates are unharmed. They are corralled together on the far right. They are simply being detained until we complete our mission."

Hunter paused before continuing. "Needless to say, your position will be extremely precarious if I call my commander and tell him that you're holding us hostage in here. It would be much better for you if you simply surrendered to us now and joined your colleagues outside. I can assure you that you will not be harmed."

"You're full of shit," Martin exploded after a brief silence. "Do you really expect us to believe that . . ."

"Hold the girl," Ed said. "I want to have another look."

Ed walked toward the window. Hunter and Julie made eye contact. "Look, someone's coming," Hunter suddenly yelled. Martin turned his head toward the door. As he did Julie jammed her elbow into his groin and hit the floor. Hunter reached Martin an instant later, grabbing and twisting his right arm and forcing him to drop the scalpel. Martin swung at Hunter with his left arm and missed. Hunter hit Martin in the face and knocked him across one of the hospital beds.

Meanwhile Ed, wielding both the wooden chair leg and the scalpel, charged at Hunter from the rear. Just before he reached Hunter, however, Julie scrambled up from the floor and distracted Ed with a tackle attempt. Ed managed to stay upright, but his wide pass with the scalpel only nicked Hunter on the back of the shoulder. While Hunter finished off the hapless Martin with two more punches, the furious Ed hit Julie in the side of the face with his club. She slumped back to the floor, blood running out of her mouth.

Hunter turned to face Ed, the chair leg, and the scalpel. The two men circled briefly and then Ed lunged and missed. Moments later, when an errant wooden leg clanged against the end of one of the hospital beds, Hunter hit Ed in the side of the head with a full right cross. The momentum of the blow carried Ed into one of the beds. He stumbled while trying to regain his balance and fell on the floor. Hunter disarmed him and bent down immediately to tend to Julie.

She was bleeding both from her neck and the inside of her mouth. "The first guy cut me when I elbowed him," she said, "but it's not serious. I think the other bastard broke my jaw."

Hunter kept an eye on the two men while he was turning on his radio. "Goldmatt," he said, "we've had some excitement in here. We've found the other two Dems, but Julie's hurt. Please send some men in here right away."

JULIE INSISTED ON sitting in the cockpit of the medical shuttle instead of stretching out in one of the rear compartments. She held her jaw in place with her left hand throughout the flight.

Hunter took off from the surface manually. He increased his altitude little by little, giving both Julie and him a long parting view of the Edison site. Below them the pirates were almost finished loading the *Darwin,* which was the third and final cargo ship.

Julie leaned forward slowly. "What an incredible day," she said with difficulty.

"Goldmatt said we took almost half a billion dollars' worth of goods," Hunter said.

"And we don't even know the value of that stuff from the sealed-off area of the storeroom," Julie said.

"Hell, I don't even know what we got," Hunter said. "By the time I was finished telling Goldmatt our story, everything was already packed into containers."

As the Moon receded in front of them, the crescent Earth appeared on the horizon. Julie and Hunter both stared at the blue planet in silence for several seconds.

"Once upon a time," Hunter said quietly, "our ancestors all lived there."

"Once upon a time," Julie echoed, "there was a land called Israel, on the shore of the Mediterranean, where the Jewish people had their own nation." She sighed. "That was my father's dream, you know. To re-create in space the Israel of Earth that flourished in the twentieth and twenty-first centuries. Goldmatt, I believe, has higher aspirations."

Hunter turned the shuttle slowly around so that the nose faced toward the stars. They flew in silence for almost a minute. "Thanks for everything," Hunter said simply.

He felt Julie's hand on his forearm. "You were superb," she said.

TWELVE

HUNTER HAD NEVER FIXED a broken jaw before. Fortunately, Julie was quite familiar with the procedure. Soon after they reached the *Solomon,* she wrote each step for Hunter to follow and showed him exactly which tools and materials to use. She also carefully explained to him how the healing process would be accelerated by the introduction of the special compounds that would cause the two parts of the bone to fuse.

Goldmatt visited Julie soon after Hunter had finished setting her jaw. The Israeli chief seemed strangely subdued after his overwhelming triumph. While they were standing together beside Julie's bed, Hunter congratulated Goldmatt on the success of the mission.

"It was almost too easy," Goldmatt said in response. "In some ways I wish that we had encountered more difficulties." He thanked Hunter for his contributions, especially for the way he handled the confrontation with the two Dems who had been hiding in the infirmary.

Following the mission design, each spacecraft in the pirate flotilla departed from the Moon in a slightly different direction. After one day, when there was no evidence of any pursuit from the Dem fleet, Goldmatt authorized each of the chiefs to change course and head for the designated postmission rendezvous location, an abandoned storage depot that had once been used as an interplanetary refueling station in the early days of space travel.

En route to the rendezvous point, a full inventory of the spoils of the raid was completed on each of the three cargo ships. Goldmatt announced on the network that the booty exceeded the mission goals "in every parameter." He then informed the pirates that the individual participation bonus from the raid would be sixty percent greater than originally promised. On board the *Solomon,* a loud, impromptu party developed soon after Goldmatt's announcement. Hunter drank so much with his new Israeli friends that he had a massive headache the next morning when he awakened.

Julie recuperated quickly. By the second day she no longer needed constant pain medication. Julie and Hunter played Intellego (she was better than he, but not by much) and when her jaw was not hurting too much, they talked about their dreams and their past experiences. A genuine friendship, doubtless strengthened by the bond their experience together on the Moon had created, developed between them. On the day before they arrived at the rendezvous station, Hunter told Julie all about Tehani, including his confused feelings for the woman who had captured his heart. Julie confided that she had never married because no suitor could compare with Goldmatt. She admitted that she had had a serious crush on the Israeli chief when she was a teenager, and had wept in her room the day Goldmatt had married.

She smiled at Hunter. "You know," she said, "he never did one single thing to encourage me, either before or after his marriage. He was always, well, just Goldmatt. Handsome, brilliant, caring—how could I not love him?"

Julie and Hunter were still talking about their personal

lives when Goldmatt called their room. He asked Hunter if he would please come up to Goldmatt's office in the control center. "I know what this is about," Julie said to Hunter. "Please listen carefully to what Goldmatt has to say."

Goldmatt's office had a window that looked out on space. When Hunter arrived, the Israeli chief was standing at the window with his back to the door. "Come in," Goldmatt said when he heard the door open. Hunter walked over and stood beside the mission commander at the window.

"That star out there—actually it's two stars, but we can't separate them from here," Goldmatt said, pointing, "is Zeta Reticulae. Do you know what's special about Zeta Reticulae?"

"Yes, sir," Hunter replied. "It's a binary star system with both stars more or less like our Sun, and at least three planets in what astronomers call the 'habitable' zone."

"Excellent," Goldmatt said with a wide smile. "And do you think there's life or intelligence living on those planets?"

"I think it's possible, sir," Hunter said. "At any rate I think it's virtually certain that there exists life and intelligence out there somewhere, but maybe not as close as Zeta Reticulae."

Goldmatt sat down in one of his small office chairs and motioned for Hunter to sit in the other. Hunter met the Israeli chief's intense gaze and recalled their first meeting on Utopia.

"Someday, Hunter," Goldmatt said, "our species will again send out interstellar explorers, just as we did in the twenty-second century. Maybe those future spacecraft will finally confirm that we are not the only putative intelligence in the universe."

"I don't know what 'putative' means, sir," Hunter said.

Goldmatt smiled warmly. "You really ARE exceptional," he said. " 'Putative' means 'supposed,' but has a tinge of irony. My use of the word in the previous context suggests that I may have some doubts about the intelligence of our species."

Hunter sat silently, returning Goldmatt's friendly gaze, for several seconds. He again had the feeling that Goldmatt's piercing eyes were seeing into his soul. "I have delayed having this conversation with you," Goldmatt said, "because I wanted to give you plenty of time to absorb your experience of the last week. What did you think of our venture on the Moon?"

"I thought it was remarkable, sir," Hunter responded.

Goldmatt chuckled. "Another perfect answer. . . . My boy, you are both a delight and an enigma. You are intelligent, capable, trustworthy, and yet . . ." He stopped, obviously thinking, and then smiled warmly again. "Your twenty-first birthday is coming soon, isn't it?"

"Yes, sir. In less than a month."

"I'm certain you remember," Goldmatt said shortly afterward, in a tone that indicated to Hunter that he was finally going to discuss the real reason that he had called Hunter to his office, "that back on Utopia I promised that if you participated in this mission, I would do everything in my power to see that you were repatriated."

"Yes, sir," Hunter said.

"I will honor my promise, Hunter," Goldmatt said, "if that is your choice, but first I would like to try to persuade you that going to Mars may not be in your best interests." He paused briefly. "I have already conferred with Lance about this. We have mutually agreed that we should do our best to convince you that you would have a better, more exciting, and more challenging life if you remained in the pirate world."

Goldmatt waited several seconds to see if Hunter wanted to say anything. "I am prepared to offer you, with the blessing of Lance and some of the other chiefs as well," he then continued, "an extraordinary opportunity as a sort of medical ombudsman for our pirate bands. You would travel from settlement to settlement, establishing the kind of clinic that you set up on Utopia, choosing and training young people to manage the clinics after your departure. . . . You could have your home base with the Utopians, or with us in Israel, or some other place if that would suit you. Your participation bonus from this mission would allow you to live comfortably for the foreseeable future."

Hunter was overwhelmed. He could hardly believe what he was hearing. His thoughts and emotions became an entangled, jumbled mess. Goldmatt was waiting for him to say something.

"Sir," Hunter said at length, temporizing, "you realize, don't you, that I'm not a legitimate doctor, just a certified paramedic?"

Goldmatt frowned slightly. "Yes, of course," he said.

That was a stupid comment, Hunter said to himself. He glanced out the window. He realized that he was not prepared to give any kind of answer. Hunter looked back at Goldmatt. "I'm flattered, sir, truly flattered," he said. "But I don't know what to say."

"Okay," Goldmatt said. "I'll take that as a positive sign. How long do you need to make a decision?"

"May I have twenty-four hours, sir?" Hunter said.

"Certainly," Goldmatt replied. "Longer if you want. If it's acceptable to you, I will not start making any arrangements for your repatriation until you have made a definite decision."

Hunter started to stand up from his chair. "Before you go," Goldmatt said, "I would like your permission to make some comments that are probably unfair, and could be construed as an attempt by me to prejudice your decision. Nevertheless . . ."

Hunter sat back down. "Okay, sir," he said.

"I have no way of knowing exactly what will happen when you reach Mars," Goldmatt said. "I presume you will still be regarded as a Covington Fellow, but that is far from certain. What is certain is that you will be interrogated by the Fed Defense Ministry, and perhaps by the ASP as well. It is highly likely that you will be forced to justify your behavior as a pirate prisoner, even though you were kidnapped, and that if you mention one word about your participation in our raid on the Moon, you will probably be indicted for treason. I presume also you do know that it's against Federation law to take part in any military operation not under Fed auspices."

Hunter didn't respond. He continued to listen carefully.

"Here's one other factor that I believe you should consider," Goldmatt said. "In our world you have been treated as an adult. You have been given major responsibilities, which you have handled magnificently. The opportunity we are offering you would be an extension of your adult role in our world. On Mars, even as a Covington Fellow, you will still be a neophyte, a learner, not a doer. Your counsel will not be highly regarded. Your opinions will not have much weight. In short, you will be a late adolescent again."

There was a protracted silence in Goldmatt's office. "Thank you, sir," Hunter said eventually. "I appreciate both the offer and your comments." The two men shook hands and Hunter left the room.

HUNTER WAS IN a daze when he returned to his cabin. Julie was out, so he had the room to himself. He plopped down on the bed on his back and stared at the ceiling. His mind was swarming with images from his life. Tehani, his father, Goldmatt, Ursula, even Chairman Covington all appeared briefly. Behind all the images a voice kept repeating, over and over, "What are you going to do?"

He had never considered purposely choosing not to return. Only occasionally had he thought that perhaps the pirates might try to entice him to stay. Several times, on Utopia, he had pondered what his life might be like if no arrangements were ever made for his repatriation, but in those moments he had always assumed that he would be remaining with the pirates because he had no choice. This was different. Goldmatt had made him an unbelievable offer. Hunter himself couldn't have designed a more perfect assignment. It was important, challenging, everything he wanted. He wouldn't have an equivalent job in the Federation for at least five years at best.

But how could he willingly embrace a life in which the likelihood that he would ever again see his family was close to zero? Hunter squirmed on his bed. *My father would never understand,* he said to himself. *My mother would be brokenhearted.* He imagined a scene in his home on Cicero in which an official informed his parents that attempts to negotiate his return had been abandoned because their son wanted to remain a pirate. His parents were dumbfounded. His mother was crying. Hunter truncated the imaginary scene because it was too painful for him.

And what about Tehani? Hunter thought. He had very strong, often contradictory emotions about Tehani. Even though he was still angry with her for her behavior on Utopia, Hunter could not contemplate not ever being with her again without sharp feelings of pain. *Is it possible that I still love her?* he asked himself. He remembered the words in Tehani's note just before she left Utopia. *And does she really love me? Or is it just convenient for her to say that in case she ever needs me again?* His thoughts trailed off. He asked himself if he were crazy. Why was Tehani even a factor in his decision? Nevertheless, Hunter knew that it would be difficult for him to make a choice that would absolutely keep Tehani out of his life forever.

But I do respect and admire Goldmatt, Hunter thought, trying to balance his evaluation process. *And the job he described would be fabulous. I would certainly never be bored. I would have an immediate positive impact on people's lives.* Hunter conjured up a picture of himself as the medical ombudsman for the pirates. He imagined an adventurous life, full of space travels and fascinating people. Goldmatt, Tristan, even Rango would all seek his advice. He would be special, now, in a fast-paced adult world.

Hunter smiled to himself. *I would marry Ursula, I guess,* he thought. *We would work together. She would bear my children.* Hunter remembered Ursula's adoring smile, her enthusiastic kisses, her desire to please him in bed. He felt a powerful surge of desire for his blonde pirate girlfriend. *If I had never met Tehani,* he said to himself, *then Ursula would be perfect.*

Hunter had not noticed that Julie had entered the room. "Sorry to bother you," she said. She pointed at the desk. "I've left something for you," she said as she departed from the cabin.

Curious, Hunter rose from his bed and went over to the desk. Julie had left a square holographic box, about eighteen inches on a side, sitting on the top of the desk. Hunter opened the lid. The still, three-dimensional scene illuminated inside the box showed a thin, gray-haired man sitting in a chair in a library. He had a book on his lap. There was something about the scene that was vaguely familiar to Hunter. He thought he had seen it before, perhaps during his secondary-school days.

Hunter activated the controls on the side of the box. The old man picked up the book on his lap and began to read in a raspy voice.

Two roads diverged in a yellow wood,
And sorry I could not travel both,
And be one traveler, long I stood,
And looked down one as far as I could,
To where it bent in the undergrowth.

Then took the other, just as fair,
And having perhaps the better claim,
Because it was grassy and wanted wear. . . .

Tears eased into Hunter's eyes as he watched and listened to Robert Frost read his most famous poem. Five hundred years had not dimmed the poignancy of the poet's words. Hunter wiped his tears away. *What should I do?* he asked himself. *What should I do?*

"I shall be saying this with a sigh," Robert Frost said, "somewhere ages and ages hence . . . Two roads diverged in a wood and I . . . I took the one less traveled by . . . and that has made all the difference."

THE **SOLOMON** WAS one of the first pirate ships to reach the depot. The depot consisted of two long docking fingers, one on either side of a spherical structure that enclosed a single large room. The fingers were 180 degrees apart. They would have formed a single line if the sphere had not been in the middle. Huge cylindrical fuel-storage tanks, empty for centuries, were attached to the sphere along a line perpendicular to the two docking extensions.

The rest of the pirate spacecraft arrived at the depot during the next sixteen hours. They docked on both sides of the central sphere. Soon after the last spacecraft reached the depot, Goldmatt announced over the network that the final celebration for the mission would be held on the *Darwin* and would begin in exactly three hours. "After the party," the Israeli chief said, "our mission is officially over. Let me congratulate each of you one more time on a job well done. We have shown that it is indeed possible for pirate bands to cooperate on a major project."

When Hunter returned to his cabin on the *Solomon* after eating dinner, he was surprised to see that not only was Julie wearing a simple white dress that accentuated her slim body, but also she was actually putting on makeup in preparation for the party. Hunter walked over beside his cabinmate, who was critically surveying her image in the tiny mirror above the washbasin. She had removed the bandage around her face and jaw that she had been wearing since the raid. "What do you think, partner?" she said lightly, turning around to Hunter.

"You look lovely," Hunter said.

She laughed. "What else could you say?" Julie said. She brushed her short dark hair back on the side. "There will be seventy men and six women at this party," she said. "Two of the women are as burly as most of the men. My odds will never be better."

Hunter smiled. "I thought you told me that romance was not important to you," he said.

"It's not, really," Julie said. She shrugged. "But every now and then I do like to be reminded that I'm a woman, and that some men find me attractive." She glanced over her shoulder at her reflection in the mirror and smoothed out the back of her dress. "It doesn't make a lot of sense," she added. "Most of the time I'm content being Julie the cantankerous medical officer. Then I'll have a short period of time where I have this yearning, as if I'm missing something." She laughed. "Maybe it's nothing more than normal sexual desire. Anyway, usually one night with a man is enough. The next day I can't remember why I wanted to be intimate with someone in the first place."

Hunter put on a clean shirt and brushed his hair. Julie and he then walked together through the lounge of the *Solomon* and retrieved their space-suit bags from the shelves near the front of the room. Menachem and another young Israeli joined them in the airlock. "It's going to be hard to return to normal life after all this excitement," Menachem said into the microphone of his space suit while the four of them were waiting for the pressure change to take place.

Outside, on the dock walkway, they followed the foot traffic toward the sphere. The *Darwin* was parked on the opposite side. Passing through the dark, empty central sphere, Hunter found himself wondering what it must have been like, centuries before, when the early interplanetary cruisers stopped briefly to refuel. He imagined a busy room, full of furniture and equipment and depot officials and travelers going from the Earth to Mars, or vice versa. The voyagers would share a drink, exchange stories, and then return to their ships. Did these ancient intrepid spacefarers ever think, even for a minute, that this depot, like most human creations, would serve its purpose only for a finite period of time and then become nothing more than a ghostly reminder of the impermanence of human endeavors?

Hunter laughed at his philosophical meanderings as he departed from the central sphere and approached the *Darwin*. He knew the reason why he was having such thoughts. It was normal for him, when he was in the throes of a major decision, to attempt to minimize the importance of his own personal life by reflecting on grand, sweeping concepts that made his own dilemma seem insignificant by comparison.

Goldmatt was stationed just on the other side of the

Darwin airlock, in the area where visitors removed and bagged their space suits. He greeted each and every pirate by name and thanked him personally for his efforts. Goldmatt gave Julie a big hug and asked about her jaw. "My, don't you look beautiful," he then said admiringly. "Your mother would be pleased."

Soon after they entered, Menachem and Julie went over to the side of the common area to obtain a drink. Hunter was left alone temporarily. Since his group had been one of the first to arrive, the room was mostly empty. While Hunter wandered slowly around the *Darwin* common area, his mind was bombarded by memories of his joyous days with Tehani immediately after the kidnapping. He had not realized that returning to the location where he had fallen in love again would trigger such vivid recollections.

Hunter walked all the way to the back of the common area and stood by the large thick door that led out of the pressurized part of the spacecraft. To his left were the computer workstations where Tehani and he had studied space history together, watched movies, and had their first passionate kisses. For a moment, Hunter was transported back to those days with Tehani and he could hear her voice, see her face, and feel her kiss. An overpowering ache spread through his body.

"Would you like to take a tour?" he heard a voice behind him say. "The stars are really fabulous from the rear struts."

Hunter spun around. Derek Sanchez was standing there, smiling. The two men hugged briefly. "How have you been?" Hunter asked Derek as soon as he had composed himself.

"Not too bad," Derek said. "The Draconians have turned out not to be total jerks, which is what I had feared. They provide me with food, clothing, and good sex as long as I do my assignments." He shrugged. "It's not perfect, but hey, what life is?"

"Any indication when, or if, you'll be released?" Hunter asked.

Derek shook his head. "I brought the subject up again about a month ago. The Draconians explained that they are doing so well in the cargo business with the *Darwin*—they use the ship to transport pirate shit from place to place—that they are going to expand and obtain other spacecraft. Naturally the two pilots I have already trained will be critical in that expansion." Derek smiled at Hunter. "Besides, at the moment I'm in no hurry. With my participation bonus from this raid, I'll be king of the hill for a little while. There's a foxy waitress at a trading post near our settlement who has promised me a week of sheer delight. In exchange for a little bauble, of course."

"Of course," Hunter said, laughing easily with his friend.

"And what about you?" Derek asked. "Are you going to be repatriated soon?"

Hunter decided there was no harm in sharing with Derek the latest developments in his life. He briefly summarized his situation, describing both the offer that Goldmatt had made for him to become a medical ombudsman for the pirates, as well as the promise that had accompanied Hunter's agreement to participate in the raid. He admitted to Derek that he was having a hard time making a decision.

"I'm impressed," Derek said. "You've obviously done well. My guess is that you'll be fine either way. But where does Tehani fit into this picture? You and she reminded me of Romeo and Juliet the last time we were all together."

Hunter described what had happened on Utopia, including Tehani's liaison with Lance and his relationship with Ursula. Derek listened patiently. "I know what I would choose," Derek said when Hunter had finished telling the story, "but I'm not as trusting and idealistic as you are. I've lived too long and known too many women."

"What would you do?" Hunter said with a quizzical expression on his face.

"I'd take the pirate offer in a heartbeat," Derek said, "and live happily ever after with fair Ursula. It's obvious she adores you. Tehani may or may not love you. But based on my experience, I can damn near guarantee that she'll break your heart. Maybe more than once."

Cooperman's voice on the loudspeaker system interrupted them before either Derek or Hunter could say anything else. "Hear ye, hear ye," the diminutive genius said. The two men walked quickly back into the main part of the common area, which by this time had become quite crowded with celebrating pirates. Cooperman was standing on top of the dining table holding a microphone in his hand.

"This is a wonderful evening for all of us," Cooperman said when the crowd quieted down, "and I for one intend to enjoy it to the fullest. We have almost everything we need to make tonight perfect. We have had a glorious victory, we're among friends, we have good booze to drink, and we have excellent drugs to heighten our pleasure. We're missing only one critical component of a night to remember—sex."

Cooperman glanced at his watch. He was clearly enjoying being the center of attention. "With apologies to those of you who either embrace celibacy and/or find prostitution distasteful, I am delighted to announce that in about an hour a spaceship will dock at this depot. Inside will be ten of the most beautiful and accomplished prostitutes in space, imported from Phobos especially for this occasion."

The roar from the pirates drowned out the end of Cooperman's sentence. It took a few minutes for order to be restored. "Listen up," he said when he could finally be heard over the noise. "It's important that everyone understands how this is going to work. Our team from Utopia has paid to transport our special guests here, and guaranteed them a minimum return, but we have not paid for their individual attentions. My friend Cho, however, with the permission of Goldmatt and the other chiefs, has set up a spreadsheet on the computer that will allow each of you to pay your sexual partners directly out of your participation bonuses. The terms for each liaison have been negotiated a priori, depending both upon the kind of sexual favor that is requested and the duration of your individual session."

Cooperman held up a few sheets of paper. "My men will be distributing these to all of you as soon as I am finished. The detailed terms, including the procedure for reserving the cabins, or the shower area, as well as photographs of our guests, are all here. Please read all the rules carefully. Note that absolutely no abuse of our guests will be tolerated. Anyone misbehaving will be fined severely and removed from the premises. The chiefs have assured Goldmatt and me that they will police their own band members. Note also that all sexual activity is to occur here on the *Darwin*. Our guests have been guaranteed safe passage to and from their spaceship, whenever they want to go, and have been assured that their vehicle will be off-limits to all mission personnel at all times."

Cooperman looked at Cho, who was sitting at the other end of the dining table with a laptop computer in front of him. "Have I forgotten anything?" he asked. Cho shook his head. "Oh, yes," Cooperman then said, addressing the pirates again, "there is one other thing. For those of you who do not want to party in this kind of atmosphere, ample liquor, as well as the usual variety of entertainments, will be available in the lounges on board the *Solomon* and the *Independence* throughout the evening."

———

"SEE ANYTHING YOU like?" Julie asked. She walked up to Hunter while he was looking at the photographs that Cooperman and his men had handed out.

"They're more attractive than I expected," Hunter said. "And younger."

Julie forced a smile. "Photographs are always flattering," she said. "And fantasies are always better than the real thing."

She looked out of sorts. "What's wrong?" Hunter asked.

"Nothing really," Julie said. "I guess I should have expected something like this at a pirate party. But orgies aren't exactly my cup of tea."

Hunter showed Julie the photos of the two males who were part of the anticipated contingent of prostitutes. "Neither of these men interests you?" he asked. "It says here that they are bisexual, and enjoy sharing pleasure with both men and women."

"They're not my style," Julie said. "The last thing my self-confidence needs is to have sex with a man who would prefer to be with a guy." She looked across the room. "Now Vittorio, that dark-haired Crocodile hunk over there avidly studying the photos with his buddies, definitely stirs my juices. He would have been worth a quick tumble. But he lost all interest in me as soon as Cooperman made his announcement."

"Sorry, friend," Hunter said.

"Hey, it's not your fault," Julie said. "It's not the last time I'll be disappointed." She pulled at her drink container. "So are you going to stay?" she asked.

"I haven't decided," Hunter said. "I thought it would be interesting to be here when our special guests arrive."

"Oh, yeah," Julie said. "There's nothing funnier than a few dozen horny bastards slobbering over some hot snatch.

And do you intend to stay for the fights, too? I guarantee you there will be a few. Sex, drugs, and alcohol are a lethal mixture for men. They revert to their most primitive states."

"You sound disgusted," Hunter said.

"Maybe a little," Julie said. "It's at times like this that I realize why I decided to remain single." She turned to listen to an argument that was rapidly escalating over at the dining table, where a Saracen and an Israeli were apparently trying to reserve the same girl at the same time. "See," Julie said, "it's already starting." She glanced at Hunter. "I'm out of here, partner. If you want to play some Intellego later, you know where to find me."

THE ARRIVAL OF the prostitutes created pandemonium on the *Darwin*. During their individual introductions by Cooperman, the pirates hooted and cheered and acted like small boys. The eight women and two men, all in their twenties or early thirties, were reasonably attractive, definitely well above average, although in general they didn't look quite as outstanding as the photographs in the brochure. One of the young ladies, a dark-haired, copper-skinned woman with wonderful eyes, appealed to Hunter. He went over to the table to reserve some time with her and found out that she was already booked for the next seven hours. Cho smiled at Hunter. "He who hesitates," Cho said with a shrug.

Hunter had another drink and cheered, along with the other pirates, as the first group headed back to the cabins with the prostitutes. One of the Crusaders, a giant of a man with a full beard and deep blue eyes, was teased as he departed with one of the two males. "Hey," he said with a smile to a friend who was taunting him, "a blow job's a blow job. At least I won't have to wait another three hours."

Hunter spent another hour at the party on the *Darwin*. He had a couple of drinks, which he sipped slowly, and was definitely among the more sober of the pirates as the evening advanced. The music and the voices around him grew louder and louder. An arm-wrestling contest began and soon became the focus of attention among the group. Men returned from their assignations with the prostitutes, most smiling broadly, and others departed from the common area, arm in arm with their chosen partners. Hunter chatted briefly with Cooperman while watching Rango win the finals of the arm-wrestling contest by defeating an equally immense Crocodile, and then had a long and involved discussion about life among the Israelis with Menachem. Lance stopped to say hello. He urged Hunter to carefully consider Goldmatt's offer, but also assured Hunter that he would support any decision he made. Hunter was finishing his last drink and thinking about leaving the party when he was approached by Rango and Hammer.

"We'd like to talk to you," Rango said, "in private."

Hunter felt his pulse rate jump. "What about?" he said.

The two Saracens looked at each other. "About Tehani Wilawa," Rango said.

Hunter said nothing for a few seconds. He was struggling with a flood of emotions, of which fear was certainly among the strongest.

"Look," Rango said, sensing Hunter's discomfort, "we're not going to hurt you. I give you my word. . . . We just want to ask you some questions."

Hunter took a deep breath. "All right," he said. "Let me find Derek Sanchez, the pilot for this spaceship. Maybe we can use his office for a few minutes."

Hunter had sobered up considerably by the time he sat down in the chair opposite Hammer five minutes later in Derek's office. He was wary about the coming conversation, but he was no longer physically afraid. Hunter had learned enough about Rango during the raid on the Moon to know that the pirate would keep his word.

"I need to verify some information about Tehani," Rango began, a scowl upon his face. The Saracen chief was standing just inside the door. He exchanged a quick glance with Hammer and then forced an awkward smile. "I would appreciate it if you would help," Rango said hesitantly. He was clearly not accustomed to being polite.

"I wanted Tehani the moment I saw her at the Andromeda trading post," Rango said at length, looking away from Hunter. "Never in my life have I seen a woman I wanted to fuck so much." He paused, his face darkening. "I was absolutely furious when you Utopians refused to sell her to me and then insulted me by fleeing from the post. If I had caught you bastards then, I would have ripped you all to shreds."

Rango was scowling again, his anger and frustration apparent. Hammer rose abruptly from his chair and stood between Rango and Hunter. The chief Saracen gestured to his colleague. "Sit down," Rango said, "I'm not going to hurt the fucking doc."

Hammer sat down. "After you guys left the post," Rango continued a few moments later, "I couldn't stop thinking about Tehani. I purposely had orgies with my normal cunts to try to wipe her face out of my mind. But it was useless. I realized that I was completely obsessed with her. I decided that Tehani would be my number one wife."

In spite of Rango's intimidating manner, Hunter was fascinated. The brute of a man opposite him in Derek's office was obviously in emotional turmoil. It was also clear that he was not at all comfortable in this kind of conversation with a virtual stranger.

"I paid a fortune," Rango said, his eyes focused on the wall behind Hunter's chair, "to copy and upgrade the security videos from that day you guys stopped at Andromeda. Day after day, in the privacy of my own quarters, I watched Tehani modeling her clothes at the post trading center. I started badgering Lance to sell her to me. I made outrageous offers. I even considered raiding Utopia and kidnapping her, even though I knew that such a raid might result in my death and the deaths of others in my band."

Rango stopped and was silent for a few seconds. Then he looked at Hunter again. "I only agreed to participate in this damn mission," he said, "and to attend the planning conference on Utopia, because I thought that I might catch a glimpse of Tehani while I was there. When I learned that she had already been returned to Mars, I cursed myself for not having executed the raid."

Hunter didn't say anything in response. As his eyes met Rango's, however, Hunter realized he was actually feeling some sympathy for the massive giant whose emotions had been thrown into such turmoil by a chance encounter with a woman at a pirate trading post.

"After Tehani was back on Mars," Rango said, "I tried again to forget her. But it was impossible. I became desperate to learn more about her. I paid several Utopians for information about her activities after the kidnapping. At considerable risk and cost, I had my contacts hire private investigators on Mars, and even on Cicero, to compile a complete dossier on Tehani. I now have several videos and dozens of photographs of her." He smiled wanly and his face then darkened again. "But the pictures are no goddamn good. They just make it worse. I want her, naked and beside me."

There was a protracted silence in the conversation. Rango's eyes were looking beyond Hunter, as if he were somewhere else. "Okay," Hammer said finally, breaking the silence, "you're probably wondering why we wanted to talk to you."

Hunter nodded.

"We would like for you to corroborate a few delicate details," Hammer said, "so that we know the information we have is correct."

"All right," Hunter said.

"Tehani became a private escort at Sybaris so that her mother and she could pay off the gambling debts accumulated by her father during his lifetime," Hammer said.

"That's correct, to the best of my knowledge," Hunter said.

"She lived as Lance's mistress during her stay on Utopia, and was frequently intimate with him."

"I believe that's correct as well," Hunter said.

"While you were on Utopia, you had little or no contact with Tehani," Hammer said, "although the two of you were lovers on the *Darwin*, before and after the kidnapping took place."

Hunter swallowed hard. "That's also correct," he said.

For several seconds none of the three men spoke. Hunter knew that Rango was staring at him. At length Hunter looked directly at the Saracen chief. "Was she an unbelievably good fuck?" Rango asked roughly.

Hunter nodded slowly.

Rango jumped up from his chair. For a brief instant Hunter thought he was going to be attacked. "Do you still love her?" Rango shouted, a wild look in his eyes.

"I don't know for sure," Hunter said after a short pause. "But I definitely still have strong feelings for her."

Rango laughed wildly. "Of course you still love her, you little shit. When an angel like that fucks your brains out, you never recover."

Hunter didn't say anything. Hammer was prepared to restrain Rango if he moved closer to Hunter.

"She must be the most amazing woman alive," Rango said, starting to pace around the room. "You still love her,

Lance still loves her, the men she has hosted at Sybaris swear she's a goddess, and I, who have only seen her on one day of my life, am totally obsessed with her."

He stopped pacing and stared out the office window. Rango suddenly turned toward Hunter. "What do you know about her affair with Lester Sackett?" he asked. The Saracen was almost snarling.

Hunter thought his mind was playing games on him. He shook his head, and repeated the question to himself. "Excuse me," he then said, looking directly at Rango. "Did you say something about Tehani and Lester Sackett? *THE* Lester Sackett, the defense minister for the Federation?"

"Of course," Rango replied. "Our reports from Mars indicate that she has been having an affair with Sackett for over a year, and that it was Sackett who arranged for her ransom."

Oh my God, Hunter thought immediately. *That would explain everything.* "I know nothing whatsoever about any involvement between Tehani and Lester Sackett," Hunter said. "In fact, I can't recall her ever mentioning his name."

There was another long silence in the room. At length Rango, who was still staring at Hunter, turned toward Hammer. "I believe the doc," the Saracen chief said. "I don't think he's that good a liar." Rango opened the office door.

"Thank you," Hammer said simply to Hunter. He stood up from his chair. He did not extend his hand. There was no pretense of friendship. A few seconds later Rango and he left the room.

THIRTEEN

IN THE DREAM HUNTER was walking gingerly along a narrow strut at the back of a large spacecraft. Tehani was in front of him. Ursula was behind. For some reason none of them were wearing space suits. Ahead of them the strut entered a small, illuminated room that looked like an igloo made of dark, charcoal metal. Hunter could see a large bed in the room.

The strut began to shake. Hunter dropped down on one knee and held on with his hands. The shaking became more violent. Both women lost contact with the strut and slipped away, both on Hunter's right side. "Hunter," they yelled nearly simultaneously. The shaking stopped.

Tehani and Ursula were floating in space not more than twenty feet apart. Hunter had a single line in his waist pack. He hooked one end to the strut and prepared to throw the rest of the line. In his dream time almost stood still. The women were drifting in slow motion. Hunter looked at first one, then the other, as he held the line in his hand.

A feeling of terror slowly crept over Hunter. He realized that he could save only one of the women. By the time the first one was retrieved and safely back on the strut, the other woman would be out of range. To whom should he throw the line? Hunter started to panic. "Help me," Tehani yelled. "Hunter, please," Ursula said.

He threw the line to Tehani. She grabbed it and wrapped it around her waist. The line became taut. Hunter started reeling it in. As Tehani drew closer to the strut, Hunter glanced over at Ursula. She was slowly moving away from the spacecraft. Tears were running down her cheeks. She blew Hunter a kiss. "I love you," she said.

"No, no," Hunter shouted, waking with a shudder. His breath was short. His heart was pounding so fiercely he could feel each beat in his wrists. On the other side of the cabin Julie was sitting up on her bed, staring at Hunter.

"What was that all about?" she asked. "You've never done that before."

"I had a nightmare," Hunter said. "Sorry I woke you up."

"It's not important," she said. She paused a few seconds. "Are you all right?" she asked.

Hunter nodded and closed his eyes. But he couldn't go back to sleep. His mind was too active. Hunter had decided the night before, after passing through the central sphere of the depot on his way back to the *Solomon,* that he was going to decline Goldmatt's offer and ask to be repatriated. Hunter had been immediately plagued by doubts. It had taken him nearly two hours to fall asleep. He had then slept fitfully, waking every hour or so from one bizarre dream after another. It was now nearly morning, not more than eight hours before the Utopian spacecraft would depart for home, with Hunter on board, and he was still not comfortable with his decision.

Is that what's bothering me? Hunter asked himself. *Or am I distressed by this news about Tehani and Lester Sackett?* One more time Hunter agonized over his decision. He made a mental list of the pros and cons of leaving the pirates. Again he listed Tehani's presence on Mars as one of the factors that favored repatriation, but an inner voice asked him if that was really a correct assessment. *If Tehani is indeed Lester Sackett's mistress,* Hunter argued with himself, *then she certainly won't have much time for me. And if Sackett knows that the two of us have been lovers, and is a jealous type, then my fellowship may be in jeopardy.*

Hunter rolled over in his bed. *But what was reported to Rango could have been only a rumor,* he told himself. *How would Tehani have time to have a protracted affair if she was working all the time as a private escort?* Lying on his bed Hunter realized that Tehani's job at Sybaris would be the perfect cover for their affair. He wondered how their liaison might have started in the first place. Hunter even asked himself if maybe Tehani and Sackett had begun their affair on Cicero, two years ago, before she had accepted the job. Hadn't the Federation defense minister visited their asteroid for a couple of days, just about that time, on a tour of the outlying territories?

He was torturing himself needlessly. *This is ridiculous,* Hunter said to himself, abruptly terminating the internal dialogue. *I have already made my decision. I'm not going to change it because of some stupid rumor.*

WHEN JULIE AWAKENED, Hunter had already laid his clothes out on his bed and was almost finished packing his bag. "Good morning," she said, sitting up and stretching. "You're certainly up early."

"I'm sorry I didn't make it back," Hunter said, turning around to face his cabinmate. "Did you find someone to play Intellego with?"

Julie yawned and shook her head. "It was pretty quiet here," she said. She smiled. "How were the girls? Did any of them send you into ecstasy?"

Hunter laughed. "Nope," he said. "I thought one of

them was fairly interesting, but by the time I made up my mind, she was all booked up."

"So we both had a sexless night," Julie said. "I guess we're pretty boring, you and I." She climbed out of bed and went over to the basin to wash her face.

"Is Goldmatt an early riser?" Hunter asked.

"Usually," Julie said. "Why? Are you ready to talk to him?"

"The sooner the better," Hunter said. He took a deep breath. "I'm not looking forward to this conversation."

"Uh-oh," Julie said, turning around to face Hunter. "It sounds as if you've decided you want to go to Mars."

Hunter nodded.

"May I ask if Tehani played a key role in your decision?" Julie said.

"Yes," Hunter said. "But my family was my major concern." He forced a smile. "And once upon a time, there was a young man from Cicero who was incredibly excited about being a Covington Fellow. It's still a great opportunity."

Julie walked over to Hunter with her arms outstretched. "Give me a good hug, partner," she said. "I will miss you very much."

GOLDMATT WAS SITTING in his office when Hunter arrived. He knocked softly and the Israeli chief waved for him to enter. "Early to bed, early to rise," Goldmatt said cheerfully as he shook Hunter's hand.

"The early to bed part's not exactly correct. At least not this time," Hunter said. "But I am usually up early."

Goldmatt was silent, waiting for Hunter to speak. He sat smiling on the other side of his desk, his intense gaze fixed on Hunter. "This has not been an easy decision, sir," Hunter said, surprised at his nervousness. "And I can't even say that I am absolutely certain I have made the right choice." He stopped for a second. "Sir," Hunter then blurted, "I would like to be repatriated."

Goldmatt continued to stare at Hunter for what seemed like forever. "All right, Hunter," he said at length. "I accept your decision, although I will tell you that I'm disappointed."

"Please understand," Hunter said, feeling uncomfortable, "that I thought the opportunity you offered me was fabulous. And I have the utmost respect for you personally—"

Goldmatt raised his hand to interrupt Hunter. "You don't need to say anything else," Goldmatt said. "You are a man, and you have made an important decision. . . . I promised you that I would arrange your repatriation, and I will keep my word. I will let Lance know when everything is set. My guess is that it will be three or four weeks."

Goldmatt stood up behind his desk and extended his hand. "Good luck on Mars," he said. "I wish you the best."

Hunter shook Goldmatt's hand firmly. "By the way," the Israeli chief said, "your participation bonus will be available to you during your last few weeks on Utopia. Whatever is left will be retained in your name in a permanent, interest-bearing account, in case, for some reason, you ever venture again into our pirate world."

"Thank you," Hunter said.

"It's the least we can do," Goldmatt said. "You have served us well."

THE FIVE-DAY TRIP back to Utopia was relatively uneventful. Hunter had some pleasant, stimulating conversations with the hyperactive Cooperman, played Intellego on three occasions with the Utopians, and told the story of his encounter with the two Dems in the infirmary several times. Most of the time, however, Hunter sat in front of the solitary large monitor on the small spacecraft, accessing Cooperman's special traveling database for information to refresh his mind about Centralia, North Mars, and both the history and the current politics of the Federation.

None of the Utopians tried to persuade Hunter to change his mind and remain with the pirates. Cooperman told Hunter bluntly, in a friendly manner, that he was making a "terrible mistake," but said nothing else about the subject. Hunter did promise Lance that he would do everything possible to leave the clinic in good shape when he departed.

They landed on Utopia in the sunlight. Through the transparent dome Hunter could see that a large crowd had gathered to greet them near the dome entrance. Hunter also noticed that five other spacecraft, a pair of which were old and dilapidated-looking, were parked in the plains area just outside the airlock.

Hunter was standing beside Lance when they landed. He pointed at the other spacecraft. "Do we have visitors?" Hunter asked.

"No," Lance replied. "But we are in an alert. According to Cooperman, who has been monitoring the Dem intelligence network for the last week, they have figured out a few things about our raid. Although they're still openly blaming the Feds, for political reasons, they have concluded that the Edison attack was a pirate operation. For the next month or two we're technically still within striking distance for the Dem fleet. The extra spacecraft are here in case we need to evacuate on short notice."

Hunter searched the applauding crowd for Ursula after he passed through the airlock. She was standing with her family and friend Janie, near the front of the crowd on the left. Hunter didn't even stop to remove and bag his space suit. When she saw him coming in her direction Ursula broke from the group and ran toward Hunter. He caught her in his outstretched arms and they hugged for several seconds.

They shared a long, delicious kiss, in front of everybody, as soon as Hunter had taken off his suit. "I'm so glad you're home," Ursula said with a radiant smile. Tears were running down her cheeks. "I've missed you very much," she added.

"I've missed you, too," Hunter said. They kissed again and then Ursula motioned for Janie and her family to come over. Her mother gave Hunter a hug. Both her father and her mother's other husband shook his hand vigorously. Congratulations came from all sides.

Before the crowd at the entrance dispersed, Lance announced that there would be a big celebration for the entire band, beginning in six hours, and that he would then brief everyone on the details of their mission. "For the moment, let me just tell you that our mission was an overwhelming success," he said, "and we now have more than adequate resources both to expand our band and to significantly improve our standard of living." The Utopians greeted his announcement with a roar of approval.

Ursula and Hunter, along with her family, walked slowly, hand in hand, in the general direction of the clinic and the permanent structures where Lance and his sub-chiefs lived. Hunter immediately noticed the many large containers stacked next to the dome, near the entrance. "We've all been packing for the last three days," Ursula said in response to his question. "We were told to be prepared to evacuate at any time."

Hunter asked about the preparations for moving the

clinic. "Jake and Gina and I have done a complete inventory of everything," Ursula said. "We've made some tentative decisions about what should be packed, and what we need to have available on a daily basis. We'll go over it all with you tomorrow."

The group accompanying Hunter slowed down when they were beside the main tent of the clinic. "Do you want to stop here, and freshen up, or have some time by yourself?" Ursula asked. "Or would you like to eat a home-cooked meal? Mom is ready to serve a feast in honor of your homecoming."

Hunter turned toward Ursula, still holding both her hands, and smiled broadly. "A feast would be great," he said. "But I had something else in mind first."

Ursula smiled broadly. "Why don't you guys go on home," she then said to her family and Janie. "Mom, you can start preparing the dinner. We'll be there in a little while."

Inside the tent, Hunter greeted Camille and gave his electronic bird a few simple commands. Satisfied that she hadn't forgotten anything during his absence, he asked Camille to leave Ursula and him alone for an hour. Accurate time measurement was one of the first features that Cooperman had designed into his creations. Hunter knew that Camille would return to her perch beside his bed exactly one hour, to the second, after she flew away.

After Camille departed, Hunter took off his dirty clothes. Ursula drew a pail of hot water and soaped Hunter's body from head to toe. She then gently, tenderly cleaned and rinsed him all over. Afterward, when Hunter tried to grab and kiss her, Ursula moved away with a coy smile. "Not yet," she said. She instructed him to lie down naked on his back on his bed. "This is my treat," Ursula said, slowly removing her clothing. "From start to finish. I don't want you to do anything but lie there and enjoy it."

She looked beautiful standing naked at the foot of Hunter's bed, her long blonde hair falling over her shoulders to just above the nipples of her firm young breasts. Ursula started by massaging his toes and feet. After a few minutes she spread his legs, putting her body inside, and massaged first his calves and then his thighs. It felt wonderful. Sitting on her knees in between his legs, Ursula touched him gently, and then leaned down and took him in her mouth. Ripples of intense pleasure coursed through Hunter's body.

He was afraid he was going to finish too soon. But Ursula stopped just in time and extended her body toward him. Hunter felt her breasts against the hair on his chest. She kissed him softly and whispered "I love you" in his ear. Ursula kissed him again, opening her mouth slightly, and Hunter felt her tongue lightly on his lips. Their tongues played together as her lips became harder and more insistent. Hunter put his arms around Ursula and pressed her against him. She pulled away, just slightly, and he felt her touching him again with her hand. A moment later they were united and she was moving ever so slowly back and forth.

Hunter's pleasure was incredible. He could not control his desire and began thrusting with his pelvis. Ursula put her right hand firmly on his chest. Hunter opened his eyes. She was shaking her head. "Remember, this is my treat. Please, darling," she said. Hunter dutifully lay still as Ursula began sliding up and down, back and forth, faster and faster. His yell of joy a minute later was probably heard all the way to the plaza next to the permanent structures.

"EVERYTHING'S ALL SET," Lance said. "You leave a week from tomorrow. Goldmatt asked me to apologize on his behalf for the delay."

"It's only been three weeks," Hunter said. "He said it might take that long."

Lance looked at the sheet of paper on his desk. "You will leave Utopia with Bailey when he makes his next trip to the trading post. At the post, you will be transferred to an Israeli spacecraft that will be carrying your escape vehicle. Several days away from the post, you will be released." Lance looked up. "That's it, I guess," he said. "Except that Tricia and I would like to have you over for a farewell dinner sometime next week, two or three nights before you leave."

"That would be great," Hunter said. "Thank you very much."

"By the way," Lance said as Hunter stood up to leave, "please stop over at Cooperman's house before you return to the clinic. He has some important issues to discuss with you."

Cooperman himself met Hunter a few seconds after the automatic interrogation at the door had begun. "Hey, Tiger, long time no see," he said. "Are you still shacked up with that nymphet of yours?"

"Yes," Hunter said, "Ursula and—"

"Ursula," Cooperman interrupted. "That's her god-damn name. I was trying to remember when I was talking with Bailey. Umm. That long blonde hair of hers is great. Is she any good? If so, maybe I'll poke her a time or two—in your memory, of course—after you're out of here."

Cooperman continued to talk at his usual high rate as Hunter followed him across the jungle of electronics that was his front room. Hunter didn't really try to pay attention to what Cooperman was saying. Much of the time Cooperman was just talking to himself anyway. Hunter did notice, however, that large containers were stacked to the ceiling in the two back corners of the room.

Cooperman waved at the containers as they turned left at the back of the room. "We may be attacked," Cooperman said, "if the Dems are really, really stupid. We're supposed to be ready to evacuate."

He stopped and opened a door in a part of his home that Hunter had never visited before. "This is my office," Cooperman said in explanation. "I only bring people here when we have something important to discuss."

Two computers were sitting on Cooperman's desk, surrounded by a jumbled mix of papers and electronic gadgets. Cooperman glanced at the computer on his right, hit a couple of buttons, and a high-speed printer built into the right wall began pumping out sheets of paper. Cooperman handed Hunter a data cube. "I'm giving you a hard copy, too," he said, "just in case you don't have access to a compatible computer on that Israeli ship." He glanced at Hunter. "Under no circumstances should any of this material be in your possession when you're rescued by the Feds. If it is, your ass will be fried."

Hunter took the data cube and looked at Cooperman with a bewildered expression. "What is this?" he asked.

"Tehani's testimony to the Feds," Cooperman answered. "Every word of it. Her official statement for the press plus what she actually told the Defense Ministry and the ASP when they interrogated her." Cooperman walked across the room and gathered up the stack of papers that had come from the printer. "Read all of it very carefully," he said, handing the stack to Hunter. "Commit the most important parts to memory. I guarantee you that any significant deviations between what she said and what you tell them will be gigantic red flags for the bastards."

Hunter glanced down at the papers. "You can read them later," Cooperman said. He was already opening the door. "I have something else to show you now."

"If you don't mind my asking," Hunter said, as he hurried to keep up with Cooperman, who was returning to his front room, "how in the world did you obtain her testimony?"

Cooperman stopped and turned around. "The Feds, and the Dems, too, for that matter, are stupid," he said. "Their so-called computer experts are old geezers who haven't learned anything new in twenty years. The security structures that supposedly guard their classified information could be penetrated by a ten-year-old."

A second later Cooperman was in motion again. In the front room he strode purposefully through the electronic chaos and stopped at a virtual-world kiosk. "Do you have a pen or pencil?" he said to Hunter as he opened one of the two kiosk doors. "You may want to write some of this down. But write it in shorthand so that nobody else can possibly understand."

"Rama world, file 48J," Cooperman said after he sat down and turned on the power in the kiosk. "I did remember that correctly, didn't I?" he said to Hunter while the kiosk computer was responding. "You're familiar with the Rama virtual world?"

Hunter nodded. He was standing outside the kiosk next to Cooperman. The little genius looked at Hunter as if he were an idiot. "Get in here," he said, patting the other seat in the kiosk, "I have something to show you.

"Here's the setup," Cooperman said after Hunter had sat down beside him. "You're in the octospider lair, at the bottom of the pit. The big subway comes. You ride it one stop, to the blue maze. You enter the blue maze, and turn to the left. Go forward until you're facing the wall. At that point, you input the following twenty-four-character alphanumeric: 3244198554KMAS3123185321. The code for the alphanumeric is easy to remember. You don't need to write it down. Reverse the order of the first twenty integers in the Fibonacci sequence and break the numbers at the mid-point, ten on either side, with the first letters of 'Kiss my ass, stupid.' Now watch me."

Although he had no idea whatsoever what Cooperman was doing, or why, Hunter dutifully made notes that would have been unintelligible to anyone else. Meanwhile, Cooperman's avatar in the Rama virtual world rode the subway to the first stop, entered the blue maze, and stopped at the prescribed spot. Cooperman spoke the alphanumeric and the game screen went blank.

Cooperman turned off the audio channel in the kiosk. "Now you must enter a four-character password. The password structure creates a different password for every day of the year and every virtual-world entry point. For this location in Rama, the password is relatively simple to derive. Take the day of the year, in Universal Time, multiply it by nine, and then enter the hexadecimal equivalent. January 1 becomes 0009, for example. January 2 is 0012, January 3, 001B, and so forth."

Cooperman looked over at Hunter. "Are you following this?" he asked.

"I think so," Hunter replied.

"Enter today's password," Cooperman said, pointing at the keyboard built into the front panel of the kiosk.

"All right," Hunter said. "Today is March 21, and this wasn't a leap year, so today is the eightieth day of the year. Multiplying by nine, the decimal number for the password is seven hundred and twenty." He stopped to think a minute. "In hexadecimal that's 2D0, I believe."

"Very good," Cooperman said. "See how easy it is. Enter 02D0."

Hunter followed his direction. On the black screen a box long enough for eight characters appeared. "Now input your code name," Cooperman said. "It's 'medicman.' Put my code name, the destination for your message, on the next screen. I'm 'smartass.' Then simply type your message. The next time I sign on at any of the virtual-world entry points, your message will be waiting for me."

Hunter went through the procedure and wrote a meaningless one-sentence message. When he finished, he looked over at Cooperman and shook his head. "What's the matter?" Cooperman asked.

"You guys are amazing," Hunter said. "You've created your own underground electronic-mail network using readily available commercial products."

"Exactly," Cooperman said proudly. "Don't ask me how we did it, or I'll be forced to reveal trade secrets. The important thing is that if you ever need to communicate with us, you have a way of doing so that cannot be traced. Goldmatt also offered his code name for your use; it's 'mattgold.' "

Cooperman opened the kiosk door. Hunter climbed out on the other side. "Aren't you afraid that I might give this information to the wrong people?" he asked.

"Goldmatt and I talked about that," Cooperman said. "We decided you were worth the risk. If you were to try to screw us, we'd close that entry point immediately. And soon thereafter the Feds would receive a full dossier detailing your participation in the Edison raid."

Cooperman headed for the door at his usual rapid pace. "One more thing," he said, after he opened the door. "I'm afraid Camille must stay here. You wouldn't be able to explain her, and the Fed agents might become suspicious. We can't risk that."

Hunter again looked puzzled. Cooperman slapped him on the back. "Don't worry about it," he said. "You don't have to understand everything. Take care of yourself. I hope our paths cross again someday."

He waved good-bye and closed the door behind Hunter.

HUNTER HEADED BACK to the clinic in a good mood. He spent most of his walk thinking about the remarkable Cooperman. A couple of times Hunter, remembering a specific moment he had shared with the little Utopian genius, even laughed out loud. As he neared his tent, however, he began to feel uneasy. Hunter knew that Ursula would be waiting for him. He was not looking forward to telling her that the date of his departure from Utopia had now been set.

Ursula rose from the chair in front of the computer monitor when Hunter entered the tent. "How was Lance?" she asked, crossing the room to give him a kiss of welcome.

"Fine," Hunter responded. He hesitated for a few seconds. "I also stopped by to see Cooperman," he said.

Ursula gave him a quizzical look. "What did Cooperman have to say?" she asked.

"He gave me some detailed information on how I could stay in contact after I leave," Hunter said. He forced a smile. Hunter was surprised that he was feeling so nervous. "Cooperman is amazing," he then added. "He has set up a secret, embedded electronic-mail system inside the virtual-world software. I should be able to send you messages from Mars."

"That's great," Ursula said without much enthusiasm.

Hunter was silent for several seconds. Ursula stared at him, waiting patiently. She knew intuitively what he was going to say next. "Lance told me that I will leave a week from tomorrow," Hunter suddenly blurted. "Everything has been arranged."

Ursula turned away slowly without showing any emotion. "Eight more days," she said softly. With her back toward Hunter, she took a few steps toward the center of the tent. He followed her and put his arms around her waist.

"I'm sorry, Ursula," Hunter said, unable to think of anything else to say. "I guess . . ."

She interrupted him by turning and putting her right index and middle fingers on his lips. "Don't say another word," Ursula said. Tears were streaming down both her cheeks. "Please just kiss me."

FOURTEEN

HUNTER'S LAST EIGHT DAYS on Utopia flew by in what seemed like an instant. Each day he would wake up, caress the sleeping Ursula beside him, and promise himself that he would take some time, that day, to savor some particular aspect of his extraordinary life with the pirates. Each night, after making love with his ardent partner, Hunter would wonder how another day had passed so quickly.

The clinic occupied most of his time during the day. The line of patients was longer than ever, especially after the date of Hunter's impending departure was circulated throughout Utopia. Anyone with any kind of chronic problem wanted to review it with Hunter before he left. Each evening, after all the patient appointments had been finished, Hunter had detailed discussions with Ursula and Jake, when Jake was actually present, about the operation of the clinic after Hunter's departure. They also discussed the major issues associated with moving the clinic in case an evacuation was ordered.

Hunter installed the data cube containing Tehani's testimony on the computer at the clinic and tried to read snippets in between appointments with his patients. He quickly realized that he was not retaining enough of what he was reading, however, and set aside an entire evening to study the material. When Ursula saw Hunter sitting in the clinic at a late hour, reading from the computer screen, she naturally asked what he was doing. In the ensuing conversation about Tehani, Hunter had his first real quarrel with his Utopian girlfriend. Hunter was astonished by a sudden outburst of anger from Ursula that he would never have expected. In tears, Ursula left the clinic, apparently headed for her home. She returned fifteen minutes later, apologetic, and made love to Hunter that night with a feverish intensity.

Ursula and her family had a surprise birthday party for Hunter three nights before his departure. Hunter shared a joint with Rebecca before dinner. Ursula declined to smoke, saying that she had a slight headache. Hunter laughingly remarked, when he was a little spiffed, that this was probably his last recreational drug experience for a long time. "I don't think," he said with a silly grin, "that Covington Fellows get stoned very often."

The food and drink were divine. Cooperman, accompanied by Loretta and some girl Hunter had never seen before, made a surprise after-dinner appearance at Ursula's family's tent and offered Hunter a celebratory orgy as a birthday present. Hunter glanced quizzically at Ursula, who seemed to be smiling her assent. Although in his inebriated state he was definitely tempted, Hunter remembered Ursula's outburst two nights previously and declined Cooperman's offer with profuse thanks. "Oh, well," Cooperman said to his two companions with his usual sardonic smile, "I guess I'm the only meat in the sandwich tonight."

Hunter and Ursula spent his birthday night in the private tent near her home. Before they made love, Ursula gave Hunter his birthday present, a handcrafted silver bracelet with his name inscribed on the top. When she turned it over, to show him what was written on the bottom in a small script, "With all my heart, Ursula," she suddenly burst into tears.

"Are you okay?" Hunter asked, putting his arms around her.

"Now I am," Ursula said, forcing a smile while wiping away her tears. She hugged Hunter tightly. "I'm just so glad to be spending your birthday with you," she whispered softly in his ear.

The next night was Lance's going-away dinner for Hunter. Ursula was invited as well, but late in the afternoon, after all the clinic patients were gone, she told Hunter that she wasn't feeling well and he should go without her. Hunter tried to persuade Ursula to attend, and suggested medicines that would relieve her stomach upset. In the ensuing conversation, Ursula reminded him that everyone who would be at the dinner was much older than she was, and that they had all been his friends before Hunter and she had become a couple. She then told Hunter that she didn't think she would be comfortable at the gathering and that he would almost certainly enjoy the evening more if he didn't need to worry about her.

Hunter argued with Ursula for awhile without success. At length, still somewhat puzzled by her attitude, he decided to attend the dinner by himself. It was a very pleasant evening. Lance was friendly and extremely complimentary. Tricia, looking gorgeous as always, teased him in private about having spurned her advances. Bailey and Renee asked questions about the Covington Fellows, and what Hunter anticipated he would be doing on Mars. When Darrell and Chelsea told him good-bye, Darrell asked Hunter to please tell his father that he was all right, and that he did indeed love his family, even if it didn't appear that way to them.

Hunter was in a good mood after he left the dinner party.

He whistled a song to himself, something he often did when he was alone, as he walked in the dark from Lance's house toward the clinic. Rounding the corner of the last of the permanent buildings, Hunter suddenly inhaled a whiff of marijuana smoke. "Finally," he heard a familiar voice say. "I thought I was going to have to wait here all night."

Ursula's mother, Rebecca, was leaning against the wall of the building on his right. She took a deep drag from her joint and approached Hunter with the butt extended. "Here," she said with a nervous laugh, "take a hit. You may need it in a few minutes."

Hunter declined the butt and looked at Rebecca with obvious astonishment. "So I surprised you," she said with another laugh. She took a deep breath. "I guess I have even surprised myself."

Hunter waited patiently while Rebecca drew on the joint again. "She made me promise that I wouldn't tell you," she said, looking away from him. "She even tried to hide it from me, but mothers know these things."

She glanced back at Hunter. "I shouldn't be doing this," Rebecca said. "It's stupid. I'm meddling." She started to walk away.

"What is it, Rebecca?" Hunter said.

She spun around. Hunter could see tears in her eyes. "She's pregnant, you fool," she almost yelled. "Ursula is carrying your baby."

"Whaaat?" Hunter exclaimed. He stared at Rebecca for several seconds. "How . . . how do you know?" he then stammered.

Rebecca cackled. "How do I know?" she repeated. "You men are so stupid sometimes." She shook her head. "Have you looked at her breasts lately? They didn't suddenly expand just because she had her seventeenth birthday. And haven't you noticed that she hasn't had a period since forever?"

Hunter continued to stare at Rebecca. His mind kept playing the same refrain. *Ursula is pregnant. She is going to have my baby. Ursula is pregnant. She is going to have my baby.*

"But why didn't she tell me?" Hunter suddenly blurted.

"Now that's a tough one to figure out, isn't it, Doctor?" Rebecca said in her most sarcastic voice. "Let's see. She probably didn't know for certain she was pregnant before you left on that mission or raid or whatever. Then, while you were on your journey back here, she was informed that you were going to be leaving Utopia. Forever. More importantly, she was told that you had been offered an opportunity to stay, and you had chosen to leave. Now why in the world under those circumstances would a young girl not tell the father of her baby, a man she obviously loves beyond any reasonable measure, that she is pregnant? Could it be that she wouldn't want him to remain with her, and their baby, out of a sense of obligation? Do you think that's possible?"

Hunter's head was spinning. His emotions were overwhelming him. He almost jumped over to Rebecca. At first she recoiled in fear, but Hunter put his arms around her in a great bear hug. "Thank you for telling me, Rebecca," he said. "Thank you very much."

He turned and ran all the way back to the clinic.

URSULA WAS SLEEPING peacefully in their bed when Hunter burst into his room. His first impulse was to grab her and shake her awake. He resisted the impulse and sat down on a chair beside the bed, on the side where he could see her face.

She was naked as usual. The sheet was pulled up to just below her breasts. He watched her chest rise and fall as she breathed easily. She was so young, so beautiful, so innocent. *And she's pregnant with my child,* Hunter thought. He waited as long as he could. Then he leaned over and kissed her softly, first on the forehead, and then on each cheek.

Ursula stirred. Hunter kissed her on the lips. Her eyes opened. "Hi, darling," she said with a smile. "Did you have a good time at the party?"

"Yes, I did," he answered. "Everyone was very nice."

She glanced at her watch. "You're home early," Ursula said. "I thought you'd stay out later than this." She reached up with her arms. Hunter gave her a hug.

"I ran into your mother on the way back," Hunter said while they were embracing.

"My mother?" Ursula said, pulling away where she could see him. She rubbed one of her eyes. "What was my mother doing up here at this time of night?"

"She was waiting for me, apparently," Hunter said.

Ursula frowned slightly and then sat up in bed. "Hunter . . ." she started to say.

"She told me," Hunter said. "I know you're pregnant."

Ursula looked at Hunter without saying anything. Tears edged into her eyes and she turned her head away. Hunter put his arms around her. "I love you, Ursula," he said, "and I love our child you're carrying. . . . I will not leave. I will stay here, and we will get a proper home, with a place for the baby . . ."

Her body began to convulse with sobs. Hunter tried to hold her but Ursula pushed him away. She stood up and put on the shirt that had been lying next to the bed. "No, no, no," she shouted, "you will not."

Ursula went into the clinic. Hunter could hear her crying. He followed her. She was standing at the entrance, looking out at the darkness. Her body was still trembling from her sobs. "Darling," Hunter said, moving toward her.

She turned around quickly. "No, Hunter," Ursula said, holding her arms out in front of her. "Please don't . . . not now . . . I can't . . ." She suddenly turned to the side and grabbed one of the thick poles next to the entrance. She dropped her head so that it was facing the floor.

"Are you all right?" Hunter asked.

Ursula nodded. "It's just a little dizzy spell," she said. When she heard Hunter take a step toward her, she again extended an arm in his direction. "I've had them before," she said. "They only last a few seconds."

She took slow deep breaths and regained her equilibrium. Hunter kept his distance. Ursula eventually looked up at Hunter. Her eyes were swollen from her tears. "You don't understand, do you?" she said in a comparatively even voice.

"No," he answered, "I guess I don't."

"It can't be this way, Hunter," she said earnestly. "It's no good. I'll always feel that you stayed out of a sense of duty. Not because you loved me."

"But I DO love you, Ursula," he protested. "I've told you that many times."

Tears were in her eyes again. "I believe you do," she said slowly. "But not enough. Before you knew that I was pregnant, you made a decision that, in all likelihood, meant that we would never see each other again." Her face suddenly contorted and Ursula broke into a sob. "Oh, Hunter, I would never, NEVER do something like that," she said through her tears. "I would do anything for you."

She stood in front of him, weeping helplessly. Ursula would not let him comfort her. At length Hunter crossed the room, grabbed some small swatches of clean cloth, and brought them back to her. "Thank you," she said, blowing her nose and wiping her eyes.

"I'm sorry," Hunter said when Ursula had calmed down a little.

"I know what you're thinking," she said after a short silence. "She's seventeen, she's emotional, she's pregnant. She'll change her mind after she thinks about it." Ursula smiled wanly. "I admit that I've been overwrought these last few minutes," she continued, "but don't be misled. I am very clear on this issue. I have thought this whole scenario through, over and over. You cannot stay here just because I'm pregnant. It's not right. You've already made your decision."

"But I didn't have all the facts when I decided to leave," Hunter said gently. "Surely you will acknowledge that. And after all, it's my child, too. It would be irresponsible for me to abandon—"

"That's the wrong reason," Ursula interrupted. She was nearly shouting. "Don't you see? I don't want you staying with me, with us, because of a sense of responsibility. Before I was hoping you would decide to stay because that was what you wanted. For you. But you didn't. You chose to return to a life that is more familiar and comfortable. You chose your family and your fellowship. I don't know," she said, starting to cry again, "maybe you even made your choice because of another woman."

Hunter and Ursula continued to talk for another hour. He tried to convince her that it was perfectly normal, and appropriate, for him to change his mind after finding out that she was pregnant. She wouldn't listen. She insisted that their relationship would be ruined if he stayed on Utopia under these circumstances, and that she would always feel that he had been forced against his will to remain with her and the baby.

No matter what Hunter said, Ursula remained intransigent. She reminded Hunter of all the special arrangements that had been made to facilitate his repatriation. She pointed out that their child would have plenty of attention and love, and that it was common for children on Utopia to have strong bonds with several adults. Toward the end, when they were both emotionally exhausted, Ursula did agree with one thing that Hunter said. She acknowledged that if Hunter left as planned, and subsequently, after having experienced the life he had chosen on Mars, decided to return to Utopia, then the situation would be different. "In that case," Ursula said, "I would welcome you with open arms. I would no longer feel that my pregnancy had forced you to stay here."

Hunter was still bewildered when they went to bed. Ursula snuggled up against him and kissed him softly. "You may not understand this now, my darling," she said. "But you will someday in the future. Believe me, I know what I'm doing."

WHEN THEY MADE   love for the final time on the morning of his departure, Hunter was full of desperation. He held Ursula fiercely, and kissed her so much that his lips were sore when they were finished. Afterward, while Hunter was packing his things, he had the feeling that he was an isolated piece of driftwood being carried forward on an immense ocean wave. Hunter knew well that everything that was happening to him was the result of his own decision, but nevertheless he felt overwhelmed by his own powerlessness.

Hunter's heart was heavy as he walked toward the airlock carrying his bags. Ursula was beside him, holding his hand, gamely smiling. He had visited her family at their tent that morning and said his good-byes there. He had said farewell to Jake, Gina, and the interns at a small gathering at the clinic the night before. There was only one good-bye left, the most important one, and Hunter dreaded it with all of his being.

Bailey and two other Utopian crew members whom Hunter knew casually were already wearing their space suits when Hunter and Ursula reached the airlock. The others passed on through the airlock, headed for the spacecraft, leaving Hunter and Ursula alone. They kissed once, then a second time. "I love you," Hunter said.

They stood, staring fixedly at each other, for what seemed like forever. "I will always love you, Hunter," Ursula managed to say. She rubbed her stomach. "If I am blessed with the birth of this child, I will see you in his or her eyes every day of my life."

Hunter could not speak. Never in his life had he felt so forlorn. Tears poured from his eyes and rushed down his cheeks. He held Ursula against his body with all of his might.

At length he turned away and began putting on his space suit. Ursula helped him. Neither of them said anything. After his helmet was on and adjusted, he hugged her one last time. He waved from the other side of the airlock, just before he entered the spacecraft. She was already walking toward the clinic.

Hunter stood at the observation window as the spacecraft slowly gained altitude. His emotions were in turmoil as he watched his pirate home slowly grow smaller and smaller. He wasn't crying anymore. Perhaps he had no tears left. Just before Utopia vanished from view altogether, Hunter heard an old man's raspy voice in his head. *Two roads diverged in a yellow wood, and sorry I could not travel both* . . .

He did not know that he had committed the entire poem to memory. Hunter listened to his mind's rendition of Robert Frost's poem until it came to the final lines. Then he substituted a change. *I took the one more traveled by,* Hunter said to himself, *and that was probably a big mistake.*

HUNTER DID NOT even enter the trading post proper when he stopped there. Bailey informed him that the Israeli spacecraft was ready to depart, and Hunter simply walked along the dock, still wearing his space suit, to the other vehicle. He was delighted to discover that Menachem had volunteered to be among the four crew members who would carry him to his release point.

He spent five days on the Israeli spacecraft. When he wasn't reliving his many experiences with the pirates in his memory, Hunter talked with Menachem, played Intellego, and carefully studied Tehani's testimony. Each time he read what Tehani had said, Hunter was more impressed by her responses to her interrogators. She identified some of the Utopians by name, including Lance, and all the kidnappers, but never mentioned Cooperman or Chelsea's husband Darrell Peabody. She described all the events at the Andromeda trading post in detail, and listed all the different band insignias that she could remember. Tehani said that she had no idea where either the trading post or Utopia were located in space, but she did report accurately the time of flight between Cicero and the kidnapping, between the kidnapping and the trading post, and between the post and Utopia.

She acknowledged that she had had an intimate relationship with Hunter aboard the *Darwin,* and that she had essentially been Lance's mistress during her entire stay on Utopia. Tehani provided a lot of information about the Utopian society and culture, based on her observations, but repeatedly stressed that she had never participated in, or overheard, any discussions of military or defense issues. She recounted accurately, and in detail, the sequence of events associated with the kidnapping and hijacking of the *Darwin.* Hunter suspected that this part of her interrogation was included to check her veracity, since each of the other passengers must have been asked the same questions after they reached Mars.

Soon after he was aboard the Israeli spacecraft, Hunter was shown the vehicle in which he would be released. It was an old, small spacecraft that had been out of operation for some time, and had been specially reconditioned for his use. The cockpit had been redesigned to be as similar as possible to the medshut that he had flown during the raid on the Moon. Twice Hunter took the vehicle out for test flights. He encountered no problems either time.

Hunter sent two messages from the Israeli spacecraft. The first went to Goldmatt, thanking him for having provided for his repatriation and for having had so much confidence in his abilities. He also asked Goldmatt to divide his participation bonus from the raid into two equal parts. Hunter requested that half the bonus be made available immediately to his girlfriend Ursula on Utopia, who was now managing the medical clinic, and that the other half be released to her when she gave birth to the child that she was presently carrying.

His second message was sent to Cooperman. Hunter thanked him for the extensive entertainment programming that had been added to the computer in his release vehicle. From Menachem, Hunter had learned that Cooperman had expressed concern that Hunter's flight to Mars, after his release, would be nine days in duration. To mitigate the boredom of such a long solo flight, Cooperman had had his staff create a special set of audio and video packages, all from the public domain so that they could not be traced, that would keep Hunter occupied during his solitude. At the end of the note, Hunter asked Cooperman to check on Ursula from time to time, "as a friend," and make certain that she was all right.

As the Israeli spacecraft approached the release location, Menachem and the other Israelis reviewed the flight manifest with Hunter. His vehicle was preprogrammed to reach active Federation flight space in nine days. His provisions and fuel were more than adequate to last for an additional two days. The spacecraft's new life-support systems were redundant, and had been thoroughly checked by Israeli engineering both before and after installation. It would not be necessary for Hunter to wear his space suit inside the small vehicle.

The communication system in Hunter's vehicle was programmed not to activate for three days, unless the onboard fault protection sensed a dire emergency, in which case an SOS would be broadcast on all frequencies. The long radio silence would make it virtually impossible for anyone to determine his release position. Similarly, the navigation system would selectively malfunction after his trajectory to Mars was established, thereby purging all pertinent historical information and leaving no clues for any Fed agents who might try to reverse-engineer his escape trajectory.

At the appointed time, Hunter carried his scant belongings to his home in space for the next nine days and strapped himself in the cockpit. As he eased away from the Israeli spacecraft, he turned his vehicle around and took one final look. Hunter felt a powerful mixture of both excitement and sadness. He was excited at the prospect of seeing his family and Tehani again, and finally pursuing his Covington Fellowship. But he was sad to be leaving Ursula, his unborn child, and the incredible characters and adventures he had encountered in the pirate world.

MARS

ONE

HUNTER TOOK A DEEP breath. He could not believe that the nine days had finally passed. In spite of his physical discomfort from having been in more or less the same position for the entire flight, he felt surprisingly good. Cooperman's music and video programs had provided sufficient entertainment to pass the time, and Hunter had slept more hours per day than at any time since his early childhood.

He turned on the radio, tuning to one of the prime space-traffic frequencies. "Hello, hello," he said. "Please help me. My name is Hunter Blake. I am somewhere inside the orbit of Mars, roughly a million miles away from the planet itself. I am a Federation citizen, originally from Cicero, who was kidnapped by space pirates several months ago. I have escaped in one of their spacecraft and am requesting assistance."

Hunter waited about a minute before repeating his call. Soon after the second transmission Hunter heard his first nonrecorded human voice in nine days. "This is Fed cruiser *Tokugawa*," a man said. "We copy you, Blake, and have tracked your transmission. We are in your general vicinity and have been assigned to provide assistance. We expect to rendezvous with you in ninety-three minutes. Repeat, ninety-three minutes."

"Copy that, *Tokugawa*," Hunter said. "And thank you very much."

Slightly more than an hour and a half later, Hunter eased his small shuttle into one of the large parking bays underneath the body of the Federation cruiser. After he was greeted on board by the crew and had a shave and a shower, the captain of the spaceship called Hunter into his office on the deck.

"Welcome back to civilization," the man said warmly, extending his hand. "I'm Captain Jeff Stiles, and I have the honor of transporting you to Phobos." The captain was in his late forties. Although he was definitely friendly, Hunter could tell from the man's demeanor that he was feeling considerable pressure. "If the flurry of activity your appearance has generated in the last two hours is any indication," he said, "you're going to be one very busy young man when you reach Phobos. I've already had calls from everyone in my line of command, including my chief of staff. The deputy director of the ASP and the governor of the Free Zone Transportation Authority have called as well."

Captain Stiles was solicitous. He first asked Hunter if there was anything that he needed that hadn't been provided. When Hunter answered that everything was fine, the captain told him that one of his officers was standing by to give Hunter a thorough medical examination. "The big brass on Mars are very concerned about your health," he said. "They have repeatedly stressed that we need both to read out all your biometry data and perform whatever additional medical testing we can on board. After all, you have been living among the pirates for a long time. You may have contracted one of those terrible diseases we've heard about."

Hunter smiled to himself. On Mars it was widely believed, based mostly on irresponsible media reports, that venereal disease was rampant among the pirates. In fact Hunter had encountered only a few isolated instances of sexually transmitted disease during his entire time at the clinic. Part of the reason for the low incidence of venereal disease on Utopia was that Lance and his subchiefs were keenly aware of the consequences of such a problem. In his first inventory at the clinic, Hunter had been pleasantly surprised to discover that the pharmacy was already adequately stocked with medicines to prevent and cure sexually transmitted diseases.

"I worked in a medical clinic while I was with the pirates," Hunter said casually to Captain Stiles, "and even though the hygienic conditions there were certainly not—"

Hunter stopped talking because Captain Stiles was waving his hand in the air with increasing vigor. "What is it?" Hunter asked with a puzzled look.

"You're not supposed to discuss your experiences with the pirates," the captain said. "Not with me and not with any member of my crew. . . . I'm sorry, I should have explained the situation to you right away. I have been asked to keep you in a communications quarantine during our flight. For security reasons. Of course you may visit with the other crew members during meals and recreation time, but all conversations about what happened to you after your kidnapping are strictly off-limits. In addition, you are to have no video or audio calls, or electronic mail, either incoming or outgoing, while you are on board. I have already informed the crew of this constraint. I hope that I can count on your cooperation."

The befuddled Hunter stood silently for a few seconds after the captain was finished speaking. "May I ask why I'm not supposed to talk about my stay with the pirates?" he said at length.

The captain explained that if Hunter had conversations

with any member of the *Tokugawa* crew about the pirates, the people with whom he talked would be subject to subsequent interrogation, and performance of the cruiser's regular assigned tasks might be impacted. "It's better," Captain Stiles said, "to avoid any problems by simply precluding all sensitive discussions."

Welcome back to the world of rules and regulations, Hunter said to himself, more amused than irritated. He indicated to Captain Stiles that he would cooperate with the quarantine. "But may I at least call my family and let them know I'm all right?" Hunter asked. "Surely that must be okay."

"We anticipated that request," Captain Stiles replied hesitantly, "and we are currently trying to obtain a ruling. The Federation Defense Ministry has already informed your parents that you have been recovered, and that you appear to be in good physical and mental condition. Your mother and father are of course very anxious to speak with you. However, there are some concerns, since nobody has any idea what you have been doing, or where you have been all this time, that even an ordinary conversation with your parents might contain classified information."

Hunter was no longer amused. He chose not to say anything, but Captain Stiles sensed that Hunter was not happy. "I'm sorry, young man," the captain said, "but this is a very complicated matter. If it were left up to me, of course you'd be able to talk to your family. But your situation is not in my jurisdiction. And I have been given strict orders to follow.

"One more thing," Captain Stiles added several seconds later. "I have also been asked to inform you that you will be met upon disembarkation on Phobos by a high-ranking Defense Ministry team. They will want to be debriefed on your experiences immediately after we arrive. My advice would be to get plenty of rest between now and then. To make you as comfortable as possible, we have vacated one of the senior cabins for you to use."

"Thank you, sir," Hunter said. He stood up, preparing to leave the office, but stopped at the door. "Sir," Hunter said after a long hesitation, "can you explain to me why the debriefing will not start until we reach Phobos? Couldn't I start the discussions with the Defense Ministry team now, over the ship's network? That seems like a much more efficient way to proceed."

"That option was discussed," Captain Stiles said, "but it was ultimately decided that it would be better to finish evaluating your medical data first, and then conduct the entire debriefing on Phobos."

Hunter wanted to ask more questions, but concluded from the captain's manner that the man thought their conversation was over. He stepped out the door and sighed. *Great,* Hunter said to himself, *I'm not allowed to speak with my parents. And I have no say on this debriefing issue. I'm probably going to be interrogated as if I were some kind of criminal. Welcome home, Hunter Blake.*

HUNTER'S   BIOMETRY   RECORDERS
had all overflowed months before. The only useful data that registered on the biometry scan were from the period that he had been sitting in the shuttle. Nothing in the data indicated any physical problems.

The officer conducting his medical examination was not very skilled, and was obviously nervous. Hunter resisted the temptation to intercede during the tests and improve the efficiency of the process. After two and a half hours of a painstakingly slow, routine examination, the officer thanked Hunter and informed him that he now had all the additional data that he needed to transmit to the doctors on Mars.

Hunter was then escorted to his cabin, where he stayed for most of the next twenty-four hours. He only left his quarters for three meals and a one-hour workout on the exercise station in the small spacecraft lounge. While Hunter was in his cabin, he caught up with the news, which was available to him on the small computer in one corner of the room, briefly reviewed what he was planning to tell the Federation authorities after he arrived at Mars, and slept for almost ten hours.

In the evening, before falling asleep in his cabin, Hunter found himself thinking about Ursula. He wondered what she was doing, and if she was having any morning sickness. In his mind's eye, Hunter saw her beautiful smile. His heart ached and he longed to be with her. Hunter tried to imagine what her life was like now that he was gone. The more he thought about Ursula, the more melancholy he became. At length Hunter forced himself not to think anymore about Ursula, or about the decision he had made to leave Utopia. *This is the life I have chosen,* he said to himself. *I must make the very best of it.*

Hunter accepted an invitation to join Captain Stiles on the observation deck of the *Tokugawa* about an hour before the cruiser reached Phobos. "Babcock tells me that you've never been to Mars before," the captain said, as Hunter and he gazed at a half-lit red planet growing slowly larger in the front window of the spaceship.

"No, sir," Hunter said. "I was on my way here for the first time when I was kidnapped."

"It's an amazing planet," Captain Stiles said. "The geological features are simply extraordinary. Seeing them firsthand is really mind-boggling." He pointed at Mars. "That huge mountain down there, slightly to the right of the center in the illuminated region, is of course Mount Olympus. It's over eighty thousand feet tall. And that long, sinuous dark line that meanders through the equatorial region is the famous Valles Marineris, the true grand canyon of the solar system. In places it is five times as deep as the Grand

Canyon of the Colorado on Earth—and our Martian canyon runs for almost three thousand miles."

"From here it looks as if someone formed that canyon by taking a huge knife and cutting into Mars," Hunter said.

"The canyon dates back to the early Martian days, when the planet was warmer and running water could still exist on the surface," the captain said, happy to share his knowledge with Hunter. He smiled. "When I was a university student," Captain Stiles continued, "I wanted to be a field geologist. But the Federation authorities thought I would make a better military officer." He shrugged. "So here I am."

The *Tokugawa* captain was silent for almost a full minute. Then he turned toward Hunter. "I have tried repeatedly during the time you've been on board," he said, a definite weariness in his voice, "to obtain clearance for you to speak with your parents before disembarking. I'm sorry to report to you that I have not been successful."

"That's all right, sir," Hunter said sincerely. "I appreciate the effort."

The cruiser began turning slowly to the left and Mars moved out of the observation window. Several seconds later Phobos came into view. It was even smaller than Hunter had imagined. Phobos was a tiny worldlet, no more than five miles long. Designated as part of the Free Zone by the Treaty of Tranquility, the Martian moon was famous not only for its uninhibited adult resorts, which featured gambling and prostitution among their many attractions, but also because it was a stopping point for all public interplanetary traffic going to and from Mars. Entry vehicles shuttled back and forth from Phobos to Mars virtually every hour, carrying passengers between the moon and one of the three spaceports on the surface of the red planet.

Several hundred miles away from Phobos, the *Tokugawa*'s approach slowed markedly. Captain Stiles explained that the cruiser had entered the Phobos space-traffic-control domain.

"The Space Transportation Board decided fifteen years ago," he told Hunter, "after a catastrophic collision between two interplanetary spacecraft, one of which, I might add, was avoiding a leisure craft piloted by a drunk, to tighten the restrictions on speed and direction of movement in this area. Violators now have their licenses revoked and pay severe fines. Government and corporate transportation vehicles can't afford not to follow the rules. Unfortunately, it's difficult to make the private spacecraft world abide by the restrictions. The individual space-yacht owners can easily afford to pay the fines, and always seem to retain their licenses except in cases of egregiously bad behavior. The resorts, unfortunately, are still major offenders. They have too much motivation to provide adrenaline bursts for their paying customers. Part of every casino package tour is a 'thrilling' afternoon out in space in a small shuttle."

"But I thought that FedEnt owned all the resorts on Phobos," Hunter said. "Surely they have the ability to make their employees and contractors follow the rules."

Captain Stiles laughed. "As you will soon discover, FedEnt is a world unto itself. It is part of the Commerce Ministry," he said, "and is accountable only to Chairman Covington and his staff. The Defense and Transportation Ministries both complain regularly about the situation here. From time to time, after a highly publicized accident, FedEnt cracks down on the casinos. But it never lasts long."

During the final approach, the *Tokugawa* passed a giant interplanetary transport headed for the Moon, a pair of cargo ships outbound toward Jupiter, and a dozen or more small leisure vehicles swooping and zooming around the larger spacecraft. One of the private craft, a four-passenger shuttle with clear casino markings on its side, came close enough to the cruiser that Hunter could actually see the faces of the people inside.

The Phobos spaceport itself, managed by the Free Zone Transportation Authority, was a gigantic complex. Its three distinct units were arranged in a linear fashion. In the center was the passenger terminal. The cargo terminal was on one side and the private spacecraft marina, a FedEnt enterprise operated on a long-term lease with the FZTA, was on the other. The spaceport, like all entities administered by the Free Zone government, was a demilitarized zone. No Defense Ministry spacecraft from either space government could land or take off without explicit permission of the governor of the FZTA. Since the *Tokugawa* was technically part of the Federation armed forces, it had applied for, and received, special permission to land at the Phobos spaceport with Hunter.

"We'll be docking at the cargo terminal," Captain Stiles explained to Hunter a few minutes before landing. He forced a smile. "I don't want to bore you with all the gory details, but that's just one of many compromises that has been negotiated since we first received your request for assistance. The FZTA didn't want a possibly destabilizing presence at the passenger terminal. And there were many reasons why it was decided not to take you to the Federation's military space station."

Hunter extended his hand to the beleaguered captain. "Thanks for everything, sir," he said with a smile. "I guess you'll be glad to get rid of me."

Captain Stiles shook Hunter's hand and then sighed. "I know it's not your fault," he said, "but this has been a real nightmare for me." He paused a moment. "I wish you well," he said. "You seem like a fine young man."

HUNTER WAS USHERED off the spacecraft, and past half a dozen photographers and reporters who had somehow learned where he would disembark, by three men in military uniforms. He was taken to a small conference room in the cargo terminal. Everything had been set up prior to his arrival. There was a microphone on either side of his chair. A glass of water was on the table on his right-hand side. Three video cameras had been mounted around the room, all focused on his position.

There was no preliminary casual conversation. Colonel Adam Webster, the officer in charge of the debriefing, introduced himself and the other two officers. He informed Hunter that the purpose of this "first session" was to obtain a general understanding of what Hunter had experienced during the months since he had been kidnapped from the *Darwin*. A "secondary" purpose, Colonel Webster told Hunter, was to determine when, or if, a press conference might be held and to establish the guidelines and constraints for that conference. Colonel Webster, a dour, efficient man about fifty years old, continually consulted his hand computer while talking to Hunter. He never smiled. Before he finished with his introductory remarks, he asked Hunter to speak clearly and distinctly, since a large audience would be watching him on the Defense Ministry network in Centralia.

"Are you ready to begin?" Colonel Webster asked.

"Sir," Hunter said, speaking for the first time, "may I ask a few questions?"

"Go ahead," Colonel Webster replied.

Hunter leaned forward on the table and smiled. "In what capacity am I here, sir?" he asked.

"I'm sorry," the colonel said after a brief hesitation. "I'm not certain that I understand your question."

"With all due respect to the three of you," Hunter said, wearing his most nonrebellious smile, "I'm really not certain why I'm here. . . . I'm not a member of the armed forces. I haven't been accused of any crimes. I'm just an ordinary citizen of the Federation, who happens to have been in the wrong place at the wrong time." He paused for a moment. "Don't get me wrong," Hunter then continued, "I appreciate very much your sending the *Tokugawa* to rescue me. And I of course understand why you gentlemen would like to question me. But nobody has asked me, not even once, if I was willing to take part in this debriefing. And quite frankly, this is not my top-priority activity during my first few hours back in civilization."

Colonel Webster was flummoxed. He and the other two officers exchanged glances without saying anything. "Mr. Blake," the colonel eventually stammered, "it may be that an aspect of this inquiry has been overlooked. We informed Captain Stiles that it was our intent to hold this debriefing immediately after your arrival. Are you saying that he did not tell you?"

"Captain Stiles did tell me, sir," Hunter replied. "But he didn't ask me. And there's a big difference."

"We also spoke with your parents," one of the other officers at the table said. "And they registered no objections to the timing of this inquiry."

"I'm sorry, sir," Hunter said. "But I am an adult. I make my own decisions. Whether or not my parents objected is really not the point."

During the ensuing long silence Colonel Webster glanced at his hand computer, which was flashing with an urgent message. "What is it you would like to do, Mr. Blake?" the colonel asked a few seconds later.

Hunter looked slowly around the table, and then at the video camera on his left. "Sir," he answered, "I would first like to talk to my family. Then, if it's permissible, I would like to have a free evening by myself. I was strapped in the pilot's seat of a tiny shuttle spacecraft for nine consecutive days before I was rescued, and then spent a day and a half in pleasant but confining surroundings on another space vehicle. Right now, a long walk, a good meal in a restaurant, and a big bed to sleep on all sound incredibly attractive. If I could have some time to unwind and relax, then I would be perfectly happy to carry on with this debriefing tomorrow morning."

Colonel Webster squirmed in his seat. His hand computer was overflowing with urgent realtime messages. He cleared his voice. "Mr. Blake," he said, "would you mind stepping outside for a moment? We would like to discuss your requests."

When Hunter was called back into the conference room fifteen minutes later, Colonel Webster told him that a reservation had been made at one of the hotels adjoining the spaceport, courtesy of the Federation Defense Ministry, and that he could charge his dinner at any of the hotel's restaurants. Hunter was also told to expect a video transmission from his parents in his hotel room in an hour, and that the circuits had been arranged for him to provide an immediate response.

"We are also prepared to grant your request for a postponement of this inquiry and a free evening, Mr. Blake," Colonel Webster said, "provided you will agree to a couple of stipulations. Because your escape and return have created such interest in the media, we are concerned that you might be approached by reporters, or just ordinary individuals who have been following your story, and asked about the details of your stay with the pirates. Since Phobos is in the Free Zone, we cannot guarantee that such approaches will not occur. We would strongly prefer that you have no discussions with anyone about what happened to you at least until after our session tomorrow morning."

The colonel paused. "Specifically, we would like you to agree to two things. First, that you will make no outside calls other than the one to your parents. Secondly, we would like to request that you accept Lieutenant Russell here as your companion for the evening, and ask that you remain with him whenever you are outside your hotel room. Are these both acceptable?"

Hunter nodded.

"All right," Colonel Webster said, almost smiling, "have a good evening. We'll see you at eight o'clock sharp tomorrow morning."

IT WAS OBVIOUS to Hunter, when he received the video from his parents in his hotel room, that the Federation authorities had talked with his mother and father after the postponement of the debriefing. After a brief and surprisingly emotionless statement expressing her happiness that Hunter was safely back in the Federation, his mother spent several minutes admonishing him about the perils of uncooperative behavior. She then entreated Hunter to remember that he was a "representative of the family" in everything he said or did. Although it was a delight to see his mother and hear her voice after all the months he had been away, Hunter was irritated that she had so readily succumbed to the pressure from the government. He had also expected to see his mother in her usual fine form, indulging her emotional proclivities, perhaps even interrupting his welcome with a few sobbing outbursts. In a way, Hunter felt a little cheated by her subdued and self-conscious behavior.

Hunter noted that his father looked as if he had aged significantly since his disappearance. Mr. Blake said that nothing that had ever happened in his life had made him as happy as the news that Hunter had been recovered and was safe and sound. He also said that he had indeed cut back on his work schedule, as he had promised, and had hoped that his heart irregularities would disappear. However, Mr. Blake informed Hunter, the peculiarities in his heartbeat had not subsided at all, and Dr. Ekanayake was now considering a major exploratory operation.

"I would love to see you, son," Mr. Blake said, "but I guess that will have to wait a while. I'm not supposed to travel and I imagine you'll be plenty busy both catching up with your Covington Fellowship colleagues and briefing all the authorities about the pirates." Hunter could tell that his father was struggling with his emotions. "I love you very much, Hunter," Mr. Blake said after a brief hesitation, "and I am, as always, incredibly proud of you."

Hunter paused the video when he realized that he had tears in his eyes. He ached with a desire to hug his father and for the first time in his life, Hunter worried that perhaps he might not have another opportunity.

The camera moved back to Mrs. Blake. She informed Hunter that, in her opinion, the reason Mr. Blake's heart was still "acting funny" was because of all the stress in his private life. "He has been worried sick about you," she said. "At first, after we were told that the Dems had hijacked your spaceship, your father actually sent an E-mail to the Federation defense minister offering his services in any effort to secure your release. After Tehani was returned home and graciously called personally to give us a report on where you were and what you were doing, your father started learning everything he could about the pirates. I daresay he's now one of the leading experts in the Federation on your kidnappers."

His mother paused and swallowed hard. "We've had some other difficulties, too," she said. "While Octavio and Amanda were separated, he went to Mars on a couple of job interviews, one of which was in the Free Zone. Then he disappeared. None of us has heard from Octavio for almost two months. That handsome ASP captain—you remember him from the shelter, I'm sure, Marco Bonesio is his name—anyway, he told Amanda and us that they suspect Octavio is involved in seditious activities. Wouldn't that be terrible? Actually Amanda seems to be recovering all right. We kept Danielle the night before last while Amanda had a date with Captain Bonesio."

Hunter smiled to himself. This was the mother he knew and loved, not the one trying to remember exactly what she had been asked to say. The rest of her news was relatively inconsequential. His mother prattled on for five more minutes about the activities of all the people he had known during his secondary-school days.

"HI, MOM AND Dad," Hunter said into the video camera in his hotel room. "Thanks for the video. It was really great to see you both. Dad, I'm sorry to hear that you're still having problems with your heart. I hope that all straightens out soon.

"As you can see, I'm fine. At least as far as anyone can tell. All my biometry recorders overflowed, of course, so no trend data were available on any of my vital functions. They did give me a physical on the spacecraft, though, so I guess they're in the process of verifying that I really am all right.

"I have had an incredible experience since the kidnapping. I'd love to tell you about it but I've been asked not to say anything just yet. I presume that after my formal debriefing I'll be allowed to tell you some of the details.

"I don't know where I'm going to be or exactly what I'll be doing now that I'm back. Nobody has told me anything yet. Right now I'm on Phobos and I'm scheduled to talk to representatives of the Defense Ministry tomorrow. As soon as I know anything about my future plans, I'll call and tell you.

"I miss you both terribly. And I hope you know that I love you very much. I am glad to be back. With any luck I'll see both of you before too long. Please take care of yourselves and stay in touch."

TWO

HUNTER ACCEPTED LIEUTENANT BRYAN Russell's invitation to join him for dinner in the Italian restaurant in the hotel. Hunter purposely ate dishes that had never been available when he was living among the pirates. His main course was a linguini dish cooked with salmon and baby squid, the seafood all grown at the Federation aquaculture center a hundred miles to the west of Centralia. Hunter also polished off more than his share of the bottle of white wine they ordered.

Lieutenant Russell was good company at dinner. Articulate and well informed, he had an easy, self-deprecating manner that belied his obvious intelligence. He was also a treasure trove of information and anecdotes about women. The lieutenant, who described himself as a confirmed bachelor, kept Hunter laughing through most of the meal.

At one point, Lieutenant Russell gestured discreetly at a newlywed couple across the room. "As far as I'm concerned," he said in a low voice, "there's only one legitimate reason for a man to marry." He paused appropriately and waited for Hunter to ask the obvious question. "A man shouldn't marry," the lieutenant then continued, "unless he wants children and has found a woman he thinks would be a good mother. Most men marry mostly for sex. They won't admit it, but it's true. How unbelievably stupid! In the first place, it's a well-known fact that sex goes rapidly downhill after marriage. I bet not one woman in a hundred still gives blow jobs to a man she's been married to for five years. But they'll do anything to please you before they have that ring."

Over dessert Lieutenant Russell told Hunter that his mother had immigrated to North Mars from Zimbabwe on Earth when he was an infant, shortly after the death of his father. Tall, handsome, and impressively built, the black-skinned lieutenant in his white Federated forces uniform drew approving stares from virtually all the women who walked past them in the restaurant.

After they finished eating, the two men walked outside the hotel for a stroll. As they passed the monorail station, where a large group of vacationers was waiting for transportation to the resort area of Phobos, a sultry young lady dressed for a night of hot dancing approached the lieutenant and put her hand on his forearm. She asked if Lieutenant Russell was "available" for the evening.

The lieutenant laughed easily. "I think not," he said. "I'm on assignment."

The young lady pouted. "What assignment?" she asked in disbelief.

Lieutenant Russell removed her hand from his forearm and kissed it lightly. "I'm an intelligence officer," he said in a low voice. "We're not allowed to tell."

Both Hunter and Lieutenant Russell chuckled as the young woman, offended by his cavalier attitude toward her advance, stalked off frowning.

"So is this resort as fabulous as I have heard?" Hunter asked his companion.

"It is definitely a unique place," the lieutenant answered. "I can do without the casinos—I can't afford to lose anyway. But Paradise, that's a whole different ballgame."

"That's the red-light district?" Hunter asked.

Lieutenant Russell put his arm around Hunter and grinned. "My boy," he said, "nobody ever refers to Paradise as a 'red-light district.' There's simply no other place like it in space. I admit that the very highest-quality girls are probably at Sybaris. But if you haven't got the big bucks, and you love the pleasure of temporary feminine companionship, then Paradise is your ticket."

The lieutenant began to extol the virtues of Paradise. When the lieutenant repeatedly suggested that it would be a great place for the two of them to spend the rest of the evening, Hunter found himself becoming suspicious. He wondered if perhaps there had been some arranged and scripted scenario for the evening. Lieutenant Russell openly admitted he worked for the defense intelligence section of the ministry. He had been assigned to Hunter for some reason. Was it possible that all of his companion's apparently natural talk about women and sex was simply part of a setup of some kind? If so, what was its purpose? Some kind of sexual-orientation litmus test? *That's absurd,* Hunter told himself, *for they have Tehani's testimony already that we were lovers on the* Darwin. Bemused by his own suspicions, Hunter was laughing at himself when he declined the lieutenant's invitation.

"Thanks for the offer, Lieutenant," he said, "but I think I'll pass for tonight. What I would like now is a long hot bath and a good night's sleep."

Lieutenant Russell didn't give up that easily. He informed Hunter that not all the girls in Paradise were true prostitutes. "A lot of them are what might be called soft hookers," he explained to Hunter. "These women may accept cash or presents for sex from a client whose company they enjoy, but most of them are simply flirts, who earn their money by talking with the clients and encouraging the men to buy more drinks. If you have limited funds and just want the company of a good-looking girl, with maybe an occasional hand on the thigh or passionless kiss, as well as a lot of overt flirtation, then Paradise is still the spot for you. It's a great place to watch a sporting event on a big-screen television, or just to spend a relaxing evening surrounded by attractive, attentive females."

Hunter shook his head and laughed. "Why don't you go ahead without me, Lieutenant," he said. "I don't want to spoil your evening."

"Can't do that," Lieutenant Russell said with a broad smile. "My orders are to stay with you tonight. After being cooped up in that cramped spaceship for over a week, I thought you would be interested in sampling a little of our local culture. It would be a lot more fun than sitting in a sterile hotel room."

Hunter walked toward the front door of the hotel. "You're probably right," he said, "but I'm really not in the mood. Besides, it would probably be a good idea for me to review everything that has happened to me since the kidnapping. I have the feeling that I'm going to be asked a lot of detailed questions tomorrow."

The lieutenant accompanied Hunter to the elevators. When they reached the fifth floor, he stuck out his hand. "All right," he said, "I guess then that this is good night. If you decide later that you want to go downstairs for a drink or anything, please give me a call. I'm just down the hall in 508." He smiled. "I hope I can count on you to make my life easy. Technically you're not supposed to be outside your room without my company. But I don't much like the idea of camping out here in the hall."

"You have nothing to worry about," Hunter said pleasantly. He shook the lieutenant's hand. "Thanks for the dinner and the conversation."

DURING HIS BATH in the hotel room, Hunter found himself thinking about Tehani. Powerful images from the time that they had shared as lovers onboard the *Darwin* insinuated themselves into his mind and filled Hunter with desire and longing. *I am not over her,* he said to himself. *No matter how much I try to convince myself that I am. In spite of Lance and now this Sackett business.*

He managed to push Tehani out of his mind until after he finished his bath. While he was brushing his teeth, Hunter noted to himself that he had agreed not to make any phone calls, but he had not been told that he couldn't send any electronic messages. On impulse, Hunter sat down in front of the computer desk in his hotel room. He tried to access his old E-mail account to send Tehani a short note saying that he was anxious to see her.

"Account no longer active" was the message that flashed on the screen.

Hunter shrugged. *That was to be expected,* he told himself.

Later, lying on his back in bed, Hunter's mind drifted at random over the events that had taken place since his kidnapping. Images of Tehani, Ursula, Cooperman, and Goldmatt floated through his mind. He relived the entire raid on the Moon in inordinate detail. Thinking about the raid reminded Hunter to review the list he had carefully prepared while he was alone in the shuttle on his way to Mars. It contained the events he would report in his Federation debriefing. He had written it in his own personal form of shorthand. For obvious reasons, there was no list, not even in personal code, of the things that he wouldn't mention to his interrogators.

Hunter didn't fall asleep right away. He was still wary of the inquiry. *Tomorrow should be an incredible day,* he said to himself just before drifting off.

———

"**MR. BLAKE. I'M** Colonel Mark Hood," the man said, extending his hand as soon as Hunter arrived at the designated conference room in the hotel. "I've replaced Colonel Webster as the ranking officer for your debriefing."

Hunter shook his hand. The corpulent Colonel Hood was in his mid-forties. He had an easy, engaging smile and eyes that were both bright and intense. "Did you have a pleasant evening?" he asked.

"Last night was fun," Hunter said. "I feel a whole lot better this morning than I did last night."

"Good, good," Colonel Hood said. "Let me introduce you now to the other people who will be in the room with us." He walked over to a tall, athletic man in an ASP uniform, who was engaged in a conversation with a Federation captain. "This is Officer Jeremy Sanders," the colonel said, "of the Anti-Sedition Police. We have asked him to join us for a number of reasons, the most important of which is that we didn't think it was fair to ask you to sit through two of these debriefing sessions."

Officer Sanders turned around and faced Hunter. For just an instant, Hunter saw a look in the man's eyes that sent a chill through him. A second later the man's expression had changed markedly. The ASP officer smiled and greeted Hunter. "My colleagues at ASP headquarters are envious of my assignment," Officer Sanders said. "Everyone wants to hear your story. It's not every day that someone shows up having just escaped in a pirate spacecraft."

Colonel Hood introduced Hunter to the other two Federation officers from the Defense Ministry, a Captain Schroeder and a Captain Tolson, and then suggested that everyone should take his seat. The setup inside the conference room was the same as the previous day. Hunter sat at one end of the small rectangular table, Colonel Hood at the other. The two Federation captains sat on Hunter's left.

Lieutenant Russell was next to Officer Sanders of the ASP on the other side of the table.

Colonel Hood announced that the debriefing had officially begun and requested that all the recording devices be initiated. "May I call you Hunter?" the colonel then asked, before launching into his preamble.

Hunter nodded. "Hunter, what you are going to experience here," the affable colonel then said, without consulting any notes, "is a standard Defense Ministry inquiry. Anytime a Federation citizen is involved in an activity that could have an impact, in the opinion of our defense intelligence staff, on the overall security of our nation, we convene a board of inquiry like this one. I think it's important that I point out to you, at the outset, that we recognize you are inconvenienced by this whole affair. We want you to be as comfortable as possible. If you don't understand a question, please feel free to ask for a clarification. You can call a recess at any time that you desire. The bottom line is that we appreciate your assistance. And of course, it goes without saying that you are under no suspicion of any kind."

The colonel smiled warmly. "Any questions before we start?"

"No, sir," Hunter said.

"Then why don't we start with your statement," Colonel Hood said. "Please summarize for us the major events that transpired between the hijacking of the *Darwin* interplanetary transport, when you were also kidnapped, and the time that you were picked up by the *Tokugawa* two days ago." The colonel glanced quickly at his Defense Ministry colleagues and ASP Officer Sanders. "Let me remind everyone on the board before Hunter starts that there are to be no interruptions or questions during his statement. You are all free to make notes on your computers, but please do not do anything that will distract the speaker."

Although he was a little nervous at first, Hunter relaxed after about a minute. He covered the events between the kidnapping and the arrival on Utopia fairly quickly, essentially repeating the story that Tehani had told in her debriefing a few months before. From that point forward, his tale was new. Hunter described his work at the clinic mostly in general terms, but also included a portrait of a typical day for him to provide more detail. He mentioned seeing Tehani briefly while they were both on Utopia, and being informed of her repatriation only after she was gone.

"Naturally, I was a little upset that she had been returned and I had been left on Utopia," he told the men around the table. "I arranged an appointment with Lance, the Utopian chief, and asked why I had not been repatriated as well. He told me that they needed my medical services for awhile longer, but would negotiate my return once I had trained someone else to take over the clinic."

Hunter spent a few minutes discussing his training of Ursula, and Jake Townsend's lack of dependability, and then started to describe his escape. "One of the biggest shortcomings of the clinic was the lack of adequate drugs and other supplies," he said. "I complained about this issue whenever I could find someone to listen. A couple of supply runs were made during my early days on Utopia, but the medicines that were brought back were often not satisfactory. In retrospect, that's understandable, for what was available at the trading post was never exactly what I had requested. The personnel who normally made the trips to the post were simply not qualified to make changes in my requisition list, for they had no medical experience.

"Eventually, Lance decided that it made sense to send me along on one of the regular trading post trips to resupply the needs of the band. By this time, because of my work at the clinic, I was no longer being treated as a prisoner. I was therefore neither confined to my cabin nor under constant surveillance. I realized soon after we were spaceborne that this would probably be my best opportunity to escape. During the first two nights, while everyone else was sleeping, I familiarized myself with the operating manuals for the shuttle. On the third night, I took enough food and water to last for twelve days, slipped into the shuttle, and zoomed away. The Utopians must not have discovered my disappearance for hours, for no attempt was made to follow me."

Colonel Hood called a short recess after Hunter had finished his opening statement. The colonel explained that the board of inquiry needed to caucus and organize the rest of the proceedings. Hunter was called back into the conference room twenty minutes later.

"We have established a rough schedule for the rest of the day," Colonel Hood said to Hunter after first thanking him for his "thorough and organized" statement. "As you have probably surmised," he continued, "we already have testimony from Ms. Wilawa covering those events that involved both of you. Thus, most of our focus in this inquiry will be on your activities during the time you were living on Utopia, as well as your subsequent escape. Captain Schroeder is a doctor himself, and will lead the initial questioning about your work at the clinic. One of our goals is to obtain a general assessment of the quality of the medical services that are available to the pirates."

For almost an hour Captain Schroeder asked specific questions about the Utopian clinic. He was particularly interested in the kinds and types of drugs and medical equipment available, not just on Utopia, but also elsewhere in the pirate world. Many of his questions were about the requisition lists that Hunter had provided to Bailey before his outpost trips, and what was actually supplied to the clinic upon Bailey's return. Hunter was completely comfortable with this entire line of questioning, and provided more than satisfactory answers for each query.

"Anything else about the clinic?" Colonel Hood asked the other board members after Captain Schroeder said that he was finished with his questions.

"I have a couple of questions," ASP Officer Sanders said just when the colonel was ready to proceed to the next subject.

Colonel Hood nodded at the ASP officer and the man turned toward Hunter. "Would you say that the pirates were satisfied with your work at the clinic?" he asked.

"Yes, sir," Hunter answered.

"Would you say that they were pleased?" Officer Sanders asked.

"I believe so, sir," Hunter said.

"Comparing the quality of the medical services provided to the Utopians at the time of your escape with the quality when you arrived, Mr. Blake," the ASP officer said, "would you say the quality was significantly higher, a little higher, about the same, a little worse, or significantly worse?"

Hunter asked Officer Sanders to repeat the question. He rephrased it slightly, but the thrust was the same. "In my opinion," Hunter said, "the medical services on Utopia were significantly better at the time of my departure. But I should point out that that was no great accomplishment. Things were in terrible—"

"Did Lance or any other pirate leader," Officer Sanders said, interrupting Hunter, "ever indicate in any way that they felt the clinic was markedly improved? Did he ever praise you, for example, either privately or in a public forum?"

Hunter thought for a few seconds. "Lance told me once that I was 'doing a good job,' " he said, "but other than that, I can't recall any explicit statements. And he never said anything directly about the clinic in his public speeches."

"I see," said the ASP officer. He paused a moment. "Would you say that the improvement in medical services during your stay on Utopia made the quality of life for the pirates there significantly better?"

"No, sir," said Hunter. "I can't say that. Too many other factors—"

"How about slightly better?" the officer said, interrupting again.

"Perhaps," Hunter replied after a slight hesitation.

Officer Sanders fiddled with his hand computer for several seconds. "Mr. Blake," he then said, "are you familiar with Article 17 of the Sedition Act of 2405?"

"No, sir," Hunter said. "I can't say that I am."

"Let me read a little of it for you," the officer said, looking up from his computer only briefly. " 'Cooperation with the enemy,' it says, 'is defined to include any and all individual actions that result in a material improvement in the enemy's ability to operate in a way that is detrimental to the Federation.' "

Officer Sanders looked pointedly at Hunter. "Would you say, Mr. Blake," he said, "that having superior medical services would materially improve the ability of the Utopians to carry out their pirate activities?"

Hunter was visibly rattled. "I don't know, sir," he said.

The ASP officer turned toward Colonel Hood. "For the record, I would like to read one other codicil from the Sedition Act of 2405. Article 11, Paragraph C." He looked down at his computer. " 'Unless this act is amended, or otherwise abrogated, all individuals, groups, and organizations involved in activities purposely designed to violate, undermine, or repudiate Federation law, or whose stated objective is to generate chaos and disorder in the Federation domain, are hereby classified as enemies for the purpose of this act. This definition includes, but is not limited to, any and all members of the bands of so-called space pirates who inhabit Federation territory but do not accept Federation law or hegemony.' "

COLONEL HOOD CALLED for a short recess after Officer Sanders finished reading from his computer. Hunter was grateful. The ASP officer's attitude, as well as his line of questioning, had both angered and frightened Hunter. He knew that he needed to calm his emotions and carefully think about his strategy for the rest of the inquiry. Hunter briefly considered objecting to Officer Sanders altogether and refusing to continue with the debriefing unless the ASP representative was removed, or at the very least, silenced. He was afraid, however, that such a combative, noncooperative stance would raise an immediate red flag and might even cost him his Covington Fellowship. Officer Sanders had not, after all, directly accused Hunter of anything. He had, however, done a masterful job of injecting suspicion into the proceedings.

It was almost an hour before the board of inquiry reconvened. Judging from both body language and the looks the two men exchanged when the group gathered again, Hunter surmised that there had been major friction between the ASP officer and Colonel Hood during the break. Colonel Hood was decidedly less affable when he asked his first question.

"Hunter," he said, "what can you tell us about the location of the asteroid on which the Utopian pirate band lives? While you were there, did you ever, for example, see any kind of a map, or reference system, that indicated where the asteroid was with respect to Mars, or the Earth, or any other known object in space?"

"I never saw any maps," Hunter answered quickly. He hesitated, and glanced around the table at the board. Only in Officer Sanders' eyes did he see any hostility. "Naturally I wondered about where I was," Hunter continued at length, "but I thought it would be imprudent to ask too many direct questions. I looked at the Sun occasionally through the dome, to measure its size, and also listened to what anybody else said that might give me an indication of where we were in space. One of my patients was the chief air-conditioning engineer, and he mentioned, while I was examining him at the clinic, that his system had just successfully withstood its maximum stress. From that comment and my own observations of the size of the Sun, I concluded that we had probably just passed perihelion. My feeling, based on everything that I heard and observed on Utopia, is that the perihelion point of the asteroid was well inside the orbit of Mars, perhaps even approaching the orbit of the Earth. But I can't substantiate that feeling with specific data."

After a few questions of clarification, Colonel Hood was apparently satisfied with Hunter's answer. He then asked the other board members if they had any other questions on the subject of the location of the home asteroid of the Utopian band.

"If I have understood what you just said, Mr. Blake," ASP Officer Sanders said, "all you knew, or thought you knew, about your location in space was a rough estimate of your distance from the Sun. Is that correct?"

"Yes, sir," Hunter answered.

"Yet while you were a passenger on that pirate spacecraft heading for some trading post," Officer Sanders said, "you planned an escape in a shuttle, obviously believing that you would be able to reach some safe haven before the shuttle's life-support and other critical systems failed. Do you really expect us to believe that you had no knowledge at all about where you were with respect to Mars at the time of your escape attempt?"

There was a brief, sharp interchange between Colonel Hood and Officer Sanders. The colonel reminded the ASP representative that the discussion of Hunter's escape was scheduled for the afternoon. Officer Sanders replied that all his current questions would be constrained to address the issue of the location of the Utopian home asteroid. Colonel Hood thought for a moment, and then asked Hunter to answer the previous question.

"I didn't really care where I was," Hunter said. "I just wanted to escape from the pirates. From the manuals, I learned that the shuttle navigation system had sufficient optical and other celestial sensors that it could precisely determine its position in the solar system, given enough time, without any initial information. The manuals also said that the shuttle could support a single passenger for twelve or thirteen days at most. My plan was quite simple. I would escape from the pirate spaceship and maintain complete electronic silence for an extended period of time. When I was safely away from the pirate spacecraft, I would activate the navigation sensors. Once the navigation system provided me with an estimate of my location, I would choose both my trajectory and the timing of my call for help. It seemed reasonable to me that I would be able to find some flight path, using the propulsion capabilities of the shuttle, that would give me a good chance of being rescued by either a Dem or a Fed spacecraft."

Officer Sanders smiled. "Very clever," he said. He paused a moment before continuing. "Did the navigation system in the shuttle have the capability of presenting maps, with reference bodies, to help you plot your trajectory?" he asked.

"Yes," Hunter replied.

"And was the home asteroid of the Utopians one of those reference bodies that could be projected on the map in the display?" the ASP officer asked triumphantly.

"Yes, it was," Hunter answered. He immediately realized that it seemed that he had contradicted his earlier statement that he had never seen any kind of a map.

Hunter looked directly at Colonel Hood, and then the other board members. "I never checked the direction to the Utopian home asteroid while I was on the shuttle. I remember that the capability was there, but I never used it. All my attention was focused on finding my way to Mars, the Moon, or the Earth."

Officer Sanders was not convinced. "Are you saying that in nine days you never once looked at a map that showed where you were with respect to the asteroid on which you had lived for several months?"

"That's correct," Hunter answered. "Soon after I planned my trajectory—"

"I, for one," Officer Sanders interrupted, "find that statement very difficult to believe. You have already made it quite clear that you are both an extremely curious and intelligent young man. It doesn't make sense to me that during all that time on the shuttle, you never once accessed the maps in the navigation system to learn where the Utopian asteroid was with respect to your position."

"As I was about to say," Hunter replied, "not long after I had instructed the navigation system to take me in the direction of Mars, the mapping display malfunctioned. For some reason, I was no longer able to display a graphical representation of my position on the monitor in the cockpit. It was even difficult for me to confirm that I was still on my proper flight path."

There was a long silence in the conference room. During the silence, Colonel Hood received a realtime message on the communication network on his hand computer. "Our engineering personnel have just informed me," he said to the board, "that the mapping capability of the shuttle navigation system was indeed not functioning when the vehicle was tested last night."

"How convenient," ASP Officer Sanders said sarcastically.

SHORTLY THEREAFTER, AFTER the ASP officer indicated that he had no further questions on the topic, Colonel Hood announced that the inquiry would now move to the next agenda item, which was concerned with the portion of Hunter's statement that dealt with his general living situation on Utopia.

Hunter was asked to describe any and all of his activities on Utopia outside the clinic. He reminded the board that he worked long hours virtually every day, and was generally exhausted by the time his medical work was finished. In that context he mentioned being invited over to people's homes for dinner, working with the children's day-care center, having an occasional meeting with Lance, and attending two or three big gatherings of the entire Utopian band.

Lieutenant Russell asked if Hunter had any special friends on Utopia. Hunter answered that the only people whom he considered to be close friends were his coworkers in the clinic. The lieutenant next asked if Hunter ever encountered anyone on Utopia whom he had known before the kidnapping, or who was connected in any way to someone Hunter had known before. Hunter pointed out that in his opening statement he had mentioned that his sister had been friends with Chelsea Dickinson, one of the kidnappers, on Cicero. Hunter then revealed that on Utopia he had also met Chelsea's husband, Darrell Peabody, who was, by an amazing coincidence, also the son of his cabinmate during his days on the *Darwin* before the kidnapping.

The revelation that he had met Darrell Peabody sparked a flurry of questions. This was new information for the board. One of the Federation captains actually knew the Peabody family. Hunter told what he knew about Darrell. Captain Tolson asked if, to the best of Hunter's knowledge,

Darrell Peabody and Tehani Wilawa had ever had any interaction. Hunter reflected for a moment and then said that he couldn't recall ever having heard Darrell speak about having met Tehani.

Colonel Hood took the questioning in a different direction. He was primarily interested in what Hunter might have learned, from interactions with his patients or other contacts, about Utopian or other pirate military activities. Hunter said that he never heard any specific action discussed, although there had once been a celebration of some successful endeavor that was never described in any detail. Were there any visits from other pirate band representatives, suggesting some kind of collaborative effort? Hunter said that he had no knowledge of such visits.

Hunter had mentioned in his opening statement the creation of the drug discussion group, and the widespread use of recreational drugs among the Utopians. Captain Tolson asked many questions about drugs, nonmonogamous marriages, and other "pathological" social behavior. Hunter's answers were factual and nonjudgmental. The Defense Ministry officers seemed pleased that he was corroborating the information about the Utopians contained in their intelligence files. Hunter had just started feeling comfortable again when he noticed that Officer Sanders was ready to ask a question.

"Mr. Blake," the ASP officer then said, smiling as he looked at Hunter, "during your time on Utopia, how many times, and with how many partners, did you engage in sexual intercourse?"

Hunter stared at Officer Sanders for several seconds, his expression clearly showing both his shock and his distaste for the question. Hunter looked at Colonel Hood. "Excuse me, sir," he said, "but if I may, I would like to object to the question. I don't think it's germane to this inquiry."

Colonel Hood thought for a moment and then turned

toward the ASP officer. "Sanders, for my edification, can you give me some reason why you think that question is important to this board?"

"Certainly," he replied. "In our dossier on the Utopian pirate band, as well as in Mr. Blake's earlier testimony, there is considerable mention about the 'different' sexual mores of these people, but no quantitative specifics. The putative sexual promiscuity of this particular band of space pirates is legendary. Mr. Blake lived among them for many months. He can provide hard data for our files."

"I cannot justify invading this young man's privacy," Colonel Hood said, "just to obtain a data point for our intelligence system. I am going to rule your question out of order."

"You may do that, sir," Officer Sanders replied in a supercilious tone, "but the question is still very much to the point. It will certainly be asked again, either by me or by someone else, at some later point in this investigation. I submit that the answer is important to understanding the very nature of Mr. Blake's experience with the enemy."

"May I remind you, sir," a red-faced Colonel Hood said, "that you are officially a guest at this inquiry. I suggest that you try to follow the protocol that was agreed upon by our respective organizations."

Officer Sanders' eyes flashed angrily, but he didn't say anything in response. Hunter was pleased, after ten minutes of comparatively innocuous questioning, that Colonel Hood announced a one-hour lunch break.

THREE

HUNTER ATE LUNCH WITH Lieutenant Russell. The lieutenant made no secret of his feeling that the ASP officer had been way out of line with both his tone and his specific questions a couple of times during the morning. "Those guys see bogeymen everywhere," Lieutenant Russell said. "Hell, they would probably even declare me to be subversive." He leaned forward and lowered his voice. "What's frightening though is that their power is still growing. Giving that asshole Tyson his own cabinet post boosted the prestige of the ASP immensely. And I guarantee you there's no love lost between our defense minister Lester Sackett and Tyson. According to my commanding officer, Sackett calls Tyson 'the number one snake.'"

For just a moment Hunter, still a little unsettled by the morning's session, asked himself if Lieutenant Russell's negative comments about Officer Sanders in particular, and the ASP in general, could have been deliberately intended to lull him into a false sense of discomfort with his Defense Ministry interrogators. He quickly convinced himself, however, that the lieutenant's remarks were almost certainly genuine.

The two men finished lunch twenty minutes before the

debriefing was scheduled to start again. Hunter spent the time in his hotel room carefully considering the kinds of questions he was likely to be asked about his escape, especially by Officer Sanders, and thinking through his answers. Hunter knew that the escape portion of his testimony was by far the easiest to attack.

When the board of inquiry reconvened, however, Officer Sanders was missing. "The two of us were unable to agree on some procedural issues," Colonel Hood informed Hunter and the other board members in the hotel conference room, "and our ASP representative chose to withdraw from the board rather than be bound by my decisions. This video is still being transmitted live to ASP headquarters, however, so I believe it still satisfies the original intent of having one debriefing for both agencies."

The afternoon session, which focused entirely on his escape, turned out to be much easier than Hunter had feared. The Defense Ministry officers accepted that five months of exemplary conduct by Hunter could very well have convinced the Utopians that their prisoner would not even consider anything as stupid as an escape attempt. That explained why he was not constrained in any way on board, and had access to the ship's computer to read the shuttle operational manuals. The board found it difficult, but not impossible, to believe that Hunter could learn enough in several hours of studying the manuals to fly a simple, outdated spacecraft. Why was the shuttle even onboard, if the purpose of the trip was a simple visit to a trading post? Hunter repeated what he had purportedly been told by Bailey, namely that the Utopians no longer had any need for the antiquated spacecraft and were taking it to the post as a barter item.

There was no hint of an adversarial relationship in the afternoon questioning. The session went smoothly, without any recess, and finished two hours earlier than originally planned. "Thank you very much for your cooperation, Hunter," Colonel Hood said after the board had completed its formal business. "You have provided us with some valuable information." He smiled. "All of us are impressed, not just with your escape, but also with the mature way that you handled these proceedings."

Hunter thanked the colonel and the board for their compliments. "There are a couple of matters we need to discuss before we break up," Colonel Hood then said, "just so there are no misunderstandings. On the subject of your personal communications, from this point forward you are no longer under any constraints. Your E-mail account has been reopened, and arrears paid, by the Federation. I daresay that your incoming mail queue is probably monstrously long as we speak.

"With respect to the press, we have decided not to conduct a formal news conference. As you pointed out yesterday, you are not a member of the military, and it is against ministry policy to sponsor press conferences that are not directly related to defense. You may deal with the media as you see fit—although I will remind you that if you tell them something new and significantly different from what we heard today, it is highly likely that this board of inquiry will be reconvened."

The colonel smiled. "If you have no questions, you are free to go. We have made a reservation for you to fly to the Centralia spaceport on the noon shuttle tomorrow. It is our understanding that the director of the Covington Fellowship program, Mr. Hans Langenbahn, will meet you upon arrival. Your hotel bill, including your dinner tonight and breakfast in the morning, will be charged to our account."

HUNTER AGAIN DECLINED Lieutenant Russell's invitation to spend an evening in the resort area of

Phobos. In the first place, he was very tired. In addition, now that the debriefing was behind him, Hunter had many other, more important items on his mind. His first priority was organizing his new life. He also wanted to contact Tehani.

Colonel Hood was correct about the large number of messages that were waiting for him. Since the Federation network had a standard policy of retaining all personal electronic transactions for at least five days, reactivation of Hunter's E-mail account recalled any message that had been sent to him since the initial news of his escape had been announced. There were dozens of messages from well-wishers, mostly from people he didn't know.

Hunter scanned through the E-mail queue in his hotel room, looking for the message that was most important to him. He found it quickly. Tehani had transmitted a video to him late the night before. Hunter opened it immediately.

"Such wonderful news!" she began. Hunter hit the pause button on the controls and a full-screen image of Tehani's head and shoulders froze in front of him. Hunter stared at her, his heart racing with excitement. Was it possible that she was even more beautiful now than the last time that he had seen her? For almost a minute Hunter just sat in his chair and stared at her picture.

"I can't believe you're actually on Phobos," Tehani said when Hunter activated the video again. "I tried calling all the hotels around the spaceport an hour ago, but none of them had you listed as a guest." She smiled radiantly. "I guess you're so famous now that you're traveling incognito. Anyway, let me hear from you as soon as you can. I can't wait to see you! Hugs and kisses."

Hunter played the short video three times. The signoff frame, which stayed on screen at the conclusion of the video, contained Tehani's new private number at Sybaris.

Without a moment's hesitation, Hunter picked up the phone, with the video mode active, and called her. During the first ring he told himself that he should have at least combed his hair, or made certain that he looked all right. The second ring was interrupted before it was completed and a recorded video appeared on the monitor in Hunter's hotel room.

"Hi, this is Tehani," the recording said. She was dressed in a casual purple blouse and a pair of black slacks. "I'm sorry I missed your call, but if you'll leave your number and a brief message, I'll get back to you as soon as I can." The camera zoomed in for a closeup. "You must be a close friend," the recorded Tehani said, "or you wouldn't have this number. In that case, you know that I want to talk with you. You probably also know that sometimes, when I'm working, I really don't have a good opportunity to chat for several days. Please be assured that I'll call you when I have some available time."

The monitor started flashing "Record your message now." "Hello, Tehani," Hunter began nervously. "I'm at the Phobos Spaceport Hotel, Room 514. I'm going down now to have dinner, but after that I should be in my room until around nine o'clock in the morning. At noon I'm leaving on a flight to Centralia. That's right. I'll be on Mars before the end of the day tomorrow. Call me if you have a moment. Even in the middle of the night. Oh, yeah, I got your E-mail from last night. You look great, but that's no surprise. I can't wait to see you in person. Hugs and kisses back."

THE RINGING OF the phone roused Hunter from his sleep. He started to climb out of bed and go to the desk, in front of the monitor and the video camera, but the modality indicator beside the bed said that the incoming call was audio only. The digital clock was flashing 4:11 A.M. Hunter picked up the receiver and said hello.

"Hi, Hunter," Tehani said in a rapid, husky whisper. "I can't talk long. Actually I'm in the bathroom with the door closed. My client would probably raise hell if he knew I was in here talking to another man. Anyway, I'll be with him another three days. Will you call me on Friday?"

"I will," Hunter said. "Are you all right?"

"Mostly," Tehani said. "Gotta run. Love you."

"Love you, too," Hunter said automatically.

Before he fell asleep again, Hunter chastised himself for responding so quickly, and affirmatively, to Tehani's statement of her love. *And what about Ursula?* a voice inside his head asked. *Didn't you tell Ursula that you loved her only two weeks ago, when you left Utopia? Isn't she going to be the mother of your child?*

It's not that simple, Hunter said in an attempt to mollify his inner voice. *In some ways I love them both. They're really completely different.*

"I'M SORRY, MR. Sparkman, but I'm not granting private interviews to anyone. I'm going to make a public statement and answer all questions in a press conference at the Phobos spaceport in about fifteen minutes. The conference is being arranged by the news department of the Free Zone Network. Please talk to them about attendance."

Hunter hung up the phone. He was exasperated. Since just before six o'clock in the morning his phone had been ringing off the hook with calls from the media. Apparently, sometime during the night a hotel computer had transferred his name and room number from a confidential list to a public one. Hunter had had three calls before he went to work out in the fitness center. When he had returned to his hotel room there were eight additional messages waiting.

Hunter had decided the previous evening that he did not want the media to be a constant distraction while he was establishing his new life in Centralia. After eating dinner in his room he had called the Free Zone Network and asked them if they could set up an open press conference at the spaceport in the morning. They had been more than willing to comply with his request.

In the corridor outside his hotel room, on his way to the elevator, Hunter encountered a reporter and a cameraman from the popular magazine with the largest circulation in the Free Zone. Initially Hunter was cordial, and politely declined to answer any questions. When, however, the cameraman blocked his pathway to the open elevator, and the aggressive reporter thrust a microphone in his face, Hunter became irritated. If he hadn't lightly pushed the cameraman out of his way, he wouldn't have been able to board the elevator.

Twenty-five members of the media, plus another dozen curious hotel guests, were already in the hotel ballroom when Hunter arrived. He was immediately approached by a lovely young woman in her late twenties, who identified herself as the Free Zone Network representative in charge of the press conference. Hunter briefly discussed the agenda for the conference with the woman and then climbed up on the raised platform at one end of the ballroom. There was scattered applause from the crowd.

"I'm going to read a short prepared statement first," Hunter said when the noise in the room finally subsided, "and then I will answer questions."

Hunter had written the statement in his hotel the previous evening before going to bed. He had initially thought that he might tell his story without a prepared text, but after careful consideration of all the possible risks, including a misquote by the media and an inadvertent comment by him, Hunter had decided that it would be wiser to have a formal written statement.

He essentially told the same story that he had told the board of inquiry, omitting of course such personal details as the nature of his relationship with Tehani onboard the *Darwin*. Hunter expected that the media would be primarily interested in the differences between life among the pirates and the way ordinary people lived on Mars, either in the Free Zone or under one of the two dominant space powers. As a result, he spent most of the time in his statement describing the aspects of pirate life that were the most foreign to his audience. Hunter downplayed his escape altogether, quickly summarizing it in a casual manner.

When he was finished with his statement, Hunter took a few sips from a container of water and opened the floor for questions. He was immediately bombarded by shouts from all directions. The first half-dozen questions all addressed the sexual mores or drug use among the Utopians. The most insightful of the first group of questions was asked by a young female reporter from an alternative-lifestyle newspaper in the Free Zone. "Based on your observation of life on Cicero and in Utopia," she said, "would you say that there was any significant difference in the degree of family harmony in the two places?"

Hunter began his answer by reminding everyone that he was only twenty-one years old, and hardly an expert on sociological issues. He then said that he had been quite surprised to discover that in Utopia, where the structure of marriage and family arrangements were free from governmental or legal restriction, there seemed to be slightly less personal dissatisfaction, especially among the women. His answer generated a flurry of related questions, some quite passionate, and Hunter eventually conceded that the necessity of survival among the pirates probably conditioned the men to be less possessive, and to be more willing to share their women.

Some of the reporters appeared to be disappointed that Hunter had neither witnessed nor participated in any sexual orgies, and had not observed a single death by drug overdose. He was asked if, based on his experience, he favored the legalization of drug usage on Mars. Hunter said that he wasn't certain, for there were many factors to be considered, but he did have the opinion that applying harsh penalties for recreational drug use and other victimless crimes was absurd.

"Eileen Young, *Free Zone Times,*" a reporter introduced herself when Hunter recognized her raised hand. "In a purported recent interview, one of the pirate band chiefs is quoted as saying that young people in particular are attracted to pirate life primarily because of their sense of alienation and disenfranchisement in the more conservative space societies. Would you care to comment on that quote?"

Hunter said that he was not familiar with either the purported interview, or the specific quote, but that he had observed on Utopia that young people had more critical roles in the society, doubtless out of necessity, than they would have had, at a comparable age, on Mars. He then mentioned that the Utopians defined sixteen to be the age of adulthood in their society, and that members of their band were expected to be responsible, contributing citizens from that age forward.

Hunter was somewhat surprised at the reaction of the reporters to his casual comment about the age of adulthood on Utopia. For the next ten minutes all the questions were about that subject. Virtually every question belied a clear prejudice that the idea that sixteen-year-olds could be treated as adults was absurd. Eventually Hunter was asked if, based on his observations, boys and girls of sixteen and seventeen on Utopia were "significantly different from" the young people he had known on Cicero at the same age.

"I would say yes," Hunter answered after some reflection. "On Utopia, the developmental process is accelerated by the knowledge that each individual must, so to speak, pull his or her weight in the society at the age of sixteen. Adolescence is therefore severely truncated. Even at what we would consider to be a very young age, the Utopian youth is aware that his contributions to the band are important. In our society, at least on Cicero, at sixteen my friends and I were still carefree students. Most of us had very little real responsibility, and we certainly didn't feel that what we did was important to our society."

Late in the press conference, Hunter finally recognized a bald-headed man wearing a business suit who had been patiently raising his hand throughout the proceedings. "Gavin Stevens, *Democratic News,*" he said. "Mr. Blake," he said, "are you aware that roughly a month ago a mammoth raid on the Dem south polar lunar ice processing facility occurred?"

"No, sir," Hunter said. "I'm not. I haven't yet had a chance to read about everything that happened during the months that I was gone."

"In that case," Gavin Stevens said, "I need to provide you with some background information before I ask my question. Is that all right?"

Hunter nodded.

"This raid was a masterful piece of work," the reporter continued. "The attackers, whoever they were, made off with half a billion dollars of state-of-the-art equipment and supplies. The Dem government originally accused the Feds of conducting the raid, and suggested that one of their elite commando groups was involved. The Feds of course have repeatedly denied it. Recently there has been a rumor that the raid may have been the work of several different pirate bands, working together. Based on your experience, do you think these space pirates are capable of the kind of collaboration that would have been necessary for such a raid?"

"I wouldn't know," Hunter replied. "I didn't see anything on Utopia that would help me answer that question one way or the other."

Soon thereafter, the young woman from the Free Zone Network informed Hunter that it was time for him to check in for his flight to Mars. Hunter thanked the members of the media, and stepped down from the platform. Again there was scattered applause.

FOUR

HUNTER'S EXCITEMENT WAS PALPABLE when he strapped himself into his aisle seat in the spacecraft that would carry him from Phobos to Mars. Finally, he was going to land on the planet that been his destination when he had first boarded the *Darwin* on Cicero so many months ago.

There were thirty-six passengers on the flight. All the seats were filled. Sitting next to Hunter was an elderly man, dressed in a conservative dark suit, who looked as if he had taken the flight many times before. The man didn't even watch the introductory video that began a few minutes before the spacecraft undocked and eased away from the passenger terminal.

Hunter, on the other hand, paid very close attention to the video playing on the monitor in the back of the seat in front of him.

The flight to Centralia will last two hours and forty-five minutes. For the first two hours, after the deorbit maneuver that will place us on a trajectory to intersect Mars, we will be coasting.

The video displayed a graphical representation of the orbit of Phobos and the path that the spacecraft would take from the Martian moon to its destination.

When we reach the upper edge of the Martian atmosphere,

attitude adjustments will be required to make certain that we will enter the atmosphere at the correct angle of attack. From then until we are deep inside the atmosphere of Mars, the ride will be very rough. It is imperative that all passengers have both their shoulder and waist belts strapped during this portion of the flight.

Hunter watched intently as the graphic display on the monitor focused on the entry and terminal descent portions of the flight.

During atmospheric entry, our speed relative to Mars will be greatly reduced. Most of the deceleration will come from the absorption of heat by the huge shield on the front of the spacecraft. During the peak deceleration, the spacecraft may bounce around wildly in many different directions. This is completely normal. Our attitude-control system will be active throughout the period, and will return us to a more comfortable flight regime once we are well within the sensible atmosphere. From that point forward, our primary engines and guidance system will take over and make certain that our landing at Centralia is smooth and safe.

An elderly couple were sitting in the pair of seats across the aisle from Hunter. From their conversation prior to the departure, Hunter had deduced that they were Dem tourists whose home was on the Moon. "Claudia said that she was terrified during the last part of her flight to Mars," the woman said after the video. "She said that it was worse than the upside-down roller coaster at Tranquility Park." Her husband took her hand and said something that Hunter couldn't hear.

Hunter was sorry that he had not been assigned a window seat. His seatmate pulled down the shade on the window soon after departure, as the spacecraft reoriented for the deorbit maneuver, and Hunter was forced to look across the aisle to see anything outside the vehicle. He had a brief glimpse of Phobos before the engines activated and he was thrust backward against his seat for several minutes.

When the maneuver was over, the ride became very gentle. Hunter scanned through the vast menu of in-seat entertainments and chose a motion picture that had been released just before his departure from Cicero. To his surprise, he found that he was not particularly interested in the movie and fell asleep after half an hour.

He dreamed that he was back on Utopia, lying in his bed in the small room partitioned off from the main tent of the clinic. Ursula was beside him. Hunter rolled over and looked at her. She was beautiful. In his dream she awakened and smiled. She yawned and stretched before giving Hunter a hug. "I think it's time for us to discuss names," Ursula said in his dream.

Hunter had no idea what she was talking about. "If it's a girl," Ursula continued, "I'd like to name her Anastasia, and call her Stacey. I've always really liked that name. Is that all right with you?"

In his dream Hunter delicately lifted the sheet and put his hand on Ursula's stomach. There was a small, almost imperceptible bulge that he rubbed gently with his hand. "That's fine," Hunter said, as he bent down to kiss the area that he was rubbing.

Suddenly the bed, Ursula, and everything in his dream seemed to be bouncing about. Hunter was jolted awake and quickly tightened both his seat belts. The spacecraft veered wildly to the right, and then began to pitch down. Someone in the cabin screamed. As soon as the pitch excursion stopped, the vehicle started to roll and the elderly couple across the aisle was temporarily below Hunter.

A calm voice on the spacecraft audio system informed all the passengers that the peak deceleration portion of the flight was occurring and that all the wild gyrations would settle down in another two or three minutes. A particularly bumpy twenty seconds forced the lady across the aisle to reach for the bag in the seat pocket in front of her with her free hand. With her other hand she was holding on to her husband's arm with all her might.

Hunter thought it would be impolite to watch the gray-haired lady throw up. He looked to his right just as the vehicle pitched violently up, throwing his body back against the seat. "This is worse than most," the man sitting beside Hunter said, "but not as bad as it can be. On one flight last month, the spacecraft pitched a full three hundred and sixty degrees before it stabilized. One of the passengers had a heart attack."

Even Hunter was feeling a little queasy when the jolts and bumps started gradually to diminish. The rest of the flight was comparatively smooth. Hunter felt the thrust when the primary engines activated, but the sensation was nothing compared to what he had experienced during peak deceleration.

The landing was perfect. Hunter barely felt the impact of the wheels on the runway. Glancing across the aisle at the open window beside the tourist couple, Hunter watched for several seconds as the spacecraft taxied toward the edge of the mammoth dome that enclosed Centralia. A landing video playing on the monitor showed the dome from above, with the many skyscrapers reaching almost to the top, and then explained that a "hermetically sealed" walkway, which was really an extension of the dome, would mate with the spacecraft and provide access to the spaceport terminal.

"For those of you who have not felt gravity for a long time," the captain said over the audio system after the spacecraft had stopped, "I want to remind you to take it easy, and let your body adjust. If you have been in orbit, or in some other weightless environment for even ten days, you will feel quite strange when you take your first steps after our touchdown."

Hunter had never experienced significant gravity before

in his life. In fact, he had never been anywhere where he
hadn't needed to keep one shoe on the ground at all times.
He was looking forward to feeling a pull toward the
ground. In fact, as the vehicle slowly parked at the gate in
the Centralia spaceport, Hunter was bursting with excitement. He was eagerly anticipating virtually everything
about his new life.

HUNTER CARRIED HIS shoes with the adhe-
sive strips in his hands as he followed the other passengers
down the aisle of the spacecraft toward the exit. Gravity
was amazing. Each step was a new experience. At one
point Hunter laughed out loud, then jumped into the air as
high as he could. He was astonished at how quickly he returned to the floor. The disembarking passengers both in
front and behind him eyed him with curiosity. "I've never
ever been in gravity before," he said to nobody in particular. Hunter put his shoes back on and said a cheery good-
bye to the flight attendant at the door before entering the
deployable, airtight walkway that led inside the terminal.

Flight arrivals and departures at the Centralia spaceport
were inside a special, secure area of the terminal. Only passengers and approved spaceport personnel were allowed inside the secure area. Departing passengers entered the
boarding area after having had their hand baggage X-rayed
and their identity cards checked. Arriving passengers were
required to pass through special individual gates that were
activated by swiping an identity card through an automatic
reader. When Hunter swiped his card through the machine
just outside one of the gates, however, a red light flashed and
an alarm sounded. The door did not open. Hunter stood
there, waiting, while the other passengers behind him
switched to other gates and passed through to the other side.

After about thirty seconds, a young man and a young

woman wearing ASP uniforms came out of an office on one side of the gates. The woman asked for Hunter's identity card. She swiped it through the side of her hand computer, then read the information on the monitor. "Come with us," she said to Hunter in a pleasant, but authoritative tone.

Hunter followed the pair into the nearby office. He was asked to sit down while the shift supervisor, who was presently on a break, was contacted by radio. A few minutes later a stocky woman in her mid-thirties, who introduced herself as Officer Melanie Windsor, came into the office. The young woman who had taken Hunter's identity card handed it to Officer Windsor, along with the hand computer displaying Hunter's information.

Officer Windsor's face brightened as soon as she read Hunter's name. "Of course," she said with genuine enthusiasm, "I've just been watching a news short about you on the network. You're the young man who escaped from the pirates. There are a dozen members of the media waiting out there for you." She extended her hand. "Welcome to Centralia," she said.

Hunter shook her hand. Officer Windsor then took him inside the only office in the room. "Your identity card was rejected at the gate because it was incomplete," she said to Hunter after she sat down at her desk and consulted her computer. "According to our records, this is the first time that you have ever passed through an entry port here in North Mars. Is our information correct?"

Hunter nodded. "For security reasons," Officer Windsor said, "every individual, including Federation citizens from the outlying territories, must receive a permit to enter North Mars. The permits are valid for one year from the date of issue. It's an easy matter, and I can accommodate you right here in this office." She swiveled the computer so that it was facing Hunter. "As soon as you fill out the information on this form," she said with a smile, "I will receive a permit number from ASP Headquarters. I will encode it on your identity card immediately, and you'll never have this problem again."

Hunter began filling out the form. There were two fields under the heading marked "Address." In the field for his permanent address Hunter inserted his home address on Cicero. The second field called for his address in North Mars, if the permanent address was somewhere else.

"Officer Windsor," Hunter said, "I'm not certain what to write for my address here in Centralia. I'm moving here for the first time, and don't yet know where I'll be staying. Should I just put the address for the Covington Fellowship Office?"

"That's right," Officer Windsor said, "I remember them saying on the network that you had been kidnapped while you were on your way to Mars to serve as a Covington Fellow." Her eyebrows raised. "Wow," she said, "you must be one smart fellow." She paused for a moment and then shrugged. "I guess it's okay for you to put the fellowship office address. If it's not, the application will be rejected and kicked back here to me in a minute or two."

After Hunter completed the application, the ASP officer dispatched it electronically to the permit office. In less than a minute a response was received. The application was rejected. Officer Windsor read the note on the computer monitor before saying anything to Hunter.

"The permit has been denied for two reasons," she then said. "You must give a home address, as we might have suspected, but more importantly, it says here that you have never been implanted with a navigation probe. Permits to enter North Mars cannot be granted to individuals who don't have navigation probes." Officer Windsor looked briefly at the information on Hunter's application. "Don't they have navprobes on Cicero?" she asked.

Hunter shook his head. "Oh, boy," Officer Windsor

said, "this is going to be complicated." She thought for a few seconds. "Is there someone meeting you here at the terminal? This could take a while and I don't want them to be inconvenienced."

Hunter told her that it was his understanding that Mr. Hans Langenbahn, the director of the Covington Fellowship program, was supposed to meet him upon his arrival. Officer Windsor activated a microphone in her computer system. "Will Hans Langenbahn please report to the ASP office in the arrivals area?" she said. After a delay of a few seconds, Hunter heard her voice on the spaceport audio system.

The young woman who had taken Hunter's identity card at the gate showed up with Mr. Langenbahn about five minutes later. He greeted Hunter pleasantly, and apologized for not having realized that Hunter would not be able to pass through the arrival security gate. Mr. Langenbahn provided a home address in Centralia for Hunter's permit application, and guaranteed personally that Hunter would be present at the navprobe installation office the following morning. It was another fifteen minutes, including the time that Officer Windsor spent talking on the phone to someone at ASP Headquarters, before an entry permit was encoded on Hunter's identity card. Before Mr. Langenbahn and Hunter departed, Officer Windsor explained that the temporary navprobe override would be invalid after the next day and that Hunter would be subject to immediate detention if a permanent navprobe indicator did not replace it in that time.

As soon as they left the secure area of the spaceport terminal, Mr. Langenbahn and Hunter were accosted by a handful of reporters and photographers who had waited during the long clearance process. They were miffed when Hunter told them that he had no additional statements to make and that he did not wish to be interviewed. Mr.

Langenbahn took Hunter aside and eventually persuaded Hunter to say something to the media. Hunter forced a smile and told the journalists how pleased he was "to be back in civilization" and how much he was looking forward to beginning his duties as a Covington Fellow. But he was adamant about not answering any questions. Hunter eventually became frustrated with the journalists and had to entreat Mr. Langenbahn to take him out of the terminal.

By the time Mr. Langenbahn and Hunter had left the spaceport and boarded the tram for the ten-minute ride to his new apartment, the enthusiasm that Hunter had felt when he first left the spacecraft had vanished completely. He hardly spoke to his companion for the first minute or two of the tram ride, except to answer direct questions. Mr. Langenbahn noticed Hunter's sour mood and attributed it to fatigue. The Covington Fellowship director reminded Hunter that he was not yet accustomed to the effects of gravity and that he should try to rest more than usual during the first week or so of his stay in Centralia.

LATER, HUNTER WOULD criticize himself for having let his impatience with both the bureaucratic security process and the media almost ruin his first day on Mars. In truth, in spite of his less-than-upbeat mood, the short tram ride fascinated him. Out his window the eclectic architecture of the modern buildings of Centralia were a feast for his eyes. Hunter had of course seen many photographs and videos of the largest city on Mars, but watching the actual buildings pass the tram window was different. Slowly but surely, his natural curiosity and the thrill of being in Centralia lifted his spirits.

He began asking questions about what he was seeing. Mr. Langenbahn, a lifelong resident of Centralia, had all the answers. He showed Hunter many maps on his hand computer and gave Hunter a quick orientation to the city. Hunter's apartment building was near the center, within walking distance of both the Covington Fellowship Office and most of the ministries. The spaceport, of course, was on the very outskirts of the area under the dome.

The most impressive complex of structures the tram passed en route was the FedEnt Headquarters. Spread out over a full square mile, the buildings dazzled the eye with both their unusual designs and variety of external decoration. The virtual-world building, for example, rose forty stories into the air before being topped with a mammoth kiosk shaped exactly like the thousands of virtual-world venues found in homes, offices, and every major public location on Mars and the Moon.

"Federated Entertainment, or FedEnt, as it is known to everybody," Hans Langenbahn said to Hunter while the tram was passing the astonishing collection of buildings, "is both the largest corporation in space and an integral part of the Federation government. Although its business endeavors are quite diverse, FedEnt is most famous for its monopoly on every aspect of entertainment in space, from networks to virtual worlds to theme parks to gambling to resorts to music and motion pictures.

"The second-most-powerful person in the Federation," he continued, "is the director of FedEnt. One of my cynical friends has suggested that the FISC government only exists to serve the interests of FedEnt."

The tram made a ninety-degree turn to the right and passed through the Centralia financial district before coming to the complex of apartments that ringed the ministries and the parliament building. Mr. Langenbahn and Hunter descended from the tram platform to the street and walked three or four minutes until they were in front of a tall apartment complex.

"All the Covington Fellows live here during their first

year," Mr. Langenbahn said to Hunter as they entered the structure. "It's very convenient. The stores and shops on these bottom two floors have virtually everything that a young single person could need. The gymnasium on the second floor is completely equipped." He pointed down the wide hall in front of them. "There's even a large entertainment center on this floor, at the far end of the building. It has a full holographic theater, a dozen different automated restaurants surrounding a lounge area, and several of those virtual-world kiosks that you young people seem to like so much."

They walked over to the elevator. "You can use your identity card to charge anything in this building to your Covington account," Mr. Langenbahn said while they were waiting. "The supermarket is right there, on the left. Reynolds and Sons is an inexpensive, but adequate, men's clothing store on the second floor. Both stores deliver inside the building if you want to order from your computer monitor. Each of the fellows has a monthly budget for charges that is generous, but not opulent. Because of your unusual situation, you will have a double allocation for your first month."

They took the elevator to the sixteenth floor, where Hunter's apartment was located. The building had thirty-four stories, with a dozen apartment units on each floor. Mr. Langenbahn told Hunter that the Covington Fellows all lived between the fifteenth and nineteenth floors.

Hunter's apartment was surprisingly spacious. There were two bedrooms, each with its own bathroom, and an open kitchen/dining room/living room that must have been six hundred square feet in size. A modern entertainment complex, with the screen built into the wall, was in the living room. Two desks, each with its own computer and small monitor, were against the wall on either side of the large window.

"Your roommate is Dallas Morrison," Mr. Langenbahn said. "He has been assigned to the Defense Ministry." He looked at his watch. "Dallas will probably return from work around six o'clock. He knows that you're arriving today and is planning, I believe, to take you out for dinner with a few of the other fellows tonight."

Mr. Langenbahn waited while Hunter surveyed the apartment. His bedroom already had sheets and blankets on the queen-size bed, and towels and washcloths in the bathroom. The large chest of drawers was more than adequate. "It's very nice," Hunter said when he came back into the living room. "Thank you very much."

"I'm going to return to work now," Mr. Langenbahn said, "if that's all right with you. We'll have a busy day tomorrow. Please be at my office at eight-thirty. We'll take care of the navprobe installation first thing, and then we'll return to the office, where I will go over your program and schedule, as well as all the administrative details. As I told you on the tram, you've been assigned to the Health Ministry. In the afternoon I will take you over there and introduce you to your sponsor, Dr. Devi Sinha, who is the Deputy Minister for Management. I guess technically Dr. Sinha is also your boss for the time being." He paused briefly. "Any questions?" Mr. Langenbahn said.

"I presume that all the maps, phone numbers, and other information I might need are stored in my computer?" Hunter said.

"Yes," said Mr. Langenbahn. "Both on your desktop over there, and on the hand computer that you'll find in the top drawer of your chest. Both computers also contain a copy of the 'Guidelines for Covington Fellows,' which covers some of the more mundane aspects of your fellowship."

"Great," Hunter said. He walked to the door with Mr. Langenbahn and shook his hand. "Thanks again for everything," Hunter said.

———

HUNTER HAD NEVER been particularly interested in clothing or fashion. However, in the bag he had carried with him on the shuttle, he had had only a barely adequate supply of shirts, trousers, socks, and underwear. His only pair of shoes were designed for a weightless environment and were a little unwieldly, as well as out of place, on Mars. After eating a quick lunch, Hunter's first stop was the men's clothing store on the second floor.

He was well aware, from all the material that he had read, that the Covington Fellows dressed formally every day. Hunter's first purchase was a simple navy blue coat, accompanied by two pairs of pants, one blue and one gray, and three different kinds of shirts to complement the ensemble. He also bought some casual clothing, plenty of underwear and socks, and an exercise outfit. Before leaving the store Hunter also picked out two new pairs of shoes, one for work and a second that could be used both for casual wear and for workouts.

The female clerk who helped him was the only employee in the small store. Twice she expressed surprise that Hunter had actually shown up in person to buy the clothing. "Almost nobody actually comes into the store," she said. "I spend most of my time every day filling the orders that are made by computer."

By the time that Hunter had put his clothes away and taken his first shower in a gravity environment, it was after six o'clock. Hunter was drying off in his bathroom when he heard his apartment door open and a cheerful voice holler, "Hello, there, Hunter Blake. Your roommate is home."

Hunter wrapped the towel around his midsection and went into the living room to meet Dallas Morrison. His roommate was a gangly young man at least three inches taller than Hunter. The pair shook hands and spoke briefly.

Then Hunter went back into his room to finish drying off and to dress.

When Hunter returned to the living room, his roommate was sitting on the couch in a polo shirt and jeans, watching a television program on the wall screen. "Want a beer?" Dallas asked.

"Yes, indeed," Hunter replied. "That would hit the spot."

Dallas brought Hunter a beer and the pair sat down on the couch. "Unless Langenbahn et al are making an exception for you," Dallas said with a smile, "tomorrow you'll start your official program. The first few weeks are intense. You'll definitely learn a lot, but I'll warn you now, some of the activities are really boring."

Dallas laughed. "To retain a modicum of sanity during your orientation process," he said, "you'll probably need support from the rest of the fellows. We can also be helpful in explaining how the program actually works. . . . Anyway, if you have the energy, I thought I'd introduce you to a couple of the other guys tonight."

"Thank you," Hunter said. "That sounds great."

"Okay," Dallas said. "Here's the tentative plan. First we're going to have some dinner with Brad McMath—he's from some godforsaken asteroid, too, like you, although I think his is bigger and more populated—and Patrick Key. Patrick is a complete and total financial genius who will probably be a millionaire before he's thirty. He wants to be the director of FedEnt. Now that's what I call ambition. Patrick is also the biggest horn dog among the fellows. His list of conquests is already longer than the lines for the best rides at New Earth.

"After dinner I thought we'd go to a special club that the fellows frequent regularly. Just for an hour or two, for all of us have to work tomorrow. Patrick guarantees that we'll be surrounded as soon as the ladies find out that we have a bona fide hero among us. He's jealous, you know. Patrick says that if he had escaped from the pirates, he'd get laid at least twice every day."

Hunter laughed easily. Dallas had already made him feel comfortable. Hunter had been afraid that his Covington colleagues might be too scholarly and serious. Dallas, at least, seemed like a normal guy. His roommate was beyond doubt exceptionally intelligent, but he had an easygoing manner and no trace of a superior attitude.

The evening turned out to be a lot of fun. The four young men ate at a nearby bistro that served a wide variety of dishes. The electronic menu was on the tabletop. Each of the meals was prepared in the automated kitchen according to a specific set of procedures. The only workers in the bistro, other than the manager, who was actually a systems engineer whose primary task was to make certain that none of the restaurant elements malfunctioned, were the girls who brought the dishes to the tables.

Patrick told Hunter that the girls were all students from the University of Centralia. "Originally," Patrick said, "the brilliant owner of this establishment had robots serving the dishes. They were functional, but dull, and the bistro was not doing very well. Then the man must have had some kind of an epiphany. He figured out that the customer base would be significantly increased if nubile females graced the place with their presence, and that college students would work for almost nothing. Now the bistro is almost always crowded, and is a big success."

Patrick was an extrovert of the first order. Soon after their arrival at the club, during an interlude between musical selections, he announced in a loud voice to the large contingent of young people present that among his group was a true Federation hero, none other than Hunter Blake, who had recently "defied death and dismemberment" by escaping from the clutches of the space pirates. Patrick then circulated around the club, approaching the most attractive young ladies, and asking them if they wanted to be introduced to Hunter. It was a most impressive undertaking. When Hunter and his new friends left the club around ten o'clock, Patrick gleefully remarked that no fewer than five of his new acquaintances from the evening were likely to occupy his bed in the not too distant future.

The four Covington Fellows were walking in the direction of their apartment when Patrick suggested that they have a nightcap together. He looked mischievously at Brad and Dallas. "Besides," Patrick said, "it's time to ask our hero here the really important question, the one that we have been too nice to mention so far."

Before their drinks had even arrived, Patrick leaned across the small table and said, in a conspiratorial tone, "All right, Hunter, let's cut to the chase. All of us have heard rumors ever since you were kidnapped. Now we want to know the truth. Did you really have an affair with that unbelievably gorgeous fantasy that all red-blooded men dream about, the one and only Tehani Wilawa?"

Hunter looked first at Patrick, and then at his other two companions. Before he could say anything, he felt himself blushing slightly. Patrick jumped up from his seat. "He did, he did, ohmygod he did," he shouted. He raised his arms and gazed at the ceiling of the bar. "I am in the presence of a man who has tasted the sweet fruit of perfection," he said.

An instant later Patrick was back in his seat. Hunter couldn't help laughing at Patrick's antics. Dallas and Brad were in stitches. "How many times?" Patrick asked breathlessly. He held up two outstretched hands. "Ten?" he said. "More?"

Hunter smiled coyly and gestured slightly upward with

the thumbs on both his hands. "Sweet Jesus!" Patrick exclaimed, a look of awe on his face. "I am profoundly humbled. Never, never again will I think of myself as a cocksman." He shook his head. "A thousand Bettys, Margots, and Olivias will not one Tehani make."

He turned toward the bar. "Bartender," Patrick shouted, "another round for my friends and me." When the drinks came, Patrick made the toast. "Welcome to Centralia, Hunter Blake," he said. "May your fortunes here be one-tenth as wonderful as the delights you have already experienced."

FIVE

EVERYTHING WENT SMOOTHLY AT the navprobe installation office, which was under the jurisdiction of the ASP. In a brief conversation with one of the officials, shortly after his arrival, Hunter mentioned that both Tehani and he had had pirate navprobes inserted in their right arms immediately after their kidnapping. The official checked his historical database and then followed the same procedure with Hunter that had been used with Tehani a few months before. First, the pirate navprobe was decommissioned by a noninvasive electronic-jamming process, and then the new, more sophisticated Federation navprobe was installed in Hunter's left shoulder.

One of Mr. Langenbahn's cousins was a middle-level manager at the navprobe office. He insisted on giving his cousin and Hunter a short tour of the facilities, including a demonstration of some of their more advanced capabilities. In a large room with electronic maps projected against one of the walls, Mr. Langenbahn and Hunter watched while a pair of antisedition detectives constructed their case against an individual suspected of treason. It was an impressive demonstration. First, based upon the stored navprobe data, the detectives displayed on the maps the suspect's location as a function of time for the previous month. Next, by searching through the location time histories for the entire database of Federation citizens, and correlating the data with the suspect's information, the detectives were able to produce a detailed time line of the suspect's activities that included every contact the individual had had with anyone else. The times and locations of each of these contacts were also included in the time line.

"With this kind of information," Mr. Langenbahn's cousin said proudly, "it is not difficult to produce evidence against a criminal. We know immediately, for example, if he or she has ever had any direct contact with any other individual who has been convicted of a crime."

On the tram ride back to downtown Centralia from the navprobe office, Hunter asked Mr. Langenbahn who had access to the data contained in the navprobe computers. "Only ASP and other law-enforcement officials," Mr. Langenbahn answered. "The information is governed by very strict laws that establish rigid 'need to know' criteria. Those criteria were tightened just last year, after it was learned that one of the deputy finance ministers had successfully bribed one of the junior computer engineers into providing incriminating evidence about his wife's activities."

At the Covington Fellowship Office, after first discussing with Hunter a wide range of administrative details including how budget allocations and reimbursements were handled, Mr. Langenbahn told Hunter that his individual program would essentially be invented as they went along. "We have never before," Mr. Langenbahn said, "had a fellow begin his tenure in the middle of the fellowship year, so we have no precedents to follow. You missed the first six weeks of testing and general orientation activities, which included introductions to all the government ministries as well as a discussion of the range of assignments that are available to Covington Fellows. Ordinarily, individual work assignments are the result of four factors: aptitude tests taken by the fellows, background experience, stated preferences, and ministry needs."

Mr. Langenbahn smiled. "When we were discussing your program," he said, "some of the more bureaucratic members of my staff suggested that we should simply move you into the next class of fellows. From my point of view, that would have been punishing you for events over which you had no control. In your case, however, a tentative assignment was not too difficult, even before we knew what you had been doing during your period as a pirate prisoner. Based on your work at the hospital in Cicero, we have placed you initially in the Health Ministry."

Mr. Langenbahn handed Hunter three data cubes. "We have told Dr. Sinha to keep your workload light for a couple of weeks, so that you have plenty of time to complete a miniorientation on your own. The videos on these cubes cover a basic overview of the workings of the Federation government, plus individual introductions to each of the ministries. You are expected to view these in your free time, but still complete whatever tasks Dr. Sinha may assign you. And of course we want you to participate, starting immediately, in all the nonwork activities that have been designed for the fellows."

Hunter was asked if he had any questions. "Not that I can think of now," he replied, "although I'm certain I will have many after I actually start doing something."

Mr. Langenbahn consulted the calendar on his hand computer. "Why don't we schedule an appointment, here in my office, after you've had some time to familiarize yourself with everything? We can discuss your initial impressions and answer any questions that might have come up."

"Sounds fine to me," Hunter said.

"All right," Mr. Langenbahn said. "I'll see you here at eight-thirty in the morning, two weeks from this coming Friday."

WHEN DALLAS MORRISON asked Hunter, later that evening in their apartment, how his first day at the Health Ministry had been, Hunter simply shrugged. "It was pretty much as I expected," he said.

Dallas opened a couple of beers and brought one over to Hunter. "That doesn't tell me a damn thing, roomie," he said. "How's your sponsor? Is he or she exciting? Do you know yet what you're going to do? Does it sound like a challenging assignment?"

Hunter laughed and took a swig from his beer. "My sponsor is about as exciting as a rock. I'm certain that Dr. Sinha is a fine administrator, and maybe an excellent doctor as well, but in three hours he exhibited absolutely no passion about anything. Even when I asked about his family, he answered in a virtual monotone." Hunter shook his head. "He seemed genuinely interested in my development, and even pleased that he had been chosen as a sponsor for a Covington Fellow, but oh my, I hope I'm not going to spend eight hours a day around him. I have no idea what I'll do to stay awake."

"How old is he?" Dallas asked.

"I don't think he's really that old," Hunter replied. "Maybe in his early fifties. But he's one of those people who was probably old when he was twenty-eight. He only laughed one time the whole afternoon. And I don't think I should really call it a laugh. It was more like an animated smile."

Dallas was amused. "So what did the two of you do for three hours?" he said.

Hunter took another long drink from his beer. "We reviewed the organization charts and functional assignments for every single department in the Health Ministry. That's right. One after another. 'This chart shows the organization of the Food and Drug Administration. Its function is to blah, blah, blah.' I couldn't believe it. We stopped for fifteen minutes for tea in the middle. Then another chart was projected on the wall."

"Did Dr. Sinha ever discuss what you personally would be doing?" Dallas asked.

Hunter nodded. "Sort of," he said wanly. "For the next two weeks I'm going to visit each of the departments and see what piques my interest. Then we'll decide on my specific assignment." Hunter finished his beer with a gulp. "Dr. Sinha told me that he had been asked by Mr. Langenbahn to make my first weeks comparatively easy, so that I can catch up on all my orientation material." He gestured over his shoulder at his computer. "I have videos covering everything that you guys did in the first six weeks after you arrived here."

"Now that stuff is truly exciting," Dallas said with a grin. "You'll probably want to start watching those videos as soon as you can." He started walking toward his bedroom. "Do you have plans for dinner?" he asked.

"No," Hunter said.

"Then why don't you join me again. My girlfriend JoAnna is coming over in an hour and we're going to have a quick bite around the corner at that little restaurant with the short, fat robots."

"Thanks for the offer," Hunter said, "but I think I'm going to take a nap before dinner. I'm a little on the tired side."

Dallas came back toward Hunter. "Cheer up, roomie," he said. "It'll get better. It was difficult for all of us at the start."

Hunter smiled. "Thanks," he said to Dallas. "I appreciate the support."

ON FRIDAY EVENING when Hunter arrived back at his apartment he went immediately to his computer to check his messages. Dallas was not yet home from work. Hunter's heart skipped a beat when he saw that he had a video message from Tehani.

"Darling," she said with a radiant smile, "I have some terrific news. I'm coming to Centralia in two weeks. I've already made my reservations. I have to do some public-relations work for Sybaris while I'm there, so I don't yet know exactly how much time we'll have together. But we'll certainly have enough time to catch up." Tehani paused for just a second. "I'm so excited, Hunter," she said. "It seems like forever since I've seen you. Give me a call when you can. I should be available today and tomorrow in the early evening."

Hunter skipped into his bathroom and combed his hair. He pulled a new shirt from his chest of drawers and returned to the living room. He adjusted the video camera and his chair until he was satisfied with his appearance. Then he phoned Tehani.

She answered on the second ring. Tehani looked stunning, as always. She was clearly delighted that Hunter had called so quickly. After expressing their mutual excitement about their upcoming rendezvous, Hunter and Tehani started talking about their families. Tehani informed Hunter that her mother and Tesoro had finally agreed to leave Cicero, and would be moving to reside near her in the Free Zone as soon as she had saved enough money to cover the costs of their move. Hunter mentioned his concerns about his father's health, and told Tehani about Amanda and Octavio's separation.

Tehani asked Hunter what he had been doing since he arrived in Centralia. He told her about his initial difficulties at the spaceport and reviewed his first three days at the Health Ministry. Hunter didn't try to hide his disappointment with his assignment. He told Tehani that it looked as if it might be a long time before he did anything of any significance. "On the positive side," he added, "I really like my roommate and the few other Covington Fellows that I've met. They've gone out of their way to make me feel like one of the group. Tonight I think they've even arranged a blind date for me."

Laughing easily, Hunter recounted the story of his first night out with Dallas, Brad, and Patrick. He toned down Patrick's comments a little, but he did explain the gist of the scene in the bar to Tehani. Her reaction was a little surprising. "I guess it's not possible," she said, her smile almost vanishing, "but I had hoped that not everyone in the world would know about us. I'm not upset with you, Hunter. I wouldn't expect you not to tell your roommate and close friends about our involvement. But there are definitely negative ramifications for me of having our love affair become public knowledge. Among other things, I'll have to endure insipid questions from reporters every time I make a public appearance for Sybaris. And my management here will doubtless tell me that my value to my clients has been significantly reduced."

Hunter was mildly apologetic. He admitted that he hadn't really thought about any difficulties that might be created for her as a result of his friends' knowing about their relationship. They talked for awhile about how to handle the issue in the future and agreed that the best policy, especially where the media was involved, was never to confirm or deny their affair, but also never to comment about it in any way.

"I'm coming to Centralia on the high-speed train,"

Tehani said a little later, "two weeks from today, on the twenty-fifth. I'm scheduled to arrive around two o'clock in the afternoon. I thought about having you meet me at the station, Hunter, but I'm having an interview with a network magazine reporter and her photographer that afternoon and they may want to begin as soon as I disembark. If you're at the station, and they're there, too, well, you understand, don't you? It just complicates things."

Hunter assured Tehani that he understood. "I should be finished by five at the latest," she said. "What time are you done with your work, or whatever it is that I'm supposed to call what you're doing?"

Hunter told her that he should be back at his apartment around six o'clock. "After my interview I'll leave you a video message with my room number at the hotel," Tehani said. Her smile brightened. "I have reserved myself for you from then until noon on Saturday," she said. "I can hardly wait."

Later in the conversation Hunter commented that in some ways he missed the clinic, where every day he had been doing something that was important to other people. He made a few more casual remarks about his life on Utopia before he noticed that Tehani's expression had markedly changed. She was, in fact, almost frowning. "What's the matter?" he said.

"If you don't mind, Hunter," Tehani said in a strange tone, "I would prefer not to talk about our time with the pirates. I would like to forget that entire ordeal, if I can. I still have occasional nightmares in which I'm back on Utopia, about to be sold to that awful Saracen chief."

Hunter was momentarily taken aback by her reaction. He stared briefly at Tehani's face on the monitor without saying anything. At that moment she looked hard and cold, not at all like the Tehani whose radiant, smiling image Hunter guarded so carefully in his heart. In the next few seconds images of Rango, Lance, and even Lester Sackett raced through his mind. *Why is Rango any worse than the others?* Hunter asked himself.

"Sorry," Hunter said, suppressing his other thoughts. "I guess I was being a little insensitive."

At that moment Dallas entered the apartment. Hunter and he exchanged greetings. Dallas saw Tehani's face on Hunter's computer monitor and started walking in that direction.

"You're now going to meet my roommate," Hunter said to Tehani. "Dallas Morrison, this is Tehani Wilawa."

Dallas thrust his face over Hunter's shoulder into the field of view of the video camera. "Hello, hello," he said. "This is indeed a pleasure. May I say that you look even more beautiful than your photos? My roommate is indeed a lucky man."

"Thanks, Dallas," Tehani said, flashing one of her patented public smiles. "Hunter has told me that you have gone out of your way to make him feel comfortable. I hope I have a chance to meet you in a couple of weeks."

"You're coming here?" Dallas said. "To Centralia?"

Tehani nodded. "I just made the arrangements today," she said. "I'm going to do some publicity work for Sybaris. Of course, I'll manage to see Hunter, too."

"Will you have time for a beer or two with some of your most devoted fans?" Dallas said excitedly.

"I doubt it seriously," Tehani said politely. "My schedule will be very crowded."

On the monitor Tehani glanced at her watch. "Goodness," she said. "I must go now." She waved at Hunter and Dallas. "See you in two weeks."

ON THE THURSDAY afternoon of the next week Dr. Sinha called Hunter into his office and asked how he was enjoying his daily visits with the various departments in the Health Ministry. Hunter decided that it was all right if he shared with his sponsor a few of his true feelings. Before he answered, however, Hunter remembered something he had read in a magazine article about the optimum way of telling a boss, or any authority figure, something that may not please him. "Always start with something positive," the book had said.

"I am very impressed with the scope of operations of this ministry," Hunter said. "There are more employees in the hospital-administration department alone than there were citizens on Cicero. The list of research topics in the pharmaceutical department absolutely boggled my mind."

"Yes," Dr. Sinha said, almost smiling, "it is an enormous endeavor. And quite a challenge to manage, I might add."

"The people I have met," Hunter said, "have been extremely nice, and have bent over backward to answer my questions. I couldn't have been treated better. And I have learned an enormous amount."

"Good," Dr. Sinha said. "I'm glad your experience is going well."

Hunter paused for several seconds. "I do have one slight misgiving, however," he then said, "not a serious one, you understand, but one that is troubling me a little."

"What's that?" the doctor asked, showing his concern.

"Well, sir," Hunter said, "everything that I am seeing is so abstract. It's charts and graphs and descriptions of projects and results. I sometimes have a hard time relating what I'm hearing to individual patients and to the actual practice of medicine. Would it be possible for me to see something a little more tangible? Understand that I think it's invaluable for me to be able to spend time with each of the departments, but—"

"Was there anything specific you had in mind?" Dr. Sinha asked.

"I have found the work of the research laboratories in each department extremely interesting," Hunter said. "In particular, there was a very articulate and intelligent woman who was describing some fascinating projects out at Masursky Center . . ."

"Dr. Bellini?" Dr. Sinha said.

"Yes," Hunter replied. "Dr. Bellini. Anyway, if I could see what's actually being done, in one of these laboratories, perhaps even with real patients, I believe that my appreciation for everything that I'm learning would be significantly enhanced."

"Yes," said Dr. Sinha. "Why not? Let me see what I can arrange."

The following Monday morning at six o'clock Hunter was standing on the platform at the Centralia station. Two minutes before the train departed, Dr. Sandra Bellini, an attractive, svelte blonde in her early thirties, rushed hurriedly toward him and introduced herself. They quickly boarded the train together.

"I guess I have you to thank for this boondoggle?" Dr. Bellini said after catching her breath. The monitors in the backs of the seats had already begun playing the safety video explaining the possible dangers of a leak in the environmental-control system.

"I guess so," Hunter said. "I told Dr. Sinha that I thought I should see something less abstract, and he arranged this trip. I'm sorry if I've caused you a problem."

"Not really," Dr. Bellini said. "I needed to go out to Masursky this week anyway. But Monday morning at six o'clock? What are you, some kind of masochist?"

Hunter laughed. "I think that Dr. Sinha didn't want to deal with the paperwork required for an overnight trip," he said. "He told me three times that he wanted me to return to Centralia tonight."

A few minutes after the train passed through the exit

from the Centralia dome and reached its cruising speed, Dr. Bellini fell asleep. Hunter gazed out the window at the magnificent landscapes of Mars. He saw sculpted sand dunes, immense rocks ejected in the formation of impact craters, and fields in which the rock population was almost impossibly dense. In the distance, after one slight turn in the train's heading, he observed a ridge of mountains that had once, hundreds of millions of years before, been active volcanoes. From time to time Hunter saw a secondary railway split off from the main track on which they were traveling, and head toward some unknown destination in the distance.

The train stopped at a pair of comparatively small outposts, both times slowing well before entering the dome that protected the outpost from the harsh Martian environment. A few passengers left the train at each stop. Others boarded. After about an hour Dr. Bellini stirred and announced that her nap was over.

"Is there anything particular you'd like to talk about?" she asked Hunter.

"Not really," he said. "I was fascinated by everything we discussed last week."

Dr. Bellini's research specialty was reproductive pathology. The previous week Hunter and she had spent an hour together at departmental headquarters. At that time Dr. Bellini had explained how she was introducing genetic alterations during the early stages of embryonic development to remove both congenital defects and predilections toward a large number of diseases. On the train journey, she explained to Hunter that her personal work was actually just one element of a large, multiyear research effort aimed at the development of "exceptional" human offspring.

"Define 'exceptional,' " Hunter said.

"Actually," Dr. Bellini replied, "we have a metric on the project, a quantitative scale by which we measure the quality of a human embryo. Without going into the details, basically the embryo scores positive points for likely intellectual acumen, physical robustness, probable longevity, inherent fertility, and a host of other factors. Negative points are assigned for birth defects, of course, as well as susceptibilities to a wide range of physical and mental disease. The project team has been tuning the metric for some years now. Once a zygote is formed, we can remove a blastomere in the early division process, analyze the genes in detail, and calculate a single number that represents, to some degree, the potential of that zygote."

Hunter frowned. "Come on, Dr. Bellini," he said, "surely you don't believe that it's that simple. To calculate a single number that somehow encompasses the whole array of human potential? That's preposterous."

She laughed. "Of course it is," she said. "I'm just trying to give you an overview of the thrust of the project. We compute many other ancillary metrics for each zygote as well, using different weighting algorithms. For example, in the prime metric a negative weight is assigned for a statistical proclivity toward manic-depression. Yet it has been demonstrated by years of research that manic-depression and creativity are positively correlated. A metric that 'turns off' the negative points for low-level manic-depression results in a different potential number for each zygote. All the metrics are valuable pointers with respect to the direction of our research."

"I don't understand," Hunter said.

"Take my research," Dr. Bellini said. "How can its efficacy be measured? How can it be compared to some other genetic intervention effort which, for example, is designed to improve the latent mathematical aptitude of the zygote? Both result in higher numbers in the prime metric—mine by reducing the negative points, and the other by raising the positive points. On which one should we spend our time and money? Computation of the metrics helps us make that decision."

For the remainder of the trip Dr. Bellini and Hunter talked about the overall project goal of producing exceptional children. Sometimes the conversation was philosophical—at one point Hunter asked, without receiving a definitive answer, if the team had tried in any way to correlate the prime metric with the degree of happiness that an individual experienced in life. Most of the time, however, the discussion centered on the biological breakthroughs that had been made by the team during the twenty years that the project had been under way.

"We have developed fantastic techniques for genetic intercession that would have been unbelievable only fifty years ago," Dr. Bellini said. "If the goals of this project are realized, and a Federation policy is implemented that each conceived embryo must be subjected to analysis and possible improvement, we could probably wipe out ninety percent of the disease humans experience in less than a century. We could certainly eliminate cancer and heart disease as major causes of death, simply by altering the genes of the unborn child to reduce significantly its tendency toward those pathologies."

The conversation with Dr. Bellini powerfully stimulated Hunter's imagination. He tried to envision a world in which disease was a rarity, but could not. To him it was almost a surreal concept. Listening to her Hunter was also buffeted by a vague disquiet, a feeling that he couldn't yet articulate. He sensed that something very important was being left out of the conversation altogether.

They entered the dome of New Austin, where the Masursky Center was located, at eight thirty-five in the morning. After their conversation, Hunter thought it was altogether fitting that New Austin was the capital of the Federation province of Utopia.

ON HIS SOLO train ride back to Centralia that evening, Hunter could not decide which of the many images that were indelibly stored in his mind from his astonishing day at the Masursky Center was the most significant. Was it the huge room where hundreds of petri dishes, each with its own fertilized human embryo, stretched out on trays in all directions, each dish standing beside a single big, blinking red number displaying the potential of that particular embryo according to the prime metric? Was it the hourlong briefing in which graph after graph demonstrated the marked superiority of a pilot group of one hundred children, conceived ten years previously as fertilized embryos at the Masursky Center, by comparing their intellectual and physical achievements with those of "average" children from the Federation population? Or was it the large circular tank with the metallic silver sheen, which Hunter felt compelled to examine, where fertilized human embryos that were no longer useful for research purposes, and had not been selected for development as part of any particular study, were unceremoniously dumped?

Early in the afternoon, while he was still reeling from all the incredible things he had seen and heard at the Masursky Center campus, Hunter had promised himself that one of his first activities after he returned to Centralia would be to read completely the International Eugenics Act of 2217. He thought he remembered that the act explicitly prohibited all research whose sole purpose was the creation of superior human beings. Was the long-term project in which Dr. Bellini and the others were participating a violation of international law? Or had the project personnel, working closely with the Health Ministry, managed to structure the research so that it fell under one or more of the loopholes in that milestone act?

Before leaving the Masursky Center, Hunter had asked if the Dems were engaged in any similar research. The director of the center, an enormously self-confident man named Dr. Shelley Kinder, told him that the Dems were almost a generation behind in understanding the power of embryonic genetic alteration.

Hunter was certainly impressed, even awed, by the talent of the scientists with whom he had visited. The work that Dr. Bellini and her colleagues were doing was on the cutting edge of biological research, and its potentially enormous impact was beyond doubt. What was going on at Masursky, Hunter realized, could change the fundamental nature of the human species. Nevertheless, as Hunter rode the train back to Centralia and the arid beauty of Mars passed by his window, he was still troubled by what he had observed. Yes, he still wanted to check the codicils of the International Eugenics Act, primarily for his own edification, but what that law specifically said, or didn't say, was no longer that important. Hunter was struggling with another issue.

He remembered a few lines from a play he had read in school in which a wise man, a principal advisor to a historical king, explained that his job was not just to tell the king what he "could do," but also to indicate what he "should do." At no time in his earlier years had Hunter ever even attempted to formulate any overriding principles to guide his life. On the train ride back to Centralia, still staggered by the terrible beauty of what he had observed during his day at the Masursky Center, Hunter developed his first major personal precept. He concluded that medicine, and science in general, ought to be as concerned about what it "should do" as it was with what it "could do."

Hunter was focused so intently on his own thoughts that he didn't even realize, until after the train had entered the Centralia dome, that his hand computer had been signaling that he had two pages. He checked the page list and saw that Mr. Langenbahn had tried to contact him twice in the last five minutes.

"Where are you?" the Covington Fellowship director said as soon as Hunter identified himself on the phone. "I've been trying to find you for almost an hour."

"I'm on a train just outside Centralia Station," Hunter said. "I went to New Austin, to the Masursky Center. Didn't Dr. Sinha tell you?"

"He was in some kind of important meeting and couldn't be interrupted," Mr. Langenbahn said. He took a deep breath. "Hunter," he said, his voice full of anxiety, "we had a call half an hour ago from Lester Sackett's office. The minister himself wants to see you. This afternoon if possible, but no later than tomorrow morning."

Hunter glanced at his watch. "It's almost six now," he said, "and we have not yet stopped at the station. I couldn't be there much before seven."

"I'll tell them it will have to be tomorrow morning then," said Mr. Langenbahn.

"Okay," Hunter said, "anytime is fine." He paused a second. "Do you have any idea what this is about?" he asked Mr. Langenbahn.

"Not a clue," said the Covington Fellows director.

AS SOON AS he reached his apartment, Hunter tried to phone Tehani. She wasn't available. She had told him that she would be working every day the week before her trip to Centralia, so Hunter wasn't too surprised, but he left her a message to call him if she had any time available. He didn't tell her in the message that he was going to have a meeting with the defense minister himself, Mr. Lester Sackett.

Hunter also didn't say anything to Dallas about his

morning appointment. He did talk at length about what he had seen at the Masursky Center, and Dallas commented that it was the first time since Hunter's arrival that he had seen his roommate excited about anything except Tehani Wilawa.

He didn't sleep well that night. Lying awake in his bed, Hunter listed in his mind all the possible reasons why the Federation defense minister might have requested a personal meeting with him. Hunter considered dozens of scenarios, most of them concerned with one aspect or another of his involvement with the pirates. He wondered, for example, if the Dems and Feds ever exchanged intelligence information. If so, had somebody from the Edison complex on the Moon, perhaps the injured Dem whom he had treated during the raid, identified him from a photograph? In that case, what should he say to Minister Sackett? Toward morning, Hunter found himself also thinking about the party after the raid on the Moon, and his discussion with the Saracens Rango and Hammer. Their contacts on Mars had suggested that Tehani had been involved in an amorous relationship with the defense minister for over a year. Was it possible that his meeting with Sackett the following day had something to do with Tehani?

SIX

HUNTER ARRIVED AT THE Defense Ministry for his eight o'clock meeting with Mr. Lester Sackett almost an hour early. He passed through all the security checks in about twenty minutes, and spent the rest of the time waiting in a small room next to the receptionist's desk. The bubbly young woman walked into the room at three minutes after eight and told Hunter the defense minister was ready for him.

Hunter's nerves were on edge. As he followed the receptionist down the hall to Mr. Sackett's office, they passed a rest room. Hunter excused himself politely and went inside. After using the toilet, he stood in front of the mirror, fixing his tie and taking deep breaths, for what must have been two minutes. He was only marginally calmer when he rejoined the receptionist.

The defense minister's office was huge. In the foreground, directly opposite the door, was a long conference table with a dozen chairs. To the left, Mr. Sackett's enormous desk, with one computer on either side, was strategically placed so that he could see out the window by looking over his right shoulder. The minister rose from his desk as soon as Hunter crossed the threshold of his office. His face broke into a wide smile as he walked across the room with an extended hand. Mr. Sackett was a handsome man, about fifty years old, with sandy brown hair and some graying at the temples. He walked with authority and had the appearance of a man in very good physical shape.

"Good morning," he said with enthusiasm. "Thank you for being so prompt."

Hunter shook the minister's hand and their eyes met. Hunter's first thought was that the only eyes he had ever seen with the intensity of Mr. Sackett's were Goldmatt's. "Can I get you anything?" the minister asked. "A cup of coffee, some juice perhaps?"

Hunter noticed that his throat was very dry and requested a glass of water. Not a minute later a man, introduced to Hunter as Mr. Sackett's executive assistant, entered the room carrying a glass of water and a cup of coffee on a tray. He set the tray on the conference table and noiselessly left the room.

Minister Sackett sat at one end of the conference table and motioned for Hunter to sit in the first chair on his right. "So how are things going for you, Hunter?" he said. "Are you getting acclimated all right?"

"Yes, sir," Hunter heard himself answer. He was certain that Mr. Sackett could tell how nervous he was. "Everything's fine," Hunter added somewhat awkwardly.

The defense minister stirred his coffee, absentmindedly taking a small sugar bag and a tiny cream container from the tray. He turned in Hunter's direction and smiled. "You're probably wondering why I asked you to come over here this morning," he said.

"Yes, sir," Hunter replied.

"Well, Hunter," he said, "to get right to the point, I'm having an unpleasant dispute with the ASP, and it involves you. They are not satisfied with the conclusions of our inquiry board, documented by Colonel Hood and his team after they met with you on Phobos, and want to conduct their own interrogation." Mr. Sackett looked directly at Hunter again. "The ASP officials have carefully studied your testimony and have identified a number of issues that they believe are significant enough to warrant opening a full investigation."

Hunter felt his heart skip a beat. "What does that mean, sir?"

Mr. Sackett took a sip from his coffee. "The ASP feels that you may have both cooperated with the enemy and purposely lied to our inquiry board."

Hunter's stomach did an involuntary flip-flop. Even though he knew his hand was shaking, he reached toward the table for his glass of water.

"Tesoro," the minister suddenly shouted. A large red electronic bird, who had been perched on a shelf near Mr. Sackett's desk, flew gracefully forward in the room and landed on the minister's shoulder. "Tell Bruce that this cream is no good," Mr. Sackett said to the bird, "and ask him to bring me another cup of coffee."

He glanced at Hunter, whose eyes were wide with astonishment. "Are you certain that you don't want anything else?" Mr. Sackett said. Hunter shook his head. "Go," commanded the minister. The bird took off and flew through the open vent at the top of the office door.

"Pretty amazing, huh?" the minister said. "Tesoro is really a fantastic technological creation. I bought him about six months ago and I'm still fascinated."

The red bird flew back into the room through the vent and hovered over Mr. Sackett. "Bruce says the coffee will be here right away," the bird said.

"Thank you, Tesoro," he said. "That will be all for now." The bird flapped its wings, lifted into the air, and returned to its perch on the shelf across the office.

The door to the office opened several seconds later and

Bruce entered with a new tray containing a cup of coffee and two creams. "I'm sorry, Mr. Sackett," his assistant said. "I should have checked the cream before I served it."

By this time Hunter was completely discombobulated. He was already imagining being ruthlessly interrogated by the ASP. Mr. Sackett did not say anything until his assistant had again left the room.

"I have myself read the key parts of your testimony," the minister then said, again smiling and looking directly at Hunter, "and although I can see the irregularities that have disturbed the ASP, it's my opinion that there is nothing there that warrants any additional investigation. Unfortunately," he added, "my opinion, although important, has not been enough to put this issue to rest."

Mr. Sackett paused. "The ASP still wants to conduct its investigation," he said, "and until yesterday was even threatening to take this matter to Chairman Covington for resolution. But I proposed a compromise, and they accepted. The compromise, however, requires your cooperation and participation. That's why I have called you here this morning." The minister stopped again briefly. "Do you have any questions so far? Is anything unclear?" he said.

"No, sir," Hunter answered in a raspy voice. He took another drink of water.

Mr. Sackett leaned toward Hunter. "Everything that I am about to tell you is classified as 'top secret,'" he said. "It is an act of treason to discuss top-secret information with anyone who does not have a legitimate need to know. It is very important that you understand this before I begin the rest of this discussion. What I am about to tell you cannot be shared with anyone that you have met so far, except me. Not with your family, not with your friends, not with anyone. Do you still want me to proceed?"

"Sir," Hunter said after a moment's hesitation, "may I

ask one question first? Just to make sure that I have understood what you have told me?"

"Of course," Mr. Sackett said.

"As I understand it," Hunter said, "you have brokered a compromise that will forestall the ASP investigation of me, but this compromise requires both my personal involvement and my exposure to top-secret information?"

"Precisely," the minister replied.

"And without this compromise it is your opinion that the ASP will continue with its efforts to conduct an investigation of my possible cooperation with the enemy?"

"You understand perfectly," Mr. Sackett said.

Hunter swallowed hard. "In that case, sir," he said, "I really don't see where I have any choice. Please continue."

"Our defense intelligence," Mr. Sackett said, "has come to the conclusion that the Utopian pirate band not only planned and implemented the hijacking of the *Darwin,* an act of war all by itself, but also carried out an unprovoked attack on your home asteroid of Cicero that resulted in at least two deaths and millions of dollars of damage. The Federation cannot allow these kinds of acts to occur without retribution. We have decided, therefore, to mount a preemptive strike against the Utopians, and to utterly destroy their ability to create any additional problems for us."

Hunter thought his heart would jump out of his chest. With all his might he struggled to remain calm.

"We have started to form a team to plan that attack," Mr. Sackett continued. "Naturally, with your intimate knowledge of the home asteroid of the Utopians, you can play a vital role on that team. The ASP leadership concurs. They have agreed that if you are willing to contribute your knowledge to this operation, they will abandon altogether any attempts to investigate you."

By this time Hunter's head was spinning and he was

feeling nauseous. It was still obvious to him, however, that he had only one course of action. "I will help to the best of my ability," he said to Mr. Sackett.

"Good," said the defense minister, reaching across and shaking Hunter's hand. "I thought you would."

Minister Sackett explained to Hunter that even though he would be a critical member of this top-secret defense team, he was to continue to participate in everything associated with his Covington Fellowship. "Mr. Langenbahn," the minister said, "will be told only that you are working a top-priority special project for me, and that he is supposed to tell nobody else anything about it. He will also be our point of contact to inform you of the planning meetings."

"How much of my time will this project take?" Hunter asked.

"No more than eight to ten hours per week, perhaps slightly more at the beginning," Mr. Sackett said.

Before Hunter left his office, the minister reminded Hunter again of the classified nature of the information that had been shared with him, and of the penalties for even inadvertent revelation of what they had discussed.

"Okay," Mr. Sackett said, standing up from his chair, "that's it." He extended his hand again and Hunter shook it.

"Thank you, sir," Hunter said as he walked out the door.

"It was my pleasure," Minister Sackett said.

As Hunter was walking down the corridor outside the minister's office, he felt as if he were going to throw up at any moment. For a brief second, he considered entering the rest room and relieving his nausea. For many reasons, however, he decided that being sick in the minister's office was not a good idea. Hunter managed to suppress his violent stomach upset until he reached the tram station.

SITTING ON THE tram heading for the Centralia Medical School, which was also the location of the Health Ministry offices responsible for licensing physicians, Hunter reviewed, over and over, the details of his meeting with Minister Sackett. His stomach and his emotions were both still in turmoil. Now he also had a headache.

Hunter clearly understood the real message of the meeting. The defense minister was telling him that they needed his information about Utopia to plan an attack. If Hunter didn't provide it, then he would be subject to a painful and embarrassing investigation.

But why had Sackett not simply asked for his help, instead of maneuvering him into a position where he had no choice? For that matter, why had the defense minister himself had the meeting with Hunter? Wouldn't it have made more sense to have had someone at a lower level, Colonel Hood perhaps, explain the situation to him? Hunter thought he understood the answer to those questions as well. Minister Sackett had had other reasons to meet Hunter personally. He wanted to demonstrate his power. *Because of Tehani,* Hunter thought.

Hunter was now absolutely certain that the defense minister had a romantic involvement with Tehani. The meeting had made that obvious. An electronic bird named Tesoro? Could it possibly have been a coincidence that the bird had the same name as Tehani's little brother? *No way,* Hunter said emphatically to himself.

Other questions swirled in Hunter's mind as he sat on the tram. Did the ASP really have any evidence, other than the fact that he had admitted doing a good job at the clinic on Utopia, that he had cooperated with the pirates? Was the entire meeting a pretense so that Sackett could size him up and give him a not-so-subtle warning to stay away from Tehani?

He didn't know the answers. He didn't know what, if

anything, he should do. All Hunter knew was that his life had irrevocably changed. And that he felt powerless.

THE REST OF the morning was boring. In some ways Hunter was glad that listening to discussions of physician-licensing procedures, handling of patient complaints, and other bureaucratic issues related to the management of the doctors in the Federation required so little effort from him. His mind was free to focus on other matters. At lunch, while his companions were involved in a heated argument about the new physician-compensation tables, Hunter suddenly remembered his last meeting with Cooperman, and his comments about why Hunter could not take Camille to Mars.

Hunter wondered if it was even remotely possible that the birds Cooperman and his team designed could contain, along with their other electronics, secret transmitters as well as listening and recording devices. *No, surely not,* Hunter said to himself, suddenly smiling. *Cooperman couldn't be that clever.*

The idea that perhaps Cooperman, and therefore the space pirates, might be listening to conversations in the very office of the Federation defense minister sustained Hunter through the rest of his day. It was the first cheerful thought he had had since learning the previous evening about his meeting with Minister Sackett. In the afternoon, when an eager bureaucrat actually spent a full hour explaining to Hunter the forms and procedures associated with approving surgeons for each specific operation, Hunter simply smiled, looked interested, and thought about his funny, brilliant friend among the pirates.

It was six-thirty by the time Hunter returned to his apartment. Dallas had already changed his clothes and was sitting on the couch, sipping a beer. Hunter greeted his roommate and went to his computer to check his messages. The first was from Dr. Sinha. The good doctor asked Hunter if he would come to his office first thing the next morning instead of going to the Food and Drug Administration. Hunter answered that he would. The second message caught Hunter by surprise. It was a weekly newsletter from a Rama virtual-world chat group.

While Hunter was staring at the newsletter on his computer monitor, Dallas walked up and looked over his shoulder. "I didn't know you played that game," Dallas said. "Who's your avatar?"

"I haven't actually played since before I was kidnapped," Hunter answered. He thought for a moment. "In my active episodes," he said, "I'm the chief of police of Beauvois. I think my name is Henri Lenoir."

"Really?" said Dallas. "I never would have suspected you had a secret desire to be a chief of police. You seem much more antiestablishment than that."

Hunter laughed. "If I remember correctly," he said, "in my most exciting game I'm down in the atrium of the old octospider lair. I'm following a trio of escaped convicts."

Dallas looked at the screen. "So you joined some formal chat group while you were still living on Cicero?"

"Actually, no," Hunter said. "I only played occasionally. I guess this newsletter must have been mailed to everybody who has ever entered the Rama virtual world."

"That's strange," Dallas said, walking back to the middle of the room. "I played Rama for a couple of hours just last month and I didn't get one."

Hunter didn't pay that much attention to what Dallas was saying. His mind was elsewhere. *What does this newsletter mean?* Hunter said to himself. *Is someone trying to contact me?* Several times since he had arrived in Centralia, Hunter had passed a virtual-world kiosk and had thought about entering. He knew that if he decided he wanted to communicate with the pirates, it would take him several minutes to move his Rama world avatar to the proper location in the blue maze. If he saved a game in that position, then he would be able to enter the portal to the pirate message system in only a matter of seconds. So far, however, Hunter had never actually gone into a kiosk.

That evening Hunter ate dinner with Dallas and JoAnna in the food court that was part of the entertainment center on the first floor of their apartment building. The couple invited Hunter to attend a movie with them, but he said that he was going to return to the apartment and study the orientation videos. After Dallas and JoAnna entered the theater, Hunter found an empty virtual-world kiosk and went inside.

He entered his personal password for the Rama virtual world and was relieved to discover that all his old files were still present even though he hadn't played for over six months. A female voice welcomed Hunter to Rama, and then a survey form was posted on the screen. A second female voice explained that whenever a player returned after a long hiatus, the player was requested to answer some questions that would help the game designers and distributors understand why the long absence occurred. "This information is used," the disembodied voice continued, "to improve all our future products."

Hunter chose not to fill out the survey. He then searched through his saved game file to find one in which his avatar was physically located close to the blue maze in the octospider lair. It took Hunter a little more than ten minutes to move his avatar into the proper position that Cooperman had shown him on Utopia. Hunter then sat in the kiosk for a long time without doing anything. He spent that time debating whether or not to input the alphanumeric that would take him out of the Rama world to the portal where a single additional password would place him inside the pirates' secret E-mail system.

Even though Hunter was fairly certain that the appearance of the Rama newsletter on the computer in his apartment indicated that he had a message from someone in the pirate world, his meeting with Lester Sackett that morning had made him extremely wary. *Up until now,* Hunter said to himself, *I have done nothing here in Centralia that could arouse suspicion. If I take the next step, and enter the secret pirate system, whether I send or receive a message or not, everything that I have done will be stored on an electronic file that could be accessed by the ASP.*

His desire to know what the message might contain was less than his fear of doing something suspicious. Hunter made five moves with his avatar in the Rama virtual world, backing away from the wall in the blue maze, then saved the game with an easily remembered designator. If he ever wanted or needed to communicate with his pirate friends in the future, it would only take him a few seconds to return to the proper location. Hunter didn't think it was a smart idea to save the game in the very location that was the portal to the pirate message system.

Hunter emerged from the kiosk and stretched his arms. He glanced over into the food court and was astonished to see Dallas and JoAnna sitting at a table eating ice cream. They waved as soon as he saw them.

"Couldn't face those orientation videos, huh?" Dallas said as Hunter came over beside them. "Can't say that I blame you. I'd much rather be immersed in a fantasy world myself."

"I thought you guys went to a movie," Hunter said, a puzzled look on his face.

"It was terrible," JoAnna said, "and really crude. We left about five minutes ago."

Hunter sat down beside Dallas and JoAnna and looked at the menu in the table. He decided that some ice cream would taste great.

"**YOU MUST HAVE** really impressed Dr. Bellini," Dr. Sinha said the next morning a few minutes after Hunter had arrived at his office. "She phoned yesterday from the Masursky Center and said that she had never met a brighter young man."

"I guess that's good," Hunter said.

"Yes, oh yes," Dr. Sinha said, looking very pleased. "Dr. Bellini is definitely a rising star in the ministry, and not just because of her outstanding research. She is very active on policy issues as well."

His sponsor sat behind his desk for several seconds without saying anything. "Dr. Bellini asked about your availability," Dr. Sinha said at length. "She said that she has just completed a portion of her research and could use some help documenting the results."

Hunter brightened. "What did you tell her?" he asked.

"I told her," Dr. Sinha said, "that I would need to talk to you about it. And to check with the Covington Fellowship Office."

"Dr. Sinha," Hunter said almost immediately, "I would love to work with Dr. Bellini. Of all my days reviewing the different departments in the ministry, Monday was by far the most interesting."

"You might be required to travel outside the city occasionally," Dr. Sinha said.

"That's all right, too," Hunter said. "In fact, I would look forward to it."

Dr. Sinha glanced down at some handwritten notes on his desk. "I had a conversation with Mr. Langenbahn yesterday afternoon," he said, "and he indicated that the proposed assignment was an excellent match with the general fellowship guidelines." He looked again at Hunter. "If you are certain this is something that you would like to do, I'll phone Dr. Bellini today and tell her you're available starting Monday."

Hunter could hardly believe what he was hearing. "Please do, Dr. Sinha," he said excitedly. He had an impulse to grab the diminutive doctor and give him a hug, but Hunter restrained himself. "Thank you, sir," he said. "Thank you very much."

IN SPITE OF his residual concern about his meeting with Minister Sackett, Hunter was in a great mood the rest of the week. Part of the reason for his good humor was, of course, that he was going to see Tehani on the weekend. But Hunter was also ecstatic that he was going to be working with Dr. Bellini. During his visits to the various departmental headquarters in the Health Ministry, Hunter had had a growing fear that he was going to be given some dreary administrative job that involved no interactions with people and no creativity or initiative whatsoever. He was fascinated by the research that Dr. Bellini and her colleagues were conducting, and he knew that he would have a chance to learn many new and interesting things.

On Thursday night Hunter sent a video message to Tehani tentatively outlining their plans for the following evening. He told her that he would come back to the apartment around six o'clock, and would wait for her call from the hotel. "I've made dinner reservations for us at eight at La Piccola Roma," Hunter said. "Dallas says it's one of the best, and most romantic, restaurants in the city." Hunter laughed into the video camera. "I'll probably be eating toast and cereal the rest of the month, but it'll be worth it."

When Hunter returned to his apartment from work on

Friday afternoon he was bursting with energy. He considered going downstairs for a quick workout in the gymnasium, but he didn't want to miss Tehani's call. She phoned at six-fifteen. "Sorry, Hunter," she said, "the interview went a little longer than I expected. I'm in Room 717 at the Tharsis Hotel. Can you meet me here in an hour?"

They talked for a few minutes and Tehani said that the plans for the evening sounded great. Then she said that she'd better start "making herself beautiful" or she wouldn't be ready when he came. After he hung up, Hunter dashed out of his apartment and had a short, but energetic, fifteen-minute swim in the gymnasium pool.

Hunter entered the lobby of the Tharsis Hotel a few minutes after seven o'clock. The Tharsis was one of the finest hotels in Centralia. One of the walls in the lobby was decorated with a magnificent mural of Mars. The mural depicted the entire mountain range containing the majestic Tharsis volcanoes. Hunter made a mental note to visit that region of North Mars at his first available opportunity.

At exactly seven-fifteen he phoned Tehani in her room. She did not have the video receiver on. "I'll be down in five minutes," she said. Hunter walked back into the lobby and sat down. He felt surprisingly nervous. He decided to go into the rest room and comb his hair and adjust his tie.

Hunter saw Tehani the moment she walked into the lobby from the elevator area. She was wearing a simple gray dress in a soft fabric with a slightly plunging neckline. The zipper down the front was partially undone. Her hair was over both shoulders in the front, and fell down to the middle of her torso. "Tehani," Hunter said in too loud a voice.

She turned, saw him, and smiled broadly. They walked toward each other until they met in the middle of the lobby. They embraced. In his enthusiasm Hunter lifted her slightly off the floor. It was a few seconds before either Hunter or Tehani was aware of the lights that were illuminating them from both sides.

Tehani straightened out her dress and looked around. She turned toward a tall, dark man standing next to one of the cameramen. "Would you please stop, Ricardo," she said. "I'd like to have a private visit with my friend."

The cameras continued to roll. Hunter was upset with himself for not having carefully checked the area while he was waiting in the lobby. By then, everyone in the large room, including all the hotel employees, was watching them.

Tehani took a deep breath and squeezed Hunter's hand. "I was afraid of this," she said in a barely audible voice. "Just smile, say nothing, and walk with me to the door."

"Is that Hunter Blake with you, Miss Wilawa?" the man she had called Ricardo yelled as they neared the hotel door. Tehani looked straight ahead.

One of the cameramen dashed in front of Hunter and Tehani just as they reached the exit. "Excuse us, please," Tehani said, lightly pushing the man aside so she could go through the door.

She pulled Hunter behind her into the backseat of one of the tiny electric taxis that were the only private transportation allowed in the center of Centralia. "Go, please, driver," she said even before Hunter had closed his door. A cameraman raced alongside the taxi until it reached the first corner.

Hunter gave the driver the address of the restaurant. It was only ten minutes away. Tehani leaned over and gave him a light kiss. "I'm sorry, Hunter," she said. "I know this wasn't exactly the kind of reunion you were expecting. It might have been better if I had simply met you at the restaurant."

Hunter shrugged. "It's not important," he said.

They stared at each other for a few seconds. "You look great," Tehani said. "I don't think I've seen you dressed up since we were teenagers."

Hunter shook his head and smiled. "Tehani," he said, "how is it possible that you are more beautiful every time I see you?"

She thanked him, and then her face became more serious. Tehani touched his cheek with her hand. "I've waited a long time for this," she said, leaning forward. They kissed. What started as a gentle touching of the lips quickly became a full, insistent, passionate kiss that consumed both of them. Hunter felt himself exploding with desire.

"Do we have to go to the restaurant?" Tehani said when they broke the kiss. "Couldn't we just go to some no-tell motel and pay the clerk with cash and sign in as Sally and Tom?"

Hunter sighed. "That would certainly be nice," he said. "But I had to guarantee the restaurant reservations." He smiled. "Besides, I assume we'll have plenty of time after we eat."

Tehani pulled back to her side of the taxi. "Okay," she said, opening her purse. "But I'll need a few seconds to fix my makeup." She grinned at Hunter. "You can mess it up again later."

AT THE RESTAURANT, the manager recognized her immediately. Hunter and Tehani were given a small table near the window that overlooked the artificial river that ran through the center of Centralia. They ate unhurriedly, holding hands across the table occasionally. They both kept the conversation light. Hunter had decided earlier not to mention Lester Sackett, or to tell Tehani that Ursula was pregnant with his child. He didn't want anything to spoil their first evening together. Once during dinner Hunter did start to tell Tehani about an incident that occurred while he was working in the clinic on Utopia, but she signaled him with her expression and a slight motion of her head and Hunter quickly changed the subject.

She suggested that they take a short walk beside the river after dinner. As they walked, hand in hand, Tehani told Hunter that she thought it was dangerous for either of them to discuss the pirates when there was any chance at all that their conversation could be overheard or recorded. "I think it is highly possible," she said, "that the ASP is watching both of us. They would like nothing better than to discover some significant inconsistency or inaccuracy in our official testimonies." She kissed him on the cheek. "So it's just better to stay away from that subject altogether."

Hunter told Tehani that he was fairly certain that the ASP had opened a file on him, but he couldn't imagine why they would have any reason to suspect her for anything. "They don't need a reason," Tehani said. "Their job is to suspect almost everybody."

On their way to the tram station Hunter started telling Tehani about his interaction with ASP Officer Sanders during his inquiry-board proceedings. She laughed out loud at the man's question about Hunter's sexual activities while he was among the pirates. "They love that kind of crap," she said. "Last year, when the ASP was investigating one of my past clients, they asked me all sorts of detailed questions about the man's sexual interests and behavior." Tehani laughed. "I just told them that I couldn't remember."

Hunter's apartment was empty when they returned. They filled two large glasses with water and took them into his bedroom. Hunter locked the door. Tehani took off her shoes and plopped herself down on the bed. "I'm a little tired, my friend," she said. She rolled over on her back. "Before you do one other thing, come down here and kiss me."

Still fully clothed, Hunter gently placed himself on top of Tehani and started to kiss her. In a very short time they were both fully aroused. "Just pull your pants down," she whispered in his ear. "I don't think we've ever done it with our clothes on before."

In the shower, while Tehani was lovingly soaping his body, Hunter apologized for being so fast. Tehani smiled knowingly at him. "Don't worry about me," she said. "The night is still young, and you're only twenty-one years old."

The next ten hours were full of unbelievable pleasure for them both. They never left Hunter's bedroom. They never put on any clothes. When they were not making love, Hunter and Tehani were still enwrapped in each other's arms, sometimes sleeping and sometimes gently touching and caressing each other.

HUNTER WAS EUPHORIC after his date with Tehani. He slept for another couple of hours after she left, and then worked out in the gym for an hour and a half. Throughout his workout and his late lunch with his roommate, Hunter smiled and even whistled for no apparent reason. That evening, after spending the rest of the afternoon reviewing some research results that Dr. Bellini had given him, Hunter ate by himself at a pub not far from the apartment building. While he was walking home, he passed a girl on the street who looked very much like Ursula.

In the next few minutes, hundreds of images of Ursula flooded his mind. Hunter smiled to himself as he remembered how beautiful she was. He felt his heart ache, and he realized that he missed his Utopian girlfriend very much. *How can I miss Ursula the day after making love with Tehani?*

Hunter asked himself. *That doesn't make any sense. Am I in love with both of them?*

Hunter had not made any progress toward resolving his emotional confusion by the time he entered his apartment. As he passed his computer, he saw on the monitor that he had a message. He sat down at his desk and accessed his mail routine.

There was a video message from Tehani that had been transmitted only about an hour earlier. "My darling Hunter," she began. Hunter paused the message and studied her face. She looked stressed, or possibly even frightened. Her smile seemed forced. Hunter had never seen Tehani look like this.

He continued to play the message. "I'm afraid I have some news that is not going to make you happy," Tehani said. "To tell the truth, it doesn't make me happy." She sighed. "My schedule has been all screwed up. I'm not going to be able to join you for dinner Sunday night. In fact, I'm not going to be able to see you again before I return to Sybaris." She paused briefly. "Last night was wonderful. Or better. I love you very much and hope to see you again soon."

Hunter phoned Tehani immediately in her room at the Tharsis Hotel. He heard her recorded audio message say that she was unavailable.

SEVEN

HUNTER WAS SITTING BESIDE Dr. Bellini at the small table in her office. She was showing him an immense spreadsheet full of data on the computer monitor that was between them. "These are the raw results of the experiment," she said. "Essentially, what you're seeing are the amino-acid sequences after the genetic alteration was completed. The previous file shows the same sequences for this embryo before the alterations were introduced. It's important that we explain every single change."

"Don't you have an automatic compare subroutine in the computer?" Hunter asked.

"Of course," Dr. Bellini said, "but that only identifies the changes. To explain them we must cross-reference each change to the fundamental genome code book."

She looked at Hunter. "Do you think you can handle it?" she said.

"Eventually," Hunter said. "At first I'm afraid I'm going to need you to point me in the right direction."

"You might begin," Dr. Bellini said, "by reviewing what the genome code book is all about. It's really a fascinating document. Basically, it translates sequences of amino-acid chains into human characteristics. When the idea was first developed, back on Earth at the end of the twentieth century, there were many skeptics. We owe an enormous debt to those pioneering scientists who first suggested that human beings could be defined, and perhaps even understood, by looking at variations in these simple chemical chains. It's a shame that their work never reached full fruition. Otherwise, what we're doing at Masursky might have been accomplished three or four hundred years ago."

"What happened?" Hunter asked. "I'm afraid I missed that part of my history of science."

"The general populace at that time on Earth," Dr. Bellini said, "was woefully ignorant about science in general. So were the policy-makers. Thus the full ramifications of mapping the human genome were not understood when the project was approved and undertaken. Once it was clear, however, that mankind was on the verge of understanding the answers to such fundamental questions as what makes each individual the way he or she is, there was a powerful backlash in society. People objected to applications of the genome research for many different reasons, some religious, some philosophical, some out of ignorance. They demanded that the governments of the time do something.

"Scientific illiteracy was so endemic in the societies of the early twenty-first century that the governmental response turned out to be a nightmarish mishmash of senseless laws that constrained and regulated all research associated with what had been learned from the mapping of the genome. Science was essentially hamstrung. Obtaining funding for applied research of the kind we're doing at Masursky was almost impossible. Then, of course, when the civilizations on Earth began to decline, fundamental research was no longer a high priority."

Hunter studied his companion. Dr. Bellini was, without doubt, one of the most intelligent people he had ever met.

During the few days that they had been working together he had been amazed more than once by the breadth of her knowledge. His job was exhilarating.

He had so many questions that he wanted to ask Dr. Bellini. Hunter wasn't timid about questioning scientific issues, yet he still didn't feel comfortable enough in his new position to ask her what he considered to be the "overwhelming questions." He had studied the International Eugenics Act in his apartment and come to the conclusion that some of the work at the Masursky Center definitely violated the spirit, if not the actual law, of that act. Did that make it wrong? Not necessarily, as far as Hunter was concerned. But he still wanted to know what Dr. Bellini and the other scientists thought was acceptable in the general field of genetic alteration of embryos.

Hunter could understand how beneficial it was to society for genetic engineering to reduce or eradicate disease. Was it also all right to reduce or eradicate low intellectual aptitude? What about bald-headedness? Or laziness, assuming that the genes for sloth could be unambiguously identified? These were the kinds of questions that Hunter hoped to discuss in the near future with Dr. Bellini and her cohorts.

ONCE A MONTH the Covington Fellows had a formal dinner, almost a banquet in fact, at a hotel or other prominent venue in downtown Centralia. At these dinners the current crop of Covington Fellows not only had a chance to compare notes with their counterparts, but also could visit with fellows from earlier years. Many of these prior fellows held high positions in the Federation government, so the monthly dinners offered an excellent opportunity for what Patrick Key unashamedly called "schmoozing."

The first monthly dinner that Hunter attended occurred

on the Saturday night of the weekend following his rendezvous with Tehani. Mr. Langenbahn formally introduced him to the gathering during the reception that preceded the dinner. At the meal itself, Hunter was seated between a supreme court justice, who had been a Covington Fellow in the second year of the program, and a FedEnt executive in his middle thirties who was very interested in Hunter's opinion of the pirates.

"What I can't understand," the FedEnt executive said after everyone was seated for the dinner and Hunter and he had exchanged a few comments about the pirates, "is why so many young people find that lifestyle attractive. They give up most of the comforts that they have known all their lives to become pirates. And for what? Just to live an unrestricted existence? Is life in either of the two space societies really that intolerable for them?"

The supreme court justice pointed out that the number of pirates was really very small, compared to the overall Dem and Fed populations, and that it was reasonable to expect, in any society, that a fraction of a percent of the people would be unhappy. He then added that a significant number of the pirates also already had a history of difficulty with authority, of one kind or another, and that they were fleeing from the consequences of their past actions.

"I believed that, too," the FedEnt executive said in response, "until one of my nephews, a bright boy who had never given any of his parents the slightest amount of trouble, suddenly ran away to become a pirate. Then I watched an excellent program on the network that featured half a dozen similar cases. It was quite an eye-opener for me."

He turned to Hunter. "You lived among the pirates for months," the executive said. "Why do you think people leave the Federation and embrace that kind of lifestyle?"

Hunter noticed that some of the conversations around him had temporarily stopped. He swallowed what he was chewing before he spoke. "Virtually every pirate," he began, "has his or her own set of reasons for being there. It's very difficult to find an easy, all-encompassing answer to your question."

He nodded in the direction of the supreme court justice beside him. "Judge Richardson is correct," Hunter said, "when he suggests that many of the pirates, especially the young ones, have had trouble with authority in one form or another in either the Federation or the UDSC. They may have violated the law, and felt unjustly punished for their actions. Or they may have wanted to live in a place where the laws were not so restrictive, as is the case for those who choose to make drug use an important part of their lives. Some, of course, grew up in wildly dysfunctional families and have always felt alienated both from their parents and the society in which they were raised. These young people embrace the pirates in an attempt to obtain a sense of belonging."

Hunter paused for a moment, thinking about what he was going to say. "But it would be a mistake to categorize all the pirates as malcontents or troubled individuals who could not function as contributing citizens in our society. Some of them, especially the leaders, are quite articulate in explaining why they have chosen not to be a part of either of the two dominant space societies. They see themselves as political rebels, not social outcasts. They attempt to analyze the Dem and Fed societies, and point out flaws that they seek to rectify in their own bands."

The number of people listening to him had steadily grown while Hunter was speaking. A voice inside Hunter counseled him to be very careful. "Apart from those who have become pirates primarily to escape the law or some other form of authority," he said, "I believe that there are three principal factors influencing those who have decided to be pirates. First, many of the younger pirates are impatient and frustrated by either real or imagined barriers to their advancement in our societies. They think that both the FISC and the UDSC are controlled by older people who, at times, purposely stymie their creativity and often force them to 'pay their dues' before being given any real responsibility. Second, some of the pirates believe that both the Fed and Dem governments, for whatever reason, have become ossified and hopelessly resistant to change. In a new setting unburdened by existing laws and the precedents of the past, they think it is easier to change situations that are unsatisfactory. And thirdly," Hunter said, "there are a small group of the pirates who believe that the values of the existing space civilizations are fundamentally unsound. These men and women are opposed to the glorification of material wealth, private property, and military power at the expense of individual freedoms, the pursuit of knowledge, and the welfare of every member of the society."

As soon as he was finished, Hunter had the feeling that he had said too much. Although the men sitting on both sides of him enthusiastically praised him for the clarity and insight of his comments, Hunter thought he could sense a general discomfort around the banquet table. He looked at his roommate for support, but Dallas appeared stunned. Patrick Key had an expression on his face as if he had just eaten something that didn't taste right. For the remainder of the meal, Hunter purposely said very little.

Just before dessert, Mr. Langenbahn made an announcement that made most of the attendees temporarily forget Hunter's comments. The Covington Fellowship director informed the group that the most widely anticipated event of each fellowship year, the annual trip to the New Earth Amusement Park in the Free Zone, would take place the following weekend. His announcement was greeted with cheers. The FedEnt executive on Hunter's right launched immediately into a set of stories and anecdotes about what had happened to his group on their trip to New Earth years before.

WHEN HE RETURNED to his apartment after the dinner, Hunter had two messages. He eagerly turned on his computer and discovered that none of them, unfortunately, was from Tehani. Hunter had spoken only once with her, briefly, during the past week and she had seemed harried at the time. He was still curious about what had happened that had caused the cancellation of their Sunday-night date a week earlier.

The first video message was from his mother. She looked very upset. She told Hunter that his father had had an "incident" and that both Dr. Ekanayake and the consulting cardiologist in Centralia believed that exploratory open-heart surgery was now indicated. "The doctor told me that it wasn't a heart attack, Hunter," his mother said, "but I couldn't begin to understand his explanation of what it really was. Dr. Ekanayake said to call him if you have any questions. Anyway, they've scheduled the surgery for the end of the month, when a certified cardiac surgeon will be in the area."

Mrs. Blake began to cry. "I'm sorry, Hunter," she said, "I promised myself that I wouldn't do this. But I'm really worried about your father. He looks bad. He doesn't eat much. He doesn't seem to be interested in anything. If somehow, some way, you could come home for the operation, I know your father would perk up. And I would feel so much better."

His mother composed herself a little before continuing. "I guess everything else here is the same. Neither Amanda nor anyone else has heard from Octavio. Captain Bonesio told her that the ASP is actively looking for him." She paused briefly. "Please call us, Hunter. I know you're very busy, but we don't even know how your visit with Tehani was. Your father looks forward to all your messages."

Hunter was both concerned about his father and upset with himself for not having sent his parents a message the past week. He immediately transmitted a detailed video message with a long description of his evening with Tehani, without the intimate parts, of course, and an up-beat report on his new assignment with Dr. Bellini. Hunter also mentioned briefly that all the Covington Fellows would be going to New Earth the following weekend and that it should be a lot of fun.

He was feeling somewhat better when he opened the second message. It was a note from Mr. Langenbahn. "Reserve next Tuesday afternoon for your special project," it said. "I'll give you more details on Monday."

Hunter had certainly not forgotten about the special Defense Ministry team that would be planning the strike on Utopia. He had simply pushed thoughts about it aside during the last ten days. As he sat in front of his computer monitor, his stomach already churning, Hunter heard a noise outside his apartment door.

"No, it's my duty as his friend," a drunken voice was saying. "I'm going to tell him whether you like it or not."

Hunter recognized that the voice belonged to Patrick Key. An instant later the door flew open and both Patrick and Dallas stumbled in. They saw Hunter immediately. "You, Hunter Blake," Patrick said, "are brilliant, but very very stupid."

Patrick lurched forward and nearly fell on the floor. "Do you hear me?" he said, waggling a finger at Hunter. "Brilliant but stupid."

THE ADDRESS THAT Mr. Langenbahn gave
Hunter for the Tuesday-afternoon meeting was a nondescript warehouse on the far side of Centralia from the
spaceport. Hunter arrived at the appointed time and
knocked on the door. A thin man wearing a polo shirt and
jeans answered his knock.

"Yes?" he said, opening the door only part of the way.

"I'm Hunter Blake," he said. "I was told to come here
for a meeting."

"Just a minute," the man said.

Shortly thereafter, the door opened again. A tall, robust
man in his mid-fifties with thick gray hair smiled and
asked Hunter for his identity card. He then invited Hunter
inside and closed the door.

"I'm General George Brougher," he said. They shook
hands and crossed the large, empty warehouse to the other
side. While they were walking, General Brougher reminded Hunter that everything about Operation Bluebeard, the name that had been given to their project, was
top secret, even the location of their headquarters.

General Brougher stood in front of a retina scanner, and
then put his right thumb and index finger inside a device
protruding from the wall next to a set of double doors on
the far side of the warehouse. When the doors opened,
Hunter followed the general inside. They were met immediately by a young woman with cropped hair whom General Brougher identified as Rhonda.

"Rhonda is the Bluebeard security officer," the general
said. "She'll go over the security procedures here and program all your personal data. On your subsequent visits, you
will pass through the warehouse and into the operations
area on your own."

Hunter spent fifteen minutes in the security cubicle with
Rhonda. When he was finished, he was led down a long
corridor into the main operations room. The room was the

size of a small theater. It was full of computers, monitors, desks, and high-technology apparatus. Eight people, all in casual dress, were scattered around the room, most of them working in front of a computer monitor. On a large wall screen at the back of the room was an animated, electronic map displaying the part of the solar system from just inside the Earth's orbit to slightly outside the orbit of Mars. Deimos, Phobos, the Earth's moon, and four asteroids that crossed inside the orbit of Mars were depicted on the display in addition to the two planets. At the bottom right of the screen was a pair of digital clocks showing both Universal Time and the local time in Centralia.

"From your testimony," General Brougher said to Hunter, pointing at the map, "and what our intelligence personnel have learned in the last two weeks, we have narrowed the list of candidates for Utopia to the four asteroids shown on the display. As you can see, all four have perihelia well inside the orbit of Mars and are presently close enough to Mars that your escape route would have been possible."

The general walked over to the closest desk and activated its control panel. A few seconds later a dozen flashing lights appeared on the large map. Each group of three lights was in a formation heading for one of the asteroids. "Late last week we launched four sets of special reconnaissance drones," the general said, "one set aimed at each of these candidate asteroids. The drones are equipped with ultrasensitive sensors that will identify the quality and quantity of electromagnetic flux from the surface. Any radio, microwave, or other electromagnetic activity at any frequency originating from the surface will be observed."

General Brougher turned around to face Hunter. "Soon after your rescue and debriefing," he said, "our intelligence department reviewed in detail all the data from our standard drone fleet that regularly performs reconnaissance operations throughout the Federation sphere of influence.

Every one of these four candidate asteroids has been observed at least once during the past year. At first we were puzzled by the fact that none of the data sets from these asteroids produced the kind of signature that is almost always associated with human settlements. Additional analysis suggested, however, that our regular drone data is possibly being corrupted by an advanced jamming process. That level of technological sophistication, which we would never, heretofore, have expected from the pirates, is not inconsistent with what would have been necessary to carry out the attack on Cicero and the hijacking of the *Darwin*."

The general smiled. "Fortunately," he said, "the drones that we just deployed carry state-of-the-art security routines, capable of detecting, and sidestepping, the most sophisticated jamming attempts. Thus if the Utopians even try to corrupt the data the drones are measuring, they will give their location away."

Hunter looked at the wall screen. The lights indicating the reconnaissance drones were roughly three-fourths of the way from Mars to each of the candidate asteroids. He felt a tightening in his stomach. *In a few more days,* Hunter said to himself, *the exact location of the Utopian colony will be known.*

"What I would like for you to do today," the general was saying, "is help us construct a detailed map of Utopia, including the locations of the landing area for the space vehicles and the permanent buildings under the dome. With this information, we can more carefully assess the various options that are available to us. We have not yet decided on the exact nature of our attack. Some members of the Defense Ministry believe that obliterating the colony is best, for it would send an unambiguous message to all the pirate bands. Others believe that seizing the colony and all its assets, both personnel and intelligence, is a better option."

General Brougher introduced Hunter to a young man

named Larry, with whom Hunter spent the next two and a half hours. Larry constructed a map of Utopia on the computer according to Hunter's specifications. As the details of the map formed on the monitor in front of him, Hunter became increasingly troubled. He described the plan of the Utopian settlement to Larry as accurately as he could, for he saw no reason not to tell the truth. But the specter of a devastating attack upon the pirate colony where he had lived sent repeated cold chills through his body.

At the end of the afternoon, General Brougher inspected the map that Larry had created from Hunter's information. The general was very pleased. He accompanied Hunter out of the operations room and thanked him for his help. As Hunter was leaving, he asked the general if a time had been scheduled for the attack on Utopia.

"We should have the correct asteroid positively identified by the end of this week," the general said. "By that same time, we will have decided on our specific course of action. The final phase of Operation Bluebeard will begin immediately thereafter."

On the tram ride back to his apartment, Hunter thought about what, if anything, he could do to stop the attack, or at least to mitigate its consequences. He understood completely that the Utopians had violated the laws of the Federation with the hijacking and the kidnapping. He did not doubt for a second that General Brougher and Minister Sackett were convinced that unilateral action against Utopia was perfectly justified. But Hunter could not stop thinking about the individual pirates he had known, and how the attack would wreak havoc upon their lives. *Even if they are not killed,* he said to himself, *they will doubtless be Federation prisoners forever, with very little chance of future happiness.*

Back in his apartment, Hunter declined an invitation to join Dallas, Patrick, and Ryan for dinner. Dallas could tell that Hunter was not his usual self. He asked Hunter if he was all right, or if something had happened at work that had disturbed him. Hunter protested that he was just tired, and that he would feel better after a good night's sleep.

When he was alone Hunter struggled again to determine some course of personal action that would not result in the destruction of Utopia. He briefly considered volunteering to serve as an emissary of some kind, to try to broker a peaceful resolution to the dispute. But Hunter knew immediately that such a suggestion would be laughed at by the Defense Ministry, and that he personally would suffer as a result.

He went to bed full of gloom and depression. Hunter found himself longing for his childhood days, when all his worries were comparatively trivial.

EIGHT

HUNTER SLEPT FITFULLY. HE awakened several
times, then had difficulty falling asleep again. Shortly after
midnight he had a terrible nightmare.

In his dream Hunter was with Ursula in the clinic on
Utopia. The two of them were having a casual chat in the
main tent when suddenly an ASP officer barged in and began barking commands. The officer ordered Ursula to undress. When Hunter protested, the ASP intruder struck
him twice with a club. Hunter fell to his knees.

Ursula took off her clothes in the dream and the ASP officer noticed her pregnancy. Still brandishing the club, the
man turned around, shouted something to unknown individuals outside the tent, and ordered Ursula to lie down on
one of the operating tables. Moments later two men entered
the tent carrying a large, open, cylindrical silver container.
They placed the container at the far end of the table, below
Ursula's legs. Hunter recognized that the silver barrel was
exactly like the one that had been a depository for unwanted embryos at the Masursky Center in New Austin.
The ASP officer ordered Ursula to spread her legs.

Hunter tried to stand up but could not move. He tried to

yell but no sound came from his voice. As he watched in horror on his dream screen, a man in a white coat carrying a strange apparatus entered the tent and stood beside the silver barrel at the end of the table. He plugged in his device. It made a loud sucking sound. The man in the white coat leaned forward toward Ursula. She started screaming and writhing. The two men who had brought in the container held her down. Hunter could not watch.

He awakened in a cold, terrified sweat. It was several minutes before he was able to convince himself that he had been dreaming. Whenever he closed his eyes, Hunter could still see Ursula lying on the table in the clinic, her face contorted in horror.

Hunter glanced at the clock beside his bed. It was one-thirty. For a few minutes he sat in the dark in contemplation. The dream faded slowly. Hunter thought again about his afternoon with General Brougher and Operation Bluebeard. *I can't let this happen,* he said to himself eventually. *I must warn them.*

He put on his clothes and walked into the living room. It was dark and quiet. Hunter walked over to the door, opened it gingerly, and slipped into the hall. He rode the elevator down to the first floor and headed for the entertainment center.

Hunter didn't see anybody that he knew in the center. Two of the virtual-world kiosks were unoccupied. He climbed inside one and activated his saved Rama game in which his avatar was only five moves away from the wall in the blue maze. With his heart pounding fiercely, Hunter moved his alter ego into the proper location and input the twenty-four-character alphanumeric that he had learned from Cooperman. The game screen went blank.

Hunter paused. He didn't move for almost a minute. During that time, he thought one more time about the possible ramifications of what he was about to do. Nevertheless, he concluded that he would not be able to live with himself if he didn't warn the pirates.

He carefully computed the proper hexadecimal equivalent of the date and entered the password. After what seemed like forever, but was in reality only a few seconds, a box that would hold up to eight characters appeared on the blank screen. Hunter wrote "medicman" in the box. Immediately a message appeared on the monitor indicating that he had three pieces of mail, two from "smartass" and one from "medicgal." The first letter from "smartass" had been transmitted on the day Hunter had had the interview with Minister Sackett and had received the Rama newsletter. Both the second letter from "smartass" and the one from "medicgal" had been sent just two days ago.

Hunter glanced furtively out of the kiosk. Nobody was watching him. He accessed the first note from Cooperman.

> Hunter, we know about your meeting with Sackett and the
> plans for an attack against Utopia. Don't worry about us. We
> will do whatever is necessary to preserve the colony.
> You, on the other hand, are in serious danger. The ASP is
> convinced they have a solid case against you already. We
> haven't been able to obtain the details, but from the high-level
> conversations it's apparent that they think they have enough
> for a conviction. The ASP was going to arrest you yesterday,
> but Sackett talked them out of it.
> Sackett believes there is some chance you might not be
> convicted on the basis of the existing evidence. He wants an
> open-and-shut case. He is jealous of your relationship with
> Tehani. It was his idea to assign you to Operation Bluebeard
> as part of an elaborate trap. Both Sackett and the ASP are
> hoping you will violate the secrecy laws, but they intend to
> trump up charges even if you don't.

> Don't trust anybody. Especially not your roommate Dallas
> Morrison. He is working directly for Sackett, and meets with
> him twice a week to provide details of all your activities. Dallas
> does not know about Sackett and Tehani, only that your
> allegiance to the Federation is suspect.
> Please let me know if and when you read this letter.

Struggling with fear and other powerful emotions, Hunter slowly read through Cooperman's first letter again. He then closed his eyes and took several slow, deep breaths before accessing the more recent letter from his pirate friend.

> Hunter, your situation is becoming more precarious. Dem
> intelligence has requested help from the Feds in identifying the
> perpetrators of the raid on the Edison complex. If that
> cooperation does indeed take place, and your involvement
> becomes known, you will almost certainly be indicted for first-
> degree treason.
> Meanwhile, Sackett is not happy about the night you spent
> with Tehani. Dallas gave him a full report. Apparently your
> roommate placed listening devices in your bedroom the week
> before she came to visit you.
> We have concluded that there is no way we could help you
> escape from North Mars. However, we may be able to manage
> an escape from the Free Zone, when you go there this
> weekend. The logistics are complicated, and expensive. We
> need to know if you will seriously consider making a break.
> Ursula has badgered me into admitting that I may have some
> way to contact you. She is coming over here later tonight to
> send you a letter herself.
> Take care of yourself, my friend.

Hunter sat quietly in the kiosk, desperately trying to quell the feeling of panic that was spreading through his body. Again he read Cooperman's most recent letter. *We need to know if you will seriously consider making a break,* he repeated to himself. Hunter sighed. *If everything Cooperman has said is true,* Hunter thought, *then I really have no options. But how can I possibly know if he is telling the truth?*

In his mind Hunter reviewed a montage of scenes involving Cooperman. Hunter smiled. It was impossible for him not to smile while thinking about Cooperman. In the end Hunter concluded that although the little genius definitely had his idiosyncrasies, he had never been anything but honest with Hunter.

Cooperman has nothing to gain by misleading me, Hunter said to himself. Still deep in thought, he accessed the letter from Ursula.

> Dearest Hunter, it is impossible to describe how much I miss
> you. I am such a fool, my darling. I should have begged you to
> stay here instead of standing on such stupid principles.
> Cooperman and Lance have both told me that you may be in
> trouble. I don't know any of the details, but I can tell that
> Cooperman is genuinely concerned. Please be careful,
> darling. I couldn't stand it if there was no chance that I would
> ever see you again.
> Our baby is fine. I am all right as well, although I am always
> tired at the end of my day at the clinic. I wish so much that you
> were here with me. I love you more than ever, Hunter, and I
> desperately hope that someday you will return to my arms.

HUNTER STAYED IN the virtual-world kiosk for another half hour. For the first fifteen minutes he sat motionless, as if he were in a stupor, and struggled with the tidal wave of thoughts and feelings that were overwhelming him. Ursula's letter had brought tears to his eyes. Now, more than ever, Hunter missed her terribly. He chastised himself vehemently for ever leaving Utopia in the first place. *But that's a useless waste of energy,* he told himself at length. *I must focus now on the future.*

Hunter read both of Cooperman's letters one more time before writing his reply.

> Thank you very much for being concerned about me. Your
> messages were shocking, to say the least. It will probably be a
> day or two before I truly comprehend the full impact of what
> you have told me.
> Yes, I am seriously interested in an escape attempt. How could
> I not be? Based on the contents of your message, my position
> here looks tenuous at best. And from what I've seen so far of
> life in the Federation, I'm not sure I would want to live here
> permanently anyway.
> Cooperman, I cannot yet make a full commitment to the
> escape, for I need to think about everything that you have
> written. By Friday afternoon, when I arrive in the Free Zone, I
> will have considered all my options. I will find a kiosk at that
> time and contact you.
> In your first message you told me not to worry about the
> pending attack on Utopia. That's impossible for me under the
> circumstances. I assume you know from your intelligence
> sources that three ultrasensitive reconnaissance drones are
> approaching Utopia and that they are equipped with state-of-
> the-art systems for identifying and sidestepping jamming
> attempts. These drones will sense any kind of electromagnetic
> activity at any wavelength. The Federation Defense Ministry is
> confident that the drones will have unambiguously identified
> the Utopian asteroid by this weekend at the latest. They intend
> to attack soon thereafter.
> Thanks also for giving Ursula a way to send me a message.
> Take care. Good luck. You are a great friend.

Hunter slowly reread his letter to Cooperman after he was finished writing. He was absolutely aware that he was committing treason by sending it. He studied the monitor for over a minute before dispatching the electronic message.

He also replied to Ursula's letter before he left the kiosk. Hunter didn't say anything about his predicament, but he did tell Ursula that he loved both her and their unborn child. Hunter added that he was now certain that it had been a mistake for him to leave Utopia. He told her that if he had known how completely the Federation intended to plan his life, he would never have accepted the Covington Fellowship in the first place.

It was almost three o'clock when Hunter disembarked from the elevator on the fourteenth floor and started walking toward his apartment. He noticed that light from his living room was shining underneath the door. Puzzled, Hunter made the final approach very quietly along the wall, stopping just before the door. He heard a voice from inside the apartment, which he immediately recognized as that of his roommate.

"It's been almost an hour now," Hunter heard Dallas say in a low voice to someone on the phone. "Haven't you idiots fixed the damn system yet?"

Even though he was speaking softly, Hunter could tell that Dallas was extremely irritated. "Yes," his roommate said sharply after a short silence, "I already told you that this is a priority-one request. Your coworker validated my priority code when I called earlier. I don't need a hassle from you. I need information."

There was no sound from within the apartment for twenty seconds or so. "Yes?" Dallas then said. "In this building? The entire time? Can you pinpoint where? All right. Good-bye. Thank you, I guess."

Hunter could tell from the fluctuations in the light coming underneath the door that Dallas was moving around. Then he heard footsteps heading in his direction. Hunter took two steps into the center of the corridor and was facing the door just as Dallas opened it.

"Oh," Dallas said, recoiling with a startled expression. "There you are. What are you doing up at this time of night?"

"I could ask you that same question," Hunter said pleasantly. He walked around Dallas and into the apartment.

"Well, I couldn't sleep," Dallas said after a few seconds. "I got myself some cookies and milk and thought maybe you'd like to play some kind of game." He smiled. "I opened your bedroom door very quietly, so that I wouldn't disturb you, and I noticed that you were gone. When you didn't come back, I became worried."

"So you were going to go out and look for me?" Hunter said with a look of disbelief. "At three o'clock in the morning?"

"Not really," Dallas said following a long hesitation. "I thought maybe I'd go down to one of the kiosks in the entertainment center. If I ran into you, then so much the better."

Hunter pulled a juice container out of the refrigerator. "That's where I was," he said casually to Dallas. "I've been playing Rama. I woke up and couldn't go back to sleep. I decided not to just lie there and toss and turn."

Hunter drank his juice and headed for his bedroom. "See you in the morning," he said to his roommate.

DR. BELLINI SAT down in the chair next to Hunter. He was working in front of a computer monitor at the small conference table in her office. A motley assemblage of papers was scattered around the table on either side of the monitor.

"All right, Hunter Blake," Dr. Bellini said in a friendly tone, "tell me what's bothering you. You haven't been yourself these last two days. What's the problem? Is it girls, work, or something else?"

Hunter looked at his supervisor. "Is it that obvious?" he said.

She laughed easily. "Oh, yes," Dr. Bellini said. "When you walked in here Wednesday morning you looked as if you were going to a funeral. And except for an occasional smile here and there, you've worn the same morose expression on your handsome face ever since." She leaned over toward him. "What's going on?"

Hunter hesitated. "It's lots of things, Dr. Bellini," he said eventually, "I'm just not certain—"

Dr. Bellini gesticulated with her hands. "Look, your personal life is really none of my business, but if anything that's bothering you is work-related, I wish you'd talk to me."

Hunter stared at her for several seconds. "Well," he said, forcing a smile, "I do have some concerns about my work. . . . Not about the assignment, or what you're doing, or anything scientific . . . I don't want you to think that I don't appreciate having this job. It's just that I have some, uh, I guess I would call them philosophical issues about this whole project."

Dr. Sandra Bellini's forehead wrinkled. "You're going to have to be more specific, Hunter," she said, "if you want me to understand." She paused a moment. "What exactly are these 'philosophical issues'?"

"Do you think it's right for scientists to try to engineer perfect, or even exceptional children?" Hunter said suddenly after a lengthy silence. He spoke very rapidly and with growing passion. "I keep seeing that scene in the big laboratory at Masursky Center," he said, "with the petri dishes spread out in all directions, and I imagine a future where possibly every single human embryo is subjected to some kind of assessment before it is allowed to grow and mature. You even said yourself that there might someday be a law requiring every Federation conception to be tested and assessed. In that future, who will be the arbiter of what kind of embryos will survive? Scientists? Politicians? Parents and other family members? Isn't it massive hubris for us to believe that we will ever be able to identify the gene combinations that create good people? Or, for that matter, happy people?"

Dr. Bellini listened carefully to Hunter's outburst. Then she smiled. "I had forgotten how idealistic the truly young are," she said slowly. "Once upon a time, before I started spending my time worrying about more mundane issues, like balancing my bank account, I too tried to grapple with such grand, sweeping concepts as the origin and destiny of the species, the planet, and the universe. I, too, wondered about what would happen when all future evolution was controlled by one of the products of the past natural evolution, the very imperfect *Homo sapiens sapiens.*"

She stood up from her chair and began walking slowly around the office. Dr. Bellini punctuated her comments with hand motions. "Your questions are absolutely legitimate, Hunter," she said, "but there are, unfortunately, no easy answers. The genie is out of the bottle. Pandora's box has been opened. You may choose whatever metaphor you like, but one fact is inescapable. Human beings now have the knowledge and the power to determine their own destiny. Should they? Probably not. Do they? Yes, indeed. Will that knowledge be used? Absolutely. Will the resultant species be, according to any metric, either happier or better? We have no way of knowing."

Dr. Bellini looked at Hunter. "The possible political ramifications are especially disturbing to me," he said. "I was told at the Masursky Center that the Federation is a full generation ahead of the Dems in understanding how to design specific attributes into unborn children. Suppose that the net historical result of all your research, and that of your colleagues, is the creation of a superior subspecies, which in turn perpetuates a less-than-perfect political system at the expense of those who are less able and less fortunate. How would you feel if . . . ?"

Dr. Bellini was holding up her hand. "This conversation has now taken a disturbing turn," she said, "and is becoming dangerous. You should be more careful, Hunter, about the way you express yourself. People will misconstrue your intentions."

She gazed at him intently, and then a mischievous grin spread across her face. "Before I give you my own personal credo with respect to this issue," she said, "I want you to answer one question for me honestly. Is this philosophical conundrum associated with our work a small, medium-sized, or large contributor to the general malaise you have been exhibiting these last two days?"

Hunter smiled. "Small to medium," he said.

"Whew!" said Sandra Bellini, almost laughing. "For a minute or two I was afraid that our work was the primary cause of your gloom and doom. In that case, I was going to recommend that you request a transfer to some nicely circumscribed assignment that would not offer you any philosophical dilemmas."

The office was quiet for several seconds. "Okay," Dr. Bellini then said, "let me tell you how I answered a set of my own, similar questions when I was young and freudened." She laughed at her own wit. "First, I convinced myself that designer children would eventually become a reality in human society whether I was part of the process or not. Second, I saw a tremendous opportunity to improve the quality of human lives by concentrating on research aimed at removing susceptibility to disease. Third, I thought that if I were a contributing member of the research team making the breakthroughs in embryonic alteration, I would have a better chance to impact the way in which the results would be used. Fourth, I found the entire subject absolutely fascinating, and clearly worth the best of my abilities." She stopped for a few seconds. "That's my justification, I guess, for what I do."

Hunter nodded at Dr. Bellini. "I understand your logic," he said. "Maybe in time my own misgivings will go away."

She put her hand on his shoulder. "They will probably never vanish completely," she said. "Mine haven't. But most of the time I believe that what I am doing is a net plus for humanity."

Hunter looked at her with admiration. "Thanks," he said.

"It was my pleasure," she said. "It's not often that I'm challenged at such a fundamental level."

THE COVINGTON FELLOWS and their chaperones occupied one entire car of the high-speed train from Centralia to the Free Zone border. The young men were in great spirits as they stored their bags in the overhead racks and took their seats. Patrick Key sat next to Hunter. He was already talking about Tehani before the train left the station.

"I have a favor to ask of you about Tehani," he said to Hunter a few minutes after the train was outside the Centralia dome. "I would love to meet her, even if only briefly. I want to see if she's as beautiful in real life as she is in her videos."

"I'll see what I can do," Hunter said. "But right now, I'm not even sure if I'll see her this weekend."

Patrick looked shocked. "Surely you jest," he said. "Sybaris is right next to New Earth. The two parks have a common boundary. She'll be only five minutes away."

"I know," Hunter said. "But Tehani has a very busy calendar. When I told her that we would be coming down this weekend, she said that she already had commitments. She said she would try to rearrange her schedule, but sometimes that's impossible."

Patrick was disappointed. *But not as disappointed as I am,* Hunter said to himself. *This may be the last time I ever have a chance to see Tehani.*

Hunter had made his decision. Sometime in the early-morning hours on Friday, Hunter had stopped searching fruitlessly for some combination of circumstances that would make staying on Mars the right choice. He intended to send a message to Cooperman as soon as they reached the Free Zone. Unless an escape was hopelessly risky, Hunter was going to make an attempt to return to the pirates.

He stared out the window of the train at the passing Martian landscape with more than casual curiosity. As he looked at one particularly unusual mountain of large boulders, Hunter wondered if he would ever again see the plains of Mars. Then he started thinking about his peculiar odyssey, from Cicero to Utopia to Mars, and how nothing had worked out the way he had envisioned it.

He would have few regrets about leaving Mars. He would, however, miss working with Dr. Bellini. Even though Hunter had decided that the scientists working on embryonic alteration at the Masursky Center had compromised their principles and ethics by performing eugenic tasks for the Federation, he still admired and liked the energetic woman who had been his supervisor and sponsor.

Hunter's feelings about his friends among the Covington Fellows were definitely colored by what Cooperman had told him about Dallas. In retrospect, even if Hunter had not overheard the conversation between Dallas and the navprobe center, he would probably have believed Cooperman's assertion that Dallas was spying on him. During the two days prior to the departure for their weekend trip to

New Earth, Hunter had remembered many instances in which his roommate had been aggressively inquisitive about his activities. At the time, Hunter had simply thought that such behavior was a part of Dallas's personality. But upon reflection, Hunter could not recall one single time when Dallas had asked similar prying questions of one of the other fellows.

Hunter no longer had any doubts about why Tehani had been unable to see him again on Sunday during her weekend in Centralia. He was certain that an angry and jealous Lester Sackett, armed with all the juicy details of Hunter's night with Tehani, had delivered an ultimatum to her. *Anyway,* Hunter said to himself as the train passed a magnificent set of tall sand dunes, *it doesn't matter anymore. Sackett wanted me out of Tehani's life. He's going to have his wish.*

A sharp heartache accompanied his thoughts about Tehani. Hunter knew that he loved her, and that she would forever occupy a special place in his heart. He allowed himself to spend a few minutes savoring his most cherished memories of their times together, but then abruptly forced his mind to think about other subjects. *I guess Tehani and I just weren't meant to be a couple,* Hunter told himself. *The sooner I accept that fact, the better.*

He fell asleep when the train was still over an hour from the border. Hunter slept peacefully, without dreaming, and didn't awaken until Patrick informed him that they needed to get off the train.

NINE

SHORTLY AFTER THEIR ARRIVAL in Lancaster, the Free Zone town that had grown up around the tourist attractions of New Earth and Sybaris, Hunter located a vacant kiosk no more than a hundred yards from their hotel. He had left Patrick, Dallas, and Ryan in the hotel bar after first explaining to them that Tehani was expecting him to call at a specific time. Hunter had taken a circuitous path to the kiosk, first riding the elevator up to his floor, then walking down the hotel stairs, just in case Dallas had decided to follow him.

Inside the kiosk, which was just outside the gates of the New Earth Amusement Park, Hunter quickly entered the Rama virtual world and moved his avatar to the proper location. He input the correct alphanumeric and the password for the day. The expected electronic letter from Cooperman was waiting for him.

> Hunter, I hope you are reading this message on Friday
> afternoon, for we need thirty-six hours to put all the elements of
> your escape plan into operation. Here's what you must do.
> Please memorize the instructions carefully. Sometime before
> eleven o'clock in the morning on Sunday, break away from

> your group and go to the Niagara Falls ride. Try to enter your
> barrel as close to eleven as you can. After you are finished,
> when the park attendants are directing everyone toward the
> pathway to the left, open and enter the gray door that's just to
> the right of the pool at the bottom of the ride. There's only one
> gray door. It is usually locked, but it will be open on Sunday
> morning.
> The door opens into the underground passageways that
> connect the various sections of New Earth. Walk down the
> stairs. An empty transport vehicle should be waiting on the
> tracks in front of the tunnel. Climb into the vehicle and enter
> "41" on the control panel. The car should activate immediately
> and wind through tunnels for three or four minutes. When it
> stops, you will be beside a long, narrow platform. Take the up
> staircase from the platform, and exit through the door on the
> first landing. Follow the path straight ahead for roughly a
> quarter of a mile and you will reach a fence on the side of the
> park. An emergency gate there will be temporarily unlocked.
> You will be approached by your contact soon after you have
> passed through the gate. The password will be "smartass."
> From that point forward you will be accompanied by someone.
> Follow their instructions. I don't need to give you the rest of the
> details of the plan. I do, however, need to remind you that this
> escape is a very dangerous undertaking. Even though you are
> not in Federation territory, ASP agents are still a threat. They
> may be watching you carefully. They are almost always armed.
> Be wary of the people around you.
> Thanks for the warning about the drones. We think that the
> Federation military planners are in for a big surprise. Good
> luck, my friend. Hope to see you soon.

Hunter read the letter over and over until all the significant parts were committed to memory. Then, without hesitation, he replied to Cooperman's message.

> I have read and memorized all the instructions and am
> prepared to implement the plan on Sunday. Thanks to
> everyone who has helped.

THAT EVENING, AFTER unsuccessfully try-
ing to reach Tehani, Hunter went out with the rest of the
Covington Fellows, just as if everything was normal in his
life. Between their hotel and the entrance to the park were
a string of bars, clubs, and restaurants that catered primarily to young tourists visiting the area. Throughout the
evening, Patrick was his usual irrepressible self, flirting
outrageously with every decent-looking female they encountered. At one club a young man in his twenties objected to an approach that Patrick made to a girl who
turned out to be his date. A fracas almost ensued.

On the street, after Hunter and Dallas dragged their
friend out of the club and away from the angry man,
Patrick loudly objected to their interference. "He was an
asshole," Patrick said with drunken conviction, "and de-
served to be pummeled."

"I don't think Chairman Covington would be pleased,"
Dallas said, "to see on the network news that one of his
fellows had been involved in a Free Zone brawl."

"There wouldn't have been a brawl," Patrick said, slur-
ring his words a little, "it would have been over in a nanosecond. The guy was a wimp."

"Patrick, my friend," Hunter said as they walked along,
"I believe your taste in women decreases in direct propor-
tion to your liquor intake. I don't think that girl was worth
even a conversation, much less a fight."

Patrick's eyes flashed. "That's easy for you to say, my
man," he said, "since the personification of feminine sexu-
ality is your personal punch." He stopped on the sidewalk

and tried to focus his eyes on Hunter. "And who are you to criticize my judgment, anyway? Aren't you the moron who praised the pirates at our monthly Covington Banquet?"

The three young men walked in silence for several seconds. "I did not praise the pirates," Hunter said at length. "I simply pointed out that not all of them were malcontents who were unable to function in our society."

"It sounded to me," Dallas said, "as if you were saying that the pirates had legitimate complaints about both the Federation and the UDSC. The man next to me, who is an officer in the Centralia Bank, came to the same conclusion."

Hunter didn't respond. He was certain that Dallas was baiting him, and would report whatever he said to Minister Sackett and the other authorities.

Patrick suddenly stopped on the street and turned to Hunter. "What I would like to know," he said, as he weaved back and forth, "is why you didn't just stay with the damn pirates? I mean, if you think they're so neat, why did you come back?"

Hunter looked first at his drunk companion, and then at Dallas. He felt his anger rise but managed to control it. "I won't dignify that absurd question with a response," he said. He then glanced at his watch. "I think I've had enough for the night," Hunter said, starting to walk back toward the hotel. "Dallas," he added, turning around, "please try not to wake me when you come back to the room."

THE NEW EARTH Amusement Park was one of the most profitable enterprises of FedEnt. It was a family destination resort without equal anywhere in space. Juxtaposed to Sybaris in the Free Zone on Mars, it offered a beautiful, and thrilling, view of the most famous locations from the planet Earth.

Inside the twelve square miles of New Earth, the vacationer could visit authentic, scaled-down replications of hundreds of places on Earth, including a typical Amazon rain forest, a pristine Hawaiian beach, a portion of the Sahara desert, a Serengeti savanna, and even, in a controlled enclosure that allowed duplication of the high-altitude weather conditions, part of the Swiss town of Zermatt and the surrounding snow-covered Alps. The flora and fauna inhabiting the different regions were also authentic in appearance, although most of the larger animals and plants had been created by the miracle of miniaturized electronics.

One full section of the park was dedicated to the cities of the Earth. A great circular plaza containing replicas of several dozen of the most famous urban monuments was at the center of this section. The avenues radiating away from the plaza cut the section into pie slices, each of which was a separate reproduction of street scenes and architecture from a specific city on Earth. Upon crossing one of the avenues, a visitor would transport himself from New York to Rome, or from Paris to Shanghai. The tourist could spend the night on a futon laid down over a tatami mat in a sixteenth-century ryokan in Kyoto, and then have a buffet breakfast at one of the garish casinos of Las Vegas.

On one side of the park were faithful re-creations of the most impressive archaeological destinations on Earth. A short ride on the Nile led past the Pyramids of Giza and the monuments of Luxor and Thebes. The Mayan zone was a potpourri of ancient artistic marvels, including pyramids from Uxmal, Palenque, and Tikal, the wall murals of Bonampak, the ball court from Chichén Itzá, and the stunning sculptures from the plaza at Copán. Ancient Rome had been compressed into a hundred acres, but the Forum, the Colosseum, Hadrian's Villa, and even four square blocks of the buried city of Pompeii were all faithfully reproduced.

For children of all ages, twenty-five percent of the park was dedicated to thrill rides. Roller coasters of all kinds and descriptions, as well as every imaginable water activity, were the highlights of that part of New Earth.

Most visitors stayed at New Earth for a week or more, which allowed them to see the attractions at a leisurely pace. The weekend trip for the Covington Fellows included only two full days at the park. On Saturday morning the young men were awakened very early, and fed an extensive breakfast at the hotel. During breakfast Patrick approached Hunter and apologized for his behavior the previous night.

"I could say that I had too much to drink," Patrick said, "but that's really not a legitimate excuse. I was really off base, Hunter, and I'm sorry."

Hunter accepted his friend's apology graciously. Nevertheless, when he returned to his hotel room briefly to finish his personal preparations for the day, Hunter found himself wondering if Patrick, like Dallas, was observing him and making regular reports to the Defense Ministry or the ASP. He smiled grimly at his reflection in the mirror as he brushed his teeth. *Goodness,* Hunter said to himself, *I'm becoming paranoid already.*

The day at New Earth began with a visit to the famous natural sciences museum, where a special guide took the Covington Fellows through exhibits, arranged chronologically, about the history of the Earth prior to the appearance of modern man. A large display in a rotunda, at the end of the dinosaur exhibit, depicted in animated detail the catastrophic impact of the asteroid or comet that smashed into the Yucatán region sixty-five million years ago, radically altering the climate of the Earth and leading to the demise of the great reptiles. Hunter was especially fascinated by the representation of the mammoth tidal wave that swept across the Gulf of Mexico and inundated more than a third of the United States.

"What is sometimes not fully understood," the guide said, "is that this enormous extraterrestrial event, which triggered the Cretaceous extinction, was absolutely essential for our evolution. The dinosaurs had been rulers of the Earth for well over a hundred million years, and had adapted to fill virtually every ecological niche available for large animals. Mammals, and therefore humans, could never have evolved to their present state if the dinosaurs had not been obliterated."

During the late morning, the fellows visited the archaeological section of the park. Hunter was the only Covington Fellow who chose the Mayan exhibition for his personal tour. After riding a slow tram through and around the great pyramids and other architectural features of the ancient Mayan ceremonial centers, Hunter was deposited, along with the rest of the passengers on the tram, on a platform adjoining a reconstruction of the central courtyard at Copán. Hunter ambled through the courtyard, stopping from time to time to admire the perfect replications of the huge, three-dimensional sculptures commissioned by one of the kings.

While Hunter was standing by himself in front of one particular sculpture, a two-sided monument about ten feet tall and slightly thicker than an obelisk, an attractive young woman with long auburn hair walked up beside him. "Pretty amazing, huh?" she said. "It's hard for me to conceive that something like this could have been created two thousand years ago in the jungles of Central America.

"This is 18-Rabbit," she said, pointing at the figure portrayed on the sculpture. "On this side he's dressed in a military uniform. On the other side he's wearing what appears to be a skirt. These glyphs underneath his portrait explain that he was a king of Copán during the fifth century after Christ, and that he commissioned these sculptures."

"How do you know all this?" Hunter asked, genuinely impressed. "Are you a guide here?"

The young woman cast a furtive glance around her and then looked back at Hunter. "Smartass," she said, slowly and distinctly.

Hunter's pulse immediately skyrocketed. "Okay," he said slowly. "I understand."

"We've had to change your plan," she said. "Do you have it memorized?"

Hunter nodded.

"Tell me what you do after the transport vehicle stops at the long, narrow platform under Sybaris," she said.

"I go up the staircase, to the first landing, and then out the door—"

"Okay," she said. "That's what has been changed. It would be too easy for someone to recognize you during that long walk to the fence." She glanced around again. There was nobody near them. "Take the down staircase from the platform. Continue down to the second landing. That's the level on which all the electrical work is done. Turn left and follow the tunnel about a hundred yards. There will be a metal spiral staircase leading to the surface. Climb up to the top and open the manhole cover. You will be no more than twenty yards from the side fence. Go through the emergency gate, which will be temporarily open, and across the park with the picnic tables. The contact will meet you in the vicinity of the building that houses the rest rooms."

The young woman had Hunter repeat the instructions until they were correct twice in a row. "All right," she said, "I guess that's it. Good luck."

"Thank you," Hunter said.

The young woman pointed at the statue of 18-Rabbit.

"Would you like to know what happened to him?" she said.

"Sure," Hunter said.

"While 18-Rabbit was focused on all the artworks you see in this courtyard," she said, "his military became lazy and complacent. When one of the vassal city-states refused to pay the customary tribute, 18-Rabbit led his army against them to teach them a lesson. Our king here was captured during the battle and immediately beheaded. His head was stuck on a stake and sent back to Copán."

"Lovely," Hunter said.

"I'm certain there's a moral in that story somewhere," the young woman said with a laugh. "Anyway," she added, "be careful. We think you're being watched."

A group of tourists from a subsequent tram was entering the courtyard. The young woman walked in that direction and disappeared.

THE ENCOUNTER WITH the woman jolted Hunter. Up until that time, the reality of his planned escape the following day had not impressed itself completely upon his consciousness. Somehow, talking about it with a live person heightened his awareness that he was about to embark on a dangerous, life-changing endeavor.

Throughout the rest of the day, although he was physically with the rest of the Covington Fellows as they toured first the Amazon rain forest and then the Serengeti savanna, Hunter's thoughts and emotions were elsewhere. He looked at his watch repeatedly, always calculating the length of time until he was supposed to ride the barrel over the New Earth version of Niagara Falls. He imagined a hundred scenarios, in many of which he was killed or injured. It was a struggle for Hunter to keep his fear from overwhelming him.

The Covington Fellows all ate dinner together at a restaurant in the Shanghai portion of the park. The Chinese food was delicious, but Hunter could hardly taste it. His mouth seemed dry even when it was full of beer or water. He avoided all conversation with Dallas, fearing that somehow just the sound of his voice might alert his roommate that something abnormal was about to happen.

Hunter declined to join his friends for a drink when, at the end of the day, they exited from the park together. As he had planned since the middle of the afternoon, when he had realized that there was no certainty that he would ever be able to contact his parents again, Hunter went straight to his hotel room and initiated a call to Cicero. Before beginning his video recording, he looked at his image on the monitor. He decided that he definitely looked frightened. Hunter stood up, walked around the room, and tried to calm himself. It was useless. At length he sat back down at the desk and began the message.

"Hi, Mom and Dad," he said in as cheery a voice as he could muster. Hunter told his parents that he was in the Free Zone with the rest of the Covington Fellows, and that they had had a spectacular first day at New Earth. He loosened up briefly while telling them how much he liked his job with Dr. Bellini, but Hunter had to stop the recording altogether when he began discussing his father's health. Twice he tried to tell his father that he would be with him in spirit during his impending heart surgery, and that he expected that Mr. Blake would be as good as new after the operation. Twice tears crept into Hunter's eyes while he was attempting to encourage his father, and Hunter had to erase that part of the recording.

Eventually he managed to keep his emotions more or less under control while talking about his father's heart problems. Hunter then chatted for a few minutes about

Covington Fellowship activities and his friends in Centralia. Hunter also mentioned that he was hoping to see Tehani while he was in the Free Zone.

When it was time to end the video to his parents, Hunter discovered that he didn't know what to say. A dramatic good-bye would be an immediate tip-off to anyone who might be monitoring his communications. He hastily scribbled some words on a sheet of paper, then revised them twice. He read them to himself, and then turned on the recording again.

"Sometimes," Hunter said, "I think that we are guilty of taking the most precious things in life for granted. Yesterday, while I was looking out my train window at the incredible beauty of Mars, I thought to myself that I don't tell you two enough how much I love you, and how much I appreciate everything you have done for me. Mom and Dad," Hunter said, his voice breaking, "I love you very very much, and I always will."

He turned off the video quickly and walked into the bathroom with tears streaming down both his cheeks.

FOR HALF AN hour after he finished his transmission to his parents, Hunter paced aimlessly around his hotel room, deep in thought about the following day. He tried to watch television, but was too full of energy to sit still. He briefly considered going down to the bar for a drink, or taking a walk outside. Hunter dismissed both options because he was afraid he might encounter one of the Covington Fellows. He didn't think he could manage small talk in his current emotional state.

On one of his circuits around the room, Hunter noticed that his message light was illuminated. How long had it been on? he wondered as he hurried to the computer. How had he missed it? On the monitor was a message that a package had been left for him at the hotel desk.

Hunter put on his shoes and took the elevator down to the lobby. He inquired about his package and showed his identity card. Less than a minute later an elderly man handed him an envelope. On the outside was written, in large black letters, "Please give to Mr. Hunter Blake personally."

Hunter managed to overcome his curiosity and not open the envelope until he was back in his hotel room. As soon as he closed the door, and made certain he was by himself, Hunter ripped the envelope open. Inside was a flat, rectangular hotel key, and a note: "Meet me at the Olympus Hotel outside of Sybaris, Room 422, at midnight. Love you. Tehani."

He looked at his watch. It was fifteen minutes until eleven. Hunter shredded the envelope and put the pieces in the wastebasket next to his bed. Then, after laying fresh clothes on the bed, he shaved and stepped into the shower. While he was in the shower, Dallas Morrison returned to the room.

"Are you going out?" Dallas said after Hunter finished showering. He was sitting on the bed next to Hunter's, looking at the clothes.

"I have a date," Hunter said brightly.

"With Tehani?" Dallas asked.

"Could be," Hunter said with a smile.

While he was dressing, Hunter responded to all Dallas's questions and comments with simple monosyllabic answers. When he was ready to leave, he grinned at his roommate. "Don't wait up," Hunter said.

"Have fun," Dallas said.

Hunter reached the Olympus almost half an hour early. He went directly to the room. As he expected, it was still empty. The room looked as if it had never been occupied.

Fifteen minutes later, when Hunter heard a sound outside, in the hall, he skipped into the bathroom and partially closed the door.

He waited, listening carefully. He heard the door lock release and the sound of someone coming into the room. After several seconds, Hunter left the bathroom and entered the bedroom. Tehani was standing near the bed with her back toward him. "Surprise," he said.

She jumped several inches off the ground. Laughing, he approached her and they kissed. "You damn near scared me to death," Tehani said.

"So," Hunter said, "what's with all the cloak-and-dagger stuff? Why didn't you simply return my E-mail message and tell me to meet you here?"

Tehani looked at him. "God, you're a wonderful sight," she said. She kissed Hunter again. "If it's all right with you," Tehani then said, "let's make love first. I'll give you an explanation afterward."

Hunter smiled and started to undress. "You're not going to get an argument from me," he said.

Twenty minutes later, while they were showering together, Tehani told Hunter that he was in trouble. "I'm afraid, my darling," she said, "that it may be mostly because of me. Or rather, because of your involvement with me."

Hunter stopped soaping her back and turned Tehani around. He looked directly into her eyes. "This couldn't, by any chance, have anything to do with your long-term affair with Mr. Lester Sackett, could it?" he asked.

She returned his gaze and smiled wanly. She didn't look surprised. "Lester told me that he had called you into his office," Tehani said. "I would have loved to have been there."

"Your name was not even mentioned," Hunter said.

"Of course not," Tehani said, "but surely you understood that I was the real subject of your meeting with Lester."

"Is that what he told you?"

"Not in so many words," Tehani said. "He didn't need to." She looked at Hunter. "Did you know that Lester has a recording containing every single sound we made that night we spent together at your apartment?"

For a split second, Hunter almost said "yes." Then the thought occurred to him that he should trust nobody, not even Tehani. "WHAT?" Hunter said, feigning indignation. "How is that possible?"

"Lester claims that the ASP is monitoring you because of a possible sedition issue," Tehani said. "I don't believe him. I think Lester had your bedroom bugged. He can be insanely jealous." She sighed. "But he definitely has the recording. He angrily quoted some of the things I said during our moments of passion."

Tehani shook her head. "Poor Lester, he was beside himself with envy. He's in great shape, of course, but he is, after all, fifty-two years old. If he can do it again after twelve hours, he's very lucky. I can't imagine what it must have been like for him to listen to all that."

She reached up for the shower faucet. "Are you all rinsed off?" Tehani asked.

"Yes," Hunter answered.

She stepped out of the shower first and handed him a towel. "Anyway," Tehani said, while she was drying off, "Minister Lester Sackett is presently a very unhappy man. He has told me that I'm not to see you or talk to you ever again. That's why I didn't send you a return E-mail message. I think he's probably recording all my communications."

Tehani suddenly became very serious. "He has threatened to hurt you, Hunter, if I don't obey him," she said.

Hunter looked at her again. "You don't seem to be too disturbed that I know about your dalliance with Sackett," he said in a measured tone. "Would you mind telling me why you haven't said anything about your involvement with him before?"

Tehani shrugged. "I was going to tell you," she said. "I was just waiting for the right moment." She reached up and kissed Hunter. "It's a long, ugly story," Tehani said. "After you and I were kidnapped, I thought that knowledge that I was Lester's mistress might cause trouble for you. When I saw you in Centralia, well, I guess I didn't want anything to spoil our reunion."

She wrapped the towel around her midriff and took Hunter's hand. She pulled him back into the bedroom. "So what are you going to do?" Hunter asked after they were lying side by side on the bed.

"I don't see where I really have much choice," she said. "I would never forgive myself if something happened to you and it was my fault." She looked over at Hunter and tears wedged into her eyes. "But let's not be melancholy tonight," Tehani said. "Let's enjoy each other while we can, and not worry about if or when we'll be together again."

Tehani removed the towel that was around her body and tugged at Hunter's. As his towel fell away, she pulled him over and kissed him, at first very softly. As Tehani increased the intensity of the kiss, Hunter started becoming aroused. Tehani reached down and touched him gently, deftly.

"Fill me up, Hunter," she said, sliding into position, "let me feel you inside me one more time."

FUGITIVE

ONE

HUNTER RETURNED TO HIS hotel room about three-thirty. Dallas appeared to be asleep on the other twin bed. Hunter undressed quietly and climbed beneath his sheets. Pleasantly exhausted from his rendezvous with Tehani, he fell asleep quickly.

Dallas shook him awake four hours later. "Let's go, roomie," he said, "or we'll miss breakfast."

When he realized that it was already morning, Hunter sat bolt upright in the bed. Immediately his mind kicked into overdrive, and adrenaline surged through his body. *Today's the day,* Hunter said to himself as he hurriedly put on his clothes. While he was brushing his teeth and washing his face, Hunter mentally reviewed all the instructions that he had received, both from Cooperman's E-mail letter and the young woman in the park the previous day.

The Covington Fellows reached the gates of New Earth a few minutes before it officially opened at nine o'clock. A special park guide met them and gave them the agenda for the day. Their first morning activity was a cable ride through the Swiss Alps, culminating with a snack and coffee on the terrace of a café that faced the mock Matterhorn.

Then they would all go to the Hawaiian beach, where they would swim and snorkel until lunchtime.

While the group was being transported across New Earth to the entrance to the alpine enclosure, Hunter studied the park map carefully. The Niagara Falls ride was almost a mile away from the Matterhorn. It should take him approximately fifteen minutes to walk that distance, including the five minutes on the footpath to reach the enclosure exit. If the line at the ride was fifteen minutes long, then he would need to break away from the Covington Fellows by ten-thirty at the latest. *Just to be on the safe side,* Hunter thought, *I'll leave at ten-fifteen.*

Just outside the alpine enclosure, a pair of friendly young park employees issued cold-weather gear to Hunter and his companions. Each of them was given a parka, a ski hat, and some gloves. Inside, before they entered the cable car, a park official explained which specific mountains in the Alps had been reproduced for New Earth. She also extolled the virtues of the park's alpine hiking trails, and mentioned that many visitors spent a day or more simply walking through the grasses, flowers, and forests covering the flanks of their mountains.

The entire Covington party fit comfortably into one of the cable cars. As the car left the station and sailed out across a deep abyss, Hunter realized that most of the area inside the enclosure was beneath the ground level of the park. The alpine towns at the base of the mountains were several hundred feet below the cable station. The tallest of the mountains rose perhaps two hundred feet, the equivalent of a twenty-story building, above the ground level, making it approximately five hundred feet high from top to bottom. Hunter remembered reading in one of the park brochures that the peak of the New Earth Mont Blanc reached within twenty-five feet of the innermost of the domes covering the parks and the town of Lancaster.

The view from the cable car was spectacular. The enclosure simulated mid-April in the Alps, so the peaks were covered with snow and the lower parts of the mountains were rich with wildflowers. Hunter had never seen real snow before, and like most of his compatriots, he immediately became engaged in snowball fights when the car made a brief stop at a high-altitude station. The group waved at a trio of cross-country skiers making their way from peak to peak before reboarding the cable car.

By the time Hunter and his companions were sitting on the café terrace with the simulated Matterhorn face directly in front of them, it was already a few minutes after ten o'clock. Hunter ordered coffee and a sweet roll and tried to force himself not to look at his watch every thirty seconds or so. He had purposely sat at a table with fellows with whom he was not that familiar, to minimize the chance that he would be involved in a conversation when it was time for him to leave.

At ten minutes after ten, just after he was served his coffee and roll, Hunter saw Patrick Key dragging a chair in the direction of his table. *Oh, no,* Hunter said to himself. *Not now.*

"Good morning, lover boy," Patrick said as he came over beside Hunter.

"Good morning, Patrick," Hunter answered, scooting slightly to the side to make room for Patrick and his chair at the table.

"I understand, from the best of sources," Patrick said with a ribald smirk on his face, "that our illustrious pirate escapee spent several hours outside of his hotel room in the wee hours of the morning last night. Could this, perchance, have anything to do with a certain beauteous creature named Tehani Wilawa?"

Hunter nodded. "Tehani left me a message last night," he said, "that she would have a few hours free."

Patrick heaved a sigh. "My man," he said with a dramatic flourish, "do you have any idea how many of your friends would gladly part with one entire testicle just to view that woman's naked body up close, much less to make love with her?"

Hunter smiled at Patrick without saying anything and took a bite from his roll. Already Hunter could feel his pulse rate increasing. What was he going to do? It was obvious that Patrick intended to stay and talk for awhile.

"Tonight, of course," Patrick was saying, "I assume you'll share her company with the rest of us."

Hunter was so deep in his own thoughts that for a second or two he had absolutely no idea what Patrick was talking about. He looked at his friend blankly, struggling both to suppress a spreading feeling of panic and to make some sense out of Patrick's comment. "Tonight?" Hunter managed to say.

Patrick looked at Hunter with a peculiar expression. "Yes," he said. "Aren't you seeing Tehani again tonight?"

Hunter reached for his roll again and knocked over his coffee cup. Some of the coffee spilled on the parka he was wearing. "No, no I'm not," he said awkwardly, standing up. Hunter glanced at his jacket. "Excuse me," he said to Patrick and the others at the table, "I'm going to go to the rest room and clean this up before it stains."

"Don't worry about it," Patrick said as Hunter turned around. "The park will take care of it," Hunter heard Patrick say as he left the terrace.

On his way through the café Hunter, his heart pounding wildly, glanced at the clock behind the bar. It was already nineteen minutes after ten. He dashed into the rest room and hastily splashed water on the sleeve of his jacket. He looked up at his reflection in the mirror. *You idiot,* Hunter thought, taking slow deep breaths to try to calm himself. *That was worse than simply standing up and walking away.*

Hunter came out of the rest room and took the wooden stairs that descended two stories to the footpath. A sign indicated the direction to the enclosure exit. Hunter walked swiftly along the path through the grass and wildflowers. At one point, he glanced over his shoulder to see if anyone was watching him from the cable-car station. Nobody was in the station.

He crossed the bridge over the abyss and then stood in a short line of people waiting to exit. As he passed through the gates, his watch said ten twenty-five. Outside the enclosure, Hunter turned to the left and increased the speed with which he was walking. He heard a shout behind him, then another. The shouts were followed almost immediately by a loud whistle. When Hunter felt a hand grab his arm from the side, his first impulse was to turn and fight.

"Easy there, young man," a park security guard said, surprised by Hunter's reaction. "We just need our clothes returned." He pointed back toward the exit from the alpine area. "Over there. See the girl waving her arms."

Of course, Hunter said to himself, slowly realizing what had happened.

He thanked the security guard and walked hurriedly back to the alpine exit. Hunter handed his parka, ski hat, and gloves to the attendant. By the time he was heading for Niagara Falls again, it was ten thirty-one.

HUNTER'S HEART SANK as he neared the entrance to the Niagara Falls ride. The line snaked out into the area adjacent to a large food court, a little past a prominent sign that said, "Thirty minutes' wait from this point." He entered the queue and checked his watch again. The time was now ten-forty. Hunter looked in front of him. The line did not appear to be very dense. Perhaps it would move quickly.

For ten minutes the line marched forward at a good pace. Hunter watched the progress of the line carefully and estimated that he would arrive at the loading area no more than five minutes late at the most. He started to relax a little. At ten fifty-two, however, when Hunter was already inside the barriers that wound back and forth immediately next to the loading zone, a tram pulled up on the side of the ride entrance and deposited a few dozen people dressed more formally than most of the other park visitors. Their guide herded them into the corral marked SPECIAL GUESTS ONLY and they immediately began entering the loading area.

Some of the special guests were quite old, and moved very slowly. The line in which Hunter was standing remained fixed while the new arrivals were accommodated. Hunter fidgeted, becoming increasingly agitated. At ten fifty-nine, people from his line started being loaded again. Hunter estimated at this point that he was ten to twelve minutes away from being placed in one of the barrel-shaped carriers that would carry him over the mock Niagara Falls.

At three minutes after eleven, as he was turning around inside the barriers guiding the queue, Hunter happened to look back in the general direction of the alpine enclosure. At the limit of his vision, maybe a quarter of a mile away, among the crowd he caught sight of a tall, thin figure in a baseball cap that looked very much like Dallas Morrison. Focusing his eyes, Hunter quickly determined that it was indeed Dallas, and that he was talking to two other men and occasionally pointing in Hunter's direction.

For a few seconds Hunter froze in fear. Then he leaped over the barrier next to him and headed directly for the loading zone. "Excuse me," he said to the other people as he dodged through the queue. "Emergency, excuse me," he repeated as he pushed people aside and hurried to the front of the line. Hunter walked right past the astonished attendants and boarded the first barrel that had an empty seat. It was already moving on its path through the water. "Emergency, sorry," he said in explanation as the door to the barrel was automatically closing.

A boy about seventeen, his girlfriend, and the boy's younger sister were occupying the other three seats in the barrel. They looked at Hunter quizzically as he fastened his seat and shoulder belts. "I've had an emergency page," he said, pointing at his hand computer. "I have to meet somebody right away."

The narrow stream on which the barrel was traveling widened quickly into a white-water river about forty yards across. Hunter's barrel was caught in the first rapids, spun around, and thrown toward the right-hand side of the river. It picked up speed and hurtled through another pair of rapids before entering a stretch of calmer water.

"Get ready," the boy said to his girlfriend. "We're almost there."

The girl clutched his arm and smiled. The younger sister looked terrified.

The barrel accelerated for several seconds and then was airborne. Both the girls screamed while the barrel was in free fall. The drop was surprisingly long in duration. Hunter turned his head, and felt a momentary disorientation, just before the barrel smacked hard against the water, dropping beneath the surface for a split second. The other three passengers in the barrel with Hunter were wide-eyed with excitement.

"That was absolutely fantastic," the girlfriend said. "Let's do it again." She turned to the boy's sister. "What about you, Andrea, do you want to go again?"

The younger girl shook her head. "Once was enough for me," she said.

The barrel slowed as it approached the narrow outlet

stream where the passengers exited. Hunter let the three youngsters climb out first, and then filed along behind them. He saw the gray door as soon as he was on the pathway. He scurried down a short cement incline, opened the door, and descended the stairs into a well-illuminated underground tunnel.

The empty car was waiting, as expected, just to the right of the bottom of the stairs. Hunter put himself in the driver's seat and entered the number 41 into the control panel. The vehicle began to move immediately.

No more than ten seconds after he was under way, Hunter's car passed a similar vehicle, going the other direction, carrying two men wearing conspicuous park employee badges. They looked at him curiously. Hunter returned their stare and smiled.

The vehicle did not move very fast. At each intersection it stopped briefly, as if it were waiting for some kind of signal to proceed. Twice more during the four-minute ride cars carrying park employees passed on Hunter's left.

When the car stopped at the designated location, Hunter stepped out onto the narrow platform. He stopped for a moment, thinking about his instructions, and then entered the down stairwell. He hurried past the first landing and had just made the turn to make the final descent to the second landing when he heard voices below him.

"I don't know why we have to replace these damn processors every six months," a man said. "The parts are guaranteed for a minimum of a year."

"The guarantee only means that Kendall Electric will replace them for free," a second man said. "Randy told me they've tested huge batches, and four percent of them fail in less than a year. FedEnt's zero-failure-tolerance policy requires a much higher reliability rate than that."

Hunter backed up to where he could not be seen if the workmen inadvertently passed the front of the stairwell.

While he was trying to decide what to do, he heard a mechanical whirring sound below him. The whir quickly increased in volume. "Finally," Hunter heard one of the men say, "I thought we were going to wait here forever." From the sounds coming up the stairs, Hunter deduced that the workmen were boarding some kind of vehicle.

Hunter waited a full minute after he no longer heard any whirring. He descended to the bottom level and looked to the left, into a narrow, dark cement tunnel with no walkway alongside the solitary track. *Turn left,* he recalled. *Follow the tunnel about a hundred yards, until you reach a spiral metal staircase.*

He stepped down on the track. As he passed the end of the landing, Hunter noticed a red arrow on the wall to his right. It was pointing in the direction opposite to the way he was going. Above the arrow was written ONE WAY in big red letters.

The tunnel became darker as he proceeded. Far in the distance in front of him, Hunter could see some additional light. He assumed that it was another boarding station like the one behind him.

Hunter counted his strides, which he knew were approximately one yard in length. He walked with his head down, placing his feet carefully in the dim light to avoid twisting an ankle. When he was sixty yards deep into the tunnel he heard a faint whirring noise in front of him. Hunter stopped momentarily and looked up. He saw a single light, in the middle of the track, heading in his direction.

He did not have much time to think. Rapidly scanning both sides of the track, Hunter saw a slight indentation in the cement wall on his left, six to eight yards in front of where he was standing, that appeared to be large enough for his body. He bolted forward and wedged himself into the indentation only seconds before the vehicle passed. The car, which fortunately was moving slowly, was no more than two or three inches away from him as it went by. There were two passengers in the vehicle. One of the workmen, who happened to be looking out the window in his direction, definitely saw Hunter pressed against the wall.

Hunter heard the brakes squealing as the vehicle slowed. He raced down the track, found the spiral metal staircase on the left, and started climbing immediately. When he reached the ground level, Hunter pushed the manhole cover up and out of the way. The Sun coming through the dome over New Earth was so bright that it took his eyes a few seconds to adjust. He looked around, temporarily out of breath, and located the fence that ran along the boundary of the amusement park.

Two security guards were standing next to the emergency gate in the fence that had been Hunter's planned escape exit. They were examining the gate, swinging it back and forth, doubtless discussing why it had not been properly locked. Hunter remained in the vicinity of the manhole cover, trying to determine what he should do next. He pulled out his park map. To reach the designated picnic area, which he could see just on the other side of the fence, he had only two options. He could go to the closest available approved exit, which would require him to walk well over a mile altogether, and pass through one of the most crowded areas of New Earth, or he could climb over the fence.

Hunter surveyed the fence carefully. It was about twenty feet high. On top of the fence were four thick black strands of metal, separated one from another by about six inches. At each major connection in the fence, the strands were marked with a double-sided sign that said DANGER, with two symbolic lightning bolts on each side of the word. The electrically charged strands were canted sharply outward, toward the picnic area. The fence had obviously been designed primarily to prevent unwarranted entry into the park, not to prevent visitors from leaving.

The sound of shoes clanging on metal coming from beneath the manhole cover spurred Hunter to action. He hurried toward a portion of the fence thirty yards to the right of the emergency gate. Fortunately the park security guards, who by this time had locked the gate, did not even notice him until he was already climbing the fence. By the time they were yelling and headed in his direction, Hunter had reached the top. He put his right leg on the thick pipe on the top of the upright fence and jumped out as far as he could. Hunter cleared the electrified strands with room to spare, but lost his balance during the ensuing fall and landed hard on his right shoulder. In spite of the sharp pain in his shoulder, he dashed across the picnic area and ducked behind the brick building that housed the public rest rooms.

He leaned against the wall for several seconds, catching his breath, and then peered around the corner in the direction of New Earth. The security guards were still standing at the spot where he had climbed the fence. While Hunter was watching the guards, two men emerged from the manhole behind them. Hunter recognized them immediately as the two men who had been talking with Dallas Morrison when he was in the queue for the Niagara Falls ride.

Hunter spun around and searched the picnic area with his eyes. A figure with a familiar gait was moving rapidly in his direction. Hunter's recognition was immediate. *Why, that's . . . that's Octavio,* he said to himself in astonishment.

His brother-in-law was beside him in a few seconds. "Smartass," Octavio said.

"Okay," Hunter replied. He started to point in the direction of New Earth.

"I know," Octavio said. "Let's run," he added. "Follow me."

T W O

HUNTER AND OCTAVIO RAN across the rest of the picnic area to the nearest street. They turned right. After they had traveled two blocks through a neighborhood of small, single-family homes, Octavio motioned to his left at an intersection. Forty yards down this street Octavio stopped beside a small, yellow electric taxi and opened the door. "Get in," he shouted to Hunter. Hunter jumped into the car only moments before Octavio started the motor and wheeled the taxi out of its parking place.

Octavio grabbed his taxi cap from the backseat and put it on his head. He made a right turn, followed by a quick left onto a broad avenue that was the main street of Lancaster. The taxi headed in a direction away from the resort areas of New Earth and Sybaris.

"Were you surprised to see me?" Octavio said with a grin.

"That would be an understatement," Hunter said. He shuffled in his seat and winced at the pain in his right shoulder.

"Are you all right?" Octavio asked.

"Mostly," Hunter replied. "I landed on my shoulder when I fell. I think I may have bruised it."

Octavio laughed. "That was an impressive leap," he said. "When I saw that the security guards had discovered the open gate, I thought our plan was ruined. I never even considered that you might try to climb the fence."

They drove in silence for several seconds. Octavio then handed Hunter a small envelope that had been sitting in the door pocket beside him. "Here's your temporary identity card," he said, "and a little background information about Mr. Lewis Smith."

Hunter opened the envelope. "Why do I need a fake identity card?" he asked.

"You're going to fly on a commercial transport from here to Phobos," Octavio said. "That's where we're going now."

Hunter quickly read through the information about Lewis Smith. He was a twenty-three-year-old medical-instrument engineer, a citizen of the Free Zone who lived in an apartment in Lancaster. The photo on his identity card looked enough like Hunter that it would pass a casual inspection.

"Is there really a Lewis Smith?" he asked Octavio.

Octavio nodded. "Yes, indeed," he said. "At this very moment he is at work in a building about a mile from here. He will report that his identity card was stolen as soon as you don't need it anymore."

A sign beside the avenue just before a large intersection indicated that the Lancaster Spaceport was two miles to the right. Octavio turned.

"How long have you been a taxi driver?" Hunter asked.

"Since yesterday," Octavio said, "when we worked out the final details for your escape." He laughed. "On my way over here, I had a slight problem. I had forgotten to turn on my 'Off Duty' sign and a lady climbed into the cab while I was waiting for a signal light to change."

The traffic in front of them suddenly slowed down

markedly. The taxi inched forward, stopping every few yards, for several minutes. Octavio began to fret. "At this rate," he said, glancing at his watch, "we won't make it in time for your flight."

A policeman was directing traffic at a major intersection, making certain that cars could move in all directions. "What's the problem, officer?" Octavio said, leaning out the window as they entered the intersection.

"Special security procedures this afternoon," the policeman replied. "Everyone entering the spaceport has to go through an identity check." He pointed down the street. "It would probably be faster if your passenger just walks from here."

Octavio pulled the taxi out of the line of traffic and turned right on the next side street. He parked a few yards after turning and looked at Hunter with a concerned expression. "This is very unusual," Octavio said. "Security here in the Free Zone is notoriously lax."

"What do we do now?" Hunter asked.

Octavio shrugged. "I don't know," he said. "If they test your retina or your fingerprints, obviously they'll know that you're not Lewis Smith. Maybe I should call in and find out. . . ."

At that moment Octavio's pager sounded. A message raced across the small screen. "Urgent, urgent. Abandon Plan A. Proceed to contingency location."

"I guess that answers our questions," Octavio said, starting the taxi.

Soon after they were under way again Octavio asked if Hunter had spoken with his parents recently. Hunter told his brother-in-law about his father's heart problems, but avoided any mention of his sister or his niece.

"I'm sorry to hear about your father," Octavio said. "He really is a fine man."

"Dad has worked too hard for too many years," Hunter said. "I'm afraid he's never taken very good care of himself."

They drove in silence for several seconds. "I'm also sorry about Amanda and me," Octavio then said with difficulty. "Sometimes these things just don't work out."

"I understand," Hunter said. "There's no need for you to apologize." He touched Octavio on the arm. "I really appreciate your helping me like this," he said.

Octavio smiled. "It seemed like the right thing to do," he said.

They drove three or four miles across Lancaster before pulling into a driveway and parking behind a small house. Octavio motioned for Hunter to follow him. Inside the house, Rachel Goldberg and another woman were watching television. On the left-hand side of the split screen a reporter was standing on the alpine grass at New Earth, with the restaurant that faced the Matterhorn in the background. He was interviewing a New Earth security guard. On the right-hand side of the screen was a photograph of Hunter above the caption "Hunter Blake kidnapped again."

Rachel kissed Octavio lightly as he entered the room. "You remember Rachel, don't you?" Octavio said. "You met her briefly on Cicero."

Hunter nodded. Rachel smiled. "See all the trouble you've caused," she said teasingly, pointing at the television.

The television program switched inside the main studio. "Here's our top story," a lovely anchorwoman said. "Late this morning at the New Earth Amusement Park, Hunter Blake, the Federation citizen who just a month ago made a daring escape from the space pirates, abruptly vanished, apparently kidnapped by the pirates again. The Free Zone police have sealed all exits from the Lancaster dome in an attempt to apprehend the person or persons who have committed this crime."

"Very clever, aren't they?" Hunter heard a familiar voice behind him say. When Hunter turned around, Cho gave him an enthusiastic hug. "You see," Cho then said, "without the pretense of some crime, the local police cannot be involved in the search for you. A suspected kidnapping gives them the excuse they need. I would be willing to bet that somebody has paid big bucks to the Free Zone police for their help." He paused, a frown crossing his face. "Your friends at the ASP obviously don't intend to let you get away. This has made your escape much more difficult."

"What are you doing here on Mars?" Hunter asked.

"I could give you a big head," Cho said, smiling again, "and tell you that I was sent here personally to supervise your escape. But that would be bullshit." He laughed easily. "Actually I brought a container load of excess electronic equipment with me—the spoils of war, so to speak—to sell or trade for items that would be more useful on Utopia."

"And has your trip been successful?" Hunter asked.

"Beyond my wildest dreams," Cho answered. "I've even sold some of the stuff back to one of the original Dem subcontractors. I guess they figured that was easier than manufacturing the parts again."

The other woman who had been watching television came over and put her arms around Cho. "I'm Sharon Pearson," she said, "Cho's girlfriend. He has told me so many things about you."

"I hope some of them were good," Hunter said.

Sharon offered everyone a beer. While she was returning from the refrigerator, Cho's pager signaled that he had an urgent message. He excused himself quickly and went into the other room.

"Okay," Cho said when he entered the room again after

several minutes, "I have just finished receiving a message from Cooperman. We now have an approved Plan B for the escape of Mr. Hunter Blake."

Cho took a huge swig from his beer. "Tonight, after dark," he then said, "Hunter will hide in the back of my truck. We'll pack it full with some of the cargo that's destined for Utopia and then drive to Arundhati's to spend the night. I owe her a new sound system for some shit she did for us two months ago anyway. Meanwhile, Cooperman has arranged for old man Leggett to move his mobile launch system across the plains and park it next to Arundhati's property. At daybreak, before the police helicopters resume their search outside the dome, Hunter will blast off for Phobos."

Cho looked around the room. "Rachel," he said, "your job is to take care of the space suits. Please measure Hunter carefully, and get two that fit him, just in case we have problems. I could use an extra as well."

Cho pulled a slip of paper out of his pocket and handed it to Sharon. "This is old man Leggett's bank account number," he said. "Take the briefcase full of cash that's in the bedroom to the Free Zone Security Bank and deposit it in his account. Get a receipt to verify that everything was done properly. Cooperman told me that Leggett wouldn't even begin to move his launching system until the money was in the bank."

Sharon was looking at Cho with a peculiar expression. "What's the matter?" he asked, after first determining that everyone understood the escape plan.

"Are you going to sleep with Arundhati again?" Sharon said.

"I doubt it," Cho replied evenly. "I'll be much too busy. Besides, I bet she'll find Hunter more enticing." He glanced down at his girlfriend, who didn't look too happy.

"Hey," Cho said to Sharon. "This is not the time for this kind of discussion. We have much more important things to think about.

"Okay?" Cho said to everybody a few seconds later. "Hunter, you probably should take a nap," he then added. "You're not going to sleep much tonight."

HUNTER SLEPT FOR three hours. He was awakened by Octavio and Rachel, who had come into the bedroom to say good-bye.

"We're going to leave now," Octavio said. "We wanted to wish you good luck."

"Your suits are over there on the chair," Rachel said. "Do you want to try them on before I go? I double-checked all the measurements."

"Thanks, Rachel," he said, giving her a hug. "I'm sure they're fine." He shook Octavio's hand. "And thank you for everything, friend," Hunter said.

"I expect we'll meet again," Octavio said, "in the not-too-distant future."

"I hope so," Hunter said.

After Octavio and Rachel departed, Hunter climbed out of bed and put on his shoes. He could smell food cooking in the kitchen and he was ravenously hungry. While he was eating dinner with Cho and Sharon, Hunter asked who Arundhati was.

"You really don't know?" Cho said, a look of surprise on his face. Hunter shook his head. "Then you must not like classical music."

Cho explained that Arundhati was beyond doubt the most famous violinist on Mars. "She's the only truly free spirit I know," Cho said. "She's fifty-two or so, and was born on Earth, in India. Arundhati came to Mars when she was a young girl and was a successful musician by the time she was twenty. She now lives out in the middle of nowhere, surrounded by beauty. She loves music first, but young men and the heavens are a close second. Her idea of a perfect evening . . . Hell, I'm not going to spoil it for you, you'll find out soon enough."

Just after dark, Hunter put on his space suit inside the house and walked out to the truck, which was parked behind the house where Octavio's taxi had been earlier. As Cho instructed, Hunter wrapped himself completely in an oversize blanket and tried to make himself comfortable lying on the makeshift wooden bed that Cho had made for him just behind the passenger area of the truck.

"Are you comfortable? Or at least not uncomfortable?" Cho asked him. "Remember, you're going to be in that position for two or three hours. We still need to load all the rest of the cargo before we're ready to leave."

Hunter's shoulder was hurting him but he wasn't going to complain. "Not too uncomfortable is a good description," he answered.

Cho and a couple of young men who had arrived at the house while Hunter was putting on his space suit began loading the truck. First they carefully packed the truck bed around him. They set boxes on all sides of where he was lying, and then arranged other containers and an assortment of miscellaneous items in the space above him so that no part of Hunter could be seen from anywhere in the truck. After Cho inspected their work, and made a few adjustments, the rest of the loading proceeded quickly.

Before the back doors of the truck were closed, Cho shouted at Hunter. "Okay," he said, "we're ready to depart. Are you all right?"

"More or less," was Hunter's muffled response.

"I'll get you out of there when we're well away from Lancaster and I'm certain we're not being followed," Cho said.

"Roger," Hunter said.

"One other thing," Cho said. "It will be really bumpy after we turn off the main road and head for Arundhati's. Prepare yourself for some misery."

For the first ten minutes the ride was comparatively smooth. Then the truck was in a stop-and-go mode for about five minutes. Hunter guessed that Cho was probably in a queue at the Lancaster dome exit. Hunter heard voices during a period in which the truck was stopped for a long time. Shortly thereafter, a huge squeak indicated that the back of the truck had been opened.

Hunter lay motionless. He felt the truck bed move, as if someone had climbed into the back of the vehicle. "All this crap is electronics?" a voice said.

"Most of it," Cho said. "There are a few odds and ends that I'm taking to one of my friends."

Hunter could hear a few boxes being moved aside. Through the blanket covering his helmet he saw a faint light. He tried to stay calm.

"You almost done, Rick?" a second voice shouted from the back of the truck. "The line's getting longer and longer."

"Yeah," Rick said. "What's at the back?" he asked Cho. "More of the same?"

"Basically," Cho answered. "Plus some blankets, a chair, and—"

"All right," Rick said, interrupting him. "That's enough."

Hunter felt Rick's steps on the truck bed and then heard the back door close. Relieved, he finally allowed himself to move into a different position.

CHO WASN'T KIDDING when he said that the road would become rough after he turned off the main thoroughfare and started heading for Arundhati's. Hunter bounced continuously, striking both the side of the truck bed as well as every object in his immediate vicinity. His shoulder was constantly being jostled, causing him discomfort with every touch. In one particularly terrible stretch of road, Hunter was certain he spent more time airborne than he did on the makeshift bed.

At last the truck came to a stop and Hunter heard the doors open. "Are you still alive?" Cho yelled.

"Barely," Hunter replied. "But I sure as hell would like to get out of here."

"Go ahead," Cho said. "Stand up and move stuff aside. I'll try to make a passageway for you."

Hunter removed the blanket that was wrapped around him and tried to sit up. Boxes were all over him. The sustained bouncing had rearranged everything in his vicinity. After about a minute he managed to dig himself out and stumble through the small lane among the cargo items that Cho had created.

His friend was standing in his space suit just behind the truck. When Hunter finally scrambled down from the truck, he reached his arms up and stretched and twisted in all directions. He also shrugged his right shoulder a couple of times and determined, to his satisfaction, that the injury was not overly serious.

"So far, so good," Cho said. "We'll be safe now until daylight. And by then, with any luck, you'll be on your way to Phobos."

"What are you going to do?" Hunter asked.

"It'll take me another two or three days to finish up," Cho said. "Then I'll come back to Utopia with the remainder of the goods."

"You don't have to worry about being caught or anything?" Hunter asked.

Cho shook his head. "Not really," he said. "I have a Free Zone identity card. A lot of us come and go several times a year." He smiled at Hunter. "We don't have the Free Zone police and a host of ASP agents looking for us."

Hunter walked out away from the truck and looked at the sky. The stars were fantastic. "Goodness," he said, "this is really beautiful."

"That's why Arundhati lives way out here in the boondocks," Cho said. "She loves to commune with the stars." He walked back to the driver's side of the truck. "You coming?" he said.

Hunter hurried over and climbed in the passenger side of the truck cab.

THEY REACHED ARUNDHATI'S after another hour's drive on what would best be described as a partially cleared track through the rock fields and sand dunes of Mars. Hunter bounced up and down in his seat, as if he had springs in his buttocks, often hitting the ceiling of the cab with his helmet. Outside the truck was darkness in every direction.

When they were still miles away Hunter and Cho saw the lights from Arundhati's property on the horizon for the first time. The lights grew in size and intensity as the truck twisted and turned along the crude road. When they finally reached their destination, Hunter was surprised both by the large size of Arundhati's house and the presence of half a dozen vehicles parked randomly outside the protective domes.

"It must be chamber-music night," Cho said as he turned off the engine of the truck. He smiled at Hunter. "You're in for quite an experience."

The outside dome door was unlocked. Hunter followed

Cho into a small, sealed area that reminded Hunter of an elevator. Cho activated the pressurization panel on the wall. Thirty seconds later, after a green light appeared on the ceiling of the airlock, Cho opened the opposite door and they stepped inside the inner of the two domes surrounding Arundhati's complex.

Cho and Hunter removed their space suits and hung them, beside eight or ten others, on hangers in an outdoor closet close to the airlock. As they started walking toward the house, which was about forty yards away, the pristine silence around them was broken by the first strains of Pachelbel's *Canon* being played by a very talented string ensemble.

The music was so magnificent, and so unexpected in this unusual environment, that Hunter was instantly overwhelmed by its beauty. He followed Cho in silence onto the porch of Arundhati's house and stood just outside the open front door. Inside, on the far side of the room, sitting in a folding chair at the top of two steps, with a kitchen and a dining room behind her, Arundhati was playing the violin with her eyes closed. She was dressed in a blue sari and sandals, with her long grayish hair in a single braid over her right shoulder. She was playing with singular intensity, totally immersed in the music. Just below her, at the far end of the living room, five other musicians, playing two more violins, a viola, a cello, and a bass, were accompanying Arundhati. Half a dozen other people were sitting on the couches and chairs closer to the door, listening to the music.

As the piece neared its famous conclusion, Arundhati's bow danced across the strings of her violin, making sounds so rich and vibrant that Hunter was deeply moved. He could not have explained what he was feeling. Later, during the grand finale of the *Canon,* a memory from his schooldays suddenly popped into Hunter's mind. He could see Tehani standing in front of a small group of students.

She was reciting a poem. " 'Beauty is truth, truth beauty,' " Tehani said. " 'That's all ye know on Earth, and all ye need to know.' "

Hunter and Cho both clapped vigorously when the piece was completed. Arundhati waved at the door. "Come in, come in," she said in a soft, mellifluous voice.

Cho opened the door and the two young men entered. Arundhati rose from her chair gracefully and came forward to greet them. "Cho, how delightful," she said, kissing him on the cheek. She turned and looked at Hunter. "And you must be the young man that everyone is talking about," she said.

She introduced Cho and Hunter to the remainder of the gathering, offered and served them cold drinks, and then returned to her folding chair above the steps. Hunter and Cho sat on one of the couches. Arundhati announced a sonata by Beethoven that Hunter had never heard before and soon thereafter, without any reference music in front of them, the ensemble was again playing.

The music continued for another half hour. Hunter could not take his eyes off Arundhati. She fascinated him. Although she was a lovely woman, with rich copper skin, intense oval-shaped eyes, and the most wonderful, outrageous dimples on both sides of her mouth, it was not her beauty that Hunter found most compelling. Arundhati was attractive to him because she projected an image of being utterly at peace with the world. Hunter had never seen anyone so totally absorbed, and so completely content, with what she was doing. Her smiles were warm and genuine, without a trace of guile or pretense. Her obvious affection for everyone in the room was contagious. The feeling in the room was one of total harmony.

When the miniconcert was over, Arundhati placed the violin and her bow in a special case and went into the kitchen. While the other musicians were packing their instruments and returning the living-room furniture to its normal configuration, she returned to the room with a large glass plate of exotic hors d'oeuvres. She asked Ray, the bass player, to serve the wine. For twenty minutes more she mingled with her guests, asking about their lives and their families with real concern. Arundhati stopped briefly to talk with Hunter and Cho, saying that she would have more time for them later, after the guests who were not spending the night had departed.

By midnight the only people left in the living room were two couples who were staying in the guest cabin, Cho, Hunter, and Arundhati herself. The two couples, one of whom was the bass player Ray and his girlfriend Zinaida, a famous ballerina in her own right, excused themselves shortly thereafter. Arundhati and Cho had a brief conversation about the new sound equipment that he had brought with him, and discussed the timetable for its installation the following day in her recording studio. Cho then yawned, and admitted he was tired. Arundhati accompanied Cho down the hall to one of the guest bedrooms.

Hunter sat in the living room, waiting. By this time he was well aware that he was Arundhati's special guest for the evening. Whatever that entailed, Hunter was delighted that he was going to have the opportunity to know her better. She was an extraordinary individual, and she appealed to him in many ways, both as a woman and as someone who almost certainly had a unique view of life.

When she returned to the room Arundhati invited Hunter to sit beside her on the couch. She asked him to tell her "all about himself." Hunter gave her the capsule autobiography, including a quick summary of his kidnapping and stay with the pirates. He did not say anything about his ongoing escape attempt, for he wasn't certain how deeply

Arundhati was involved with the endeavor. As it turned out, from her questions Hunter quickly determined that she was really more interested in what he thought and felt and valued than in his specific activities.

In the ensuing half hour Arundhati asked Hunter about his family, his schooling, his religion, what he thought happened after death, whom he would invite to dinner if he knew he was going to die tomorrow, in what circumstances he would take another person's life, how many times he had been in love, and what were the three happiest and unhappiest days he had ever experienced. Her curiosity about him seemed inexhaustible. After only a few minutes, Hunter felt completely at ease talking with her. He shared with her feelings and ideas that he had never told anyone else before.

Just before the forty-two minutes of extra time were over, Arundhati went to the kitchen and brought back salmon caviar, crackers, and a new bottle of wine. When Hunter picked up the fork and spoon to help himself to the food, she gently restrained him. "It's delicious if you feed yourself, Hunter," Arundhati said with a marvelous, feminine smile, "but it's even better if I feed it to you."

She picked up a cracker and placed some of the red eggs on top. With her left hand she softly touched both his cheek and his chin. Her eyes never leaving his, she slowly placed the caviar-and-cracker combination in his mouth. The explosion of taste and texture in Hunter's mouth was exquisite. He smiled. "That was great," he said.

During the next hour the conversation became more intimate. Hunter talked freely about Tehani and Ursula, admitting to Arundhati that he loved them both, for different reasons, and that his feelings confused him. She took his hand and kissed it. "There's no reason to be confused," she told him. "It's perfectly appropriate that you love both these exceptional girls. I congratulate you. You are in the process of learning one of life's fundamental truths at the tender age of twenty-one."

She caressed his face with her free hand. "You see, Hunter," Arundhati said, "love is not a consumable resource. You, and every other human being, possess an essentially infinite capacity for loving. It is one of the best attributes of our species."

Arundhati told Hunter about her early childhood in Delhi and Agra, and of her visit to the Taj Mahal when she was seven years old. "I had never even imagined that a building could be so incredibly beautiful," she said. "My father took me there at sunrise, and I was absolutely captivated. I could have stayed all day. I cried when my parents forced me to leave. On our way home my mother told me that the Taj had been built by the emperor Shah Jahan as a memorial to the woman he loved, a special wife who died giving birth to their fourteenth child at the tender age of thirty-eight." Arundhati sighed. "Ever since," she said, "I have remained utterly fascinated by all the different manifestations of human love."

She leaned over and kissed Hunter on the lips. It was a soft, delicate, satisfying kiss that sent tingles through him. "Tonight, perhaps," she said, "you and I, total strangers before three hours ago, will share our love and give one another the great gifts of pleasure and self-validation. It does not matter if we do or don't ever see each other again. If we are able to free ourselves from the self-imposed constraints that tell us under what conditions we are supposed to express our love, we can make each other's hearts and bodies sing with joy."

Her eyes, only inches from his, were both beautiful and enchanting. Hunter kissed her back. Arundhati's lips remained soft and yielding. When they broke the embrace, she took his hand and stood up from the couch. "Come with me," she said, "I want to show you my world."

She led him up the staircase to her private bedroom. Her bed was large and round. On the wall directly behind the bed was a magnificent photograph of the Taj Mahal. To the right of the bed was a long, deep bathtub. The left wall of the room was entirely transparent glass. The rest of the walls were tastefully adorned with fine paintings. The furniture was all dark wood, with inlaid mother-of-pearl, in a very Asian motif.

Arundhati lit candles at both ends of the bathtub, and then switched off all the other lights in the room. She looked at Hunter with her beatific smile as she pushed a button on the wall behind her bed. Slowly, steadily, the panels covering the entire ceiling withdrew, pulling back to expose the sky and stars in all their majesty.

Hunter had goose bumps as he looked up at the profusion of stars. He felt as if he were among them. "It's fantastic," he mumbled.

"The dome material above my house has the highest transparency possible," Arundhati said proudly. "The seeing, right here in my bedroom, is the best that exists anywhere on Mars."

"Wow," said Hunter, his head craned backward. "This is amazing."

She came over beside him. For five minutes Arundhati pointed out constellations, telling Hunter synopses of each of the mythological stories. He was entranced. Then she went to the refrigerator and poured two glasses of water, putting one on each end table beside the bed. "Lie down," she said, unbuttoning his shirt. "The view is even better from the bed."

Hunter allowed her to undress him completely. When he was completely naked, Arundhati kissed him again. "You are magnificent," she said softly.

She motioned toward the bed. Hunter stretched out on

his back while Arundhati, standing in front of the candles near the bathtub, pulled the sari slowly over her head. Underneath she was wearing only tiny black panties. Looking directly at him with a soft smile, she pulled her pants off and dropped them on the floor. Her body was firm and lithe. Hunter felt himself becoming aroused as she walked around the end of the bed.

Instead of getting into bed beside him, however, Arundhati took a violin and a bow from a case over beside the wall. "Do you like Mozart?" she asked.

Hunter nodded in the candlelight. Arundhati began to play a Mozart violin concerto. Hunter, lying on his back, alternately watched the brilliant heavens spread out above his head and the naked goddess playing divine music beside the bed. His senses were filled to overflowing. "Beautiful," he murmured, "absolutely beautiful."

He felt a slight shake when Arundhati climbed onto the bed. She finished the concerto on her knees, just to the left of Hunter's body. She set the violin and bow gently on the floor, and came over beside him. "That was superb," he said.

She put her finger on Hunter's lips and gently hoisted herself on top of him. With her body pressed against the entire length of his body, Arundhati kissed him. It was a marathon kiss of promise and passion, with its own themes and counterpoints and nuances. It was a kiss that Hunter would never forget. When Arundhati finally broke the embrace after several minutes, Hunter was aching with arousal.

She leaned back with her hand and fondled him. She smiled coquettishly, and taunted him with occasional kisses. "Are you ready yet?" she said teasingly. She rubbed him against her, causing her breathing to become heavier and more uneven. "Just a little more," she said. She closed her eyes and increased the speed of the rubbing.

"Don't hold anything back," Arundhati said as she rose to receive him. "I want every bit of your love and energy."

She was an artist at lovemaking as well. She modulated the intercourse to make certain that she, too, was pleased. Hunter barely controlled himself until Arundhati began to moan. He then exploded inside her.

THREE

CHO WOKE HIM UP while it was still dark outside. "Let's go, Hunter," he said from beside the bed. "Old man Leggett is getting nervous."

Cho was already in his space suit. Arundhati stirred and opened her eyes while Hunter was sitting on the side of the bed. She leaned over and kissed him on the back. "Good luck, Hunter," she said. "And thanks."

Hunter turned around. "I'm the one who should be saying thank you," he said. "The entire evening was fabulous."

She smiled and said nothing. Hunter dressed hurriedly, then slipped into the space suit that Cho had laid on the chair beside the bed. "Good-bye, Arundhati," he said into the microphone in his helmet. He blew her a kiss before following Cho down the stairs.

"She's something else, isn't she?" Cho said as they exited from the house.

Hunter nodded. "That's the understatement of the year," he said.

"Everything's all set," Cho said while they were waiting for the pressure change inside the airlock. "We've already loaded the cargo and the rocket fuel. Denise finished the prelaunch check just before I came to get you." He glanced at his watch. "She has scheduled the launch for fifteen minutes from now."

"Denise?" Hunter said.

"Denise Leggett," Cho said. "She's the old man's daughter. She's the best freelance pilot in the Zone."

Cho had parked his truck right opposite the door to the dome. They drove to the east just as the first light from the coming sunrise began to spread into the sky from the horizon. "All right," Cho said to Hunter while they were driving, "let's go over what you're going to do once you reach Phobos. Denise will land at the noncommercial flight terminal, among the casino space yachts and the private shuttles. You will stay in the spacecraft while she enters the terminal to fill out the required paperwork. Roughly five minutes after she has departed, you will come down the ladder. Stay out on the field and walk toward the center zone. One of the technicians, wearing a blue space suit with FZTA on both shoulders, will approach you with the password. Follow him to your escape shuttle."

Cho glanced at Hunter. "Any questions?" he asked.

"Is the password still 'smartass'?" Hunter said.

"Yes, indeed," Cho said, chuckling. "Cooperman really likes that word."

Hunter repeated all the escape-plan instructions to Cho. Shortly thereafter, he saw his launch spacecraft for the first time. It was mounted vertically, with its huge rocket tanks in the rear, on top of a mobile launchpad in the middle of the Martian plain. A pair of large trucks with mostly empty trailers were parked several hundred yards away. As the light improved, Hunter could also see four people milling around the trucks.

A peculiar queasiness settled in Hunter's stomach when he realized that he was about to blast off from the surface of Mars, headed for Phobos tens of thousands of miles away, in that strange vehicle directly in front of him.

"Is this flight dangerous?" he said to Cho.

His friend laughed. "Compared to what?" he said. "For you, it's much less dangerous than if you stay here." He glanced over at Hunter. "Are you having cold feet?" he asked.

"Maybe," Hunter said. "My stomach doesn't feel so good."

"Don't worry," Cho said. "It won't last long. You'll be out of here before you have time to freak out."

As they drew closer, Hunter's anxiety increased. His mind was tormenting him with images of crashed spacecraft from the network news. He compared the setup here with his flight to Mars from Phobos just a month before. For that flight, there had been trained technicians all around the spacecraft prior to its flight, checking and verifying all the critical parameters. Here he was, out in the middle of nowhere, trusting his life to four people he had never even seen before.

For the first time since he had committed to the escape plan, Hunter realized clearly that there was a very real chance that he might die. He tried unsuccessfully to push the thought out of his mind. The discomfort in his stomach increased.

"Leggett has the best reliability record of any of the unscheduled launch providers," Cho said, as if he was reading Hunter's mind.

"Do I dare ask what that reliability record is?" Hunter said.

Cho glanced over at him. "Do you really want to know?" his friend said.

No, not really, Hunter said to himself. *The die is already cast.*

Hunter was suddenly angry with himself for not having written notes to his family, Ursula, and Tehani. Just in case. He took a deep breath. "Cho," he said haltingly into his helmet microphone, "if something happens . . . Will you make certain that my family is told in a proper fashion?"

"Of course," Cho said, "but nothing is going to happen."

"And ask Goldmatt," Hunter said as an afterthought, "to please give Ursula whatever I have left from my raid bonus."

"Okay," said Cho, a slight frown on his face, "but let's stop this kind of talk now. You're about to meet your pilot and crew and we don't want them to think that you're petrified. That could spook them."

Cho parked the truck beside the other vehicles. Hunter and he climbed out of the cab and Cho introduced Hunter as Lewis Smith to the Leggetts, father and daughter, and the two engineering technicians.

"Everything in good shape?" Hunter asked brightly.

"One of the gyros is acting kind of weird," the technician named Barney said. "But I don't think it's going to be a major problem."

"We can fly with only two gyros if we have to," Ralph Leggett said. "Denise can pull it off-line during the flight if necessary."

Ralph Leggett's unwieldy gray beard filled most of the bottom of his faceplate. He was a large man with sharp eyes and a pockmarked face. His daughter Denise, who Hunter guessed was about thirty, was petite and blonde.

Denise was clearly impatient. During the small talk that followed the initial introductions, she kept looking at her watch. "We're ready to go if you are," she said to Hunter and Cho during a break in the conversation.

When Hunter learned that only Denise and he would actually be walking over to the spacecraft, he thanked Cho, Mr. Leggett, and the two technicians.

"Be safe," Cho said. "I'll probably see you in about two weeks."

Hunter turned and followed Denise toward the launch

area. While they were walking, he struggled mightily with his apprehension and his fear. At one point he hurried up beside Denise. "How many of these flights have you made?" he asked.

She looked at him curiously. "This will be my seventh," she said.

BY THE TIME Hunter had climbed up the long ladder and strapped himself into the passenger seat of the cockpit, he had acknowledged to himself that he was not going to be able to overcome his fear. Nothing about the situation gave him confidence. On close inspection the rocket tanks and external equipment at the back of the spacecraft looked old and weather-beaten. Denise told him that the vehicle had been decommissioned by the Dems eight years previously, after twenty-five years of service, and that her father and she had reconditioned it themselves at their hangar outside a small town a hundred miles to the west of Lancaster. The critical guidance computer had a new processor—the old one had failed toward the end of her last flight, fortunately after she had already achieved orbital velocity. Denise herself had applied for flight school with Free Zone Transport, but had not scored high enough on the mathematical sections to gain entrance.

"Have you ever flown in a high-gee environment before?" Denise asked Hunter a minute before their scheduled liftoff.

"Only on the descent from Phobos to Mars," Hunter said.

"That was a piece of cake," Denise said with a grin. "The first thirty seconds of our flight will be pure hell."

Great, Hunter said to himself. *I can hardly wait.*

Denise next explained that when she flipped the launch switch, two "hypergolic" fuels would feed into the rocket tanks, causing an instant explosion upon contact. "That explosion is what creates the thrust that propels us upward," she said.

When the digital countdown clock in the cockpit reached fifteen seconds, Hunter fought against a desire to close his eyes. Denise released the metal arms holding the spacecraft in place and it started shaking slightly in the light wind. At launch time, she flipped the fuel switch and an enormous roar behind Hunter was followed by a powerful upward thrust.

He was pinned against his seat by an unbelievable force. He could not move, or even breathe, the force was so overpowering. Hunter became afraid that his helmet would shatter, or that his eyes would be forever damaged by having been forced back into his head. The ride was too terrifying to be thrilling. He didn't dare look out the side window, for fear that he would see that they were off course.

The vehicle continued to accelerate upward. The force pressing him against his chair did not abate. Hunter became disoriented, then thought he was going to pass out. He closed his eyes and started slowly counting to himself.

Eventually, after what was actually only a few minutes, the pressure began to ease. Hunter realized that he had been holding his breath the entire time and started inhaling deeply.

"Don't hyperventilate," Denise said. "It will make you giddy." She smiled. "And please don't throw up. You look a little green."

The spacecraft rolled slightly and Hunter could see the surface of Mars far beneath him. It was an awesome sight. "How far are we off the ground?" he asked.

She looked at her altitude readout. "Forty-eight miles," she said. "The rest of our flight is simply a navigation problem. We need to match our position and velocity with that of Phobos. The exciting part is over."

Denise turned on the audio system. "Would you like to listen to some music?" she said. Hunter nodded. "Jazz, soft rock, or wild stuff?" she asked.

"Soft rock, please," Hunter said.

As the music began playing in the cockpit, Hunter realized that he was absolutely exhausted. He looked out the window beside him. Far below the spacecraft the planet Mars looked peaceful and serene. While Hunter was gazing out the window, he thought about what he was going to do when he reached Phobos. A few minutes later, Hunter closed his eyes. Much to his surprise, he soon fell asleep.

DENISE WAS TALKING with the traffic controllers at the Phobos spaceport when Hunter awakened. Out the front window Hunter could see nothing but stars. Denise pointed across him, to his right, at one of the brighter lights in the black heavens. "That's Phobos," she said. "We should land in about fifteen minutes."

The spacecraft was slowly turning. After about a minute Mars moved into view on Hunter's side of the spacecraft. It was half-illuminated, an impressive reddish-brown sphere nearly filling his window. Hunter could easily identify Mount Olympus and a few other prominent main geological features on the lit half of the globe.

Denise displayed the spacecraft trajectory on the monitor between them. Hunter noticed that they would be outside the orbit of Phobos for the remainder of the flight. Denise explained that all private spacecraft were expected to approach the Phobos spaceport from outside the moon's orbit.

Denise glanced at Hunter and smiled. "You all right now?" she said.

"I guess so," Hunter said. "For several seconds during the launch, however, I wasn't certain I was going to survive."

Denise laughed. "Everybody feels that way on their first trip." She paused for a second. "What did you do, anyway?" she then said. "Kill somebody important?"

Hunter looked at her with a quizzical expression. "I know it's none of my business," Denise said, "but I am curious. Somebody was willing to pay a hell of a lot of money to get you from Mars to Phobos in a hurry."

"You don't know?" Hunter said.

"Nope," Denise said, shaking her head. "And I guess I really shouldn't be asking. If I don't know anything, I can't get into any trouble."

Hunter was quiet for several seconds. "I didn't kill anybody," he said at length into the microphone in his helmet. "That much I can tell you."

"Thanks," Denise said. "I feel much better."

The traffic controllers at Phobos asked Denise to delay her arrival by a minute and forty-two seconds. The guidance computer recomputed the trajectory instantly. Shortly thereafter the spacecraft made a slight attitude adjustment.

As they approached, Phobos changed from a single light to a set of lights and then into an oblong feature whose surface was covered by illumination from man's architectural creations. The spaceport, the resorts, and the new residential areas made the moon's largest natural feature, Stickney Crater, virtually unrecognizable from space.

Just before their vehicle reached the spaceport, they passed several other spacecraft, including a large interplanetary transport well off to their right. When Denise received her permission to land, she lowered the six adhesive wheels of the spacecraft, four of which were attached to the fuel tanks at the rear. The horizontal landing on the short runway at the edge of the spaceport was reasonably smooth, for Denise had negated most of the vertical velocity during her descent. Still, they had a few minor bumps before the wheels finally grabbed on to the landing surface.

Denise taxied the spacecraft for a couple of minutes, ending up in a parking area where several dozen small spacecraft were sitting around and beside a T-shaped terminal. Only the larger private vehicles, which could accommodate twelve or more passengers, had an individual entryway connecting them directly with the terminal.

"As I understand it, Lewis, or whatever your real name is," Denise said, while the transparent shield over the top of the cockpit was folding back, "this is where we part company." She deployed the tethers from the cockpit to the ground. "Good luck," Denise said to Hunter, awkwardly extending the hand of her space suit.

"Thanks a lot," he replied, shaking her hand. He grinned behind his faceplate. "It was quite an experience, especially the first minute after launch."

She leaned behind her seat and grabbed her flight bag. Several seconds later Denise climbed out of the cockpit. She slid gently down to the asphalt surface holding on to the tether. Hunter watched her until she entered a terminal door about a hundred yards away.

Hunter glanced at his watch. Cho had instructed him to wait approximately five minutes before leaving. He spent the time surveying the other parked spacecraft, wondering which one would soon carry him away from Phobos. When it had been nearly five minutes since Denise had left, Hunter rose from his seat with his small bag and used the tether on his side of the spacecraft to guide him to the ground.

When he reached the surface Hunter looked around for somebody in a blue FZTA space suit. Ten seconds later, he saw an official in a blue suit approaching him from the general direction of the terminal.

"You just arrive from Mars?" the man said.

Hunter nodded. He waited expectantly for the password. The man, however, pointed toward the terminal door that Denise had entered. "Please go inside over there," he said. "We're monitoring all passenger traffic today."

Hunter thanked the man and started walking toward the building. He looked around the field as he walked, hoping that his contact would soon appear. Hunter stopped briefly about halfway to the terminal, when he passed two technicians apparently going out to service one of the space-craft. He glanced furtively back in the direction from which he had come. The official was still watching him.

What am I going to do now? Hunter asked himself, again moving toward the door to the terminal airlock. He knew that actually entering the terminal would be a terrible mis-take. *Someone will certainly recognize me as soon as they ver-ify that I'm not really Lewis Smith,* Hunter told himself. He fought against the fear that was growing rapidly with each step.

Just before he reached the door, a group of ten or twelve passengers from a corporate space yacht approached from the left. Hunter slowed his pace and fell in behind them. Since the airlock could only hold six to eight people at a time, part of the group remained outside for over a minute. While he was waiting, Hunter noticed that the official who had spoken to him soon after his arrival on Phobos was no longer in view. Relieved, Hunter moved away from the others, and walked several yards along the side of the building.

In less than a minute a short man, also in a blue FZTA suit, emerged from behind a large parked truck and ap-proached Hunter with a rapid gait. "Smartass," the man said, turning around immediately.

Hunter followed him. The man walked straight out onto the asphalt, away from the building. He turned right between two of the larger space yachts and headed toward a blue shuttle that had five stars painted just below its two windows. It was sitting at the edge of the parking area. As they drew closer, Hunter could see a tether hanging from the passenger side of the cockpit to the surface. When they were about fifty yards from the shuttle, the man pointed. "That's it," he said brusquely. He then turned and hurried back toward the terminal.

Hunter walked over to the shuttle and put his hands on the tether. He climbed easily up the side of the spacecraft. He had almost reached the cockpit when he saw two men running toward him. One of the men was the FZTA official who had told Hunter to go inside the terminal. The other man was wearing a black space suit with a large badge and the Free Zone Police insignia on his right shoulder.

HUNTER DUTIFULLY FOLLOWED the policewoman down the hall. "You'll be staying here for awhile," the woman said, opening the door to a small room, "until we decide how to proceed with your case. Your space suit and other belongings have been marked and stored in one of the lockers in the main office."

She handed Hunter a container of water and glanced at her watch. "If you're still here in two hours," she said, "we'll serve you some lunch."

Hunter entered the room without saying anything. The policewoman closed and locked the door behind him. He looked around. The room was small, but comfortable. There was a bed with two end tables against one wall. A chair was positioned right in front of the television set. The bathroom was in the back right corner of the room.

Hunter sat down in the chair and stared numbly at the blank wall above the television. A jumbled stream of images from the previous hour and a half swarmed through his mind. With difficulty, attempting to overcome his pervasive feelings of doom and hopelessness, Hunter forced himself to organize the images in his short-term memory into a coherent sequence.

He remembered vividly entering the spaceport terminal, accompanied by the two men who had accosted him while he was climbing the shuttle tether, and being greeted there by a pair of Free Zone Police officers. They had demanded and taken his Lewis Smith identity card, asked him a few questions, and then had moved Hunter temporarily to a small empty office.

During the fifteen minutes that he had been alone in that office, Hunter had realized that it was certain that the Free Zone Police would conclude that he was not really Lewis Smith. Fighting against a growing feeling of panic, Hunter had struggled to concoct a kidnapping story that would explain to the police, without any glaring inconsistencies, both his presence on Phobos and his possession of the false identity card. Hunter had decided that his best hope was to say that he had been drugged and asleep from shortly after he had entered the rest room at the Matterhorn Café at New Earth until just before he had boarded the spacecraft that had carried him from Mars to Phobos. In his story, soon after he awakened somewhere on the Martian plains, Hunter had been given both the Lewis Smith identity card and explicit instructions to follow after arriving at the Phobos spaceport. The instructions had been accompanied by threats.

Hunter had known at the time that any serious investigation would have found all kinds of problems with his kidnapping tale. Too many witnesses had seen him during his escape route across the park. They could testify that he had not been in the presence of any abductors. *But what other options do I have at this point?* Hunter had asked himself in desperation during his wait in the police office. *If I wasn't kidnapped, how do I explain what I'm doing here? If I admit now that I was trying to run away to join the pirates to escape a possible Federation indictment, my fate will be sealed and I will be imprisoned for life. Or worse.*

A Free Zone Police captain had eventually entered the office where he was being kept and informed Hunter that he was under arrest for possessing a false identity card. During the ensuing conversation, Hunter had told the captain who he really was. He had then asked if he could make an official statement. The policeman had taken him to a processing room in the spaceport where, after having had his photograph taken from every angle, his fingerprints recorded, and his retina scanned, Hunter had told his kidnapping story on video both to the assembled Free Zone Police and to their counterparts on Mars.

After his statement, the police captain had asked Hunter why he had not simply identified himself as soon as he was inside the terminal. "I was still afraid," Hunter had said with a shrug. "And confused. I really didn't know what to do."

I still don't know what to do, Hunter said to himself in his small room inside the police building at the Phobos spaceport. *But I'm not certain it even matters.*

Reviewing all the details surrounding his arrest had not done anything to improve Hunter's mood. Feeling utterly forlorn, he walked into the bathroom and washed his face. Hunter stared at his reflection in the mirror for a long time, trying not to think about the future. But his mind was already tormenting him. Hunter winced as he imagined how his parents would react when they were told that he had been arrested. *This might kill my father,* he said grimly to himself. He was unsuccessfully attempting to suppress an image of his mother weeping desperately when he heard the door to his room open.

Hunter walked back into the room. The Free Zone Police captain was standing just inside the door. He looked very serious. "It appears," he said to Hunter, "that this case is more complex than we originally thought. We have already been contacted by both the UDSC and Federation authorities. They both want to question you. After some conversation, we have agreed to their requests. A pair of ASP representatives will be here in less than an hour."

FOUR

THE NEXT HOUR WAS absolute torture for Hunter. He had never experienced such fear and anxiety. He was no longer concerned about possible inconsistencies in his kidnapping story. Lying in a statement to the police was a comparatively minor crime. Hunter was worried that the Dems had positively identified him as having been a participant in the Edison raid, or that the ASP had already figured out that he had sent a warning message to Cooperman about Operation Bluebeard.

The punishment for treason under both governments is death, Hunter said to himself with a shudder. For a grisly moment he tried to imagine what it would feel like in the last seconds between a lethal injection and the unconsciousness preceding death. The thought made him squirm uncontrollably.

In the middle of his agitation, Hunter suddenly remembered his conversation with Arundhati the previous evening about the best and worst days of his life. "Today," he said out loud. "Today," he repeated, laughing frenetically, "is by far the worst day of my life. Or any life."

He went to the bathroom to urinate every five minutes.

He could not sit down at all. Hunter paced about the room like a caged animal. He knew that he should try to remain calm, and think about what he was going to say to his interrogators, but it was impossible for him to think logically.

Hunter tried pushing against the wall with all his might to alleviate the tension. That helped a little. He decided to repeat the action a few minutes later. Hunter was standing with his arms pressed against the wall when the police captain returned.

"We're moving you to another facility," the captain said, "where the audio and video capabilities are better. You'll have your interviews there."

Hunter followed the captain out into the hall. A policewoman, also wearing a captain's badge, was in the hall waiting. When Hunter and the two officers passed the main administrative desk, the receptionist asked the captain if he wanted to take Hunter's space suit and other belongings. "Yes, of course," the man answered absentmindedly, motioning to the other captain to grab Hunter's things.

They descended in an elevator to the basement. Several steps to the right of the elevator exit the trio passed through a door that was the entry to an underground tram system. The female captain explained that the tram connected all the police facilities on Phobos. "We're going now to our main headquarters," she said. "It's between the spaceport and the primary resort area."

The tram was a small, open vehicle. Hunter sat beside the male captain in the front seat. The woman officer sat in the back with Hunter's belongings. The vehicle began moving slowly forward after the control panel was touched.

Hunter's fear and hopelessness returned with a vengeance as the tram moved through the tunnel. He found himself wondering if he would ever again have a happy moment in his life.

The tram began to slow down as it was making a long turn to the left. A message on the control panel indicated that the tram's safety system had detected some kind of irregularity in the pathway ahead. The puzzled police captain beside Hunter stood up in the open car. He saw the large metallic object partially blocking the path just before the tram came to a complete stop.

The captain suddenly recoiled and slumped down in his seat. An instant later the policewoman in the back was hit by some kind of projectile and she, too, collapsed. A bewildered Hunter glanced up and saw two men wearing the blue space suits of the FZTA standing on the narrow walkway next to the tram path. They had apparently been hiding in a small equipment area beside the pathway. They were both holding pistols.

"Hurry," one of them said to Hunter. "Put on your space suit."

It was a few seconds before Hunter recognized the two men. "Bailey?" he said, the astonishment in his voice obvious. "And Snyder?"

They both smiled briefly without saying anything. Bailey glanced at his watch. "Hello, Hunter," he said. "We have two minutes at the most before someone shows up. You will need to follow me as fast as you can."

Snyder started running down the tram pathway. While Hunter finished putting on his space suit, Bailey explained that Snyder was going to open the emergency exit a hundred yards up the pathway and enter the airlock password. As soon as he was dressed, Hunter jumped out of the tram onto the walkway. Bailey put his pistol in his pocket and started to run.

Hunter followed Bailey. Before they reached the short

set of stairs on the left, they could already hear the Klaxon siren initiated by the opening of the emergency exit. They raced up the stairs and into the airlock. Bailey pulled the door shut behind them.

"Our spacecraft is only fifty yards or so outside this door behind me," Bailey said while the airlock pressurization routine was active. "Everything's ready to go. The tethers are down on both sides. Whatever happens, you go to the spacecraft. Snyder and I will take care of anyone who tries to stop us."

The moment that the digital readout indicated that the pressure had essentially reached zero and the airlock door released, Bailey pushed the door open and went outside. Hunter was on the landing asphalt half a second later. "There," Bailey said, pointing at a sleek white spacecraft with no markings. "Go. Now."

Hunter ran across the field and grabbed the tether on the passenger side. He was in his seat in a few seconds. Bailey and Snyder joined him almost immediately. Bailey activated the control that pulled in the tethers. He then lowered the shield over the cockpit. He started the spacecraft engines and began taxiing in spite of the fact that spaceport personnel were waving their arms frantically on both sides of their vehicle.

A large police truck with flashing lights came barreling toward them on the landing surface. "Well," Bailey said with a grim smile, "I guess we aren't going to use the runway after all. Hold on, I haven't done this in a long time."

He retracted the back landing wheels, pointing the spacecraft slightly up, and nearly simultaneously engaged the main thrusters. The vehicle took off immediately, blasting through the gaps between the spaceport buildings, as the ground personnel scrambled for cover.

Bailey narrowly missed hitting two other spacecraft as he increased his speed and raced away from the spaceport.

"David Henry 052, this is Captain Owens of the Free Zone Police," a voice on the spacecraft radio said. "Your takeoff was both unauthorized and dangerous. You are hereby ordered . . ."

Bailey abruptly switched off the radio. His eyes were full of excitement behind his faceplate. He looked over at Hunter. "Most of the things that I like in life," he said, "are either unauthorized or dangerous."

BAILEY FLEW THE shuttle through the most densely crowded region around the Phobos spaceport. Throughout a wild ten-minute ride, he was constantly changing directions without warning, at times terrifying the other spacecraft pilots. Twice he saw a police patrol shuttle in the distance, and immediately took off in the other direction. When Bailey spotted a large cargo ship moving away from Phobos, he zoomed underneath it, and then hovered just on the other side, no more than twenty-five yards away from the much larger craft.

"We won't be seen on anyone's radar here," he said, grinning at Hunter. "We're protected for the time being by our huge neighbor."

"Do you think they're following us?" Hunter asked.

"Unlikely," Snyder said from the backseat. "The Free Zone Police are not prepared to act that swiftly. My real concern is the Federation fleet. They're spread out all over and may have orders to interdict us if they can."

Their shuttle continued flying in formation with the huge cargo ship. During a moment of comparative calm, Hunter thanked the two Utopians who had risked their lives on his behalf. "I can't tell you how grateful I am," he said. "I will be forever in your debt."

"Not a problem," Bailey said. "We think of you as one of us."

Snyder suddenly leaned forward. "Off to the right, Bailey," he said hurriedly. "Unless I miss my guess, that's a Federation fighter squadron."

Bailey looked out Hunter's window and immediately hit the throttle. The shuttle blasted forward, quickly leaving the cargo ship behind. Snyder kept an eye on the fighter squadron until it could no longer be seen. He observed no unusual behavior.

As their distance from Phobos increased, the density of the space traffic fell off markedly. After two hours the shuttle radar screen showed only two other blips within a radius of a hundred miles.

"Where are we going?" Hunter asked during a lull in their conversation.

"That depends," Bailey answered.

"Depends on what?" Hunter said.

"On whether or not anyone is following us," Bailey said. He looked at the digital time on the control panel. "Which Cooperman will tell us in another hour or so."

SLIGHTLY OVER AN hour later Bailey received a message from Cooperman. The little Utopian genius confirmed that the Federation fleet had been alerted to be on the lookout for their shuttle, but that no pursuit force had been dispatched. The remainder of his message was a listing of the current locations of the Federation spaceships and space sectors that should be avoided. Cooperman had also transmitted the fleet-location information directly into the shuttle navigation system, so that their flight path automatically steered away from any possible encounters.

"You know," Snyder said to Hunter, "Cooperman engineered this whole crazy escape plan."

"Why, I wonder?" Hunter asked.

"He thinks you're one outstanding young man," Bailey

said. "Cooperman was furious when he learned that Sackett was going to hang you out to dry. He hates that bastard. Your escape became a personal vendetta for him."

"So tell me," Hunter asked after a short silence, "how did you know that I was going to be on that tram?"

"Curious, are you?" Bailey said. "I was wondering when you would ask."

"Cooperman has friends everywhere," Snyder said.

"Even inside the Free Zone Police department?" Hunter said.

"Especially there," Bailey said. "That thirtyish receptionist with the big teats in the Phobos spaceport office is passionately in love with a dashing young Crusader. She can't become a full-time pirate because she needs to care for her ailing mother. It's a perfect situation. She provides access to information and Cooperman arranges her trysts with the young Crusader."

"We knew where you were at every moment," Snyder said. "As long as you stayed with the Free Zone Police, we were not worried. But when we heard they were going to allow the ASP and the Dems to interrogate you, well, we knew we had to act."

"Why didn't you simply overpower the policeman and the FZTA official who confronted me when I was climbing into the first shuttle?" Hunter asked.

"We thought about it," Bailey said. "But it would have been very complicated. Perhaps even foolhardy. There are always lots of eyes, both human and electronic, watching the spaceport parking area."

"The blue shuttle with the stars was only a decoy," Snyder added. "We would have moved you to this spacecraft anyway."

Hunter shook his head. "Such an elaborate arrangement, just to help me escape," he said. "I'm flattered beyond belief."

APPROXIMATELY EIGHTEEN HOURS
after their wild takeoff from Phobos, Bailey steered the
white shuttle into the parking bay of the same Israeli spacecraft that had transported Hunter to his release point a
month earlier. Hunter was delighted to discover that both
Menachem and Julie were among the crew on board. Julie
gave him an enthusiastic, sisterly embrace, and told him
that she was "overjoyed" that he had escaped safely from
the Feds.

Soon after his arrival, Menachem informed Hunter that
the ship had received two personal video transmissions addressed to him. Hunter sat down at the familiar computer
system in the lounge and accessed the videos. The first was
from Ursula. She was transmitting from Cooperman's
home, Hunter was certain, because the background was
cluttered with miscellaneous electronic equipment.

"Hello, my darling Hunter," Ursula said with a huge
smile. She was positively radiant. "I am so excited and so
happy. Cooperman has just told me that you have safely escaped from Mars, and that you're on your way home to us.
I can't believe it."

She paused for a moment and the camera zoomed in on
her face. Hunter could see tears in her eyes. "Baby Blake
and I will be waiting for you with open arms," Ursula continued in a halting voice. She stopped again and wiped the
tears from her cheeks with a tissue that someone handed
her from offscreen. "I love you," she then said, "and I can't
wait to see you. Be safe, my love."

Hunter replayed the short video three times. Each time,
when he was finished, he wondered how he had ever left
Ursula and his unborn child in the first place. Hunter remembered something that his father had told him when he

was a boy. "Everyone makes mistakes," he had said. "The smart man never makes the same mistake twice."

The second video was from Cooperman. "Hi, guy," he started. Cooperman was wearing an undershirt, a pair of boxers, and white socks. "Hey, thanks a lot for the info about the drones." He laughed. "We completely screwed up your friend Sackett and his minions," he said in his normal breathless manner. "We sent a flotilla of tiny electronic packages to one of the other, uninhabited, asteroids, and programmed them to transmit massive amounts of cyclical garbage at a range of frequencies for a full week. The Feds took the bait. As we speak, they are preparing to mount an attack against a gigantic, uninhabited rock."

Dirk flew into the picture and landed on Cooperman's shoulder. "Say hello to Hunter, Dirk," he commanded. The bird looked at the camera. "Hello, Hunter," it said.

"Anyway," Cooperman continued, "Camille is waiting for you at the clinic. Ursula's been training her in her spare time. Not that the girl has any spare time. Sorry, but I didn't think to have Camille brought over here tonight. I had too many things on my mind, I guess."

He paused. "We've missed you here," he said. "Glad you're coming back. I need a decent challenge at Intellego."

During dinner Hunter entertained the crew with the detailed story of his escape from Mars. He handed out kudos to everyone involved, especially Bailey and Snyder, and thanked the cruiser crew for helping him to return to the pirate world. Afterward, he composed short videos to both Ursula and Cooperman. He told Ursula that he couldn't wait to hold her in his arms, that he loved her, and that he was a fool for ever having left her in the first place.

Hunter had more difficulty with the video for Cooperman. *What do you say to someone who has saved your life?* Hunter asked himself. He knew that Cooperman would not be comfortable with any kind of an emotional display, yet Hunter felt, in his heart, that he had to make certain his peculiar, wonderful friend knew how much Hunter appreciated what he had done.

"Yo there, Cooperman," he said at the beginning of the video. "It looks like you're not rid of me after all. I'll be glad to see you again, my friend, and to thank you personally for not letting the Feds send me to the big sleep.

"I'd love to be watching when Sackett gets the report that he has launched an attack against a big rock. By the way, is that bird of his one of yours? Do you have it programmed, you sly dog, to send you shit directly from his office?

"Anyway, we'll have plenty of time to catch up when I get back. I guess I'll even let you annihilate me at Intellego, as long as Loretta is playing with us." Hunter laughed. "Thanks again, Cooperman, you are one amazing human being."

HUNTER SPENT SEVEN days on the Israeli cruiser. Although he visited frequently with his friends on board, and thoroughly enjoyed some extended games of Intellego, he had plenty of time for reflection.

Almost every evening, before he went to bed in his cabin, Hunter set aside an hour or more of solitude so that he could think about what had happened to him, and what he had learned, from his extraordinary experiences.

He reached very few overwhelming conclusions during his soul-searching. Hunter thought that perhaps he was wiser and more mature than he had been a year before, but he could not cite any specific examples of altered behavior as a result of his new wisdom and maturity. He also thought that he now understood much more about sex and love as a result of his intimate relationships with Tehani,

Ursula, and even Arundhati. However, when he sat at a computer and tried to encapsulate what he had learned about these difficult subjects, he found himself writing vapid clichés that were devoid of any real meaning. He could not capture his complex thoughts and feelings in a few words.

Hunter knew that he was much more politically aware than he had been before he left Cicero. He also knew that his decision to return to the pirates had really not been a political choice, that in truth it had been no choice at all. Although Hunter now could say that he preferred the freestyle lives of the pirates over the more constrained, more secure existences of the citizens of the established space governments, it was, in actuality, a moot point. Circumstances had made him a pirate. There was very little chance that anything would ever happen to change that fact.

He had very few regrets. Sure, it was obvious now that he should have accepted Goldmatt's offer when it was made, but that was a judgment based on hindsight. And if Hunter had never gone to Mars in the first place, would he have understood and appreciated so keenly the differences between the two lifestyles? Would he, for that matter, ever have accepted in his heart being separated permanently from either his family or Tehani?

His estrangement from his family still bothered him. Hunter knew that his parents would both suffer immeasurably once the true story of his disappearance was made public. One of his top-priority activities, while he was establishing his life among the pirates, would be to find some way to send a communication to his mother and father explaining what had happened. Hunter believed that Cooperman would be able to help him do that.

He would miss Tehani. She would forever be the great passion of his life. But Hunter already knew that he would be perfectly happy to be married to Ursula. His love was not a consumable resource, as Arundhati had pointed out. He would not love Ursula less because he retained feelings for Tehani.

Hunter wondered what would happen to Tehani. Would she continue to work at Sybaris even after she had paid back all the gambling debts her father had accumulated? Or would she perhaps eventually marry someone who idolized her so completely that he could overlook her past? Hunter asked himself if Tehani's relationship with Lester Sackett was just one of convenience for her, or if the two of them shared a true connection. *It doesn't matter,* he told himself eventually. *That's her life, and has little or nothing to do with mine.*

A large welcoming party greeted Hunter at the trading post where the Israeli cruiser docked at the end of its mission. In fact, there was even a banner affixed to the dock itself. "Welcome home, Hunter Blake," it said.

The party had obviously begun a couple of hours before the cruiser arrived. Everyone inside the post was already in a joyous mood. An ecstatic Ursula hugged and kissed Hunter as soon as he passed through the airlock. Cooperman saluted Hunter throughout the evening and made certain he was properly supplied with intoxicants. Lance and Goldmatt took Hunter aside for twenty minutes. The three of them discussed, in considerable detail, how his new position as medical ombudsman would actually work. Hunter told the two chiefs that he would like to have two or three weeks to rest, recuperate, and make arrangements before he began the job.

Cooperman had converted the largest room at the post into a bedroom suite for the evening. With great fanfare, and a dozen or more people in attendance, he led Hunter and Ursula into the suite around midnight. "Now I don't suppose I need to tell you guys what to do," Cooperman said, patting Ursula on the stomach. Everyone laughed.

When the others had gone, Hunter and Ursula kissed. He had forgotten how intense her kisses were. She held nothing back.

"Would you like to take a shower first?" she said.

He nodded. She undressed him slowly. *This is going to be wonderful,* he thought.

ABOUT THE AUTHOR

GENTRY LEE has been chief engineer on Project Galileo, director of science analysis and mission planning for NASA's Viking mission to Mars, and partner with Carl Sagan in the design, development, and implementation of the television series *Cosmos*. He is the author of *Bright Messengers* and *Double Full Moon Night*. Gentry Lee was also the co-author of *Cradle, Rama II, The Garden of Rama,* and *Rama Revealed.* He lives in Dallas, Texas.